THE INGRID SKYBERG THRILLERS

BOOKS 1 – 3

EVA HUDSON

VENATRIX

FRESH DOUBT

BOOK ONE

EVA HUDSON

PROLOGUE

Dear Lauren,

They make you write letters here. One to your parents. One to mine. One to my future self, that sort of thing. Apparently, the fact you're dead is supposed to free me to write the truth about my feelings. The doctor running the rehabilitation programme has fewer psychology qualifications than me—fewer than you, in fact—so it's fun to play with his head. And let's face it, he's the only one who's going to read this, isn't he?

So how do I feel, Lauren? I believe they want me to say I'm sorry, or remorseful, or sad. But the truth is I'm angry. Angry with you for putting me here. If I'd never met you, I honestly think I could have been happy. But you had to come along and ruin everything.

At the beginning it was fun, I'll admit. It was just the two of us against the world, remember? We had this crazy, intense connection but when the spell was broken you couldn't keep your mouth shut, could you? I warned you to keep it to yourself, to hold your tongue, but you didn't, did you? So what happened was... inevitable.

There's something that really bothers me. Can you guess what it is? It was that look you gave me when you were lying on the floor. You were still alive then—I checked your pulse—and there was this moment when you seemed to see me and recognize what was happening. I want to know if that look—that narrowing of your pupils, that tightening of your features—was that you hating me, or thanking me?

I picture that scene often. Your head at an odd angle, the gash in your skull

3

starting to glisten. God, the sound you made when you fell. It was almost metallic, like the crunching of a car when it goes into the back of another. Although that wasn't the last sound you made, was it? There was that wheezing rasp as the air left your lungs.

I don't know if you care, but I thought you should know I didn't hate you when I killed you. Like I said at the time, I only wanted to shut you up, to put an end to things. But by God I hate you now. You've caused me so much trouble.

This is such a ridiculous exercise. It's not like you're going to write back is it? And how am I supposed to sign off a letter like this? Best wishes? That's all for now? Rest in peace? Ah. I know…

See you soon,
Prisoner A2441AC

1

"Somebody stop him!" the woman shouted. "Please, someone!"

Special Agent Ingrid Skyberg saw it all happen in slow motion as she ran past on her early morning run along the Thames river path. A moment to shove the woman sideways, another to drag the straps of the bag from her shoulder, then a second to snatch and scoop the bag into his arms. The young Caucasian male sped away, barging into a crowd of commuters near the London Eye. The woman fell hard onto the concrete path, her mouth forming a wide silent O as she hit the ground.

Ingrid had just been getting into her stride, feeling her muscles warm, absorbing the faint heat of the early morning April sun on her face. She pulled up fast—the man was escaping behind her—turned on a dime and ran back under Jubilee Bridge toward the Royal Festival Hall. She accelerated through the crowd.

"Stop!" she shouted, pumping her arms faster. "FBI!" Then she remembered herself, threw a glance over her shoulder and yelled at the mugging victim to call 9-1-1. The woman looked at Ingrid blankly. "I mean nine nine nine, call nine nine nine!"

Ingrid turned face front again and scanned a sea of disgruntled faces to find the thief.

"Get out of my way!" she yelled, but most had headphones in and didn't hear. She scrutinized the edge of the crowd and spotted him again, his shaven head appearing bright white above the throng of commuters. She memorized his description for later. White, male, five eleven, one-seventy pounds, bald head, no more than twenty years of age. And fast. Really fast. Her cell phone vibrated, tingling against her bicep. Whoever it was would have to wait.

The crowd cleaved in front of her, opening a central channel. Ingrid pumped her arms harder and dragged air down into her burning lungs. Thirty yards ahead, the perp darted quickly right, pushing a tourist out of his way before roaring up a concrete staircase to the terrace above.

Ingrid dug deep, gaining on him with every stride.

"Stop! Police!" she yelled.

She took the first four steps in a single leap, drove the balls of her feet hard into the concrete and propelled herself upward. A bottle of water hurtled down toward her. She ducked left, and the half liter of Evian bounced harmlessly off her shoulder.

"Son of a…"

Ingrid reached the top of the steps and located her quarry as he crossed an expanse of concrete paving. This part of the Southbank was home to an arts complex built in brutal, bare concrete, with walkways and staircases connecting concert halls, galleries and theaters on several stories. Ingrid knew the center well: she met other parkour athletes here once a week for training sessions, jumping from level to level to find new and inventive ways to get from A to B. She smiled: she hadn't been this exhilarated since her last Bureau fitness assessment. She'd been training for something like this for years. She was going to enjoy herself.

He ran toward a narrow passage leading between two buildings, discarding items from the woman's bag as he went, briefly disappearing from sight. Ingrid ran after him, spotting him as he headed for another concrete spiral of steps down to street level. She lengthened her stride, reached for the waist-height wall and vaulted over it, twisting and holding onto the other side before dropping down to the flight below. He appeared at the bottom of the staircase and showed no sign of flagging. Ingrid jumped over the wall and dropped down, landing a few feet behind him.

"Fuck off, bitch."

Ingrid rolled to disperse the impact and sprang up to give chase. He reached into the handbag, fetching a pink leather wallet then discarding the bag as he ran. It caught under Ingrid's foot. Her ankle twisted, and she stumbled, but she kept on running. Her phone buzzed again. She was five yards back now. He ran into a graffiti-covered undercroft where skateboarders practiced their jumps. They zigzagged around each other, not paying any attention to her or the thief. The noise of the wheels on the hard standing echoed off the walls.

He darted between the boarders. Ingrid was within lunging distance now. She ran up one of the ramps and launched herself up into the air, cycling her legs before bringing her right foot down on the back of his calf, sending his face crashing into the hard concrete below and forcing the pink wallet out of his grasp.

She rolled him over; a huge graze covered his face from chin to ear. The skateboarders gathered round. One picked up the wallet.

"Who the fuck are you?" the thief managed.

"Ingrid Skyberg," she said, breathing heavily. "Special Agent Ingrid Skyberg to you, Federal Bureau of Investigation."

"FBI? Is this a joke?"

A uniformed police officer riding a bicycle came to a stop at the edge of the skate park, ditched the bike and scrambled over to them. He spoke urgently into his radio. "Suspect apprehended." He turned to Ingrid. "Where'd you learn to do that?" Behind him another cop ran over, and behind her was the woman whose bag had been snatched. The cops bent down and yanked the youth up to a seated position.

Ingrid's phone was still buzzing. She lifted it out of her armband and answered. "Agent Skyberg."

"You sound terrible." It was her boss.

"What's up, Sol?" She breathed heavily, her chest heaving with exertion.

Sol Franklin cleared his throat, then coughed. He really needed to stop smoking.

"Sol?"

She heard a deep inhale. "Got a case for you. An American citizen has been murdered. I'll text you the details, but you need to get there super quick."

"I'm on it."

The male police officer, with help from one of the skaters, had the thief in restraints. Ingrid approached his colleague. "I'm real sorry," she said, still out of breath, "but I don't have time to give you a statement right now." She pulled out a business card. "Call me this afternoon if you need one."

The officer looked at the card. "For real?"

"Phone the US Embassy after lunch. They'll patch you through to me."

The cop looked up and down the river path, searching for something. "FBI? Where are the cameras?"

"What?"

"You're filming something, right?" The cop nudged her colleague, whose mouth dropped open. "Is this another parkour video for YouTube?"

One of the skaters turned to her. "No. You're that... erm... that actress... the one who—"

"No." Ingrid tucked her short blond hair back under her baseball cap. "I'm not." She forced a smile.

The mugging victim stared at her intensely. "I can see it myself. You do look a bit like her. Except for the short hair, of course. What's her name? Charlize... thingummy..."

The skaters already had their phones out and were filming her. She really didn't need to end up on a viral video on Facebook. "Call me," she shouted, and accelerated back along the river path to continue her run. If it wasn't for the huge smile on her face, it was almost as if nothing had happened.

Her phone buzzed as she was slipping it back into the armband, and she glanced at Sol's message. Her smile quickly disappeared: the murder victim was only twenty-two. She didn't have time to waste: she took the steps up to Westminster Bridge three at a time and flagged down a black taxi.

2

Ingrid reached her hotel in Marylebone in fifteen minutes. After a quick shower, she chose a somber dark gray pantsuit from her small collection of work clothes. Yet again, she made a mental note to visit Banana Republic to purchase one or two alternative suits. She had only intended to stay in London for five days, and living out of a suitcase was getting tiresome. Her posting to the FBI's overseas Legal Attaché Program was supposed to be temporary, but it had stretched out to four months, and she was bored of wearing the same clothes. She was also over the glamor of hotel living. Ingrid dabbed a smudge of mascara under her left eye and promised herself she'd do something about her wardrobe and her living arrangements soon.

Ingrid picked up her helmet and belted leather jacket and took the stairs down into the hotel's underground parking lot. Her Triumph Tiger 800 didn't compare to her beloved Harley back home, but it was perfectly suited to weaving in and out of rush-hour traffic in central London.

The GPS led Ingrid to New Cross, a suburb she hadn't been to before, south of the Thames. She parked the bike at one end of a wide side street lined with cherry trees in full blossom. Fifty yards from where she stood, blue and white police tape fluttered in the stiff breeze outside a large, detached, five-story Victorian villa.

Her cell phone buzzed in her bag, vibrating noisily against her metal water flask. She swiped it and checked who was calling. Marshall, her fiancé. Not for the first time in the past few weeks, Ingrid didn't feel like talking to him and let it go to voicemail.

She locked her helmet into the top box and smoothed down the pants of her suit. A few feet from the police tape was a frizz-haired, middle-aged woman in a dark raincoat and patent leather boots arguing with a weary constable. The woman wagged a finger in his face, and Ingrid heard her shout something about press freedom. Ingrid recognized her from her very first assignment at the embassy: Angela Tate, an investigative journalist for the main London newspaper, the *Evening News*. Tate, Ingrid had learned, had a knack for finding out about stories before any of her colleagues. Press freedom? Tate seemed to have plenty.

Ingrid approached the police cordon and flashed her ID. None of the officers were armed. Strict UK laws meant only specialist firearms officers carried weapons, a rule that also applied to Ingrid and her Bureau colleagues.

"Don't I know you?" Tate said.

Ingrid pushed through, keen for the hack not to remember who she was.

"I never forget a face," Tate shouted after her.

In the entrance of the house, standing at the top of wide stone steps, was a familiar face Ingrid was much happier to see. Detective Inspector Natasha McKittrick was the closest Ingrid had to a friend in London. They had met at a training session Ingrid had delivered to the Metropolitan Police on child protection, the area of law enforcement she had specialized in before her deployment in London. The two women had discovered a similar sense of humor and taste for tequila and had enjoyed several 'putting the world to rights' sessions. She beamed at the detective.

"You got here fast," McKittrick said.

"I've been trying to tell you to get your motorcycle license."

"And I've tried to tell you how much I like my limbs in their current unbroken state."

Any anxiety Ingrid had about working with her friend instantly evaporated. "So what have we got?" Ingrid asked. "Murder one?"

"Pathologist says it's too close to call. Could just be an accident. We'll have to wait for the preliminary autopsy report."

Ingrid peered beyond McKittrick into the main hallway of the house. There were two doors on the left, another on the right, with a flight of stairs in the center leading up to the next story. The walls were scuffed, and a bicycle leaned against the banister.

"Cause of death was most likely severe loss of blood," McKittrick said as they turned to go inside. "Victim has a huge gash in her head. Seems a hard, sharp object went into her temple with a lot of force."

"You found the murder weapon?"

"If you can call a glass and steel coffee table a weapon, sure."

"She fell and hit her head on a table?"

"You sound disappointed."

Ingrid checked herself. She was a little.

"The next question I'm sure you're itching to ask me is 'was she pushed, or did she fall?'" McKittrick said.

"And?"

"That's what we're here to find out." McKittrick stopped on the stairs. "It's not that I'm not pleased to see you, but why exactly are you here?"

There wasn't a quick answer.

"Please don't say 'protocol.'"

"Well, when an American citizen dies in mysterious circumstances, it's diplomacy," Ingrid said, deliberately avoiding the word *protocol*, "for us to assist local law enforcement in any way we can."

"So you're not here to spy on me?"

She kind of was. "Of course not. I'm here to look out for the interests of American citizens, and that means ensuring the crime, if one has been committed, is thoroughly investigated."

They reached the top of the stairs. "So you are here to spy on me!"

Ingrid cleared her throat. "The US Embassy has total confidence in the investigatory competence of the Metropolitan Police."

"You rehearsed that." McKittrick gestured toward a pile of overshoe bootees and all-in-one Tyvek suits. "We'd better get togged up."

Togged up? Ingrid imagined she could live in England for the rest of her life and still not understand everything that came out of Brits' mouths. Once they were in the protective clothing, McKittrick filled her in on what they knew about the victim.

"Her name is Lauren Shelbourne. Twenty-two. Postgrad psychology student at Loriners College, which is part of the University of London." McKittrick led Ingrid up to the third-floor landing, then through a narrow door into a single-room apartment. Bright lights bathed the studio room in a magnesium glare, making every surface and object look strangely artificial, as if on the set of a horror movie. The CSI team fussed round the crumpled body lying next to the low coffee table, taking photos and collecting samples.

Ingrid was engulfed by sadness when she caught sight of Lauren Shelbourne's body. She was fully clothed, her arms flung out in front of her,

her legs folded awkwardly beneath. A dark red pool of congealed blood had spread across the floor. A piece of her forehead was missing. Ingrid pulled herself together. "Estimated time of death?"

"Some time between midnight and four a.m."

"You've spoken to the other residents?"

"Working through them, one by one. They're not all home."

"Inspector!"

Angela Tate was hovering by the door.

"Care to make a comment, detective?" Tate said. "Or perhaps the US Embassy would like to make a statement?" She smiled insincerely at Ingrid.

"How the bloody hell did you get past the cordon?"

The reporter took a step inside the room.

"Stay exactly where you are!" McKittrick rushed toward her. "You're contaminating the crime scene."

"So you are treating this as murder?" Angela Tate held her ground.

McKittrick grabbed the reporter's arm. "Mills!" she hollered.

A flush-cheeked face appeared in the doorway, an embarrassed, almost pleading look in his wide brown eyes. "Sorry, boss. I thought the uniforms had everything under control."

Tate snatched her arm away from McKittrick and pointed at the tall man. "You lay a hand on me, Ralph Mills, and I swear my paper will sue the arse off you."

The apologetic detective held his hands up high, palms facing toward Tate.

"Are you linking this death to the suicide at Loriners last week?" the journalist shouted before Mills herded her toward the stairs.

"Get her out of my sight, Mills," McKittrick said.

"I'll just be outside, Agent Skyberg," Tate said. "You can speak to me later."

Ingrid admired the reporter's determination, but she had absolutely no intention of telling her anything.

After talking to the crime scene investigators, Ingrid followed McKittrick downstairs and back out into the front yard. "Who called the police?" Ingrid asked her. "Who actually discovered the body?"

McKittrick nodded toward a shell-shocked, ghostly-white young woman sitting half-in, half-out of a police car. She was shivering despite the foil blanket wrapped around her shoulders.

"Have you questioned her yet?"

"Not beyond the preliminaries. We'll interview her formally down at the station."

"She lives here in the house?"

"No. A few streets away, apparently."

Ingrid watched as the young woman rose unsteadily to her feet. She seemed completely disoriented. She was wearing a blue Tyvek suit like Ingrid's.

"She's not a suspect?"

"Not at this stage, but her clothes are covered in blood. She found her, so I'm not ruling anything out. We'll find out more when we question her." McKittrick turned to Ingrid. "I suppose you'll want to sit in when we do."

Ingrid frowned, not taking her eyes from the staggering figure wrapped in the silvery blanket. The young woman got out of the car and wandered toward the house. She stared directly at Ingrid and McKittrick. A uniformed female officer attempted to guide the girl back to the police car.

"Madison Faber—also studying psychology at Loriners," McKittrick explained. "Also an American citizen."

"Really?"

That meant Ingrid had to offer her consular assistance. "Are you planning to arrest her?"

"I expect her to come to the station voluntarily."

"Does she understand that? Maybe I should speak to her." The young woman in the blanket wriggled her arms free from the cop. "Looks as if she isn't about to volunteer to go anywhere."

Madison Faber dragged the foil blanket from her shoulders and threw it at the feet of the female constable, who glanced toward McKittrick for help before Faber shoved the uniformed cop, who staggered backward.

"What the hell does she think she's doing?" McKittrick ran out onto the street.

Two more officers tried restraining the ashen-faced student, who batted their hands away and drove her fist into the face of the nearest officer. "Don't touch me!" she screamed.

Ingrid ran toward her as Angela Tate fired questions from the cordon. Faber looked up at Tate, the confusion on her face obvious. "Who are you?" Faber yelled.

A male officer stepped forward and grabbed both Faber's arms. The bewildered student kicked out at him, her right foot hitting hard against his shin.

"Let me go! I have to get out of here!" She struggled, kicking him again to slip from his grasp. She ran down the street.

"How was she when you first spoke to her?"

Ingrid and McKittrick hurried into the road.

"Shocked. Quiet. Traumatized."

"Let me speak to her."

McKittrick held firmly onto Ingrid's arm. "It's OK. We have this under control."

Her friend's expression told her she was in danger of taking over. Ingrid nodded.

Two more officers ran toward the distraught young woman, arms held out wide, as if capturing a wild animal. One grabbed her shoulders, another held onto her arms, and a third attempted to attach wrist restraints. Faber screamed at them to let her go.

McKittrick looked at Ingrid. "Contrary to my earlier statement, it seems we are indeed arresting her. You might want to sort out legal representation for her."

3

The interview suite in Lewisham police station smelled of freshly laid carpet. Ingrid sat next to a blank-eyed Madison Faber now wearing a gray sweatshirt and pants the police had given her. She hadn't spoken since Ingrid had introduced herself over an hour ago. They were waiting for the embassy-appointed attorney to show up, even though Ingrid had put the request in while she was still outside Lauren Shelbourne's apartment.

Faber had sat perfectly still for over twenty minutes, staring straight ahead at a bulletin board crammed with local notices. She was prim look-ing, with a neat mousy bobbed hairstyle and single pearl earrings. Her large blue eyes gave the impression of seeing everything while revealing nothing. There was something owl-like about her.

"Can I get you anything?" Ingrid asked her. "A glass of water?"

Faber turned and stared at her as if seeing her for the first time. She tried to speak, but only managed a low croak. "I've got to get out of here."

"You will, don't worry. Just as soon as—"

"No! I mean now." She stood up.

Ingrid pulled her back down. "Everything's OK. A lawyer will be here real soon, and I'm here for you in the meantime."

"How can you say that? Everything's not OK!" She struggled against Ingrid's grasp.

"You don't have to answer any of their questions if you don't want to." Ingrid was deliberately trying to sound calm. The girl had just been through one of the most traumatic experiences of her life, and she implicitly understood why Faber had lashed out when the cops restrained her. "You have the right to remain silent, just like back home. Is that clear?"

Faber's face was expressionless.

"It's important you understand me. Are you clear about the questioning?"

Faber nodded slowly.

"Good." She patted Faber's arm. "I'm on your side. Everything is going to be OK." She regretted the platitude the moment it left her lips.

"Everything is *not* going to be OK! My friend is dead." Faber pulled away from her and got to her feet. "I have to get out of here. I need to call Lauren's parents. They should hear the news from a friend, not some English cop." She could not keep the sneer from her voice when she said 'English cop.'

Ingrid stood up. "The embassy has that under control. Lauren's parents have already been informed." She kept her voice low, gentle, reassuring. "Right now, my job is to worry about you."

"Me?" Faber's eyes widened. "I'm fine."

She was anything but. "You don't seem it, Madison. You've seen something awful this morning; it's bound to have an impact."

The girl peered into Ingrid's face, scrutinizing her. Ingrid found her impossible to read.

"I'm scared." Faber dropped her voice to a whisper.

"That's understandable. You want me to call someone for you? Your parents?"

Faber clenched her jaw. "No."

"I can stay with you just as long as you need."

Faber slumped back onto the couch.

"The lawyer should be here any minute," Ingrid said. "He'll explain your rights, but like I said, you can remain silent if you choose to."

"Why would I want to do that?" Faber's eyebrows knitted together. "My friend is dead. I want to help the police all I can."

"They've arrested you, Madison. Yes, you want to help them with their enquiries into Lauren's death, but you hit a police officer."

The girl sniffed and stuck out her bottom lip.

"Though I'd say it's likely they'll drop the charges, given your evident distress."

Ingrid stared into Faber's face, and an unbidden image filled her mind. She screwed up her eyes in an attempt to banish it. In an instant she was back in Minnesota, fourteen again and feeling more helpless than Faber did now. *Not this, not here.*

"Are you OK?" Faber asked her. "What just happened?"

Ingrid forced a smile. "I'm fine."

"You don't look fine."

"It doesn't matter."

"Obviously it does. You said I could trust you, but now you're scaring me."

Ingrid placed her hand on Faber's knee. "I'm sorry. Old memories."

Faber looked puzzled. "Oh my God, this happened to you, didn't it?" Those eyes didn't miss much.

"Not quite," Ingrid said. "But I did lose a friend."

"I'm sorry."

"It was years ago."

"But you're not over it."

"Creeps up on me sometimes."

"Was your friend murdered?"

Ingrid had said too much. "This isn't about me. Let's focus on what you need."

"But I thought—" The door to the interview room opened, and McKittrick entered with Ralph Mills, the tall detective who had escorted Angela Tate from the house in New Cross.

"Feeling calmer?" McKittrick asked Faber. There was no trace of sympathy in her voice. Ingrid had never worked with McKittrick before, so had no idea how her friend operated professionally. "We won't talk about the assault charge without your solicitor here—"

"Go ahead. Agent Skyberg is looking after me." Faber grabbed Ingrid's hand.

"—but I would like to get a statement from you about what happened this morning. Are you up to that, Madison? I can call you Madison, can't I?"

"Sure." The girl shrugged.

"Thank you." McKittrick sat down and opened a fresh notebook. DC Mills did the same. "Can you tell us the exact time you discovered Miss Shelbourne?"

Faber nodded almost imperceptibly. "I went to her apartment early. We'd arranged to meet before class. So I guess it must have been eight. Certainly no later than eight thirty."

"This morning?"

Faber glanced at Ingrid, her confusion evident. "Of course this morning."

"How did you gain access to the property?"

"I have a key. We used to be roommates. Lauren has—had keys to my apartment too."

"So you were close?"

"We looked out for one another, you know? Us 'Yanks' gotta stick together." She made air quotes with fingers raw from the forensics swabbing process.

"So Lauren was expecting you this morning?" McKittrick asked.

"She wanted to discuss her thesis with me. She was getting a little anxious about it, and I said I'd help."

"And the apartment door was locked when you arrived?"

Faber nodded. "I went straight up to the third floor. Banged on the door, waited. When there was no response, I used the key. The door was stiff, sticky. I had to force it open."

"Then what did you do?"

"I called her name from the hallway outside the apartment."

"And she didn't answer?"

Faber wrinkled her nose. "Of course she didn't."

"I'm sorry if my questions seem obvious, but we do have to be very precise."

Faber took a shaky breath and swallowed. "I stepped into the apartment and called her name again, louder this time." She blinked. "That's when I saw her. Just lying there." She snatched a Kleenex from the box on the table. "Who would do something like that to her?" She stared at McKittrick, her eyes wide, as if she were actually waiting for an answer.

Faber's hands dropped into her lap, and she picked at the Kleenex. She hadn't dabbed her eyes or blown her nose.

McKittrick pressed ahead. "Do you know if Lauren had fallen out with anyone recently?"

"What?"

"Did Lauren have any enemies?"

Faber snorted. "No way. Not Lauren. She never fought with anyone."

"How about boyfriends?" McKittrick asked. "Was Lauren in a relationship?"

Faber wriggled in her seat and pulled a face.

"What is it?"

"I don't know if she was seeing anyone. Whenever I asked, she got evasive. She'd change the subject. But she had that look sometimes, like she was keeping a secret. And sometimes she had that other look." She turned to stare at Mills. "Like she was getting laid."

The detective's face blushed, and Mills looked down at his notepad.

How could a thirtysomething homicide detective be so easily embarrassed?

"Can you hazard a guess?" McKittrick asked. "Someone she studied with, perhaps?"

"Why do you want to know? Do you think he could have killed her?"

McKittrick took a deep breath. "In a case like this, we're particularly interested in her close relationships. Can you think of any reason she wouldn't want to tell you who she was dating?"

Faber shrugged. "Maybe she just wanted to keep it a secret. Maybe she was embarrassed."

"About what?"

"Whoever was screwing her."

Ingrid flinched. She had been expecting Faber to say 'sleeping with.'

"What about other friends? Would they know who she was seeing?"

Faber shook her head. "If she was going to tell anyone, it would've been me."

Ingrid was taken aback by her certainty.

"Can you give us a list of her friends' names at college? We will need to speak to all of them." McKittrick scribbled something in her notebook.

"You can find them on her cell phone," Faber said. Her tone was now infused with a teenager's snark, a brooding petulance.

McKittrick's nostrils flared ever so slightly. "A list from you would be very much appreciated."

"Sure, it won't take long."

"Are you saying Lauren didn't have many friends?"

Faber pinged the elastic cuff of the Tyvek coverall. "She didn't really click with many people. She could be a little... What's the word you Brits use?" She played with the stitching while she tried to remember. "Brittle. That's it."

"Brittle? Lauren had mental health issues?"

"Not exactly. At least... none I know of. She could just be a little... off beam now and then."

McKittrick scribbled more notes. "Thank you, Madison, we really appreciate your cooperation. Now, when was the last time you saw Lauren?"

Faber's mouth dropped open. "You know when."

McKittrick drew a breath. "I'm sorry, I meant *before* this morning."

"You mean when was the last time I saw her alive?" Faber shuddered.

Ingrid had heard enough. "I think we need to take a break."

McKittrick gave Ingrid a stern stare and raised an eyebrow. Where was her compassion?

"I'm fine to carry on," Faber said in such a way that it sounded like a rebuke to Ingrid's concern. "We had lunch together on campus yesterday." The girl wasn't helping herself: she was coming across as cold and uncaring. Ingrid remembered her own odd behavior when she lost her best friend. She understood that shock can make a person appear unhinged.

"How did Lauren seem to you?" Mills asked.

Faber pursed her lips as she considered her answer. "Fine. No, more than fine, actually. Happy even. Maybe the happiest I've seen her."

McKittrick made more notes, then flipped back through the notebook. After a few moments of concentrated reading, she looked up and stared at Faber. "When did you and Lauren stop being roommates?"

McKittrick's sudden change of direction took Faber by surprise. She turned to Ingrid for guidance, and Ingrid nodded encouragingly.

"In January. I went away for a long weekend. When I came back, she'd moved out."

"Why?"

Faber shrugged. "She said something about wanting to be more independent."

"What did she mean?" McKittrick asked. She was questioning Faber like a murder suspect, and Ingrid's concern was mounting.

"She didn't really explain. But I guess, if I think about it, I had assumed the big sister role. I took on most of the responsibilities. You know, making sure the rent got paid on time, settling the bills, cooking. I guess she wanted to prove she could survive on her own."

"And how did that make you feel?" McKittrick's questions were taking advantage of the late arrival of Faber's lawyer.

"Feel? It didn't make me feel anything. I was a little surprised she hadn't discussed it with me in advance."

"You weren't at all upset by her departure?"

Ingrid didn't want to tread on her friend's professional toes, but she would be handling this interview completely differently. After four years working in the Violent Crimes Against Children Unit, Ingrid knew how to handle adolescents. Faber might legally be an adult, but she was nevertheless vulnerable.

"It's almost as if she was snubbing you," McKittrick continued, "throwing everything you'd done for her back in your face?"

"No, I was happy for her." Faber bristled: McKittrick was getting to her.

After a pause, Mills picked up the questioning. "Did you ever fight with Lauren?"

"Why are you asking me that?"

"Please answer the question, Madison." His tone was gentle but urgent.

"What are you trying to say?" Faber jumped up. "We never fought!"

Ingrid and Mills also got to their feet.

"We are taking a break now," Ingrid said. She turned to McKittrick. "Madison is a young woman experiencing one of the worst days of her life. I must insist you wait for her lawyer to arrive."

McKittrick, still seated, looked up at Faber. "Just one last question."

"She was like a sister to me. I can't believe you're suggesting—"

Faber's flow was interrupted by the door bursting open. A steel-haired woman in a power suit and dangerously high heels marched into the room, a bewildered uniformed cop trailing in her wake. She pushed past Ingrid and Mills and stopped next to Faber. She slipped an arm around the student's shoulders. "That's quite enough, detective. This interview is now terminated."

4

―――――――

"Mr Brewster?"

Ingrid flashed her ID toward the narrow gap. The door closed and opened again. Ingrid slipped in from the hall to see a shoeless fat man padding down the plushly carpeted interior hallway of his luxury hotel suite.

"Well, come on!" Brewster yelled over his shoulder. "I don't have all goddamn day."

On the phone Sol had told her to 'play nice': he was aware of Brewster's reputation and wanted to make sure Ingrid didn't rise to the businessman's bait. From what she'd seen of Brewster already, it was going to be a struggle. She wasn't happy being taken away from chaperoning Faber, but Sol said it was important Brewster knew the embassy was taking his case seriously.

She entered the bedroom and found the red-faced businessman tying a dressing gown over his fleshy belly, the fat undulating like Jell-O. Diabetes and heart failure were just waiting to happen. The lack of wrinkles on his doughy face made it hard to determine his age. He could be anywhere between thirty-five and fifty.

"How long is this going to take?" Brewster barked. "I have better things to do with my time."

You and me both. "I'm sure you want this dealt with thoroughly, sir."

"I don't want it 'dealt with' at all." He tapped his watch, the leather strap secured on the very last hole.

"You called us, sir."

"Not through any choice of my own. I have an obligation to inform the authorities when something like this gets stolen. Let's get on with it, shall we?" He gestured toward an empty space on a narrow desk opposite the bed. A power cord snaked into thin air.

"Your laptop has been stolen?" Ingrid had meant it to sound more like a statement than a question.

"You don't know?"

"Just confirming the facts, Mr Brewster." She was pushing a boulder up a steep incline.

"Laptop, credit cards, cash."

"And you won't report this to the police, is that correct?"

"It's a diplomatic incident, not a criminal one." His sneer was threatening to turn into a snarl.

"I see." She didn't. She was grasping in the dark. "I'm going to need a bit of background, Mr Brewster. What line of business are you in?"

"What level of security clearance do you have at the embassy?" Brewster looked her up and down.

"That's not something I can discuss."

He shook his head. "Well, that tells me plenty."

"Sir?"

"Unless you have level five clearance, I cannot tell you what I do, or what was on the laptop, but there are documents on there of a sensitive nature."

"National security?"

"It would be more accurate to say commercially sensitive with security repercussions." He looked out the gothic arched window of his hotel down onto the busy four-lane highway of Euston Road. "The content is encrypted. I'm confident the information is completely secure, but there are people in government who need to know about the potential for a breach."

"Sir, I work for the FBI. I understand embassy officials are informing relevant parties via the regular channels. I am a criminal investigator, and as it is my understanding there was information on your laptop that belongs to the United States government, it is my job to retrieve it."

He huffed.

"Do you have the make and model? The serial number?"

"I can get my secretary to email you that sort of thing."

"That would be helpful. Now, do you know an approximate time your possessions were taken? I'll need to interview the staff on shift."

"No, you don't."

Her cell phone buzzed in her bag, vibrating noisily against her metal water flask. No doubt it would be her fiancé again. They hadn't spoken for days, possibly weeks. She ignored it.

"The robbery had nothing to do with the hotel staff."

"How can you be so—?"

"I had a... guest last night." He leaned his plump forearms on the window ledge. "It's an agency I've used every other time I've visited. I've never had any trouble before." He held up a hand, his wedding ring digging into the flesh of his finger. "Before you ask, I've already been in touch with the agency. All the contact information they have is fake."

"An escort agency?" His dressing gown made him look like a sleazeball.

"I'm a businessman on a long trip from home." He turned to face her. "It's not exactly unusual."

Ingrid took a notebook out of her bag. "Can you give me a description of your visitor? I should be able to track her down."

Brewster's shoulders tensed.

"A description?"

"What did she look like?" She joined him at the window and caught sight of a skyline of modern glass spikes and ancient religious spires. His eyes were screwed tight shut.

"I can assure you I will be discreet." *You cheating bastard.*

Brewster let out a long sigh. "Dark short hair, mid to late twenties. Six feet two, one-eighty pounds, muscular." He opened his eyes and studied her face, daring a response.

Ingrid fought hard not to appear surprised. "Ethnicity?"

"White."

"Nationality?"

"How the hell would I know? I wasn't paying to make chitchat with him."

"Did you notice an accent?"

"He sounded British; that's the best I can do."

"I'll need the name of the escort agency and a complete list of what was taken."

He glanced at a large flight case shoved beneath the narrow desk.

"What's in the case?" she asked.

"Nothing was taken from it." He stepped between her and the case. He was hiding something.

"How long are you in London?" she asked him.

"Another forty-eight hours. And then I will be back again in a week."

"And you're sure no one else had access to your room? Only the escort?"

"Correct." He was getting agitated.

"I have to ask you, sir. Is there anything personally compromising on the laptop?"

His eyes narrowed. "It is my *work* laptop."

"I'm trying to ascertain a motive for the theft, Mr. Brewster. If, as you suspect, the thief wants to access whatever sensitive information is on the device—and if that's the case, I imagine he'll be easier to find—but if his intention is merely to blackmail you"—she looked deliberately at his wedding ring—"he might be harder to track down."

Brewster said nothing.

"I need to ask: were you conscious the entire time the escort was in your room?"

She could tell he wished he hadn't called the theft in. "I may have nodded off."

"Might you have been drugged?"

He looked puzzled.

"Rohypnol," she explained. "The 'date rape' drug. There may be other crimes he could be charged with if we can't prove the theft."

Brewster had had enough. He looked at his wrist. "Dear God, is that the time?" His flesh bulged around his watch strap. "I really do think you should be going, Miss Skyberg."

The man was objectionable.

"It's *Agent* Skyberg." She dropped her notebook into her bag and turned for the door. "I'll show myself out."

When she reached the door, she glanced back and saw Greg Brewster crouching down for the aluminum flight case. She paused, suddenly needing to straighten her collar in the mirror.

He looked up at her. "You can go now."

She let herself out. Ingrid had no desire to help him out, but every single piece of her wanted to know what he was hiding.

5

Ingrid arrived at the embassy building in Grosvenor Square shortly before lunch. She fired up her computer, determined to do a bit of background research on Greg Brewster. While she went through the long-winded log-in procedure, her mind drifted back to the scene in Lauren Shelbourne's apartment. She saw again the lifeless body and was overwhelmed with sadness. She wondered which of the embassy staff had told the girl's parents.

Ingrid closed her eyes, and inevitably an image of her lost school friend appeared, the way she'd looked the last time Ingrid had seen her. The last time anybody had seen her. Ingrid took a moment to offer up a silent wish. *One day I'll find you.* Then she puffed out a breath, snapped her eyes open, and focused on her computer monitor. She tapped Brewster's name into the database search field and tried hard to concentrate on something other than dead girls. There was no record of him. She tried another database, and this time an alert flashed up: 'access denied.'

On her way through the bullpen to Sol's office, Ingrid passed a couple of other agents. One acknowledged her politely with a nod; the other totally blanked her. She knew her role in the criminal division was seen as lowlier than the counterterrorism work her colleagues were involved in, but sometimes the way she was treated felt like more than rudeness.

She reached the end of a wood-paneled, airless corridor and rapped on the frame of Sol's half-open door. The office was empty. She checked the hallway both ways. No sign of Sol. Or anyone else. After one last glance up and down the empty hallway, she slipped inside the office and behind Sol's desk. She looked for a scrap of paper and a pen. Sol's computer woke from sleep mode. Ingrid stared at the cursor flashing enticingly at her from the search field in the center of the screen. Maybe Sol had a higher clearance level—he was bound to, wasn't he—and she wouldn't get the access denied message if she searched for Brewster on his computer? Her fingers hovered over the keyboard.

"Can I help you with something?"

"Sol, hi." She swallowed hard. "I, um, thought you always ate a sandwich at your desk."

"I'm not sure that's the correct way to address a superior officer." He folded his arms and glared at her. A moment later his face broke into a wide grin, but as he walked toward her, Ingrid got the feeling he was scrutinizing the merest flicker of movement in her expression. He slipped behind his desk and checked his monitor. He glanced up at Ingrid and narrowed his eyes.

"What was it you needed, agent?" He reeked of cigarettes. He always did.

"I don't think I have sufficient security clearance for this Brewster assignment. I can't find out who he is, or what he does."

Sol raised an eyebrow. "You don't actually need to know, Ingrid. All you have to do is find his laptop."

"Which would be much easier if I knew what someone's motivation for stealing it was."

He scratched his salt-and-pepper beard. "I appreciate that, but it's national security. Need-to-know. Just put a trace on the serial number and do your best."

Ingrid felt her fury rising. "Is there something I've done, Sol? Some reason I don't have clearance?"

He pulled off his wire-frame glasses and cleaned them with a cloth. "What makes you say that?"

"Am I still on probation?"

He leaned back in his chair. "You shouldn't be. We've made your appointment permanent, haven't we?"

"Not as far as I know."

He replaced his spectacles. "Are you happy here? At the embassy? In London?"

Where the hell had that come from? She thought about the dark looks she got from her colleagues. "Mostly."

"Good. We should probably do something about finding you an apartment."

It would be nice to leave the hotel. "I'd rather you did something about my clearance level."

Sol laid his hands flat against the desk and stared at them for a moment. "I'll see what I can do. But in the meantime, find the laptop. Impress the people who need to be impressed."

He might as well have said 'run along, little girl.' Ingrid had warmed to Sol. He was usually an avuncular, easygoing presence who was slow to anger and didn't rush to judgment. But if he didn't have her back, if she wasn't sure he was on her side, then she should think about moving home to DC. Ingrid wandered slowly in the direction of the criminal division office. Jennifer, her assistant, had returned from lunch.

"Hey," she said brightly. "Did David Eustace turn up at the interview this morning?"

Ingrid, still rattled from Sol's stonewalling, sat down heavily. "Who's Eustace?"

"He's, like, the embassy criminal lawyer." Jen was a total Valley Girl, down to her sunny Californian personality and the inclusion of the word *like* in every sentence.

Ingrid pictured the smartly dressed woman who had terminated the Met's questioning of Madison Faber. She definitely didn't look like a David. "No," she said. "A woman turned up."

"Strange. He's normally very reliable."

"Can you give me his number?" Ingrid said. "I'd like to give him a call."

"Sure thing." Jen swiveled breezily in her chair and flipped through an old-fashioned Rolodex. It matched the rest of the office, which could easily be described as 'vintage.' It could also be called 'dated.' It looked like the set of an '80s cop show.

Ingrid nudged her mouse, and her computer flicked into life. The 'access denied' alert was still in the middle of her screen. It was clear Sol wasn't going to give her any more information, but there had to be another way to discover what Brewster's business trip was really about.

All she had to do was figure out how.

6

The arrival of Faber's high-powered lawyer, paid for by the girl's family, had resulted in Madison being released without charge. Now that Faber no longer needed embassy assistance, Ingrid's job was to ensure Lauren Shelbourne's death was investigated properly.

Ingrid made an early start, arriving a little after nine at Loriners, the college where Lauren Shelbourne had been studying. The young woman's grieving parents wanted her body repatriated, and for that to happen, all the paperwork—including Ingrid's report—had to be completed.

Loriners was a mix of impressive twentieth-century brick buildings and ultramodern concrete, glass and steel structures, haphazardly stacked cubes, their doors and windows painted in bright primary colors. A network of walkways at various levels connected the muddle of architectural styles together. It was a glorious spring day, and the students were in short-sleeve tees, with a handful braving shorts and cutoffs. The weather was in contrast to the mood on campus: everyone seemed quiet and subdued, speaking in hushed tones and moving slowly.

Ingrid claimed her visitor's badge from the administration block and memorized the map of the campus. She surveyed the piazza in front of her and spotted the building she was interested in. Just to the left of it was Detective Constable Ralph Mills chatting to a uniformed colleague. She ducked behind a tree: she was there to report on the thoroughness of the Met's investigation, and she'd rather they weren't aware she was on site.

There was a quality about Mills Ingrid had warmed to. He was tall, slim, with collar-length hair and substantial sideburns. He looked like he could have been the bass player in one of the Britpop bands that had dominated the charts in the 1990s. Maybe that was who he reminded her of—there was definitely something unnervingly familiar about him. Unlike most homicide cops she'd known, Ralph Mills gave the impression he was caring and compassionate. She imagined he was very good at dealing with bereaved families. His height gave him presence, but his slight stature and easygoing nature meant he wasn't intimidating. He would probably be a good person to ask for the preliminary autopsy report.

When Ingrid had called Natasha McKittrick the previous evening to request it, the person who'd answered the call transferred her not to the detective inspector, but to a press officer, who told her precisely nothing and treated her like a journalist rather than a fellow law enforcement officer. When she'd complained, she was told to go through 'proper channels.' Which was what she'd thought she'd done calling McKittrick in the first place. She could understand why McKittrick was keeping her at arm's length—no one likes another investigator scrutinizing how you run a case—but it was as if their friendship counted for nothing.

With Mills safely occupied on another part of campus, Ingrid made her way to the large cafeteria housed in one of the traditional Edwardian redbrick buildings. Inside, it was furnished with long wooden refectory tables and benches, coats of arms decorating the walls below the high ceiling. Despite the dark wood and stone floors, the cafeteria was actually quite a welcoming space. The students were more relaxed than they had been outside, most of them chattering noisily to one another, raising their voices to be heard above the general din. She grabbed a plastic tray and joined the line waiting for a cooked breakfast, hoping to tune in to any conversations where Lauren Shelbourne's name was mentioned. She didn't have to wait long. Two excited teenagers lined up behind her. They were already in full flow, speculating about the death.

"Martina said they found her naked. Raped, Martina said. The police think it might be a serial killer."

"Who else has he killed?"

"Well, no one yet—no one we've heard about. But all serial killers have to start somewhere, don't they?" She shuddered.

"Makes me glad I'm still living at home. I bitch about the commute, but being two bus rides away actually makes me feel safer."

"I wonder who's going to be next." There was a mawkish thrill in her tone.

Ingrid took a good look at them. They were ordinary students, even a little bookish. One sported Harry Potter–style spectacles, the other had a wild head of red hair stuck up in a ragged bun held together by an HB pencil. Nice girls. Why were they talking about the suspicious death of a fellow student as if it were an episode of their favorite soap opera?

Ingrid reached the bakery display and helped herself to a rubbery-looking raisin pastry. It didn't really matter if it tasted as bad as it looked, she had no intention of eating it. She paid and found a place at the center of one of the long wooden tables, where she could listen to as many conversations as possible while she played with her food.

As soon as she sat down, the surrounding chairs were vacated. Just as she was wondering whether she'd forgotten to apply deodorant after her run that morning, a gawky, geeky teen shoved his food tray onto the table and sat heavily on the hard wooden bench directly opposite her. His plate was stacked high with fries, eggs, and a pie buried beneath a landslide of baked beans. He definitely wouldn't be starting class on an empty stomach. She watched as he smothered the whole lot in tomato ketchup and dove and attacked the fries as if they were an enemy army. She looked away as soon as he shoved the first forkful into his baby-bird gaping mouth, and considered switching tables. She picked a flake off her pastry and popped it into her mouth. She chewed slowly and glanced up at her uninvited companion.

"What's in the pie?" she asked.

When he'd recovered from the shock of her dialog opener, he answered with a full mouth, "Steak." He swallowed. "And mushrooms. Thankfully though, not many. Mushrooms make me gag."

"Then why did you choose the pie?"

"Halal, innit? Only meaty thing on the menu that is."

"But it's OK?"

He shrugged back at her. "S'all right."

She smiled at him, taking a proper look at his face. His greasy complexion mirrored the fatty mess on his plate.

"Is the campus usually this... subdued?" she asked.

"Is it? Hadn't noticed." He carried on shoveling his food, barely chewing it before each noisy gulp. "Might be something to do with that girl who died."

Ingrid sat up straight. "You knew her?"

"Do you?"

"Me? How would I know her?"

"You're American, aren't you? She was American."

"Hey, it's a big place." She smiled again. "I've just heard a few people talking about her this morning."

"You're new here. I would definitely have noticed you before otherwise. Are you a lecturer?"

She shook her head.

"Admin staff?"

"I'm just checking the place out. Prospective PhD student."

"Mo," he said and nodded at her. "Short for Mohammed."

"I figured it wasn't short for Maureen."

"Nice—an American with a sense of humor." He narrowed his eyes. "What's your name?"

Ingrid paused a beat before answering. "Sarah." She glanced down at her visitor's badge and quickly shoved it inside her jacket.

"OK, Sarah... so what can I say to persuade you to come here?"

"I'm not sure you can say anything. I've heard people talking about a serial killer on the loose."

"You shouldn't listen to rumors. Most of the students here are complete morons."

"That's not exactly a glowing recommendation."

"Not all of us!" He put down his knife and fork. "The postgrad stuff is all right. But I wouldn't be here if I'd got the grades for Imperial."

Ingrid tore off a corner of pastry and rolled it between her fingers like a ball of modeling clay. "So far you're not convincing me."

He shrugged and grabbed his cutlery from the table. "Shame. You'd improve the scenery round here a bit." He stared unashamedly into her face.

Ingrid eyeballed him until he dropped his gaze to his plate. "Just saying," he mumbled.

"I'll take it as a compliment."

"How many other colleges are you visiting?"

Ingrid paused before answering, she hadn't gotten that far working out her cover story. How many would sound right? "Oh, um, a few."

"Which ones have you rejected?"

"None so far."

"I suppose... if you're gonna make an... informed decision..." He stared at his plate. "I should tell you about the girl who died last week."

"Another girl?" Ingrid remembered the question Angela Tate had fired at McKittrick when the reporter had barged into Lauren Shelbourne's apartment. "So there *is* a serial killer?"

"Nah, nothing like that." He shoveled another quivering pile of meat, gravy and pastry into his mouth. "It was suicide. I saw it happen. She jumped from the top of the admin block."

"You saw her jump?"

"I saw her fly. Until she stopped. Splat! Guts and brains all over the shop. They still haven't managed to clean it all up." He shook more ketchup onto the remains of his pie.

"Must have shaken you up."

"Not really. I don't mind the sight of blood. I'd be a useless doctor if I did, wouldn't I?"

"You're studying medicine?"

"I like cutting stuff up."

Ingrid glanced at the knife he was wielding over his plate.

"Did you know her? The girl who jumped?"

"No."

"But as far as you're aware, her death isn't connected to the one that happened yesterday?"

"There isn't a serial killer—you don't need to worry."

"I don't suppose you knew… what was her name… Lauren?"

"Depends on your definition of 'knew.' I'd seen her face around. The psychology grads like to put themselves about a bit. But they're a stuck-up bunch. Especially the Americans. No offense."

"None taken."

"They're all too important to speak to lowly undergrads. Until they need another recruit for one of their Mickey Mouse experiments. Always looking for volunteers for them. Then it's all 'Hi, Mohammed, how are you? Come and have your testicles wired up to an electrical current and we'll measure how loud you scream.'"

"Wait a minute—you're not telling me they're *torturing* students?" Ingrid leaned forward.

"No, I was exaggerating." He chewed another mouthful of fries. "But not by much."

"What kind of experiments, then?"

The young medic inched toward her, clearly excited to have anyone listen to what he had to say. "I know for a fact that they—" He pulled away suddenly, distracted by something or someone across the room.

"What is it?" Ingrid turned to follow his gaze and saw two male students deep in conversation. They were wearing matching green and purple polo shirts.

Mohammed slumped in his seat, making himself smaller. "Nothing."

"You were telling me about the experiments."

He pulled a face. "I don't really know anything about them. Don't listen to me. Loriners is a good college. You should definitely do your PhD here." He shoveled the last of his fries in his mouth and stood up. "Are you planning on finishing that?" He nodded at the pastry.

"Be my guest."

He produced a used square of aluminum foil from his bag, smoothed out the wrinkles on the table and carefully transferred her uneaten breakfast onto it. He wrapped it up in a neat cylinder and slipped it into his backpack. "I'm not a big fan of the sugary stuff, but there's no point in wasting it."

"Those two guys…" Ingrid gestured to where the students wearing the purple and green shirts had been standing. "What are they, in a sports team or something?"

"Don't know what you're talking about. I didn't see anyone." He nodded a goodbye, weaved quickly around the table and disappeared through the main door.

Ingrid shoved her dirty tray onto a nearby stack and followed him out. But by the time she'd reached the exit, Mohammed had melted into the crowd. There was no sign of the purple and green shirts either. Ingrid wondered what they might have done to have gotten Mohammed so spooked.

She crossed the piazza in search of the psychology department where Lauren Shelbourne had studied. Her attention was snagged by a man in overalls up a ladder, scrubbing at a scrawl of graffiti on one of the gray concrete walls. As she approached, she saw the first two words painted in bright yellow paint, previously obscured by the workman's ladder.

She froze.

lauren shelbourne = whore

7

Ingrid asked the janitor to stop: he was destroying evidence in a potential murder. He refused, and without UK powers of arrest, she had settled for him wiping some of the paint onto a tissue so she could get it forensically analyzed. She carefully folded the tissue, stored it inside a candy wrapper and went in search of the office of Lauren Shelbourne's psychology professor. She knocked on the door and opened it quickly without waiting for a reply.

"Can I help you?" A forty-something white man, with close-cut silver hair over his head and most of his face, stared up at her from his perch on the edge of a desk. He was lean, long-limbed and held himself with an athlete's poise and the confidence of a man used to students hanging on his every word. His eyes were red, as if he'd been up all night.

"I'm so sorry to interrupt." Ingrid nodded to the four young students, three men and a woman, sitting in a tight semicircle of chairs. One chair was vacant. "Professor Younger?"

"That much you must have gleaned from the brass plate on my door." He sounded irritated.

Ingrid flashed her ID at him. "Special Agent Skyberg. From the US Embassy."

Professor Younger tensed at the mention of her title, then again at the word *embassy*. She sensed a general stiffening in the students' postures.

"We were just finishing up, anyway." He glared at the students, who scraped back their chairs and got to their feet.

"Actually, if it's not too inconvenient, I'd like to speak to all of you." Ingrid smiled at the four suspicious faces, all of them scrutinizing her just as closely as she was studying them. The woman folded her arms across her chest and looked at the floor in embarrassment. Two of the young men wore Chinese-style collarless gray shirts and plain black corduroy pants, almost like a uniform. The third was more interesting to Ingrid. He was the only student to return her gaze, making eye contact for much longer than was polite. He was also wearing a purple and green polo shirt. She smiled and stared back at him, determined he should look away first. When he did, she said, "I want to talk to you about Lauren Shelbourne."

All four students mumbled at once, making vague noises that at no point threatened to coalesce into actual words.

"I'm sorry, what was that?" Ingrid stared directly at the female student.

"I didn't really know her," she said.

Ingrid pointed at the extra chair. "The registrar's office told me this was Lauren's study group. I'm supposing the empty chair is hers?"

The girl looked imploringly at Professor Younger.

"The whole group is very shaken by what has happened," he explained. "I'm not sure firing questions at them is entirely appropriate. They're clearly still in shock. Can't it wait?"

"So you did know Lauren?"

The students nodded and mumbled again.

"It's terrible, what's happened," the student in the polo shirt said. "Do you know if the police are treating it as murder?"

Professor Younger threw the young man a warning look.

"I'm sorry, I can't discuss that with you."

Younger levered himself off his desk and opened his arms wide. He moved forward slowly, shepherding his flock toward the door. "They should really be getting back to their studies."

Ingrid stood to one side and watched the students shuffle out of the room. The man in the polo shirt was the last to leave. "Which sport do you play?" Ingrid pointed at his shirt.

For a moment he was confused.

Younger came to his rescue, butting in before he could answer for himself. "Hockey. Thomas represents the college in the university league."

"Isn't this the off-season?" Ingrid had no clue which season the Brits played hockey. She just didn't want to let him off the hook that easily.

"We play all year round," the bemused student finally managed before leaving the room.

"Good luck!" Ingrid called after him.

He turned back. "I'm sorry?"

"In your next match."

"Right, yeah. Thanks."

Ingrid closed the door. "I'm hoping you have a few moments for me, Professor?"

"Please." He gestured toward a leather chair close to the desk. "Call me Stuart."

Ingrid remained on her feet. "I'm trying to get some background information. Perhaps you could paint me a picture of Lauren's life here at Loriners?"

Younger let out a long, quiet sigh.

"I guess it's hit you hardest of all," Ingrid said.

He blinked at her. "Why do you say that?"

"Lauren was effectively in your care during her time here."

"It's not as if I could have done anything to prevent what happened." He lifted a trembling hand and ran it over his short hair.

"Even so."

He nodded, bit his lip then made deliberate eye contact. "Why is the American embassy involved? Surely the police are investigating the circumstances of her death?" He scratched the side of his face, the pale skin beneath his beard reddening in long streaks.

"It's a matter of routine."

He frowned at her. "I've already spoken to the police, a chap named... Mills, I think. I answered all his questions. Can't you liaise with him rather than asking me the same things all over again?"

"My role is to make sure the police investigate thoroughly, that if a crime has been committed, they deliver justice for American citizens."

"I see. I didn't know you did that sort of thing." He blinked nervously.

"Tell me about Lauren."

"I'm confused. Are you saying Lauren was murdered? The police didn't give that impression."

"I really can't comment." Ingrid moved toward him. "What kind of student was Lauren?"

He blinked again. "Lauren was, um, an exceptional student. Quiet. Reserved. Always impeccably polite. Her parents brought her up that way." His eyes focused on an invisible distant object. "She'll be missed."

Ingrid smiled at him. "As far as you're aware, Lauren hadn't made any enemies here at college?"

"Enemies?" His eyes bulged. "What makes you say that?"

"You must have seen the graffiti?"

"Graffiti? I don't understand."

"On one side of the science block. It was—"

At that moment the door burst open so hard and fast Ingrid had to jump to avoid getting hit.

"Why are you ignoring my calls?"

Madison Faber stomped into the room, and Younger held up his hands defensively. Following his gaze, Faber spun round.

"Oh," she said.

"Hello, Madison," Ingrid said. "How are you doing?"

Faber cleared her throat. "Why are you here?"

"Actually, I'd like to talk to you. We didn't really get the chance yesterday. After the lawyer arrived." She smiled warmly at the student. "I'm glad to see you're well enough to come into college."

It took a few seconds for the scowl on Faber's face to soften. She turned back to the professor. "We have to talk," she told him. "I'll find you later."

8

Ingrid thanked Younger for his time and raced to catch up with Faber as she crossed the piazza. The girl was very pale, her large eyes bloodshot through lack of sleep. Ahead, the janitor had water-blasted all but the final *r* and *e* of the word *whore* from the concrete facade.

"That must have really upset Lauren. Did she speak to you about it?"

Faber raised an eyebrow. "It was new this morning."

"It was?" Ingrid hoped Mills and his colleague had spotted it before the cleaning operation started.

Faber studied the janitor as he water-blasted the *r* of yellow paint. "It's the first time I've seen it."

"Any idea who would have written it?"

She shrugged in response. "How would I know?"

Ingrid shook her head. "Who would want to say something like that about Lauren, in these circumstances?"

Faber stared at the wall. "People never fail to appall me. The more I study, the more convinced I am in the limitless human capacity for cruelty. Some people are just plain evil. Surely I don't need to tell you that, with your job?"

Ingrid turned to her. "You still believe Lauren had no enemies?"

"Everything I've learned tells me that says more about the person who wrote it than Lauren." Faber inhaled sharply, her nostrils narrowing. "They heard her name on the news and decided to make a little news themselves. Make a mark. Shock the college authorities."

"You're the psychology student," Ingrid said. "You'll no doubt have some insights."

"Are you making fun of me, Agent Skyberg?"

"Absolutely not. No."

The girl looked offended.

"No, I meant it. I wasn't being glib." Ingrid needed to change the subject. "I'm glad I ran into you today. I wanted to make sure you felt you were treated properly by the Metropolitan Police yesterday."

Faber's pace slowed. "I guess they were only doing their job."

"Was it tough?"

"Finding Lauren was horrific enough." Ingrid's thoughts seized on the image of Lauren's crumpled body, emptied of blood, and the gaping wound in her forehead where she had smashed into the coffee table. "Reliving it for the cops was almost as bad."

Ingrid pushed her hands into her pants pockets. "I hope they were gentle with you."

Faber bristled. "Like I say, it's their job."

"That's a good attitude to have. It'll help with future interviews."

Faber pulled up. "How many more are there likely to be?"

"Um, well, I'm not entirely familiar with procedures here in the UK, but given you were the one who found Lauren, they will want to rule you out as a suspect. That's standard in every case."

"But Miriam said there was no need for me to worry."

"Your attorney? I'm sure she's right. But nine times out of ten, the perpetrator is either the boyfriend or the witness who reports the crime. Don't take it personally if they want to speak to you again. And the autopsy may well say it was an accident, anyway." Ingrid rested a hand on Faber's shoulder. "Between the embassy and your attorney, we have everything covered. You don't need to be overly concerned." She tugged gently on Faber's arm.

Faber wouldn't be budged. She was staring into space, chewing her lip. "You don't think I had anything to do with Lauren's death, do you?"

"Of course not."

Faber put her hand on top of Ingrid's. "It helps to know you're in my corner."

"You have no need to doubt that. Come on, let me buy you a coffee."

"I guess... after losing your friend... you understand what I'm going through."

Ingrid said nothing. She didn't like that Faber knew, and she certainly didn't like that the girl had brought it up, but Ingrid wasn't about to give her a hard time. Faber was alone in a strange country, thousands of miles from home: at least when she had lost Megan, Ingrid's mom and grandma had been around to look out for her. "I'm here for you." She pulled out a card from her jacket pocket. "However I can help."

"Thank you." Faber tucked Ingrid's contact details into her bag, and they walked to the cafeteria. "Can I tell you something?"

"Sure."

"I've been thinking things over since yesterday," Faber said, withdrawing her hand from Ingrid's arm. "There is something I forgot to mention to the police."

"Whatever it is, you should definitely tell them about it. The smallest of details can help."

"I'm not sure what made me think of it, but it just didn't make any sense."

"Go on."

"The desk in Lauren's apartment was empty. Where was her laptop? Or her iPad? We were supposed to discuss her thesis. She would have been using her computer, surely?"

"Maybe she left her stuff somewhere else?"

"Or maybe they were taken. What if it was a robbery gone wrong?"

"I can mention it to the police if you like?"

Faber, lost in thought, didn't answer. "Poor, poor Lauren. Her parents must be devastated. It puts my pain into perspective."

"Don't underestimate the impact losing Lauren, and finding her, will have on you. Has the college talked to you about counseling?"

Faber nodded vigorously. "That's what I went to see Younger about."

"Oh." Ingrid wasn't sure she believed her. "I'm glad. He seemed pretty upset too. Was Professor Younger close to Lauren?"

Faber shrugged. "I guess tutors and students form a special bond."

"And is he, I'm not sure how they phrase things in the UK, like your personal supervisor? Is that why you were talking to him about counseling?"

They neared the refectory block.

"The exact opposite, in fact."

Ingrid looked blank.

"I don't agree with his research methods. I have my own way of approaching the work. I don't want him getting involved in my personal affairs."

Ingrid hadn't warmed to the professor either. He exuded arrogance. The exterior wall of the cafeteria had a large patch of cleaned concrete.

Ingrid pointed at it. "Do you remember what was written there before it was cleaned off?"

Faber shrugged. "No idea. You see a lot of graffiti in this neighborhood."

They entered the large refectory, and Ingrid ordered them both large black Americanos.

"For here or takeaway?" the barista asked.

"To go," Faber said firmly before Ingrid could answer. Ingrid looked over at the table where she'd spoken to Mohammed. "You're not the first person to comment about Younger's methods. What is it he does that you don't agree with?"

"You should ask Professor Younger himself. My work is paper based: I research other people's research. A lot of people think it's dull, but I happen to consider it groundbreaking." She was displaying more than a little arrogance herself. Ingrid marveled at the girl's confidence. If only she'd been so self-assured in her early twenties.

"I've heard he uses other students in his experiments."

The barista placed two paper cups on the counter. Behind him, a colleague scrawled the word *tonight* across a poster for a music gig.

"Students are cheap and eager. They'll do pretty much anything for a pizza and a few beers."

"What kind of experiments are we talking about?"

"As I said—you'll have to ask Professor Younger. I'm really not that interested in what my peers are doing. I need to be focused on my own studies." Faber locked eyes with Ingrid, her large blue irises catching the light. "Talking of which, I should get to work."

"Already? I'm sure the staff here would make allowances if you took some time off."

Faber took a sip of very hot coffee. "I'd rather keep busy."

"It's as good a strategy as any," Ingrid said. "You've got my card. Call me if there's anything I can do to help."

"Thank you. And thanks for the coffee."

Ingrid watched Faber walk away. The girl's gait was heavy, determined, and she didn't look back or wave. It was as if she'd switched from friendly chat mode to serious academic mode in a heartbeat. There was a Jekyll and Hyde split in Faber's personality, and Ingrid imagined that prickliness made friendships difficult: Lauren's absence would leave a huge hole in her life.

Before Faber reached the door, a tall, familiar figure stepped into the cafeteria. Faber pretended not to have seen DC Mills, but he reached out one of his long arms and placed a palm on her shoulder. Ingrid was too far away to hear what he said to her, but her response was to slap him out of the way and push past him out the door. He ran after her. Ingrid ditched her coffee and did the same.

In the piazza, Faber had been apprehended by Mills and his uniformed colleague. "What's going on?" Ingrid asked. "Has there been a development?"

"I've been leaving messages for Miss Faber all morning," Mills said.

The girl shrugged. "My cell phone must be out of juice."

"I was beginning to fear you'd left the country." He smiled at each woman in turn. "Which wouldn't be a good idea: you need to come with us to the station. Right now."

9

Detective Inspector Natasha McKittrick wheeled round, arms raised ready for a fight, when Ingrid tapped her on the shoulder. She was waiting in line in a sandwich shop five minutes from Lewisham police station.

"Easy!" Ingrid held up her hands, surprised at McKittrick's extreme reaction.

"Christ almighty. What are you doing creeping up on me?"

"Just saying hello." Ingrid smiled at her. "But I can go again. If you'd like."

What was up with McKittrick? Ingrid had got to know her as an easy-going, sharp-witted woman who wasn't scared of an opinion or an extra drink. But for the past two days she had been weirdly uptight.

"How did you know I was here?"

"The desk sergeant told me you were between shifts." Ingrid peered at the chalkboard above the counter. She'd forgotten to eat lunch again. "Your boy Mills just picked up Madison Faber. Thought I'd sit with her till her lawyer came, but one of your team said she didn't want me hanging around."

"You've pissed her off too?"

Ingrid was taken aback. "I take it that means I've pissed you off?"

McKittrick curled a lip. "I know you're just doing your job."

"Sorry. No one likes anyone second-guessing the way they run a case." She thought about the paint-soaked tissue in her bag and decided to hold back from handing it over.

McKittrick studied the menu, giving Ingrid a chance to notice how run-down her friend was looking. Whenever they met for an after-work drink, McKittrick turned up in a tailored power suit, kitten heels and a designer handbag. She wouldn't be described as glamorous in any APB profile, but her hair was always fixed and her lipstick was always freshly applied. Right now, however, McKittrick looked considerably older than her thirty-five years and a bit scruffy. She reached the front of the line and ordered tuna salad on whole wheat. "Do you want anything?"

Ingrid nodded a hello at the weary woman behind the counter. "Make that two." She turned her attention back to McKittrick. "If it makes you feel better, you've not been singled out for special treatment. We do it for every American citizen who dies in unexplained circumstances."

McKittrick said nothing.

"It's just a box-ticking exercise," Ingrid explained. "I'm not keeping tabs on you."

McKittrick's shoulders finally dropped. "You're probably the only one who isn't, then."

Ingrid's eyebrows narrowed. "What's going on?"

McKittrick grimaced. "It's nothing I can talk about."

"No? My lips will be forever sealed."

"I'm sorry, but I've got to get back." McKittrick paid for both sand-wiches, shoved one at Ingrid and pushed her way between the tightly packed tables to the door. Ingrid joined her on the sidewalk.

"Another time, then," Ingrid said. "Before I let you go, anything I should know about why you questioned Faber again? Has something been flagged on the autopsy?"

"We call it a postmortem. And no, we're just eliminating her from our inquiries," McKittrick said. "We've spoken to a couple of neighbors and just need to make sure she gives us the same information. If she does, she can sign a statement and we'll let her go."

"Has someone corroborated her time of arrival at Shelbourne's apartment?"

McKittrick sank her teeth into one half of her sandwich, took a messy bite and chewed vigorously for a few moments before answering. "A downstairs neighbor said she arrived at eight twenty. She had trouble opening the main door to the house. The key wasn't working properly. She buzzed all the other apartments until someone answered."

Ingrid handed her a paper napkin. "You have a little..." She pointed to her own chin. McKittrick quickly wiped the spot of mayo away. "So Faber shouldn't expect a four a.m. call from the boys in blue?"

"Not unless we discover something specific to link her to the death."

"And when will you be getting the *postmortem*?" Ingrid pulled a shred of lettuce from between the slices of bread and popped it in her mouth.

"This afternoon. I'll ask one of the lads to get it to you by close of play."

"You must have had a preliminary report by now?"

McKittrick swallowed another rushed mouthful and nodded. "No surprises. Apart from the massive trauma to the head, there were only insignificant injuries. It's looking like an accident to me."

"But that was one hell of a head wound."

"I know, so we're keeping an open mind."

"You have a time of death?"

McKittrick finished her sandwich and tossed the messy bag into a trash can at the curb. "Pathologist puts it between midnight and two a.m."

"Toxicology? Had she been drinking? Or taking drugs?"

"We'll get the bloods back later too." McKittrick's shoulders crept up toward her ears.

"Sorry, I'm adding to your stress. Wasn't my intention. Had thought maybe we could have a nice catch-up."

McKittrick sighed. "I think what we have here is a case of this being a higher priority for you than it is for me. You know how many cases I'm overseeing?"

Ingrid didn't.

"Five murders, and one of them is really, horrifically complex. For as long as it looks likely the girl tripped on her landlord's Axminster shag pile and collided with his chrome and smoked-glass coffee table, I've got other things that need my attention."

"Understood." Inside though, Ingrid was furious. The first twenty-four hours are crucial in every investigation. If the pathologist suspects foul play, the Met will have squandered a precious opportunity to gather evidence.

Ingrid looked down at her sandwich bag; the greasy mayo had started to leech through the paper. Suddenly her appetite vanished. McKittrick was already walking away, heading back to the station. Ingrid raced to catch up with her. "Lauren's parents are flying in tomorrow. I'm meeting them at Heathrow in the afternoon. They'll want to know if their daughter was murdered, the local police are doing everything possible to find her killer."

"I'll do my best to see you've got the latest developments by the time they land." McKittrick had picked up her pace.

Ingrid remembered the tissue. "Natasha, slow down."

She didn't. "And there's also something you can do for me."

"Name it."

"Stop teasing my constable."

"Your constable?"

"Mills. He's been asking about you. Wondered if it'd be OK to give you a call."

"Really, I've not spoken more than two words to him."

"Well, your movie-star good looks have done the trick, then." McKittrick smiled mischievously. At last, a little of the Natasha Ingrid was used to had made an appearance.

"You did tell him I was engaged?"

"No. Not really. Must have slipped my mind." Another smile. "Besides, the way you talk about Marshall, I don't really see you as the marrying kind."

McKittrick's throwaway comment almost winded Ingrid. "Really?" She was rooted to the spot while McKittrick marched on. She caught up with her on the police station's front steps. Ingrid grabbed her friend's arm. "There's something Faber mentioned earlier."

McKittrick turned. "Oh yeah?"

"Lauren's laptop. Did you find it? Faber said it wasn't on the desk where she usually kept it."

"No, there was no laptop. Or tablet. We haven't even located a mobile phone. In the apartment or at the college. Perhaps you could ask her parents if they have receipts for her devices. The serial numbers would be extremely helpful."

"But you've put traces on her number, her email?"

"I'm sure my team are doing all of that. The moment anyone switches Shelbourne's phone on, we'll know about it." McKittrick turned to go. "So"—she looked over her shoulder—"what should I tell lovestruck Mills?"

Ingrid smiled. "Tell him I've got an appointment at an escort agency."

10

Ingrid's trip to Escort Angels, the agency who supplied Greg Brewster's nighttime companion, wasn't exactly fruitful. The address they had for Barry Cline was fake. The number they had for him rang and rang without diverting to an answering service. And the woman running the agency couldn't be entirely sure the photo they had on file for him was a good likeness. When Ingrid got back to the embassy, she unsurprisingly discovered 'Barry Cline' wasn't in any database because it was almost certainly a fake name. Ingrid arranged for the phone number to be monitored, and checked to see if the laptop had been handed into the police, or London Transport lost property, or a branch of Cash Converters. She had very low expectations of finding it. She still wanted to know, however, what the hell was on it that required it to be reported to the embassy. More than that, she really wanted to get to the bottom of why she didn't have sufficient security clearance to access Brewster's files in the archives.

Unable to face another night in her hotel room and a long conversation with Marshall or her mom, Ingrid got on the bike and returned to Loriners. She was meeting Lauren Shelbourne's parents in the morning and wanted to be able to tell them as much as possible about the circumstances around her daughter's death. She kept seeing the gash on Lauren's forehead and couldn't believe such a wound could be inflicted by simply falling over. Ingrid fully expected the autopsy report to indicate she had been murdered. The suicide of the girl the week before and the whore graffiti meant Ingrid wanted to do a little digging. She remembered the poster for a music concert on campus and thought it was a better use of her time than another self-flagellation session in the hotel gym.

After the gig—a poorly attended cacophony of discordant experimentation—Ingrid found herself on an almost deserted campus and decided to take a look around. Apart from the odd camera, there was no obvious sign of a security presence save for occasional signs warning of dogs and specially trained staff.

Ten minutes after the musicians left the stage, she seemed to be all alone on the campus. The main piazza was deathly silent. When she reached the science block, she stopped: even in the dim light cast by the distant streetlamps, she could see fresh paint dripping down the facade. She checked left and right, but the campus appeared to be deserted. The vandals had dispensed with words and chosen to spray three identical symbols on the newly scrubbed concrete:

$$\backslash / \backslash / \backslash \quad \backslash / \backslash / \backslash \quad \backslash / \backslash / \backslash$$

She'd never seen anything like it before. Was it a symbol from some ancient language studied in the linguistics department? She got her phone out to take a photo, when the silence was broken by a clang of metal hitting metal, the sound echoing around the piazza. She turned toward the noise and saw a spray can bouncing off walls and steel handrails as it fell earthwards. A level up from the ground, two dark-clad figures leaned over the walkway wall.

"Hey! What are you doing?" Ingrid ran toward them. They just stood there watching her, making no attempt to escape, no doubt confident that the only way up onto their level was via a long ramp at the far end of the piazza. They laughed as she approached. Determined to wipe the smiles from their faces, Ingrid accelerated and launched herself at the lower wall, landing cleanly on top and using her momentum to leap upward, high enough to grab the metal rail on the next level up. She swung her right leg out and up, the rubber toe of her sneaker catching the edge of the walkway wall. Though she couldn't see them, she heard the unmistakable shuffle of feet sliding over cement. They weren't laughing anymore. Using both arms and her right leg for leverage, she pulled her body over the rail and rolled onto the walkway. In the gloom she could just make out the two graffiti artists at the end of the walkway.

One turned left, the other right.

She got to her feet and ran. She went after the heavier of the two, thinking a slower man would be easier to catch. Ingrid leaped onto the wall running alongside the walkway, intending to jump on him from above, but in the dark she hadn't seen the wall was way too narrow to run at full speed. The vandal started to pull away. She stopped and was about to drop back onto the walkway when something slammed into her calves, pushing her forward into thin air. She struggled to stay upright. A second later she hit the ground feet first and rolled quickly, spreading the impact of the landing. The second vandal peered down at her from the walkway above, a short length of wood in his hands.

She scrambled to her feet. Her left ankle rolled sideways as she put her weight on it, forcing her back onto the ground, searing pain shooting from her foot up her leg toward the knee. She grabbed her ankle and watched helplessly as the black-clad figure escaped, disappearing into the gloom.

A sudden bright flash lit up the walkway. Ingrid turned. Another flash blinded her momentarily. It was quickly followed by another and another. Ingrid held a hand up to her eyes and tried to blink away the purple stain on her retinas. With each blink a shadowy figure that had materialized in front of her became more solid. She recognized the boots first: shiny black knee-lengths. Then the raincoat came into focus. Angela Tate. The journalist.

Goddammit.

After another bright flash, Ingrid realized Tate was taking pictures of her with her cell phone.

"What do you think you're doing? Stop that." She grabbed at the phone, but Tate pulled away swiftly and slipped it safely into her coat pocket.

"That was quite a display," Tate said. "Isn't that what the kids do? Parkour, isn't it?"

"Did you get a photo of them?"

"It was too dark. Besides, their faces were covered." The journalist held out a hand to Ingrid, which she batted away.

Ingrid slowly stood up and tested her left ankle, gradually easing her weight onto it. It was sore but still functioning. "What are you doing here?"

Angela Tate looked Ingrid up and down. "I could ask you the same thing."

A set of lights came on over the main concourse below them. Tate peered over the walkway wall. "It appears the security firm, dogs included, have chosen to make an appearance."

Ingrid grabbed the journalist and dragged her further into the shadows. She dropped her voice to a whisper. "What are you doing here?"

"Research. I'm working on a story about Loriners. You know about the suicide last week?"

"Why don't you tell me about it?" Ingrid folded her arms and nodded encouragingly.

"Not here. I was rather hoping you'd give me a ride home. I doubt I'll pick up a cab at this hour. Presumably your car's parked nearby?"

"Motorcycle."

A dog barked in the distance.

"I think it's time we made a swift exit. A motorcycle, eh? Sounds like fun. Haven't been on a bike for years."

"Sorry. I only have one helmet."

"Even better. I like to feel the wind in my hair."

"No way."

"Do you want me to tell you what I know about the suicide or not?"

Without another word, Ingrid led Tate through campus, managing to avoid security guards and their dogs, to where she'd parked the Triumph Tiger. Ingrid unlocked the top box and handed the helmet to the journalist. "You wear it. Just in case we have an accident."

"Let's just make sure we don't, shall we?"

11

After an uncomfortable ten minutes of the journalist squeezing her hands so tight around Ingrid's waist she thought her dinner might find its way back up her digestive tract, they finally arrived at Tate's home in Kennington, just a few miles from Loriners in south London. Tate led Ingrid down a flight of stone steps to the basement apartment of a tall, narrow house in the middle of a row of identical properties.

Ingrid hesitated on the threshold. "Should I take off my sneakers?"

"God, no. We don't stand on ceremony here."

"We?"

"Figure of speech. We're quite alone."

She joined Tate in a narrow kitchen at the far end of the hallway. The woman dropped her coat and gloves onto a chair and lined up bottles of liquor on the kitchen bench. "What are you in the mood for? A drop of brandy to keep out the cold? Or a shot of tequila to get the gray cells firing?"

"A glass of water is just fine."

"Don't be a party pooper. What about a wee dribble of whiskey in that water?"

"You were going to tell me about the suicide last week." She watched as Tate poured herself a triple brandy then downed the lot in one.

"My God, that's better. Are you sure I can't tempt you?"

Ingrid shook her head.

"Please yourself." Tate pushed past her, bottle in hand, and disappeared into another room off the hallway. She hollered, "Well, come on, then."

Ingrid hurried into the room, scanning it quickly, taking in the artful decor and antique pieces of furniture. Angela Tate might be an alcoholic old hack, she thought, but the woman certainly had taste. The journalist was standing over an old oak table in the corner of the room, busily rearranging photographs and sheets of paper that covered most of its surface.

"Tuesday last week. It happened in the afternoon. I think that's what shocked people the most—the extravagant and very public nature of it. You expect people to have suicidal thoughts in the early hours, don't you? Not on a bright spring day. Sun shining, birds singing."

"What do you know about her?"

"Young. Canadian. Studying fine art. Loriners has something of a reputation for the arts. Places are highly sought after. She was only twenty years old. Quite a talent by all accounts."

"How did she die?" Ingrid would have to ask McKittrick for the official report; the graphic version Mohammed had given her wasn't exactly illuminating.

"Top floor of the admin block. It was a miracle she didn't hit anyone on the way down."

"Did she have mental health problems? Was there a note?"

"No and no. According to her friends at college and the ones back home in Montreal, she could sometimes display an 'artistic temperament,' but any depressive episode lasted no longer than a day."

"Maybe she was going through one when she jumped."

Tate refilled her glass and took an unhealthy slug. "It's possible, but there's something not quite right about the whole thing. People at the scene said they thought she was drunk. Properly off her face drunk. Yet no one I've spoken to since can even remember seeing her so much as take a sip of the hard stuff."

Ingrid wasn't sure the Canadian student's death was relevant to Lauren Shelbourne's death unless it demonstrated criminal neglect of students' welfare by the university hierarchy. If it did, then it was something Lauren's parents might want to take action over. "Is there anything else you can tell me? Anything unusual you've discovered about Loriners?"

"I've been working bloody hard on this story for weeks; I'm not just going to hand it to you on a plate."

"Oh, come on. You might be working on a story, but I'm investigating the violent death of a young woman."

"Interesting way of putting it." Tate drained her glass and shoved it on a nearby bookshelf.

"I don't follow," Ingrid said.

"You would have said 'murder' if that's what the evidence has shown. What's the pathologist saying?"

"I honestly don't know. I haven't received the report yet."

Tate folded her arms. "Why are you investigating Lauren Shelbourne's death, violent or otherwise? Is that something the FBI would normally get involved in?"

"If a US citizen dies in a foreign country of something other than natural causes? Sure, we investigate."

"Can't trust the local plod, is that it?"

Plod? She meant the police. "I have full confidence in the Met."

"You must be the only person in London who does. Should we have called nine nine nine about the graffiti?"

Ingrid remembered the paint-covered tissue: she forgot to give it to McKittrick. "I'll mention it to the investigation team in the morning."

Tate returned her attention to the documents on her desk. "What did you make of their artwork?"

"The symbols?"

"Ever seen anything like it before?"

"Have you?"

"I asked first."

Ingrid's cell buzzed in her pocket. Relieved to escape the back-and-forth with an increasingly brandy-fueled Tate, she made her excuses and took the call.

"What is it? Has something happened?"

"I need to speak to you. Urgently." Madison Faber sounded scared.

"I'm listening."

"Not over the phone. Face-to-face. It's a matter of life and death."

12

Despite her initial demand that Ingrid meet her right away, Madison Faber had reluctantly agreed to a rendezvous in Hyde Park early the next morning. She had been quite insistent that they not meet on campus. Ingrid had told Faber her run route, and they had decided to meet at the Serpentine Café.

"I don't feel safe there," she'd whispered into the phone, her voice catching partway through.

Ingrid slowed as she approached the café on the shore of a long lake in the middle of the park, and checked her time and distance stats on her watch. The pain in her ankle had slowed her down considerably, but it seemed to be holding up. Faber was already waiting at the entrance, puffing impatiently on a slim cigarillo.

"I didn't know you smoked," Ingrid said.

"I didn't. Seems to help." Faber clocked Ingrid's look of disapproval. "For now."

There was a coffee cart outside the café, which didn't open until ten a.m.

"Can I get you anything?" Ingrid asked.

"An Americano?"

Five minutes later, coffees in hand, Ingrid found Faber pacing up and down the wooden decking beside the lake, obsessively checking her phone every few seconds. "Sorry about the wait. You take it black, right?" She handed Faber the cardboard cup. "Shall we find somewhere to sit? It's such a lovely—"

"I want to keep moving." Faber set off toward a path running east-west through the park. "What's happening with the case?"

"I won't know any more until I get into the office. How did it go yesterday, with the police?"

The girl was walking briskly, her gait deliberate as if the placement of each foot required concentration. Madison Faber was a serious young woman. "The police told me not to leave the country. Can you believe that? They let me go, but then lay that on me."

Ingrid wanted to reassure her. "It's nothing personal. They need you as a witness at the coroner's hearing. Now, you said you were scared. Has something happened?"

Faber ignored the question. "When are Lauren's parents arriving?"

Two lines of kindergarten children walking in pairs appeared around a kink in the path, all dressed in gray and yellow uniforms. Ingrid ducked out of the way, but Faber didn't seem to notice them and stood in the center of the path, forcing the pairs to walk around her or unlink hands. She was buffeted and banged on both sides by the tide of tiny bodies. When the final pair had negotiated the unwelcome obstacle, Faber squeezed her eyes shut. Ingrid put a hand on the student's shoulder.

"I think you need to sit down." She guided her to a nearby bench bathed in dappled sunshine.

Faber allowed herself to be led and set her coffee on the wide wooden slat beside her. "You haven't answered my question. When do they get here? I'd like to speak to them."

"They're due in this afternoon. They might not feel up to visitors. And there's a lot of ugly official business they have to deal with."

"It wouldn't be a social call. I need to talk to them about Lauren."

"I'll have a word with them—pass on your condolences."

"No!" Faber's eyes widened, and Ingrid was caught off guard by the power of her gaze. "I mean really talk to them, not spew out platitudes. I'm sure they've had enough of those already." Faber checked her phone again, reached for her coffee, brought the cup to her lips and returned it to the bench without taking a sip. The girl was on edge. Faber seemed more distressed than after discovering Lauren Shelbourne's body.

"You haven't told me why you wanted to see me." Ingrid kept her voice low and gentle, trying to sound as soothing as possible. "What's happened?"

"You'll only think I'm crazy."

"Try me?"

Faber stared at two women, nannies judging by their age and ethnicity, pushing bulky three-wheel baby strollers along the path. The women chatted happily to one another in Russian. Ingrid tried to stop her ears tuning in to their chat, something she always did when she heard people speaking in her mother's native tongue. One woman shrieked a high-pitched laugh that made Faber jump. Ingrid placed a hand on Faber's knee. "What's going on, Madison?"

The girl nodded vigorously. "There's something at college. Something bad." She lifted a hand to push a stray lock of hair from her forehead. It was trembling. "The atmosphere in the psychology department is really jumpy. Especially Professor Younger's group."

"Really?"

"I said you'd think I was crazy."

"Jumpy in what way?"

"Really tense, like they're waiting for something bad to happen." She stood up abruptly. "I've got to keep moving." She checked her phone.

"Are you expecting a call?"

"No, just checking the time." She walked in the direction they'd just come. "Do you think whoever wrote that graffiti has something to do with Lauren's death?"

"What makes you mention that?" Ingrid asked. "You weren't taking it very seriously yesterday."

"I've had more time to think about it since then." She quickened her pace, glancing at her phone again.

What had gotten into the girl to make her this nervous? "Is there something you're not telling me?"

"I just... I'm scared."

"There's no need to be. The police have eliminated you from their inquiries."

"I'm not scared of the police."

"Then what is it?"

"I'm scared for my life."

"Has someone said something?"

"I think I'm next." Faber broke into a jog. Ingrid ran after her, grabbed her arm and pulled her to a stop.

"Next? What are you saying?"

"First that Canadian girl died last week, now Lauren..." Her eyes widened and she stared blankly at the ground.

"The student last week committed suicide. And Lauren... well, the police aren't connecting last week's suicide and Lauren's death."

"Well, they should. They're linked. I know they are."

"Even if they are, why would you be next?"

"I found Lauren, didn't I? Maybe whoever did that to her is worried I saw something, and they can't risk me telling the police."

Ingrid wondered if she could persuade Faber to see the embassy doctor. "You're in shock. What you're feeling right now is completely natural."

"You're patronizing me." Faber pulled away and hurried back toward the café.

"Please, Madison. I'm not. I'm really not," Ingrid called out. She jogged to catch up with her.

"You said you were here for me. I thought you meant it." Faber was speaking in an urgent whisper.

"I am here. I've got your back."

"Your friend—the one you lost..."

Not this. Not again.

"How did she die?"

"It's really not relevant."

"Why won't you tell me?"

Because it's none of your goddamn business!

Ingrid took a steadying breath. She needed the girl to trust her. "She was abducted. And never found."

"So she could still be alive somewhere?"

"It was eighteen years ago."

"But she could be? And what if the police looking for her hadn't turned over every stone? Wouldn't you want to know they did everything to find the truth?"

Ingrid stared into Faber's pleading eyes.

"You have to find out what's happening at college." Faber took hold of Ingrid's arms and squeezed tight. "You have to take me seriously."

"And you have to tell me what's happened to you since the last time I saw you."

Faber let go of Ingrid and visibly sagged, all the pent-up energy leaving her in one simple gesture. "If I tell you, you have to swear not to tell anyone else."

"That depends on what it is."

"Promise me!" Passersby stared, making them both realize Faber had been shouting.

"OK, I promise."

Faber dropped her gaze to the ground. "It happened last night. I was at college, in the psychology lab. I left my workstation for a few minutes, and when I returned from the restroom, there it was, just lying there, its guts spilling out onto the desk."

"What are you talking about?"

"A white laboratory mouse. Partially dissected." Her owlish eyes widened. "There was no one around. I'd assumed I was alone in the whole building. But someone must have been there, just waiting for me to leave my desk for a moment."

"What did you do?"

"I panicked. I ran. That's when I called you."

"Did you call the police?"

"I was too scared."

"So the mouse could still be there?"

"I doubt it. Whoever put it there got the result they were after. It terrified me." Faber chewed the inside of her cheek.

"Is it possible it was just a prank? A practical joke?"

"At close to midnight? With no one else around?" She blinked deliberately then looked into Ingrid's face. "It was a warning. I know it was."

"What kind of warning?"

"It's obvious, isn't it? They're making it clear that what happened to Lauren will happen to me. If I don't keep quiet."

"I don't think it's clear at all."

"The mouse on my desk... they hadn't just disemboweled it." She pulled a pained face. "They'd stitched its mouth shut."

13

The embassy car was stuck in traffic on the freeway. Ingrid's frustration was rising. If she'd taken the bike, she'd be waiting in Terminal 5 by now, in plenty of time for the Shelbournes' flight from JFK.

"There must be a faster route," she said from the back seat. It was all she could do not to grab the steering wheel.

"This is the only way to get to Heathrow. I have been there before."

The driver had already explained, repeatedly and at great length, he used to drive a black taxi, which he called a 'cab,' and that Ingrid gathered was some kind of badge of honor. She squeezed her fists into tight balls and took a few deep breaths as the line of traffic ahead ground to a halt yet again.

Madison Faber's revelation was preying on her mind. Ingrid hadn't been able to persuade the girl to go to the police about the incident in the psychology lab. Faber was convinced the police secretly thought she was involved in Lauren's death, but without having the mouse as evidence, Faber was worried they would take it as a sign of her mental instability. On reflection, Ingrid agreed: Faber's behavior and demeanor had been understandably erratic since she'd discovered Lauren's body, and without the mouse, even she wasn't entirely sure she believed the student.

Ingrid's priority for the next few hours was chaperoning the Shelbournes and bringing them, tactfully, up to date with the investigation into their daughter's death. When the driver finally dropped her off, she ran all the way to the arrivals lounge, aware of the soreness in her left ankle. She pulled down the bottom of her jacket and combed her fingers through her hair to tidy it as the first few passengers from flight 489 trickled through. She held up a printed card with the Shelbournes' names and directed it toward any couple who were vaguely the right age. Her research had revealed Anthony and Lisa Shelbourne lived in Greenwich, Connecticut. He owned an ad agency in New York City, and she collected art and good causes.

Ingrid hadn't needed the card.

Lauren's parents were easily identifiable by their strained expressions and gray complexions. Though they had dressed for first class, their clothes were crumpled and disheveled. Mrs. Shelbourne had done her best to refresh her makeup, but her eyes were puffed and lined. No amount of cosmetics could hide her distraught features.

Ingrid set her face somewhere between a concerned frown and a sympathetic smile, not at all sure she was pulling it off, and approached the couple with an outstretched hand. "Ingrid Skyberg, from the embassy," she said and steeled herself for her first platitude. "I'm so sorry for your loss."

Anthony Shelbourne squeezed her hand in his and nodded. His wife held onto him as if she might slide right onto the floor if she let go.

"We have a car waiting," Ingrid told them. "If you'd like to follow me?" She gestured toward the exit.

"We have to wait for my daughter," Mrs. Shelbourne said. "She's bringing the bags."

"Your daughter?" Ingrid hoped she'd managed to suppress her surprise, struggling to keep her expression and tone neutral.

"We left her at the baggage reclaim," Mr. Shelbourne explained. "Alex volunteered to wait for the suitcases."

A full ten minutes of awkward silences and painful small talk later, Alex Shelbourne emerged from the customs channel, pushing a baggage cart stacked high with suitcases and carry-ons. The girl had to be no more than sixteen or seventeen, a little over five feet five and less than a hundred pounds. She was struggling with the weight of the cart. Ingrid hurried to help her.

"It's OK—I can manage," the girl told her firmly.

She wore thick eyeliner, dark purple lipstick and had lilac streaks in otherwise jet-black spiky hair. Alex Shelbourne had cast herself as the rebel of the family.

Ingrid planted a restraining hand on the uppermost bag and guided the Shelbournes through the busy arrivals hall, navigating a channel through the crush of bodies. The embassy limousine was waiting at the curb.

"We can go straight to your hotel or deal with the formalities at the embassy first, if you'd rather," Ingrid told them as the driver loaded the bags into the trunk.

"Take me to the morgue. I want to see my baby." Lisa Shelbourne's voice was surprisingly clear and strong.

"I'll, um, I'll need to make a few calls to arrange that for you. At this time of day it may be difficult."

"Make as many calls as you like. We're going to see my daughter."

Ingrid sat next to the driver, who buzzed up the glass partition between the front and back seats. Each time she turned to check on them, the Shelbournes were gazing out their respective windows, never once looking at one another or exchanging a word.

Once they were making good progress on the freeway, Ingrid called Sol and told him about the unexpected arrival of the Shelbournes' youngest.

"I get the impression she's the type of teenager who can't be left at home alone," Ingrid told him.

"It's going to be tough on the kid."

She caught sight of Alex Shelbourne in the wing mirror. She was staring at her smartphone, earphones snaking from the device and disappearing into her ears. So far she seemed to be coping with the situation remarkably well.

"I need you to make some calls for me," Ingrid said.

"Can't Jennifer do it?"

"I need your help. Mrs Shelbourne is insisting we visit the mortuary first. I figure they might listen to you. I really need the body in a viewing room in ninety minutes."

Sol was good to his word. When they arrived, an orderly was waiting for them at the entrance of the hospital mortuary. Anthony and Lisa Shelbourne followed the earnest man in scrubs into the single-story building while Alex hung back.

"Is it OK if I don't come in?" the teenager asked her mother. "I feel like I need some fresh air."

Lisa gently rested a hand on Alex's arm. "You're sure you don't want to see her?"

"Not here. Not like this."

"OK. Don't go wandering off."

"I'll stay with her," Ingrid said. "You'll need some privacy."

"Thank you."

Ingrid watched the ashen-faced couple disappear through the sliding doors.

"I don't need a babysitter," Alex Shelbourne said.

"Good, because that's not my job." Ingrid gave her a smile.

"I'm just fine by myself."

"I know that."

The teenager, instead of taking herself for a walk, pulled the earbuds from her ears. "Was she murdered?"

The bluntness of the question caught Ingrid by surprise.

"Well? Was she?"

"The police are still investigating." Ingrid still hadn't had the final autopsy from McKittrick.

"You must have an opinion." Alex Shelbourne fished a pack of cigarettes from one of the many pockets of her black combat pants. She offered the pack to Ingrid, who declined.

"Do your parents know you smoke?"

"Give me a break." She lit a cigarette and inhaled deeply.

"It must be very difficult for you, coming here like this."

"I wanted to come."

"Were you close to your sister?"

"You're trying to change the subject. Do *you* think someone murdered Lauren?"

An ambulance parked nearby. Two EMTs opened up the back and pulled out a gurney. A black body bag was strapped to the guardrails. The EMTs wheeled the gurney toward them, so Ingrid grabbed the teenager's arm and walked her away from the entrance.

"It's OK—you don't have to shield me from it. I do know what happens in a morgue."

Ingrid wondered how long it would be before the hard exterior the girl was doing her best to project started to crack.

The teenager took a deep drag on her Marlboro. "You still haven't answered my question."

"You're asking the wrong person. Only the Metropolitan Police can tell you."

Alex Shelbourne shrugged her dissatisfaction at Ingrid's answer. "So what happens now?"

"That depends on what the police find."

She ground her half-smoked cigarette under her sneaker. "Do you trust the local cops? To do a thorough job?"

Where did her cynicism come from? "I have every confidence in the ability of—"

"Don't give me the official crap."

Ingrid made deliberate eye contact. "I do. I trust them."

"You don't sound too sure."

"They're doing a good job. Believe me." This time, Ingrid heard the doubt in her own voice.

Alex Shelbourne put the earphones back in her ears. "They'd better be. Otherwise my dad's gonna hire a private investigator to do the job for them."

14

"Look, can this wait? We're up to our eyeballs." DI McKittrick shoved Ingrid out of the way and hurried from her office in Lewisham police station, her arms full of case papers and card files.

"I've just come from the morgue. They need answers." Ingrid followed her down a long corridor and into the elevator.

"Number six."

Ingrid punched the button with a knuckle. "Where are you taking all this stuff, anyway?"

"The main incident room is being remodeled. All the case files have to be transferred."

"Don't you have people to do that for you?"

"Supposedly." The elevator arrived at the sixth floor and the doors slid open. McKittrick hurried through. "Only it's much faster if I do it myself."

Ingrid felt much the same way about delegation. By the time you'd prepared for it, explained the situation, then dealt with whatever was thrown back at the end of the process, it was just simpler and more effective to do everything yourself. She tried to get a glimpse of the file on the top of the pile.

"Do you have the final autopsy report?"

McKittrick inhaled slowly. "I do."

"Great—"

"But I can't let you see it until my boss has approved it for release."

"And how long will that take?"

"You can see how busy we are."

Ingrid tried to see what case files McKittrick was carrying. "Is that the Shelbourne case?"

"I'm sorry to say this, but in the scheme of things, Lauren Shelbourne's death barely registers as an event. It's certainly not worthy of a dedicated incident room."

"You make it sound like you've closed the investigation."

"We're not far off." McKittrick, more harassed than ever, marched down another long corridor lined with closed doors glazed with opaque glass on either side.

Ingrid matched McKittrick's pace stride for stride.

"Lauren's parents have arrived."

"I know. Who do you think organized the viewing at the mortuary?" McKittrick stopped abruptly and kicked open a door. It swung wide to reveal Detective Constable Mills standing at the far end of the large, brightly lit office. He was rubbing marker pen off a wide whiteboard with a paper towel. He turned as they approached.

"I'll take those, boss."

McKittrick dumped the files into his arms, and Mills let out a grunt, his forehead puckering as he concentrated hard on not letting any of the loose paperwork slide to the floor. In that instant, Ingrid realized who the detective reminded her of and blushed.

Clark Swanson.

Her first crush in junior high. The boy who broke her heart without knowing it. He hadn't even known she existed. The extra forty pounds she was carrying at the time effectively made her invisible to all but the geeks and weirdos. Geeks and weirdos like her. She found herself involuntarily smiling at the memory. Mills made eye contact and quickly looked away. Was he blushing? She definitely was and she didn't like how it felt.

Ingrid turned back to ask McKittrick a question and discovered the overworked inspector disappearing into the corridor. She ran after her, her left ankle still complaining. "I spoke to that journalist yesterday," Ingrid told her as she caught up with her again. "Angela Tate."

"Not someone I'd recommend having cozy chats with. What did she want?"

"I just happened to run into her."

"Knowing Tate, I expect she planned it that way. I suppose she wanted the details on the Shelbourne investigation?"

"She's writing about the suicide on campus. Thought you'd want to know."

McKittrick wiggled her nose.

"She thinks the girl didn't kill herself."

"Well, there'd be no angle for Tate if she had."

"Did you hear anything about it?"

"Didn't get as far as my team. The detectives on duty called it in as a suicide. No one else involved. Cut and dried. No need for HSCC to wade in with our size nines."

"There'll be an inquest though?"

"That's a formality."

"Tate told me she was drunk."

"Hardly surprising, she's a gin-soaked old hack."

"She meant the student, as you well know."

"So?"

"So the girl never drank."

"And your only source of information is Tate?"

The elevator doors opened and three uniformed officers stepped out with a nod of acknowledgment for McKittrick. Ingrid and her friend stepped back inside. Ingrid reached into her bag and pulled out a candy wrapper.

"What's this?"

Ingrid opened it to reveal the paint-soaked tissue. "It's a sample of the paint used in the graffiti on campus. The one that said Lauren Shelbourne is a whore?"

McKittrick peered at the tissue. "You're serious. You're handing me an old tissue?"

"I meant to give it to you yesterday. The janitor cleaned it off before your team would have had a chance to take a sample."

"You know I can't take that, Ingrid." She glowered at her. "A Twix wrapper is hardly an evidence bag. It would be inadmissible."

Ingrid scrutinized her friend. "But you're tempted though, aren't you? You suspect there's something odd going on at Loriners too, don't you?"

The elevator reached McKittrick's floor and the detective shot through the half-open doors as if a starter pistol had just gone off.

"The only thing worth looking at was the fact security around the admin block—the building the Canadian girl jumped from—was found wanting. It's the highest point on campus."

"Found wanting?"

"A maintenance crew inadvertently left a door unlocked. The incident was fully investigated. Why are you so determined to link the suicide to the Shelbourne case?" she asked Ingrid. "Please don't tell me it's a hunch."

Ingrid was still holding the tissue. "I'm just following the evidence."

McKittrick rolled her eyes. "I can't spare anyone to investigate a teenage prank."

"Lauren's parents want to repatriate her body as soon as possible. I want to be sure we know what happened to her before we lose a vital forensic asset." She hated referring to Lauren that way. "You might not have the manpower, but I do. And if I don't look into it, Lauren Shelbourne's father is going to hire a private detective."

With a long, exasperated sigh McKittrick opened a nearby file cabinet and picked out a slim folder. She placed it carefully and deliberately on her desk, then held Ingrid's gaze. "I need to visit the ladies'. You'll be OK waiting in here for me, will you?"

Ingrid glanced down at the file, saw Lauren Shelbourne's name printed on a neat label in the top right-hand corner, then nodded her understanding to McKittrick. Natasha was still in her corner after all.

"I won't be long." McKittrick left the room, opening the door wide on her way out, and made a point of leaving it open.

Ingrid checked the hallway outside. The coast appeared to be clear. She returned to the desk and flipped open the file, her back toward the door, obscuring what she was doing from anyone passing. There was no time to read the contents now. She opened the camera app on her phone and snapped a picture of the first page. The flash went off as she did.

Damn.

Ingrid disabled the auto-flash function and moved on to the second page. She had photographed all but the final sheet when she heard a noise behind her. She spun around and saw Mills standing in the doorway. Ingrid slumped heavily onto the edge of the desk, at the same time reaching an arm behind her back. She groped for the switch on the side of the phone and clicked it, hoping she'd captured an image of the last page.

"Hey! Ralph, isn't it?"

The detective nodded slowly.

"Natash—I mean DI McKittrick has slipped out for a moment." She smiled at him as innocently as she could.

He narrowed his eyes, tilting his head sideways to get a better view of the surface of the desk. "Everything OK?"

"Perfectly." In a single smooth movement she stood up, flipped the file closed and took a step toward him. "How are you?" He was still frowning at her, looking more and more like Clark Swanson from Middleton Junior High.

"Can I help you with anything?"

"No, I'm fine." She folded her arms.

"I'm glad we've got a few moments on our own." He closed the door behind him.

"You are?"

He glanced again at the desk. "I've been really interested in the FBI since I was a kid."

Ingrid's heart sank. "Don't tell me—*The X Files*, right?"

"Am I that much of a cliché?"

Ingrid threw her arms out wide. "Hey—it was a great show. I was a fan of it myself." *Geeks and weirdos.*

"Is that why you joined up?"

"Kinda." This was neither the time nor the place to reveal the real reason.

"I don't suppose you could tell me a bit about it? The training and all that? Maybe over a coffee or something?"

Was he actually hitting on her?

"I'm so busy these days. Work pretty much takes up all my time."

He shifted his position and stared pointedly at the desk. "Perhaps we could... pool our knowledge."

"Knowledge about what?"

"Any of our current cases you might be interested in."

Was he offering to keep her updated on the Shelbourne investigation? "I suppose I might be able to find some time in my calendar." She pulled a business card from her pocket and handed it to Mills. "We'll set something up. Call me."

He smiled at her, his cheeks showing just the hint of a blush. "Excellent." He turned and opened the door, but didn't leave. Instead he stood beside it and looked at her expectantly.

"It's all right. The inspector said I could wait for her in here."

"No. That's why I'm here. The boss specifically asked me to escort you from the building." He smiled and she was suddenly looking right at Clark Swanson.

"She did?" He knew exactly what she'd been doing in McKittrick's office, and now Natasha was giving him the nod to help her out. That's what friends are for.

Outside, Ingrid waved an awkward goodbye to Mills, already inventing excuses to turn down whatever date he suggested for their meet-up. She retrieved her cell phone from the back pocket of her pants and opened the photo gallery, enlarging specific parts of images that seemed relevant. Everything was more or less what she suspected until she reached the final page. The picture was a little blurred, and the left-hand side of the page cut off completely. But as she enlarged and brightened the image, the information she needed came into focus.

According to the Metropolitan Police toxicology report, at the time of her death, Lauren Shelbourne's bloodstream contained 'significant' amounts of LSD and methamphetamine.

15

Ingrid tied a double knot in the lace of her running shoe and scooted out of the embassy building, along Upper Brooke Street, across the eight-lane highway of Park Lane and finally into Hyde Park. Her second visit in as many days. Despite the soreness in her left ankle, she cruised along somewhere between a fast jog and a sprint. She eased up as soon as she saw the outline of her boss fifty yards away. Or rather her boss's boss. Amy Louden was further up the food chain than Sol. She was only forty-three years old, yet was already the Deputy Special Agent In Charge of the FBI's legal attaché program in the most prestigious US Embassy in the world. Ingrid was coming up to thirty-two. She was running out of time to have a meteoric rise of her own.

Louden had insisted their meeting take place in the park while she ran. Two birds with one stone, she'd said. "Let's show the boys how to multi-task, shall we?"

Ingrid watched Louden's uneven gait as the woman ran holding a cell phone in one hand, a wire trailing out of the top. Ingrid stepped up her pace a little and effortlessly caught up with the DSAC, pulling in alongside and quickly mirroring her stride pattern. Louden glanced at her from the corner of her eye without turning her head. She finished up her call and navigated to an app on the phone without missing a stride. It seemed looking where she was going wasn't a priority for Louden.

"Steady at ten miles an hour; metabolic rate increased fifteen percent," she told Ingrid. "Three hundred forty-six calories burnt."

"Impressive."

"Three miles a day, rain or shine." Louden pointed a thumb toward her own chest. "For me it's just a part of my daily routine, like taking a shower. It's a matter of discipline. Like anything else."

Ingrid had decided long ago never to compete with a superior officer. She kept her five-mile minimum and parkour routines to herself. She was just glad Louden hadn't suggested racquetball: somehow Ingrid's hand-eye coordination got stuck on automatic, and she found it completely impossible to throw a game, no matter how hard she tried.

"We haven't had a chance to speak properly since you first joined us. How are you settling in? Enjoying London?"

"Yes, ma'am. One of the best postings I've had." It wasn't exactly true, but she knew it was what Louden wanted to hear.

"Good, good. We like to make new arrivals feel welcome."

Ingrid had to suppress a smile. Apart from Sol, no one had bothered to make much of an effort to extend a friendly hand.

"So, these assignments you're working on at the moment," Louden said while checking her running stats again. "Sol tells me you're not making much headway in the Brewster case."

So that was why Louden had ask to meet with her.

"The trail goes cold at the escort agency. I've been contacting other agencies with a description of the suspected perpetrator, but so far it seems he's simply disappeared. I'm sure I'd have better results if I knew more about the victim." Ingrid glanced briefly at the DSAC to check her reaction. Her boss kept her eyes front and center. "I take it there's a reason why you're asking me about it?"

Louden slowed slightly and inclined her head toward Ingrid for the first time. "Somebody leans on me, so I lean on you."

"Do you know who Greg Brewster is? Or what he does?"

Louden took several strides to answer. "I can tell you that's not his real name. But, no, I don't know what his legal name is, before you ask."

Ingrid was intrigued. "And this alias is approved by…?"

"I'm not entirely sure we should be discussing this."

"Due respect, ma'am, you want an update on a case I can't give you because I can't investigate it properly. Could you at least see if my security clearance could be raised?"

Louden didn't answer.

"Just for this one case?"

Still no response.

"I'll get you the answers you need if you let me know who Brewster is."

They rounded a corner of the path and found themselves running between flower beds alive with spring bulbs.

"I can't. I don't know. But I'm getting pressure from the Department of Defense, so I'm guessing it's military. That enough for you?"

It was a start.

"Thank you. I appreciate that." It was a lot less than she'd hoped for, and Ingrid felt a spike of anger erupt in her chest and travel to her legs. She wanted to take on a fast sprint or throw herself over a wall, burn away the fury, but neither of those two options was open to her in present company. She settled for clenching her teeth instead.

"Good. I hear the Shelbourne case is almost wrapped up. Such a tragedy."

"I've seen the toxicology report. She'd taken LSD and methamphetamine."

"She sounds like a very unfortunate individual." Louden was distracted by whatever her fitness app was telling her.

"Don't you think it's strange to find that combination of drugs in her system?" Ingrid skirted around a fresh pile of horse dung and landed heavily on her left foot. Fireworks of pain shot upward into her knee.

"She was obviously a young woman with serious problems."

"There's no record of previous drug offenses."

"That doesn't mean she was clean."

"I'm seeing her parents again later. I just want to be able to tell them it was a tragic accident."

"But you have reservations?"

They reached an enormous plane tree and Louden pulled up sharply. She tapped something into her smartphone and nodded with satisfaction. She looked at Ingrid. Ingrid hesitated.

"Well?"

"I have a few causes of concern. About the investigation. I want to make sure the Met hasn't missed anything before they release the body for repatriation."

"Tread carefully, agent. The Shelbournes have suffered enough. I don't want them upset needlessly." She tore her gaze away from a long list of 'missed call' alerts and turned to Ingrid. "Do I make myself clear?"

Ingrid suppressed a sigh. "Perfectly."

"Do everything you can to repatriate the body in the next few days."

"I'm not sure the inquest will happen that fast."

"Let's ensure it does, shall we?"

"It feels like we're rushing things when there's no need."

"You don't have children, do you, Ingrid?"

"No, ma'am."

Louden leveled a stare at her. "Try to imagine what those two souls are going through."

Ingrid only just managed to unclench her teeth to speak. "I'll do my best." She forced a smile and left her superior officer to continue with her carefully planned warm-down exercises. Ingrid sprinted back to the embassy as quickly as she could.

———

Showered and dressed, with a strong strapping of elastic bandage on her left ankle, Ingrid returned to her desk to collect her bag. She retrieved her cell and did something she should have done days ago.

Marshall picked up immediately. "Hey, sweetie. I was about to call your boss to find out what had happened to you."

"Sorry. It's been crazy here the last few weeks." Ingrid walked through the bull pen toward the elevators.

"I've been calling."

"I know. I got your messages."

"Why didn't you call back?"

Ingrid didn't have a good enough answer. Absence, it was turning out, wasn't making her heart grow fonder. She reached the elevators, then pushed through the doors to the emergency exit and took the stairs.

"I'm sorry, Marshall, but this isn't a social call. Can you see if you can find something out for me, on the down low?"

He sighed heavily.

"You're more senior than me; your clearance level is higher than mine. Can you run a search for me on someone called Greg Brewster?"

"You know I can't do that." He was such a stickler. Marshall Claybourne would never do anything that threatened to blemish his reputation and slow his progress up the Bureau's greasy pole. "How would I explain it? What if it raises a flag?"

You'd make something up. "Well then, can you do something else for me? Apparently my predecessor works in the DC office now. Dennis Mulroony."

"Never heard of him." The FBI's headquarters employed tens of thousands of people. Not even an uber-networker like Marshall could know everyone.

"Well, could you keep an eye out, and an ear out, for him? I'd like to swap notes, but don't want to alert anyone we're in contact. Can you find him for me?"

"Sure, but you've got to do something for me."

"Name it."

"Give me a date."

"We've been engaged for two years, Marshall. I think we're a bit beyond dating." She knew exactly what he'd meant, and she also knew how insincere she sounded.

"I mean a date for the wedding. My mom keeps asking."

Ingrid sucked on her teeth. "We discussed all this when I took the job. You agreed the posting will help with my promotion prospects. We can't all be highflyers like you." Her voice echoed in the stark, empty stairwell.

"Come on! Don't give me a hard time for getting lucky."

"You get lucky every time there's a vacancy."

"You don't resent me for that?"

Ingrid pulled the phone from her ear. *You bet your ass I do.* "Of course not! It's not like we're in a competition with one another." They always had been. Ever since Quantico.

"I want a date for our wedding. Can't we at least be working toward it?"

"We'll have to talk about this later. I have an appointment."

"What should I tell my mom?"

Tell her to butt the hell out of your business. "Tell her I was asking after her." She'd reached the lobby and decided to walk the short distance from the embassy to the Shelbournes' Mayfair hotel.

"But I miss you," Marshall said. "How about you come home for a couple of days? A long weekend?"

"I'm in the middle of two very important investigations."

"But you always are." An irritable whine had infected his tone, exaggerating his Southern drawl.

"We had an agreement."

"Sure, but an agreement needs an end date."

"I can't speak about this now. I'll call you back." She ended the call before he managed a rejoinder, then shoved her phone in a pocket. She puffed out her cheeks in frustration. He always made her feel this way. Always wound her up. Dating someone on the job had made so much sense in the beginning: a mutual understanding of the pressure of work, the sacrifices that had to be made, the last-minute cancelation of long-standing arrangements. They never needed to apologize, never needed to explain. Now that seemed all he ever wanted her to do. Her cell buzzed and she grabbed it, tempted to tell Marshall where he could shove his end date. But it wasn't him. It was a UK cell number she didn't recognize.

"Hello?"

"Ralph Mills here. I was wondering if you had a spare five minutes, maybe later today?"

When she'd given Mills her card, she'd wondered just how long it would take him to call her. She thought he'd take a little longer. If it came to it, she'd just throw Marshall into the conversation. He could still be good for something.

"Are you still there?"

"Hi, yes, I'm here."

"Mutually beneficial cup of coffee or glass of wine, I was thinking," Mills said, embarrassment detectable in his tone. Was he offering something on the Shelbourne investigation?

"Do you want to speak to me about the case?"

"Let's talk about that when we meet up, shall we?"

16

When she approached the five-star hotel, Ingrid was sure the BMW pulling away on the other side of the road contained McKittrick and Mills. He hadn't sounded like he'd been in a car when they'd spoken. Ingrid felt wrong-footed: if the Shelbournes had been briefed by the Met, they would know more about the case than she did, and she risked seeming a fool. Ingrid took the elevator up to the top floor with a certain amount of reticence. When she reached the family's suite, she heard raised voices coming from inside. Anthony and Lisa Shelbourne were shouting at one another. Ingrid leaned a little closer to the door.

"I never wanted her to leave the country in the first place," Mrs. Shelbourne said. "This would never have happened if you hadn't insisted that—"

The unmistakable trill of a cell phone cut her off.

"For God's sake. Ignore the goddamn phone for once, can't you?"

"I need to take this."

Ingrid stepped away from the door and raised her fist as if to knock, knowing from the loudness of his voice that Anthony Shelbourne was heading her way. The door swung open, Shelbourne took a moment to recognize her, then held up a silencing finger. His face was drawn, a dark shadow of stubble covered his chin, and his hair stuck out in cowlicks. He marched down the long, subtly lit hallway, shouting into his cell.

Ingrid tapped on the already open door and stuck her head inside. "Mrs Shelbourne, Agent Skyberg from the embassy."

"We only met a few hours ago. I'm hardly likely to forget. Despite appearances, I do still have some control over my faculties."

"I'm sorry, ma'am."

"Let's get this over with, shall we?" She ran a shaking hand through her hair. Her eye makeup had smudged beneath her eyes. Long dark trails of mascara slithered down her face.

Ingrid glanced around the room. There was no sign of Alex. Lisa Shelbourne dabbed at her eyes, making them even more of a mess.

"Please take a seat. I can order some fresh coffee if you'd like?"

Ingrid raised a hand. "Not on my account." There was a tray of dirty cups sitting on a low table between two formal chairs upholstered in maroon silk.

"The police were just here," Mrs. Shelbourne explained. "You've seen their report, I take it?"

"I realize it's been a very long day for you. I'll take up as little of your time as possible."

"How long have you been working here in London?"

Ingrid was taken aback by the change of subject. "Around four months, why?"

"And are you aware of a serious drug problem in the city?"

McKittrick must have disclosed the blood test results. No wonder Lisa Shelbourne looked so wrecked.

"Not in the course of my duties."

"I've never thought of England in that way before." She collapsed onto one of the silk-covered chairs, folding her stockinged feet beneath her. She grabbed a lilac angora sweater from the arm of the chair and clutched it to her breast. "I'm not naive. London is a major world city; I accept it must have a seedy side. But those aren't the circles I expected Lauren to move in. You've been to the college?"

Ingrid nodded.

"It has a good reputation. If I'd thought for a moment Lauren would be at risk from… undesirable influences while she was there—" She looked past Ingrid toward the door, an admonishing expression on her face. Ingrid turned to see Anthony Shelbourne standing in the doorway, his face paler and damper than it had been only moments before. "—I would never have let her go."

He quietly closed the door behind him and slipped his cell back into the breast pocket of his shirt. "You couldn't have stopped her," he told his wife.

"She may have listened to you. But you didn't even try to dissuade her."

"How many more times? She wanted to come. The research program here is one of the best in the world. Didn't she tell us that over and over?" He turned to Ingrid. "She wanted to be part of something important. I remember her face when she found out she'd been accepted in the course. It was the happiest I've ever seen her."

"There are colleges just as good at home. You should have made her stay." Lisa Shelbourne's voice was brittle.

Anthony Shelbourne started to speak but checked himself. His jaw muscles flexed. He began again. "We don't know what Lauren might have gotten into wherever she'd gone to study. We'll never know."

"Had Lauren..." Now it was Ingrid's turn to check herself. "Do you know if your daughter might have... experimented with drugs at home?"

"What?" Lisa Shelbourne leaped to her feet. "How dare you—"

Her husband grabbed her arm to stop her before she barreled straight into Ingrid. "Calm down, Lisa, the kid's just doing her job."

Kid?

Lisa Shelbourne snatched her arm away.

"The truth is we don't know," her husband admitted. "We've both been a little distracted the past couple of years. My business, Lisa's charity work. I can't say for sure what Lauren may or may not have done, even when she was still living at home."

"Don't you dare lay any of the blame at my door." Their daughter's death had blown apart the cracks in their marriage. "I only started my work because I saw nothing of you."

A door opened behind Ingrid. She turned to see Alex Shelbourne hesitate on the threshold of the adjoining room. "I need some air," she announced.

"Don't stray too far," her mother told her.

Alex made a point of walking past Ingrid, rolling her eyes as she did, like a truculent teenager. Which, Ingrid supposed, was exactly what she was.

When the girl had left the room, Anthony Shelbourne cleared some space on an antique wooden bureau pushed up against the wall that divided the two rooms of the suite. "Let's just get this paperwork finalized, shall we?"

"Paperwork?"

"The inspector explained earlier—we need to complete the forms for the repatriation of... of..." He let out a long faltering sob.

"We can't do that yet," Ingrid said. "Then there's the inquest. And then the final coroner's report."

"Yes, I know. But the detective said the matter could be expedited. Fast-tracked somehow."

"I want to take my baby home," Lisa Shelbourne said. "She's lying in the morgue. In the dark and the cold."

"I can complete the appropriate forms with you when the time comes."

"If you don't have the paperwork now, why are you here?" Mr Shelbourne asked.

Ingrid looked from Anthony to Lisa Shelbourne. She cleared her throat. "In addition to the police investigation, the embassy has to complete its own report. I'm here to gather a little background information—"

"Why? Is there some doubt about what happened?" Mrs. Shelbourne got to her feet.

"It's just standard procedure, ma'am."

A phone rang. This time it was Lisa Shelbourne's. She answered and disappeared into the bedroom.

"That's her mother," Mr Shelbourne explained. "She'll be on that call for hours."

"They have a lot to discuss," Ingrid said.

His cell phone lit up in his pocket. "Excuse me," he said on his way out to the corridor.

Talking to grief-stricken parents was something Ingrid had plenty of experience with. In her four years in the Violent Crimes Against Children unit, she'd seen relatives behave in all sorts of ways from denial, to anger, to wailing and ululations: the Shelbournes' reaction to tragedy was not unusual. They were still trying to carry on with life as normal, not yet accepting that their lives would never be the same again.

She sat on the couch for a few minutes. When it was clear neither would be talking to her soon, Ingrid went in search of Alex. She passed Anthony Shelbourne in the corridor and said she would make contact to rearrange for a more convenient time, then opted for a swift jog down the twenty or so flights of stairs to ground level to shake some of the tension from her muscles. Her best guess was sixteen-year-old Alex would be walking in the direction of Oxford Street, but she found Alex Shelbourne standing by the main entrance, waiting for her.

The girl stubbed out her cigarette on the sidewalk, choosing to ignore the metal trash can right beside her. "You know it's bullshit, right?" Alex said, folding her arms across her chest.

"I'm sorry?"

"How can they swallow all that? Everything the policewoman said. They listened like a pair of morons, believing every line they were being fed."

"I'm not sure I understand—"

"The drugs? The drugs they say they found?"

"I've seen the toxicology report myself. I realize it must have come as a shock for you all, but the drugs were in your sister's bloodstream."

"Oh, cut the crap. Someone, somewhere is spinning you a line." She reached into her pocket and retrieved her pack of cigarettes. She waved them at Ingrid. "Lauren didn't even smoke. Not even a joint now and then, like any normal person. There is absolutely no way she would ever willingly take drugs."

17

Ingrid looked at Google Maps on her phone and selected a green space at random for her morning run. Twenty minutes later, she found herself on Hampstead Heath, breathing in the crisp spring air. From Parliament Hill, she looked down across the city and picked out all the landmarks she recognized, trying to assign a date and time she'd visited them.

Her ankle seemed completely healed, so she picked up her pace and focused on the Shelbourne investigation, attempting to untangle fact from fiction. She ran flat out for a solid forty minutes, which was enough to clear her lungs but not her mind. Too much about Lauren Shelbourne's death wasn't adding up. She thought about something Faber had said. When Ingrid had told her about losing her friend when she was fourteen, Faber had talked about the cops at the time leaving no stone unturned. Ingrid had been unable then, or since, to get closure for Megan and her family, but she could make amends by making sure Lauren's death was properly investigated.

When she arrived at Madison Faber's building later that morning, the student met her at the front door, grabbed Ingrid's hand and physically dragged her over the threshold. "Thank God! I thought you'd abandoned me." She led Ingrid into a wide hall then straight through an internal door and up a steep, narrow flight of stairs. The house was very similar to the one where Lauren had lived, though with slightly grander proportions. At the top, Faber guided her through another door into a bright, cheerful apartment.

"Did you see anyone on the street outside when you arrived? Anyone waiting?"

"Waiting? For what?"

"For me to come out." Faber scratched her arm. "I don't feel safe. Not even here."

Ingrid walked Faber to a chair and pushed her gently into it. "Has something else happened? Have you been threatened again?"

Faber bit her lip. "Every time I close my eyes, I see that fucking dead mouse."

Ingrid crouched down in front of her, choosing submissive body language to help soothe Faber's anxiety. "Have you figured out who left it there?"

"It has to be someone in the psychology department. Someone with access to the laboratory." She paused, then locked her imposing stare onto Ingrid. "You were going to look into it for me."

"I plan to. I will. But you must have an idea who's threatening you?"

Faber pressed her lips together; her eyes darted left and right. She dropped her voice to a whisper. "There is someone…"

"Then tell me."

Her eyes widened. "I can't give you a name." She sounded manic, unhinged. "What if they find out I've spoken to you?"

Ingrid pulled a footstool over in front of the armchair and sat down. She leaned forward, her elbows on her knees. "Tell me exactly what you know. Everything."

Faber slumped back into the chair, putting distance between her and Ingrid. "I can't believe the police are saying it was an accident."

The pathologist's findings had been reported in the press. The official line was accidental death caused by a fall while under the influence of drugs.

"The pathologist's conclusions were reasonable, given the drugs in Lauren's system. You know I share some of your concerns about what's been going on at Loriners, so if you want me to continue looking into things, you have to tell me why you think Lauren was killed." Ingrid grabbed a blanket from a couch and wrapped it across Faber's shaking shoulders. "Why would someone want to hurt Lauren?"

Faber rattled her head from side to side. "I'm so scared." Slowly, the movement changed and the girl began nodding.

"I want to get answers for you, Madison, but you have to give me more information."

A cell phone rang and Faber froze. "Every time it rings, my heart stops."

"Please, Madison. Tell me what you know."

"You promise you can protect me?" The girl was terrified.

Ingrid couldn't promise anything. The Met weren't treating it as a priority, the Shelbournes wanted things wrapped up so they could take their daughter home, and as far as Louden was concerned, Ingrid should be concentrating on finding Brewster's laptop.

"What I can promise you is that no one will ever find out where I got my information from. Whatever you tell me will never be repeated. Understand?"

For the first time, a tiny smile crept onto Faber's lips. "It's making sense to me now."

"What is?"

"Why Lauren moved out. That must have been when she started using drugs. She knew I would disapprove, so she had to hide it from me."

Ingrid thought about Alex Shelbourne's comments: she didn't know which young woman knew Lauren best. "Why is this making you scared, Madison? I don't understand."

"Don't you see?" Faber's voice was getting stronger.

"Join the dots for me."

"Well, I know who her dealer was, don't I? And if he was the killer, well…"

"What? He'll want to silence you?"

Faber nodded vigorously.

"Did you mention Lauren's habit when the police interviewed you?"

"No!" Her tone suggested she thought Ingrid was stupid. "I didn't know for sure she was using drugs until I heard about the postmortem."

"But you know who her dealer was?"

Another nod.

"You have to tell me a name. If I don't know who he is, I can't protect you from him."

"But what if he finds out I've been speaking to you?"

"The only way for that to happen is if you tell him." Ingrid felt like she was getting somewhere. "Come on, Madison. You can trust me."

"He's a student at Loriners. I don't really know him."

"A name is all I need."

"You promise me he'll never find out I told you?" Faber scratched her arm again, raking her fingernails hard across the skin.

How many more times did she have to tell her?

"I promise."

Faber closed her eyes for several seconds. "Timo Klaason." She spelled the name out for Ingrid. "When you find him, you should be careful. I don't know him, but I've heard he likes to hit girls."

18

The subdued atmosphere Ingrid had noticed on campus on her last visit seemed to have disappeared completely. Students hurried between buildings, chatting and laughing, heavy bags of books swinging from their shoulders. Although she looked carefully for it, Ingrid failed to spot any trace of graffiti on the wide gray concrete facades. She had sent the tissue with the paint sample on to the Bureau's lab in DC. Just because it was inadmissible in a court of law, it didn't mean it couldn't help identify who had labeled Lauren a whore.

She had called ahead and arranged to meet Madison Faber's research team leader after the first lecture of the afternoon session. The harassed tutor arrived late and insisted they talk on the way to her next meeting. She hugged an armful of files to her chest like a protective shield.

"I really appreciate your seeing me on such short notice, Ms—."

"Please, call me Rebecca. I'll feel a hundred years old otherwise." She nodded a greeting at a couple of students lounging on the grass next to the path. "You've seen Madison today?"

"I saw her this morning, as a matter of fact. She is extremely distressed."

"She must be taking it hard. Not something you get over easily."

"No—it was a traumatic experience for her."

"And to be accused of—"

"I don't think anyone was ever accusing her."

"No—no, of course not. Even so—to be in police custody. In a foreign

93

country. Must have been terrifying." The woman checked her watch. "I really don't have long. You said you wanted to discuss her welfare. Doesn't sound like the sort of thing I'd expect the American embassy to take an interest in."

Ingrid slowed her pace, forcing the tutor to match her speed. Ingrid's assessment was that Faber was at more risk from self-harm than anything the mysterious Timo Klaason might do to her. She also knew how much support she had needed when her friend Megan had been abducted. "I just thought, after the suicide last week, after Lauren, the university might not want another young woman to come to harm. She was extremely agitated. How has she seemed to you?"

"Seemed?"

"Anxious? Depressed? Has she been getting along with other students in the psychology department?"

"Why wouldn't she?"

"There's been no evidence of… bullying, for example?"

"She's a postgraduate student, not a kindergarten pupil. Why would she want to bully anyone?" The lecturer lengthened her stride.

"I mean has Madison *been* bullied?"

"Of course not. That's just ridiculous."

"I take it she hasn't come to you with any problems?"

The tutor stopped abruptly. "I'm not the person she would come to."

"You aren't?"

"Madison has only been part of my research group for a short while. I really don't know the girl. Personally or academically." She squeezed the files tighter in her arms.

"I thought—"

A shrill whistle sounded at the other end of the path. Ingrid looked up to see Angela Tate with one hand to her mouth. She whistled again then gestured urgently to a man holding a long-lens camera. What the hell was Tate doing here?

"Madison Faber switched research groups just before the spring break," the tutor explained. "She was in Professor Younger's group before that."

"Are you sure?"

Tate whistled again. With some effort, her photographer jogged toward her. Ingrid scanned the wide piazza to see what the journalist was so interested in. She followed Tate's gaze upward and her breath stalled in her throat. Five stories above Tate's head, on the top floor of the main admin block, a girl stood at an open window, one foot resting on the window ledge, her arms braced against the window casement on either side. She threw back her head and let go with one hand. A collective gasp went up from the students gathered outside the building. The girl looked down at them and waved. A few hands waved back at her.

The girl let go with the other hand. She wobbled.

The crowd held its breath.

Behind the girl a figure approached the window. Tall, broad-shouldered. Definitely male. He reached a hand toward the girl. She half-turned her head. The man took another step forward and the girl tensed. The crowd gasped in unison.

Tate's photographer made long swooping arcs with his zoom lens, predicting the girl's downward trajectory.

Ingrid ran toward the crowd, not taking her eyes from the girl's slim frame in the window.

For God's sake, somebody grab her.

As if he'd read Ingrid's mind, the man hovering behind her lurched forward, grabbing her left shoulder and knocking her off balance. Her left foot swung out over the ledge. The man wrapped his other arm around the girl's waist and leaned away from the window. They both fell backward inside the room and dropped to the floor.

The crowd exhaled. Then a cheer went up.

Ingrid pushed into the building and threw herself up the stairs, leaping three, four steps with each stride. She reached the fifth floor to see the man and girl slumped against the wall, the man's arms wrapped tightly around her. He looked toward Ingrid, his face pale and sweating.

It took Ingrid a moment to get her breath back, then another moment to recognize him.

19

The waitress took their order and slowly returned to the kitchen. Ingrid leaned closer to Angela Tate. "If this is going to work, we need to trust one another."

The reporter raised her eyebrows and studied Ingrid from the other side of the table. They were sitting in a café that Tate had described as a 'greasy spoon' a couple of streets away from Loriners.

After the excitement in and around the admin building had subsided and the agitated student had been taken to the campus medical center, Ingrid had decided there was very little to be achieved by hanging around. Angela Tate had suggested they adjourn to the nearby establishment to 'compare notes.'

"Trust, yes. But you can't expect me to just hand over information without getting something from you in return," Tate said. "I'll show you mine if you show me yours."

Ingrid took a sip of coffee and quickly set her cup back down. Instant. It tasted like an infusion of pencil shavings. "We share the same goal, and if there is something fishy going on at Loriners, I will certainly help you expose it."

"So you do think something's going on?"

Ingrid pressed her hands against the table. "It's fair to say I wouldn't still be at the campus if I didn't think there was something that needed investigating." Ingrid waved to the woman behind the counter and ordered an orange juice, hopeful it would at least taste of oranges. "So what have you sniffed out about Professor Younger?"

"The hero of the hour? Quite dashing, wasn't he, in his tight shirt and designer pants? My photographer got some lovely shots as Younger helped the girl to the medical center. We'll probably run a feature tomorrow. Why are you interested in the good professor?"

"He was Lauren's research group leader. I'm following up on all her college contacts."

The waitress dumped a small carton of OJ on the table and wandered back to the counter. Ingrid stuck the plastic straw into the carton and took a tentative sip. The journalist arched an eyebrow. "And who else have you spoken to?"

"Mostly people outside the psychology department."

"Well, that's because the professor and his research are a closed shop." Tate wrinkled her nose. "There's a protective firewall around him and his inner circle that so far I haven't found a way of penetrating. And believe me, I've tried everything."

"And what have you found out?"

"You first."

"Excuse me?"

"You tell me what you've found out," Tate said, "and then I'll reveal all."

Ingrid had thought things had been going a little too well. She sucked on the plastic straw. "I take it you know about the drugs being taken on campus?"

"Students taking drugs is hardly news," Tate said, searching for something on her phone. "Lecturers taking drugs wouldn't even make it into the paper these days." The journalist pulled an irritated face. She placed her phone on the table and proceeded to scroll through her picture gallery. She stopped at a dark, blurry photograph. "It doesn't do you justice."

Ingrid caught a brief glimpse of herself, lying in an awkward heap on the walkway at Loriners, before Tate swiped a finger across the screen.

"Here we are." Tate tapped twice and an image of the graffiti symbols filled the screen. "I haven't had any luck trying to find reference to the symbols anywhere. I've had the paper's librarian dig into it, and she's come up with nothing. And believe me, if there was something out there, Rita would have sniffed it out." She tilted her head as she gazed at the image. "Have you found anything out?"

Ingrid hesitated. Feeding Tate a crumb couldn't do any harm. "I sent my own hand-drawn version of the symbol to Quantico. There was some excitement initially—an agent thought there might be some ancient hieroglyphic connection, but it came to nothing."

Tate narrowed her eyes, obviously trying to gauge whether or not Ingrid was telling her the truth. "I'm not surprised. As I said, Rita would have found something otherwise." She swiped at the screen again and stopped at a photo of two students, one male, one female, both sporting purple and green polo shirts. "Now this I find interesting," Tate said. "I've gone through all the clubs and societies listed at the college—even extended it to the rest of the University of London—and none of them uses this particular combination of colors." She shifted her gaze to Ingrid's face. "Don't you think that's peculiar?"

Ingrid shrugged.

"You must have noticed them, but have you also noticed they've disappeared from campus completely? Not a trace. The graffiti's miraculously vanished too."

Ingrid tried to recall when she'd last seen a student in one of the polo shirts.

"Take a look at these two." Tate tapped the screen, enlarging the image of the students.

"Let me see."

Tate handed her the phone. Ingrid scrolled through a selection of images. She spotted the student in Younger's tutorial group, but didn't know any of the others. But there was something striking about them. "Notice anything about them?" Ingrid asked.

Tate took the phone and peered at the images like a woman who needed reading specs. "What have you spotted?"

"It might be nothing." Ingrid slurped loudly as she reached the bottom of the carton. "Within a normal group, you'd expect a bit of... irregularity. Short, fat, spotty, ugly, older, balder. Some imperfection or other. These students are all perfect. Look at their hair. Their skin. Their smiles. All blemish-free and perfectly proportioned. They look like they've stepped out of a glossy brochure."

"And that means...?"

"I'm not—" Ingrid was cut short by her phone buzzing noisily on the table. "I need to take this call." She jumped up and ran out onto the sidewalk. "Jennifer, thanks for getting back to me so fast. What have you got on Timo Klaason?"

"I've got an address for you."

Ingrid clenched her fist. "Excellent. Well done."

"I'm texting it to you now."

Ingrid glanced through the window at wily old Tate. She hoped she'd get considerably more out of Timo Klaason.

20

Ingrid arrived at the pub early. After a brief survey of the exits, front and back, and the restrooms, she settled on a stool at the long bar. The bartender stopped wiping down the woodwork and stared at her quite openly. From the corner of her eye she could have sworn his mouth was gaping. He cleared his throat and ambled over to her.

"What's a nice girl like you—"

She cut him off with a wave of her hand. "Don't even think about finishing that sentence. I'll have a ginger ale. No ice."

"Only trying to be friendly. Jesus."

The glass was warm when he dumped it on the bar, fresh from the dishwasher. She saw no benefit in getting into a fight with him, so chose not to ask for a replacement.

Detective Constable Ralph Mills arrived ten minutes later. Right on time. So punctual, in fact, Ingrid suspected he'd been pacing up and down outside, just waiting for the big hand to hit twelve.

"Am I late? Have you been waiting long?" He slipped onto the stool next to hers. "Would you like another?"

"I'm fine." She gestured to a free table on the other side of the room. "Shall we?"

Mills ordered a pint of cider on draft and joined her, carefully tucking his long legs beneath the low table. "Cheers," he said and then proceeded to drink half his cider in three gulps. His nervousness was endearing. He wiped a hand across his mouth and attempted to suppress a belch. He almost succeeded. "So. This is nice. You found it all right?"

"Obviously."

"Sorry, stupid question." He looked so much like Clark Swanson, the motorcycle-riding bad boy of Middleton High, that Ingrid would swear they were related if they weren't so completely different in temperament. "I suppose you're wondering why I suggested getting together like this?"

Ingrid said nothing, preferring to watch Mills twisting himself further into his embarrassment.

He drank another quarter of his cider. "I don't want you getting the wrong impression. I mean, it's not as if I make a habit of this."

"It seems quite simple to me. You asked me out; I said yes. And here we both are." She smiled again, less fulsomely this time.

"But it wasn't as if this was my idea."

"It wasn't?"

"See? I knew I was right to clear things up straight off the bat."

Ingrid lifted her drink to her mouth, felt the warmth of the glass against her lip and put it down again. "Are you trying to tell me this isn't a date?" She couldn't decide if she was relieved.

"God, no. Is that really what you thought?" His face colored in an instant. A shade somewhere between crimson and beet.

"Ah," she said. "McKittrick."

His right eye twitched in reply. "Boss wanted to keep things strictly off the books."

And she also wanted to set us up.

"She said she'd liaise with you herself, but"—he lowered his voice—"she asked me to speak to you because she's under a lot of pressure at the moment. From high up. Plus she's being scrutinized." He pulled a face.

"Scrutinized how?"

"Can't say exactly—it's not really my place to. There's stuff going on."

"What kind of stuff?"

"All kinds. Thing is, she can't throw resources at the Shelbourne case because, well, the scrutiny."

"But?"

"But she isn't happy about the situation."

"She didn't seem to have a problem with the accidental death verdict when I spoke to her about it."

"See." He inched in further. "She's being leaned on... and well... that's made her curious. Now she wants to probe a little more."

"I still don't see how I fit in."

He ran a pale hand through his thick brown hair. "The boss was hoping you'd share anything about the case that you happen to dig up. She can't be seen to do it herself."

"And in return?"

"I help you out on the QT."

"QT?"

"The down low." He smiled shyly at his use of teenspeak, lifting the corners of his mouth a fraction. He had never looked more like Clark Swanson, and Ingrid's cheeks prickled with heat. *You're engaged,* she told herself. *To be married.*

Mills's smile disappeared. He furrowed his brow, a knot of tension forming between his eyebrows. "It's just occurred to me... you thought I'd actually asked you out on a date... yet you still agreed to come."

"'Mutually beneficial' you said." She was smiling at him.

His frown deepened. "So, how can I help?"

She told him about the paint sample that she had sent for analysis, and he told her from now on he would help with that sort of thing. When she got the results, he could run it on their database to see if the same paint had been used by known graffiti artists, though whoever wrote *lauren shelbourne = whore* wasn't exactly Banksy. But it was a start.

"There is something else you could do for me," Ingrid said.

"Of course."

Ingrid wasn't at all sure that what she was about to suggest was a good idea. "Can you run a name through your databases for me?"

"Sure."

"Greg Brewster." A chill spread over her skin. She wasn't used to flagrantly breaking the rules.

"You think he's a suspect?"

Ingrid took a long mouthful, giving herself time to think. "I don't even know if it's his real name. All I know is he's from Tulsa, Oklahoma, and fifty-one years old. Though both those pieces of information could be as fake as the name."

"And you're interested in him because?"

She'd played everything by the book for so long this minor transgression felt like treason. She was terrible at lying. "It may be nothing."

"Is he related to Lauren Shelbourne or something?"

"Not exactly." Ingrid rummaged around in her bag for the printout of Barry Cline's photograph. "And if you can, see if any of your colleagues recognize this guy."

Mills looked at the already tattered sheet of A4.

"His name may or may not be Barry Cline."

"Same drill? Trawl the databases?"

"Not for this guy—I've done that much myself. I'm figuring he's a petty criminal, working over vulnerable tourists, and hoping he's known to the Met."

"Tourists from Tulsa, Oklahoma, for instance?"

"That's the idea. Now… let me get you another drink."

21

The GPS guided Ingrid and her Triumph Tiger 800 to a dark little side street in Deptford, a district of south London not far from Loriners college. She climbed off the bike, stowed her helmet and gloves, and pulled a dark blue beanie over her head, tucking her short blond hair inside.

The narrow street was lined on both sides by seven-story black-brick warehouses, the facades looking like ominous cliff faces in the dark. The road was paved with smooth, rounded cobblestones, slick with rain from a recent downpour. It was like stepping into another century. The buildings were run-down with broken windows and rusting ironwork. Surely it wouldn't be long before they were converted into luxury apartments, like the rest of the old buildings in the city. She checked the address Jennifer had given her for Timo Klaason, as these buildings were so dilapidated it didn't seem possible anyone could actually live inside.

She'd already tried calling the cell number Jennifer had provided. The line was dead, her call not even diverting to voicemail. Timo Klaason was a hard man to pin down.

Ingrid peered up and down the street. A single streetlamp at the far end emitted a weak yellow glow, illuminating no more than a circle beneath it ten feet in diameter. She pulled a Maglite flashlight from a pocket in her vest and flipped on the bright beam, tracing it up the buildings on both sides of the street. She walked slowly toward the streetlamp, stopping regularly to listen. Despite the busy main street just a hundred yards away, the noise of the traffic was no more than a distant hum. She aimed the flashlight in the direction of a scuttling, rustling noise, letting out an involuntary gasp when she saw what was making it. A rat the size of a cat, sitting on its hind legs, was watching her with beady eyes. It sniffed the air. Two more rats appeared, even bigger than the first. Ingrid feinted a step toward them, jabbing the flashlight in their direction, her arm extended. Unafraid, they continued to regard her with something approaching curiosity. A shiver crept up her spine. She was just a few hundred yards from a small creek that emptied into the Thames: this close to water, there were probably dozens of rats. She rolled her shoulders to shake some of the tension from her arms, then carried on walking along the street. She trained the light beam onto the warehouses on either side, looking for an entrance.

Painted in untidy, whitewashed brushstrokes on the wall of a building were the same symbols she'd seen on campus. Three zigzagging lines. She aimed the beam immediately below the graffiti and discovered a doorway set inside a twelve-inch-deep recess. Attached to the side wall of the recess was a broken intercom buzzer hanging from a single screw. Stuck to the intercom was a yellowing scrap of paper with the number 32 printed on it in faded black marker. This was the property she was looking for. She tried the handle. The door was locked. The frame was made of steel, the door opening outward. There was no way to kick or shoulder it open.

There was more scuttling and scraping. Expecting to see another half-dozen giant rats, Ingrid poked her head out of the recess. Two figures were standing by a dumpster, one holding open the lid, the other throwing an armful of rectangular packets inside. It was close to midnight: far too late for putting out the garbage. She stepped into the street, shining her torch toward them.

"Hey! Can you help me?"

Two men, early twenties, tall and trim, spun around, holding up their hands against the glare of the flashlight. The metal lid of the dumpster clanged shut.

"Hi. I'd like to speak to you for a minute. I'm looking for somebody who lives here. You might know him. His name's Timo Klaason."

They looked at one another, then turned and ran. Ingrid shoved the flashlight into her waistband and gave chase, pumping her arms and stretching her legs. "Hey! Mr. Klaason? I only want to talk to you!" she hollered.

After a few strides she was gaining on them, but a third man suddenly appeared from the other side of the dumpster. He dropped his head low and ran toward her. She checked right and left, looking for somewhere to go. Her momentum continued to take her forward, but still he kept coming straight toward her like a freight train.

She grabbed for the flashlight, ready to jab it into his face, but before she could retrieve it, the running man slammed into her, knocking her off her feet. She fell hard on the cobbles, and her attacker drew back his leg before driving his foot into her ribs. Intense pain radiated around her back one way and into her chest the other. He drew back his foot again and kicked hard. Her head buzzed; darkness crept into her vision. He lifted his leg a third time, and this time she rolled out of the way.

"Come on, man!" A shout from one of the other two. "We have to get out of here."

Breathing hard, she watched them run off. She lay on the ground for what seemed like minutes before she felt able to roll onto her side. *This,* she said to herself, *is why cops in the States carry firearms.* No one else about, she could have put a slug in his thigh and stopped him.

Eventually, the pain eased slightly and she could draw a deeper breath. Then another. Ingrid pressed a hand against the wet cobbles and levered herself into a sitting position. Then, inch by excruciating inch, she got to her feet and staggered down the road toward the dumpster. She leaned against it, steadying herself before she attempted to move again. With one hand flat against the body of the big metal cube, she used all her strength to lift the lid, flipping it right over. She peered inside and retrieved one of the rectangular packets the men had discarded.

Within the transparent plastic wrapper, she could see, even in the faint glow from the distant streetlight, a perfectly folded purple and green polo shirt.

22

Aware she was listing to one side, Ingrid adjusted her posture. Each time her foot hit the ground, an electric shock of pain jolted around her ribs. The embassy MD had prescribed nothing stronger than Tylenol. No strapping, no binding, just a handful of over-the-counter painkillers and the unhelpful suggestion she 'take it easy' for a few days.

Sure.

Ingrid made her way slowly across the main piazza at Loriners, carefully avoiding groups of students not looking where they were going or anyone who appeared to be in a hurry. Another blow had the potential to bring tears to her eyes.

She hadn't reported the incident the night before to the local cops. She hadn't seen any of the men well enough to give the police a helpful description, so it would have been a futile exercise. She suspected one of the three men was Timo Klaason, but she had absolutely no way of proving it. Her presence in the deserted street close to midnight would have taken some explaining too. No need for that to get back to Sol or Louden.

Jennifer hadn't been able to dig up much about Klaason, but Faber had said he was a student at Loriners. She had visited the registrar's office and wasn't entirely surprised to find out Timo Klaason had been studying under Professor Younger. Unfortunately, the staff in the office also told her he'd left college the previous semester. Armed with directions, Ingrid set out to find the lecture theater where Younger was teaching: there was an outside chance he would be able to guide her toward Klaason's friends and acquaintances at college. One of them might know where to find him.

Ingrid slipped quietly into the cavernous space, taking a seat right at the back. On stage, Younger leaned on a lectern, looking up at a young student who was standing to attention on top of a table.

"OK, you can come down now." Younger snapped his fingers.

The young man on the table staggered slightly to one side and an 'ahhh' erupted from the audience of rapt students.

"And that, ladies and gents, is the power of suggestion." Younger stepped toward the table and held out a hand. The student ignored it and clambered down unaided. He patted down his clothes as if he was half expecting a vital garment to be missing.

Younger took a bow and was rewarded with a round of enthusiastic applause. He held up both hands and turned his head to one side, feigning embarrassment. He was enjoying every moment. When the applause died down, the students got to their feet and shuffled toward the exits. Ingrid fought her way to the front against the tide of chattering young men and women, taking care to skirt around the gesticulating arms as she went. She reached the lectern as Younger packed the last of his notes into a battered leather satchel. He glanced up, frowned at her for a beat, then smiled. He looked more youthful without his beard. But his eyes were still bloodshot, his forehead crisscrossed with deep lines. Something was keeping him up at night.

"Agent Skyberg." He drew down the corners of his mouth.

"Do you have a moment?"

"Ten whole minutes before my next... performance." His shoulders slumped. "I do sometimes feel like a vaudeville entertainer. But it's just the sort of thing that keeps the students interested. Stops them switching courses. Got to keep the faculty full of fee payers."

Ingrid pointed to the first row of seats. "Can we sit down?" Her aching ribs were affecting her energy levels more than she'd expected.

"If the sun is still shining, I think we should take full advantage, don't you?" Younger headed toward the exit.

Outside, the professor dropped onto the verdant lawned quadrangle, his long legs splaying out in front of him. Ingrid lowered herself to the ground, her ribs screaming in protest every inch of the way.

"Are you all right?"

She forced a pinched smile. "Perfectly." She blinked, conscious her eyes were prickling. "That was an impressive performance."

"A cheap end-of-pier hypnotist's trick, believe me."

"No, I meant what you did yesterday." Ingrid gestured to the roof of the tall administration building. "Quite a feat of strength. And fast thinking."

"Ah. I did what anyone would have done in the circumstances. Right place, right time."

"Is the girl a student of yours?"

"Emily? No—she's a medic."

"Where is she now?"

"Gone home to her parents, I believe. Best place for her. Seems end-of-year exams stress really got to her." He picked a stalk of grass from the knee of his pants.

"Will the college offer her counseling?"

"Most definitely."

"And have you arranged a counselor for Madison Faber yet?"

He froze. "Not really my job."

"Oh. Sorry." Ingrid observed him for telltale micro-expressions. "I'm sure Madison said that was why she was coming to see you the other day."

Younger said nothing.

"You remember, when we were talking in your office?"

His Adam's apple plunged and rose in his newly shaved neck. "Yes, of course I remember. I should check with the office. Make sure she's getting support. Is that what you wanted to speak to me about?"

Ingrid shifted her weight so she could straighten her spine and put less strain on her bruised ribs. "I actually wanted to speak to you about another student of yours."

He narrowed his eyes. "Who?"

Ingrid stared into his face, not wanting to miss the merest flicker of emotion. "Timo Klaason."

There it was—a definite tightening around the eyes.

"Timo?" He scratched his head. "It's not ringing any bells. You'd think it would—an unusual name like that." He screwed up his eyes. "Are you sure he's one of my students?"

"I just checked with the registrar's office."

"I hate to be disloyal, but they do operate on a skeleton staff over there. It wouldn't be the first time they've made a mistake. It's not their fault; budget cuts, I'm afraid."

"The staff were very thorough. They showed me the paperwork."

"Ah. Well… I shall have to put on my thinking cap. Clarkson, you say?"

"Klaason. He's Dutch. I'm supposing you don't have too many Dutch students here."

"It's quite a mixed bunch, actually. Budgets again, of course. Overseas students are our bread and butter." He pursed his lips and patted an index finger against his chin. Another performance, Ingrid suspected. "Timo… Do you know what he looks like? So many students pass through this place."

Ingrid pulled out a printout the registrar's office had given her, a blurry black-and-white version of Klaason's passport picture. Younger squinted at the image.

"Perhaps," he said eventually. "He's not in the faculty now; I'd definitely know him otherwise."

"He left just before the spring break."

He nodded and handed the sheet back. "Well, there you are."

"Can you tell me anything about him? What kind of student he was? How he got along with his classmates? Who he hung around with?"

Younger shrugged. "I know he can't have excelled academically. Or indeed been struggling terribly. In either case he would have come to my attention."

"You're absolutely sure you don't know him?"

Younger got to his feet. "One hundred percent. I'm really sorry I can't shed any light." He held out his hand. "Would you like some help getting up?"

Ingrid ignored his hand and did her best to stand without grimacing.

"My audience awaits. Another two hours of spinning plates and fire-eating. Please excuse me." He smiled at her then strolled toward the lecture theater. A moment later he stopped and turned back. "If you happen to… I mean…" He puffed out a breath. "If you see Lauren's parents, would you tell them all of us here at Loriners—staff and students alike—miss her terribly. She's a great loss to the field. She really might have made a difference."

Ingrid watched his loping gait until he disappeared inside the building. She wasn't sure what to make of Stuart Younger. Her research revealed a man who appeared to have led a blameless existence. He didn't even have a record for weed possession when he was at college himself. Or a speeding violation in the two decades since. He was squeaky clean. Too damn clean for comfort.

"Hello!"

The voice in her ear made Ingrid jump. She stepped back and found herself staring into the eager face of the medical student she'd met on Tuesday morning.

"So you must be *seriously* considering coming here to study, then?"

Ingrid quickly tucked her visitor's badge into her jacket.

"Second visit in four days. That's keen," Mohammed said. "You got over the whole 'serial killer' thing?"

"I, um, haven't made a final decision yet."

"Good job you weren't here yesterday. That would've put you right off."

"Why?" she said innocently. "What happened?"

"We almost had another jumper splatted across the square." He shook his head. "I thought Emily would have more sense than to get herself mixed up in all that crap."

"Emily?" Ingrid walked him away from the lecture theater building, concerned Younger might come back out and blow her cover.

Mohammed fell into step with her. "The girl who nearly jumped."

"You know her?"

He nodded. "She's in my year. Studying medicine, like me."

"What 'crap' is she mixed up in?"

"If I tell you, you might decide not to come here. Like I said before, you improve the scenery round here, innit?"

"What if I promise you right now that anything you tell me won't affect my decision one way or the other?"

"OK. You swear, yeah?"

"Cross my heart."

Mohammed stared at her finger as she dragged it across her chest.

"Emily was a volunteer. I was telling you about the experiments when I spoke to you before. She was a guinea pig in the psycho department. I reckon whatever twisted shit they did to her must have pushed her over the edge."

"You think the research program had something to do with what happened yesterday?"

"Emily's sound. Not my type, like." He smiled slyly at Ingrid. "But she's a good sort, you know? Maybe too good. Maybe that's why she agreed to take part in the research; she was too nice to say no."

Ingrid frowned at him.

"What I'm trying to say… Emily's solid. Smart. Sensible. She wouldn't try to throw herself out of a window without someone or something influencing her."

"Someone?"

Mohammed shrugged. "There's a bunch of them running the experiments."

"You're sure about Emily's involvement in the research?" she said.

Mohammed nodded vigorously. "I told you it was twisted."

23

Madison Faber yanked hard on the black Labrador's leash and the dog immediately stopped pulling.

Ingrid gingerly bent down and squeezed the dog's ears. "You're quite the disciplinarian."

"You have to be firm with him, or he'll take advantage. Sorry about just now, but I needed to get out of the apartment. Miriam, my mom's college friend, is driving me crazy. Fussing over me, wanting to talk about anything that happens to pop into her head. Walking the dog gets me a break from her. Though I'm actually quite allergic to his fur." She gave a little sniff as if to prove it.

Ingrid had been wondering how Faber was managing to resist petting such a cute canine specimen. "But you feel safer now you've moved out of your apartment?"

"A little, I guess."

"Good. And your mom's friend is happy to let you stay for as long as you want to?"

"She is. If I don't wring her neck first."

Ingrid smiled. She was pleased Faber was up to making a joke. The girl was much calmer than their previous meeting. "You've got to admit Hampstead is a nicer suburb than New Cross."

"I feel like I'm on the set of a Hugh Grant movie."

"And having access to the Heath"—Ingrid gestured to the almost rural landscape surrounding them—"is great for clearing your mind."

Faber pulled the dog away from a French poodle he'd taken a shine to. "So, what did you want to talk about? Did you speak to Klaason?"

"Not yet. I'm having some… issues tracking him down. I was hoping you could tell me a little more about him."

Faber inhaled sharply. She was marching up the same hill Ingrid had run up two days previously. "Like I said before, I don't really know him. Not personally." Her voice sounded strained. She lengthened her stride, and the dog trotted along obediently beside her. Then she suddenly pulled up and did a three-sixty turn, scanning the horizon in all directions. "You're sure no one knows you're meeting me here?"

"No, nobody. You're quite safe."

"You can't guarantee that."

Ingrid held onto the young woman's arm. "I'm not going to let anyone hurt you."

The dog barked once and buried its nose into Faber's thigh.

"And you've got this guy looking out for you too." Ingrid held Faber's gaze.

Faber pulled away, changing direction toward a lake at the bottom of the hill. The dog's tail wagged in anticipation. "No!" Faber told him. "No swimming for you." She turned to Ingrid. "He got me drenched when I let him in the pond yesterday. Scared the shit out of the ducks too."

They walked several yards in silence as Ingrid tried to find the right words to get what she wanted out of Faber. "Do you know why Klaason left Loriners last semester?"

"Left?"

"Just before the spring break."

"He hasn't left."

"He has, according to the registrar."

A gaggle of schoolgirls in dishevelled school uniforms pushed past them, teasing one another and shouting and giggling as they went. Faber tensed at the noise. When they were gone, she bent her head close to Ingrid's, as if she wanted to make sure their conversation wasn't overheard. "The registrar's office must have made a mistake. Klaason is a psychology undergrad though he spends more time partying than studying. Somehow he still manages to pass all his assignments."

"And he's running a drug-dealing operation on the side."

"I never said he was a drug *dealer*. I get the impression he's more of an *enabler*. Though he did try to sell me some coke once at a party. He got really angry when I refused."

"You should tell the police."

Faber shuddered, then said softly, "I shouldn't even be talking to you about him. There's no way I'm going to the police." She grabbed Ingrid's arm. "And you promised me you wouldn't tell anyone."

Ingrid patted her hand. "I know. I won't." They started walking again. "How well did Lauren know Klaason?"

"Um. I'm not really sure. But they were in the same research group."

This time it was Ingrid's turn to grab Faber's arm. "Wait a minute. Professor Younger's research group? *Your* research group right up until the spring break?"

Faber's expression remained fixed.

"You were all in the same group together?"

"It's a big group. Around thirty people or so."

"I thought Klaason was an undergrad."

"He is. But…" Faber's right eye twitched as she surveyed the distant horizons again. "I don't know if I should tell you this."

"Haven't we moved beyond that by now?"

"Klaason's useful to the professor, so Younger lets him assist in the research. Klaason's practically his right-hand man."

"Younger knows him that well?" Ingrid was careful to keep the tone of her voice neutral.

Faber wriggled her arm free of Ingrid's grasp and walked ahead. "I've just said, haven't I?"

Ingrid pushed her hands deep into her jacket pockets. Faber was too relaxed about contradicting herself, and this wasn't the first time she'd remembered a fact when it was convenient to do so. She caught up with her. "Why didn't you tell me you were part of Lauren's research group before? Working with Younger."

"I'm sure I did. I definitely told you I don't agree with his methods, and that was why I left his group."

That was true, but it still felt like a lie. "Yes, I remember. So does that mean you have some mutual friends? People who can help me track him down."

Faber stood a little straighter. "I can give you one or two addresses. Friends of friends of friends. But you didn't get them from me—is that clear?"

"Crystal." What was less clear, however, was why Madison Faber was suddenly trying to be more helpful.

24

After a fruitless night keeping vigil outside one of the addresses Madison Faber had given her, Ingrid was not in the best shape to handle an early morning meeting with Louden and the Shelbournes. Two double espressos and a couple of Tylenol weren't enough to deal with the pain in her side and the intense fatigue fogging her head like a thick wad of cotton.

At least a dozen CIA field officers and their superiors huddled in groups of twos and threes in the bull pen outside her office. There were faces she didn't recognize. They lowered their voices or stopped conversations altogether as she approached. It was as if someone had called a crisis meeting at the embassy and hadn't bothered to mention it to her. Sol was waiting for her outside Louden's office when Ingrid arrived, pacing up and down, his face grave.

"Hey—I thought Saturdays were sacrosanct for you. What're you doing here?" Ingrid's smile wasn't returned. She lowered her voice. "Is it something to do with whatever the hell is going on around here?"

He said nothing.

"Imminent invasion? National emergency? Help me out here. I've never seen so many spooks outside Langley."

Sol gnawed his bottom lip.

"You're scaring me now. What is going on?"

"It's nothing that concerns you. Or me, really, just some high-level CIA stuff."

Ingrid folded her arms. "You mean you can't tell me because my security clearance is too low."

"Something like that."

"Should I be buying canned goods and a year's supply of batteries?"

Sol ignored her flippancy. "I'm looking into it, by the way. Raising your clearance."

Well, that was a surprise.

"But there are issues."

"Such as?" she asked, suspecting he was giving her the brush-off.

"It's nothing to do with you."

"Then who is it to do with?"

He bit his lip, then leaned in. "Your predecessor."

"Mulroony?"

Before he could elaborate, the elevator doors opposite Louden's office opened and the Shelbournes emerged.

Ingrid set her face in what she hoped was compassionate understanding, doing her best not to tilt her head to one side. Lauren Shelbourne's parents stepped into the corridor and both acknowledged her with a nod. They didn't look at one another. There was no supporting arm from Anthony Shelbourne for his wife to lean on today.

"Have you met my colleague, Sol Franklin?" Ingrid asked.

Sol stretched out his hand. "I am so sorry for your loss."

The Shelbournes nodded mutely. Alex Shelbourne curled her lip, tired of the platitudes.

"I hope you've got some news for us," Anthony Shelbourne said.

"It's this way," Ingrid said, guiding them toward Louden's office.

Alex didn't move. "I need the bathroom."

"Yes, of course," Ingrid said, "it's just along there." She pointed out a door a short distance down the corridor, and when Alex brushed past her, she pressed a folded square of paper into her hand. Ingrid slipped it into her pocket, glancing uncertainly at the girl's parents.

Alex emerged a few moments later, her face glistening with moisture. "Just needed to freshen up," she said pointedly.

They knocked on Louden's door. Alex Shelbourne glowered at Ingrid as they waited for the DSAC to open it.

"Mr. and Mrs. Shelbourne." Amy Louden outstretched her hand. "I'm so sorry we're meeting under such sad circumstances. You must be Alexandra. Won't you all come in."

Louden ushered them toward two couches facing each other across a low mahogany coffee table laden with a selection of international newspapers and huge photo books about America. *New York From The Air. A Journey Through Yellowstone.*

"Thank you for agreeing to meet with us on the weekend," Lisa Shelbourne said, still studiously ignoring her husband.

"It's the least I can do."

For the next fifteen minutes, Louden painstakingly went through the police report with them, patiently answering the Shelbournes' questions whenever they needed something clarified. Alex Shelbourne remained silent throughout, occasionally throwing Ingrid a look. Something was preying on the girl's mind.

"Is there anything else you need to know? Any ground I haven't covered?" Louden said as she closed the file on her desk.

"You've been very thorough," Anthony Shelbourne assured her. "Thank you for taking the time to go through the report. The police offered to do it themselves, but I feel... more reassured hearing the details from you."

Alex shifted in her seat, cleared her throat, then said, "Is it possible they've made a mistake?"

Immediately her parents turned in their seats and the temperature in the room dropped. Louden did no more than raise her perfectly threaded eyebrows.

"Alex?" her mother said, "where has that come from?"

"I'm just saying..." She leaned forward in her seat, ignoring both her parents and Ingrid, and leveled her gaze at the DSAC. "Do you really trust that the local cops know what they're doing?"

"I can understand your feelings, I can, really," Louden said in a voice so gentle Ingrid couldn't quite believe the words were coming out of her mouth. "You want to know nothing has been overlooked, no piece of evidence, however small, has been missed. Rest assured, the Metropolitan Police Service is one of the best in the world." She patted the file to reinforce her point. "But, as you know, we have our own officer carrying out an independent investigation." She turned to Ingrid. "Agent Skyberg, what's your opinion?"

Ingrid thought about the note Alex had slipped her. What did the girl know? Was she about to drop a bombshell? She glanced at Sol, who was pulling his gravest face, his eyes urging her not to cause the Shelbournes any unnecessary pain, and mostly not to contradict her DSAC. Louden steepled her hands and leaned her chin on the tips of her fingers. The Shelbournes leaned forward expectantly. The room was painfully silent.

"I have full confidence in the Met." Ingrid's stomach muscles tightened. She watched as Mr and Mrs Shelbourne slumped back in their chairs, relieved. Everyone seemed to exhale at once. "There was no evidence of a break-in at Lauren's apartment, no evidence of a visitor, and given the level of drugs in your daughter's body and the lack of other wounds, I wouldn't expect the inquest next week to alter the preliminary findings of accidental death."

"I'm sensing a but," Louden said, her face sour with frustration.

"But…" She stopped herself. "I don't want to cause you any more pain, but I do think there may be some scope for accusing the university of being negligent in their duty of care to your daughter."

Lisa Shelbourne stiffened.

"I've been spending some time on campus," Ingrid said, "and I'm hearing things about drug dealing and also extreme pressure being put on students." She told them about the most recent suicide attempt. Sol's expression collapsed: he really didn't want his lone criminal investigator wasting her time on this. "I think, until the inquest has taken place, there are a few enquiries I can make. They will not, of course, bring your daughter back, but they may begin to answer why Lauren's life unraveled so quickly."

"See, I told you," Alex said. Neither of her parents looked at her.

Ingrid remembered something Faber had said, about Lauren being the happiest she had ever seen the day before she died. It wasn't the behavior of someone whose addiction had gotten so out of control they lose consciousness the next day. She wanted an explanation. She looked at the Shelbournes' ashen faces and was momentarily floored by their loss.

"And might," Anthony Shelbourne began, "might this lead to charges? To a prosecution of some sort?" He had balled his fists so tight his knuckles were white.

Louden intervened. "I wouldn't want you to get your hopes up."

"But it might?" Lisa Shelbourne asked.

Ingrid scratched her forearms. "A slim chance, yes, depending what I find out."

"It sounds more like," Sol said, his eyes boring into Ingrid, "the basis for a civil case against the college."

She understood the subtext: this is not a criminal matter, move on, agent, and don't waste the Bureau's time. She nodded at Sol, then turned to the Shelbournes. "With your blessing, I'd like to use the next few days before the inquest to gather more evidence. But you should know that if I do find something, and the coroner accepts it, it may mean Lauren's body is not released for—"

Lisa Shelbourne gasped before Ingrid could say the word *repatriation.*

A smile stretched Alex Shelbourne's lips. Anthony's hand—finally—reached for his wife's arm. "Yes, please, Agent Skyberg, please continue your work."

Ingrid tried hard to keep the satisfaction from her expression: Louden and Sol wouldn't stop her now the Shelbournes had endorsed her plan. "I will let you know what I find out," she said.

"Thank you," Lisa Shelbourne said. She had not responded to her husband's timid show of affection.

"If that's it..." Anthony Shelbourne shuffled forward in his seat.

"I'm sorry we don't have more for you at this stage," Louden said, "but Agent Skyberg will keep you up to date."

Shelbourne got to his feet and stuck a hand out toward Sol. He shook it, encasing Sol's hand in both of his. Then he extended the gesture to Louden. He turned to Ingrid. "We really do appreciate everything you're doing."

Lisa Shelbourne grabbed Ingrid's arm on the way to the door and gripped it firmly. She went to say something, but she didn't need to: her eloquent eyes expressed more than words. Find who did this. Ingrid nodded that she understood.

"I'll show you out," Ingrid said.

"Actually," Louden said, walking back to her desk, "Sol, would you please escort the Shelbourne family to the lobby."

He raised an eyebrow but said, "Of course."

He held the door for Lauren's family, then followed them out of the room.

"Ma'am?" Ingrid turned to Louden.

Louden looked at something on her monitor, then at Ingrid. "I was just wondering what progress you've made in the Brewster case? Any closer to that laptop?"

Ingrid took a moment before answering. "Ah. Not much." What was Louden's interest in Brewster? "Without knowing the victim's real identity, or the likely thief's, I'm at a serious disadvantage."

Louden frowned.

"But I have a meeting later today." It was a weak lie, and if interrogated further, she'd have nothing to reinforce it.

"With whom?" The words shot out of Louden's mouth with the force of a bullet.

"A... another escort agency. And I'm interrogating other databases." Or rather, the pliable Ralph Mills was.

"Good... good." Louden was distracted by whatever was on her screen.

"Sol mentioned my clearance level was being looked at." Ingrid stood a little straighter, sending a spasm of pain across her ribs. "If it's going to take a long time, perhaps you want to assign this investigation to an agent with the appropriate authority?"

Louden looked at her as if she hadn't understood. "I'm sorry. I really have to deal with this."

Ingrid nodded. "Of course. I'll keep you updated."

Louden had already picked up the phone and wasn't listening. Outside in the hallway, Ingrid exhaled very slowly and shoved her balled fists into her pockets. She felt the folded piece of paper Alex Shelbourne had given her and quickly retrieved it.

There's something you need to know about Lauren.

25

Ingrid stabbed the 'B' button inside the elevator and willed the metal doors to close. But by the time she reached the parking lot in the basement, there was no sign of the Shelbournes' car. She considered racing to the exit at street level, but the car was probably long gone. She had no means of contacting Alex Shelbourne short of turning up at the hotel. Not something she wanted to do unless she knew Lisa and Anthony Shelbourne were elsewhere. Whatever it was, Alex didn't feel she could reveal it in her parents' presence.

She returned to her desk and checked her emails. Brewster's laptop hadn't shown up on any of the registers of secondhand computers. She entered the make and model into eBay but didn't find a match. Just about the only thing she knew for sure about the theft was that whoever had stolen the laptop was interested in its contents, not in blackmailing Brewster. In any normal investigation, knowing the motive would make it easier to identify potential suspects. But unless someone told her what was so valuable, she was fighting blind. Hopefully Marshall would track down Dennis Mulroony and she could swap notes.

Mulroony. Sol had been about to say something, hadn't he?

Energized, Ingrid leaped up and hurried to Sol's office, her bruises rubbing painfully against her pullover. His door was locked. She tried his phone. Voicemail. She wondered how long it would take him to call her back.

With a renewed sense of purpose, Ingrid called the embassy garage and requested a car. They only had limousines, which weren't the incognito vehicle she was hoping for. So she found a local car-hire company and picked up a dinky Chevy Spark that she drove to one of the addresses Faber had given her, not far from the warehouse she'd visited two nights previously. Feeling decidedly conspicuous in a quiet residential street, she wriggled further down in the driver's seat. She'd promised Madison Faber she'd do everything she could to find out what really happened, and now she had made the same pledge to Lauren's family. She had a snowball's chance of finding Brewster's laptop, but was confident a little diligent police work could explain Lauren's death. She might not be able to get the Shelbournes justice, but she could damn well get them answers.

Memories from the past surged, thrusting painful images to the fore. *Not here. Not now.* If there was one thing the experience of losing Megan had taught her, it was that without answers, you remain lost. It had been eighteen years since Ingrid's best friend had been abducted in front of her, never to be seen again. When the local police closed Megan's case without a conviction and without finding her, Ingrid had vowed to uncover the truth about her friend's disappearance. It was why she joined the sheriff's department. It was the reason she had gone on to become an FBI agent. But she was no closer to finding Megan, and she was still living with the void that might have been healed had the original investigation turned over every stone.

So far, every lead she'd followed had led her back to Loriners, the psychology department and Professor Younger. Maybe Timo Klaason had nothing to do with Lauren Shelbourne's death, but if he was dealing drugs, and he was connected to the polo shirt wearers within the psychology faculty, she was going to pay him a visit.

She focused her attention on the blue door of the two-story house. The drapes were drawn at all the windows, even though it was well after midday. She was hopeful Klaason was yet to crawl out of his bed. Assuming, of course, he was even inside. She shook another couple of painkillers from the bottle and swallowed them dry.

Two hours later, as the effect of the pills was beginning to wear off, she considered getting out of the car to stretch her legs. She had just popped the lock when the drapes fluttered in the downstairs window. She sat very still and held her breath, but there was no further activity for another five minutes. Her patience was finally rewarded when the blue door opened and a tall, slim white man, early to mid-twenties, closed it behind him and stood for a moment on the low stoop. Ingrid slipped further down in her seat. The man placed a pair of headphones on his shaved head, fiddled with his iPhone, then set off at speed, striding out of the front yard and down the street, heading north toward a network of equally respectable residential streets.

Ingrid quickly checked the passport-sized portrait of Klaason she had on her phone. It had to be him. It was also possible it was the man from the warehouse who'd played football with her ribs. She eased herself gently out of the car, and by the time she'd locked the door, Klaason was already nearing the end of the street. A good distance for a tail. She reached the corner and spotted him heading west. Then he stopped abruptly and started patting his pockets. He had forgotten something.

Crap.

Ingrid looked around for some place to hide, but short of launching herself over a wall into somebody's front yard, she had few options. She tensed, waiting for Klaason to turn around and look straight at her. She jammed her cell phone to her ear and angled her body away from him, keeping her head half-turned. A moment later, he retrieved a small packet from the rear pocket of his pants. He lit up a cigarette and Ingrid exhaled. He was on the move again, stretching his long legs, forcing her to trot along behind in order to keep up.

A half mile later, he turned into the cobbled street where she had been kicked the night before last. In daylight, she could see the businesses that plied their trade from the ramshackle collection of buildings and derelict warehouses: a health food wholesaler, a vehicle repair shop and a clothing recycling business. Only the clothing operation was in operation on a Saturday afternoon. A large truck pulled through a set of metal gates, which clanged shut behind it.

Klaason stopped at a building immediately beyond the clothing business and reached into a pocket. He pulled out a key and unlocked the door. Ingrid crept closer, hiding behind a truck. The door opened and Klaason stepped inside. Ingrid raced across the street, toward the closing door, and just managed to shove a foot between it and the frame before it shut. Three painted zigzags told her she was in the right place. She got her breath back and tried to ignore the nagging pain in her side, then ventured inside.

26

At the end of a long corridor, Klaason turned right. Ingrid traced his steps, reaching the corner just as the doors of an old-fashioned industrial elevator cage clanged shut. The elevator ascended, and she watched the numbers above the door light up one after the other, finally stopping when it reached number 7.

Not wanting to alert anyone to her presence, Ingrid made her way up a narrow staircase as quickly as she could, stopping on each landing to draw painful breaths. At the top, she pulled open the heavy spring-loaded door that led to the corridor. She counted a half dozen doorways, three on each side, though she couldn't see the doors themselves, as they lay in shadowy recesses set back from the hallway. She listened for a moment, heard nothing beyond the low hum of the fluorescent strip lights, and moved out into the corridor. The first door she came to was padlocked with three solid steel locks. She checked the opposite door, and again it was padlocked. More businesses that didn't open on the weekend. She ventured slowly down the corridor.

She froze at the sound of distant voices. Ahead, the elevator door slid noisily across its rail. Ingrid was in no-man's-land between doorways. She retreated, running backward, keeping her eyes on the elevator. A man stepped out, his head turned away from her. He laughed, throwing back his head. He was wearing combat pants tucked into black boots and a purple and green polo shirt.

Ingrid's heart thumped hard against her ribs.

Another man pushed past the first one, knocking a hand against his shoulder.

"Later. There's plenty of time for that," the second man said.

She pressed herself into a recess just as they turned her way.

"Did you see the look on his face?" one voice said.

"He's all right. He knows what he's doing."

There was a loud bang, fist against wood. A door creaked open. Another voice, deeper than the first two, mumbled something indistinct. Ingrid risked a glance into the corridor in time to see the two men disappearing inside the door furthest on the left, nearest the elevator. It had to be where Klaason was. She waited for a minute before making her way stealthily down the hallway. There was no name plate or number on the door, just the three symbols she'd seen before scratched into the paintwork. She could hear voices on the other side of the door, but wasn't able to pick out specific words. A light flickered in the corridor, a warmer glow than the fluorescent glare. She looked up to see narrow windows set high into the wall, just below the ceiling. Klaason or his new visitors had switched on more lights inside the room. She stared at the high windows, knowing the only way to get a glimpse inside the room would be through one of them. She stepped back to inspect the wall. It was rendered in smooth concrete. A few feet from where she was standing, she spotted a pipe running from floor to ceiling. It was three inches in diameter and attached to the wall with metal brackets large enough to use as climbing toeholds. The big question was whether it was strong enough to take her weight.

There was only one way to find out.

Ingrid stood with a foot on either side of the pipe. She reached up and clamped her left hand around it, braced herself for the inevitable surge of pain in her ribs, and lifted her right leg. She rested the toe of her boot on the first bracket, grabbed the pipe with her right hand and heaved herself up.

The pipe was solid.

She repeated the process the other way, right hand grab, left foot against the next bracket. Again she hauled herself up. Took a breath. Listened. If anyone chose that moment to open the door, she would be completely exposed with nowhere to go and no possible explanation. She stretched up with her left hand and saw the next bracket had only one loose screw attaching it to the wall. It was doing nothing to secure the pipe to the wall, and the smallest amount of force would wrench it from its moorings and send the metal ring and screws, and quite possibly her, clattering to the ground. She reached as far as she could, her fingertips finding the edge of the nearest window ledge. She tried to pull herself up, her hand grabbing tightly on the ledge, but the throbbing in her ribs was too great. She blew out an agonizing breath.

She needed to get a look inside the room. Maybe she could wait for Klaason and his two visitors to exit the premises. But she had no idea how many other people might be inside. She risked walking into a situation she would be unable to extricate herself from. She reached for her pocket for her phone. If she stretched enough, she might be able to get a photograph of the interior of the room. She disabled the flash function and, holding the phone by its bottom edge, reached up again. The pain in her side made her head buzz. She bit into her bottom lip. With effort, she positioned the phone higher than the window ledge. She squeezed the button on the side of the phone, but heard no reassuring shutter click.

Damn.

She reached up higher and squeezed again. This time a bright white flash reflected off the windowpane.

27

Ingrid dropped from her perch like a stone, landing hard, both ankles taking the full force of her weight, her knees bending a fraction too late to distribute the shock wave. Despite the pain, she gathered herself quickly and ran for the stairway, the shouting voices inside the room getting louder as the occupants approached the door.

Shit.

She flung open the door to the stairwell and started to head downward. *No. Mistake. They'll head down too.* She turned quickly and bounded upwards, her head spinning from the pain in her ribs. She reached the next landing and heard the door below being yanked open. She waited till she heard their footsteps going down, then dragged herself up another two flights until she was out of steps. She had two options. The first was waiting for them to leave the building.

"Where are you, bitch?"

"She must have gone up!"

The second option was a fire exit that she guessed led onto the roof. She tried the handle. It turned, but when she leaned her weight against it, the door wouldn't budge. The door frame was damp and swollen.

Footsteps thundered up from below.

Ingrid leaned harder against the door, stifling a scream as her ribs slammed into the wood. The door burst open, sending her flying out onto the roof. It was empty apart from another door on the opposite side, identical to the one she'd just come through, about forty yards away. There was nowhere else to go, so she headed for it as quickly as she could. She pumped her arms and drove her feet into the ground, pushing herself forward.

"There she is!"

She threw a glance over her shoulder. Klaason stormed out of the doorway and ran toward her. She gasped for every breath as she ran for the other door. She was ten feet away when it flew open.

Shit, shit, shit.

Two men, both wearing the signature polo shirts, bundled through the doorway and ran toward her. She couldn't go forward. She couldn't go back. She checked left and right. The rooftops of the neighboring buildings were a good fifteen feet away. Too far to jump with her injuries. But she had no choice. She swung left and drove herself forward, picking up momentum. She gripped the cell phone, which was still in her fist.

There was a low wall at the edge of the roof. She aimed for it, adjusting her stride so she could launch herself from it and clear the sixty-foot drop. Anything other than a clean jump down onto the next rooftop and she was finished.

She lengthened her stride. The edge was coming up fast. She kept her head up, her gaze focused on the perimeter wall. She gritted her teeth. Her right foot hit the top of the wall perfectly; she threw out her arms and thrust both legs in front. There was nothing beneath her but air. She swung her arms backward, propelling her hips forward.

Her feet hit the roof, but her weight fell backward, away from safety, toward the drop. She curled her torso, and her buttocks hit the asphalt, followed quickly by her upper back and shoulders. Her cell phone flew right out of her hand. She watched as it somersaulted through the air.

"Get over there!" Klaason yelled.

Ingrid scrambled onto her side and looked at him. He couldn't believe what she had done, and his face was a picture.

"Five years of parkour," she shouted, her chest heaving with deep, heavy breaths.

His companions peered over the rooftop edge at the sheer drop. Ingrid tried to get to her feet, but the soreness in her ribs forced her back down. One of the polo-shirted men jogged back across the roof to the far side then turned. He started to run toward the edge, his speed nowhere near fast enough to carry him over.

"Go on!"

"Get her!"

Ingrid tried to get up again and made it onto her hands and knees. She watched in horror as the man on the opposite building hurtled toward the edge.

"No!" she shouted, her voice getting lost on the wind.

He pulled up. Just a few yards from the drop, his arms swinging wildly to stop his momentum. In slow motion, Ingrid saw him slide toward the low wall hemming the roof, his feet slamming into the bricks. He dropped backward.

Klaason shouted something in Dutch. He grabbed the prostrate man by the collar and hauled him to his feet. Then he shoved him at the rooftop door.

"Get over there!" he yelled.

Ingrid had to get moving. Little by little, she pulled herself vertical, her head spinning as soon as she was upright. She blinked, then staggered. She scanned the roof for her phone, praying it hadn't gone over the edge. She spotted its cover first. A moment later she located the phone. She bent down, letting out a yelp, and scooped it up. There was no door on this roof, no obvious way down. She limped to the edge of the building and peered down at the street. A rusting metal fire escape zigzagged down as far as the second floor. Klaason's henchmen burst out of the warehouse next door and ran toward her only obvious means of escape. One of them jumped up, grasping for the bottom rung. Ingrid crossed to the other side of the roof. The rear of the building looked out onto a goods yard, a tall metal fence protecting it from the street beyond. There was no way down. No access hatch. No roof ladder.

Directly beneath her, a truck belonging to the recycled clothing business was parked in a loading bay. It was piled high with rags and old clothes. Not a bad option. She stood on the edge, pressed her elbows into her sides, laid her forearms across her chest and stepped off.

She hit the clothes, rolled sideways and tucked her knees into her chest. Then she lay completely still, assessing the damage. Nothing seemed to hurt more than it had before.

She pulled her cell from her pocket and found the picture she'd taken of Klaason's premises. The image was blurry and dark. She stared at it until she could make sense of the strange shapes. She'd seen those shapes before. But not for years. Not since she was a rookie agent working out of a field office in Cleveland. It had been her first big bust: a methamphetamine factory.

28

The crime scene investigators removed the last of the meth-making equipment from Klaason's makeshift laboratory: a large set of kitchen scales wrapped in a huge plastic evidence bag. Ingrid had been interviewed by the senior investigating officer from the London Crime Squad at length and had arranged to make a formal statement in the station on Monday morning. From what the SIO had told her, the squad was responsible for most of the drug busts across the whole of London.

"You look like you just crawled here from a war zone."

Ingrid turned slowly to see Natasha McKittrick, burger in one hand, can of soda in the other, hurrying toward her.

"Jeez, what is that?" The aroma of the beef fat and burned onions had Ingrid's stomach roiling. "It smells like yesterday's garbage."

McKittrick tipped her head to one side. "If I'd known you were going to nag me about my eating habits, I wouldn't have come." She took another bite. "I can't walk past a burger van without buying something. It's the onions." She waved the offending meat sandwich under Ingrid's nose. "Want a bite?"

"I'll pass."

McKittrick shrugged, took another mouthful and tossed what was left in a nearby trash can. She took a swig of soda. "Takes me back to my childhood."

It did the same for Ingrid, which was why she never drank the stuff.

McKittrick wiped her hands on a paper napkin. "So... what was so important you couldn't tell me about it over the phone?" She dabbed some ketchup from the corner of her mouth. Ingrid took a moment to study the off-duty detective. In the four months she'd known her, she'd only ever seen her this upbeat on tequila.

"Are you OK?" Ingrid inquired.

"You're asking *me* that?" She stepped back and looked Ingrid up and down. "You need to get yourself down to the nearest A&E department."

"I'll be fine." A CSI closed the doors of a nearby truck, making Ingrid flinch.

"Some people go to the cinema on a Saturday afternoon, you know, settle down with a big box of popcorn and while away a couple of hours. Are you auditioning for the part of a superhero?"

"I thought you'd want to be updated if I discovered new evidence connected to the Shelbourne investigation."

McKittrick's face sank.

"Why else did you think I'd get you here on your day off?"

"I dunno, maybe you wanted to see a friendly face, a shoulder to lean on? Instead I see you've added to my workload."

McKittrick blinked, her eyes swimming slightly as she stared at the front of the building. "I take it you think this meth factory supplied the drugs Lauren Shelbourne took?"

"It's run by a student in Shelbourne's study group. Timo Klaason, the man responsible for this... enterprise, was, or is, in Professor Younger's research program at Loriners."

"He was Lauren's supplier?"

"According to Madison Faber."

McKittrick's eyebrows shot up. "Didn't know you were still in contact with her." She licked the last of the ketchup off her fingers. "I'm sure I don't need to remind you the cause of death wasn't an overdose. The girl hit her head. That's what killed her."

"I thought you weren't happy with the findings."

"Never said that."

"I thought that's why you sent Mills to help—"

"I'm not happy being leaned on. Being told what I should be delivering and by when, especially when you're not my boss, and extra especially when it makes me look bad."

Ingrid let out a sigh. "That's why I figured you'd want to see it. This way you can let your Crime Squad colleagues take the bust, or you can send in your CSIs and see if there's anything that relates to Lauren."

McKittrick tapped her foot rhythmically. She didn't seem to be concentrating. She was hyper. "Jesus, Natasha, are you high?"

McKittrick whipped round so fast Ingrid took a step back, fearing she might actually slap her. McKittrick nodded at her Met colleagues, all of whom were out of earshot. "What did you say?"

Ingrid was in no mood for another fight. "Nothing."

"Good. Because it is my day off. Or at least it was meant to be."

She didn't know Natasha that well. She liked her. They'd been out for a few drinks, but Ingrid realized she knew very little about her friend. And she had enough experience with addicts and users to think McKittrick wouldn't pass a blood test. Her cell phone bleeped twice. The vibrate function hadn't survived being dropped. She retrieved it from a pocket and scanned the text message. It was from Mills, suggesting they meet. He had 'discovered something' about their 'American friend.'

"Anyone I know?" McKittrick asked.

Ingrid glowered at McKittrick, suddenly very unsure where she stood with the inspector. "It's personal."

McKittrick raised her hands and took a step backward. "Sorry I asked. You said Faber put you onto this Timo fella?"

Ingrid nodded.

"Why?"

"She said she was scared. Scared that Lauren's dealer would seek to silence her." Ingrid thought better of mentioning the mouse.

McKittrick rubbed her chin. "She called the station yesterday, wanting to know if we'd found Lauren's laptop and mobile."

"You seem to be implying there's something wrong with that. What am I missing?"

"I thought she was smarter than that."

Ingrid wasn't catching Natasha's drift. "What point are you making?"

"Faber's pushing you; she's nagging us—doesn't she realize she could be putting herself back in the frame? She was covered in Shelbourne's blood when we found her."

"That doesn't make sense," Ingrid said. "Why would she be so insistent we look into her friend's death if it could backfire on her?"

McKittrick shrugged. "Don't you think there's something odd about that girl?"

Ingrid was exasperated. "She just found her best friend in the country dead in a pool of blood. Trust me, none of us know how we'll behave in those circum —" She was cut off by sudden shouting on the other side of the police cordon.

McKittrick's lip curled. "Christ, not her."

Running toward them, pursued by a uniformed policeman, was Angela Tate. "Just a brief statement," Tate shouted. "The people of Lewisham have a right to know what's happening on their streets." She reached McKittrick and Ingrid just as the constable caught up with her. "Don't even think about laying one of those fat-fingered paws on me." She scrutinized McKittrick, a sudden sparkle in her eyes. "What are you doing here? Do we have a homicide to report as well as a drug bust?"

"How did you find out about this so quickly?" McKittrick asked her. "Does the *Evening News* have spies on every corner?"

Tate caught Ingrid's eye. Ingrid tensed. She'd called the journalist right after dialing nine nine nine. She'd decided she needed to keep Tate on side, in case she needed a favor later. With only three days before the Shelbournes were due to return home with their daughter's body, Ingrid needed all the help she could get.

"Spies on every corner? Hardly. But keen-eyed members of the public with camera phones at the ready are happy to tell us what's going on," Tate said, still looking at Ingrid. "So—*have* you found a dead body in there?"

"Detective Inspector McKittrick isn't here in a professional capacity," Ingrid told her.

Tate raised her eyebrows. "What? Is this what you do at the weekend for kicks?"

"Something like that." McKittrick pulled Ingrid to one side. "Anything new, let me know. Else my hands are tied."

"Ma'am?" The uniformed police officer was still hovering nearby. He nodded toward Tate.

"Oh, leave her be. Just don't let her get inside the building."

Ingrid and Tate watched McKittrick leave. "What do you make of her?" Tate said when the detective was far enough away.

"What do you mean?"

"There's something... not quite... I don't know. Journalist's nose. Something about her doesn't smell right."

"Can't say I've noticed." There was definitely something up with McKittrick—Mills had said as much—but Ingrid was far too faithful a friend to voice her concerns to a reporter. Especially this one.

29

Ingrid ordered an orange juice. When she put her change back in her wallet, she saw the photograph of Marshall. She found a table with a view of Greenwich Market and considered giving her fiancé a call.

We look so young.

The photo had been taken at the finish line of a half marathon. They looked exhausted but elated, covered in mud. Ingrid remembered the day well. Marshall had said he would run with her for the first few miles but intended to push himself. He hadn't reckoned on Ingrid's extra hours of preparation and her absolute determination not to be beaten. When they'd crossed the line together, everyone said how well matched they were. And for a couple of years she had believed them. She stared down at the photo, unable to unsee the indignation behind Marshall's smile. The hand that held the photo wasn't wearing an engagement ring. It hadn't left her hotel safe for months.

She didn't even reach into her bag for her cell. An impromptu conversation with Marshall was likely to make her feel even more unsettled. He'd only ask her again about a date for the wedding. Instead she fished out a packet of painkillers and administered two more pills. She closed her eyes and relived her jump onto the roof. The rush was electric. She would never forget the look of astonishment on Klaason's face. She opened her eyes to see the tall, slim figure of Ralph Mills standing in front of her.

"I've kept you waiting again. I'm so sorry." Mills grabbed her shoulder.

She winced and he pulled back his hand as if he'd been electrocuted. "What did I do?"

"I'm a little worse for wear. I'll get over it."

He pointed to her orange juice. "Can I get you something stronger?"

"I'm driving. I've got a rental car to deliver back to Mayfair."

An expression of intense disappointment cast a shadow over his face. He had hoped this might be more of a social meeting. "Oh, OK. I'll just get myself something."

Ingrid heard him charming the woman behind the bar with his schoolboy banter. He was the polar opposite of Marshall. It took her a while to realize she was gawping at his skinny ass and admiring his slender torso. No preening muscles. No tight tee shirt. There was a modesty to Mills she was finding attractive.

You're engaged.

She turned in her seat, sending a wave of pain from her hip to her shoulder. Maybe McKittrick had been right; perhaps she should go to the hospital. Mills returned with a pint of Guinness. His first sip left him with a white mustache.

"That's the trouble with these things," he said, producing a handkerchief and dabbing his mouth.

The silence that followed was awkward.

"Ah. Um. You had some information, I think, that you wanted to share?" Ingrid prompted.

"Oh yes. Of course. The whole reason you're here."

Not entirely. The logo on his tee shirt was for a band she'd never heard of. It had been years since she'd been to a gig. Damn, now she was staring at his chest. "So, you got something on Greg Brewster?"

He smiled one of the Clark Swanson smiles. "He's an arms dealer."

"Really?"

"Honestly. All above board and everything. Works for a major arms manufacturer in Florida. I wrote the name of the company down somewhere…" He patted his pockets.

"It's OK—that can wait. What else did you find out?"

"It seems his… entertainment preferences… I mean…" He pulled a face. "I'm not really sure how to say this in the right way."

"I know about his taste in men."

"Right. OK. Good. Well, it turns out the company he keeps when he's over here isn't the most… wholesome."

"How d'you know that?"

"He's been robbed before."

Ingrid said nothing. She'd expected as much by the casual way Brewster had reacted to the loss of his laptop.

"Less than twelve months ago he was over here for some big trade show—an arms fair. Can you believe that? They actually have shows at conference centers where regular punters can just wander round and gawp at automatic machine guns and ground-to-air missiles." He frowned, staring right into Ingrid's face. The frown disappeared and his face softened. "Where was I?"

"Brewster was robbed last year."

"Yes. His wallet. Cash, credit cards, everything. He reported it to the local borough force—the Belgravia uniforms dealt with it. I was a uniform there once. Seems like a million years ago now." He stared out the window at the bargain hunters and tourists browsing the market stalls.

"Ralph?"

"Hmm?"

"You got distracted again."

"Sorry. Anyway, one day he gets his wallet taken—mugged in St James's Park two o'clock in the morning—the next day he's withdrawn his statement. Said he was mistaken. The wallet wasn't missing after all. My ex-colleague at Belgravia said he wasn't that surprised, given the circumstances."

"He was with a guy in the park?"

"That's what he'd said originally. Then he said he'd been mistaken about that too." He took a sip of his pint and managed to avoid a frothy upper lip this time. "You'd expect he'd be more careful. I mean in this day and age, there's no need to be skulking around public lavatories and parks after dark. There are apps for that kind of thing now. You can just tap something into your phone and Bob's your uncle, or... whoever you want him to be."

"You seem to know a lot about it." Ingrid decided to distract herself from the pain in her back by teasing him. He didn't rise to the bait. Another way in which he was so very different to Marshall.

"Me? I'm an expert. Another ex-colleague of mine keeps me up-to-date on all that stuff." He smiled to himself. "You should meet Cath. You'd like her."

Was he so easily distracted because he was nervous?

"Brewster obviously thought he was being careful this time," Ingrid said, yanking the conversation back to Brewster. "He went to the trouble of using an escort agency."

"But they're not exactly… reputable, are they? They can't afford to ask too many questions in their line of business."

"Did your friend at Belgravia have anything else to say?"

"It wasn't the incident itself that he said was interesting, which is why it stuck in his mind so much. It was the way Brewster withdrew his statement. My mate said he seemed really twitchy when he saw him the second time. Anxious, like he was looking over his shoulder constantly. You'd think he would have been more anxious straight after being mugged by the strange bloke he'd picked up in the park. But apparently he was quite defiant about the incident just after it happened. Throwing his weight around. Not embarrassed in the slightest. He was a different man the second time my mate saw him. Meek as a lamb."

"Did your friend have a theory why Brewster had changed his attitude so much?"

"No, he just thought it was strange. What do you make of it?"

"Not sure. Did you have any luck tracking down information about the escort?"

"Didn't really have much to go on. False name. False address. Throwaway phone."

It had been a long shot asking Mills for help, but he'd delivered. "Talking about phones… did you ever find Lauren Shelbourne's cell phone and laptop?"

"No. We've not managed to track them down. We've checked the phone company records, obviously, but her phone hasn't been switched on since she died. We're still monitoring it." Mills took a long drink of his Guinness and sat quietly for a moment. "The thing I mentioned before, about our meeting being mutually beneficial?"

Ingrid shifted in her seat. What was he going to suggest?

Mills swallowed noisily. "I'd be really grateful if you could do me a favor."

"Name it." She braced herself.

"I'm worried about the boss."

"Natasha?"

"She's going through a tough time at the moment. She's not been in London that long. I'm not sure how much support she has in this part of the country. She worked out west before—Bristol. I'm doing my best to keep an eye out for her, but I think she might need a mate, you know? Someone to confide in."

Ingrid considered her erratic behavior at the meth bust. "You think she'd confide in me?"

"I know she respects you."

Didn't seem that way earlier.

"I just saw her, actually."

"You did?"

She filled him in on the afternoon's action. "She wasn't in much of a confessional mood. She certainly didn't seem to relish the prospect of reopening the Shelbourne case."

He screwed his face up. "There's a lot of stuff going on at work at the moment."

"You mentioned as much before. What kind of stuff?"

"I can't say what." He pushed away his glass. "Maybe you could go out with her? Let her know she can speak freely to you."

"I can try. But Natasha isn't really the talking kind." She wondered if McKittrick thought exactly the same thing about her. Perhaps they should go out and sink a few tequilas.

"My hunch is she puts on a good front."

Jeez, you're a nice guy, Ralph Mills.

"I'll call her. I promise."

Ingrid's phone buzzed and she glanced at the screen. "I should take this."

"Sure. I'll get us another drink."

Ingrid turned away to answer the call. "Madison, how are you?"

"I have to see you. Now. I'm at my apartment." She hung up.

30

Ingrid slammed the car door. She turned toward Madison Faber's building and froze. Painted across the front door in wide brushstrokes were the words *faber* ☐☐*whore*. The bright yellow paint had dripped messily down the door and onto the step.

Ingrid looked up and saw a twitch in the wooden window shade at the second-floor window, then glimpsed Faber's face at the glass. A moment later the face disappeared and the buzzer sounded on the door. Ingrid hurried up the steps, doing her best to ignore the grinding pain in her side and back.

Inside, Faber was waiting for her at the top of the flight of stairs within her apartment.

"What took you so long? I've been going out of my mind."

"I came right away."

"You've seen what they've done to the door?"

"Did you call the police?"

Faber marched into the living room and Ingrid followed.

"Sit down, Madison. Big, slow breaths."

"Don't patronize me!"

"Did you call the police?"

"I can't speak to them. I've got to get out of here. I only hung around because I need to show you something." She stopped abruptly and studied Ingrid's face. "What happened to your cheek?"

Ingrid lifted a hand to her face, lightly tracing her bruised cheekbone with her fingertips. "It's nothing. Madison, listen. We need to tell the police. They need to take a sample of the paint. They need to take prints. You understand?"

Faber got up and paced the room. "I should never have told you about Klaason. My God. What if I'd been here when he did that to the door?" She shivered.

Ingrid held up her hands, only just managing to stop herself telling Faber to calm down. "Why did you come back?"

"I needed fresh clothes."

"And the door onto the street was already vandalized when you arrived?"

"Yes."

"Do you know when it might have happened?"

"The woman downstairs told me it wasn't there last night when she came in around eleven. She asked me what I was going to do about it? As if it were my fault. My mess to clear up." She started shaking her head and biting her lip. "Stupid bitch."

"And you think Klaason is responsible?"

"Who else would do that?" She was squeezing her hands together, the knuckle bones straining her delicate skin. Faber's fingers looked raw, as if she'd been scrubbing them obsessively.

Ingrid sat down, hoping to set an example for Faber. "There is no way Timo Klaason knows you've spoken to me."

"I tell you where you might be able to find him, and less than twenty-four hours later, that message gets painted on my door." Her head turned at whiplash speed, her fierce eyes locking onto Ingrid. "That's one hell of a coincidence, wouldn't you say?"

Ingrid sat back, attempting to look as nonconfrontational as possible.

"Please tell me you've found him," Faber said, still pacing.

"Klaason hasn't been apprehended yet. But I did find his meth factory."

Faber didn't appear to have heard her. "I've got to leave." Her voice was jittery.

"I'm confident the police will track Klaason down soon."

"I told you not to go to the police!" Faber flung her arms in the air. "Jesus."

"I didn't have much choice in the matter. I discovered his laboratory."

"His what?"

"He was manufacturing methamphetamine."

"Manufacturing? Jesus—no wonder he's so fucking angry with me. I really need to get out of here now."

"Are you still staying with your mom's friend in Hampstead?" She had the car for another twelve hours at least: she could give the girl a lift.

A sob escaped from Faber's mouth. "I only wanted justice for Lauren, and all I've done is make myself even more vulnerable. I've put myself at greater risk and for what?" She looked at Ingrid, an accusing glint in her eye. "The police have no intention of reopening their investigation. Why haven't you convinced them?"

"How do you know I haven't?"

"I know Lauren's parents are taking her body home in three days."

Where was she getting her facts?

"When were you going to share that particular piece of information with me?" Faber said. "After she'd arrived back on American soil?"

"Who told you about—"

"I went to see her parents."

"When? How did you even know where to find them?" She remembered the note Alex Shelbourne had passed her. She still hadn't managed to follow it up.

"It wasn't that much of a challenge. I called every five-star hotel in central London until I got lucky."

The prospect of a distraught and paranoid Faber trampling over their grief, telling them things they didn't need to know about how much blood their daughter had lost, alarmed Ingrid. "What did you say to them?" she said warily.

"What did I say? My God, I wanted to scream at them to open their eyes. They've just accepted everything the police have been feeding them." Spittle collected at the corners of her mouth. She dabbed it with the back of a hand. "Poor bastards." She sniffed loudly.

"When did you see them, Madison?" Ingrid needed an answer.

"Oh? Yesterday," she said offhandedly. "But anyone could see they were hurting too much for me to tell them that their daughter was murdered."

Ingrid exhaled, relieved Faber hadn't seen them since her meeting with them. "There's no proof she was murdered, Madison. You're right to keep your suspicions to yourself." She reached for Faber's arm and pulled her down onto the couch.

"You saw her body, Ingrid."

An image of the crime scene thrust its way into Ingrid's vision.

"And her laptop is still missing! Why am I the only one who thinks she was murdered?" Faber stared wide-eyed at Ingrid. "Will it take them killing me for you to believe me?"

Ingrid was starting to feel no amount of effort would be good enough for Madison. The girl needed counseling. She needed support. It was surprising her parents hadn't flown over to take care of her, or insist she recuperate at home; it was no wonder the girl was falling apart.

Ingrid took a deep breath. "If you tell the cops about the graffiti on your door, maybe they would offer you some protection."

Faber's gaze hadn't wavered. "I am done with the Metropolitan Police."

"If you don't tell them, they can't help you."

The girl finally blinked. "I have no faith in them. They're all useless."

Ingrid wasn't going to respond. She felt responsible for Faber, she shared some of her concerns, but she couldn't let herself be drawn any further into her delusions. Ingrid spread her hands into stars and pressed them against her thighs. "Was the graffiti why you called me, Madison?" She made an effort for her voice to sound level, reasonable.

The girl leaped up. "Gosh! No!" She was smiling.

"What is it?"

"I found something!" Her voice had become girlish, almost squeaky. "Come with me!"

Wary, Ingrid followed the increasingly unstable Faber down the hallway and into Lauren's old room. The window was wide open, a light voile drape billowing in the breeze. Beneath the window was a black trash sack. Faber saw Ingrid looking at it.

"A few of Lauren's clothes. She left them behind when she moved out. I thought I'd give them to her mother. I don't know how much of Lauren's things the police have given to her parents." She picked up a ragged sheet of paper from the dresser opposite the window and held it up to Ingrid. It looked as if it had been folded and unfolded several times. There was a brown stain in the middle where it must have gotten damp and dried out again, leaving an inch-long hole near one edge. Untidy block capitals were scrawled across the page. A dozen or so lines of what Ingrid supposed was poetry.

"What is it?" Ingrid asked.

"I opened the window when I came in here—the room smelled musty —I thought it needed airing. This was folded and wedged between the window and the frame. To stop it rattling in the wind, I suppose."

"I don't see how it's relevant."

"It's Lauren's handwriting."

"Really? How can you tell?"

"Believe me, it is. Besides, the content proves she wrote it."

Ingrid looked more closely at the sloping scrawl. "A poem?"

"It's a sonnet. A love poem."

Ingrid scanned the text. English lit had been her worst subject at high school.

"It's based on an Emily Dickinson poem. You must recognize it."

Ingrid shrugged an apology. "You still haven't explained how this is relevant to Lauren's death."

"Don't you see? It's a *love* poem. Written to her lover."

"So?"

Faber jabbed a finger at the end of one line where three capital letters had been made to rhyme with 'lie.' "Look at that."

"S-M-Y?"

"Stuart McKenzie Younger. Don't you see! She was having an affair with Younger. With her *tutor*, for God's sake. There's the proof you need to reopen the case."

Ingrid took a moment to work through the implications. Even if this were a poem to Younger, and even if they were having an affair, it didn't prove he had anything to do with Lauren's death. She hesitated, not wanting to voice her misgivings to Faber. She was close enough to hysteria already.

"You can take that to the police." Faber pressed the piece of paper into Ingrid's hands. "They wanted to know who she was seeing, didn't they?" Faber's eyes were shining with tears. "Because, you know, nine times out of ten, the boyfriend is the killer." She looked expectantly at Ingrid. "Stuart Younger murdered Lauren."

31

Ingrid thought long and hard about involving Natasha. If she had been drinking at three in the afternoon, she didn't hold out much hope of an enthusiastic response to Faber's revelation at eight o'clock in the evening. Like the tissue in the candy wrapper, the poem's forensics value was minimal. And the mistrust on both sides between Faber and the Met had reached such a level she decided to take a different approach.

She drove Madison to Hampstead, returned the rental car, then installed herself in a quiet pub not far from her hotel in Marylebone. She then called the one person who was very interested in Stuart Younger: Angela Tate. The journalist pushed open the door, and Ingrid plastered a friendly smile on her face.

"Wow, the bruising has really come out since this afternoon," Tate said.

You should see my ribs.

"What can I get you?" Ingrid offered.

"Oh, um, just a ginger ale, thanks."

Angela Tate not drinking? That was a surprise.

Ingrid got up carefully; the effects of the painkillers she'd taken had long worn off.

"My God, you really are in the wars."

Ingrid returned with a ginger ale for Tate and a neat double vodka for herself. The moment she put the drinks on the table, Tate pulled out a silver flask from her coat pocket and slipped a brazen measure of whisky into her drink.

"No point you paying for what I've already got," she said. The pub—pastel colors, uniformed staff and blackboard menus—was part of a national chain. During the week, it would be busy with after-work drinkers, but on the weekend it had a lackluster, insipid corporate vibe. "I think the shareholders will survive without my contribution. To be honest, when you suggested this place, I thought about not coming." Tate slipped the flask back into her purse. "I've got principles."

"You said it was urgent on the phone."

"Well, I wanted to make sure you had all the information before you go to print."

"All the information on what?" Tate asked.

Ingrid leaned in. "Stuart Younger."

Tate's eyebrows did a high jump. "You have my attention."

"And you have mine. You tell me what you've dug up about the esteemed professor, and I'll give you a killer final paragraph." Ingrid regretted her choice of language the moment the words left her lips.

"Killer, eh?"

Ingrid left her hanging.

"OK, I'll go first, but if I say anything you know not to be true, you have to correct me, understood?"

"Completely."

Tate shuffled her chair closer to Ingrid and took a theatrically deep breath. "I finally managed to get through the force field Younger has constructed around his research. It's genius, really, what he's done."

Ingrid took a long sip of her vodka and prayed the journalist would get to the point soon.

"So are you sitting comfortably? It might take a while."

Ingrid shifted in her seat. She doubted she'd sit comfortably for weeks.

"How familiar are you with CIA history?" Tate asked her.

Ingrid had the feeling a good night's sleep was a little further away than she had hoped.

"The Agency? Can't help you. But feel free to ask me anything about the FBI."

"How very loyal of you." Tate pushed her glass out of the way and set a file in front of them. "Do you know about the psychological experiments the CIA undertook in the fifties?"

"A little before my time."

"Mine too—believe it or not." Tate removed a sheet from the file. "MKUltra—ring any bells?"

It did. "Keep talking."

"From as early as 1953, the CIA conducted experiments in mind control, using electroconvulsive therapy, torture, hypnosis... and... wait for it—"

"The administration of LSD."

"Go on, steal my punch line."

"What's this got to do with Younger's research program?"

Tate raised her eyebrows. "Everything."

"You're not seriously suggesting he's been using MKUltra techniques at Loriners? That would be totally unethical."

"I'd wager a year's salary on it."

"Drugs? Hypnosis?"

"I don't know exactly how many of the techniques Younger has decided to employ. As I said, he's been quite rigorous in covering his tracks. Though I would imagine even he would draw the line at strapping electrodes to students' temples."

Ingrid remembered the claims of torture Mohammed had made. Maybe they weren't so far from the truth after all.

"The girl who supposedly jumped to her death last week?" Tate continued. "She was a participant in the program. And the near miss two days ago? Same with her. Strange how Younger was right there to save the girl from jumping, don't you think?"

Ingrid didn't answer. She sat very still and attempted to work through the ramifications. "No," she said finally. "I don't buy it. Younger would never be able to hide that from the college authorities."

"He's a very smart man. I was actually looking for something and I had a tough enough time finding anything out. How would the college discover anything amiss if they didn't suspect something in the first place to even go looking for it?"

"But the students who take part—why haven't they come forward to report him?"

"He's got some sort of hold over them."

"Now that sounds a little far—"

"Please don't accuse me of being a conspiracy theorist."

Ingrid said nothing.

"I've been trying to make contact with the girl he *rescued* on Thursday afternoon, but I'm getting stonewalled. Maybe you could help me with that?"

Ingrid could only admire Tate's tenacity. "I'll see what I can do," she lied. "I still don't buy it. There would be too many people involved to keep something like that secret."

"You're having trouble believing it because I've only given you half the story." The journalist's eyes were sparkling. She wriggled in her seat and pulled out a blank sheet of paper from the file then quickly drew the spiky symbols they'd both seen painted on the wall at Loriners.

"You found out what it means?"

"Look at this." Tate proceeded to draw the lines again, but this time made them much less angular. "What do they look like now?"

Ingrid was reminded of countless physics experiments at high school, wavy lines just like these flickering on the screens of a dozen oscilloscopes. "Sine waves."

"Waves, exactly. Three waves." A satisfied smile spread across Tate's face. "The Third Wave. Heard of it?"

It rang a distant bell. "Go on—I can see you're itching to tell me all about it."

"It was a highly controversial psychological experiment carried out in the sixties. Never to be repeated. Until now, that is."

"Controversial in what way?"

"I'm just getting on to that." Tate cleared her throat. "Picture it—1967, Palo Alto, California."

Tate certainly knew how to string a story out.

"Am I boring you, agent?"

"No, not at all."

"Good. Where was I?"

"Palo Alto."

"Ah, yes. A high school history teacher was having trouble convincing his students of the inevitable rise of fascism in Germany in the 1930s. They were skeptical otherwise ordinary people could turn against their fellow citizens. That they could lose their humanity quite so comprehensively."

Ingrid nodded encouragingly.

"So... rather than teaching them from textbooks, he decided to demonstrate the phenomenon in action." She pulled out another piece of paper and read aloud: "Strength through discipline, strength through community, strength through action, strength through pride."

"Is that supposed to mean something to me?"

"It's the manifesto the teacher invented for the experiment. Naturally, none of the students knew they were participating in an experiment at all."

"How did he manage that?"

"It was the start of a new week. The class had been discussing Nazi Germany the week before. But on the Monday the teacher started his lesson not even mentioning history, but talking about the beauty of discipline." Tate paused and sipped her drink. "You know, how an athlete or an artist has to be focused and hardworking to achieve success. You're part of an organization that runs on a similar basis—doesn't FBI training involve drills and routines a bit like an army?"

"Something like that, I guess."

"I'm too much of a bloody-minded old bugger for any of that to wash with me." She slipped the hip flask from her pocket and drained its contents into her glass. "The teacher got them all sitting up straight, eyes front, no talking, and asked them how much better they felt. How it was easier to breathe, easier to concentrate. Then he got them doing drills, marching in and out of the classroom in double quick time and in silence. And the surprising thing was, the students loved being told what to do." She paused for a moment and Ingrid took her opportunity to interject.

"The high school students were what, fifteen, sixteen? Impressionable. I can't see anything like that working with twenty-year-olds."

"Just let me tell you the rest. The teacher invented three simple rules the class had to follow to the letter." She started to count them off on her fingers. "One, they always had to carry a notebook and a pencil—now that's a rule I'd subscribe to myself—two, they had to sit to attention before the class bell rang, and three, they had to answer questions in three words or less, standing beside their desks and prefacing each response with the teacher's name."

"That doesn't sound sinister."

"But the students got into it. Suddenly they wanted to please the teacher, and each other. Quiet or badly performing students started to participate for the first time, supported by their peers. The whole class found it empowering."

"Which encouraged them to carry on."

"Exactly. And the teacher assumed the role of dictator. After he got them enthusiastic, he was really smart—he talked about the importance of community, about supporting the members of the class, taking action to preserve and protect it from outsiders. He even distributed membership cards and invented a salute." Tate brought her right hand up to her right shoulder, the palm facing outwards, the fingers curled. "The cupped hand is meant to symbolize a wave." She uncurled her fingers and picked up her glass and took a large mouthful of whisky. "As news spread of the exclusive group, more students wanted to be part of it to enjoy that sense of belonging. After just two days there were over two hundred active members, a lot of them prepared to report any of their group for rule-breaking. After four days the experiment had got completely out of hand.

Students were adopting fascist-like behavior with no prompting from the teacher. It was like an organism that had taken on a life of its own."

"Are you suggesting Younger is doing the same thing at Loriners? That he's appointed himself as some sort of benevolent dictator?"

"I'm not sure there's anything benevolent about that man."

"But you really think he's brainwashed the participants of his research program into some kind of… Hitler Youth?"

"There's no need to sound so skeptical. Not just the participants. The whole of his research group too. It was something you said the other day, about how perfect they all looked in their exclusive purple and green polo shirts. There is something deliberately homogenous about them. They're part of Younger's group, fiercely loyal to him and the research program. They'd do anything to protect it, and they shun people who aren't like them."

Ingrid now wondered if it really was possible Younger was linked to Lauren's death. He might not have done it, but maybe she was about to expose him? "And you think it's gotten out of control at Loriners?"

Tate shrugged. "In California the experiment was halted after five days. God only knows how long it's been going on at Loriners." She pulled a pack of cigarettes and an antique lighter from her purse. "Two student deaths and one near miss? Yes—I'd say it was out of control."

Ingrid took a moment to take everything in, to order the information in her mind.

"Looking at your face," Tate said, "I would say you're starting to believe me."

She was. But unless they could prove a link between the experiments and the suicides, and possibly also to Lauren's death, there was no point in going to the police. "Do you think anyone you've spoken to would be willing to testify?"

"Christ no! I've got one or two students who are prepared to break ranks, but they need very careful handling. They've effectively been brainwashed into a cult and need to be deprogrammed gradually. If I mentioned the police to them at this stage, they'd totally freak out."

Ingrid leaned back in her chair and drained the last of her vodka. She would put nothing past Younger. He was sly, he was vain, but she couldn't just accuse him of involvement with Lauren's death. Angela Tate waved a hand in front of her face.

"Earth to Skyberg, come in, agent."

"Sorry."

"So." Tate rested her elbows on the table. "Now it's your turn."

32

Ingrid stepped off the train in the East Sussex town of Lewes and was immediately struck by the sweetness and warmth of the air. It was the first time she'd left London for months, and it felt good to be out of the city. A big part of her would always be a Minnesota farm girl. Small-town life was in her blood.

In the interests of road safety—she was too badly injured to handle the Triumph on the freeway—Ingrid had opted for the train to convey her to Emily Taylor's parents' home fifty miles south of the capital. The journey had given her time to think about what Angela Tate had told her. If Stuart Younger really was running some kind of cult at Loriners, it would fit the charismatic-leader playbook if he was sleeping with his students.

Overwhelmed by the softness and fragrance of the air, she decided she should breathe as much of it as possible and set off on foot from the station as fast as her battered body could carry her. She realized her error when, after following the route suggested by the GPS app on her phone, she encountered a steep cobblestone street rising at an alarming gradient. She drew in a deep breath and started the near-vertical march, taking her time to admire the dinky little cottages lining both sides of the street. Her legs were aching as much as her ribs when she reached the top. Ten minutes later she approached her destination. A middle-aged man dressed in tweed pants and a woolen vest over a crisp white shirt was clipping a neat yew hedge that ran the length of the front yard.

"Mr Taylor?"

The man stopped clipping but didn't lower the large and menacing shears. He eyed her suspiciously, his lined forehead puckering into a network of deep furrows.

"I spoke to your wife on the phone," Ingrid continued, countering his grave expression with a much sunnier one of her own. "My name's Ingrid Skyberg—I work at the US Embassy. I explained everything—"

"Yes, yes, I know. I thought for a moment you might be a reporter. I've already seen two off this morning." He waved the shears at her by way of demonstration.

"John! What do you think you're doing?" A woman dressed in a wrap-around apron appeared at the open front door, wiping her hands on a dish towel. "I'm sorry. He's just thinking of Emily."

"Of course—it's only natural." Ingrid smiled broadly and followed Mrs. Taylor through the door and into an interior lobby. The place smelled of furniture wax and lavender. As they walked further down the hall, the unmistakable aroma of roast beef filled the air. Ingrid's mouth started to water. She'd forgotten breakfast again and wished she'd had time to pick up a sandwich at the train station before leaving London.

"I'll pop the kettle on. Make us a nice pot of tea." She smiled at Ingrid. "Unless you'd prefer coffee, of course."

In Ingrid's experience, all home-brewed coffee she'd been offered in the UK was pretty much undrinkable. "Tea would be perfect."

After being shown into a light-filled living room, a room that looked out over a backyard stuffed with plants of all kinds and a cherry tree in full pink blossom, Ingrid waited for one of the Taylors to reappear. Finally John Taylor materialized at the door, hovering on the threshold of his own living room, apparently reluctant to be alone with her.

"Your house is beautiful," she said.

"That's Julia's doing. I can't take the credit for it."

"The garden too—really lovely."

He pulled back his shoulders and stood a little taller. "Oh yes. Well. There's always something to do. Especially this time of year. I can spend the whole weekend tending to it."

"Your efforts are certainly paying off."

He offered her a begrudging smile. "I should see how my wife's getting on in the kitchen." He started to turn.

"How's Emily today?"

Taylor flinched as if he'd taken a physical blow. His nose twitched and he stared at the carpet. "Well as can be expected, I suppose."

"Mind out of my way." Mrs Taylor appeared at his side, holding a tray.

She squeezed past him and carefully unloaded the contents of the tray onto a side table. Bone china tea service and a large round walnut-encrusted cake safely transferred, she shoved the tray at her husband. "Make yourself useful." She turned back to Ingrid as her husband wandered toward the kitchen. "Has John been bending your ear?"

"We didn't really get a chance to—"

"I'm teasing you. He's not great with strangers. Especially not in his own house. He goes into caveman mode: protect and survive."

Ingrid thought that sounded like a pretty good strategy.

"Though I suppose he's got good reason to at the moment." She let out a sigh. "He blames himself for what happened."

"He does?"

"He thinks he's been pushing Emily too much to do well in her studies. Putting too much pressure on her."

"Do you think that's true?"

"Good grief, no. He's just a proud dad who wants the best for his daughter."

"How is Emily?"

Another sigh. "I only wish I knew. She's been holed up in her room ever since she came home."

"Do you think she might speak to me?"

"You can try. But like I said on the phone, she's not really talking to anyone. Not even us."

"How about her friends?"

Mrs. Taylor shook her head. "All her friends are at uni. I haven't even heard her speaking on the phone. I suppose she might have been texting them." She poured tea into one of the neat china cups. "Milk and sugar?"

"Just as it comes. Thank you."

"Carrot cake? It's a new recipe I'm trying out."

"I'd love some." Ingrid smiled again. "But first, do you think I might be able to speak to Emily?"

"Why would she speak to you if she won't talk to her own mother and father?" Mr. Taylor was in the doorway again.

"I'll show you where her room is." Julia Taylor led Ingrid out of the room, scowling at her husband on the way. "I really don't think she'll respond," the woman said when they were standing on the second-floor landing. She tapped lightly on a door still adorned with an 'Emily's room —DO NOT ENTER' plaque. "Emily, sweetheart. There's someone here to see you. She'd like to speak to you about Lauren Shelbourne."

Ingrid and Mrs. Taylor both held their breath and listened for sounds on the other side of the door. There was a definite creaking of floorboards. Then nothing. Ingrid exhaled.

"May I?" she said. Mrs Taylor stepped to one side. "Hello, Emily. My name's Ingrid. I'm from the American embassy in London. Did you know Lauren?" She turned to the girl's mother. "Could I have a moment alone with Emily?"

"Be my guest." She raised her voice. "I'll be in the kitchen, if you need anything, love."

Ingrid watched the woman trudge wearily down the stairs. "I know about the experiments, Emily. There's nothing to be afraid of. You're quite safe." She heard a noise from within the room. A crash of something being dropped on the floor? "Emily? Why don't you open the door and we can speak more privately?" Silence for a moment followed by the boom of dance music at top volume.

"I did tell you." Mr. Taylor was standing at the bottom of the staircase. "But you wouldn't listen."

Back in the living room, half a cup of tea and a few crumbs of carrot cake later, Mr Taylor was in full swing, berating the welfare services at Loriners College. "Students are in their care. They should be keeping a closer eye on them. One look at her and you could see she's in a terrible state. Do the tutors just leave them to their own devices? First time away from home, they're not more than schoolchildren, really. It's a dereliction of duty. I've a good mind to sue." He paused for breath and Ingrid took the opportunity to broach the subject she'd been avoiding.

"Does Emily have any history of…"

"Depression? Is that what you want to know? It's none of your bloody business!"

"Don't be like that, John. Miss Skyberg's come all this way," Julia Taylor said. "Emily's always been a happy child. She never even went through that difficult teenager phase. You couldn't have met a sweeter girl. I don't know what happened. She was fine at Christmas. Spent time with us. And her friends. Went out riding on Boxing Day."

"How was she during the spring vacation?" Ingrid asked, keen not to get sidetracked.

The Taylors looked at her blankly.

"The, ah… Easter holidays?"

"She didn't come home for Easter. She stayed up in London. She said her friends were staying at college, so she would too," Julia Taylor said. "They were taking part in some experiment or other. She said it was important she didn't miss it."

"Experiment?" Ingrid did her best not to sound too interested.

"Something in the psychology department, she said."

"Not part of her medical studies?"

"She wants to specialize in neuroscience," Mr Taylor said. "Apparently, participating in the research program helps with that." He stared blankly into space. "Though God knows how all this will affect her degree. She might have to repeat this whole year. She should be preparing for her exams right now."

"Have you met any of the teachers at Loriners? Do you know Professor Younger?"

"Younger?" Julia Taylor said and rolled her eyes. "At Christmas she wouldn't stop talking about the man. Stuart this, Stuart that. How brilliant he is. Such an important pioneer in the field."

"And has she mentioned him or the research program since she's been home this time?"

"She hasn't spoken about any of it."

"I'd like to see Younger," her husband added. "Shake him by the hand. Buy him a bloody big drink. If it wasn't for him and what he did..." He shook his head. "I can't even think about what might have happened."

"The professor hasn't made contact with you?"

"No—and we haven't had any luck reaching him. But then if he's as brilliant as Emily says, I don't suppose he has much spare time." Julia Taylor started to clear away the tea things.

"But you'd think he might have made the effort," Mr Taylor said, "in the circumstances."

With some difficulty Ingrid got to her feet. "I should let you folks get on with your Sunday lunch. Thank you so much for seeing me." She handed Julia Taylor a business card. "If Emily changes her mind about speaking to me, please call me. Anytime."

Back on the tree-lined sidewalk, Ingrid looked up toward the second floor of the building. A drape fluttered at a small side window, a figure in shadow quickly moving away from the glass.

33

"Do you ever take a day off?" McKittrick said when Ingrid approached. Not the response she was hoping for. McKittrick set down the 1950s butter dish she was holding and moved on to the next table of secondhand objects. The flea market, or as McKittrick insisted on calling it, the 'car boot sale,' was the biggest Ingrid had ever seen, taking up most of a two-acre high school field in Kentish Town, the district of London where McKittrick lived. McKittrick had invited her to similar events before, but rummaging through other people's unwanted castoffs was not something that appealed to Ingrid, and she'd always made the excuse of a prior engagement.

"You never know what little gem you might stumble upon," McKittrick had said, in an attempt to convey what Ingrid was missing. So far they had stumbled on trash fit only for the garbage truck. "So. Why are you here, Ingrid, or do I need to report you to the ambassador for interfering with a Metropolitan Police investigation?"

Ingrid was taken aback.

"It's a joke."

"Right." Ingrid exhaled. "Phew."

McKittrick gave her a playful slap on the arm and Ingrid winced.

"Serves you right for jumping off buildings."

Ingrid didn't know how to respond.

"Think we're having a communication breakdown here. That was another attempt at humor."

"Ah."

As McKittrick browsed the stalls, Ingrid told her most of what she'd learned about Stuart Younger. The inquest into Lauren Shelbourne's death had been scheduled for first thing on Wednesday morning, and that meant they had sixty hours to present any evidence that would cast doubt on the accidental-death verdict.

"Can you at least go talk to Stuart Younger?" Ingrid asked the detective before McKittrick sifted through the next pile of random junk.

"Why? I'm not sure you've mentioned which law he's broken."

"You don't think appointing himself dictator of the research program, setting up controversial experiments that have driven at least one student to her death, is worth investigating?"

"From what you've told me, the experiments sound... unscrupulous maybe, unethical at worst. Not illegal. You should report him to the university, but it's not a matter for the police. Unless you have hard proof of Younger administering Class A drugs to the research participants, or brainwashing them to jump from tall buildings."

"Hard proof? What about the Canadian student? Are you telling me there wasn't either LSD or meth... or both in her bloodstream when she died?"

"I can't tell you that. Not because she did—I'm not saying that—but because I don't actually know. Like I explained to you before, it wasn't my case. The Homicide and Serious Crime Command didn't pick it up. There was no need. It was called as a suicide at the scene." She wandered over to the next table. "I can have a quiet word with my colleagues in CID, if you like. See if I can get hold of a blood-analysis report." She turned to Ingrid. "I'm not promising anything, mind."

"Thank you."

"But you don't have any evidence of an affair with one of his students, do you? All you've got is hearsay."

"No, but you could put Faber on the stand—"

McKittrick snorted. "No jury would believe her. She's obviously got mental health issues."

Ingrid wasn't going to be shut down so easily. "In a few weeks, I'm sure Emily Taylor will be up to being interviewed. And you could try talking to Younger's wife. She might have plenty of evidence of his affair. Wives often do."

"Alleged affair."

McKittrick had a point. She picked up an unopened rusty tin of crackers. They looked as if they'd survived the Second World War. "They'd go down a treat with some foie gras and a glass of claret."

"But if it is true," Ingrid said, determined to make her case, "the affair could be a motive for murder. What if Lauren was going to expose his experiments?"

"This isn't an episode of *Miss Marple*, Ingrid."

"You really think I'm that..." Ingrid searched for the right word. "Inept?"

McKittrick looked shocked.

"I'm an FBI agent, Natasha. I do know how you build a case, how you need evidence for a conviction, but there's a clock ticking here. Once the coroner releases Lauren's body on Wednesday, we've lost our chance to... we've lost our strongest piece of forensic evidence. Right now, I think there are enough loose ends to put the inquest on pause."

McKittrick examined a bright green teapot.

"Have you even questioned Younger?" Ingrid asked.

"Saw one of these at my first crime scene," she said, and put it down.

"Natasha! Stay with me here. If this were the States, we'd be questioning Younger."

McKittrick's expression turned icy. "Would you now?" She had found a pair of long earrings made of orange, red and yellow glass. She held them up to her ears. "What do you think?"

"They match your eyes." Ingrid managed a smile.

"Charming. Remind me never to ask for your opinion again."

Ingrid stared directly into McKittrick's face, forcing the detective to make eye contact. "What do I have to get you for you to take this seriously?"

McKittrick considered the request. "OK, from what I'm piecing together here, you're suggesting Younger buys drugs from Klaason to give to students as part of his experiments. Have I got that straight?"

Ingrid nodded.

"I'd need proper, solid evidence proving Younger has received drugs from Klaason—LSD and methamphetamine specifically—then I'd have no choice but to consider the impact on the Shelbourne case. I'd at least suggest my colleagues in the London Crime Squad invite Younger in for questioning."

"You would?"

"I'm not deliberately setting out to be obstructive, you know. You get me the evidence. I'll follow it up."

"Thank you." A firework of elation burned and fizzed inside her. She wasn't an idiot. She did know what she was doing. And if someone was killing kids, there was no way in hell she would let them get away with it.

McKittrick picked up a black-and-white photograph, the edges ragged with age. She held it up to show Ingrid. "Look at those sad eyes. I bet she had some stories to tell." She flipped over the picture. "1941. Wow, middle of the Blitz. No wonder she looks sad."

Ingrid wasn't familiar with McKittrick's sentimental side. Perhaps it was the right time to speak to her about whatever 'stuff' was going on at work. She had promised Mills she'd broach the subject. They wandered to the next table, which was selling home-baked pies and cakes. Only a few items remained so late in the afternoon. Ingrid selected a slice of cold pizza, piled high with goat cheese, sun-dried tomatoes and olives. It was gone in two bites. McKittrick raised her eyebrows.

"Want anything?" Ingrid asked her and bought the last slice of cheesecake before she'd had a chance to answer.

"I'm fine."

"Really? Are you *really* fine?" Ingrid could have kicked herself for sounding like such a klutz.

"I had a late lunch."

"No... I mean..." This wasn't going the way Ingrid had hoped. She took a bite and tried to chew the mouthful of sweet, vanilla-flavored cream cheese and dark, caramelized cookie base slowly, but the whole thing melted on her tongue. She swallowed and started the sentence again. "When I spoke to Mills yesterday, he said—"

"Mills?"

Ingrid nodded.

"Oooh."

"Not like that!"

"Ralph and Ingrid sitting in a tree..."

"Stop it!"

"K-I-S-S-I-N-G!"

Ingrid said nothing.

"You should know you're blushing."

Ingrid gathered herself. "He said he was worried about you. And, well, you were a little off-kilter at the meth bust yesterday." Ingrid shoved what was left of her cheesecake into a nearby trash can.

McKittrick was seething.

"Look, he barely said a thing. He certainly didn't betray any confidences, but if you need someone to talk to, consider me a pair of ears."

McKittrick's nostrils flared. "Bloody Mills. He's way too soft to be a copper."

She headed for the exit and Ingrid hurried after her.

"I'm sure his intentions were honorable. He's just watching your back."

"I suppose you might as well know." McKittrick finally slowed down as they reached the gate. "Professional Standards are investigating my... *conduct* at the moment. I've got to keep a low profile. Keep my head down to prevent it being shot off. I'm this far—" she held up her finger and thumb, leaving a tiny gap in between "—from being sent on gardening leave. I have to play everything by the book." She ran a hand through her hair.

"I had no idea—"

"So apart from chasing CID about that blood test, I really can't help you." She stared Ingrid hard in the face. "As far as Lauren Shelbourne is concerned... you're on your own, kid."

"Understood." Now wasn't the time to question why Natasha was being investigated, but she could guess. "There is one more favor I have to ask."

McKittrick narrowed her eyes. "Before you do, can I just remind you, this is meant to be my day off."

"It's a small thing. A favor for me, nothing to do with the Shelbourne case." Ingrid paused. "Don't agree to do this if it'll cause you any problems. I don't want you getting into trouble on my account."

"I think you know by now I have absolutely no problem saying no." McKittrick smiled at her.

"That's certainly true."

"Come on, then. Spit it out."

"My predecessor at the embassy, a guy named Dennis Mulroony... I'd really like to speak to his main contact in the Met. I'm not sure who that is. All I need from you is a name."

34

The two women said an awkward goodbye at the high school gates, neither of them quite making the 'to hug or not to hug' decision before the moment had passed. Ingrid at least felt she was getting her friendship with the detective back on track. Like McKittrick had said, she wasn't being obstructive over the Shelbourne case. Just objective. Which only highlighted how much her own objectivity had been tested. She knew she'd let her judgment be influenced by events from the past. And that was unprofessional.

Ingrid's cell buzzed as she walked toward the Tube station on Kentish Town Road. When she saw Madison Faber's number, she considered not answering. But with only two and a half days till the inquest, now wasn't the moment to shut down on Faber.

"Hi, Madison, are you OK?" She braced herself for a panicky rant.

"I have something I need you to see." Faber sounded calm.

"What is it?" She wasn't sure she could face another meeting with Faber right now. Calm or not. She felt like she needed a little distance from the student. Get some of her objectivity back.

"I have proof," Faber said, her voice even and quiet. "The proof you said you needed. To take me seriously."

Ingrid didn't remember asking her for anything. "Proof of what?"

"Come see—it's much better if I show you."

Ingrid approached the Tube station. She was pretty certain the

Northern line train would take her straight up to Hampstead, so, wearily, Ingrid agreed to another trip to the house where Madison was staying near Hampstead Heath. She didn't have the energy to even begin to imagine what Faber might want her to look at. She didn't suppose it would be anything that useful. But she felt obliged to check it out.

Down on the platform at Kentish Town Tube station, Ingrid discovered she'd have to travel south to Camden Town, then switch to the Hampstead branch of the Northern line, making this particular endeavor seem like even more of a wild-goose chase. The thought of soaking in a soothing warm bubble bath that would ease her battered ribs and aching back was suddenly overwhelmingly appealing.

She emerged from the deep station in Hampstead grateful for air and daylight. Ten minutes later she arrived at Faber's impressive temporary home, and when the front door opened, an excited Madison Faber grabbed her by the arm and guided her to an annex at the rear. She was being put up in considerable style and had been gifted her own suite decorated with mid-century modern furniture. It looked like something from a magazine.

"You know I was getting some clothes from home?"

"Yes." Ingrid was being slowly engulfed by tiredness.

"That's when I noticed it." She nodded at a short red cocktail dress laid flat on a large rectangle of tissue paper spread carefully over the bed.

"This belonged to Lauren?"

"She only wore it on special occasions."

Why would Lauren leave it behind, if it were that special? Ingrid's heart sank. Maybe she should have ignored Faber's call after all. "I'm sorry, Madison, I really don't see how this is relevant."

"Special occasions—like dates. Don't you see? Dates with Stuart… with Professor Younger."

"We don't know for sure the poem was about him."

"But we will!" There was a trill of excitement in her voice. The calmness Faber had demonstrated on the phone had vanished completely. Ingrid steeled herself for whatever revelation was coming next.

"Look at that mark, down at the bottom there." She pointed to a dried white stain, a patch roughly two inches by three.

Ingrid hoped this wasn't about to go in the direction she feared it was headed. She said nothing.

"I couldn't believe it when I saw it. I'd almost finished getting Lauren's things collected together—to send them to her parents—when I discovered it."

Ingrid remained silent.

"It's the evidence we needed. All you have to do now is get it analyzed."

"Are you suggesting the stain is semen?"

"It doesn't take a genius to work it out."

"And you think it's Stuart Younger's?"

"Of course I do! Who else's would it be?"

Ingrid took a moment to work out the best way to dampen Faber's excitement as gently as possible. She needed her to calm down. "Even if I get this analyzed—"

"What do you mean, 'even'?"

"Please—just let me finish. I get this analyzed and prove it's semen. I prove it's Stuart Younger's semen. And from that I assume that Lauren was having an affair with him?"

Faber was nodding at her vigorously. "You can more than assume it! You'll know it for an indisputable, incontrovertible fact."

She laid a hand gently on Faber's arm. "But even if it is, how does that prove Younger had anything to do with her death?"

"Don't you see? It's obvious. Lauren *kept* the dress with the stain on it. This was her best dress, remember. She didn't take it to be dry cleaned. Yet she wrapped it in tissue paper. Why would she keep a dirty dress carefully wrapped up like that? It's not like this doesn't have a precedent."

Ingrid waited for Faber to draw the inevitable comparison.

"Didn't a certain White House intern do exactly the same thing?"

"Maybe Lauren just hadn't gotten around to taking it to the dry cleaner's."

"It was carefully wrapped in tissue paper, laid flat in plastic on top of her closet. She wanted to keep the dress just as it was, *with* the stain. She even left it at my apartment when she moved out. She wanted to store it someplace safe. Somewhere Younger wouldn't find it."

This wasn't adding up, but Ingrid was so fatigued she wasn't able to figure it out. "Why?"

"Why else? To blackmail him. She wanted to blackmail him into leaving his wife."

She sounded delusional. "Don't you think that all sounds a little… extreme?"

"I told you Lauren could be off beam sometimes. This was her insurance policy. If the relationship didn't go the way she wanted… if Younger proved to be reluctant in choosing Lauren over his wife, she had this stored away to persuade him." Faber had worked herself up so much her cheeks had flushed and her eyes were wet. "Only it didn't persuade him. Not in the way she'd intended. Lauren blackmailed Younger and he had to silence her." She pointed at the dress again, quite breathless. "There's all the proof you need."

35

Ingrid's exhaustion was such that she fell asleep in her clothes. The pain in her ribs woke her up at five thirty when she undressed and got under the covers, but she didn't go back to sleep. There was something creepy about Faber's glee at the stain on the dress, and it bothered Ingrid. The girl couldn't believe Ingrid wasn't taking it away for testing. Once she explained that, under UK law, only a British investigator could do that, Faber was equally exasperated Ingrid didn't call the Met.

"The thing is, Madison, that dress has your DNA on it. It was found by you in your apartment. Even the greenest, most newly qualified defender in the country could create enough doubt in a jury's mind for the dress to be worthless to a prosecution."

Faber's features had pinched and her lips pursed like she was sucking on a lemon slice. "Oh." But her deflation only lasted a second. "But you believe me, don't you?"

Wearily, Ingrid had said that she did, and as she lay awake in her hotel bed, she hated herself for lying. She had been so focused on getting justice for Lauren that she had failed to arrange some support for Faber. When the college office opened, she would report her concerns and suggest they urgently get her a counselor. She would also ask Jennifer to research therapeutic options for the girl in case the embassy could help. Given everything Faber had been through since finding Lauren's body, her odd and erratic behavior was understandable, but Ingrid was fearful the girl was on the cusp of some kind of psychiatric episode.

She arrived at Loriners just after eight. The place was quiet: it was far too early for most students to be up on a Monday morning, but the cafeteria was open, so she got herself a coffee then sat in the early morning sun in the piazza. When three tall, blond, unusually handsome men entered the science building together, Ingrid's curiosity meant she followed them. She reached Professor Younger's office to discover the door half-open. Through the gap she saw the men removing files from cabinets, shifting piles of CDs from shelves into waiting cardboard cartons, and feeding sheets of paper into an industrial-sized shredder. Such was their industry that they didn't notice her until she tapped lightly on the door.

"I'm looking for Professor Younger. Is he in yet?"

The young man hunched over the shredder looked up and eyed her suspiciously. For a long and agonizing moment, she wondered if he recognized her. Although he wasn't wearing the trademark green and purple uniform, it was possible he'd been one of the men pursuing her across warehouse rooftops on a Deptford industrial estate. She didn't recognize him.

"Who're you?" he said finally.

Ingrid let go of the breath she'd been holding. "Sarah Charles. Prospective PhD student." She smiled warmly at him, eager to make the lie more believable.

"Stuart didn't mention anything to me about a meeting."

"And you are?"

He didn't answer.

The other two men had stopped what they were doing and studied her as closely as the first. Again, she hoped neither of them had been at the meth factory on Saturday.

"Stuart's in the lab all morning."

"Really? I'm sure our meeting was today."

"He's busy."

"That's a shame. I've heard so many exciting things about his research. I was looking forward to meeting him."

"I can pass on a message." The man threw an armful of files into a box at his feet.

"Never mind. I can rearrange for another time."

Ingrid turned on her heels and headed toward the exit, keen to get to the lab while Younger was still there. Assuming, of course, the shredding man was telling her the truth.

The cleanup operation was puzzling. Angela Tate's story about Stuart Younger's research methods wasn't due to hit the streets for a while yet.

Had Younger found out about her plans for publication? She picked up her pace, grateful her sore bones were complaining just a little less than they had the day before.

She found the research laboratories and followed the signs to the psychology section, peering into rooms as she went. Each one she passed was empty, the lights off. Younger and his merry gang of industrious students were the only people on campus. She came to the end of a corridor and stepped into a larger space lined on both sides with small booths. She opened the door of one of them. The booths were no more than ten feet square. A single chair was tucked beneath a waist-high workbench. On the bench sat a pair of headphones connected to a socket in the wall. She supposed this was where some of the experiments took place, a willing volunteer isolated in each booth. She closed the door and continued toward a bank of file cabinets that divided the space in two. Professor Younger appeared suddenly from behind one of the cabinets, his head turned away from her.

Ingrid crept a little closer and watched as he opened a drawer, retrieved a handful of files and dumped them with a *thwump* on the floor.

Was this all part of the cleanup operation she'd witnessed in his office?

"Professor!" she called.

Younger spun round, saw it was her, then looked past her, over her shoulder. He seemed relieved to discover she was alone. He'd aged ten years since she'd last seen him, his face grayer, the skin around his eyes more lined, the eyes themselves bloodshot. With some obvious effort he managed to smile at her. "Agent Skyberg, to what do I owe this unexpected pleasure?" He looked at his watch. "I'm afraid I don't have much time for you. I'm very busy at the moment."

Ingrid looked at the pile of files by his feet. "A spring clean?"

"Something like that. I do like to get my house in order as we move further into the summer term. Clear the decks."

"Seems like quite a clearing out. At least you got some help."

He gave her a puzzled look.

"I was just over at your office."

"You were?" He touched his shirt pocket, running his fingers along the outline of his cell phone, no doubt wondering why no one had warned him to expect a visitor. "Look—I really am up to my eyeballs with all this. What do you want?" He slammed shut a cabinet drawer.

"I was wondering if you'd seen anything of our Dutch friend lately— Timo Klaason?"

"He doesn't study here anymore. We discussed that the last time you were here."

"You told me you didn't know him. Yet it turns out he was actually part of your research group."

"You're mistaken."

"I have it on good authority."

"Whose?"

"One of your other students. Madison Faber."

He flinched at the mention of her name. "She is, as usual, mistaken. Don't you think I'd remember him if he was part of the group?"

"The police are pursuing Klaason in connection with a drugs offense." She watched Younger's reaction.

He paused before answering. Calculating. Judging the best way to respond, maybe. "Drugs? One of my students?" He tilted his head to one side. "I suppose that sort of thing goes on within every student body."

Ingrid folded her arms schoolmarmishly.

"Are you telling me you never experimented while you were at college? A little weed?"

"Never appealed."

He gave her a wry smile.

"They want to question him about a *serious* drugs offense. We're not talking about smoking the odd joint here and there."

"Just as well he left the college. We don't want that kind of thing at Loriners." He wetted his dry lips with his tongue. "How serious?"

"You don't know?"

"How on earth would I? I don't even remember him." He glanced at his watch. "Look, if we're done here, I really must ask you to leave." He opened a drawer in the next file cabinet. "I take it you can see yourself out." He didn't bother to look at her.

Either he wasn't even curious about Klaason's offense, or he knew about it already?

"I'm not sure that we are… done, that is," Ingrid said.

He blew out an irritated sigh.

"When we spoke before, you told me Lauren Shelbourne was an exceptional student."

Younger tensed slightly but recovered quickly. "She was. She'll be greatly missed." His shoulders slumped, his hands dropping inside the drawer. "By everyone."

"By you in particular?"

"What do you mean by that?"

"I got the impression Lauren was a favorite of yours."

"She was intelligent, hardworking, energetic. Students like Lauren don't come along that often. It was a pleasure to work with her." He straightened up, pulling back his shoulders, and fixed Ingrid with a cold stare. "Where are you going with this?"

"So much of a pleasure you… made it personal?" She stepped up close. She could smell coffee and a metallic tang on his breath.

"What?" He leaned toward her.

"Were you having a sexual relationship with Lauren Shelbourne?"

His mouth dropped open and his eyes widened. "You've really got the gall to ask me that? Incredible. Is that what the US government is paying you for? To harass British citizens?"

"I'm just pursuing a line a of inquiry—"

"How dare you!" He fumbled in the rear pocket of his pants and retrieved a wallet, then pulled out a small square color photograph of a dark-haired woman in her late thirties. She had perfectly proportioned features. Full lips, straight nose, chiseled cheekbones. Younger prodded the picture with a finger. "That, if you're in any way interested, is my beautiful wife. The mother of my children. We've been together fifteen years. Claire is my best friend, closest ally and confidante. Do you think I would jeopardize a relationship like that for the sake of… what? A sordid little affair with a research student?"

She had certainly hit a nerve. He glared at her, his chest rising and falling rapidly. "Get out!"

Ingrid stood her ground.

"You have no jurisdiction here. I've only been speaking to you out of courtesy. Leave now before I get security to escort you from the premises." He squared up to her. "Get. Out."

"I'd think about your answer very carefully when you're asked that question again."

"No one in their right mind would even ask it." He grabbed the phone from his pocket and waved it at her. "What's it to be? You leave now, or I have you forcibly removed?"

Ingrid backed away. She scanned the rows of file cabinets. "This cleanup of yours…"

"What about it?"

"You're wasting your time. It'll be impossible to destroy all the evidence."

"What are you talking about?"

"I think you know."

"You're out of your mind." He swiped the screen of his phone and tapped in a number.

"It's OK—I'm leaving."

As she passed the long row of narrow booths, Ingrid heard Younger raise his voice.

"For Christ's sake," she heard him say into his phone, "please tell me you're about to leave the country."

36

She reached the main piazza and dialed Angela Tate's number. The journalist answered after a half dozen rings.

"What?"

She had obviously woken her up.

"This is Ingrid Skyberg. Have you coaxed your sources to go on the record yet?"

"What?"

"Is your story about Younger's program about to hit the streets?"

There was a silence on the line. "Why are you asking?"

"I've just seen Younger. He's covering his tracks. What isn't being moved is being destroyed. Files, CDs, paperwork, you name it. I could practically smell smoke coming out of the shredding machine."

"Shit."

"Maybe one of your sources told him. Perhaps his hold over them is stronger than you thought."

Ingrid kept a close eye on the main entrance of the research block, expecting to see more of Younger's acolytes arrive to help with the cleanup operation. What she didn't expect to see was Younger himself racing through the doors, his cell phone clamped to one ear, a dark gray baseball cap pulled low over his head. She snuck into a doorway.

"You've got to stop him destroying the evidence," Tate said.

"I'm not in a position to do that."

"Inform the college authorities."

"I'm kinda busy right now." Ingrid hung up, and when Younger had crossed the square, she emerged from her hiding place. The professor exited through the main gates, and Ingrid followed, staying a good fifty yards behind him. Where did he have to be so urgently he could abandon the task of sanitizing his office and laboratory?

Ingrid trailed Younger all the way along the street, watching and waiting as he stopped at three different ATMs, withdrawing cash from each one. He stuffed the money in his pocket and continued until he reached the next cross lights, where he turned right. When she reached the corner, she scanned the sea of faces for Younger, but couldn't pick him out. This street was busier, lined with stores on either side, and full of rush-hour commuters. She'd lost him.

Dammit.

She stared at the bobbing heads, but the professor had vanished. Her heart thudded. He could be in any one of the stores. She headed up the street, hoping she was still going in the right direction, praying he hadn't hopped on a bus. Mostly she hoped he hadn't already spotted her. She kept her eyes peeled and her legs moving. Then she spotted his baseball cap. He had picked up his pace. Wherever he was headed, he needed to get there fast. Younger took the next left, and Ingrid hurried to the corner.

It was a residential street and much quieter. There was only a handful of people on the sidewalk, and Ingrid had no choice but to let the gap widen between them, even if it meant the risk of losing him again.

She followed him for a half mile through a network of quiet roads until his pace slowed. Younger was checking the numbers of the large duplex, two-story houses as he passed them. Each house had a garage out front and a narrow alley running alongside it. Most front yards were neat and clean. Smart cars on the driveways. After another fifty yards Younger stopped abruptly, and Ingrid ducked behind an SUV. She peered through its windows and saw him glance left and right before walking up the front path of a house that had a bright red motorcycle parked on the driveway. Younger banged a fist against the door, which was opened almost immediately. Younger slipped inside, the door closing quickly behind him. Less than a minute later he was back out on the street, adjusting his cap and retracing his steps.

Ingrid waited behind the SUV until Younger reached the end of the street. Then she watched the house and the corner for another five minutes until she was happy the professor wasn't returning.

She hurried across the road and made straight for the alleyway that ran along the side of the house. She pushed open a wooden gate to discover a ramshackle backyard. A square lawn overgrown with weeds took up most of the space, discarded plastic toys strewn over it. She stopped for a moment. Was this a family home? Would there be children inside? She continued into the yard, where she found the back door, a cigarette smoldering in a saucer on the ground beside it. She crept up to the door and tried the handle. It wasn't locked. She pushed it open a fraction then waited for a response from someone inside. There wasn't one. She held her breath and stepped over the threshold, feeling exposed without a weapon. All she could do was work quietly and slowly, listening and watching as she went. She entered a long, narrow galley-style kitchen. Pots and pans were stacked high in the sink and on the drainer. Empty cans of beer littered the counter. The room smelled of tobacco and Chinese takeout.

She stopped. Listened. No sign of activity.

She continued through the kitchen until she reached a gloomy hallway. A staircase to her right, with a low, narrow door set into some wooden paneling. On her left was a closed door—the living room presumably—and straight ahead was the front door leading out onto the street. She crept forward and listened at the door on the left. All she heard was her own heartbeat banging in her ears.

Someone had to be in the house. Judging by the silence of the room on her left, that someone was upstairs. She inhaled. Listened again. Somebody coughed. The sound came from somewhere above and behind her, perhaps on the second-floor landing.

"Now's as good a time as any." A woman's voice.

"No, it'll wait until tonight." A man's voice.

"What's there to hang around for?" The woman again.

Both voices English. Not foreign. Not Dutch. Not Timo Klaason.

Dammit.

She'd been so sure. She continued to listen, but the conversation had ended. She moved toward the front door. No point in staying now. She tried the door. It was locked. No sign of a key. She turned back to the kitchen, but before she could take a step, the door beneath the stairs opened. She froze for a microsecond before instinct kicked in. She levered down the handle of the door into the living room and ducked inside. In the gap between the door and frame, a tall figure emerged from the cellar door under the stairs.

Timo Klaason. No question.

He had a small duffel bag slung over one shoulder, a motorcycle helmet in his other hand. He leaned over the banister and shouted up the stairs, "Hey, you guys! I'm leaving now. Thanks for everything, yeah?"

Scraping and thumping overhead was swiftly followed by heavy footsteps clattering down the stairs. The leaving committee. Ingrid pushed the door further toward the jamb. She heard the sound of a key in the lock, then the front door opening.

"Send us a postcard, yeah?" the woman said.

"Sure—I'll upload my holiday photos to Flickr for you."

"All right, whatever. Take care of yourself, though, I mean it."

"I always do," Klaason called from outside.

The motorbike in the front yard started to roar. Ingrid reached for her cell phone and dialed 999. Without hanging up, she shoved the phone in her pocket and threw open the door.

"What the fu—"

The woman and man wheeled around toward her, their jaws dropping wide. Ingrid pushed a path between them and threw herself through the front door. The bike revved again. Ingrid leaped toward it, clawing at Klaason's back. He half turned, his right arm swinging at her, making contact with her ribs. She flinched but tightened her hold. She felt a pair of hands grip her shoulders, trying to yank her off the bike. She gripped him even harder.

"Help! Police!" she shouted. "I'm being attacked!" She screamed the address of the house at the top of her voice, hoping she was still connected to emergency services. The hands on her shoulders let go.

The engine revved again and Klaason accelerated out of the front yard and into the street. Ingrid held on tight. Klaason couldn't control the bike, but she clung on.

They went twenty yards down the street, thirty, forty. He started swinging the bike, trying to throw her off. This wasn't going to end well. She pressed her thighs against the bike, freeing her hands. She reached forward and grabbed his right arm. He accelerated harder. She didn't even want to look at the speedometer. He took his left hand off the clutch and whacked her right hand, but she tightened her grip. They were coming up to a junction. They were going too fast to take the corner safely. He braked hard and the bike slid sideways beneath them. Ingrid let go and slammed, shoulder first, into a parked car. Her body thumped down onto the road. She heard sirens in the distance.

And then everything went dark.

37

The embassy staff doctor typed up his medical report, alternately sucking his teeth and sighing as he pecked at his keyboard.

"Bed rest," he said after he'd tapped the final key with a flourish. "It's all I can suggest. Painkillers every four hours, every two if you switch between ibuprofen and acetaminophen." He looked at her over the top of the glasses balancing on his thick nose. "I'll sign you off duty for the rest of the week."

Ingrid shook her head. "Not possible. I'm in the middle of an investigation."

"Tough."

Two hours earlier, much to the dismay of the medical staff at King's College Hospital, Ingrid had discharged herself shortly after arriving there by ambulance. The doctors had wanted to keep her in overnight for observation, a precaution for all concussion sufferers, they'd explained. They told her how lucky she had been to have escaped such a serious accident with no broken bones or ruptured organs. She'd listened politely to them until they were done, then demanded they give her back her clothes so she could get out of there.

As she sat staring into the embassy MD's rheumy eyes, she felt anything but lucky. Every part of her was either bruised or grazed, and every time she moved, she set off a new tsunami of pain through her entire body. Lucky or not, she sure as hell wasn't going to be confined to quarters.

"Really, Doc, I look a lot worse than I am. It's my coloring—I bruise easily. I'm fine to carry out desk duties, wouldn't you say?"

The doctor pushed his glasses onto his head and noisily drew in air through his teeth. He sat back in his chair and folded his arms. "Very well. But make sure you perform light duties only. Here in the embassy, where I can keep an eye on you."

When she walked into the criminal division office, Jennifer's mouth fell open, making her look even younger than her twenty-three years. She looked like she should still be selling Girl Scout cookies.

"Don't ask."

Jen got up. "I, like, have to ask. Did you come off your motorcycle?"

"Not exactly."

Ingrid gave her the basic outline of what had happened. Jen perched on her desk, peering at the grazes on Ingrid's face, her luscious strawberry-blond hair framing increasingly concerned features.

"I don't understand," Jen said. "This guy is Dutch, right?"

"Correct."

"And he's a drug dealer, like, in the UK? Selling drugs to British students?"

Ingrid fired up her computer. "He doesn't care about their nationality."

"But, like, this might sound really stupid, but what's it got to do with us? First you find his... his *factory*, then you track him down. Are the British police paying you or something?"

Jen was not being stupid. Her summary was totally correct. It didn't really matter that Ingrid was after answers in the Shelbourne case, the Klaason thing had been an unnecessary detour. The whole reason she'd checked out of the hospital was to stop Sol and Louden finding out just how far off track she'd gotten.

Among her emails was one from the forensics lab in DC with the subject line Sample request ready. The paint analysis. She clicked on it. Ingrid scanned through the explanatory notes, registered something about the delay due to the sample not matching US databases, and found what she was looking for. The paint used to write *lauren shelbourne = whore* on the walls of Loriners the day after her death was made by Dulux, and the shade was Sun Dust 2.

Her desk phone rang. Normally calls to the department went to Jen's phone.

"You want me to get that?"

Ingrid waved her away. "Criminal Division, Agent Skyberg speaking."

"Hi, sweetie."

"Marshall! Did someone call you?"

"I don't understand."

"It's nothing." Ingrid had thought maybe someone had let him know about her hospitalization. No need to tell him she was OK. "How are you?"

"Sweetie, listen." He was talking very quietly. "You need to leave the building. Go for a walk. And take your cell."

"Marsh?"

"I can't say any more."

"Marsh, I—"

"Just pick up your coat, and go. You've got five minutes, OK?"

What the hell was going on with him? It was not like Marshall, which was why she was going to do as he said. "Jen, I'm just heading out to pick up some painkillers, OK?"

"You want me to go?"

"Thanks, but I think a gentle walk would do me good."

"I've got Tylenol," she said as Ingrid reached the threshold.

There was no way Ingrid was up to taking the stairs, so she punched the button and called the elevator. Two minutes later, she passed the security barriers in the lobby and walked out into Grosvenor Square. It was almost dusk, and the spring warmth had gone from the air. She buttoned up her coat, checked for traffic and stepped into the garden square, where crocuses and primroses welcomed her. The cinder path led her past several empty benches, but it was a little too cold to sit down. She breathed as deeply as her battered ribs would allow, and held tightly to her cell.

An out-of-area message flashed on her screen. She hit the connect button.

"Agent Skyberg."

There was a slight delay on the line. "Hi. Is that Ingrid?"

"Speaking."

"I have some information for you."

She kept walking. "Who is this, please?"

"You made an inquiry about an agent called Mulroony."

"Is that you?" Ingrid's mouth was dry. She pushed a finger in her ear, determined not to miss anything.

"We have only one record of a Dennis Mulroony." The voice was male, East Coast, and educated. He sounded middle-aged, but with the quality of the line, it wasn't possible to be sure.

Ingrid's pace had picked up. She still couldn't quite believe Marshall had come through for her. "And what is that record?"

"London, Legal Attaché Program, April till December 2012."

"That's it?" Mulroony had only worked at the embassy for eight months? She was sure, when Sol had recruited her, he'd said her predecessor had been there for years.

"There are no other records." He paused. "No college records, no public records, no birth or death certificate."

"You're kidding." Ingrid strode out of the square and walked north toward Oxford Street. "He's disappeared?"

"Right off the map. You have any other questions, agent?"

"Any idea what his security clearance was when he worked in London?"

"Negative, agent."

Ingrid's thoughts were spinning, trying to work out which questions to put forward, but leery of asking any when she did not know whom she was speaking to. "Thank you. Were you also asked to research Greg Brewster—" she stopped herself, considered the ramifications of revealing she knew his occupation, then proceeded "—the arms dealer?"

"Affirmative. Gregory James Brewster is an alias for Sidney Joseph Baxter. He is booked on a flight from Oman to London, arriving Heathrow twelve twenty-five tomorrow." The line went dead.

Ingrid checked the last-number feature on her phone. It only said 'international,' but she dialed it anyway. She wasn't surprised to get a message saying the company was unable to connect her call, with the helpful suggestion she should check the number and try again. Her stride had slowed to a shuffle as she absorbed not only what she'd just been told, but also that Marshall had put himself out for her. She should call him. She was scrolling for his number when an incoming call vibrated her phone. It was Ralph Mills.

"Hey, Ralph."

"How are you? I heard about what happened."

"I'm fine." She shifted the phone from left hand to right, the soreness in her left arm suddenly too painful to ignore.

"I have some news. Thought you might like to know Lauren Shelbourne's mobile phone has become active."

38

"I had no idea your injuries were so bad." Ralph Mills rushed toward her. "Should I take you to the hospital?"

It was her face, Ingrid realized. Her hip, right thigh and ribs were in much worse shape, but a woman with a grazed cheek and bruised eye was guaranteed to attract the wrong sort of attention.

"Really—it's nothing." Ingrid was tempted to say 'stop acting like my mother' except Svetlana Skyberg had never shown as much sympathy and concern in all the years she'd raised her. Mills offered her his hand, and reluctantly she took it. The visitors chairs in Lewisham police station were particularly low, and she was actually grateful of the gesture. He led them out of reception and swiped them through into a network of corridors that was starting to be familiar.

"Tell me about Lauren's phone."

"Like I explained earlier, it was switched off again before we had a chance to triangulate."

"Do you have a rough idea where it was used?"

"Greater London."

"Oh. How long was it on for?"

"Less than five minutes. And it didn't make any calls or send any texts."

"But Natash… DI McKittrick has called off the inquest?"

Mills pushed open a door. "I haven't had confirmation, but I imagine that's a formality. If Lauren's phone was stolen, that puts a whole other spin on the crime scene. We'll go over everything again."

Part of Ingrid was elated—she'd always thought there was enough about Lauren's death to suspect foul play—but she also knew the pain that knowledge would inflict on the girl's parents.

"And any sign of Younger? Do we know where he went after visiting Klaason?"

Mills shrugged apologetically. "We've got officers watching his house and the college."

"What about airports and train stations?"

"We don't have that kind of manpower available. But his wife has surrendered his passport, so we don't think he'll try to leave the country." He pulled an apologetic face. "Right now the London Crime Squad, whom I am about to introduce you to, are trying to match up the serial numbers of the twenty-pound notes Klaason had on him with the cash withdrawn using Younger's bank card. As soon as they've proved that link, they'll issue a 'perverting the course of justice' arrest warrant." He held open another door for her and they entered a corridor lined with doors and plastic seating. "Delivering cash to a known felon to aid his escape is serious enough for us to lock him up for a while."

That was something.

"Millsy!"

Ahead of them a short, female detective with a huge smile bowled over to them and slapped a hand on Mills's, shaking it hard.

"You might have to be gentler with Ingrid," Mills said. "Agent Skyberg, this is Detective Constable Cath Murray. We used to work together."

"Ooh, yes, you do look a bit ropey." Cath had a northern accent and scruffy short hairstyle that made her look like she was up to no good. Ingrid took an instant liking to her. "Call me Cath. It's a real pleasure to meet you. I've heard so much about you."

"Really?" Ingrid was incredulous.

"Ralph's been singing your praises nonstop."

Mills's cheeks reddened. "I'll, um, be next door. If you need anything at all, Cath'll sort you out."

"I'm sure I'll be fine—thank you."

Mills shut the door behind him, and Murray led Ingrid into an observation room. She pulled a chair out from under a wide desk, with two huge TV monitors set on top. "You look like you need all the rest you can get. Take a seat."

Ingrid eased herself onto the chair, careful to avoid any sudden jarring movements. "Ralph mentioned you were part of the initial interviewing team when you brought Klaason in."

"I work in the London Crime Squad. Just started, as a matter of fact." She beamed at Ingrid. "I sat in while the SIO questioned Klaason about his industrious little setup in Deptford."

Ingrid focused her attention on the left-hand TV monitor.

"But now Homicide and Serious Crime Command—"

"McKittrick's team?"

"Exactly. They want to talk to him about the girl they found in New Cross."

The monitor showed Klaason sitting very calmly at a three-foot-by-four-foot table. He had a shaven head, sallow skin and broad, dark features. His ethnicity was hard to determine, but Ingrid would guess he had ancestors from central Asia. There were no obvious signs of injury from falling off the bike. But then Klaason had been wearing a motorcycle helmet and a thick leather jacket when they'd hit the ground. His face was completely blank. The right-hand monitor displayed a wide shot of the interview room. Sitting next to Klaason was a neat woman in a smart suit. Her face was set in a scowl. Neither of them spoke.

"What did Klaason tell you during the first interview?" Ingrid asked.

"Bugger all. It was as much as we could do to get him to confirm his name and date of birth. He didn't even give us an address."

"And you're here in case he says anything relevant to your investigation?"

"Correct." Murray shuffled in her seat. "Great detective work, by the way, finding him like that. Not to mention brave. Really impressive."

Ingrid smiled. "Thanks."

The monitor showed McKittrick and Mills enter the interview room. They made their preliminary introductions, stated clearly that the interview was being recorded—Klaason glanced up at the camera and blinked —and McKittrick kicked off the interview.

"When did you start supplying narcotics to Lauren Shelbourne?"

For an opening gambit, it was nothing if not direct. Klaason stiffened. But remained silent. It was a bold move by McKittrick.

"OK," McKittrick said, "let's start with something easy. How long have you known Professor Younger?"

"I'm sorry, my English is not so good. Can you repeat the question?" She did and Klaason responded with: "No comment."

The microphones in the interview room were very sensitive—Ingrid heard McKittrick failing to suppress a sigh.

"He did the exact same thing with us," Murray said, her voice low, as if the four people in the room at the other end of the corridor might hear her. "His English is perfect—he refused an interpreter."

McKittrick cleared her throat, then said, "We've checked with the college's admission records. You started at Loriners last October. Studying psychology. Under Professor Younger."

"If you already have the information, why are you asking me?"

"Where were you on Monday the fourteenth of April between the hours of midnight and eight a.m.?"

"How would I know that?"

"The date may have stuck in your memory, given it's the day Lauren Shelbourne died."

Again there was a definite tensing across Klaason's shoulders. Ingrid leaned forward, closer to the monitor, wishing she were conducting the interview herself.

"I don't see why." Klaason stretched his neck left, then right, then rolled his shoulders.

"You knew Lauren Shelbourne?"

"No."

"You were a member of the same research group."

"It's a big project. Lots of people take part."

"Are you denying you met Miss Shelbourne?"

Klaason folded his arms and stretched out his legs under the table, kicking Mills's feet in the process. He didn't apologize. "I'm not *denying* anything. My English, sorry… I mean I didn't know Lauren well."

"Did you ever visit her in her flat?"

Klaason started to answer, but his lawyer grabbed his arm. "No comment," he said.

"Here we go again," Murray chimed in. "We had nothing but 'no comments.' Even when we told him we had masses of forensic evidence placing him at the meth factory. But at least that wiped the smile off his face."

Ingrid pulled back from the monitor and turned to Murray. "Do you know how many DNA samples were collected from Lauren's apartment?"

"No, I'm not on that team."

"So we don't know if Klaason's DNA was found in her apartment?"

"Don't quote me on it, but I doubt it. When the pathologist said it was accidental death, the lab wouldn't have prioritized samples from that investigation."

"But now the case has reopened, there might be samples to test?"

"Not my area, I'm afraid." Murray nodded at the screen. "You'd need to ask those two."

Ingrid switched her attention back to the monitor, aware the conversation had restarted in the interview room. She caught the final few words of a sentence. "… my client has already been answering questions for several hours."

"Not answering them, more like," Murray said.

McKittrick forced a smile. "He had a lengthy break between interviews."

"My client hasn't eaten."

"Answer a few more questions and we'll get him a sandwich, how about that?"

"Make sure it's no more than two."

McKittrick rolled her eyes. "I'll decide how many questions I ask. Mr. Klaason, I realize your solicitor has advised you to assert your right to silence, but you have to remember that if you fail to tell us something that may help your—"

Klaason held up a hand. "It's too complicated. My English… I told you…"

"Is good enough to study a degree course at one of the UK's top universities." McKittrick forced another smile. "If we discover you have visited Miss Shelbourne in her home, it won't be—"

"I never did!"

"So you didn't provide a delivery service when Miss Shelbourne requested more drugs?"

"You're crazy. I never supplied her with drugs."

"Is that so?"

The lawyer grabbed Klaason's arm again; he batted her hand away.

"Ask Younger—he knew her better than anyone."

"What do you mean?"

Klaason slumped forward, resting his elbows on the table. "He was screwing her."

"How do you know that?"

"He told me."

"So you and Professor Younger are quite close?"

"I wouldn't say that."

"But he told you about his sex life. Isn't that quite an admission, given he's a married man?"

"I'm sorry, my English…"

"Change the bloody record!" Murray shouted unhelpfully at the monitor.

"You say you never supplied Lauren Shelbourne with drugs?"

"That's right."

"So how do you explain the high levels of methamphetamine in her bloodstream at the time of her death?"

"What?"

"You're the man manufacturing the stuff, not two miles away from her home. You studied with her. You can understand why we might think there's a connection."

"I never gave her anything. If she was taking meth, it has nothing to do with me."

"Nothing?"

"No comment."

"I think we've moved beyond that now, Timo." McKittrick sniffed loudly, then spread her fingers flat against her notes. "Let me ask you a different question. Did you supply Stuart Younger with LSD and meth-amphetamine?"

Klaason didn't reply.

"Mr Klaason, a young woman has died. A brilliant young woman, by all accounts, a woman whose life revolved around Loriners College. Her only friends in London study at the college. Her Oyster card shows she hasn't moved more than a mile from the college in the past month. Her mobile phone records show she had not made or received calls to any person we have not been able to speak to—"

A flicker of alarm on Mills's face confirmed that McKittrick was lying about that.

"—so as far as we have been able to establish, it is extremely probable that she obtained the drugs that killed her from the campus. A campus where you appear to be the main dealer—"

The lawyer interrupted. "My client is highly unlikely to be the only dealer at the college."

McKittrick ignored her. "—and it seems worthy of my time to see if you can help me find out why this bright and brilliant woman, with no previous history of substance misuse, had such large quantities of drugs in her system."

Klaason was silent.

McKittrick circled something in her notes. "Mr Klaason, you are looking at a minimum of eight years in prison for the production of meth-amphetamine, but I am willing to put in a good word with the London Crime Squad if you tell me what you know about Lauren Shelbourne and how she came to have drugs—very likely *your* drugs—in her system."

His lawyer cleared her throat and whispered something to Klaason, who nodded.

"I have nothing to do with Lauren dying, OK?"

McKittrick and Mills said nothing.

"But I did give stuff to the professor." The lawyer held onto his arm. He pushed her away. "Ask Younger how come she was taking meth. Ask him why she ended up dead."

There was a knock on the interview room door and a uniformed PC stuck her head through the door. McKittrick got up and spoke to her. They exchanged a handful of words before the inspector returned to the table and officially suspended the interview. Mills followed her eagerly out of the room.

The observation room door opened a moment later and the two of them walked in.

"What a result!" Murray said. "Great work."

She high-fived a beaming Mills. "It gets better than that," he said.

Ingrid's eyes widened. "What's happened?"

He looked to McKittrick. "Can I?"

She was smiling too. "Go for it."

"Uniforms say Lauren Shelbourne's phone is active again."

"And this time they've got a location." McKittrick paused for dramatic effect. "It's within a fifty-meter radius of Stuart Younger's house."

39

Jen got such a shock seeing Ingrid at her desk, she almost dropped her coffee.

"Sorry, didn't mean to scare you."

"Please tell me you didn't sleep here last night." Jen took off her coat, opened her umbrella to dry, and switched on her computer. It had been raining hard since Ingrid had got up at six.

"Do I look that bad?"

"Jeez, no. Totally no. Except for, you know..." She gestured to the bruising on Ingrid's cheek, which was now deepening from mauve to eggplant. "How come you're in so early?"

Ingrid explained she was in no state to go for a run, and even lying flat was painful. There was also the small matter of Greg Brewster's return to the UK at lunchtime, and she had much to plan. "Also, the Deputy wants to see me."

Jen turned round, her mouth agape, her eyes wide. "What have you done?"

Ingrid scrunched up her face. "I find out at eight thirty." She looked at the clock: she still had fifteen minutes to put her pieces in play. She called the St Pancras hotel and asked to be put through to the concierge.

"Good morning, I'm hoping you can assist me today."

"Of course, madam."

"My boss, Mr. Greg Brewster, is checking in with you this afternoon, and I would like to make some reservations for him."

"Of course."

Ingrid was calculating that whoever had stolen Brewster's laptop had not got what they wanted. Its encryption had almost certainly held up to attempts to access the information they had stolen it for. What they needed was the passwords that would unlock the laptop's secrets. The other calculation she made was that Brewster always stayed at the St. Pancras hotel because he felt well taken care of by the staff there. It was her guess that the reason they took such good care of him was because someone at the hotel was tipping off the people who were targeting him. If she was right, the appointments she was lining up for him after he checked in would make him the victim of a second crime, and this time she would be there to intercept the criminal. Getting him to play along might prove impossible, but she would cross that bridge when she met his plane at lunchtime.

At exactly eight thirty, Ingrid knocked on Amy Louden's door. She straightened the collar of her shirt while she waited to be told to come in. When she entered, Louden couldn't keep the surprise from her face.

"My God. The medical report was comprehensive, but I couldn't have guessed you'd look so... beaten."

"Just a few superficial injuries. I heal quickly," Ingrid said. "A couple of days before I'm back to full strength. Max. I promise I won't scare any members of the public between now and then."

"The MD authorized desk duties."

"Yes, ma'am."

"So where were you yesterday afternoon?" She indicated Ingrid should take a seat opposite her desk.

A flash of fear engulfed Ingrid. Did Louden know about her anonymous call?

"I came looking for you about five o'clock."

"Oh. Right. I was at Lewisham police station. The investigation into Lauren Shelbourne's death has been reopened."

"Ah. Have you told her parents?"

"Not yet, no." Ingrid chewed her lip. "Why did you want to see me?"

"I received a call from the senior investigating officer in the London Crime Squad yesterday afternoon."

"You did?"

"He called to thank me for your intervention. Explained how useful you've been to his investigation."

Ingrid blinked. She'd assumed she was going to be rebuked.

"But I thought I should point out that jumping off a roof isn't very smart. You're needed here, Ingrid, and you can't go putting yourself in danger or taking unnecessary risks."

Louden had called her 'Ingrid' and not 'agent.' That was a first. "I didn't have much choice. If I hadn't jumped, I could well have been pushed."

"And jumping on the back of a drug dealer's motorcycle? Was your life in danger then?"

Ingrid fidgeted awkwardly. "I guess that Quantico training just kinda kicked in."

At least that dragged a smile onto Louden's lips. "Listen, it's clear you are a very committed investigator, but this is just a friendly reminder to take better care of yourself. I'm all for awarding bravery medals to my agents, but I'd prefer not to hand them out posthumously, you understand?"

"Got it."

Louden walked over to her window and looked at the torrential rain. "Now, what about Mr. Brewster's laptop? Are you getting anywhere?"

Ingrid outlined her plan to set a trap for the thief—or more likely whoever had hired the thief—when they came back to complete the job. Louden listened without interrupting.

"If we had the manpower," Ingrid said, "we could also set up meetings for Sidney Baxter, an alias used by Brewster—"

Louden turned sharply away from the window. "Where did you find that out?"

Ingrid felt heat rising up her neck. "It was something that came to light during the course of my investigation."

Louden returned to her desk, positioned herself within inches of Ingrid and leaned against it. "Yes, but someone must have told you that information?"

Sweat formed between Ingrid's shoulder blades. "I interrogated Met archives. It wasn't the first time Brewster has been the victim of a crime in London. Ma'am?"

"Yes?"

"What's really going on? Why are you so personally interested in Greg Brewster?"

Louden pressed her lips together.

"I have been trying to investigate this robbery with one hand tied behind my back. I have a great deal of respect for you, and for your rank, and I know that you know how hard it is in these circumstances to find evidence and unmask the perpetrator." Ingrid paused to assess from

Louden's expression if she had gone too far. "Yet you keep pushing me for more information. I just want to understand why."

Louden nodded slowly. She walked round to the other side of her desk, sat down, then steepled her fingers under her chin. "You're right. We haven't made this easy for you. Let me reassure you that you are doing excellent work."

Ingrid waited for her to say more, but that was it. "Thank you. If there's nothing else, I should go and speak to the Shelbournes, update them on the case."

Louden nodded.

"Thank you for your time." Ingrid winced as she got to her feet. By the time she had reached the door, Louden had picked up the phone. She waited until Ingrid had left the room before she dialed.

Ingrid closed the door behind her and leaned against the wall in the corridor outside, trying to work out her next move. The painkillers were wearing off and she felt a little nauseous. She needed air. She would walk to the Shelbournes' hotel.

It wasn't until she reached reception she remembered it was raining. She was about to go back upstairs to borrow Jen's umbrella when she saw a familiar face standing on the sidewalk in the pouring rain. She grabbed a magazine from a rack and headed out to join her.

40

Alex Shelbourne was drenched. By the looks of her, she'd been standing in the rain for hours. Ingrid held the magazine over her head and raced toward the girl.

"What did you do to your face?" the teenager asked as she approached.

"Had a fight with a parked car."

"You've got blood on your cheek."

"It's just a graze."

"No, I mean fresh blood. It's running down your face."

Ingrid lifted a hand to her cheek and it came away pink, where the blood had mingled with rainwater.

"Here." Alex Shelbourne handed Ingrid her scarf.

"It's OK—it'll stop soon enough."

"Take it." She thrust the scarf at her and Ingrid blotted her cheek.

"Why didn't you get security to call me? How long have you been here?"

"I didn't want anyone else to know I was here. So I waited."

"You'll catch cold. Let's get you inside." Ingrid started back toward the embassy, but Alex tugged on her arm.

"Not there."

They headed down North Audley Street and stopped at the first café they came to. Ingrid threw the sodden magazine into the trash and handed Alex back her scarf, scooping up a handful of paper napkins from a nearby table. She pressed the wad of tissue against her face.

A hot chocolate and double espresso ordered, they took the table furthest from the window.

"How long have you been waiting?" Ingrid asked.

"A couple of hours."

"You must be soaked."

"I'm OK."

She didn't look it.

"Do your parents know you're here?"

Alex stared into her hot chocolate. She scooped the froth backward and forward across its surface with a teaspoon. "I told them I wanted to visit the Apple Store." There was no attitude now. The goth makeup had gone, to be replaced with a palpable sadness. Alex Shelbourne seemed a completely different girl.

"They were relieved to get me out of the way so they could fight some more without an audience. They've never been like this with one another before. Mom blames Dad. And Dad…"

"Blames himself?"

"I don't know. Maybe. But mostly he just pretends it's not really happening."

"I'm so sorry."

"Me too." Alex Shelbourne shivered as she gazed blankly at her hot chocolate. Ingrid wanted to tell her the case into her sister's death had been reopened, but she needed to tell the parents first. Alex put down the spoon and looked up suddenly at Ingrid. "Why did you ignore the note I gave you?"

"I didn't. I would have gotten in touch. But events kind of overtook me."

The teenager pointed to Ingrid's face. "You mean your fight with a car?"

"Among other things. Plus I had no way of contacting you without going through your parents first. I'm guessing that's the last thing you wanted me to do."

The girl nodded slowly. "I hoped I'd get a chance to speak to you after the meeting on Saturday."

"I was kept behind by my boss."

"You make it sound like she's your teacher or something."

"More like the principal." Ingrid gave her a smile. "What was it you wanted to tell me about your sister?"

Alex took a deep breath, her shoulders rising almost to her ears then slumping down again. "I wasn't one hundred percent sure I should even tell you, but when she came to the hotel, pretending to be so upset, I knew I couldn't keep it to myself. I wanted to scream at her."

"Who?"

"Madison. She's a two-faced bitch."

"Madison Faber? You saw her when she visited your parents?" Why had Alex Shelbourne taken such a strong dislike to a woman she didn't even know?

"I saw her—but she didn't see me. I stayed in the room next door. No way was I going to speak to her. She hated Lauren. And Lauren hated her right back. How could she cry like that in front of Mom and Dad? She's so fake."

"Are you sure? Weren't Madison and Lauren good friends?"

"If they were, why did Lauren move out of the apartment? She should have made that bitch leave instead."

"I'm sorry, I don't follow." Ingrid's head was foggier than she'd realized.

"The apartment, it was Lauren's. She should never have let Madison move in."

"Lauren's? Are you sure about that?"

"Yeah—why wouldn't I be?"

"So you're saying Madison moved into *Lauren's* apartment?"

"Yes!" The girl sniffed. "I'm sorry—I didn't mean to shout."

"That's OK." Ingrid took a sip of coffee. "Is that what you wanted to tell me about Lauren?"

"No—I thought you should know why she and Madison had such a big fight."

Ingrid blinked. Where the hell was this going? "I want you to take this slowly. Make allowances for me, I've taken a lot of painkillers. I want to be clear exactly what you're saying."

"Lauren and Madison had a big fight. Lauren asked her to leave, but Madison refused. She's such a spoiled bitch. She wouldn't move out."

"So Lauren was forced to leave instead?"

"She didn't want to stay a moment longer with that weirdo."

"Weirdo?" Ingrid wasn't going to correct the kid's language—she was only sixteen—but it was a reminder to arrange proper support for Faber.

A sob erupted from Alex's throat. Her eyes started to water.

"It's OK—take your time."

"She told me they had a fight over some guy she was seeing."

"A man your sister was seeing?"

Alex nodded. A tear dropped into her cup.

"Did she tell you who that was?"

"Lauren never said who she was dating. Not even when she lived at home. She always kept her boyfriends secret." She sobbed again. "I mean, I thought for about a year she was gay she was so damn secretive."

Ingrid laid a hand over the girl's. "Drink some hot chocolate—you're chilled right to the bone. I'm going to sit here and watch you drink it."

"I don't really want any."

"Just a little, come on."

With shaking hands, the girl lifted the wide cup to her lips, took a sip and put the cup straight back down. She dabbed her mouth with a paper napkin. "It was weird Madison knew who the guy was because I don't think Lauren would have told her. I guess she must have found out some other way."

Faber had always said she didn't know who Lauren was dating, but Alex Shelbourne seemed sure of her facts.

"And that's why they fought?"

Alex nodded. "Madison was jealous as hell. She wanted to go out with the same guy. She accused my sister of stealing him from her. Lauren told me he couldn't even bear to look at Madison. When I saw her crying at the hotel with Mom and Dad, I just wanted to punch her. I wish I had."

Ingrid wished there was a pause button she could press. She needed time to think. "Drink some more hot chocolate, Alex. Just a little."

Faber had told the police she and Lauren never fought. Not once, she'd said. The inconsistencies were mounting up. Why would Alex make any of this up? What could she gain from fabricating something like this? The girl looked up and saw Ingrid staring at her.

"What is it?"

"You are sure about what you've told me? You couldn't have misinter-preted what your sister said?"

"She was clear enough. I think she needed someone to talk to about it all. She didn't really have many friends here." Her bottom lip quivered.

Ingrid's phone buzzed in her pocket. She took it out and glanced at the screen. It was Ralph Mills.

"I'm OK—you should take it," Alex told her.

"I won't be long." Ingrid turned away to answer the call. "Ralph." She got to her feet and headed toward the exit. "What have you got?"

"We've picked up Professor Younger."

41

Ingrid waited in the embassy limousine. She decided it was better if the driver was the one holding up the sign that said 'Greg Brewster.' She saw them approach, Brewster on the phone, and realized her palms were moist. First, the driver opened the trunk and placed Brewster's bag in the back, and then he opened one of the rear doors. Brewster ducked his head inside.

"You?"

"Good flight?" Ingrid gave him a smile, certain the ten-mile journey into central London was going to feel more like a hundred.

Brewster's podgy face reddened with fury. "I will have to call you back." He sat down beside her, carefully placed a laptop case between his feet, and the driver pulled away. "Is this a trap?"

Had he already been in contact with the concierge?

"Well, sort of."

He looked puzzled. "I don't understand."

Ingrid explained her theory that someone would attempt to complete the job by trying to get hold of his passwords on his return trip to London. She then told him of the appointments she had arranged with the concierge.

"But I have appointments of my own," he blustered.

"I appreciate that, sir, but when I put this plan into action, you were already in the air and uncontactable." She breathed in deeply, sending pain spiraling round her torso. "I was hoping we could use this journey to work out which of the appointments you would be able to keep. I will then, posing as your assistant, shake the tree a little and see who falls out."

"Shake the tree?"

"Let it be known where you'll be at what time, and then I'm going to watch you like a goddamn hawk and see who turns up."

The driver navigated the limousine through the parking lot barriers and, once in the open, the rain hammered down on the roof.

"My bet is at some point on this trip you're going to be asked to set up a password to use the Wi-Fi, or asked to authorize a card payment, or to access the gym in the hotel—" she glanced at his corpulent belly as he stared out the window: Greg Brewster was not a user of hotel gyms "— and one of the people doing the asking is going to use the information you give them to de-encrypt your laptop."

Brewster said nothing. Instead he breathed so heavily it sounded like light snoring. "Are you saying that you are actually trying to investigate the theft?"

Ingrid pursed her lips. "Of course I'm investigating it. Why wouldn't I investigate?"

He turned to her. "Because no other fucker in the past few years has bothered."

On the remainder of their journey into the center of London, they went through Brewster's appointments for the rest of the day. A visit to the Iranian embassy. A private meeting at the Reform Club with a representative of the Malawian army. An opening night at an art gallery, where he hoped to meet a member of the Kazakh government. It was a snapshot of how central the UK capital was to the international arms trade. Ingrid got on the phone and, posing as Brewster's secretary, started to give the tree a shake. When she had finished, Brewster turned to her.

"There is, of course, one major problem with your plan."

Just the one?

"With those bruises on your face, you're a little, well…" He struggled to find the right words. "The thing is, no one is going to believe you're my secretary. There is no way anyone in my industry would let you come to work like that—" He leaned forward and tapped the glass screen separating them from the driver. "This isn't the right way. I'm staying at the St Pancras."

The driver nodded.

"Then you can't leave at this junction. It's straight ahead."

The driver turned south.

"You need to turn back." Brewster was agitated. He looked at Ingrid for an explanation. "Where are we going?"

Ingrid met the driver's gaze in the rearview mirror. His eyes were smiling. "Heavy traffic on Marylebone Road," the driver said. "Taking a detour."

Ingrid knew the area well—they weren't far from her own hotel—and she could see the driver was taking them on a very long detour. He accelerated, moving them quickly south down Edgware Road.

"What's going on?" Brewster demanded.

The driver said nothing.

"Answer me!"

The car came to a halt at a set of traffic lights. "Sorry." The driver turned round. "There's been some kind of incident. I need to take you the long way round."

"What sort of incident?" Ingrid asked.

The driver shrugged. "Think a truck has tipped over. Whole road's blocked. Probably take another ten minutes."

The road ahead hadn't looked blocked. The traffic hadn't been grinding to a halt.

The lights changed and the driver carried on south, quickly reaching the Marble Arch oneway system. Ingrid was familiar with the route: it was one of her regular runs into the embassy. When the driver didn't turn left onto Oxford Street, she got suspicious. She hadn't checked him out. She'd just assumed the embassy had approved him. She swallowed hard. Her skin shivered. They had just spent the entire journey laying out their plan. Shit. She hadn't even considered the driver might be the one to try to get the password. She got out her phone surreptitiously, ready to call the police and report a kidnapping, when the limousine turned sharply off Park Lane and into the back streets of Mayfair. They passed the Shelbournes' hotel at speed then swung right into the street running along the rear entrance of the embassy. The barriers lifted and the car descended urgently into the embassy's underground parking lot.

Brewster turned to Ingrid. "What the hell?"

She didn't know what to tell him.

The car screeched to a stop and the rear doors of the limousine were yanked open. Sol Franklin bent down and introduced himself.

"Sidney Joseph Baxter, you are in the US Embassy. That means you are officially on American soil, and as a federal officer I am arresting you on suspicion of selling privileged information given to you by the Department of Defense. Will you please step out of the car?"

Brewster didn't know what to do. Behind Sol was a Marine. An armed Marine.

"Sir," Sol said, "please step out of the car."

Dumbfounded, Ingrid turned to see that Amy Louden was holding open the door on her side. "Do you want to come with me, Ingrid? I think we need to have a little chat."

42

Deputy Louden took Ingrid straight to her office, asking her assistant to make sure they weren't disturbed. Louden gestured to a couch facing a coffee table and indicated Ingrid take a seat.

"So much for 'desk duties,' eh?" Louden said.

Ingrid eased herself onto the couch. She still had no idea what was going on. "Am I in trouble?"

Louden sat on the couch opposite. "Good grief, no! Gosh, you've not been thinking that the whole way up here, have you?"

"You said we needed to talk privately."

"Well, I'm sorry you got that impression." Louden smoothed down her skirt. "I thought you deserved a proper explanation."

Ingrid was disoriented at the turn of events and chose careful silence instead of the nervous small talk she often ended up spewing in situations like these.

"Yesterday, when we were sitting in this office, you said you'd found out Greg Brewster was an alias for Sidney Baxter. You also said you had been informed this wasn't the first time Brewster's property had been stolen." Louden paused. "I'm sorry, I didn't offer you a drink, did I? Would you like a coffee?"

"No, thank you."

"I need to ask you how you found out that Brewster and Baxter were the same person."

Ingrid held her gaze and snapped her brain out of the disbelief she was experiencing to come up with an answer. When she remembered, she felt a stone fall from her throat to her stomach. "I cannot tell you that."

Louden stiffened. "Why not?"

Ingrid thought about the anonymous call in Grosvenor Square, five minutes after Marshall had instructed her to leave the office. "I received that information from an anonymous informer."

Louden's chest heaved as she inhaled sharply. "I see. Do you mean anonymous to you? Or is that you are not prepared to reveal their identity?"

Ingrid scratched her forearms, a nervous tic. "Anonymous to me. Why are you asking me this?"

Louden stretched her fingers, then curled them into fists. "That is rather delicate, I'm afraid. If your source was anonymous, what reasons did you have for thinking he or she was a credible source of information?"

Ingrid looked down at her hands, trying to avoid Louden's scrutiny. She had to keep Marshall's name out of the conversation. She couldn't recall any other time he had put himself out for her, and their relationship was on shaky ground at the moment. Revealing his role had the potential to... well, she wasn't prepared to consider the consequences. Ingrid ran through what she was about to say in her head and, reckoning it stacked up, gave her response. "I'd put out a few feelers, asked around for background—"

"From who?"

"Oh, um." Ingrid's train of thought had been interrupted. "Contacts in the Met, here in the building, associates elsewhere in the Bureau." Damn. She'd said too much.

Louden looked at her intensely. "And then what happened?"

"My phone rang. Out of the blue. It was a short conversation." Ingrid's discomfort was mounting. She couldn't just sit there and take the inquisition. "You told me I haven't done anything wrong, which I appreciate, but I would like to know what is going on."

Louden paced over to the window. "You will have gathered, from what Sol said when he arrested Baxter, he is believed to have sold defense secrets."

Ingrid had indeed worked out that much.

"It is suspected"—Louden adjusted the wooden slats of the window shade—"one of the intermediaries he used was..."

Yes? Ingrid willed her to tell her.

"And this is completely confidential."

"Yes."

"Never to be repeated outside this room."

"Of course."

"Dennis Mulroony." Louden turned to check Ingrid's reaction.

Ingrid felt a little dizzy. "My predecessor?"

"Which makes sense of why I was getting pressure from above to keep asking you about the Brewster case."

Ingrid's thoughts spiraled. It also explained the hostility Ingrid had gotten from other agents and CIA officers since her move to London. "And you thought, what, that I was... what? Going to take Mulroony's place?"

"There was a possibility Baxter would have tried to recruit you—"

"He wouldn't have stood a chance."

Louden almost laughed. "I think we know that now, Ingrid. You've been here for four months, maybe five, and we're all getting to understand your tenacity and dedication. You're gaining a lot of fans here, Ingrid, both among the London police and your colleagues at the embassy."

Ingrid wasn't used to flattery. "Thank you."

"I suppose it was a test of your loyalty." Louden perched herself on the arm of the couch Ingrid was sitting on. "Am I right in thinking your mother is a Russian national?"

Ingrid blinked: she had not been expecting that. "My mother is a US citizen. She defected from the Soviet Union in 1976."

Louden nodded. "I've read your personnel file, Ingrid. After she competed at the Montreal Olympics, am I right?"

"Yes." What the hell was going on?

"And I can see nothing in your career that would explain the scrutiny you've been under since you arrived in London." Louden grimaced slightly. "Mulroony's behavior got everyone nervous about double agents."

Ingrid felt a fire burn in her chest. "And because my mom grew up in Russia—"

"I think it's more likely to do with the fact that you speak Russian, fluently, I believe."

Ingrid had joined the FBI as a languages expert. French, Italian and Russian. She was too mad to speak any of them right at that moment.

"I mention it as something to keep in mind. You probably haven't had this sort of... oversight... before. But now that you're working overseas... Well, I wanted to give you a heads-up."

"What? That I've been earmarked as a potential traitor?" Ingrid needed to rein in her fury.

Louden got to her feet. "I didn't mean to upset you."

Ingrid wasn't upset, she was angry.

"I may be completely wrong, but I sense that someone, somewhere, was setting a trap for you with this Brewster thing." Louden walked over to the door. "And I wanted to alert you to that fact."

Louden opened the door. The meeting was suddenly over. Ingrid wriggled forward and pushed herself painfully to standing. "Thank you, ma'am."

"For the record," Louden said as Ingrid approached, "I think you're a real asset to the team here. I'm sorry the actions of your predecessor have impacted on you in this way."

"Thank you."

"And your behavior with Brewster… Baxter this afternoon has been exemplary. I'll be letting that be known."

"Thank you again."

"But"—Louden stopped Ingrid as she was leaving—"I will have to report something about ignoring doctors' orders. Desk duties, remember?"

"Yes, ma'am."

"Please," Louden said, holding out her hand, "call me Amy."

When Ingrid got back to her office, she was relieved Jennifer wasn't around. She needed to process what she'd just heard. Her predecessor, of whom almost all records had been destroyed, was some kind of double agent? And her bosses way up the food chain, higher than Louden, had potentially set a deliberate trap for her? She felt blindsided, hollowed out, stunned. Her head slumped into her hands.

"Hey there!" Jen was as bright and breezy as ever. "Looked what I picked up for you."

Wearily, Ingrid lifted her head to see Jen deposit a copy of the lunchtime edition of the *Evening News* on her desk.

"Thought you'd like to see it."

Ingrid stared at the headline. It was something to do with a delay to a new underground line being built. "I don't get it," she said to Jen. "What am I missing?"

Jen put down her take-out coffee and donut and pointed to a strap line printed above the newspaper's masthead. 'College scandal: prize-winning professor arrested. Turn to Page 5'. "That's your investigation, isn't it?"

Ingrid turned to page five, eager to see what Angela Tate had written. She scanned it quickly. It didn't even mention Stuart Younger by name. It

said nothing about Lauren Shelbourne. It was all about his close relationship with a drug dealer who was referred to as 'a Dutch national now in
custody.' Ingrid checked again. There was no mention of his experiments
either. And certainly no mention of Lauren's phone being used within a
fifty-meter radius of his house? What was Tate playing at?

"Damn."

"You need help?" Jen asked, now beavering away at her desk.

"No. Thank you."

If Younger's arrest was in the papers, she really had to speak to the
Shelbournes. They shouldn't be getting their updates from the *Evening
News*.

"Well, actually, maybe," Ingrid said. "Could you get me the number for
the hotel the Shelbournes are staying at?"

"I have it right here."

Jen was efficient, but that was ridiculous. "How come?"

"Sol asked me for it a couple of hours ago. Said he wanted to update
them on the investigation."

"Oh." Ingrid knew it should have been her to make the call, but she
was grateful—and a little embarrassed—that Sol had stepped up.

"Still need it?"

"I guess not."

However, there was still someone else who needed an update: Madison
Faber. Ingrid guessed the girl would know by now Timo Klaason was in
custody and not likely to walk free for several years. But now that Younger
was being questioned, Ingrid thought Faber might feel free to say more
about the egotistical professor. Ingrid dialed her number. Voicemail.

"Hello, Madison, Ingrid Skyberg here from the embassy. Just checking
up on you. Am assuming you've heard the news that Stuart Younger has
been arrested, but as far as I know, he is only being questioned in relation
to the distribution of methamphetamine, not Lauren. If I hear any more,
I'll let you know. In the meantime, you have my number if you have any
questions." Ingrid ended the call and instantly relaxed. She exhaled loud
enough for Jen to check over her shoulder and make sure she was OK.
Why had leaving a message for Faber got her so tense? Her body was
sending her a message and she needed to pay attention.

Ingrid picked up a pen and flicked it between her fingers. Something
had been bothering her about Faber for some time. The girl's focus
changed every time they met. First she was worried about Lauren's
parents, then about Klaason, then about Stuart Younger. Particularly about
Younger. She only had Faber's word that Lauren had been sleeping with

the professor, and she only had sixteen-year-old Alex Shelbourne's word that Lauren and Faber were dating the same man. Ingrid had cut Faber a lot of slack—she was a young woman living through a horrific trauma without a support system—but it was definitely time she did a bit of digging on the mercurial Madison Faber. If Ingrid was limited to desk duties, she was going to use her time wisely.

Her initial search for a criminal record for Madison Faber drew no results: Faber was completely clean. Ingrid then searched the alumni records for the major colleges in the US. Luckily, there was only one Madison Faber of the right age listed. The search returned results for two colleges. The first in upstate New York and the second just outside Boston. Faber had excelled academically, finishing top of her year in both institutions. A disappointingly blemish-free record. Ingrid trawled further back to Faber's school career.

And things got a lot more interesting.

According to the records, from the age of sixteen, Faber was home-schooled. Given both her parents, lawyers with major firms in New York, had hectic work schedules, Ingrid supposed she must have been tutored by someone other than her mother or father. Homeschooling was an unusual choice. Not something she expected. She trawled back a few more years and found out why.

Madison Faber had been forced to leave her private school just a few days after her sixteenth birthday. Three weeks before that she had made a complaint about a member of the faculty that led to the teacher's dismissal. She made a note to find out exactly what became of him after she'd finished looking into Faber's past. According to a teenage Madison Faber, her chemistry teacher, a young man fresh out of college himself, had kept her late after school one day, trapping her in the lab technician's room —the only room with a lock on its door—and sexually assaulted her. As soon as she reported the assault, he was suspended from duties awaiting criminal investigation. He was never reinstated even though just a week after Faber made her initial complaint, she withdrew it. Along with the statement she'd given to the NYPD.

Ingrid sat very still, trying hard to shut out the sound of Jen's eighty-word-a-minute typing frenzy.

Ingrid went over the reports again, trying to work out what motivations Faber would have for withdrawing her claim. She had been fifteen when she made the complaint against the teacher, and it was entirely possible the school put pressure on her, eager not to have their otherwise excellent reputation tarnished. But would Faber's parents have allowed that to happen? Another trawl revealed that the chairman of the board of trustees of the exclusive school was none other than Faber's father.

Now Ingrid didn't know what to think. Was Faber an innocent student forced to back down because of school board politics? Or the instigator of a nasty lie that had caught up with her?

43

The next morning, Ingrid lasted till midday before she felt compelled to abandon her desk duties and headed to Loriners. She wanted to test how many of Faber's outrageous claims stacked up to a little investigation. Still not strong enough to handle the bike, she made her way to southeast London on public transport. Her phone rang when she was on a surprisingly packed lunchtime train. It was DC Ralph Mills. Just seeing his name on her phone made her smile.

"Was wondering if I could buy you a drink? Got something you might like to hear."

When she told him she would shortly be in what he called 'his manor,' Mills sounded childishly excited and said he would meet her at the train when it arrived at New Cross. He was holding two paper cups of coffee, a bag of sandwiches from a local shop and a Clark Swanson smile.

"I guessed you took it black?"

She took the cup from him. "You guessed correctly." Eye contact was a little more difficult than it ought to be.

"So what brings you to the hood?" he asked, leading her out of New Cross station and into the sunshine.

"Still have a few loose ends to tie up."

"Relating to?"

There was a chance her plan would do more than ruffle feathers at Lewisham police station. "Just getting some answers for Lauren Shelbourne's parents." It was bland and opaque, but it was true. She changed the subject. "You made it seem pretty intriguing on the phone," she said. "I didn't realize you were letting me in on state secrets." They came to a pedestrian crossing—for some unfathomable reason the Brits called them 'pelican crossings'—and she pressed the button that started a countdown to the traffic lights changing color.

Mills took a sip of coffee and licked his lips. "The boss has given me the OK, but you have to understand she's sticking her neck out for you."

"Tell Natasha I appreciate it."

"She reckoned she owed you a favor, not letting go of the whole Shelbourne thing."

The lights changed and they crossed the road.

"Where are you headed?" he asked.

"Loriners."

"I know a shortcut."

He led her down a side street where once grand houses looked ashamed of the mattresses and broken appliances littering their front yards. Even in broad daylight it was menacing.

"So. What was it you wanted to tell me?"

"I'm an idiot," he said. "I haven't asked you how you are."

"I'm healing. Ralph, what is it you need to say?"

He raised his eyebrows. "Right. Yes. Remember the Canadian student who died at Loriners week before last?"

"Of course."

"It's taken a while, because suicides aren't high priority, but we got her blood tests back."

Ingrid stopped herself from taking a sip of coffee. "And?"

"High levels of methamphetamine and LSD."

"Really?" Somehow it wasn't much of a surprise. "What does that mean for Younger?"

He guided her through a back alley running behind several neglected backyards. It was the kind of shortcut only a cop or a drug dealer would know about.

"He's still in custody. We get seventy-two hours before we have to charge or release him."

"And what are you going to charge him with?"

Ralph chucked his empty coffee cup onto an aluminum trash can overflowing with food waste. "Assisting an offender."

"I don't get it."

"For assisting Timo Klaason's attempt to leave the country."

"Come on! You've got to be able to pin more on him than that?"

"We can, and we will. I'm sure. The DI's going gently with him. We still have another forty-eight hours for him to panic and incriminate himself."

They came to the end of the alley and Ingrid recognized where they were. A high brick wall ahead of them marked the perimeter of the college grounds.

"And what has he said about Lauren Shelbourne?" An image of the wound taking a chunk out of the girl's skull flashed through Ingrid's thoughts. "Are you questioning him about her?"

"Ah, yes, there's quite a lot I need to bring you up to speed on. We actually recovered Lauren Shelbourne's phone from Younger's house."

"When the hell were you going to tell me that?" She slapped him on the arm.

"Sorry. It's all been moving pretty quickly." He nodded at a narrow gate in the wall. "See, told you it was quicker." They entered the campus grounds and followed a signed path that led to the main piazza.

"Tell me about the goddamn phone, Ralph."

"Ah, yes, right." He really needed to get out of the habit of stringing out a story like a comedian building up to a punch line. "The phone was discovered by none other than Mrs Younger herself. She found it in Professor Younger's underwear drawer."

Ingrid held fire on her questions to prevent Mills from taking hours to get through his story. She took a sip and let him continue.

"So here she is, dutiful and faithful wife, putting away the laundry, and voilà, she discovers a strange mobile phone nestling amongst his underpants and woolly socks. Odd, she thinks, what's this? She then proceeds to turn the phone on and read all the text messages stored in the memory." They came to a bench that was neither covered in bird mess nor chewing gum. "Shall we?"

"Sure."

They sat down and Ralph handed her a sandwich out of the paper bag. A steady stream of students poured through a gap in the buildings and disappeared into their accommodation blocks. No doubt the poor kids who couldn't afford lunch in the canteen.

"So," he continued, "she's shocked to discover over ninety percent of the texts are *from* her husband. She's even more shocked by the nature of their contents. Once she's got through all of those, she takes a look at the 'sent' folder. In here we have such X-rated missives that they make her husband's texts look positively tame. Understandably, she's getting a tad angry over all of this. Angrier with each new description of what the phone's owner—whose identity, remember, is still unknown to her—has planned for the good professor next time she gets her hands on him. By now Mrs Younger wants to get her hands on him herself, but we're talking X-rated horror movie, not soft porn."

He paused for breath, but Ingrid thought it wise not to interrupt and ate her sandwich. BLT. Good choice.

"Then things get even worse. Mrs Y reads texts that mention her in a less than flattering light. How fantastic her husband's and his mystery lover's lives will be when he dumps his nagging wife and runs away into the sunset—I'm paraphrasing—with said lover." He stopped again and picked a slice of tomato out of his sandwich and threw it onto the patch lawn. Pigeons descended on it within seconds. "That's the final straw. Next thing, she's marching out to the two uniformed officers sitting in the squad car parked outside—I wish I'd been there—telling them she's ready to answer any questions they might have concerning her husband, and offering to provide an exhaustive list of the places the professor might be. And this was all playing out just about the same time we'd pinned down the location of the phone."

He paused again and Ingrid took her chance to interject. "Yet it still took a couple of hours for you to pick Younger up."

He lifted his eyebrows.

"I'm yanking your chain."

"Right." His face gradually broke into a smile.

"So there's no doubt Younger was having an affair with Shelbourne. You've got so much proof now, he can't deny it." Madison Faber's lurid allegations had been proved right. Just because she was excitable, it didn't mean the girl was wrong. She really didn't know what to make of Faber's reliability as a witness.

Ralph nodded.

"So are you talking to him about Lauren's death? Do those texts give him motive to get her… out of the way? What's he got to say for himself?"

Ralph rapidly swallowed a mouthful. "Nothing at all. Not a murmur."

"Even his connection to Timo Klaason?"

"His prints are all over the money we found in Klaason's possession. Klaason has confirmed Younger gave him the cash. But still Younger won't say anything. His lawyer's a hot shot from a firm in the city, and he's advising the professor to keep quiet."

"And you haven't charged Younger with anything yet?"

"Like I say, we've still got plenty of hours on the clock before we have to do that."

"And what might you be able to charge him with?"

"Assisting an offender. Definitely perversion of the course of justice. It'd be hard for him to get off that one."

"But nothing to do with Lauren's death? Or the drugs used in his experiments?"

"We've got him on the line and we're reeling him in. Be patient with us. We're using his phone data and diary to piece together his movements the night Lauren died. DNA samples from her flat will almost certainly confirm his presence there, but that won't be a surprise—he must have visited her there loads of times—so wouldn't necessarily be helpful with implicating him in killing her."

"But you think he might have?"

"He's an arrogant twat, so I'd put nothing past him, but..."

"Yes?" Ingrid was electrified at the prospect of nailing the bastard.

"There's nothing in the texts he exchanged with Lauren that suggested their relationship was on the rocks."

That was true. The phone could just as easily exonerate him. Ingrid thought about things for a second. "He explained how come he had Lauren's phone?"

"Nope."

Ingrid wanted desperately to be in on the interrogation. "Is DI McKittrick doing the interviews herself?"

"Yep—I'm her number two." He looked at his watch. "I should get back over there. Our next crack at him starts in fifteen minutes." He drummed his fingers on his knees.

"Well, thanks for the update. And lunch."

He stood up. "I almost forgot. Your predecessor's main liaison in the Met?"

Ingrid looked up at him. Now wasn't the time to tell him it didn't really matter anymore. "You have a name for me?"

"Not exactly." He screwed up his face. "McKittrick told me to tell you your predecessor's primary contact was a high-ranking officer in SO15— Counter Terrorism Command. She couldn't get his name. For reasons of national security, apparently. You want a hand up?"

She didn't, but accepted his offer, wincing as she got to her feet. "Thanks so much. Hope it didn't get you into any trouble."

He gave her a Clark Swanson special. "I hope so too."

"Say thank you to Natasha for me," she called after him.

"Will do."

She turned toward a gap between buildings that she hoped would lead her to the administration block. Out of the sunshine, the spring air was cool. The atmosphere on campus was febrile, with students and staff hurrying between buildings as they gossiped. Ingrid found the administration block and was given a map marking out where she would find the buildings used by the medical faculty. A few minutes after that, she was outside the lecture theater she was looking for. She was about to let herself in when her phone buzzed in her pocket. It was Ralph again.

"Hi." She spoke quietly, keen not to disturb the students on the other side of the door.

"Hi." He was a little out of breath. "You'll never guess who was in reception when I got back to the station."

She could.

"Madison."

No surprise there.

"She wants to give us a statement. She's claiming Stuart Younger confessed to killing Lauren Shelbourne."

44

"When?" Ingrid asked, her voice rising several decibels.

"She says he came to her two days ago."

"Why the hell did she wait two days?"

"Listen, I don't know. I have to go. I thought you'd want the heads-up."

Mills hung up, leaving Ingrid stunned. She leaned against the wall; the lecturer's drone permeated through the door. She was more than willing to believe the sly Professor Younger was involved in Lauren's death, but somehow Faber's allegation undermined that belief. The revelation that she had withdrawn the accusation of assault against her teacher made Ingrid doubt every word that came out of Faber's mouth. She could no longer put her erratic behavior down to recent trauma.

The doors to the lecture theater swung open and students filed out, chatting excitedly, talking over one another, as if they'd just been released from a silent order of monks. Or more accurately, nuns. Almost all of the people emerging from the hall were women. A few moments later she saw the person she'd been waiting for and hurried toward him before he was lost in the stream of bodies.

"Mohammed!"

The medical student pulled up sharply and quickly turned his head left then right.

"Mo," she said again when she was just a few feet away.

"Hello. Man!" He reared away from her. "What did you do to your face?"

"It's OK—it's not as bad as it looks."

"I never expected to see you again. I thought you wouldn't want to get anywhere near this place after what's happened. You'd be better off getting your PhD somewhere else."

"Ah... yes. About that." She explained who she was and apologized for the earlier deception.

"You're kidding me. FBI? No way, man."

She pulled out her badge. He snatched it from her and inspected it closely, front and reverse, only reluctantly handing it back to her when she wrapped her fingers around it.

"Are you here because of Younger? Did you suspect him all that time?"

"I can't discuss the details of the police investigation."

"I won't say a word. Honest."

Ingrid told Mohammed the bare minimum to get the result she needed. Ten minutes later she was climbing the stairs of a small accommodation block just around the corner from campus.

"Jamil probably won't want to talk—you'll have to use your best inter-rogation techniques to get him to open up. He hardly even told me what happened to him. And we've been mates since, like... infants. We go way back." He stopped at a door halfway along a corridor on the third floor and thumped his fist against it. "Jamil! It's me, man. I know you're in there."

They listened for noises inside the room. There weren't any.

"Jay! Come on! I got a hot lady out here desperate to speak to you." He glanced sideways at Ingrid and smiled at her with one corner of his mouth. "No offense—any means necessary—you get me?"

"Piss off," a muffled voice called from the other side of the door. "I'm busy."

"Seriously, man. She ain't gonna take no for an answer."

"Jamil?" Ingrid raised her voice. "I'm Special Agent Ingrid Skyberg. I work out of the US Embassy here in London."

The noisy metal rattle of a lock unfastening was followed by the creak of the door. A sliver of face appeared and a single eyeball inspected first Ingrid, then Mohammed. "Ouch! Who mashed your face?" Jamil said, opening the door wide.

Ingrid followed him into a dark study-cum-bedroom, a podlike bath-room right next to the door, a narrow single bed along one long wall, a desk against the other, drapes drawn shut at the window. The room stank of toasted cheese and adolescent sweat. Two laptops sat on the desk, glowing in the dark.

"Jamil here is a regular Mark Zuckerberg. He makes apps in his spare time. He's an entrepreneur, innit." Mohammed pulled out the chair so that it stood in the narrow space between the bed and the desk. "How about some light in this dungeon, yeah?" He opened the drapes and bright sunshine came streaming in. Jamil held up a hand to shield his eyes.

"And maybe some fresh air too?" Ingrid suggested.

Mohammed pushed open the window a crack while Jamil threw a cover over his unmade bed. He and Mohammed sat down. Ingrid smiled at them both. "Mo tells me you took part in the psychology department research program last semester."

Jamil glared at his friend.

"It's all right, bro. Nothing can happen to you now, can it?"

Ingrid showed him her badge. "Anything you tell me will be treated in the strictest confidence."

Jamil stared at the badge with wide eyes. "Why are the FBI interested in what I've got to say?"

"It's in connection with an ongoing investigation. I can't share the details, I'm afraid."

"But I signed a nondisclosure agreement—I don't want to get sued."

"Jamil's loaded," Mohammed said. "He's been stashing away millions, innit. He thinks I don't know."

"A nondisclosure agreement signed under duress wouldn't stand up in court." Ingrid kept her voice as gentle as she could. "Trust me."

"Yanks know everything about all that legal stuff, suing and that—they practically invented it," Mohammed offered. Ingrid wished he'd shut up.

"I'm curious—why did you sign up for the experiment in the first place?"

Mohammed started to answer for his friend, but quickly stopped when Ingrid held up an admonishing finger.

"The researcher was really nice to me. Girls normally just ignore me. Or take the piss. She was different." He sighed. "And gorgeous. She said she'd selected me specially. Because I wasn't like the other students. She told me I would be part of something really important. It was an exclusive group, she said." His head dropped into his hands. "I can't believe I fell for it."

"Who was this?" Ingrid pictured one of Younger's acolytes dressed in her green and purple shirt, ingratiating herself. Preying on a vulnerable student.

"Her name's Madison Faber. She's American."

Faber? Ingrid took a deep breath, her mouth suddenly dry. She moistened her lips with her tongue.

"You know her, don't you?" Jamil said, reading Ingrid's face. He was trembling, a faint tremor making his upper body vibrate.

"You're sure it was Madison Faber who enrolled you in the program?" Ingrid asked.

Jamil nodded. "She told me she was running a side project of her own. She made me..." He stopped himself.

"It's OK—take as long as you need."

"There was this one experiment where I had to... *hurt* somebody." He blinked rapidly, as if he were reliving the event in his head. "There was this machine. It electrocuted people. I actually heard them scream in the next room. But Madison said it was OK—the pain only lasted a fraction of a second. She said it was important for me to carry on. To put the person in the other room out of my mind." His breath caught in his throat.

"I'm not in a hurry, Jamil."

The experiment he was describing wasn't new to Ingrid. Anyone studying psychology 101 would have heard of the Milgram Experiment. And most of them would know it was no longer carried out due to ethical concerns. Faber would have known it too.

"How could I put them out of my mind when I actually had to speak to them? I had to ask them questions. If they got the answer wrong... that's when I flipped a switch on this big machine. They were wired up to it. They got a shock if they didn't know the answer." He shuddered. "I had to stop. I told Madison I couldn't go on. She got really angry. She told me I was putting her project in jeopardy. Then she said if I was so concerned about the person in the next room, maybe I'd like to take their place. I'd be connected to the machine, and she'd ask the questions." He swallowed another wet gulp.

"You're certain it was Madison who was running the experiment? Not Professor Younger?"

"She told me Younger was in overall charge. She carried out other experiments for Younger. I'm not sure exactly what they were. I didn't ask. I didn't want to know."

"Can you tell me what happened next?"

He started gnawing at one of his fingernails.

"You're doing really well. What you're telling me is really helping my investigation."

Jamil looked at his friend, who urged him on, nodding encouragingly.

"I said I'd report her to the college authorities. Tell them about her twisted experiment."

Ingrid nodded. "And how did Madison react to that?"

"She went mental. Told me I didn't understand anything. Called me a moron. She said no one would listen to a loser like me." He shook his head. "Maybe I was a moron—to actually believe she liked me in the first place."

"Did she say anything else?"

"She threatened me." He shivered more violently. Mohammed jumped up and closed the window. "She said she'd get the guardians to come and speak to me, see if I might change my mind about ratting on her then."

"The guardians?"

"It's a private group in the psychology department."

"Private army more like," Mohammed added. "You spoke to me about them in the cafeteria when I first met you. I said I didn't know what you were talking about. You remember? The blokes in the polo shirts? You don't see the shirts anymore, but the guardians are still around. I steer well clear of them."

"Me too," Jamil said. "And Madison. Every time I see her, I get the shits. I ran right into her after my tutorial last week. She threatened me again."

"Man, I'm sorry," Mohammed said, "you should have told me. I didn't realize it was that bad. Is that why you've been locked up in here since Thursday?"

Jamil nodded. "After I saw her, I came straight back. Been living on pot noodle ever since."

No wonder the room smelled. Ingrid had heard enough and she didn't want to make Jamil relive any more of his pain. "Jamil, you've been incredibly helpful. I really appreciate it." She handed him a card. "You should know, the experiment you took part in? I've seen it before, and you don't need to worry about what you did to the other students."

"You didn't hear them scream."

"Really—it's OK. You weren't torturing anyone. You were the *subject* of the experiment. Madison Faber was testing just how far she could push you. And from what you've told me, that wasn't very far at all. You've done nothing wrong."

"You're sure?"

"Absolutely." She offered him her hand. "Thank you, Jamil. You too, Mo."

Ingrid got to her feet. Mohammed did the same. "I'll walk you down to the street."

"It's OK, I can find my way." Ingrid opened the door and stopped just outside the room. She turned back. Something Jamil had told her wasn't right. "You said you've been holed up in here since last week?"

The student nodded at her. "Since Thursday."

"Last Thursday, that's when you ran into Madison? You're certain?"

"Why wouldn't I be?"

Ingrid smiled at him. "No reason. Don't worry about it. Thanks again." She closed the door quickly and hurried in the direction of the exit.

What was Madison Faber doing at Loriners on Thursday when she'd told Ingrid on Wednesday morning that she was too terrified to set foot back on campus?

45

Ingrid stood on the street for over ten minutes waiting for a black London cab with its light on to drive past. She told the driver to take her to Lewisham police station. With any luck, she could get there while Madison Faber was still giving her statement.

Her phone rang. It wasn't a number she recognized.

"Ingrid Skyberg."

"Miss Skyberg, is that you?" A polite, male voice.

"Speaking."

"This is John Taylor." He paused. "Emily's father."

Ingrid's brain trawled through its databases, trying to place him.

"You came to our house in Lewes the other day."

Ah! "Yes, yes of course. How is Emily?"

"She's much better, thank you for asking. My wife and I are just bringing her back to Loriners College, so I think that's a good sign."

"That's excellent news. I'm so pleased to hear that." Ingrid still had no idea why he was calling.

"She said she would like to talk to you." There was some chatter in the background. "Now, if you're free."

Ingrid asked the driver to turn around and take her back toward Loriners. Emily had rented a room in an apartment in a street identical to the one Ralph had walked her down earlier in the day. The buildings were large, five-story houses with bay fronts and would once have been respectable family homes. But in recent decades, they had been bought up and divided by landlords seeking to exploit the transient student market. Ingrid wasn't able to stop herself from thinking that, if Emily had been living somewhere a bit nicer, she might not have found herself standing on a window ledge contemplating suicide.

John Taylor opened the door before Ingrid got a chance to knock. "That didn't take long."

"I was in the neighborhood."

He showed her into a tattered kitchen at the rear of the house. Cabinet doors were hanging off their hinges; dirty dishes were stacked in the sink. Ingrid remembered the nice, well-maintained house she had visited in Lewes with its clipped yew hedge. Coming back to such a student dive would be hard on Emily's fragile psychology.

The girl smiled when Ingrid walked into the room. "Hi," she said. "I'm Emily."

Ingrid noticed a tattoo of an infinity symbol on the girl's wrist as they shook hands. "Ingrid, nice to meet you."

"Would you like a cuppa?" she asked.

Ingrid looked at the counter, imagined the dirt in the cups and the Legionnaires' in the pipes and declined. Emily's father hovered in the doorway, just as he had done in Lewes.

"We're OK, Dad," Emily said.

"Right, yes. I'll bring some more things in from the car."

Ingrid joined Emily at a small square dining table that wobbled. "Sorry about the state of things. Mum's gone to the supermarket to buy a year's supply of cleaning products."

Ingrid smiled nervously.

"I know, we still have to use them."

"Perhaps your mom will draw up a cleaning roster for everyone too?" Ingrid reached out a hand toward Emily, stopping short of touching her. "How are you doing?"

Emily's eye twitched. "Good, I think. The worst bit was the drugs. I feel like they're out of my system now, so almost back to normal, really."

"And," Ingrid lowered her voice, "have you spoken to a therapist or a counselor?"

"Nah. I would never have tried anything like that if it hadn't been for the drugs. That's why I wanted to talk to you, and also kind of why I came back."

Ingrid waited for her to explain.

"I read that Younger's in prison—"

"Not yet. He's been arrested, but they haven't charged him yet."

"So he's in police custody, is that what they call it?"

"Yes, that's right."

"So he hasn't actually been found guilty of anything yet?"

"No, that would require a judge and a court case." Ingrid was amazed at how naïve the girl was about criminal proceedings. It was one of the hallmarks of a middle-class upbringing where no one she knew had ever been in trouble with the police. "But it seems very likely that he will be charged, and he will serve time. Do you think you know something pertinent to his case?"

The girl nodded and gave her a brief, weak smile. "I'm not sure where to start."

"How about I ask some questions, and we'll see where we get to? Why don't you start by telling me how you got involved in Professor Younger's research program?"

Emily shook her head.

"You don't need to worry. He can't hurt you anymore."

Emily Taylor frowned. "Why would he want to hurt me?"

Ingrid was confused. "I assumed you felt able to speak to me now because he's not around."

"No! It's the opposite of that. You have to tell the police they've made a mistake. I don't suppose they'll listen to me; that's why I thought you could help. They've probably labeled me as unstable or unreliable. Or just mad. I want you to tell the police that Stuart's not a bad man. He shouldn't go to prison. You have to believe that."

Ingrid pressed her palms against her thighs. "He systematically gave drugs to students, Emily. It was part of how he controlled everyone."

"No." She tapped the table firmly for emphasis. "I went into it with my eyes open. I knew exactly what was involved. So did everyone else. Look, I'm interested in the brain, right? It's what I want to specialize in. Psychology is all part of the same whole. Being involved that closely with live experiments was a fantastic opportunity for me. It's why I chose Loriners in the first place. There are better colleges in London to study medicine. But none of them has a psychology department that even gets close to Stuart's."

Emily was yet another student with a crush on the handsome professor. Which made her testimony dubious at best, useless at worst. "So tell me about the experiments."

Emily craned her head close to Ingrid's. "It's the drugs you're really interested in, isn't it? That's the important thing as far as the investigation is concerned, isn't it?"

"It's almost certainly what he'll be charged with."

"Then you need to understand the drugs were why I was taking part. They produce transformative results. Groundbreaking."

"You took drugs voluntarily?"

"Of course I did. Did you think they were forced down my throat?"

Ingrid rubbed her chin. "How were they administered?"

"I swallowed them with a glass of water. How else? No one forced me to do anything. I knew what I was doing." Emily's eyes were bright and alert. "I can't be sure whether I was given real drugs or a placebo—these were proper robust trials—but I certainly felt the effects. The whole experiment was carefully designed and properly monitored. I didn't leave the lab for four hours after I took the pills. I was under observation the whole time."

"So what happened this last time? How did you end up—"

"You want to know how come I was on the top floor of the admin block, dangling out of the window?"

Ingrid nodded.

"I'm not sure. I don't understand what happened, and I've been trying to analyze it myself. Maybe the purity of the drugs was different. Maybe it was a new batch. Or I was given the wrong dose."

"Is that possible? That something could go that wrong?"

The girl shrugged. "With Lauren not around to double-check everything? Sure. I nearly didn't continue in the program after she died. I thought it would be disrespectful to her somehow. But then if I hadn't, it would have messed up all the results."

"Who was supposed to be watching you?"

"They were short-staffed. Stuart popped in at regular intervals to make sure I was OK."

"Did he give you the drugs himself?"

"No, it was another of the researchers."

"And was there a staff shortage the week before? When the other student jumped from the same window? Could she have been administered the wrong dose?"

"I spoke to Lauren about that right after it happened. Jessica—the Canadian student—was taking a placebo. It couldn't have been the drugs that made her jump."

"She had high levels of LSD in her system."

"What?"

"According to the blood tests the police carried out."

"She couldn't have. She was definitely taking a sugar pill."

"Not before she died she wasn't."

"That doesn't make any sense. That means someone switched her from the control group to the active group without letting Lauren know. Who would do something like that?"

Ingrid took a moment to figure things out. "Is it possible someone was deliberately trying to meddle with the experiment?"

"It's possible, I guess."

"Is it possible you were previously on the placebo, but your dose was also switched last week?"

Emily covered her mouth with her hand. "I guess."

Ingrid felt she was getting somewhere. "Do you remember which researchers gave you the drugs the last time?"

She nodded. "Yeah. I don't know her name, but I'd seen her around the lab now and then. I got the impression she was more senior than the other researchers. She certainly acted that way."

"Can you describe her?"

"Oh, you'd be able to track her down if you need to speak to her, I'm sure. She was the only other American in the program."

46

Ingrid left Emily Taylor and called Natasha McKittrick. When she got her voicemail, she called Ralph Mills and left a message for him too. She thought about calling Madison Faber on the pretense she was concerned for her welfare, but the girl was smart, she was manipulative, and Ingrid wasn't convinced she could keep her ulterior motive out of the tone of her voice.

If Madison was at Lewisham police station, Ingrid was willing to risk that at some point while she was in the neighborhood, she would pay a visit to her apartment, so that was where she headed. Ingrid wanted to see her face when she confronted her.

The street Madison Faber's apartment was on felt like genteel suburbia compared to the house share Emily Taylor had rented. The cars parked in the street were newer and larger, and the front gardens were tended and abundant. Either Faber was taking on a lot of debt to get her master's, or her parents were footing a sizeable bill.

Ingrid looked up at Madison's apartment from the sidewalk. The shades were open, but that didn't mean Faber was at home. She rang the bell, one of four buttons on the intercom panel. No answer. She tried all the other buttons.

"Hello?" A woman's voice.

"Hi." Ingrid leaned into the intercom. "I'm from the American embassy. I need to get hold of the girl who lives on the top floor."

"Sorry, haven't seen her."

The woman disconnected. Ingrid buzzed again.

"Hello."

"I'm so sorry to disturb you, but I think she might be in trouble."

The crackle on the intercom ceased, and Ingrid was ready to turn.

"Who did you say you were?"

"Ingrid Skyberg. US Embassy."

The locked clicked and Ingrid pushed the door open. Ahead of her was a neatly decorated hallway, a table on the right-hand side with mail in piles, a staircase straight ahead. A door on her left opened and a middle-aged white woman in pajamas and a heavy cardigan stood in the doorway.

"I'm sorry, did I wake you?"

The woman smiled. "I work from home."

Ingrid smiled at her. "Thanks for letting me in. So you haven't seen Madison?"

"No, I don't really know her. Only know her name from the post." She didn't open the door further.

"When was the last time you saw her?"

She shrugged. "I'd have to think. Day before yesterday maybe. When you work from home, the days sort of merge. Why are the embassy interested in her?"

"We think she might be in some difficulty."

"Is it to do with what's going on at the university?"

Ingrid dodged answering directly. "It may be adding to her stress. Have you ever seen her come home with anyone?"

"What kind of trouble?" the woman asked. "Should we be taking precautions?"

"I think she's in danger more than she's in trouble, which is why I want to trace her." Ingrid reached into her pocket and pulled out a business card. "If you do see her, would you please give me a call? No matter what time of day."

The woman looked at the card. "You work for the FBI? Really?"

Ingrid smiled apologetically. "Yup, there's a bunch of us in most embassies around the world."

"So she's committed a crime?"

Ingrid didn't reply.

"Is she dangerous? I've got a kid."

"Mostly I'd say she was a danger to herself. The moment you see her, please call me."

The neighbor looked at the card again. "OK. You need me to do anything else?"

"You don't have the number for a local taxi company, do you?"

The woman nodded to the table where the mail was. "You'll probably find a flyer amongst that lot."

Ingrid leaned against the wall separating the front yard from the sidewalk and called herself a taxi. It would be a ten-minute wait. She tried calling Ralph Mills again. This time his phone didn't go straight to voicemail, but rang and rang until she got the automated message. Neither he nor McKittrick had returned her calls. She left another message for Natasha, saying she had spoken to credible witnesses and that she had concerns Faber had deliberately sabotaged Younger's experiment.

When her phone rang, she was disappointed to see it was an embassy number.

"Ingrid Skyberg."

"It's Sol."

Ingrid ran her fingers through her short hair. "Hi, Sol."

"I notice you're not at your desk." His voice rasped with forty years of cigarette addiction.

"Ah. About that."

"Where are you?"

"Outside Madison Faber's apartment."

"Who's she?"

Ingrid was taken aback. She had been so consumed by Faber and her erratic behavior over the past few days it seemed impossible that Sol wouldn't know who she was. "The girl who found Lauren Shelbourne's body."

"And why are you there?"

That wasn't an easy thing to explain. "I'm helping the Met."

He said nothing.

"But I'm taking it easy. No motorcycle. In fact, I'm waiting for a taxi. Is there a reason you're checking up on me?"

"It's called pastoral care, Ingrid. Just checking you hadn't jumped off another building or a moving vehicle."

"All limbs still in working order."

"Also."

Ingrid knew that hadn't been why he was calling.

"The Met have been in touch. Concerned there may have been a security breach. Counter Terrorism Command. Starting to ring any bells?"

Ingrid's blood turned to ice. "Is this to do with Mulroony?"

"You tell me."

Ingrid closed her eyes, silently hoping she hadn't got McKittrick or Mills into trouble. "I was only hoping to speak to his Met handler. I never even got a name."

Sol inhaled audibly. "Do yourself a favor, agent, when it comes to your predecessor, ditch your tenacity, lose your curiosity and discover a blind eye that will stand you in good stead. You hear me?"

"Do I get to ask why?"

"It's better if you don't."

Neither of them said anything for several moments.

"My taxi's here." It was a lie, but she hung up anyway, too annoyed to talk anymore to her boss. She scrolled for Mills number, but stopped herself from calling him. Leaving three messages might just send the wrong signal, even if all three were genuinely about work. She was, she reminded herself, engaged, and that came with certain obligations she intended to honor.

The taxi came and took her toward Hampstead. She wanted to speak to the family friend Faber was staying with. Perhaps she could shed more light on the young woman's mental stability. Her phone illuminated in her lap with a text. It was from Mills.

Sorry. Not ignoring you. Been flat out. Big news. Stuart Younger has been charged with Lauren Shelbourne's murder. He was remanded in custody about an hour ago.

Ingrid dropped the phone onto the seat and gazed out the window. She didn't know how to feel. A tiny bit proud that she had been the one who hadn't let it lie? Pleased the smug smile would have been wiped off Younger's face? Desperately sad a young woman's life had been ended not by misadventure, but by force? Her head fell against the window and she watched the traffic.

If Younger had been charged, that meant Natasha and the Crown Prosecution Service felt there was sufficient evidence. They wouldn't just be taking Faber's word for it. Maybe he had even confessed.

Damn.

There was somewhere else she needed to be.

"Excuse me," she said to the driver. "Can you take me to the Ixion Hotel in Mayfair?"

He looked at her in the rearview mirror. "It'll be extra."

"Whatever."

Somebody had to tell the Shelbournes their daughter had been murdered.

47

Ingrid walked slowly back to the embassy. Lisa Shelbourne had screamed when she'd told her. Alex had remained perfectly still apart from the tears rolling down her cheeks. Anthony Shelbourne had paced like a caged animal. Ingrid absorbed as much of their pain as she could, but she had to put up a barrier. Their grief, their anger, added to her own about the friend she had lost. She didn't know what had happened to Megan after her abduction, but every crime scene, every murder report she read, Ingrid could never quite stop herself from imagining her friend was the victim. She made her apologies and her excuses and left them to their anguish and heartbreak.

By the time she got back to her desk, most of the civilian staff had gone home. A few other agents were still working, but the place had a weekend feel. She closed her office door and signed in to the computer network, pulled up a browser and logged in to her personal Skype account. An icon told her Marshall was online. But that wasn't whom she had arranged to call. She tapped in the details, and her call was answered almost immediately, and the Skype window was filled with the surprisingly healthy features of an ex-schoolteacher from Washington Heights.

"Hello, Mr. Timms," she said.

A beat later the tanned face beamed back at her. "Agent Skyberg, please, call me Kevin."

The years had been kinder to Kevin Timms than she had been expecting. After being forced out of his chosen profession by the false claims of a fifteen-year-old Madison Faber, his reputation ruined, Ingrid had supposed the man would have turned to drink or drugs. According to the records, Timms had moved to Mexico shortly after leaving the school and hadn't returned to the US. She'd only managed to trace him by searching social media sites.

"OK," he said, "you have to put me out of my misery. My mind has been racing since you first contacted me. What does the FBI want with a simple man eking out an honest existence south of the border? I'm assuming you don't want to haul my ass back to the US, else you wouldn't have gotten in touch first." He smiled at her again and leaned back in his seat. Behind him, through the glass of patio doors, Ingrid spotted a generously proportioned swimming pool, two very tanned children playing noiselessly. It seemed Kevin Timms had done very well for himself in the last seven years.

"Don't worry, sir—you're quite safe."

"Good, because I've no intention of *ever* coming back." He picked up a tall glass of yellow liquid, an umbrella sticking out the top, and lifted it toward the webcam of his laptop. "Giving up teaching was the best thing that could have happened to me." He took a sip of his juice. At least she assumed it was juice. It was just after lunch in Lake Chapala.

"That's why I'm calling. I'd like to talk to you about Madison Faber."

He put down his glass with a clunk. "Why, what has she done now, murdered somebody?"

Ingrid's heart missed a beat, but she ignored the remark. "I wondered whether you could go over the details of—"

He cut her off. "Do you know, I thank that twisted bitch every single day of my life. If it weren't for her, I'd probably still be teaching."

"I've read the report of what happened, but I was hoping you'd be able to fill in the blanks for me."

"I'd really rather not relive that time in my life," he said. And then spent the next ten minutes doing exactly that.

When he reached the part of his story Ingrid hadn't heard before, she stopped him. "Wait a minute, are you saying Madison Faber was stalking you?"

"She was always waiting for me after school. At my house on the weekend. Dressed like a whore, might I add. Then, when I'd made it clear I wasn't interested, she turned on me. Twisting reality so that suddenly it was me stalking her day and night. Harassing her any chance I got. Until finally I supposedly attacked her one afternoon in the chemistry lab."

"She withdrew all her claims."

"Too late for my career. Still, as I say, I've never looked back. I make more now in a month than I did in a year." He waved a paperback book at the webcam. "Romantic fiction. Quite ironic, don't you think? I can churn out one of these every two months. More than covers my extravagant lifestyle."

"Do you know why she withdrew her story?"

"Not for certain. Though if you put a gun to my head, I'd guess the school leaned on her. And her family."

Though the image of his face on her screen had started to break up a little, Ingrid couldn't mistake the change in his expression. Gone were the toothy grin and raised eyebrows, replaced by a thin-lipped scowl and furrowed brow. A few moments later he snapped himself out of whatever reverie had come over him, and he clapped his hands together. "So, what do you need from me, Agent? A character reference for Miss Faber? A report on the standard of her high school chemistry?"

"I think you've given me enough information for now, thank you."

"You're kidding me. I've only just gotten started." He lifted his glass. "You still haven't told me what she's done to come to the attention of the FBI. Must be some serious shit. *Did* she murder somebody?"

Ingrid glanced away from the screen, aware someone was standing at the threshold of the office. "Mr Timms, I'm sorry, but I have to go." She thanked him again and turned to the woman in her doorway. "Hi."

"Hi. I'm Christine. I work with the counterespionage group."

"Hi, yes, come in."

Christine, a robust-looking woman in her thirties with a formidable power suit, strode toward her with a piece of paper in her hand. "I've taken a couple of calls for you today."

"That's weird."

"I know, I think there's a divert on the system, so I couldn't put this through to you." She placed the paper on Ingrid's desk. "This man was quite insistent you call him back."

Ingrid looked down at the name. Julian Granger. "Who is he?"

"An arrogant asshole is all I can tell you."

"Well, thanks for bringing it to me."

Christine called out a 'you're welcome' on her way out.

Ingrid picked up her phone and dialed.

"Julian Granger." The man was upper class. He sounded like he was in a BBC adaptation of a Le Carré thriller.

"Ingrid Skyberg. I understand you wanted me to call."

"Ah, yes, Miss Skyberg, where have you been?"

Christine's description of him was so far wholly accurate.

"I only just got your message."

"Hmmm."

"Mr Granger? Why are we speaking?"

"I am Stuart Younger's solicitor. He is asking to see you."

"What?"

"In fact, he is insisting."

48

Early the following morning, Ingrid got off the Triumph, pleased her body had healed well enough to handle being on two wheels again, and walked up the steps of Lewisham police station. With any luck she could have a quick word with McKittrick before visiting Stuart Younger in the cells. She unzipped her motorcycle jacket and realized she had got a smudge of engine oil on the pants leg of her shabby suit. She really did have to buy some new clothes.

"Miss Skyberg?"

"Yes?"

"Julian Granger." She had already guessed as much. He looked as upper class as he sounded with a double-breasted pinstripe suit and a perfect triangle of a silk pocket square poking out of his suit jacket. It was almost impossible to tell his age, as his outfit was so old-fashioned, but she'd hazard he was early thirties. His gold watch rattled as they shook hands. "I hope you don't mind, but I've taken the liberty of signing you in. If you would come this way."

A uniformed officer led them into a stairwell and took them down two flights. So much for getting the latest from McKittrick.

"He's being transferred to Thameside later," Granger said.

"What's Thameside?" Ingrid asked.

"A category B prison. I'm very grateful you came. The professor is convinced you can help."

Ingrid gripped the chin guard of her helmet as they trotted quickly downwards. "What has he been charged with?"

"You don't know?"

"I want to hear it from you."

The constable opened a door that led into a waiting area. "Desk sergeant will sort you out," he said before leaving.

An aroma of stale body odor mingled with the more subtle scent of disinfectant and overcooked food. They were now underground in the bowels of the Victorian building, and there were no windows and no phone signal. The tile floor beneath their feet gleamed only in patches: decades of shuffling footsteps had scuffed and scraped the surface so badly that no amount of polishing could fix it.

"Mr Granger," the sergeant said from behind a counter, "I see you have company this morning."

Granger made the introductions and Ingrid signed a succession of forms the sergeant put in front of her. Once the paperwork was out of the way, the sergeant gestured for Ingrid to follow him.

"What about you?" she said to Granger.

"He wants to speak to you alone."

At the end of a long corridor lined with cells, Ingrid was shown into a visitor room, where she was patted down by a female constable. "I need to take that." She nodded to the helmet. "You could knock him out with that."

Ingrid handed it over and opened her shoulder bag for inspection. Satisfied she was free of offensive weapons, the constable told Ingrid to take a seat. "We'll bring him out in a minute."

Ingrid sat on an orange plastic chair on one side of a wooden table that was covered in graffiti and scratched messages. Protestations of innocence, profanities and women's names predominated. She heard footsteps.

Stuart Younger appeared in the doorway, accompanied by an officer.

"I'll be right outside," he said. "Knock when you want to leave."

Younger was dressed in his own clothes, presumably the ones he'd been arrested in, and the pants were grimy, his shirt crumpled and creased. His hair was damp against his scalp. His eyes were puffed and red-rimmed; a slick of sweat covered his forehead. "Thank you so much for agreeing to see me," he said, his hand outstretched as she approached.

Ingrid ignored the hand. She didn't want him to think she was doing him any favors. Younger took his seat and she waited for him to speak.

"She's out to destroy me. You know that, don't you?" Younger leaned in close. "My work, my career, my marriage." The last word snagged in his throat. For a second Ingrid thought he might cry. "It's a tissue of lies. Everything she told the police."

"Take a moment," Ingrid told him. "Breathe slowly. Then back right up and start at the beginning. Do you need a glass of water?"

"No, I'm fine. I just need you to listen to me. The police won't take me seriously."

She wasn't sure she would either.

"I started to tell them about her, how evil she is, but they weren't interested. They insisted on repeating the same questions over and over. Like a stuck record. My solicitor advised me to stay silent. I've provided a written statement about her. But the way things stand, I can't be sure anyone in authority has even read it." He rubbed a hand over his head. "Why are they listening to her?"

Ingrid studied him carefully.

"Why would they believe her and not me?" He clasped his hands together and stared with wild, wide eyes into Ingrid's face.

"If you need me to listen to you, then you have to do what I say." Ingrid spoke very clearly and slowly, as she might to an overexcited child. "Do you understand?"

He nodded, his face pinched.

"Good. Now—tell me who you're talking about."

"It's bloody obvious, isn't it?"

"I need to hear you say the name."

"Madison fucking Faber. Is that clear enough for you?" He squeezed his hands into tight fists and thumped the table.

"Take it easy," Ingrid said.

"For Christ's sake, they've charged me with murder."

"I can get up and leave, anytime. Walk straight out that door and not look back. Give me a reason to keep listening—start from the beginning."

He sat back in his chair and shoved his fists under his arms. "I've got to get out of here."

"Then start talking."

He closed his eyes for a moment then gazed down at the tabletop. "Madison Faber started at Loriners in October last year. She was enrolled on the MSc course. It became clear very quickly she was a gifted student— a sharp, forensic mind, hardworking, energetic. Before the end of the first term, she was working with me and a handful of other postgraduate students in my research program. A program I began five years ago. A program all my previous work has been leading towards." He let out a sarcastic snort. "My life's work." He glanced up at Ingrid.

"Who else was working with you?"

"Shouldn't you be taking notes? Or recording our conversation?" She stared at him until he realized he hadn't earned the right to ask questions. He bit his lip. "It's vital you get the details straight."

"No, it's vital you do. Right now you're shoveling a load of horseshit."

He swallowed hard and looked at his hands. "Everything seemed to be going along swimmingly right up until the middle of the autumn term. Then Faber's attitude changed. She wanted to be given more responsibility in the program. Said she'd like to take a leading role in the planning of experiments, be more hands-on with the subjects."

"What triggered the change?"

"I think she may have been bored. As I said, she's a very bright young woman." He sighed. "Unfortunately for me."

"And you agreed?"

"I got the impression she wanted to compete with Lauren, prove herself smarter, more industrious and so on—a healthy rivalry can lead to greater discoveries. It's happened many times in the history of experimental science. I'm sure I don't need to tell you that. So, yes—I agreed to her request, hoping the other students would up their game."

"And did that happen?"

"After a short while one or two of the others came to me, complaining about the way Madison was behaving. The way she was treating them. Using them as if they were *her* research assistants."

"And was Lauren one of them?"

"I'm forgetting—you never met Lauren. She was the sweetest... She wasn't the complaining type."

"So what did you do about the complaints?"

"I had a quiet word."

"And did Madison modify her behavior?"

"Initially. But she's a clever manipulator. On the surface things seemed to have changed; meanwhile Madison was busy devising other plans. Obviously I had no idea at the time."

Ingrid would have labeled Younger paranoid if she hadn't had so many misgivings about Faber herself.

"Things came to a head in January. Madison wanted to work more and more closely with me. Normally I would have been thrilled to be sharing the work with such a talented student, but... well, I didn't really *like* her. She was brilliant... and enthusiastic, but difficult. Too intense. Too demanding. Of my time. Of my attention."

"Why January?"

He buried his face in his hands and shook his head. "I was so bloody stupid." He pounded a fist on the table. "Stupid, stupid, stupid."

"Did something happen over Christmas?"

He hesitated.

"You have one chance to tell me everything. I'd seize the opportunity if I were you."

"I... Oh God. I... slept with Madison."

49

Ingrid had suspected a liaison ever since Alex Shelbourne's revelation her sister and Faber had fallen out over a man.

"I don't need you to judge me. It was a mistake. One I bitterly regret." He sniffed. "My God, that's an understatement."

"How did it happen?"

He was bewildered by the question. "How do these things usually happen? We got together at the end-of-term Christmas party—you know the sort of thing—too much booze, a letting off of steam... a slow dance." He opened his eyes wide. "Jesus, if I'd known then..."

"How often did you see each other... romantically?"

"We didn't! It was a one-night stand. Instantly regrettable. Quickly forgotten. For me at least. But Madison had other ideas. All over the holidays... she wouldn't leave me alone. Texts, phone calls. Visits to my house."

"Your house? How did you explain that to your wife?"

"Madison's clever. She made sure to come round when she knew my wife would be out. Which means she must have been watching the house. I mean... watching the house, for God's sake."

"What did she do?"

"She'd bang on the door, scream at me through the letterbox until I let her in. She said she just wanted to talk. She was interested in my mind, she said. But the number of phone calls increased. She started calling me in the middle of the night. I told Claire the phone calls were from marketing companies. Claire threatened to answer my phone herself, give the marketers a mouthful. It was a constant struggle to get to it in time. I couldn't risk my wife speaking to her." He ran a hand over his face. "In the end I agreed to meet with Madison—to spend some time with her on New Year's Eve—it was the only way I could think to get her to stop... harassing me."

Ingrid despised him. An arrogant man in a position of power over young women thousands of miles from family and friends. A bit of her admired Madison for standing up to him. "What did you say to her?"

"I explained I couldn't see her again. I mean, sleep with her. I told her I wouldn't betray my wife. She seemed to accept it. She was very mature about it, in fact. She even apologized for the calls and visits. I was so relieved." He rubbed his eyes. "Unfortunately the relief was short-lived. When the new term started, she kept her promise to leave me alone. But went too far the other way—she was positively hostile towards me." Younger sounded rehearsed. "Her treatment of the other students in the program deteriorated, generating more complaints than before. The only way to deal with it was to let her work alone. She devised her own experiments and executed them quite separately from the rest of the group."

"But in a way the situation was resolved? She'd stopped harassing you."

"It was resolved temporarily. As I said before, things came to a head in January. It all... it all got out of control."

"What did?"

"I take full responsibility. I should never have let it happen. I'm weak. I know I am. There's absolutely no excuse." He looked down at his hands resting on the table. "In the middle of January—the twelfth, to be precise—I started seeing Lauren."

"Seeing her?"

"Do you need me to spell it out?"

"It was a sexual relationship?"

"Of course it bloody well was!"

He was a pitiful sight. A once mighty alpha male slayed by his own libido.

"No one knew," Younger said. "We were very discreet, Lauren and I. Such a sweet, sweet girl. I fell for her. I hated myself, yet could do nothing to stop it. I still love my wife."

Ingrid made no comment.

"I know what you're thinking. I know how pathetic I must sound... I'm not going to blame a midlife crisis. There was something very special about Lauren." He sighed. "Oh God, if I'd known... Somehow Madison found out about us. I don't know how, Lauren swore she never told her. Madison probably spied on Lauren, going through her mail, her text messages. Who knows what else? I wouldn't put anything past her."

"What did Madison do?"

"That's the incredible thing. I would have expected her to go straight to the college registrar—report me for gross misconduct. Or worse—tell Claire about it. But she did nothing. Absolutely nothing. Nothing to me. She let rip with Lauren though. They had a huge row. Madison started throwing things, breaking Lauren's stuff. Lauren had to move out of the apartment in a hurry. It was obvious Madison wasn't going to leave. I'm not even sure Lauren managed to pack all her things before she left."

Something was nagging at Ingrid, some fact that didn't fit. "So that was it?" Ingrid pushed back her chair, indicating she would leave if he didn't come up with something that resembled actual facts and believable evidence.

"Far from it. She was just biding her time. She visited my house—actually had tea with my wife. Chatted with her as if she were an old friend. Claire said she practically had to throw her out. But Madison never breathed a word about my relationship with Lauren. She was planning something though. It's amazing how clear hindsight is. I realize now that annoying little things that were happening then must have been her doing."

"Such as?"

"Items of clothing going missing. Expensive things: a silk tie, a cashmere sweater, some kid leather gloves. I still don't know what she's done with them. Maybe she has something else planned." He blinked rapidly as if he were imagining what that something might be.

"When did those things go missing?"

"I don't know for certain."

Ingrid was getting fed up. "When was the last time you saw Faber?"

"She..." He gulped and stared into space for a moment. "I still find it almost impossible to believe."

The constable opened the door and looked at them both. "You need anything?"

Ingrid eyeballed him. "No. Thanks."

Alone again, Younger continued. "Madison Faber is evil. She's trying to frame me. You have to trust me. I have nowhere else to turn."

"The last time you saw her?" Ingrid prompted.

"She arrived at the lab long after all the other students had gone and...

Madison tried to *seduce* me. Right there in the lab. What was going through her mind? I told her in no uncertain terms that I wasn't interested in her, not then, not ever." He stood up. "God—especially not then. Maybe she thought she'd strike while I was vulnerable. While I was still grieving."

"Wait." Ingrid got to her feet. "Grieving? When was this?"

"Just a day after Lauren's death."

Ingrid had seen her that day. The girl was still numb from discovering the body. They had walked across the campus—it had been the morning the whore graffiti had appeared—they had drunk coffee. The girl had seemed detached, but not deranged.

"She said that now that Lauren was dead, there was no reason we couldn't be together."

Ingrid planted her elbows on the table and interlocked her fingers. She stared hard at Younger.

"What she actually said was 'Now that Lauren is out of the way.'" His eyes bored into hers. "You have to believe me, I've got no proof, but I've gone back over that night again and again, and there was something in the way she said 'out of the way'…" His words trailed off.

Ingrid rested her chin on her hands, bringing her head closer to Younger's. "Are you saying Faber killed Lauren?"

A tear fell from his left eye. "I'm convinced of it."

50

Ingrid asked the desk sergeant to phone Detective Inspector McKittrick for her. When the call was connected, he handed over the receiver.

"Natasha, hi, it's me."

"This is Detective Inspector McKittrick's office." It was a young woman's voice.

Oh. "Can I speak to Natasha? This is Special Agent Ingrid Skyberg from the US Embassy."

"The inspector is in a meeting right now."

Damn. "Is Ralph Mills around?"

"One moment."

Ingrid rested her head on the counter while she waited.

"He's in the same meeting. Can I take a message?"

"Please ask DI McKittrick to call me urgently. It's to do with the Shelbourne case. I may have more evidence."

Ingrid grabbed her helmet and ran up the stairs to ground level to get a phone signal. She reached reception and dialed McKittrick's cell and left a message. While she was speaking, her phone bleeped with an incoming call. She didn't even check the number before answering.

"Hi."

"Is that Ingrid Skyberg?" The woman's voice was tentative.

"Speaking."

"This is Gail Mooney, Madison Faber's neighbor."

"Yes, hi."

"You wanted to know if she showed up. Well, she's here. Just bolted up the stairs."

Ingrid ran her fingers through her hair. She wasn't expecting that. "Great. Right. Thank you for calling."

"You want me to give her a message?"

Ingrid thought for a second. "No, probably best not to."

Ingrid looked at the doorway she knew led toward McKittrick's incident room. She considered making a run for it. Slipping past the reception staff and tracking her down, yanking her out of her meeting and… and what? She had no evidence Faber killed Lauren. McKittrick had interviewed the girl herself. As she said, Faber was found covered in Lauren's blood but had been eliminated from the investigation. The neighbor had confirmed her arrival at the apartment at eight in the morning, hours after the time of death. Ingrid couldn't tell an inspector in the Metropolitan Police, even if she was a friend, that she had let the killer go without giving her some proof.

Ingrid pushed on the door and stepped into the bright spring sunshine. She texted Mills as she walked. *Are you with Natasha? I really need to speak to her about Lauren Shelbourne.* Ingrid unlocked her bike, pulled on her helmet and kicked the Triumph into life.

Ingrid didn't know if Faber had killed Lauren, but she thought it was entirely plausible she had used Lauren's death to put Younger in the frame for murder. She didn't know if Faber was capable of smashing Lauren's head against a coffee table, but she was convinced she was more than able to persuade her former roommate to take a cocktail of drugs that contributed to her death.

She accelerated through the streets of south London, fairly sure she could find her way to Faber's apartment without checking the route. Her phone rang and she tapped the Bluetooth headset attached to her helmet to take the call.

"What's so bloody urgent?" McKittrick's voice.

Ingrid needed to concentrate on the traffic. "Hi. I've just spoken to Younger. He asked to see me."

"Uh-huh."

"Do you think he did it?"

McKittrick sighed. "That's why we charged him. You know how it works." She sounded fed up.

"Listen, I've been doing some background checks into Faber. You know she has a history of making allegations against her teachers?"

McKittrick said something to someone, her hand over her phone. "I've got about two minutes before I need to go back into this meeting. It's a major case review for a multiple homicide."

"Do you think there's any chance Faber was involved in Lauren's death?"

McKittrick came back quickly and emphatically. "No."

Ingrid filtered down a line of cars and came to a junction she didn't recognize.

"We eliminated her from our inquiries. The postmortem report exonerated her. Her story was confirmed by the neighbor. She didn't get to Shelbourne's apartment until eight hours after the estimated time of death."

"But that doesn't mean she didn't visit the night before, does it? Just because no one saw her the first time doesn't mean she wasn't there. Have you even found a witness confirming Younger was at Lauren's apartment that night?"

"We're still checking the CCTV recordings."

"So you don't have confirmation Younger was there at the time of death either?"

"No. Listen, mate."

Ingrid didn't like the way she said 'mate.'

"I know you like to be all superhero about this stuff, but we do know what we're doing. If you think we've charged Younger on the basis of hearsay, you can fuck off."

"Shit." Ingrid braked hard to avoid a pedestrian stepping out between parked cars.

"What?"

"I know you've got more than that, Natasha, and I appreciate you're very busy, but there's something about Faber that isn't stacking up."

"Ingrid, I like you. I consider you a friend, but you are pushing our friendship to the absolute fucking limit right now." She was in fearsome form. "Yesterday, we carried out a second search of Younger's property. With dogs this time."

"A second search, why?"

"Something that came up in Faber's statement prompted us to check again."

"But you can't trust anything she says. Whatever she's told you—"

"Enough!"

Ingrid was gripping the throttle too hard. She was going way too fast.

"There's some shit you don't know," McKittrick said, fury soaking her words. "At the back of Younger's garden, in the vegetable patch, sniffer dogs found a half-burned cashmere sweater."

Ingrid was listening.

"The burned remains of Younger's sweater was drenched with blood. The case is closed, Ingrid, a slimy predator of vulnerable young women is behind bars, and I really don't need your shit right now."

McKittrick hung up, leaving Ingrid in no doubt how close she'd come to burning their friendship. It took a few blocks for her to calm down, but she eventually got her bearings and found Faber's street. There was no answer from Faber's intercom. She tried the ground-floor apartment.

"You just missed her," Gail Mooney said.

Ingrid slammed her hand against the wall of the house before the locked clicked and Ingrid pushed open the door. Gail Mooney was standing in the open doorway to her apartment. "You might want to come and take a look at this."

She beckoned Ingrid inside and led her into her kitchen at the rear of her flat.

"See that?" She pointed out the window to a large garden. A row of fruit trees lined the edge of an overgrown lawn.

"What am I looking at?"

"The smoke."

Beyond the trees, a narrow plume of smoke curled up into the sky.

"She was out there for about twenty minutes, and then a cab came and took her away."

Gail Mooney unlocked her back door and Ingrid ran down some stone steps, across the lawn and dashed between the fruit trees. In the middle of a neglected vegetable garden was a trash can, flames licking up the sides. Ingrid rushed over to it and peered in. The heat pushed her back. She looked round for a stick.

"I was right to call you, then?" Gail Mooney appeared between the trees in her slippers.

Ingrid pulled out a bamboo cane that might once have supported beans and prodded the fire. The flames leapt higher. Shielding her face, Ingrid looked again. A hunk of smashed metal smoldered, its surface blackened. It took her a moment to realize she was looking at a hard drive.

Ingrid turned to Gail. "Is there a hose here, a pail?"

"I don't know. The garden's not really my thing."

Ingrid pushed past her and ran toward a dilapidated shed. She almost ripped the door off its hinges. She searched for a watering can or a bucket of some kind. She scanned a selection of rusted tools and half-used tins of paint. On the floor she looked for anything she could put the fire out with, any way she could preserve evidence. For some reason her eyes were drawn back to the paint tins. Why am I staring at the goddamn paint?

Sun Dust 2. By Dulux.

Ingrid wheeled round. *Damn you, Faber*. She ran down the side of the house. There had to be a faucet. Or a hose.

She found a brass spigot and used all her strength to turn it.

"I've got this. If it helps."

Gail proffered a washing-up bowl. Ingrid swiped it from her and shoved it under the flow of water. Why wasn't it filling more quickly? Come on! Half full she grabbed it and dashed back to the trash can, trying not to lose too much water. She sloshed it into the can, releasing a geyser of sizzle and steam.

"Can you fill this again?"

Gail ran back to the outdoor tap. Ingrid picked up the bamboo and prodded. Definitely a motherboard. There was no way she could lift anything out without burning the skin off her fingers. She thought she could see bits of broken keyboard. She grabbed her phone and snapped away, hoping a forensics team could confirm it was the make and model of Lauren's laptop. Maybe they'd be able to read the serial number. Gail came back and tipped more water onto the dying flames.

"What's going on?" she asked.

Ingrid scratched her scalp. "You said a taxi took her away. Any idea where she was going? Did you speak to her?"

Gail pulled her cardigan tight around her. "No, but it wasn't the local cab company, if that helps. Had a sticker on the passenger door. Heathrow Transfers."

Ingrid felt the air escape her lungs. She bent over, resting her hands on her knees. "She was heading to the airport?"

51

Ingrid told Gail Mooney to put the fire out and make sure no one touched the trash can. Ingrid ran back through Gail's apartment and out onto the street. She clasped her phone, wondering who to call first.

"Jen, it's me."

"Hi, Ingrid. Where are you?"

There was no time to answer. "I need your help. Madison Faber is booked on a flight out of Heathrow. I need you to find out which airline, which terminal and text me, OK?"

"I'm on it."

"You're a star."

Ingrid switched her phone to Bluetooth settings, pulled on her helmet and sat astride her bike. She dialed McKittrick and got her voicemail yet again. She didn't want to sound like an idiot, and she didn't want to piss off her friend.

"Natasha, it's your favorite FBI agent. I'm sorry about earlier, but I have new information. Madison Faber is leaving the country. Right now." Ingrid worked out what to say next. "I'm at her apartment. She's been burning things, evidence, I believe. You need to speak to her downstairs neighbor. Ground floor. I can't be sure, but I think she's destroyed Lauren Shelbourne's missing laptop." Ingrid turned the key in the ignition. "Also, you know that tissue with the paint on it? Well, I had it analyzed. There's a tin of the exact same paint in Faber's garden shed." She knocked back the stand and kicked the bike into life. "I'm going to Heathrow. I'm going to try to stop her getting on a plane, but, Natasha, that's all I can do. I've got no powers of arrest here. If you want to stop her leaving the country, you're going to have to send someone to the airport."

Ingrid tapped Heathrow into her satnav app, pulled down her visor and roared out into the road.

Faber's taxi had no more than a twenty-minute head start on her, probably more like fifteen minutes. The sort of lead an 800 cc motorcycle could eat up. She was in central London within ten minutes, back on familiar roads. So long as she avoided roadworks and accidents, and she didn't get stopped for speeding, Ingrid was confident of beating the taxi.

Ingrid ran through all the ways to detain Faber without the authority to arrest her. Without a request from the Met, she couldn't get the Border Agency to detain her. As an FBI agent, she could make sure she was stopped at immigration in the US, but without an extradition request from the UK, they would have no reason to prevent her from entering her own country. Of course, Ingrid reminded herself, Faber might not be going home. She could be flying anywhere.

Ingrid kept an eye out for any taxi with a Heathrow Transfers logo. It was likely the driver was taking the same route, and it was just possible she would intercept Faber on the road. She didn't know what she would do if that happened.

She desperately wanted to check her phone, she wanted to call Natasha or Ralph and find out what the hell they were going to do, but it was tucked in her pocket, and she needed to keep both hands on the handlebars. She hadn't heard a bleep to tell her Jen had messaged her back either.

The traffic in Earl's Court was glacial. A bus had blocked a box junction, and cars were having to wait for the lights to change several times to get through the intersection. Even on the bike Ingrid had to pick her way through, weaving between stationary cars and irate van drivers, who all thought they had right of way. With any luck, Faber's car was somewhere in the snarl-up.

Ingrid cleared the traffic jam and swerved up onto the Hammersmith Flyover, a raised freeway that carved an elevated path over roundabouts and junctions, easing her way west toward the airport.

It wouldn't be enough to find Faber, she had to somehow stop her from boarding her plane. Persuading the police at the airport was a possibility, but a faint one. By the time she had explained who she was and what she suspected Faber of doing, the girl would be through security. Ingrid had a credit card on her: she had the means to buy a ticket if necessary and follow her through the gates, but her passport was in her hotel safe: there was only so far she could go. What she really needed was for McKittrick to pick up the phone and authorize the airport cops to arrest Faber. But for that to happen, Natasha had to leave her meeting, listen to her messages and take Ingrid seriously. The last of those things, given her tone earlier, seemed the least likely.

There were other options, but almost all of them involved breaking the law whether that was calling in a bomb scare or flying a remote control drone. There was no way Ingrid was going to shut down the entire airport and inconvenience thousands of passengers. If she'd had more warning, there were plenty of things she could have tried. She could have slipped something into Faber's bag, drugs or a weapon; she could have submitted her passport number and requested an intercept. The way she saw things, the only advantage she had was that Faber didn't know she was coming. The girl thought she was free and clear. Younger had been charged, and while the Met congratulated themselves for getting him held on remand, Faber was making her escape. The girl was as smart as Younger claimed.

Ingrid reached the outskirts of the city where the freeway began. From there it was just fifteen minutes to the airport. Her phone rang and she tapped her Bluetooth headset to answer.

"Hi." She accelerated into the fast lane.

"It's me."

"Hi, Jen."

"Sorry it's taken me so long, but there was no record of a Madison Faber booked on a Heathrow departure."

Maybe she planned to buy a ticket at the airport? Ingrid overtook a succession of cars, her speed well over the limit.

"So I thought she might use another name."

"And?" Ingrid was in danger of losing concentration.

"And then I checked the other airports. Ingrid, she's flying from Gatwick."

"Fuck."

"She's booked on a Virgin flight at fourteen forty to Las Vegas."

Booking a Heathrow taxi to take you to Gatwick? That was smart. That was *devious*. It also told Ingrid Faber was deliberately leaving a false trail. She wouldn't put anything beyond Faber, including murdering her roommate. Ingrid peeled off the freeway and took the exit for the M25, an orbital superhighway that encircled London, famous for its traffic jams and backups. But on two wheels it was also a very quick route to Gatwick, London's second airport, about thirty miles south of the city. Ingrid estimated the journey would take her twenty-five minutes, and when she got there, she was taking Madison Faber down.

.

52

Ingrid ran into the terminal building clutching her helmet. She checked the display boards and headed for the check-in area for Virgin.

She hung back, not wanting Faber to see her. The line of passengers waiting to dump their luggage was at least a hundred people long. Several flights were using the same check-in desks. She scanned the faces. Faber was not there.

Ingrid checked her phone. No messages. It was twelve twenty. An hour since she'd left Gail Mooney's apartment. The chances she had beaten Faber's taxi were extremely low, and in all likelihood the student had already gone through security. Ingrid turned and ran, darting between jet-lagged passengers and precariously stacked luggage carts. A public-address over the loudspeakers informed everyone that, due to unforeseen circumstances, several gates had been closed, and they needed to check the departure boards for accurate information. Ingrid kept running till she saw what she was looking for.

A sales desk. There were three people ahead of her. She didn't need to panic. Faber's flight wouldn't board for another hour. All she had to do was buy a ticket to somewhere in the UK that didn't require a passport, go through security and wait for Faber to arrive at the gate. Easy. She checked the electronic display boards and saw there was a flight to Edinburgh in two hours. That was good enough. She called Ralph while she waited. She couldn't remember how much she'd already told him.

Damn. Voicemail. *Again.* It was like they saw it was her calling and refused to answer.

"Ralph, hi, it's Ingrid. I'm at Gatwick airport. Madison Faber is getting on a plane to Las Vegas in two hours, and I am going to stop her. I know you all think Stuart Younger killed Lauren Shelbourne, but I'm damn sure Faber is framing him. I think he can prove it, which is why she's leaving the country before you realize what she's done."

The people in front of her turned their heads, making it obvious they were listening in.

"Ralph, I have no powers of arrest. I don't have time to work the diplomatic channels. I need McKittrick to authorize her for detainment. I need you to call the Gatwick police."

She hung up, then texted him. *PLEASE LISTEN TO YOUR MESSAGES.*

Maybe she should have sent a different kind of text. One offering to meet for a drink. He'd probably reply to that.

"Can I help you?"

Ingrid put her helmet on the counter and asked for a seat on the Edinburgh flight. Out of the corner of her eye, she saw two armed police officers carrying MP5 semiautomatic carbines. Airports and government buildings were the only places in the UK where the police were routinely armed.

"Let me see if there's any availability for you." The man behind the desk had long, pointed sideburns, dyed black hair and a spray tan. His bored demeanor betrayed how much he hated his job. His words were polite, but his tone was acidic. "That will be two hundred and thirty-five pounds, please."

Ingrid pulled a bank card out of her jacket pocket and placed it next to the helmet. A few minutes later, the ticket agent placed her card, a receipt and a boarding pass in front of her. She grabbed them and ran straight to the security gates. While other passengers emptied bottles of water or sorted their liquids into plastic bags, she dashed past them. She presented the boarding pass at the electronic barrier and was allowed into the security hall, where a uniformed guard ushered her toward one of ten conveyor belts.

The hall was rammed with vacationers and travelers. Ingrid checked her bag to make sure she didn't have anything that would get picked up by the scanners. The helmet was bound to attract attention, as would the fact she was wearing a leather jacket over her tired business suit. She looked a mess. If they stopped her, she needed an explanation. A friend in need, she would say. A mercy dash. Her embassy ID should cover all eventualities.

The line moved slowly as inept travelers took off their belts and shoes and forgot to take laptops and iPads out of their bags. *Hurry up!* Ingrid had to remind herself it didn't matter: all she had to do was get to the departure gate before Faber. *Don't panic. You've got time.*

One of the other lines appeared to be moving much more quickly, adding to her frustration. She looked at them enviously, and that was when she saw her. Faber. Ingrid turned away, keen that the girl didn't recognize her. Ingrid stooped, hiding her five-foot-ten frame behind a family of Dutch tourists. She didn't want to draw attention to herself, but judiciously peered over their heads. Faber placed her bag in a shallow plastic tray, then took off her jacket and folded it before placing it another tray along with her watch. She then lined up to go through the metal detector.

Ingrid's line shuffled forward and she lost sight of Faber, but when she spotted her again, she saw the student was putting her coat back on and slipping her passport into the right-hand pocket. *That's what I have to do,* Ingrid told herself, *I need to steal her passport.* Without it, she wasn't flying anywhere.

Ten minutes later, Ingrid left the security hall and snaked her way through the endless duty-free area, searching for Faber. She wasn't browsing the perfumes or the whisky; she wasn't looking at discounted electronics. A public-address announcement issued a reminder about the late change to departure gate numbers. Once through into the lounge, Ingrid scoured the seating area. If she was really, really lucky, she would find a seat behind Faber and somehow distract her enough to get access to her jacket pocket. But Faber wasn't in the seats. Ingrid did a three-sixty. There were so many shops, countless food outlets, prayer rooms, restrooms: Faber could be anywhere.

People stared at Ingrid's helmet. It was an unusual thing to see in a departure lounge. She thought about dumping it, about making herself less conspicuous. And then she wondered if she could use it to her advantage. Could she leave it somewhere that would create an incident? Hope someone reported a suspicious item? It still wouldn't be enough to get Faber's flight delayed. She carried on through the departures lounge, hoping to spot her.

Ingrid checked the aisles in WHSmith. She scrutinized passengers at the checkouts in Boots. She studied the diners in Café Rouge, but she couldn't see Faber. *OK,* she told herself. *Back to plan A.* Intercept her at the gate. She scanned the departure board to see if the Las Vegas flight was boarding. It still said 'wait in lounge.' Ingrid searched for a place to wait, somewhere out of the way where she wouldn't be noticed. Her ears tuned in to yet another announcement over the PA system.

"Would passenger Skyberg, that's passenger Ingrid Skyberg, please proceed to gate thirty-nine, where your friend is waiting for you. That's passenger Skyberg..."

Ingrid stopped listening. She hadn't spotted Faber, but evidently the girl had seen her.

53

Ingrid followed the signs to Gate 39 down corridors, travelators, escalators and stairs. It was warm under her leather jacket and she unzipped it as she ran. The crowds thinned. The tannoy announcements faded away. Faber was leading her to the closed departure gates. A 'caution: men at work' A-frame sign kept guard, but there was no sign of maintenance workers.

Ingrid slowed down. She came to a lounge with a central rectangle of seating surrounded by four departure gates. The place was deserted. The LED signs behind the desks were blank. There was no lighting. The Coca-Cola vending machine wasn't humming. A power failure must have caused the airport to close the annex. It suddenly felt like an ambush. Sweat trickled between her shoulder blades, sending a shiver across her skin as it snaked down into her waistband. Ingrid reached into her pants pocket for her phone.

Something moved behind her and she spun round.

There was no one there.

If the power was out, that meant the CCTV cameras weren't recording. There was no surveillance. Ingrid checked the lounge again. It was almost a perfect square with a gate on each side. In front of each set of doors leading to the jet bridges were desks where airline staff would normally check passports. The only exits were the alarmed gate doors out to the empty plane stands, or the corridor she had just run down. Apart from the vending machine and trash cans, the only furniture was several rows of rigid plastic seats forming a neat square. Faber had to be hiding behind one of the desks.

Ingrid gripped the chin guard of her helmet, ready to swing it at Faber's head. "I spoke to Kevin Timms yesterday," she said, her voice surprisingly clear. "You remember Mr Timms, don't you, Madison? Your old chemistry teacher?"

There was no reply.

"He remembers you. Wanted me to thank you on his behalf. Losing his job was the best thing that ever happened to him. That's what he said. He's very successful now. Rich, happy." Ingrid's voice echoed through the empty chamber. If Faber was watching her, she might see her leg was trembling.

"It's remarkable how similar what happened seven years ago is to what's gone on with Stuart Younger. The stalking, the obsession. It's like history repeating itself. I'm sure your friends in the Met will be very interested to hear all about it."

There was a loud whacking sound behind her as a door was yanked open. Ingrid turned in time to see it close. Ingrid ran over, pulled it back open and found herself in a stairwell that led down to the airport apron. The staircase formed a series of descending U-shapes around a central void. The cinder block walls were painted white. The steps were concrete edged with steel protectors. The drop in temperature suggested the door at ground level was open.

It took Ingrid a moment to notice she couldn't hear Faber's footsteps. She turned just as Faber was revealed by the closing door. She smiled before lunging at Ingrid, pushing her against the metal railing. Ingrid yelped as her bruised ribs erupted with pain. She brought up her hand, aiming the helmet at Faber's head, but she wasn't quick enough and Faber ducked.

Madison pushed Ingrid again, sending spikes of agony through her body. Faber, sensing Ingrid's weakness, grabbed the helmet from Ingrid's grasp, lifted her arm and took a swing at Ingrid's head. Ingrid curled out of the way, and the helmet flew out of Faber's hand and clattered down the stairs. Ingrid reared up, leading with her elbow, and pushed Faber back against the wall.

"Is that your plan, Madison? You think if you silence me, you'll get away with it?" Their faces were inches away from each other. Ingrid kept her forearm against Faber's neck, pinning her against the cold wall. "You think you've been so clever, don't you?"

Faber maintained eye contact as she stamped down hard on Ingrid's toes, making her recoil before leaning in harder and pressing Faber against the wall. Faber spat in her face, but Ingrid barely blinked.

"You're not going to beat me, Madison." Ingrid stared into the girl's livid eyes. "This is going to end one of two ways." Faber relaxed and attempted to slide down, out of Ingrid's grasp, but she wasn't fast enough. "The thing you don't realize is the Metropolitan Police have found Lauren Shelbourne's laptop."

Faber's eyes widened.

"You shouldn't have left that fire unattended, Madison."

Faber's lip snarled.

"And really, if you were as smart as everyone thinks you are, you'd have added that can of yellow paint to the bonfire."

Was there a slight tensing of Faber's upper body? Was Ingrid starting to get to her?

"I'll take it one stage at a time." Ingrid paused, quickly checking Faber's impassive expression. "After all, I wouldn't want to misrepresent what happened."

"You don't know what you're talking about."

"So you are talking to me, then?"

Faber bared her teeth, and Ingrid jabbed her forearm a little harder against the girl's throat.

"Because I wouldn't want you to think I'm not impressed, Madison. Before you spend the rest of your life in prison, it's important I acknowledge how special you are."

Faber scowled.

"I mean, really, you've been so clever it's a shame you haven't gotten away with it. First, when you call the cops and tell them you've found your roommate in a pool of blood, you make damn sure you get into a fight with one of them so you get arrested. And that means the police scrutinize your story even harder than they might otherwise. But that's just what you wanted, wasn't it? That way, when they release you, you're completely exonerated. They'll never suspect you again. Why would they? Lauren was your friend. They could see for themselves how devastated you were by her death."

Faber wriggled under the force of Ingrid's restraint. "You saw it too, agent." Faber managed a smile that released a rush of anger in Ingrid's chest. Heat radiated up into her throat and face. She kept her forearm pressed against Faber's neck. Her other hand, still gripping the phone, pushed into her stomach.

"The police released you, accepting you arrived at Lauren's apartment for the first time at eight twenty a.m., the morning *after* she died. So now you're free. And clear. So you pay Professor Younger a visit. You offer him a shoulder to cry on in his time of need. You suggest that with Lauren dead, the two of you can be together."

Another flicker of reaction. Faint, but unmistakable. Distant engine noises roared up the stairwell.

"But Younger rejects you again. Again, Madison. You've removed the main obstacle between you, but he tells you where to go. And that is unforgivable. So you move to phase two of the plan. And for this you need someone on your side. Someone, perhaps, whose job it is to support US citizens in the UK. And how lucky for you this person also lost someone. What great leverage that gave you. And what an easy mark I was. Your years of studying psychology really paid off, didn't they?"

Faber raised her eyebrows, a smile faintly playing across her lips.

"Oh, you should feel smug. I went all out for Younger. Like he was public enemy number one. Choose between an American citizen in fear for her life and an arrogant, egotistical English college professor with dubious morals? It was no contest. I almost admire your cunning and inventiveness."

"My inventiveness? You're the one making the whole thing up."

"I'm congratulating you, Faber. Can't you at least congratulate me on finally working it all out?"

Faber looked right and left, but no one was coming to her rescue. "An imagination like yours is wasted at the FBI. Aren't you trained to deal in cold, hard facts?" She balled her right hand and slammed a fist into Ingrid's ribs, inflicting enough pain for Ingrid to loosen her stance. Faber wriggled free and headed for the stairs. Ingrid took a second to suck down as deep a breath as she could manage and gave chase, taking the steps three at a time. Faber reached a half-landing and pulled a fire extinguisher off the wall. It was heavier than she was expecting, and instead of aiming it at Ingrid's head, she swung it at her shins, sending her toppling downward. Ingrid's tight grip on her phone meant she couldn't break her fall properly, and she let out a yelp of pain before clambering onto all fours. She looked up at Faber. She held the fire extinguisher in both hands and brought it down hard. Ingrid rolled out of the way, making Faber lose her balance. Men's voices drifted in from outside. Maintenance workers most likely. Ground crew.

"Is that what you did to Lauren?" Ingrid was breathing hard; her entire torso was circled with pain. She forced herself to stand upright. "Did she put up a struggle too?" Ingrid lunged at Faber, holding her against the banister with her body weight, arching Faber's back over the handrail. A fall from this height was either life-changing or life-ending. "You know what always bothered me about your testimony?" Ingrid said. Her chest rose and fell with each painful breath. "It took me a while to work it out. Can you guess what it was?"

A flicker of something flitted across Faber's face. Fear or curiosity?

"You told the police you had a key to Lauren's new apartment. But why would she give you a key? She loathed you by then." Ingrid shifted her weight, pushing Faber further over the handrail. "So either you got it from Stuart Younger when you were planting her phone in his house and stealing his sweater or, much more likely, is you took it the night before. Lauren was high because you'd made sure she hadn't received the placebo. I can imagine you saying to people at college, 'Don't worry, I'll make sure she gets home OK.' And then when you're alone, something happens. Either she trips and falls, or she says something about Younger, something that makes you flip, and you shove her so hard she falls. She hits her head. She loses consciousness."

The fight went out of Faber's body. She slackened. Softened. But Ingrid held firm.

"Instead of calling the EMTs, you start planning. You wait until you're sure she's dead. You take her key. You take her phone. Her laptop. Maybe you thought you'd make it look like a robbery. Am I close, Madison?"

Faber arched her back, then brought her head forward sharply, slamming her skull into Ingrid's cheek, sending her backwards. She slipped free of Ingrid's grasp and turned on her, pushing her against the banister and bending her over the rail. Ingrid winced as it dug into her rib cage. Faber pressed her advantage. Ingrid knew Faber's only hope was to silence her and get on her flight. No one would find Ingrid's body until the annex was reopened, and by then Faber would be in the air. Ingrid stared at the concrete floor two flights down: it was plenty high enough for a fatal fall.

Faber brought up her knee. The force of the blow pressed Ingrid harder into the metal and finally ejected the phone from her hand. Ingrid watched it fall through the air and clatter to the ground below. She released the breath that had stalled in her throat, emitting a deep, guttural cry. Madison relaxed her grip and Ingrid turned painfully. Faber picked up the fire extinguisher and swung it up toward Ingrid's head. Ingrid leaned out of its path, but her momentum took her over the top, and she tumbled into the void. She reached out and managed to grab the banister with one hand, then the other, as her legs dangled below. Faber raised the fire extinguisher and brought it down hard with both hands, aiming for Ingrid's fingers.

Ingrid tucked her knees and dropped down. She aimed her feet onto the handrail below, turned and jumped again, this time reaching out for the handrail opposite. With every ounce of strength she had left, she repeated the move: tuck, drop, grab until she hit the concrete floor, rolling on impact to disperse the force. *Five years of parkour.*

Faber's footsteps echoed as she ran upward, toward the exit, toward escape. The door opened and slammed shut.

Ingrid picked up her phone. "Please tell me," she said between breaths, "you heard all that?"

Was that cheering on the other end of the line?

"The airport team have instructions to arrest," McKittrick said. "Nice work."

Ingrid stared up at the steps and took a deep, weary breath. She swiped her dented helmet from the floor and began climbing, one agonizing step at a time. Ingrid reached the top and yanked open the door into the departure lounge. Three uniformed airport police officers, two holding MK5s, had surrounded Faber. The other placed her in hand restraints.

"You do not have to say anything," he said, "but it may harm your defense if you do not mention when questioned something you later rely on in court. Anything you do say may be given in evidence."

Ingrid caught Faber's eye and the girl smiled at her. "This isn't over."

Ingrid slumped against the wall. She wanted to answer back. She wanted to tell Faber it was indeed over, that the game was up and to see the smile permanently wiped off her face. But she wasn't worth it. She could let the kid have the last word: after all, nothing Faber said now would make any difference.

The cops led Faber away. She yelled something about her father. About how they didn't know who they were dealing with. She shouted that Inspector McKittrick would explain everything. Ingrid stopped listening. She collapsed onto a plastic seat and let her head fall into her hands. As the tension left her body, she felt sobs rise up from her chest.

Her tears weren't for Lauren or the Shelbournes. They never were. She was crying for Megan and for her fourteen-year-old self, who had never given up the search for answers. Every time she figured out a new case, it was a painful reminder she was no closer to solving the one crime that really mattered. But she would, she told herself.

"One day," she said out loud. "I promise."

In KILL PLAN, the next book in the series, Ingrid is on the trail of a serial killer. Trouble is, he's also hunting her.

READ IT NOW

KILL PLAN

BOOK TWO

EVA HUDSON

1

Special Agent Ingrid Skyberg peered more closely at the dead man. His light brown hair fell loosely across his forehead. His haircut had been styled by an expensive hairdresser rather than a barber. His suit jacket was open, revealing the deep maroon lining: a touch of flamboyance in an otherwise somber gray two-piece. Ingrid supposed he was trying to prove he had a personality. His right hand was shoved up into his left armpit. He must have fallen clutching that side of his chest. His left arm was flung over his head, the hand bent into a claw-like curl. His face was unlined, his skin clear. His lips already had a bluish tinge to them. He couldn't have been older than late twenties.

She pulled a pair of nitrile gloves from her pocket, quickly snapped them on and stepped over the makeshift cordon of blue and white police tape strung across three office chairs.

"What do you think you're doing! You can't touch him!" A uniformed police officer lunged forward and grabbed Ingrid's arm.

Ingrid stared into the woman's face. It was criss-crossed with deep lines. Her cheeks were flushed. No doubt a result of years working the beat in all weathers. "I have no intention of compromising your crime scene, officer," Ingrid said.

"Who said it was a crime scene?" The middle-aged officer glanced toward her youthful male colleague, as if she wanted his support. But he didn't seem to be listening. He'd been staring at Ingrid from the moment she'd shown the two cops her FBI badge.

"If it's not a crime, why are you here?" Ingrid asked.

"The paramedics called us in." The cop gestured toward the two EMTs who were standing near the elevator, deep in conversation with a gray-haired man dressed in a suit even smarter than the corpse's.

"Why did they call you in?"

The cop puffed out an irritated breath. "Why don't you ask them?" She started to walk away and beckoned to her colleague to follow her. They disappeared around a corner at the far end of the corridor.

Ingrid stood up, pulled off the gloves and looked through the glass wall separating the corridor from the large open-plan office of Fisher Krupps bank. The morning sun was streaming through the floor-to-ceiling windows. There had to be about seventy or so individual work stations on the trading floor. Over two-thirds of those were currently occupied by traders. Most of them had a phone cradled between shoulder and ear, their hands moving fast over computer keyboards. They were clearly still working despite the fact that the dead body of their colleague was lying just yards away in the corridor outside.

She approached the two men in green jump suits, an empty gurney standing between them.

"Hey," she said and flashed her badge at the EMTs and the smart-suited man they were talking to. "Special Agent Ingrid Skyberg, from the US embassy. Can I ask you a couple of questions?"

The man in the smart suit shoved out his hand. "Richard Wennstein, I'm the manager of the trading floor—I called the embassy." His accent was East Coast, probably New Jersey.

Ingrid shook his hand. "Thank you for your vigilance, sir."

He shrugged. "It's company policy here at Fisher Krupps. Anything happens to one of our US employees, we call the embassy." He stood back a little and unashamedly scrutinized her from head to toe. "I saw you just now looking at the body. What's an FBI agent doing here anyway? I expected some administrative clerk to arrive and make me fill out a dozen forms."

"We should really get going," the first EMT said.

"I'm sorry, Mr Wennstein. Would you mind if I spoke to these gentlemen before they leave?"

Wennstein shrugged again. "Be my guest."

One of the EMTs glanced at his watch.

"I promise I won't keep you," Ingrid told them. "Why did you call in the police?"

"Standard procedure," one of them said.

Ingrid nodded at him. "It is?"

"If someone dies unexpectedly we always inform the police. It's up to them to decide how to proceed."

"What are the options?"

"There are basically two: call the coroner's office to request an autopsy and let them come and collect the body. Or, if foul play is suspected, call in the detectives. Full forensics examination of the victim and the scene."

"You think this could be foul play?"

"I couldn't tell you one way or the other."

"Any idea what he might have died of?"

"It's down to the pathologist to determine the cause of death," the other EMT chimed in and glanced toward Wennstein, who was hovering a few feet away, well within earshot.

"How about an educated guess? Help me out here, fellas."

The first EMT leaned toward her, almost conspiratorially. "If I was a betting man, I'd put fifty quid on it being a massive coronary."

"Based on what?"

"The sudden onset, the way he was clutching his chest when he keeled over."

"He's a little young for a heart attack," Ingrid said.

"Which is why we called the police."

Ingrid glanced down the corridor. The two uniformed cops still hadn't returned to the body. Where the hell were they? "Thanks for your time, guys," she said.

They looked at one another, said goodbye to Wennstein, then shoved the gurney toward the elevator. The first EMT punched the down button and let out a long sigh.

Ingrid turned to Wennstein. "You manage the trading floor?" she asked him.

He nodded.

"So that's maybe seventy, eighty people?"

"Ninety-two."

"How well did you know Matthew Fuller?"

Wennstein glanced over her shoulder down the corridor and toward Fuller's stiffening body. He sniffed. "No better than anyone else here. He worked hard, always made good numbers every month. He was a stand up guy. What do you want me to say?"

"Was he healthy?"

"I guess—he worked out."

"The bank must have something on file about his medical history."

"Sure. Look—he was a fit, young guy. Not heart attack material if that's what you're asking." He took a step backward. "Exactly what are you asking? I mean, why is a federal agent getting involved with something like this?" He stuck a finger between his collar and his neck.

In Ingrid's experience, the presence of a Bureau agent often had this effect on people. Especially those working in financial institutions. It was as if they were all hiding some guilty secret they were worried was about to be exposed.

"Unexplained death of a US citizen in a foreign country? An FBI agent from the Criminal Investigation Unit always gets involved."

"Criminal? You think somebody killed Fuller?"

"I'm not saying that at all." Not at this stage, Ingrid thought. "Whatever this is, I'm here to represent the embassy and the Bureau. If there's a criminal investigation into Mr Fuller's death, I'll be assisting the police any way I can. I'll also write a report on the way the investigation is handled."

"Is that something we get to see?"

"It's more for the family of the deceased."

Wennstein closed his eyes for a moment.

"What is it?"

"Fuller's girlfriend. She works here at the bank. She's in New York, working at HQ for a couple days. How am I going to tell her about this?"

"Would you like someone from the embassy to contact her?"

"Could they?"

"Sure—I'll take her details before I leave. What about his parents?"

"I... I don't know anything about them. Maybe you should talk to Kristin."

"His girlfriend?"

He nodded.

"Would it be possible to see Mr Fuller's medical records? Would he have had a medical exam before he started at the bank, for insurance purposes?"

"Every employee does."

"So, can you get me the records?"

"I should really be getting back to the floor, see what's going on."

"Maybe you could make a couple of calls? Get the personnel department to do the legwork?"

Wennstein stared forlornly through the glass wall of the corridor toward his busy team of traders, like an anxious father peering into a room full of newborns at the hospital. He reluctantly pulled his phone from his pocket.

Ingrid was about to return to Matthew Fuller's body and continue the examination she'd started before the uniformed cop told her to stop, when she heard a loud crash sound from further down the corridor. She looked up to see a man wearing dark blue coveralls stagger out of a door. For a moment she was transfixed by the six feet tall man's strange lurching gate. She glanced at Wennstein, who was speaking in hushed tones into his cell phone. He shrugged back at her.

The man in the coveralls leaned a hand against the corridor wall to steady himself. Ingrid ran toward him. As she approached she could see he was blinking rapidly and sweating like he'd just stepped out of a sauna.

"Hey, are you OK?" Ingrid asked him, just a few feet away now.

The man dropped heavily onto his knees, remained in a kneeling position for a few moments, then pitched forward onto his face.

2

Immediately, Ingrid hollered back to Wennstein, "Call reception down-stairs. See if those EMTs are still in the building. We need them back up here fast."

"What's wrong with him?"

"Make the call, goddammit!"

Wennstein tapped a number into his phone.

Ingrid turned her attention back to the guy on the floor. She pushed two fingers into the soft flesh of his neck, trying to feel for a pulse. It was fast, but faint. His eyes flickered open. "Hang in there, buddy," she said.

"Help me," he said feebly.

"Don't worry. Help is on its way."

"Help me get up."

"You just rest there, the ambulance guys will be here any second."

He ignored her, and, still lying face down, reached out his right arm and leg and hauled himself a foot or so sideways. He writhed, snake-like across the tile floor until he reached the wall of the corridor. Then he started to haul his upper body upright. Ingrid pulled one of his arms around her shoulders and together they managed to get him into a slumped sitting position, propped up against the wall.

He looked down toward his hands and flexed his fingers, then relaxed them. Then he started tapping the tips of his fingers against his thumbs. He swallowed. The perspiration had made his hair stick flat against his head.

"Pins and needles," he said and took a sharp, shallow breath. "My arms are going numb too. My legs feel like rubber." He turned his head to one side and stared into Ingrid's face. "I'm so cold." The sweat continued to drip from his eyebrows into his eyes. He shivered. "Freezing."

Ingrid glanced up toward the elevators. She saw Wennstein standing with his hands on his hips, looking up at the illuminated display above the elevator doors, no doubt thinking the same thing she was: where were the goddamn EMTs? Behind him Ingrid could see the prone body of Matthew Fuller. She bent close to the sweating guy's head.

"Do you have pains in your chest?" she asked him.

He nodded. "Can't breathe."

A few moments later Wennstein stepped back from the elevator as the doors opened. The gurney came crashing out ahead of the two EMTs. They ran toward Ingrid who was waving frantically at them. When they reached her, Ingrid quickly described the man's symptoms.

"So cold," he said again and his torso slid sideways to the floor as he passed out.

Ingrid stepped away and let the medical guys do their thing. One EMT was shining a light into the man's eyes while the other snapped an oxygen mask over his mouth and nose. There was nothing she could usefully do, so she set off in search of the two uniformed cops. The last time she'd seen them was at the opposite end of the long corridor. She started to hurry toward it. A few feet from the end she heard the raised voice of the female cop.

"For God's sake, Mark, it's not murder just because you think it's exciting."

She turned the corner to discover the two police officers sitting on a low window ledge, steaming cardboard cups of coffee in their hands. They looked up at her, guilty expressions on their faces.

"You have to call in your homicide detectives," Ingrid said. "Right now."

"Have you been listening to our private conversation?" The female cop stood up. Coffee slopped over the edge of her cup.

"Come with me." Ingrid headed back around the corner, hoping the police officers were following.

When the female cop finally appeared at the end of the corridor her mouth dropped open. The EMTs were lifting the tall man in the coveralls onto the gurney. "What's happened to him?" She eyed Ingrid suspiciously as if she'd had something to do with it.

"I guess the same thing that happened to Matthew Fuller," Ingrid told her.

"Bloody hell," the male cop said and started to jog toward the elevator.

"You need to call in your homicide and serious crime team, CSIs, pathologist, whoever else needs to be here. And get somebody to go with that poor guy to the hospital."

"I'll be the judge of that." The female officer hurried toward the moaning man strapped to the gurney. "What's wrong with him?" she asked the EMTs.

"I've got no idea." The lead man in the green jumpsuit pushed her out of the way and dragged the gurney to the elevator.

"Maybe you should get the whole building evacuated," Ingrid told the policewoman.

"I don't have the authority to do that."

"Then get somebody who does. You've just watched a second victim get stretchered out of here. Don't you think it's time to call in a little help?" Ingrid looked up and down the corridor in search of Wennstein. Maybe the manager of the trading floor could close down the building for her.

A few moments later the door to the men's restroom opened and Wennstein appeared. Ingrid strode toward him.

"We need to get this floor evacuated," she told him.

"Stop trading? There is no way that's going to happen." He winced a little.

"Are you OK?"

"I'm perfectly fine." Beads of sweat had broken out across his top lip.

"Do you know what that maintenance guy was doing here?" Ingrid asked him.

Wennstein ignored her question. He seemed distracted. "What?"

The guy the EMTs just took away—what was he doing here in the building?"

Again, he didn't answer. He was staring at his hands. "That's the weirdest thing." He started to shake his hands, as if he were flicking water off them. "Hey—didn't that guy say his hands were tingling?" There was a definite strain of panic in his voice. He balled his hands into fists then folded his arms.

"The maintenance guy?"

He blinked at her. "Servicing the hand driers in the restrooms."

Ingrid glanced at the restroom door. Wennstein had emerged from there just a few moments ago. "What were you doing in the restroom?" she asked him.

"What do you think I was doing? Taking a crap, if you must know."

Ingrid ran to the restroom and flung open the door. A man was standing at one of the urinals at the far end of the room.

"Get out of here—now!" she hollered.

He didn't move.

"I said now." She marched over to him.

"Jesus Christ—I'm mid-piss. I'm not going anywhere."

Ingrid kicked open the doors of each of the three cubicles in the washroom. All the stalls were empty. She raced over to the wash basins just as the man was zipping his fly. "Forget about washing your hands."

He raised his eyebrows at her. "Don't tell my mom."

Ingrid hurried him outside into the corridor. "I want the restroom sealed off," she told the policewoman. "And the floor evacuated."

"No way!" Wennstein said. He was rubbing his fingertips together. "I can't lose a day's trading."

"You can't lose any more of your employees either."

3

Thirty minutes later the trading floor was still trading, but at least the men's restroom had been cordoned off. Five minutes after that, the detectives emerged from an elevator, together with a half dozen CSIs already suited and booted.

The man leading the team of four detectives had a determined expression on his face. He looked like a quarterback squeezed into a suit two sizes too small. His biceps were bulging through the cheap material. Beneath a close-cropped beard, Ingrid noticed his chiseled jaw and cheekbones. The hair on his head was even shorter, no more than a black stubble against his dark skin. Ingrid hurried toward him.

"Special Agent Ingrid Skyberg, from the US embassy." She extended her hand.

The detective glanced toward the policewoman, who was currently standing sentry outside the men's restroom. Her colleague had gone in the ambulance with the maintenance guy. The cop pulled a face then looked down at her shoes.

"Detective Inspector Patrick Mbeke," he said and shook Ingrid's hand. "You're from the embassy?"

"Standard procedure," Ingrid said, and smiled warmly at him. "I work out of the Criminal Investigations Unit."

"And your role here?"

"To assist in the investigation, any way I can. I report back to the embassy."

"You don't trust the City of London Police to get the job done?"

"It's not like that at all. I'm just looking after the interests of American citizens."

"And American banks?" His tone was sarcastic.

She chose to ignore it. "City of London Police? Is that part of the Met?"

"No it bloody well isn't. The Met have no jurisdiction in the City."

Dammit. Why didn't she know that already? Since she'd arrived in the capital, four and a half months ago, she'd been aware the Met weren't exactly the most popular police service in the country. With the public or the media. Now she'd pissed off a potential ally.

"Hey—can I use the excuse that I'm new here? Shall we back up and start over?" She smiled her broadest grin at him, hoping it might work some magic.

Two of the CSIs were moving the temporary cordon surrounding the corpse of Matthew Fuller, and had started to create a new, much larger no go zone around the body. Two more disappeared inside the men's restroom.

"How much have you been told already?" Ingrid asked Mbeke.

"Practically nothing—I only got the call from my DCI ten minutes ago."

"Are you the senior investigating officer?"

"No—DCI Simmons is. She'll be here shortly."

Ingrid got Mbeke up to speed as they both quickly pulled on protective overshoes and gloves and ventured into the restroom.

"So you think the problem is in here?" Mbeke said when Ingrid had told him everything she knew. He glanced around the bathroom. "Should we even be in here? I mean—it might not be safe."

The two CSIs, who were busy bagging up anything that wasn't bolted to the floor or the walls, froze and glanced at one another.

"I'm guessing we're not dealing with an airborne pathogen, otherwise every guy who'd had a piss today would be in the hospital by now." She raised her eyebrows at the CSIs, who got back to work. "Just as long as we don't touch anything, I think we'll be OK."

"There are three casualties, is that right?"

"One fatality, one hospitalization."

"And the third?"

"He seems OK now. At least, he refused to leave the trading floor."

"He's still here?"

"I get the impression he thinks he's indispensable."

Mbeke turned in a slow circle then headed for the door. "We'll let them get on with it, shall we?"

Back in the corridor, Mbeke stared through the glass wall toward the busy trading floor. "It's a bank holiday," he said. "Don't they get any time off?"

"It's not a public holiday in Japan, or Hong Kong. The New York Stock Exchange will be opening in a few hours."

"There's a dead man in the corridor."

"Hey—I'm with you on this one. I want to clear the whole floor. But I need you guys to authorize that for me."

"That's a bit above my pay grade, I'm afraid. I'll have a word with the DCI, but I wouldn't be surprised if Fisher Krupps won the argument. Got to keep our international corporations happy, otherwise they might just up sticks and move somewhere else."

Ingrid thought it wise not to comment.

"You've been on the scene the longest. Come up with any theories?"

"Maybe some kind of anti-banking extremist? Or a disgruntled investor."

"You think someone would go this far to make a point?"

"I've seen people do a lot worse, just because someone pissed them off in the post office line."

Mbeke ran a hand over the stubble on his head. "But this would have taken some planning. I mean, how did they even get into the building?"

"You've sealed it off?"

"No one in or out unless I've personally approved it."

Ingrid was relieved someone was taking things seriously, even if Fisher Krupps didn't seem to be. She turned in response to the elevator doors pinging open. A woman dressed in a navy blue suit and pink shirt stepped into the corridor. She glanced left then right, spotted Mbeke and hurried toward him. "Patrick, what have you gleaned so far?" She ignored Ingrid completely.

"This is Agent Skyberg, boss. FBI, from the American embassy. Agent Skyberg this is DCI Anna Simmons."

The woman looked at Ingrid with narrowed eyes. "I'm sure you've done absolutely sterling work, agent. Rest assured, we have everything under control. You can return to the embassy."

"I'd rather stick around, assist if I can." Ingrid glanced at the team of CSIs buzzing around Matthew Fuller's body.

"That really won't be necessary." The DCI turned to Mbeke. "Do you have any business cards on you, Patrick?"

Mbeke reached into his breast pocket and handed Ingrid a card, his face a picture of apology.

"I'm sure Patrick will be in touch just as soon as we have anything to report." DCI Simmons smiled blankly and planted her hands on her hips. "Would you like one of our uniforms to give you a lift back to the embassy?"

"Thanks for the kind offer, but that won't be necessary, Anna." Ingrid reluctantly made her way to the elevator. She could have chosen to hold her ground, do a little flag planting, but if her experience of working with UK cops had taught her anything, it was when to choose her battles.

4

The embassy seemed eerily quiet when Ingrid returned there from Fisher Krupps. Apart from a little congestion around the main shopping centers, traffic had been pretty much nonexistent and she had made it back to the underground parking lot beneath the nine-story building in Grosvenor Square in under fifteen minutes. She jogged up the emergency stairs two steps at a time, feeling the need to give her heart rate a little jolt. Since her motorcycle accident two weeks ago, Ingrid's lack of regular training was making her body feel heavy and sluggish. Any extra exercise she could incorporate into her day was very welcome.

She reached her floor and carried on up until the pleasant burn in her legs was matched by the one in her lungs. Rather than turn around and go straight back down again, Ingrid took the opportunity, seeing as the building was emptier than usual, to take a peek at the view from the top floor. She'd only made it halfway down the dark wood-paneled corridor before a woman's voice called after her.

"Hello there. You drew one of the short straws, huh?"

Ingrid spun on her heels and found herself face to face with none other than the US Ambassador. "Yes, ma'am. I mean... I guess..." Ingrid doubted she'd have been more tongue-tied if the president himself had stopped her in the corridor.

The ambassador took pity on her. "It's such a lovely day to be cooped up inside."

"Actually, ma'am, I just got back. I've been working on a new case. I came up here to take a look at the view."

"I find myself staring out of the window all the time. Especially during particularly tedious teleconferences!" Smiling, she walked toward Ingrid. Then straight past her to the end of the corridor. "Well come on then, if you want to take a look at the view."

Ingrid hurried to the window.

"And you are?"

"Special Agent Ingrid Skyberg, ma'am. Criminal Division."

"Ah yes—you pretty much hold the fort all by yourself, I hear."

"I work with a great team."

"That's very loyal of you. I meant you're the only investigating agent."

"Yes, ma'am. I like to keep busy." Ingrid was surprised the ambassador had the first clue about her role.

"And what is this new case of yours?"

Ingrid wasn't sure how to respond. Right now she didn't know exactly what she was dealing with. "Sudden death of a young trader in the City."

"Oh dear. Do the police suspect foul play?"

"Yes, ma'am. It's possible that Fisher Krupps bank has been targeted by some extremist organization."

"Oh my." She stared directly into Ingrid's face, her clear, brown eyes filled with concern. Up close the woman looked more like Jackie O than Ingrid had noticed before. "I suppose the police have notified other major investment banks in the City?"

Although Ingrid was tempted to explain how she'd been thrown out of the bank, and didn't know if it had even occurred to the investigating team to inform the other banks, she knew it would be totally inappropriate, not to mention unprofessional, to complain about the City of London Police's obstructive attitude. She gave the ambassador a non-committal nod.

"How young is the victim?"

Ingrid hadn't gotten chance to see Matthew Fuller's personnel records before she'd been dismissed. "Late twenties," she said, hoping she didn't sound too vague.

"Tragic." The ambassador turned toward the window. "His poor family."

"Yes, ma'am." Ingrid stared through the glass. She'd only seen the view once before—on her second week at the embassy, when Sol Franklin, her boss, had finally gotten around to giving her the guided tour. It was so clear today she could see all the way across town to the City, where she'd just been.

"I mustn't keep you from your work. It was lovely meeting you, Ingrid." The ambassador held out a small, pale hand. Ingrid was careful not too squeeze it too hard.

"The honor is all mine, ma'am." She trapped the ambassador's fingers inside hers for a fraction of a second too long and awkwardly pulled her hand away.

Goddammit.

Ingrid turned and moved as fast as she could down the corridor without actually breaking into a run. Her hands were sweating and her heart was beating hard and fast. When she reached the stairway she silently cursed herself for being such a klutz. She'd been even worse with the Secretary of State a few months ago. The memory of her clumsy interactions with her sent a shiver across her shoulders.

Jogging down the stairs, she managed to shake a little of the tension from her limbs. She was thirty-one years old, for God's sake. What was she doing feeling like a teenager at their first pop concert?

She reached the office a little flushed and forced herself to take a couple of deep breaths before opening the door. Jennifer, the Bureau's civilian administrative clerk, was at her desk, speaking animatedly to someone on the phone.

"I know, I know! She was so nice to me! Said I was making a big difference. Said US citizens could sleep a little easier in their beds with me here to support them. Can you imagine that?" She glanced up and finally spotted Ingrid. "Listen, mom, I gotta go." She gave Ingrid an embarrassed smile. "No, of course I didn't ask for her autograph! I'll call you later, when I get home." She slammed the phone down. "Hey! Can I get you anything? Coffee maybe?"

"I'm fine. I'm guessing from what I just overheard you were graced by the presence of the ambassador?"

"Sorry about that—I just couldn't wait to call my mom." Jennifer suddenly looked much younger than her twenty-four years. She could have been fresh out of high school.

"I don't care who you call." Ingrid was a little relieved someone else had reacted to an audience with Frances Byrne-Williams the same way she had.

"She was so charming. Came right in here, and introduced herself to me. Can you imagine?"

Only too well.

Ingrid glanced around the office. It looked pretty much as she'd left it. Jennifer hadn't taken the opportunity to switch desks in her absence. Even though she had been making noises about a reorganization of the office furniture since the departure of her fellow clerk a few days ago. They were still waiting for his replacement to arrive. For some reason it was taking a while for the State Department to assign one of their embassy clerks to the FBI Criminal Investigation Unit. "Apart from the excitement of meeting the ambassador, how have things been here?"

"Oh real quiet. A couple stolen credit cards to deal with. A road traffic accident—no serious injuries. Nothing you need to worry about." She stood up. "Sure I can't get you that coffee?"

"Actually I'd like you to run a check on the trader who died this morning."

"How'd it go at the bank? How did the trader die?"

Ingrid wondered if the pathologist had arrived at the bank by now. "Too early to say." She fired up her desk computer. "I should know more later."

Jennifer tapped something into her keyboard. "Matthew Fuller… social security records, school records, college… employment… medical. Have I forgotten anything?"

"Criminal," Ingrid added helpfully.

"You said he was the victim?"

"Still worth looking into."

"Of course. I wasn't thinking." Jennifer, always eager to please, twitched an embarrassed smile in Ingrid's direction.

Ingrid's online search was a little less clearly defined. She wanted to know which substances might trigger a heart attack in an otherwise healthy victim.

After ten minutes of surfing, she had compiled such a long list of possible agents, some everyday innocuous household substances, some rare and highly toxic chemicals, that it would take a lab months to test Matthew Fuller's tissue for all of them. She got up and wandered over to Jennifer's desk. "Have you checked his medical records yet?"

Jennifer swiveled in her chair to another computer screen. "I can do that for you right now." She ran her fingers over a second keyboard in a blur of typing. A moment later a half dozen windows opened on the monitor. Ingrid started reading over the clerk's shoulder. When she was halfway down the first list of information, Jennifer closed the window.

"I hadn't finished," Ingrid told her.

"Sorry—I can scan text stupidly fast. You want me to bring it back up?"

"No—you carry on."

"What am I looking for exactly?"

"Any evidence of heart disease. Or a history of it in his family." Ingrid had been wondering why Matthew Fuller had died and, as far as she knew, the maintenance guy had survived. An underlying weakness in Fuller's heart might explain it.

"Not getting any indication of that so far."

"Let me know when you're done."

Ingrid returned to her desk and did a little research into the organizational structure of the City of London Police. As far as she could work out, the force's main responsibilities within the Square Mile were investigating cyber crime and corporate fraud and dealing with threats of terrorism.

"Ingrid? Can you take a look at something?" Jennifer was frowning at her computer screen. "I haven't seen anything like this before," she said. "I don't know what it means."

Ingrid hurried to the clerk's desk. "What is it, have you found something in his medical records?"

"Nothing connected to heart disease. But look at this." She pointed at her screen. "In 1992 the records just stop. There's nothing here about him before he was eight years of age. Looks like it's all been redacted."

"No record of his place of birth? Inoculations? Childhood illnesses?"

"He had chicken pox aged nine. From birth to seven, your guess is as good as mine. Have you seen records just stopping like this before?"

"It's weird, isn't it?" Ingrid said innocently and peered more closely at the information on the computer monitor. She had indeed come across something very similar before. But never for someone so young. In her experience, there was usually just one explanation for it, but it certainly wasn't something she wanted to share with Jennifer right now. Not until she had more information. "And no sign of heart disease after 1992?" Ingrid asked.

"Nope."

"Family medical history?"

"I've only been checking on Matthew Fuller himself up till now—so the information I have is what appears on his insurance applications. His dad died in 2003, but he was involved in an accident. Nothing to do with his heart. I guess Matthew Fuller was a pretty healthy guy." Jennifer gazed eagerly at Ingrid. "So if he wasn't sick, does that mean he was murdered?"

"Ask me again tomorrow, when we have the autopsy report."

Jennifer's shoulders slumped a little.

Ingrid searched the FBI database and brought up the same records for Matthew Fuller that Jennifer had, plus another couple that the admin clerk didn't have the security clearance to access. Ingrid stared at the screen, wondering what this revelation meant to the investigation into Fuller's death. The records she was looking at now, from the US Marshals database, confirmed her hunch. For some reason, at the ripe old age of seven, Matthew Fuller had been enrolled into the Federal Witness Protection Program.

5

Ingrid had eventually asked Jennifer to fetch her a coffee from the local Italian coffee shop, rather than the embassy cafeteria, hoping that in the time it would take the clerk to walk there, wait for her order, and walk back again, she would have gleaned all the information she needed from the US Marshals Service. She'd been wrong. Fifteen minutes later, she was on hold, having been transferred a half dozen times. Each person she'd spoken to had refused to give her any details about Matthew Fuller's former identity, or the reason he'd been enrolled in the Witness Protection Program in the first place. Every time she'd been rebuffed she'd insisted on speaking to that person's superior. Now she'd just been left hanging. She was just about to slam the phone down when Jennifer appeared at the door. Ingrid listened to another second of hold music then gently returned the handset of the phone to its cradle. She smiled up at Jennifer.

"They insisted on calling it an Americano, even though I asked for a long black," the clerk said. "But I watched the barista as he was making it. He poured the espresso into the water, just the way you like it." She carefully placed the cardboard cup on Ingrid's desk.

"Thanks, it's exactly what I need. Now you're back, I might stretch my legs." She shoved her cell and DI Mbeke's card into a pocket, picked up the coffee and strode toward the door. "I won't be long."

She made her way to the emergency stairwell at the end of the corridor, where she knew she wouldn't be disturbed, and sank onto a cold concrete step. She tapped Mbeke's number into her contacts list—she had the feeling she might be speaking to the man a lot—and called him.

"DI Mbeke." He sounded a little irritated. Maybe he was having as frustrating a time as she was.

"Hello, this is Agent Skyberg, from the embassy?"

"I don't really have any developments to report, I'm afraid," he said, his tone mellowing a little. "I'll get in touch just as soon as I do."

"Actually I have something to tell you," Ingrid said quickly, concerned Mbeke was just about to hang up on her. She told him everything she'd uncovered so far about Matthew Fuller.

"Witness Protection?"

She'd kept that morsel until last, hoping it would pique his interest.

"Why was he put into the program?" Mbeke asked her.

"I'm still waiting for the US Marshals Service to get back to me on that." It was only the smallest of lies.

"You think he may have been specifically targeted?"

"It's a possibility, right?"

"But if someone wanted Fuller dead, why go to those lengths? Why not choose a baseball bat to the back of the head on a dark street? Why endanger other people?"

"Maybe the killer doesn't care about collateral damage."

"Do you really believe that?"

"I'm not ruling out any possibilities at this stage of the investigation."

"You think I am?" The irritable tone was back.

The last thing she wanted to do was piss off the investigating detective. "Not at all. I just thought I should let you know about anything I dig up, Stateside."

He paused a beat before answering. "Look, it's been a long day, we've got dozens more people to interview... I didn't mean to be short with you."

"Has anyone else complained of the same symptoms as Wennstein? The tingling fingers, numb hands?"

"Not to my knowledge. Could be we just haven't spoken to them yet."

Ingrid grabbed the handrail and pulled herself up. "How is Wennstein?"

"He seems fine. He's still working."

"And the maintenance guy?"

"Still waiting to hear back from the hospital about him. I'll let you know when I get an update." He hung up without saying goodbye.

Ingrid wandered back to the office, an untouched cup of coffee in her hand.

"Matthew Fuller has no criminal record," Jennifer announced as soon as Ingrid stepped in from the corridor. "No misdemeanors, major or otherwise."

"Good work, Jennifer, thank you."

The clerk smiled a self satisfied grin. "So, what's next?"

"Find out everything you can about Fisher Krupps Bank. The police are working on the assumption that someone has targeted the bank. I need to know why Fisher Krupps may have been singled out. What have they done that's any worse than any of the other banks? I need you to find out everything you can about them."

"You know for sure no other banks have been targeted?"

Ingrid thought about calling Mbeke back to confirm, but there was no way he would have forgotten to mention something like that to her. "Concentrate on Fisher Krupps for now—we can widen the search later if we have to."

Ingrid then trawled FBI intelligence herself to see if any anti-capitalist threats had recently been intercepted. After about an hour of intensive searching, she discovered that apart from the usual general social media chatter, no specific threats, about either Fisher Krupps, or the City of London in general, had been issued. Which made her more inclined to believe Matthew Fuller had been the target. For some reason, someone had decided to kill him in the middle of his place of work, using a method that meant collateral damage would be pretty much unavoidable.

"Ingrid?"

She looked up to see Jennifer had swiveled in her seat to face her.

"Something to report?"

"Thought I'd give you a little summary of what I've found so far."

Ingrid found a notebook and pen in her desk drawer. "OK—go for it."

"Fisher Krupps are a little different from other banks."

"Really?"

"If it hadn't been for a buyout back in 2011, they wouldn't even exist today. They were on the verge of bankruptcy."

Ingrid tried to square that statement with the expensive interior decor she'd seen at the bank. Fisher Krupps must have recovered significantly in the past two years. "The banking crisis was in 2008. Why did it take so long to hit Fisher Krupps?"

"Their trouble wasn't caused by the meltdown in '08—they survived it almost unscathed. In 2011 they almost went bankrupt because of a rogue trader. He lost the bank nearly a billion dollars through bad investments. Then Wall Street lost faith in them and their share price bombed."

"So what saved them from going under?" Ingrid wasn't at all convinced Fisher Krupps' previous financial troubles had any bearing on what had happened today in their London office.

"A shale gas billionaire bought the company for a dollar. From what I've read, it seems he'd always dreamed of owning a bank."

"The way some guys want to own a football or baseball team?"

"Oh, this guy owns those things too. He's very, very rich."

"And in all your research, have you discovered any reason why somebody might want to target his bank?"

"Not so far. But I'm just getting started."

"Thanks. Let me know if you do dig up any major enemies who might want to see Fisher Krupps suffer."

"Sure." Jennifer turned back to face her computer and started typing.

Ingrid felt a little sorry for the clerk, it would be a long and tedious task. Unless Jennifer dug up some specific threat to the bank, Ingrid was still more inclined to suspect Matthew Fuller was the intended victim. Discovering the reason for his involvement in the Witness Protection Program was vital to prove or disprove her hunch. Tomorrow she would speak to her boss about the situation. The US Marshals Service might be able to decline her request for information, but they'd have a much tougher time denying an official request from the Deputy Special Agent in Charge.

6

At 7:30 p.m., after putting in a call to DI Mbeke and learning the man had nothing new to report, Ingrid decided there was nothing more to be usefully done and started to pack up her things. Hopefully tomorrow would yield more success. Right now she was too frustrated and hungry to concentrate on anything more than getting back to her hotel and ordering something from room service.

She had been staying at the four star hotel in Marylebone ever since she'd arrived in London, back in December. It was convenient more than luxurious, and lately she'd seriously been considering looking for an apartment to rent. The Bureau offered a pretty generous relocation package and she figured it might make sense to take advantage of it. But first she had to decide whether or not she was planning to stay.

A decision she had managed to avoid making for the last four and a half months.

She grabbed her jacket from the back of the chair and headed to the exit. Her cell phone started vibrating before she'd reached the underground parking lot. She hoped it was Patrick Mbeke, calling to tell her about some vital new piece of evidence his team had uncovered, but when she glanced at the screen she was disappointed to discover the call was from an unlisted 'out of area' number. Which meant it was an international call. She hadn't given her cell phone number to Witness Protection, so it was most likely her fiancé calling. She quickly dismissed the call. A conversation with Marshall Claybourne on a poor quality trans-Atlantic cell phone connection wouldn't be good for either of them.

As she reached her motorcycle in the parking lot, the phone buzzed again. Again the unlisted out of area number. She thought about switching off the cell, but in a moment of rashness answered the call.

"Hey, Marsh. I'm kinda in the middle of something. Can it wait?" She opened the box on the back of the bike and removed her helmet and gloves.

"I need you to get some place fast. Do you have the bike?"

Ingrid looked down at the Triumph Tiger 800 and thought about telling Marshall it was at the garage for a repair. Instead she said nothing.

"Something's being flagged over here," Marshall continued, "somebody's trying to access a bank account that's on a watch list. I need you to check it out. I have an IP address and a location."

"What kind of watch list? Are we talking terrorism? If we are, then you should go through the counter-terrorism division. Those agents would be better qualified than me to—"

"He's not a terrorist."

"Who is he? What's he done?"

"I can't get into the details right now. Just trust me, OK?"

In Ingrid's experience, whenever Marshall asked for her unquestioning trust, things never turned out well.

"We're wasting time. Check it out—don't identify yourself as a federal agent, come up with a cover story."

"What?"

"Report what you find and we'll decide how to proceed. No need to alert him the FBI are on his trail."

"Shouldn't I get some back up?"

"It's probably nothing. Just check it out. I'm texting you the address."

And with that he hung up.

Less than a half hour later, Ingrid had arrived in Dulwich, an area in southeast London roughly seven miles from the city center. She kicked down the prop stand and climbed off the bike. She'd parked fifty or so yards from the address Marshall had texted her, in a regular residential street. As far as she could see, the houses were a mix of large, smart detached properties with well-maintained gardens and even larger double-fronted buildings that had been converted into apartments. Some of the houses had shiny new SUVs parked on their driveways.

Once she'd stored her helmet and gloves, she made her way slowly up the street, doing her best to look like a lost tourist. According to her GPS, the property she was looking for was around the next corner. She approached it cautiously, checking the street for any signs of activity. Apart from a dog walker at one end and a guy washing his car at the other, the street was surprisingly quiet for a sunny evening on a public holiday. She sniffed the air and detected a definite tang of grilled meat and supposed people were enjoying barbecues in their backyards.

Marshall had called her back just after he'd texted her the address and reminded her that under no circumstances should she identify herself as an FBI agent. But he still refused to answer any of her questions. She'd worked out a fairly lame cover story on the ride over. Hopefully it wasn't so lame it would arouse suspicion.

Number twenty-three was the third property on the right. She walked purposely up the driveway of the wide, white stucco house and rang the door bell for apartment two. She waited for thirty seconds or so then rang again, keeping her finger on the buzzer. After another half minute the door creaked open a crack, a suspicious face peered at her through the gap. The woman at the door was probably late twenties or maybe early thirties, thin and very pale. Her hair was piled on top of her head in a haphazard French pleat. It was the color of cherry Kool-Aid. A small, dark green tattoo of a crucifix decorated the left side of her throat. It was a classy look.

Marshall had told Ingrid she was looking for a man in his mid-thirties.

"What is it? Who are you?" The woman's accent was eastern European, one of the Baltic states, Ingrid reckoned. Estonia or Latvia, maybe. The crucifix tattoo danced as she spoke.

"I'm so sorry, ma'am. I wonder, could I use your bathroom?"

The woman looked Ingrid up and down and narrowed her eyes until they were no more than heavily mascaraed slits. Then she looked over Ingrid's shoulder, toward the street.

"I wouldn't ask, only I'm desperate. You're the fifth house I've tried. Seems no one is in."

The look of suspicion still hadn't left the woman's face.

Ingrid reached into her purse and retrieved a tampon and held it up between thumb and forefinger. "You see, it's kinda embarrassing."

The woman raised her eyebrows. "OK—you make it quick, yes?"

"Thank you so much."

The woman ushered her into the house, pointed toward the half-open door of her apartment a few feet away, then stuck her head outside again, before she finally came in and closed the door.

"Quickly!" the woman told her. "Through door, bathroom is on right."

Ingrid scurried toward the tiny room and locked the door. She quickly checked the cabinet above the sink. It was full of the usual bathroom paraphernalia, a collection of various painkillers, deodorant, depilatory cream, tampons. No sign of any male presence. She unlocked the door as quietly as she could, and opened it a crack, half expecting to see the woman waiting for her outside. Thankfully she wasn't. Ingrid stopped for a moment and listened. She heard the woman's voice coming from another room. Then the talking stopped, there was silence for a few beats, and then the machine-gun fire Latvian—Ingrid was pretty sure that was the language she heard—started up again. The woman was having a very one-sided conversation on the phone.

Ingrid crept out of the bathroom and along the narrow, dingy hall and peered into the kitchen and discovered no one lurking inside. The room next to it, a bedroom, was also unoccupied. She was just about to check the closet for men's clothes when she heard the woman's voice call from the only room she hadn't seen inside. "Hello? Are you OK?" came the thick accented voice.

Ingrid hurried back to the bathroom, flushed the toilet and closed the door noisily. Then she strode down the hall and met the woman in the doorway of the sparsely decorated living room.

"Thank you so much—you are a life saver." Ingrid noticed an open laptop sitting on a table at the other end of the room, together with four cell phones of varying sophistication.

The cherry-haired woman followed her gaze, the suspicious expression on her pale face deepening. "You must go now."

"I'm just so glad you answered the door, rather than your husband." It was a long shot, but Ingrid thought she may as well try.

"Husband?" The look of suspicion was quickly replaced by one of confusion.

"You see, in the circumstances I would have felt too uncomfortable to ask a man for help." Ingrid smiled innocently.

"No husband."

"Oh—my mistake—I just assumed you lived here with your husband, or boyfriend. I didn't mean to pry."

"Please—you go now. I am very busy."

Ingrid glanced at the laptop again, its sleep light gently pulsing bright white every second or so. Why did this woman need four cell phones?

The Latvian redhead spread her arms wide and ushered her unwanted visitor to the door of the apartment.

"Thank you again. You're very kind." Ingrid was hustled to the main front door of the building and out onto the driveway. The woman stood at the open door and watched Ingrid return to the street before she went inside.

When Ingrid got back to the bike she called Marshall back.

"Well? Did you see him?" he barked at her as soon as he picked up.

"Can we work this another way? You know, the way where you're really grateful for all my help and ask me nicely."

There was silence at the other end. Then a noisy inhale. She knew Marshall was busy counting to ten to control his frustration.

"I'm sorry, honey. I'm just a little pressured at the moment." Another deep exhale. "Of course I'm grateful for any help you can give me. I really appreciate your taking time out to—"

"Enough! Now you just sound phony." She reached into the box on the back of the bike and pulled out her helmet without saying anything for a long few moments.

"Honey?" She could hear the strain in Marshall's voice. "Honey? Are you still there?"

"I'm here. I met a woman at the property. Latvian, twenty-five to thirty, dyed red hair, tattoo of a cross on her neck. Description mean anything to you?"

"Zip. No man at the address?"

"No man and no sign of one."

"Notice anything interesting at all?"

"The woman was using an expensive laptop. I saw four cells too."

"Four?"

"As far as I could tell, one was a smart phone, the other three no-frills bottom of the range. I assume they were burners."

"Did you ask her about them?"

"There wasn't exactly a way to work them into the conversation."

"See what was on the laptop?"

"It was on sleep mode."

Marshall went quiet.

"What do you want me to do? Call for reinforcements?" she asked him eventually, tired of waiting while he devised her next move.

"No. Seems you may just have stumbled on an internet scammer who got lucky with one of the accounts on the watch list."

"Is that likely?"

"It's not impossible."

"If she's a scammer, the local cops might be interested in her. I should call them."

"No—stand down. Do nothing."

"So who is this guy you're so interested in?"

"It doesn't matter, I don't think you found him."

"What are you doing monitoring watch lists, anyhow? Have you been demoted?"

"Demoted? Very funny."

Marshall's meteoric rise up the ranks was almost legendary. He had a knack of being in the right place at the right time, willing and eager to scoop up any glory on offer.

"So what are you doing? Looking for easy wins?"

"Look, I have to go. We'll talk later, OK?" He hung up.

Ingrid stood for a moment just staring at her phone. She must have hit a nerve. Marshall had to be trawling intelligence for fast turnaround cases. More notches to add to his belt. She wondered for a moment why that notion made her more mad than envious. Then she remembered just how hungry she was.

7

The next day Ingrid left her hotel shortly after dawn. She jogged around the Outer Circle of Regent's Park: a simple run followed by a few reps of squat thrusts, lunges and chin-ups. It felt good to really test her muscles.

As she headed back to Euston Road, running along the eastern edge of the park, she realized she was running toward Winfield House, the official residence of the US ambassador. She relived her awkward encounter with Frances Byrne-Williams. An embarrassed glow warmed her cheeks. Automatically, her speed increased as she passed the armed cop on the gates—she wasn't exactly dressed for another impromptu meeting with the ambassador.

She managed to maintain the same speed all the way back to the hotel and by the time she stepped out of the shower, she felt a little more human, and ready for the day ahead.

After a breakfast of Bircher muesli and a double-shot espresso, she was pretty much ready for anything the day could throw at her. She arrived at the office to discover Jennifer already at her desk. In her four or so months at the embassy, Ingrid had never seen the clerk so keen. Perhaps her conversation with the ambassador had made her more eager to impress. She was tentatively poking a dessert spoon into a bowl. Ingrid peered at the gray-tinged mixture specked throughout with bright crimson pomegranate seeds.

"What have you got there?" Ingrid asked her.

"Quinoa and fruit porridge." She lifted the spoon to her nose and sniffed. "It's super healthy."

"Are you supposed to spread it on your face or eat it?"

"I was talking to Frances about it yesterday."

"The ambassador is taking an interest in what you have for breakfast?"

"Not exactly. We got to talking about the new chef. And how all the food is organic now, and locally sourced. It's a passion of hers. She wants the embassy staff to stop eating junk."

"Locally sourced?" Quinoa and pomegranate—most probably from South America and northern Africa.

"Wherever possible." Jennifer prodded the gray mixture again. The spoon seemed to bounce back at her. The porridge was showing signs of resistance.

"Good luck with that. What's for lunch?"

"There's a tofu stir-fry I liked the sound of."

Ingrid felt her own breakfast stirring in her stomach. Thankfully her phone started to ring to take her mind off it. She snatched up the receiver, gave her name and waited for a response, but all she heard was a strange mumble at the other end of the line.

"Hello? Is there someone there?"

She heard a cackling laugh, following by a cough. "Agent Skyberg! How are you this fine spring morning?" It took Ingrid a few moments to place the voice. Once she had, she wished she'd let the answering service take the call.

"Ms Tate?" Angela Tate was a grizzled investigative journalist working for the main London newspaper, the *Evening News*. She had an uncanny knack of turning up at a crime scene just moments after the police. The woman had a fierce reputation for getting the story she wanted, no matter what she had to do to get it.

"I'm calling to claim my prize."

Ingrid closed her eyes. Tate played a major role in her last big investigation. Such a major role that Ingrid owed her a favor. This was payback time. "What do you need?"

"You!" The cackling laugh erupted again. Ingrid wondered if maybe Tate were drunk. The woman seemed to go nowhere without her own private supply of alcohol. "You promised me a fly-on-the-wall, unfettered access, day-in-the-life profile. And today's the day! Aren't you the lucky one!"

"Not today—I'm way too busy."

"Busy's great. I can work with busy. It'd be no fun for me watching you catch up with your paperwork, would it?"

"Call me tomorrow and we'll fix a date. I'd need to clear it with security."

"But I'm here now, why not just throw protocol out of the window and go for it?"

"You're here?"

"Downstairs, sitting on the desk of a very handsome man in uniform. Oh look—I've made him blush."

"I'm sorry—it's just not convenient today."

"Wait a minute." Tate dropped her voice. "I do hope I don't have to remind you of our little agreement."

Ingrid clamped her bottom lip between her teeth. Tate could cause so much trouble for her, if she set her mind to it. The journalist's role in her last case was unconventional to say the least, downright dishonest and immoral might be a more accurate description. Tate had a reputation for tenacity and dogged determination. Once she sank her teeth into a project she wouldn't let up until she was good and ready. Ingrid would have to succumb to her demands eventually. But maybe she could put her off just a little longer.

"Of course you don't need to remind me," Ingrid responded in a whisper, keeping her eyes trained on Jennifer, hoping the clerk's breakfast was enough of a distraction to stop her listening in. "I promise you we'll fix up proper access at a later date. I just really can't do today."

There was a long silence at the other end of the line. Then a lengthy intake of breath. "Oh, all right! But I want you to understand—I won't be fobbed off a second time. Is that clear?"

"Crystal."

Tate hung up, leaving Ingrid listening to the dial tone for a moment, wondering how the hell she was going to handle Tate when the time came.

"Hey, everyone! If you have a moment."

Ingrid looked up to see her boss, Sol Franklin, standing in the doorway of the office with his arm around the shoulders of a tall, slim black man in his very early twenties.

"Listen up, folks." Sol removed his arm and took a step away from his young companion. He cleared his throat. "I'd like to introduce you all to Isaac Coleman. Isaac here is part of the International Mission Graduate Program. He's aiming to specialize in the personal safety of US citizens abroad, and he has the good fortune to have been assigned to the Criminal

Investigation Unit for the next part of his training. Say hello, people," Sol ordered.

Jennifer jumped up from her desk and warmly shook the new arrival by the hand. "I'm Jennifer Rocharde. Good to have you on board, Isaac."

"Thank you." Isaac smiled broadly as Jennifer pumped his arm practically off his shoulder.

"Welcome to the embassy, Isaac. I'm Ingrid." Ingrid's gaze switched from the new recruit to Sol. She raised her shoulders at him in an almost imperceptible shrug. Another pair of hands to help Jennifer would be great, but she had an uncomfortable feeling there was more to it than that. A moment later Sol made his intentions plain.

"Isaac here has completed the victim counseling training course and he's eager to apply what he's learned to a 'real-life' situation. So, next US citizen in peril, I want Isaac in the thick of the action. OK?" He turned from Jennifer to Ingrid then quickly looked away. "Good. That's all settled then." He put his arm around the new man's shoulders again. "Now—as promised—the guided tour. And you must remind me to fix a date for you to come to my house for dinner. It's customary for new recruits. And I won't take no for an answer." He swung Isaac around and back through the door, hurrying away before Ingrid or Jennifer could ask any questions about Isaac's responsibilities.

Ingrid supposed her request for Sol to contact the US Marshals Service would have to wait until after he'd completed Isaac's tour.

Jennifer closed the door behind them. "No one has ever asked me if I want to learn victim support skills. The closest I get to supporting US citizens is passing on their temporary passport requests or arranging for a money wire."

"If you want to get more training, I'm sure you can put in a request."

"I get rejected every time I ask for training. It's like I don't count or something."

Ingrid grabbed her purse and jacket. She didn't have the time or the patience to stay in the office listening to Jennifer complain about the shortcomings of the embassy's professional development program.

"Where are you going?"

"Back to Fisher Krupps."

"The dead trader?"

Ingrid nodded. She'd decided to tackle the obstructive DCI who had thrown her out of the bank head on. If the detective complained, Ingrid would escalate the matter with Sol or someone higher up the food chain. "Can you arrange for a driver to meet me in the parking lot?"

"You need him to wait at the bank for you till you're finished?"

"No—I could be there a while."

By the time Ingrid had skipped down the stairs to the underground parking lot, a driver, dressed in traditional G-man garb—right down to the dark glasses, even though the lighting was dim in the basement—was holding open the door of a black BMW sedan. He was embassy rather than FBI personnel, but the black suit and white shirt look was pretty much universal. They were out of the embassy compound and onto the street less than a minute later.

It wasn't Ingrid's habit to use an official vehicle to carry out her tasks, but finding a convenient place to park the bike in the City of London would have been more hassle than she needed. After ten minutes or so the driver let out a heavy sigh and hit the steering wheel with the flat of his hand in frustration.

"It's not just me then," Ingrid said.

"Ma'am?"

"Please—call me Ingrid. I'm guessing you've noticed the tail too?"

"I've been trying to shake him off for the past five minutes. If he's a genuine taxi driver, he's in the wrong business. He's pretty damn good."

Ingrid stared into the passenger side mirror and took a good look at the black London cab. She could barely see the driver. No way could she make out who was in the back.

"Let's just continue to the destination, shall we? I'll deal with our unwanted escort when we get there."

8

As soon as she'd spotted the cab herself, Ingrid had a pretty good idea who might be tailing her. If it was supposed to have been a covert operation, then the mission had failed spectacularly. Fifty yards from the entrance of Fisher Krupps on Leadenhall Street, Ingrid told her driver to pull over.

"Will you need any assistance?" he asked, turning to her as he switched off the engine.

Looking at him, Ingrid saw two miniature versions of herself reflected back in the dark rectangles of his shades. She needed a haircut. Her hair was hanging limply over her ears. "I think I'll be able to manage," she told him. The driver seemed to deflate a little. Even if she'd needed help, no way would she get a non-Bureau member of embassy staff involved. "You can get back to base now." She opened her door and climbed out, flagging down the cab as she walked into the road. The taxi pulled in just in front of the embassy sedan. Ingrid strode toward it and rapped on the nearside window.

After a long pause, the door opened and Angela Tate stuck her head through the gap. "How'd you know it was me?"

"I took a wild guess." Ingrid should have known Tate wouldn't just accept being fobbed off without putting up more of a fight. "What exactly did you hope to achieve, following me here like this?"

"I thought there was a chance you'd change your mind."

"Trust me—I haven't forgotten our... arrangement. I'll do what I can. Please, just leave it with me."

Tate sniffed in a long breath, obviously unconvinced.

"I'll call you just as soon as I can with an alternate date. I promise."

Tate peered over Ingrid's shoulder, to the street beyond. "Square Mile? What is it? Cyber fraud? Anti-terror? Give me a clue at least."

Ingrid was surprised the sleuthing reporter hadn't already heard about the mysterious death of an American trader. "Nothing so interesting. Please, Angela. Cut me a break here."

Tate pursed her lips and screwed up her face. "I've got a lunch meeting anyway. So I can't stop. But I warn you—I won't let you off the hook."

"Believe me, of that I have no doubt." Ingrid stepped back and watched as Tate slammed the door. A moment later the cab pulled into the busy stream of traffic. A few seconds after that, the embassy car did the same. The driver flashed his rear warning lights at her to say goodbye.

Already later than she had wanted, Ingrid jogged toward the entrance of the bank, glancing around the street as she approached, just to make sure the journalist wasn't still spying on her. After checking in with the main reception desk and collecting a visitor badge, she made her way straight to the trading floor in search of Mbeke, hoping she wouldn't run into DCI Simmons first.

She stepped out of the elevator on the third floor and checked up and down the corridor. The place where Matthew Fuller had died was still cordoned off, as was the men's restroom. Ingrid peered through the glass wall of the corridor into the open plan trading floor area. She spotted Mbeke addressing a group of five detectives in a small conference room immediately opposite her position. She waited for him to finish up before approaching. The grave-faced detectives—three men and two women—filed past her in silence.

"Hey," Ingrid said, "are things going that badly?"

Mbeke blinked at her.

"Your team look a little low. Has something happened? Is the maintenance guy OK?"

"What are you doing here?"

"My job. How's the maintenance guy?"

"His doctors have decided to put him into an induced coma, until they find out what's wrong with him."

"Poor guy. When is Matthew Fuller's autopsy happening?"

Mbeke paused before answering, as if weighing up whether he should even answer her at all. "This afternoon. The mortuary's a little backed up because of the bank holiday."

Ingrid scanned the trading floor. "No DCI Simmons today?"

"She's coordinating back at the station. I'm managing things here."

Ingrid nodded slowly, relieved she didn't have to get into a messy, time-wasting battle with the senior detective. "And you're OK about my being here?"

Mbeke folded his arms. He scrutinized her face. "You promise you won't interfere with my investigation?"

"Interfere? How about assist and consult?"

The merest hint of a smile flickered across Mbeke's face.

"How many staff members are yet to be interviewed?" Ingrid asked him, pleased he might be a little more amenable than his boss.

"We've already interviewed all of the traders on this floor. We're spreading out to the rest of the building today, concentrating on anyone who was in the building yesterday. More staff are in today. The process will take a while."

"What about the maintenance and cleaning staff who had access to the restroom?"

"There's just one man we haven't been able to talk to. He didn't show up for work today."

"And he is?"

Mbeke consulted his notebook. "Miguel Hernandez, thirty-five, originally from... actually, nobody is completely clear about his country of origin. The cleaning agency say Columbia, but a couple of the cleaners here think he's from Spain."

"He was here until when yesterday?"

"Still trying to pinpoint the exact time."

"And he would have had access to the men's restrooms?"

"Just like everyone else in the building."

"You've tried his home address?"

"A couple of uniforms visited his flat about an hour ago. There was no answer."

"Do you have any more intel on him?"

"Surprisingly little. He doesn't have much of a profile on any level."

Ingrid felt a knot tighten in her stomach. "Are you treating him as a potential witness or suspect?"

"Witness at this stage."

She tried to disguise her surprise. "Are the uniformed cops staking out his place?"

"I'd need to put in a special request for a surveillance team. Jump through a lot of hoops. I thought I'd just send them back out there later." He shoved his hands in his pants pockets and stuck out his chin, as if he were challenging her to question his decision.

Ingrid chose not to rise to the bait. "So what's next?"

"According to the cleaning agency, one of the cleaners is quite close to Hernandez. I was just about to speak to her."

"Mind if I tag along?"

"In an observational capacity?"

"Whatever works for you."

A few minutes later, the elevator doors opened onto the eighth floor, bright sunshine flooded the corridor, coming from a floor to ceiling window at one end. Halfway toward the other end, Ingrid spotted a cleaning cart. The cleaner couldn't be too far away. Mbeke picked up pace a little so that he was a couple of steps ahead of Ingrid.

"Hello!" he called. "Patience Toure?"

A heavy, middle-aged woman appeared from a doorway next to the cart. She was dressed in dark pants that were too tight for her and an unflattering sage green tee shirt. "Who is looking for her?"

Mbeke introduced himself and showed her his badge.

Immediately the woman narrowed her eyes and drew in a sharp breath. "Is this about the man who died?"

"I'd like to ask you a few questions," Mbeke said, his voice softening noticeably.

"I wasn't here yesterday—I don't know anything about what happened." She glanced toward Ingrid.

Ingrid stepped forward. "Agent Skyberg, American embassy," she said. "The man who died was a US citizen." Ingrid sensed Mbeke wasn't happy about the interruption. She smiled at Toure and shuffled sideways, leaving the floor to the detective. She glanced into the room Toure had just come out of. It was some sort of closet for storing cleaning materials and equipment.

"We're interested in speaking to one of your colleagues," Mbeke continued, "Miguel Hernandez?"

"So?"

"I understand you know Mr Hernandez quite well."

"Who told you that?"

"Do you have any idea where he might be today?"

Toure shrugged. "How would I know?"

"Is he your friend?"

"I hardly know the man. Why are you asking me about him?"

Mbeke blew out a frustrated sigh. "He's not in any trouble, we just need to ask him a few questions."

"He is in the country legally. You have no right to harass him."

"Like I said, he's not in trouble. I just need to know what he saw when he was here yesterday. I'm not interested in his immigration status."

Toure snorted a laugh. "I need to get back to work. I don't have time for this. I don't know him and I can't help you." She turned away and ducked back into the cleaning closet.

"Mind if I try?" Ingrid asked Mbeke under her breath.

"Be my guest." Mbeke turned and headed back toward the elevator.

Ingrid stepped into the cramped space of the cleaning closet and lightly touched Toure on the arm. "Patience... may I call you Patience?"

Toure shrugged back at her.

"I really don't care about Miguel's immigration status. That has nothing to do with the embassy. The only thing I'm interested in is Matthew Fuller—the young man who died yesterday. Miguel may have some information about what happened."

"Miguel is a good man. He wouldn't have anything to do with the man's death."

"I'm not saying he does, but he might know something that helps us. I promise you, if you can tell us where we might be able to find him, I'll make sure the police don't pursue any immigration issues."

"You expect me to believe you? He speaks to the police and the next thing he knows he's at Heathrow airport waiting for the next flight home."

"I promise you that won't happen."

Toure shook her head. "I don't know where he is. I can't help you." She bent down and picked up a large plastic container from a low shelf and heaved it onto the cleaning cart. It landed with a thud. "I have to work now." She started to push the cart toward the ladies' restroom.

Ingrid looked at the large container Toure had just dumped onto the cart. According to the label it was a ten liter box of liquid soap. "Do you refill the soap dispensers in the restrooms every day?" she asked.

Toure stopped. "Why?"

"Is fresh soap added every day?"

"In the ladies' toilets I refresh the dispensers twice a day. Men don't wash their hands so much. Maybe once every other day."

"It's possible new soap would have been added yesterday to the restrooms on the third floor?"

Toure nodded and looked at Ingrid as if she were crazy.

"Thank you for your help." Ingrid raced toward Mbeke, who was still waiting for her at the elevators. "Call your forensics lab," she said when she reached him.

"What?"

"Get them to test the soap dispensers as a priority. We may have found the source of the toxin."

9

Mbeke turned away from Ingrid as he put in the call to the forensics laboratory. She clearly heard him make the request that the soap dispensers should be tested first. She felt as if maybe they were actually starting to make some progress.

"What do you mean?" Mbeke raised his voice. "Are you telling me they've been lost?" He turned back toward Ingrid and momentarily made eye contact with her, raising his eyebrows. "Then what are you saying?" He started to shake his head. "Dear God, what a balls-up. Who's responsible for this?" As he listened to the reply the muscles in his jaw flexed. After a few more seconds he hung up.

"What's happened?"

"There were no soap dispensers," he said and shoved his phone into a pocket.

"I don't understand."

"The lab can't test them because they were never recovered from the scene."

"They had to be."

"All the evidence from the gents' toilets was carefully bagged up and labeled by the CSIs. According to the forensics manager, there were no dispensers to bag up."

Ingrid tried to remember what she'd seen in the restroom when she'd gone in there herself. She would have noticed if the dispensers had been missing, wouldn't she? If they were there when she was in the restroom, what the hell had happened to them? "They must have been removed by the perpetrator, some time between Wennstein visiting the restroom and your uniformed officers sealing it off."

"That wouldn't have been much of a window—ten, maybe fifteen minutes?"

Ingrid pulled a face. She wasn't one for telling tales, but she couldn't just let it go.

"What is it?" Mbeke pressed the down button with a knuckle.

"I'd say closer to twenty minutes, maybe a half hour. I had to do a lot of persuading to get the restroom sealed."

"Do you remember seeing anyone going in or out?"

"I didn't have my eye on the door all the time. I was a little busy fighting with the police constable."

"Which one?"

"I don't want to get anyone in trouble."

"It's OK, I can find out without you telling me."

The elevator arrived. Ingrid glanced up and down the corridor, looking for CCTV cameras. "Is there footage some place of the corridor on the trading floor?"

"I've got a DC with security right now running through all the footage for yesterday morning. There's nothing for the exterior or interior of the toilets." He stepped into the elevator and Ingrid followed him. "But there are cameras in all the lifts." He pointed toward the shiny black hemisphere attached to the center of the ceiling of the elevator. "And the reception area and all the exits have good coverage." He punched the button labeled 'LG'. "Let's go and see what they've uncovered so far, shall we?"

The elevator doors seemed to take an age to close.

"If the toxic agent that killed Fuller and put the hand drier engineer in the hospital was in the soap," Mbeke said, "that blows your theory about Fuller being targeted specifically. Unless you've heard something from Witness Protection?"

"Still waiting for them to get back to me." Ingrid hated having to admit she didn't have the necessary intel. As soon as she got back to the embassy she'd insist Sol Franklin contact the US Marshals Service.

"So there's just as much chance that the hand drier man was the intended target. But still more likely that Fisher Krupps has been targeted in general."

"The maintenance engineer is still alive. Fuller's dead."

"That makes him unlucky, not a target."

The elevator doors opened and two smart suited young men stepped in. Ingrid made sure to drop her voice. "If it was the soap, then we have to assume the toxin was absorbed through the skin. Maybe that might speed up the process of identifying it."

"We'll hopefully find out more after the autopsy." Mbeke looked at the two men, obviously uncomfortable about discussing the case. He remained silent until the elevator doors opened again and they exited. "If it was in the soap, anyone could have been affected. Surely there would have been more casualties."

"Maybe not." Ingrid braced herself to ask an awkward question. "Tell me—and I really need you to answer honestly—do you wash your hands, with soap and all, every time you use the bathroom?"

Mbeke shifted his weight from one foot to the other. "Maybe not *every* time."

"Wennstein complained about tingling in his fingers after he went for a crap. I'm supposing he washed his hands. The maintenance guy would have gotten pretty dirty hands pulling apart a hand drier and reassembling it, so he must have used plenty of soap to clean up afterward."

"And Fuller? What possible reason would he have for being so meticulous about his hand hygiene?"

"That I haven't worked out yet."

"So either the hand drier engineer was the intended victim, or Fisher Krupps was targeted."

"Why remove the soap if someone wanted to do as much damage as possible?" Ingrid felt as if they were chasing around in circles, getting nowhere. "I guess you should look into the background of the maintenance guy. I feel bad calling him that all the time, what's his name?"

"Colin Stewart."

"So—a full profile of Stewart might help."

"I'll get one of the DCs onto it."

The elevator finally reached the lower ground floor. Ingrid followed Mbeke down a maze of corridors to a dimly lit room full of TV monitors, a different image of part of the building on each one. A uniformed guard was showing a plain clothes detective some footage.

"How's it going, Craig?" Mbeke asked the cop.

"Not sure we've got anything worthwhile yet."

"Can we take a look at the elevator footage between 10:20 and 10:50 a.m.?" Ingrid asked.

Rather than answering her, both the security guard and the detective looked at Mbeke for approval.

"In your own time," Mbeke said.

Within five minutes the appropriate footage was lined up on the monitor. The image was split in two—the left side showing footage for 'elevator north' and the right side displaying what was captured in 'elevator south'. All four of them crowded around the screen as the guard ran the recordings at eight times normal speed.

"Stop it there!" Ingrid said, after she saw a figure appear dressed in dark pants and the same color long-sleeved green tee shirt Patience Toure had been wearing, a baseball cap pulled low over his face. The still image on the left hand side of the screen clearly showed a bag shoved under the man's arm.

"Ten thirty-seven," the young constable read from the screen.

"Dammit—I might have been able to stop him." Ingrid shook her head. "You think it's Hernandez?"

Mbeke peered at the screen and shrugged.

"Outside agency staff are issued with temporary security passes," the guard told them. "So that means we don't have a photograph of him on the system."

"You can't see his face, anyway," Craig said.

"But it's enough to keep his place under surveillance?" Ingrid turned to Mbeke. He had already pulled out his cell phone.

"Just about to get that organized," he told her.

It seemed Miguel Hernandez had just switched from being a potential witness to a possible suspect.

10

Ingrid ducked out of the way, narrowly avoiding a group of three tottering women who had burst through the door of the tequila bar. She checked her watch. It was already a quarter after nine. Her friend was late, as usual. If Detective Inspector Natasha McKittrick didn't turn up in the next ten minutes, Ingrid would head for the Tube at Old Street. She'd already worked out her route: Northern Line to King's Cross then Circle or Metropolitan to Baker Street. Her hotel was five minutes away from Baker Street Tube. She moved a little further away from the door and, to keep her mind occupied, replayed the events of her day.

Before she'd left Fisher Krupps, she had discovered a few things that she wasn't sure helped the investigation into Matthew Fuller's death or hindered it. On the surface, DI Patrick Mbeke's request that she liaise more closely with his team should have been a good thing. Unfortunately, the reason for his sudden desire for cooperation didn't leave her feeling too confident that the case was in entirely safe hands. After he'd sent a surveillance team to Miguel Hernandez's apartment, Mbeke had taken her to one side for a private chat.

"I'd like you to be more hands on with the investigation," he'd said.

"Great—the Bureau will do everything we can to assist."

"Do you know how many murders there were in London last year?"

Ingrid saw the earnest look on his face and waited for him to tell her.

"Ninety-nine."

That seemed pretty low. She hoped he wasn't going to move on to a discussion about gun control. She preferred to avoid politics in the work-place at all costs. It only ever ended badly.

"Do you know how many of those were within the City of London?"

Again, Ingrid waited to be enlightened.

"Just one. And I didn't investigate it."

She wondered where the conversation was going.

"How many homicide investigations have you worked on?" he asked her.

"Really not that many. The cops only call in the Bureau under special circumstances."

"How many, ball park figure?"

"Twenty-five, thirty, maybe. I've been working in the Violent Crimes Against Children program the past three years. I haven't worked any murder cases there."

"This is my first. Same for DCI Simmons too."

At the time, Ingrid hadn't been able to understand Mbeke's sudden confessional mood. But now she'd had time to think about it, she supposed the reality of a potential suspect had brought his insecurities to the surface. She felt a little sorry for the guy. Their little tête-à-tête had been abruptly curtailed when the detective inspector took a call from the pathologist. As the EMTs had suspected, Matthew Fuller had died of a massive coronary. However, the pathologist's initial investigation had found no evidence of poisoning in Fuller's major organs. But they would know more tomorrow.

Ingrid checked her watch again. McKittrick had precisely three more minutes to make an appearance. She crossed the narrow cobbled street and took a good look at the exterior of the bar. Apparently, it had only opened the weekend before and had created quite a buzz. Ingrid had been reliably informed that it was situated in the 'Williamsburg of east London'. That was Williamsburg, New York, rather than Williamsburg, Virginia, she presumed. Even if it were true, she wasn't sure it was recommendation enough. She just hoped it sold a good range of tequilas. After her nights out with McKittrick, she was becoming quite a connoisseur.

"Hello!"

Ingrid turned to see her friend ambling toward her.

"You look vaguely suspicious loitering on the pavement like that," McKittrick said. "Different shoes and a short skirt and you might get arrested."

"That's hilarious." Ingrid grabbed McKittrick's arm and dragged her across the street. "Let's get inside, I'm really ready for a drink."

"I can't stay long."

"What?"

"Sorry—I've got more crap to deal with from Internal Investigations. They sprang a seven a.m. meeting on me just as I was leaving tonight. I've got to get to bed at a reasonable time. And I can't get too bladdered either."

Ingrid let her silence tell McKittrick how disappointed she was.

"I'm sorry OK? If it had been anything else I'd say sod it, let's party. But we are actually talking about my future career here."

"Are we?" Ingrid pushed open the door into the bar. Immediately the noise of dozens of excitable twenty-somethings swallowed up McKittrick's reply.

It took a full ten minutes to get served at the bar. After nine of those, Ingrid got so pissed off with the wait that she stooped to using what her dad was fond of calling her "feminine wiles" to jump to the front of the line. She felt a little pathetic, flirting her way to a jug of margarita and two large salt-rimmed glasses, but at least it got the job done.

"We're not doing shots then?" McKittrick sounded disappointed when Ingrid arrived at the table the detective had secured in a slightly quieter corner of the bar. Ingrid suspected McKittrick had used her warrant card to stake her claim to the bench and two stools.

"You said you didn't want to have a big night. Margarita is a good compromise." Ingrid found herself shouting against the din. Was she really so old the atmospheric trance track sounded more like noise than music? She hoped to hell she wasn't.

"There's big and there's enormous." McKittrick filled their glasses.

"So are you finally going to tell me what Internal Investigations are actually investigating?"

McKittrick shrugged. "It's just a pain in the arse. A suspect I arrested has made an allegation about me. Says I pocketed some of the drugs we recovered. Claims he saw me slip a few packs into a pocket before we bagged up the evidence."

"Why are your bosses taking him so seriously? Surely they won't believe his word against yours."

"They have to be seen to take every allegation seriously. The Met's had enough scandal to deal with lately, they can't take any chances."

"What was it? Cocaine? Heroin?"

"God no, just some prescription drugs—your usual range of uppers and downers. We weren't even arresting him for possession. He's an accessory in a murder investigation. The drugs were just a distraction."

"When will it all be over?"

"Tomorrow may be my final grilling before they finally accept my word over the scumbag's."

"I had no idea you were going through so much crap." Ingrid squeezed McKittrick's arm. "You should have told me."

McKittrick quickly pulled her arm away. "The irony is I've been clean for ages. I wouldn't have taken his poxy drugs if he'd paid me."

Ingrid stared into her friend's face, not sure how to take that last statement. McKittrick's expression was deadpan. Then she smiled a little, a twinkle in her eyes.

"I'm kidding! God—you need to know when you're being wound up." She topped up Ingrid's glass. "Anyway—enough about me and my crap, how's your latest case going?" McKittrick quickly swiped a dish of tortillas from the tray of a passing waitress. Ingrid scowled at her. "I'm sure they're complimentary," McKittrick said. "They bloody well should be, upmarket place like this. Besides, I'm ravenous."

Ingrid quickly updated her with everything that had happened so far.

"And what's the DI like to work with?"

"He's fine. I get the impression he's feeling a little out of his depth."

"Well it's a bit beyond your average credit card fraud or case of embezzlement, isn't it? Out of his depth? I'm surprised the poor bugger's not drowning."

"It's his first homicide. Twelve years a cop and never seen a murdered body before."

"You need to be gentle with him, then." She wiped a little chili powder from the corners of her mouth.

"It's not my job to hold his hand."

McKittrick raised her eyebrows. "What's he look like? Is he fit?"

"Why are you even asking?"

"Might add a little more interest to the investigation."

"I'm engaged to Marshall."

"But he's over three thousand miles away. A bit of harmless fun while you're in London would hurt no one."

Ingrid lifted her glass to her face and swallowed a large mouthful of margarita before she felt able to comment. "I'm not about to betray Marshall's trust, how many times do I have to tell you? I still haven't forgiven you for trying to set me up with your DC."

"But Mills is practically besotted with you. I thought you might appreciate a little adulation."

"Well your little matchmaking exercise didn't work. We had a perfectly pleasant brunch and went our separate ways."

"What did you talk about, work?"

"Actually, I spoke a lot about Marshall."

"Well that explains Mills' stinking mood for the last week. You really know how to crush a bloke's dreams."

"I didn't want him to think I was… available."

"Well you've obviously made that quite clear."

Ingrid wasn't sure how the conversation had veered in this direction. She attempted to get it back to neutral territory. "From everything I've told you about the case, what's your hunch? An attack on Fisher Krupps or something more personal?"

McKittrick chewed thoughtfully on a nacho for a few moments before answering. "This Witness Protection fella… when did you say he entered the program?"

"Nineteen ninety-two."

"I bet you didn't share that particular nugget of information with Mbeke. Doesn't exactly promote your theory, does it? How likely would it be that someone would have been holding a grudge against him all these years?"

"It's not impossible."

"What about the engineer who's in the hospital? Would anyone want to target him?"

"We haven't uncovered any information to suggest that. I think the poor guy was just in the wrong place at the wrong time."

"Why would the toxin have affected the City trader so badly? Is it possible he had an undiagnosed heart condition?"

"I'm hoping the full autopsy report will offer some kind of explanation."

"And you're no nearer locating the missing cleaner?"

"Even his neighbors don't ever remember seeing the guy. Apart from the cleaning agency, no one seems to have heard of him."

"So he's got to be the prime suspect?"

"I'd put money on it."

"I never had you pegged as the gambling type."

"I'm not—I'm just so damn sure Hernandez has to be responsible."

McKittrick drained her glass and refilled it. "Enough shop talk. There must be something else we can discuss."

Ingrid raised her eyebrows.

"OK, OK, I realize we both have nothing else in our lives. What a couple of saddoes. It's what happens when you dedicate fifteen years of your life to the force."

"Fifteen? That beats my eight. I feel like an amateur in your company." Ingrid lifted a glass to her.

"And just you remember that—treat me with the respect a senior law enforcement officer deserves."

"Yes. Ma'am." Ingrid sat to attention.

"But don't take the piss."

"What made you join the police in the first place?"

"Oh God—that's far too boring a story."

"Try me."

McKittrick gulped another mouthful of margarita. "OK, the edited highlights: parents wanted me to be a lawyer—my dad's one—he works for good causes, you know, Amnesty International, Liberty, Reprieve. All a bit too worthy for my liking at the time—I decided I wanted to be the opposite of an idealist, whatever that's called, and I rebelled. I studied criminology at uni then went straight into Nottingham Police graduate scheme and got fast tracked. Never looked back." She was staring blank-eyed into her half-empty glass. "Your turn."

Ingrid got the impression McKittrick had edited the story just a little too rigorously, but the forlorn look on the detective's face warned her not to pry.

"Me... oh now that's too long a story. You said you needed to get home early."

"Just give me the headlines."

Ingrid could feel her nose tingling. She thought it might be the chili powder on the tortillas, but suspected it was the usual cause. She took a deep breath. "I lost someone close to me when I was a teenager. A school-friend. My best friend. After she went I promised I'd do everything I could to prevent what happened to her happening to any other fourteen-year-old girl. When it comes to clearing the filth of the streets, I guess I haven't even scraped the surface during my eight years as a Fed."

"She was murdered?"

"Abducted. Never found. The Bureau ran the investigation into her disappearance. But they came up with no leads at all in over eighteen months of searching. After three years they wound the case right down." She shoved a triangle of deep-fried corn into her mouth and started to chew slowly.

"Still hard to talk about?"

"Always—that's why I avoid the subject."

"And here I am asking you to rake over it." She filled Ingrid's glass. "Sometimes though, getting it out of your system is the best thing you can do."

"I was in therapy for years afterwards. Believe me, the only thing that made me feel better was being accepted into the Bureau Academy."

"Well here's to that achievement." McKittrick chinked glasses with her. "Just make sure tomorrow you kick arse with this new case of yours."

11

Up a little later than usual the following morning, Ingrid tried to convince herself it wasn't the margaritas making her limbs feel sluggish and her head as thick as cotton, but the high dose of deep fried corn. Whatever the cause, she nevertheless forced herself to complete a three mile run, and felt a little better at the end of it. Skipping the strength and flexibility workout was her one concession to the factory of hammers pounding in her head.

When she reached her desk at the embassy, there was already a message waiting for her. She unstuck the Post-it from her computer monitor and tried to decipher Jennifer's handwriting. Jennifer herself was conspicuously absent. The new recruit, Isaac, was studying something intently on his computer screen in the far corner of the room.

"Hey, Isaac—you came back today, huh? We didn't scare you off."

"Good morning, Agent Skyberg—I'm sorry I didn't see you come in."

"Call me Ingrid." She wandered over to his desk.

"Sure."

"How did you enjoy the grand tour of the embassy yesterday?" she asked him.

Immediately he grew more animated and his eyes lit up. "It was awesome. I didn't realize there are actually *three* basements under the building. Have you seen the bunker?" He paused a beat then carried on without waiting for her reply. "Stupid question, of course you've seen it. Agent Franklin showed me this huge closet of canned and dried foods. It's got its own independent air and water supply too. I'm sure there must be preppers back home who'd go green with envy for all that stuff!"

Ingrid smiled at his enthusiasm. Hopefully the crushing reality of boring admin work wouldn't squeeze it out of him too fast.

"Then we went to visit the gym and the steam room," Isaac continued, almost sounding a little breathless, "Agent Franklin said I should ask Jennifer to organize a pass for me—he said I can use the facilities any time I want—even on the weekend."

"I'd give it a couple of days before you ask for that. Jennifer's a little busy doing work for me at the moment." Ingrid remembered just how pissed Jennifer had seemed at her own lack of training opportunities. No point in adding salt to the wound.

"Sure. OK. I don't use the gym much anyhow." Already a little of his enthusiasm seemed to have leaked out of him. "I'm worrying maybe I've upset Jennifer in some way. She was a little... distant with me yesterday."

"I'm sure she was just concentrating a little too hard on her work. Don't take it personally."

"OK." He sounded anything but convinced.

"Hey, how'd you like the view from the top floor?" she asked, hoping to get him a little excited again. It seemed to work.

"The views are amazing. You can pretty much see the whole of London from up there. Agent Franklin took me up onto the roof. The roof! I stood right next to the flag pole. I wanted to take a photograph, but Agent Franklin said it wouldn't be a good idea."

Ingrid felt a slight twinge of envy. Sol hadn't taken her onto the roof when she'd done the tour. Maybe he'd only recently added it to the itinerary—after all, it'd give him the excuse to smoke a cigarette. Sol rarely missed an opportunity to get a nicotine fix. "Sounds like you got the VIP tour," she said.

"I'm just so pleased to have the chance to work here. Let me know if there's anything I can do for you. I really want to help."

"I'll be sure to." Ingrid smiled at him and returned to her desk. She stared at the message Jennifer had written but was no nearer deciphering it.

The phone on Jennifer's desk started ringing. Isaac jumped out of his seat, eager as a puppy to do something useful. He reached the phone at the precise moment Jennifer reappeared. She threw him a glowering look. He backed off.

After Jennifer was finished with her phone call, Ingrid wandered over to her desk. She bent low and leaned in close to the clerk's ear. "I don't know what is going on with you and Isaac, but you need to get a grip. He's young, inexperienced. He needs our support. He's done nothing wrong."

"But I've been working here for two years and every request I've made for professional development has been denied."

"So you told me yesterday."

"You think I'm complaining too much?"

"You need to speak to human resources about training. If you need me to approve a request, I'd be happy to do that for you."

"You would?"

"Sure, but in the meantime, we've all got to get along, OK?"

Jennifer nodded reluctantly, still keeping her eyes trained on her new rival.

"Good." As Ingrid straightened up, something on the 24-hour news channel Jennifer had playing permanently in the corner of her monitor caught her eye. It was an artist's impression of a young woman with a ghostly pale face and a peculiar shade of red hair. Ingrid pointed at the player window. "Can you make that full screen and turn up the volume?" Jennifer's fingers flew over the keyboard and suddenly Ingrid was staring at a large portrait of the woman she'd seen two nights ago in Dulwich.

According to the reporter, the police were appealing for anyone who might know the identity of the victim of a vicious knife attack. The picture changed abruptly to show divers on a river police boat peering into a murky, churned up River Thames.

"What is it?" Jennifer was staring at Ingrid rather than the news report.

Isaac was hovering uncertainly next to Ingrid. "You know her?" he said tentatively.

Ingrid ignored their questions and grabbed her cell from her desk. She quickly punched in McKittrick's number and waited for the DI—who probably felt as hungover as she did—to pick up. Finally the detective answered, slightly out of breath. It was only at that moment Ingrid remembered McKittrick had an early morning meeting with Internal Investigations. "Can you speak?" Ingrid asked her.

"I'm out of the Spanish Inquisition, if that's what you mean."

Ingrid left the office and quickly explained both her trip to Dulwich on Monday night and what she'd just seen on TV.

"If you think it's her, why are you calling me and not the incident line?"

"I need you to check something for me. The woman I saw had a distinctive tattoo on her throat, in the shape of a crucifix."

"Where was she found? I need to know which murder investigation team to contact."

"In the river, beneath one of the bridges, London Bridge, maybe... I didn't catch it. The body had gotten tangled in some mooring chains of the boats there. According to the report, if it hadn't, it might not have shown up for weeks. Or ever. The body might have washed right out to sea, if the tide was moving in the right direction."

"Leave it with me. I'll see what I can find out."

Ingrid hung up and quickly called Marshall. It was early hours of the morning in D.C., but she figured this was something he should know about as soon as possible. He answered the phone with a mumble.

"It's me."

"Jesus! Honey!"

Ingrid heard the rustling of bedclothes.

"Is everything OK?" he asked.

"I'm fine. Sorry to wake you, but I thought you'd want to know. That address I checked out for you? I'm pretty sure the woman I met there has turned up dead."

There was a pause. Ingrid wondered if she should repeat what she'd just said. Was Marshall even properly awake? Finally he broke the silence. "How did she die?"

"Stabbed—I don't have all the details—I figured you'd want to know right away."

"How many stab wounds?"

"What's that got to do with anything?"

"How many?"

"I don't know, enough to be described as 'vicious'. Why is that important?"

"It's not our guy."

"How can you be so sure?"

"That's not his M.O., is all. He wouldn't kill in that way. It's not his style. He doesn't like to get his hands dirty."

"Maybe he's changed. Who is 'your guy' anyway? You didn't actually give me his name."

"It doesn't matter, because it's not him."

"Why won't you tell me?"

"Because it doesn't concern you." He let out an impatient breath. "Listen, I have to go. I have an important briefing this morning. I can't be late." He hung up.

Ingrid checked her watch and counted back. It was four-thirty a.m. on the East Coast. Any meeting Marshall had would be hours away. He was lying to her. He was notoriously bad at it. The question was, why? Why wouldn't he give her any information about the case? Her desk phone rang.

"Do you want me to get that?" Jennifer started to get up from her chair.

Ingrid held up a hand to stop her. "Agent Skyberg, US Embassy, Criminal Investigation Unit."

"Do you know, I didn't actually realize that's what your little outfit was called." The unmistakable tones of Angela Tate. "So, when are we going to fix up this interview?"

"Don't you have better things to do than harass me?"

"Harass? I haven't even started. It'd be much easier for you to give me what I want, believe me."

"And what is that? You still want to do this damn fool fly-on-the-wall thing?"

"It'll be fantastic, trust me."

"OK! Friday. Ten a.m. I'll meet you at the embassy gate."

"Fine."

"Good."

Ingrid slammed the phone down. It took her a few moments to realize the two clerks were staring at her. "What's the matter with you? Don't you have work to do?" Her cell phone started to buzz. She jumped up from her desk and answered the call outside in the corridor. "Hey, Natasha, that was quick. Does that mean there was a tattoo?"

"No."

"Oh." Ingrid had felt certain the portrait she'd seen on the news report was the cherry soda haired Latvian from Dulwich. "Are you sure?"

"Not at all."

"Wait a minute. Then what are you saying?"

"There was no tattoo on the victim's throat because there was no skin there either."

12

As soon as Ingrid ended the call from McKittrick, she tried Marshall again. This time her call went straight to voicemail. She cursed him silently and started back toward the office. If she just had the identity of the suspect he was monitoring, she could decide for herself how significant his M.O. was.

Jennifer and Isaac were both looking up at her expectantly when she entered the room.

"What's happened?" she asked them.

"Shouldn't you be leaving about now?" Jennifer said. She pointed to Ingrid's desk. "Kristin Floyd said she had a window between eleven and twelve. It's in my note."

Ingrid glanced down at the indecipherable scrawl and tried to remember who Kristin Floyd was. She wasn't sure it was a name she'd even heard before.

"Matthew Fuller's girlfriend—she's back in London. You wanted to speak to her. I arranged it for you yesterday evening."

"OK—thank you. Can you text me the address? Is it some place I'll be able to park the motorcycle?" She noticed Isaac had grabbed his jacket from the back of his chair.

"We're going on a bike? Awesome!"

What the hell was going on? "Wait a minute. *We* are going nowhere."

"Agent Franklin said I should accompany you the next time you interview someone. To use my victim support skills."

Ingrid vaguely remembered Sol mentioning it the day before. *Dammit.*

337

Isaac's skills better be worth it. "Could you book me a car, Jennifer? I'd really appreciate it."

A half hour later they arrived at an upmarket glass and steel apartment block in Bankside, just a couple hundred yards from the Tate Modern art gallery.

"Do you want me to lead on this?" Isaac innocently asked Ingrid as they ascended the building in an external glass elevator.

"As it's your first case, why don't you just observe on this one? Let me do all the talking."

"But I really want to be able to help."

"Trust me, a sympathetic smile can make all the difference in the circumstances."

His shoulders slumped and he stuck his hands in his pockets. Ingrid wondered if he might sulk his way through the entire interview.

"This isn't about what we want. It's all about Kristin Floyd. We're putting her needs first, OK?"

He nodded his head rapidly and stood a little straighter. If he'd put up any kind of argument, Ingrid would have told him to go wait in the car.

The elevator arrived at the twenty-first floor and Ingrid straightened her jacket. She turned to Isaac. "Ready?"

"Sure."

They walked the length of a thickly carpeted corridor—it seemed more like the hallway of a five star hotel than an apartment block—and Ingrid leaned on the buzzer of apartment 210. The door opened right away, as if Kristin Floyd had been waiting just behind it for their arrival.

"Thank you for fitting in with my schedule," Fuller's girlfriend said. "It's much appreciated." Her accent was pure upstate New York.

Ingrid introduced herself and Isaac as she studied the woman's face. The eyes were red-rimmed, as were her nostrils. She wasn't wearing any makeup and her hair hung loose over her shoulders. It looked slightly damp from the shower.

Isaac stuck out his hand and said, "I'm so sorry for your loss."

Ingrid flinched a little.

"Thank you." Floyd closed the apartment door and led them down a wood-floored hallway to a large, light-filled living room. The room was sparsely furnished, just two couches, a low coffee table sitting on a ten feet by twelve cotton rug, and a large TV mounted on the wall.

"Do you mind if we speak outside?" the woman asked. "I need a little air." She grabbed a pack of cigarettes and a lighter from the coffee table and stepped outside onto a balcony that ran the length of the room.

338

By the time all three of them had settled themselves around a small circular aluminum café table, Floyd's cigarette was already an inch shorter.

"What is it you want to speak to me about?" Floyd's voice was steady, as was her gaze. She looked first at Ingrid, then glanced in Isaac's direction. Isaac wriggled back in the seat and sat a little taller, the sympathetic smile Ingrid had mentioned earlier plastered across his face.

"I'd like to get a little background on Matthew, if you feel strong enough to talk about him."

"Oh I'm plenty strong enough." Floyd raised an immaculately threaded eyebrow. "Ask me anything you need to. I want to help." She took a long drag on her cigarette. "Although I may not have all the answers."

Ingrid smiled gently at her. "We appreciate any help you can give us." She pulled out a notebook.

"Do you know how the police investigation is going? Have there been any threats toward Fisher Krupps?"

"I'm afraid I can't comment on the investigation. I only have an overview. I believe the police are making progress."

"Who would do a thing like that? Sick bastards."

"That's what the police hope to find out. I'm sure they will." She flicked through her notebook to a fresh page. "How long had you and Matthew been together?"

"Just over..." Floyd stopped and looked up toward the early May sky, fluffy white clouds skudded across the blue. "Eight months."

"So you knew him well?"

"Gosh, no, I wouldn't say that. I barely knew him at all."

Ingrid didn't comment, but leaned in a little closer.

"Matthew was a very private man." Floyd almost whispered the words. "He didn't even really open up to me. It frustrated the hell out of me. We fought about it sometimes." She took a long drag on her cigarette. "I guess I shouldn't say things about him like that. Makes me sound a little callous."

"Not at all." Ingrid tried a sympathetic smile of her own. "Did he speak about his family at all?"

"He doesn't have one."

"He doesn't?"

"Not much of one, anyway. He was an only child. His dad died when he was still at school. I guess he's still pretty close to his mom. Have you spoken to her?"

Ingrid couldn't admit they still hadn't tracked down contact details for the woman. "Not personally, no."

"She must be taking it so hard."

"You haven't spoken to her yourself?"

"I don't have her number. I've never met her. Matthew and I didn't really have a 'meet the folks' relationship."

"You weren't planning to make things more permanent?"

"Gosh no. We both knew it was a temporary thing that would end when one of us went back to the US. Or maybe even before." Her voice caught in her throat. "I guess that's exactly what's happened. Never thought it would be under these circumstances."

Ingrid paused a beat to allow Floyd to regain her composure. "So you hadn't considered moving in together while you were both based in London?"

"No way! I like my own space. Matthew likes…" She wriggled her shoulders as if she were trying to cast off an unwelcome arm. "I mean Matthew *liked* his."

"So you split your time between both apartments?"

Floyd hesitated. "Actually, you know, I don't think Matthew spent a single night here. We always went to his place."

Ingrid jotted down a few notes. "Would you say that Matthew was happy at work?"

"I guess. He was quite driven. You have to be in our business. It's not for the faint-hearted." She stubbed out her cigarette into a dirty saucer on the table. "I'm so sorry—I haven't offered you anything. Would you like tea or coffee?"

"We're fine, thank you."

Floyd lit another cigarette. "What was I saying?"

"You were telling me how driven Matthew was."

"He worked so damn hard. He never really relaxed. He was always twitchy about something. I guess that was all part of his condition."

Ingrid tensed. "His condition?"

"The anxiety and all." She drew on her cigarette and slowly exhaled. "You don't know about it?"

Ingrid said nothing.

"But then, how could you? I only know because I stayed over at his apartment. He kept the whole thing very private. Made me promise I'd never tell anyone. I guess that doesn't matter now."

"What condition did Matthew have?"

"General anxiety disorder. He's had it ever since his dad died. He took it really badly. The OCD was Matthew's coping mechanism."

"He was suffering from obsessive-compulsive disorder?"

Floyd nodded and took another puff on her cigarette. "He was a complete control freak. Everything had to be just the way he liked it. I have to admit—it drove me crazy. My place was way too messy for him. Everything had to be super neat and clean. Like, for example, the towels in his bathroom were always perfectly folded, all facing the same way. Same for the mugs in the kitchen cabinets, all the handles had to point to the left. Or was it the right? Jesus—you'd think I'd remember, he drummed it into me so often." She turned her head and stared toward an oblique view of the Thames. "I'd always get it wrong. And if I ever used any of the special cream he had for his hands…" She shook her head. "Listen to me, bitching about his OCD. What kind of person am I?"

"Tell me about the hand cream."

"It was perfume-free, had extra vitamin E in it. His hands used to get so raw."

"Raw?"

"He washed them over and over. I think maybe he counted how many times. If I ever interrupted him, he'd have to start over. I learned not to interrupt pretty quickly." She let out a shaky breath.

"How did he manage to keep the hand washing thing a secret at work?"

"He learned to be strategic about it."

"But he'd still wash his hands many, many times?"

"He didn't have a choice. Poor bastard."

Ingrid stood up. "Would you excuse me a moment—I need to make a phone call."

"What did I say?"

"It's OK. Nothing to worry about." Ingrid shot Isaac an encouraging look before she went back inside the apartment. She hoped he understood now was the time to put his recently acquired victim support skills to good use. He nodded back at her. Ingrid quickly found Mbeke's number in her contact list.

"I don't have any new developments to report. I'd call you straight-away if I did, I hope you know that."

"Sure, sure. Listen, something came up I thought you should know about. I think maybe Matthew Fuller might have been the intended target."

"You've heard from Witness Protection?"

"No—I've just been speaking to Fuller's girlfriend. She told me Fuller had OCD—one of the ways it manifested was in repeated hand washing. We're talking dozens of times every time he visited the bathroom."

"Which is why the toxin affected him so much more than anyone else?"

"It's what I'm thinking. Say he was the intended target. The killer hangs around, watches Fuller die. Then removes the evidence from the restroom, having done what he intended to do."

"Doesn't explain the delay. Fuller died approximately 9:25 a.m. Colin Stewart was taken ill over forty minutes later. Why leave the soap around to do collateral damage once the job was done?"

"Like I said before, maybe the killer doesn't care about collateral damage."

"Like some kind of sadist?"

"I couldn't possibly make that kind of judgement."

"But it's what you're thinking."

"I'm thinking we're dealing with a sick bastard who needs to be tracked down as soon as possible." Another thought occurred to Ingrid. "If Fuller was the target, the killer had to know about Fuller's OCD. According to his girlfriend, no one knew except her."

"So?"

"So Hernandez—let's just agree for the sake of argument right now he's the most likely suspect—must have been observing him closely. He must have been working in the bank planning his move for weeks or maybe even months. This had to be a meticulously prepared attack."

13

The morgue in Westminster wasn't open by the time Ingrid arrived there early the next morning. She'd decided to walk from Marylebone to Horse-ferry Road through the back streets, feeling a need to clear her head and work through some of the frustration she felt.

After she'd gotten off the phone from Mbeke the day before and wrapped up the interview with Kristin Floyd, Ingrid had returned to the embassy and gone on a hunt for Sol Franklin. She still hadn't managed to have a conversation with him about contacting Witness Protection and forcing them to reveal the details of Matthew Fuller's former identity. In the end she'd had to settle for leaving a longwinded voice message for him, justifying her request as well as she could. He hadn't gotten back to her before she left the embassy for the night. DI Mbeke had, however, and the news he had to share didn't give her much hope they would ever track down Miguel Hernandez. The officers staking out his apartment finally managed to track down one of the property's occupants only to discover that Hernandez didn't live there and never had. At least not for the last five years. The tenant's story was confirmed by the landlord of the prop-erty. It seemed Hernandez, or whatever his real name was, had given the cleaning agency a false address.

Ingrid sat down on a wall outside the main entrance of Westminster Public Mortuary and waited, driving herself crazy mulling over the facts of the case and getting nowhere. On the stroke of eight-thirty, she jumped off the wall and banged on the main door until the woman on reception begrudgingly opened up.

"I have an appointment with Jeremy Moorecroft. I spoke to him yester-day. I'm here to see a Jane Doe."

"Jeremy's not in today."

"What?"

"Are you Ingrid?"

Ingrid nodded.

"The pathologist's agreed to see you herself. Take a seat."

Five minutes later, a man emerged from an interior doorway. He was dressed in a dark suit, his tie a little skewed, his top button undone. His face was sweaty and blotchy. He seemed harassed. Ingrid had been expecting to be greeted by a woman in scrubs and rubber boots. "Ingrid Skyberg?" He held out his hand. "I'm Detective Constable Fraser. I'm working on the Jane Doe case."

Ingrid shook his hand.

"I believe you might be able to tell us something about the victim?" he said.

"Only if I can positively ID her. I won't be able to do that until I've seen her."

"No—of course not. Suppose we should get on with it then." He seemed decidedly reluctant to move.

"Shall we?"

She followed Fraser down a series of featureless corridors, each one looking identical to the last, until they finally reached a set of transparent swing doors.

"God, I really hate this part of the job," the detective said. "Never gets any easier, does it?" He screwed up his face as he applied some sort of menthol rub to his nostrils. That approach didn't work for Ingrid. The menthol made her feel more nauseous than the smell of dead flesh and formaldehyde. He pushed open one of the doors and stood to one side. "After you."

The examining room was like every other she'd ever seen, on the other side of the Atlantic or this. White tile floor, blinding overhead lights, lots of stainless steel. The body was laid on a steel table, uncovered. Even from just inside the door, Ingrid could tell it was the woman she'd met on Monday night. The build was identical, same weight, same height. Plus there was the wild cherry-colored hair. There could be no mistaking that. Ingrid ventured closer to the examining table. A woman appeared from a side door. She was wearing scrubs and rubber boots. She pulled on a pair of nitrile gloves.

"Ruth Freeman. I won't shake your hand." She gave Ingrid a tight little smile. "Would you like to take a closer look?"

Ingrid managed to swallow the saliva that had gathered under her tongue. She joined the pathologist next to the body and saw the cadaver's face for the first time. It was a mess.

"The killer has—rather clumsily, I'm afraid—removed any identifying features. The teeth have been smashed, the pads of her fingers sliced off… and of course, so has the skin around the neck and upper chest. Frankly someone's butchered her to remove any identifying features. Mercifully, post-mortem."

"Is this the woman you met?" The detective constable was staying close to the door, his face had already gone a little green.

"I'm pretty sure it is. Yes."

"How sure?"

Ingrid stared at the halo of red hair, then down the pale arms toward the mutilated hands. "I'd be prepared to testify to it in a court of law. Will that do?"

"But you don't know her name, is that right?" Fraser said from the other side of the room.

"I know where she lived before she died. I guess that's somewhere for you to start."

"It's more than we had five minutes ago. Is there anything else you can tell me? Anything at all?" The detective had retrieved a note book from his pocket.

"She's Latvian. I'm pretty sure. I have a good ear for accents. Especially former Soviet ones." She was transfixed by the synthetic color of the woman's hair. It looked even brighter now under the harsh light of the autopsy room.

"And what's your connection with this woman?"

Ingrid hesitated. She thought it wise to be as vague as possible. Marshall wasn't answering her calls and until she had more information about the watch list and who it was Marshall was actually monitoring, she should tell the local cops as little as possible. "Following up on an unrelated case. An FBI matter."

The pathologist cleared her throat. "If you're finished with me… and her, perhaps you could continue your conversation outside? I do have a lot of bodies to get through."

"About the skin on her neck that was removed," Ingrid said. "She had a tattoo of a crucifix on the left hand side."

"As I said, the killer wanted to remove all identifying marks."

"Sure, I get that. I was just wondering how… professional the work was. You said he butchered her, but do you think it's possible this killer knows how to use a knife?"

"Judging by the untidy nature of the incisions, he's not been medically trained. Or if he has, he was in one hell of a hurry."

"Time of death?"

"Some time between midnight and four on Tuesday morning."

Ingrid took a moment to let that information sink in. The woman was killed just a few hours after she'd seen her.

"That it?" The pathologist looked from Ingrid to Fraser.

"Sure, thank you for your time," Ingrid said.

The pathologist gave Ingrid a nod, one seasoned professional to another, and covered the Latvian's body with a green cotton sheet.

DC Fraser swallowed noisily. "Thanks, Professor Freeman." He was out the door before the pathologist could respond. In the corridor, Ingrid found him leaning up against a wall taking deep breaths.

"Tough, huh?" she said and gave him a sympathetic smile.

"Always." He unwrapped a stick of gum and popped it in his mouth, without offering her any. "So, all I need from you is the deceased's address and I won't take up any more of your time."

Ingrid stared at the cop, his pen poised over his notebook. The green hue had left his face and the red blotchiness had returned. She hesitated. She couldn't help but feel some sense of connection with the woman lying on the cold metal table not twenty feet away. To this cop, she was just another corpse. An immigrant at that. Ingrid suddenly felt the need to protect her. From God only knew what. She couldn't just walk away. Besides, she still wasn't convinced her death wasn't connected to the man Marshall was pursuing. She must have hung up after being transferred to his voicemail over a half dozen times. Why was he ignoring her calls? The more he did, the more curious about the case she became. She was aware the cop had started tapping his pen against his notebook.

"Don't you have it written down somewhere?" he said. "In your phone, maybe?" He was getting visibly frustrated with her—the red blotches had joined up to form an angry flush.

"I want to be there," she said.

"What?"

"When you search the apartment. I want to be there."

"I don't think that's something the boss would go for. I'm sorry."

"Why don't you ask him or her?"

"Are you refusing to give me the address?"

"Not at all—I'm making a friendly request to observe the search—one cop to another."

Ingrid could see the muscles in Fraser's face working overtime as he chewed his gum and considered her request.

"If it's something you can't agree to yourself, maybe I should talk to the SIO myself? Or maybe get my superior at the embassy to do that. It's completely up to you." She smiled sweetly at him.

14

Walking up and down the driveway of the house in Dulwich, phone pressed hard against her ear, Ingrid listened to Marshall's outgoing voicemail message. Again. This time she'd decided not to hang up in frustration, but actually leave him a message.

"Hey... honey, it's me. I have some news on your watch list guy... maybe. Give me a call when you get this." She hung up and shuffled sideways to allow a pair of white suited CSIs to get past. More CSIs were heading in her direction, so she moved to the edge of the police cordon, the blue and white tape fluttering against the brick wall separating the front yard from the sidewalk. The senior investigating officer hadn't said more than a few words to her since he'd arrived. Ingrid had the distinct impression he resented her presence and wasn't afraid to show it. From her marginal position at the edge of the cordon, Ingrid looked up and down the street. Uniformed officers were conducting house to house inquiries. Tedious, but necessary work. She didn't envy them. One cop was standing on the path of the house next door, looking up at the second floor windows.

A car pulled into the curb on the other side of the road. Detective Constable Fraser climbed out. He spent a few moments talking to a uniformed officer then hurried across the street. Ingrid met him at the front gate. "Good morning, detective. Thank you so much for arranging this."

"No worries. We like to help out our American cousins." He gave her an insincere smile. He hadn't been too keen to help her a couple of hours ago.

"That's good to know. What have you managed to find out about the occupants?"

"I'm not sure I can discuss that with you, not before I've okayed it with the boss." He stuck his chin out defiantly.

"Oh come on—you and I are both foot soldiers. We both know what it's like. We do all the legwork while the superior officers get the credit. Surely sharing a little intel wouldn't hurt any."

The detective looked toward the house. Another two CSIs were just emerging from the front door. As far as Ingrid could see, they always moved around in pairs.

Fraser ran his pale tongue over his bottom lip. "I suppose you'll find out anyway," he said, grudgingly. "The property is owned by a private company that's registered overseas. We haven't been able to contact the directors of the company."

"But you have names for them?"

"And we have phone numbers and a P.O. Box. The phones have either been disconnected or they weren't valid numbers to start with."

"You think the owners were living here?"

"No—the property is let via a lettings agency. An online one. There's no local lettings agent to talk to about the flat, unfortunately."

"Have you managed to speak to anyone from the agency yet?"

"They said they never met the tenant. The whole thing was done via the internet."

"Isn't that a little risky? What if tenants didn't pay the rent, or trashed the place?"

"Didn't seem to bother them. But then it's not their flat, is it?"

"So you must have a name for the person the apartment was let to?" Ingrid wondered whether Fraser was telling her the whole truth or keeping something back. Had he really uncovered so little intel?

Fraser peered at a notebook. "Abdul Al-Ala Shehadeh. He's on their books as the tenant. He's been paying the rent regularly, but not always on time." He had a little trouble pronouncing the name. Ingrid repeated it, putting the stresses on the correct syllables.

"Yeah—that's what I said, didn't I?"

"So you think he may have sublet the apartment to our victim? Or maybe they lived there together?"

Fraser glanced toward the house.

"Come on—foot soldiers, remember?"

"I've got absolutely no idea. All I know is, a Latvian name hasn't cropped up on any official documents so far."

"So you're no nearer finding out her identity?"

"It's early days. The name on the tenancy agreement hasn't popped up anywhere else yet either: you know local doctors' surgery, dentist, that kind of thing. But it's not as if we've completed a comprehensive trawl. I do know the registered council tax payer for the property is the same overseas company that owns the flat."

"What about the neighbors? Do they know if there was a man living at the property? Do they know the victim's name? What she did for a living?"

"No one's mentioned a man as yet. And nobody seems to know very much about the victim. But again—we haven't completed our house to house inquiries." He folded his arms across his chest defensively. "You still haven't told me why the FBI is so interested in this case."

"I can't go into the details with you."

"I thought we were both foot soldiers. I've got to tell my DCI something."

"Why don't you leave that with me? The embassy will square everything with your boss. Or, most likely, your boss's boss."

Fraser raised his eyebrows.

"Standard procedure."

"If you say so."

Ingrid watched another CSI lingering just inside the front door of the building. This one was on his own. The man looked exhausted.

"Look—I've got to go," Fraser said. "I need to report back to the DCI."

"Any chance I could take a look inside?"

"I'll ask him, but I wouldn't get your hopes up."

She watched Fraser stride toward the front door. He reached it just as the CSI was coming out. The man in the Tyvek suit snapped off his gloves and shoved them into a large plastic trash can standing on the driveway. Ingrid wandered over to him. "Tough gig, huh?" she said.

"Bloody impossible."

"Really?"

He stepped back and studied her face. "Shit. You're not a reporter are you?"

She showed him her badge.

"You're a long way from home."

"I work out of the American embassy here in London."

"Why are you here? There's no US connection, as far as I know."

"It's a long story—I won't bore you with it." She flashed him a big smile and he seemed to relax a little. "Any signs of a man having lived there?"

"Not as far as I can see, but there's very little of anything. Place is practically empty."

"It is?"

He put his hands on his hips and leaned back, stretching his spine. "Looks like whoever was living there has moved out."

"That must have happened pretty fast. I was here Monday night. I didn't see any packing boxes."

The CSI shrugged at her.

"According to the pathologist, the woman died some time in the early hours of Tuesday morning. There's no way she could have packed up all her stuff."

"Maybe the dead woman they dragged out of the Thames didn't live here. Maybe this is all a waste of bloody time."

"No—it was definitely her. I'm certain."

"Well then, I've got another puzzle for you." He leaned his neck one way then the other before he spoke again. "We're getting no samples at all. Not a single one."

"What have you been looking for, specifically?"

"No—I mean no samples *at all*. Of anything. No hairs, no fingerprints, no clothing fibers, nothing."

"How can that be?"

"Exactly what I've been thinking. If this place was where the victim was living, she not only found the time to pack up and remove all her stuff before she copped it, but also managed to arrange for the whole flat to be industrially deep-cleaned."

15

After a rushed sandwich she'd picked up from a Brooklyn-style hipster deli in Dulwich, Ingrid returned to Grosvenor Square. It wasn't until she'd reached her desk and smelled the delicious aroma emanating from Jennifer's desk that she remembered the clerk had told her about the fabulous new menu in the embassy cafeteria.

"What is that?" Ingrid pointed to the steaming bowl.

"I'm sorry—I should have eaten downstairs, but I've got such a lot of stuff to do, I thought I'd work straight through."

"I was admiring it, not criticizing your eating habits."

"It's a vegan pad thai. Organic tofu."

Ingrid screwed up her nose.

"That's not as bad as it sounds. And it tastes as good as it smells." She lifted a spoon toward Ingrid's face. "Wanna try?"

"I'm good—thanks. Is Isaac around? I asked him to do a little research for me."

"I haven't seen him in a while."

"Never mind, I'll catch him later." Her cell started to buzz. Out of area. She hurried out the office and answered the call. "Hey—what the hell happened to you?"

There was a long pause at the other end of the line.

"I've been in the middle of a special operation," Marshall said. "Complete communications blackout."

"Did you even listen to the messages I left you?"

"Just about to. Is something wrong? Are you OK?" His concern sounded sincere. But she could hear the tapping of computer keys in the background. Was he attempting to multi-task?

"I want you to tell me about the guy whose bank account is on the watch list."

"I can't believe you're still talking about that. I told you to drop it." He said something away from the phone. It sounded like he was giving someone his breakfast order.

"Where are you?"

"At the office."

Ingrid distinctly heard the rattle of cutlery and clatter of dishes. "Sounds like you're in a diner."

"Nope. At my desk, working hard." Lying again, badly.

"What's this guy suspected of doing? You still haven't told me."

"It's not important—come on, you said some Latvian woman lived at the address."

"I ID'd her at the morgue."

"You did what? Why are you getting involved?"

"A watch list bank account was accessed from her address, is that reason enough? I don't understand why you're not interested."

Marshall let out a long sigh. "This is strictly between you and me, honey, OK?"

That depended on what he was about to tell her. She made a non-committal 'hmm mmm' sound.

"Lately I've been monitoring a whole heap of watch lists, keeping my eyes and ears open. You never know when you might stumble over something—a quick win. Something to impress the bosses with the minimum amount of effort from yours truly. This was just another example where I got zero results. Happens practically every day. I'm sorry I dragged you into it."

"I wouldn't call a woman's mutilated body a zero result." She went on to describe exactly what she'd seen in the morgue in graphic detail. She pictured Marshall sending his pancake stack and rashers of bacon back to the kitchen.

"But our guy didn't kill her. That's just not his style." It sounded as if he were speaking with his mouth full. "He's not a butcher. I told you—he doesn't like to get his hands dirty."

"Don't you think that the whole thing is way too coincidental? The bank account is accessed by Jane Doe and just forty-eight hours later she's found dead, all identifying marks removed?"

"She must have just been a scammer who stumbled on one of our monitored accounts. You know as well as I do those people keep pretty bad company. I hate to repeat myself, but whoever was responsible for her death, it wasn't our guy." He gulped down some liquid then tried to suppress a belch. "I appreciate your trying to help me, but really, all it's doing is wasting my time."

"Oh really?"

"I'm sorry, honey. That came out all wrong."

"OK—I won't waste another precious second—just tell me his name and I'll do a little digging of my own." Ingrid had marched all the way to the rear of the building and along the main corridor, her pace increasing the madder she got at Marshall. Now she was so pissed at him she wanted to punch something.

"Listen, honey, why don't you just leave the investigation into the Jane Doe's murder to the local cops? It's not FBI business."

"You can't know that for sure. Where's the harm in my pursuing it?" She reached the end of the corridor and started to head back toward the office.

"If you find anything pertinent, you will let me know?"

"Sure—I wouldn't leave you out of the loop, Marsh. We're a team, huh?"

He blew out a noisy breath and mumbled something inaudible. "OK—it's Darryl Wyatt. But don't complain to me when you find out how totally wrong you are."

"What did he do?"

"He murdered a woman in a restaurant in Savannah, Georgia."

"If he doesn't like to get his hands dirty, how did he kill her? What is his M.O.?"

"Our guy's a poisoner."

16

Ingrid pulled up sharply. "Poisoner?"

"Yes—that's what I said—not some knife wielding maniac."

"What kind of poison did he use?"

"I really don't have time for this—check out the details for yourself."

"Please, Marshall, just tell me—"

A fraction of a second later, the disconnected tone bleeped in her ear. He'd hung up on her.

Really?

She was just about to call him back when she thought better of it. Damn Marshall and his 'quick win' watch lists. She'd just have to work this case without any help from him.

A poisoner. What if Darryl Wyatt *was* right here in London? What if the Latvian had gotten too close to discovering his true identity and he'd had to kill her to eradicate the threat. Was it possible he'd had something to do with Matthew Fuller's death?

She started to run.

Ingrid quickly reached the office and hurried to her desk, aware her speed had aroused the interest of both Jennifer and Isaac.

"Is there something wrong?" Jennifer asked.

"Nope. Everything's just fine," Ingrid snapped back at her. She'd been more curt than she'd meant. "Sorry, Jennifer, just really busy right now."

"Can I help at all?"

"I'll be sure to holler when you can."

The clerk shrugged her shoulders a little theatrically and went back to her computer. Ingrid fired up her own desktop PC and waited for long agonizing seconds while the machine went through the slow start-up routine. Then she logged into the main FBI database and tapped Darryl Wyatt's name into the search box. Three records came up for that name, but only one was a murder suspect last seen in Savannah. Ingrid quickly scanned the information for the name and contact details of the investigating detective. She could read plenty of dry facts on the database, but they would constitute just a fraction of the intel gathered by the team on the ground. Only the barest details would have been keyed into the database—Ingrid hadn't met a cop or a Fed yet who enjoyed typing.

A few moments later Ingrid was on hold at Savannah-Chatham Police Department, waiting to be put through to a Detective Trooe. When he finally took the call, Ingrid quickly introduced herself and told the detective what she was calling about.

"The peanut poisoner?" Trooe said as soon as she'd finished. His voice was rich and deep and strangely comforting.

"I'm sorry?"

"Darryl Wyatt, right?"

"I know practically nothing about the case. I was hoping you could enlighten me. Do you have the time right now?"

"Sure. Hang on a second."

Ingrid heard the sound of the receiver clunking down onto a hard surface, then a door close, then the creak of a leather chair. While she was waiting, she scrolled through the records on the database until she found a photograph of Darryl Wyatt.

"That's better," Trooe said, "a little quieter."

"We have a picture of him here," Ingrid said. "It's a little indistinct, but Wyatt is white, thirty-three years of age, dark hair, with a beard. Is that right?"

"I can send you through a better photograph than that. Sounds as though you're looking at his drivers' license picture."

"Just now… you called Wyatt—"

"The peanut poisoner. That's what he did—he killed that poor lady by feeding her peanuts. She had a real bad allergy."

Ingrid felt a sudden sense of disappointment. It seemed Wyatt wasn't quite the 'poisoner' Marshall had suggested. "He hasn't poisoned anyone else?"

"Not as far as we know." The leather chair creaked a little more. "So, you think Wyatt is in London?"

"That's what I'm trying to find out. How well do you remember the case?"

"Oh it's crystal clear. It was only twelve months ago."

With his slow southern drawl, Ingrid wasn't sure whether Detective Trooe was being sarcastic. "I guess you've investigated plenty of other homicides since then?"

"A few, but nothing like this one. This one kinda sticks in the memory."

"Can you go through the highlights for me?"

"I guess you like using the computer about as much as I do, huh?"

"You can give me the background I won't find in the official records."

"I sure can. Where do you want to start?"

"Tell me everything you can about Darryl Wyatt."

She heard the detective sniff. "That particular request won't take real long to answer. He was using a false identity. The ID of a dead man. I can't tell you a whole lot about him. He did have a girlfriend while he was working at the restaurant, he was dating the restaurant manager. I can give you her contact details when we're through, if you want."

"That'd be really helpful." Ingrid wriggled into her chair, it felt like she might be in for a long session. "He worked at the restaurant where the woman died?"

"He was the maitre d', had the job there for a couple months before he made his move." There was a clunk and a buzzing on the line for a few moments. "Tell me your email address, I'll send you the photograph we have of Wyatt that his girlfriend gave us."

Ingrid spelled out the address. "So Wyatt was early thirties, white... dark or fair skinned?"

"Depends how much time he spent in the sun I guess. See for yourself when the picture comes through. He was a little under six feet tall, medium build, maybe even a little athletic, if you're talking tennis player rather than football." He made a sound as if he were sucking his teeth.

"That's it?"

"Real charming with the ladies, by all accounts. He had good dental work, they all seemed to remember."

"Any distinguishing features?"

"He did as a matter of fact. Something only the girlfriend reported—a tattoo on his left forearm."

"Of what?"

"A dark red rose with the word 'MOM' written across it."

Ingrid sketched something similar in her notebook. "Sentimental."

"Not a word I'd use to describe him."

"What was his connection to the victim? Why did he want her dead?"

"We just don't know enough about the guy to work it out. Mind you, Mrs Highsmith musta made plenty of enemies over the years." He sniffed again. "You really haven't looked at the details on file at all, have you?"

"I'm sorry. I guess I was a little eager."

"I'm just joking with you, I'd do exactly the same thing in your position."

"Thanks for being so accommodating. Why did she have so many enemies?"

"Barbara Highsmith was a congresswoman for Georgia. Not when she died, she didn't get re-elected a second time, but before she was elected to the House, she was the District Attorney here. Any number of disgruntled convicts or disappointed voters could have been lining up to take potshots at her."

"Can there be any doubt that Wyatt was responsible for her death?"

"Only three people in the restaurant knew about the allergy: the chef, the restaurant manager and the maitre d'. We interviewed the chef and the manager extensively. We couldn't interview Wyatt because he skipped town right after she was killed."

"Maybe he left for some other reason."

"Highsmith carried around two of those special auto-injectors—just in case she came into contact with peanuts accidentally. She kept both of them in her purse. Her purse never left her side. Except on that day. A number of witnesses confirmed they saw Wyatt remove the purse from under her table. They thought nothing of it at the time. They just assumed he was taking it to the cloakroom. The purse was never found."

"How soon did he leave? Did he stay to watch her die?"

"The sick bastard sure did. While everyone else was screaming for help, looking for the missing purse, calling 9-1-1, he just stood there and watched while she gasped her last breath."

"What did you find at his address when you searched it?"

"The address he gave the restaurant was fake. Just like every other piece of information they had about him. We couldn't track down an address for him hard as we tried. It was as if he didn't really exist. The whole thing musta taken some careful planning." The creaking leather noise sounded again, louder than before. "Listen, I've got a briefing I got to be at in precisely two minutes."

"Thanks for your time, detective. Would it be OK if we spoke again later?"

"Sure. And the name's Carl. I'll send over the girlfriend's details."

Ingrid put down the phone and sank back in her seat, thinking about what she'd just learned. Wyatt was a poisoner who was aware of a weakness in his victim that wasn't widely known. He used that vulnerability to kill her. Matthew Fuller had kept his OCD and excessive hand washing secret. Very few people knew about his vulnerability.

The similarity between the Highsmith and Fuller cases might be slight, but too significant to ignore. Now more than ever she had to know who had wanted Matthew Fuller dead. And the best place to start was Witness Protection. For any hope of success she'd have to bring in the big guns.

She grabbed her cell from the desk and ran out of the office.

17

Ingrid reached Sol's office to discover it was empty. There was no sign of his cigarettes on the desk, so she guessed he was out back in the embassy compound getting his nicotine fix. She headed back downstairs.

Sure enough, she found Sol standing on his own, keeping his distance from a nearby group of kitchen and janitorial staff. It wasn't like Sol to act so aloof, he could talk to anyone about pretty much anything. Then she saw the reason for his enforced isolation. He had a wire trailing from his ear to his cell phone. He obviously didn't want anyone to overhear his conversation. As Ingrid approached, she noticed he was nodding every few seconds, but not saying anything. She supposed it was another conference call. He seemed to be spending more and more time on trans-Atlantic calls and less and less managing his agents. Ingrid wondered idly why the big cheeses in D.C. were so interested in the Bureau's International Program and whether it might have any impact on her own work. She sure as hell hoped it wouldn't.

When he saw her, Sol held up a finger, then hit a button on his cell.

"Bureaucratic bullshit," he said, and smiled at her. "Hey, I hope you're getting excited about dinner at chez moi?"

"What?"

"I thought it'd be a chance for Isaac to get to know you a little, outside the office environment. I get the impression he looks up to you."

Ingrid had been forced to endure Mrs Franklin's cooking shortly after she'd started working at the embassy. She wasn't keen to repeat the experience. "I think I'm busy that night."

"I haven't even finalized a date yet. Tell me when you're free and we'll work around your... commitments." Sol knew very well that her social engagements were few and far between. She was more likely to be at her desk than anywhere else most nights. He had her. There was no way she could politely back out now.

"This week is completely full. What about next month?"

"It's a welcome to the embassy dinner for Isaac, don't you think next month may be a little late?" Before she could answer, Sol held up his finger again. He un-muted the phone, said, "I couldn't agree more, Jason." Then hit the mute button again.

"You're listening to them and me at the same time?"

"Incredible, isn't it? Multitasking, huh? Meanwhile you still haven't come up with an excuse to wriggle out of your dinner date."

"Monday!" she said without thinking.

"Good. I'll tell Maddy. She'll make us a feast."

That was exactly what Ingrid was afraid of.

"What can I do for you?" Sol asked.

"You listened to the message I left you about my new case?"

"The dead trader?"

"I need you to try again with Witness Protection."

Sol pulled a pained face then shook his head. "I'm sorry—I just can't. They're acting completely within their remit. If they responded to every request for information, they wouldn't be doing a real good job of protecting their witnesses, now would they? The system works—let's not screw with it."

"Did you even speak to them yet?"

"I didn't think it was appropriate."

"You might have let me know."

"I'm telling you now."

"But Fuller is already dead. His dad's dead. He didn't have any siblings. There's no one to protect except his mother."

"Doesn't she deserve protecting?"

"Oh come on, Sol. You know what I mean."

"I'd look for a motive for his murder a little closer to home if I were you. Dig a little into Matthew Fuller's life here. Something that happened to his family when he was a small child isn't likely to have come back to haunt him so many years later."

"But he's been here less than a year. How likely do you think it is he's crossed someone so badly they'd want him dead?"

"Hey—he's a City trader. They can't go anywhere without crossing somebody. And according to your message, the local cops still haven't ruled out the possibility that the attack was on the bank rather than specific employees."

"Only officially—that's just a political exercise to make Fisher Krupps feel as if they're taking a potential threat seriously. There's been absolutely no intel on possible extremists targeting the bank. It seems the toxic substance was removed shortly after Fuller's death. How does that square with doing as much damage as possible to Fisher Krupps?"

"But isn't that scenario still much more likely than someone from Matthew Fuller's dim and distant past coming all the way to London to kill him?"

For a moment Ingrid considered mentioning a possible link between Fuller's death and the murder of the ex-congresswoman in Georgia. But she knew the similarities between the two cases weren't strong enough to convince Sol of any connection. He'd just tell her to dig up more intel.

A first few drops of rain started to fall, fat and heavy. Sol pulled up his collar and sucked on his cigarette.

"You'll catch pneumonia," Ingrid told him, and realized she must have sounded just like his wife.

"Don't worry about me—I've located myself a quiet little closet inside the building that's warm and dry. No smoke detectors, no nicotine police. This turns into a downpour, I can still carry on smoking."

"Maybe the rain is a sign you should stop."

"Oh sure. If I didn't smoke, I'd never be able to get through these interminable conference calls."

"Fine, you carry on." Ingrid held up both hands in surrender, said goodbye and returned to the office.

Back at her desk, she punched the number for the Savannah-Chatham Metropolitan Police Department into her phone. She got through to Carl Trooe a lot faster this time.

"Detective Trooe, S-C-M-P-D." There was that rich tone again. Ingrid hadn't realized before just how much he sounded like her father. The accent was all wrong, but the honeyed tones were just the same.

"Good morning, Detective Trooe, I'm Special Agent Ingrid Skyberg, we spoke earlier."

"Now I'm not likely to forget your lovely voice, am I?" He chuckled a little. "Did that photograph come through OK? And the contact details for Wyatt's girlfriend?"

Ingrid quickly scanned her inbox. "They did—thank you so much for that. Now you're out of your briefing, can you spare me a little more of your precious time?"

"As you ask so nicely…"

"I appreciate that—thank you… Carl."

"The pleasure is all mine. What do you need to know?"

"I have a case I'm investigating here at the moment, also a poisoning, very different circumstances to the Barbara Highsmith murder, but—"

"Similar enough to make you want to dig a little deeper, huh?"

"That's right, I figure, if Wyatt was responsible for both murders, and it's a really big stretch, no more than a dumb hunch at this stage—"

"Hey, no hunch is so dumb it doesn't deserve a little attention."

"If he did murder this guy in London, I need to know as much as I can about him. I need to know why he targeted an ex-congresswoman and a City trader. What did he have against them both to want them dead? Do you know if Wyatt had any connection to high finance or big business?"

"Like I told you before, we know very little about the guy. He covered his tracks too damn well. We did recover some DNA samples from the girlfriend's apartment. But the DNA didn't match anything on record, so that didn't help us any. You got DNA from your crime scene over there?"

Ingrid remembered the Latvian's apartment in Dulwich that had been industrially deep-cleaned. She supposed it was just possible Miguel Hernandez had left some trace of his DNA behind at the bank. She'd have to speak to Mbeke about it. Was it really possible the same man was responsible for killing an ex-congresswoman, a City Trader and an internet-scamming Latvian? "I'd need to talk to the local cops about any DNA evidence. Wyatt's girlfriend… earlier you said you interviewed her intensively."

"We did. She was real pissed at Wyatt for duping her the way he did. She was happy to cooperate."

"But still she couldn't tell you anything about his history?"

"Nothing he'd told her about himself turned out to be true."

"Can you tell me anything about her?"

"She was seriously freaked out by what happened. I think she was a little scared of what Darryl Wyatt might do to her. I tried to reassure her he was long gone. But then she told us about his temper. He'd hit her a few times. Never where it'd show, he was real clever about it."

"Why did she stay with him?"

"Too scared to end it. I think she was mighty relieved when he skipped town."

"How long had they been together?"

"Not long—she got him the job at the restaurant."

"She did?"

"She blames herself for the whole thing. Like I say, you're better off speaking to her directly. She might remember something relevant she didn't even tell us."

"I'll do just that, thank you, Carl."

"Anytime."

Ingrid exchanged direct dial numbers with Trooe then and immediately called Darryl Wyatt's ex-girlfriend. Her call transferred straight to voicemail. At least the woman was using the same cell phone number. Ingrid left a short message and spelled out her email address—she didn't want the cost of a trans-Atlantic call to deter the woman from getting back to her. As soon as she put the phone down, her cell started to buzz.

It was Patrick Mbeke.

"Can you spare an hour or so?" he asked.

"You've got a lead?"

"Not exactly. Just an appointment with the pathologist. He wants to show me something. Thought you might like to take a look too."

18

Before she left the embassy, Ingrid emailed a copy of Darryl Wyatt's photograph to DC Fraser, together with strict instructions for him to ask the Latvian's neighbors if they'd seen Wyatt at the property. It was a long shot —Wyatt had probably altered his appearance since his time in Savannah, but it was just possible the picture might jog somebody's memory. She also told Fraser about the rose tattoo on Wyatt's left arm.

Detective Inspector Mbeke met her at the main entrance of St Pancras Public Mortuary and escorted her to the autopsy room. "I haven't been in one of these places since I was in uniform," he said.

At that moment Ingrid realized it was her second morgue of the day. God it had been a long one. "Will you be OK?"

"Don't really have much choice." He managed a smile. It was possibly the first time Ingrid had seen him properly smile. Even though it flashed across his face for a matter of moments, it brightened his whole expression so much she felt she was looking at a completely different man.

"Thanks for bringing me in on this," she said.

"You make it sound like a visit to the mortuary is a pleasant afternoon excursion."

"Some of the local cops I've worked with here in London find it a little hard to be… inclusive."

"You're referring to my SIO?"

"Not specifically." She was actually thinking more of Detective Constable Fraser.

When they reached a set of double doors, Mbeke stopped and stepped to one side. "I was about to say, 'after you', but I suppose that would be a very *un*gentlemanly thing to do."

"Don't worry about me." Ingrid pushed through the doors and saw Matthew Fuller's naked body laid out on a steel examining table. His chest was open, the ribs pulled apart on each side and the skin clamped down, away from the gaping hole. She pulled up quickly. A man in scrubs on the other side of the room turned to look at her. In his hands he was holding a bloody organ. From the shape and size, Ingrid guessed it was a heart.

"Ah good, you've arrived," the pathologist said. "I'm Colm Anderson." He carefully laid the heart in a steel dish. "Sorry to get you down here, but I thought it made sense to show you, rather than try to explain it over the phone."

"What are we looking at, exactly?" Ingrid stepped closer to the examining table and forced herself to peer into the corpse's thoracic cavity. It was just that—a hole where his organs should have been.

"It's easier to demonstrate." The pathologist held up the steel dish containing Fuller's heart. "Look at this."

Patrick Mbeke shuffled a little closer. He seemed even more reluctant to be in an autopsy room than DC Fraser had been earlier. He screwed up his eyes and nose and glanced toward the dish, all the while angling his head away from it.

Anderson prodded the heart with a gloved finger. "I've rarely seen a healthier example." He pulled a green cloth from another dish with a flourish, as if he were a conjuror snapping a table cloth beneath a full set of dinnerware. In the dish was a large liver, deep maroon in color and smooth in texture. "Same with this. In fact all his organs are in perfect working order."

"And you wanted us to see this for ourselves because..." Mbeke swallowed repeatedly. Ingrid wondered whether he might be forced to excuse himself from the room altogether.

"The healthy nature of the deceased's organs got me thinking. We're looking for a toxin that left no visible trace."

Mbeke swallowed again. "OK. But would you mind saying whatever else it is you have to say in your office?"

"I have something else to show you first." The pathologist strode toward the body. He lifted Fuller's left hand and gently laid the fingers over his, more like a lover than a medical examiner. With the little finger of his left hand he traced around the edges of Fuller's fingernails. "See how red they are? And the skin on the knuckles too?" If I didn't know this man was a City trader I would have sworn he worked in an old-fashioned laundry, his hands immersed in strong detergent all day long."

"And?" Mbeke was edging back toward the door.

"The broken skin on the hands is key. Even with repeated washing, if a poison is absorbed through the subcutaneous layer of skin, one wouldn't normally expect its effects to have quite the impact it had on this chap. But the broken skin meant that he absorbed much more of the poison than the other victim and at a much faster rate." He pressed a fingertip against one of the corpse's knuckles as if to reinforce his point. "The skin on the hands signifies something else too. There's no blistering or ulceration. That means we can rule out the obvious substances— sulfuric or hydrochloric acid. Which prompted me to do a little research of my own. Having dismissed the possibility of harsh chemicals, I decided to look for something a little more... natural. And I think I've hit on the culprit. It's consistent with the symptoms and the ultimate fatal outcome."

Mbeke had made it half way to the door by now. "Fascinating. Would you mind sharing that information with us?"

"Aconite."

Mbeke shrugged and looked at Ingrid. She shrugged back at him.

"I've requested it's fast-tracked, ahead of any other tests, I'm so sure. As soon as it's confirmed, the doctors can set about helping that poor chap in the hospital."

"Aconite?" Mbeke said.

"You might know it by another name: monkshood or wolf's bane?"

"Still not ringing any bells. Is it easy to get hold of?" Ingrid said.

"Common as anything. In fact I think I may have some in my garden. Tall stems with bell-shaped purple flowers. Beautiful... but rather deadly. As this unfortunate gentleman can testify." He snapped off his gloves and marched toward the doors, pushing one open with his behind. "Now, I rather think you may need a cup of hot, sweet tea, inspector."

Ten minutes later, Patrick Mbeke seemed to have completely recovered. He thanked Anderson for his time, even though, Ingrid thought, it should have been the other way around, and they made swiftly for the exit.

All the while the detective had been drinking his tea, Ingrid had been wondering whether or not to mention the poisoning case in Savannah. Like Detective Trooe had said, no hunch was so dumb it should be ignored. So when they reached the front entrance and stepped out into the fresh air, Ingrid launched into an abridged version of the Barbara Highsmith investigation not forgetting to mention the fact that the perpetrator had given his employers a false address. She spoke so rapidly she barely paused for breath. When she was done she stared at Mbeke expectantly.

"And you think your... what do you call them... your *unsub* is here in London?"

Ingrid supposed Mbeke was basing his information on some American cop show he'd seen. "He's not strictly speaking an *un*sub, as we have identified him."

"But you don't know his real name."

"True. But we do know what he looks like. We have a pretty good photograph of him."

"Even if it is a long shot, I suppose we should at least rule it out." He pointed his key fob toward a black BMW parked in the lot outside the morgue. The alarm chirruped and the doors unlocked. "You need a lift down there or do you have your own transport?"

"Why, where're we going?"

"Fisher Krupps. See if your unsub looks like our missing suspect."

19

Ingrid had Jennifer send the best quality photo of Darryl Wyatt to both her cell and Mbeke's. First stop was the cleaning supervisor's office. Even if the woman wasn't that familiar with Hernandez's features herself, she could point them in the direction of Patience Toure, who had to know what he looked like. Hopefully Toure was on duty today.

"Nope, don't know him," the supervisor said after glancing at Ingrid's phone for barely two seconds.

"Please take a closer look, madam," Mbeke asked, and shoved his phone under her nose. She stared at the image for a little while.

The picture of Darryl Wyatt showed a youngish man with short cropped dark brown hair and a tightly shaved beard. His faced was slightly turned away, from the camera, as if he hadn't been aware his photo was being taken. His skin was tanned, but hardly lined at all.

After a few more moments studying the picture, the supervisor's answer was exactly the same. "Sorry—that's not a face I've seen before."

"How well do you know the cleaners who work here, in general?" Ingrid asked.

"We don't go to bingo together, if that's what you mean."

"But it's possible you're not that familiar with his face?" Mbeke gave her an encouraging smile.

"S'pose not. You'd be better off speaking to Patience."

"She's in the building?"

The supervisor grabbed her schedule from beneath a half-empty cup of coffee and studied it carefully. She sniffed. "You're in luck. Kind of."

Mbeke raised an eyebrow.

"She's here, but she's on toilet duty today. She could be anywhere in the building. I've got a mobile number for her, I can give her a call." She reached toward the phone on her desk.

"That won't be necessary, I have it too." Ingrid didn't want the cleaner to get spooked and decide to flee. "Thank you for your time, ma'am."

"Do we really have to trawl through all the lavatories in this building?" Mbeke said when they emerged from the elevator onto the main reception area.

"Hey, come on—it's only sixteen stories. The exercise will do us good."

He looked her up and down. "I think neither of us particularly need it." He folded his arms across his chest, his biceps straining against the material of his jacket. Ingrid felt her face warming.

"So, how about I take the ladies' restrooms and you take the men's?"

Mbeke started to move away then stopped. "What if we miss her? What if she's in the lift while we're in the toilet?"

"Maybe we'll get lucky." Ingrid let out a breath. It was a stupid idea. "OK, rather than call in a whole army of cops to do this—"

"Believe me, the SIO is not going to approve that much manpower."

"Why don't I call her cell while you wait at the rear exit, just in case she decides to leave the building. The guy on the front desk can watch the main doors."

"Give me five minutes to get down there," he said, but made no attempt to move. "Unless we do this the other way round. It is my investigation, after all." He planted his feet more firmly on the marble floor of the lobby.

"I think she's more likely to speak to me. You represent authority here. I'm just some schmuck from the US embassy with no ax to grind and no powers of arrest. And anyway, I'll be showing her a picture of *my* unsub." She pulled her phone from a pocket. "Before you go, you should call the personnel department to circulate this photograph to all members of staff. I'm guessing they all have smart phones. The traders at least. See if they recognize the guy."

"Any more orders?"

"You know I really appreciate your help."

He raised an eyebrow before swiftly turning around and heading toward the security guy sitting on the reception desk. "I'll text you when I'm in position," he called over his shoulder.

Less than ten minutes later, Ingrid's phone bleeped with Mbeke's message. She called Patience Toure. To Ingrid's surprise, the woman didn't hesitate in telling her where she was. Ingrid headed for the fifth floor ladies' restroom.

When she found Toure waiting for her in the corridor outside the bathroom, leaning heavily on her cleaning cart, Ingrid texted Mbeke.

"You still looking for Miguel?" Toure said as Ingrid approached. "He's a good man. You are wasting your time."

"We only want to speak to him, ma'am. If he hadn't just disappeared, we'd have found out for ourselves whether he's good or bad."

Toure shook her head and muttered, "Wasting your time."

Ingrid found the photo of Darryl Wyatt on her phone and showed it to the cleaner.

"What's this?"

"Please take a good look, ma'am."

Toure squinted down at the image. "One second." She produced a pair of glasses from a pocket and stared at the photograph good and hard.

"You recognize him?"

"Never seen him before."

Ingrid studied the cleaner's face carefully. Her expression remained blank. Too blank. As if she were struggling to keep it that way. "You're saying this isn't Hernandez... this isn't Miguel?"

Toure shook her head.

"Please take another look. Try to imagine him without the beard and maybe with darker hair. Or paler skin."

"It's not him."

"Is there any way you could be mistaken?"

"I may need glasses, but I'm not blind." Toure shoved the cell back at Ingrid and muttered to herself in French. "You are wasting your time looking for Miguel. He's a good man. I have met plenty of bad ones. Miguel is not one of them."

"I look forward to discovering that for myself."

"When you find Miguel. What will you do to him?"

"We just want to talk. He may know something important. Can you think of anywhere he might have taken himself?"

The cleaner blinked her disgust at the question and turned her head away, as if answering was the last thing she would dream of doing. "He's not a bad man. That is all you need to know."

Out of the corner of her eye, Ingrid noticed Mbeke appear at the end of the corridor. He'd taken his time. Maybe he was keeping his distance so that he didn't freak Toure so much she'd stop talking altogether. But Ingrid doubted anything the detective could throw at this woman would scare her. She was made of sterner stuff. Ingrid saw him shrug his shoulders. "I appreciate your help, Madame Toure, I really do." She said goodbye and jogged toward the detective inspector.

"Make any progress?"

Ingrid shook her head.

"It was worth a try."

"I'm not convinced she's telling me the truth. Seems she thinks a lot of the guy. Maybe she's protecting him."

"Got any ideas?"

"If she does know something about Hernandez, she's decided not to talk, and I don't think anything I can say would persuade her to." She looked down at the picture of Darryl Wyatt then shoved the phone in her pocket. "You'll let me know if Fuller's tissue tests come back positive for aconite?"

"I'm surprised you even need to ask." He gave her a smile.

Ingrid stopped at the exit and turned to the inspector. "What's your next move?"

"We're still in the process of interviewing everyone Fuller knew here in the UK. He doesn't seem to have been the most popular of blokes—he pretty much kept himself to himself—but so far we haven't found any evidence that he made any enemies either."

"So we're no closer to discovering a motive?"

"Not by a long way. You will let me know if you come across any evidence that connects my case with the one in the US?"

"Of course," Ingrid said.

All she had to do now was find some.

20

Ingrid returned to the embassy to do a little more digging. Even if the two poisoning cases weren't linked, in theory it was still possible the man on Marshall's watch list was right here in the UK and was responsible for the murder of the cherry-headed Latvian.

She reached her desk to discover another note from Jennifer. This one had to have been written in less of a hurry. It clearly informed her she had an appointment in Kilburn at ten-thirty a.m. the next morning. A woman had reported her husband missing to the local cops, but was frustrated they hadn't taken her seriously. She wanted the embassy to do something about it.

Ingrid slammed a hand down onto her desk and cursed under her breath.

Angela Tate was due to arrive at ten to conduct her 'fly-on-the-wall' interview. Ingrid had been hoping it'd be a really slow day and the journalist would get so bored watching her sitting at her desk, maybe helping Jennifer a little with her filing, that she'd give up on the idea and leave of her own accord. An actual missing persons interview might be just a little too interesting. Then there was the whole issue of client confidentiality.

Screw it.

Keeping the hack away from the embassy could only be a good thing. She decided to leave both arrangements just the way they were. If Tate misbehaved, Ingrid would have the perfect excuse to terminate their little 'arrangement' and hopefully the debt she owed the journalist could be written off.

She tapped the woman's details into her phone and screwed up Jennifer's note. For some reason Jennifer liked communicating on paper when Ingrid wasn't at her desk. Maybe she thought an actual physical message was less likely to be ignored.

Maybe she was right.

Judging by the lack of coats and bags on and around Jennifer and Isaac's desks, Ingrid figured they'd both left for the night. Which meant she had all the time she needed to investigate the Barbara Highsmith case without interruption. She dialed Detective Trooe's number.

"Detective Trooe, how can I help?"

"Detective, hi. This is Special Agent Skyberg, I wonder, do you have time to speak to me about the Highsmith case?"

"I just finished my shift."

"Oh, I see." She couldn't mask her disappointment. "I can call back tomorrow."

"No—I meant you got as much time as you need. Nothing to rush home for except a leftover pizza and a couple cans of beer. They sure ain't going anywhere. You spoken to the girlfriend yet?"

"I left her a message."

"Keep trying. She'll get back to you eventually, I'm sure."

Ingrid settled back into her seat. "I'm guessing, given the high profile nature of the victim, you investigated who she might have crossed so badly they wanted her dead?"

"Sure. I looked into who she put away when she was a District Attorney. Then narrowed it down to anyone who had been released from jail. Then reduced the list again, to those matching even a vague description of Wyatt."

"And?"

"No one of interest fitted the bill. Just when I thought I'd gotten a little closer, I'd discover the ex-con had died, or was built like a quarterback, or couldn't string two sentences together. You gotta remember, Wyatt was civilized and charming enough to get himself a job as a maitre d'."

"So you found no likely candidates at all from Highsmith's past?"

"No one she put away. So then I moved on to her new profession as a congresswoman. Again—lots of potential enemies in politics. I just wasn't prepared for how many. She had a lot of fights during her time in Congress. Just a little too outspoken to stay the course. It's incredible she ever got re-elected. Folk are real conservative here in Georgia, even the Democrats."

"She was elected for the first time in November 2006, is that right?"

"Re-elected 2008, then lost in November 2010."

"And the people she fought with? Did she make any of them mad enough to want to plan her murder?"

"Plenty mighta wanted to strangle her right there in the House, but nobody who'd bear a grudge so strong they'd actually do anything about it."

"So pretty much all your leads came to nothing?"

"It's heartbreaking. We put in so many man-hours. And came up with diddly."

It didn't give Ingrid much hope she'd find a potential enemy lurking in Highsmith's past. She let out a sigh. Trooe must have heard her.

"It ain't all bad. There's one little thing you might find interesting." He paused. "I'm sorry, I got another call coming in, give me a second to get rid of them."

Ingrid had been doodling thoughtlessly on a notepad as she listened to the detective. She glanced down at the page to discover she'd drawn a cube with lots of arrows pointing toward it. The inside of the cube was empty. It reflected the conversation she was having pretty accurately. She tore out the page and threw it in the trash.

"Sorry about that. My ex-wife," Trooe said. "Doesn't do to ignore her." He sucked in a breath. "Where were we?"

"Something I might find interesting."

"Sure. Well, maybe not that interesting. But anyhow, back in 2008, the congresswoman had a pretty close call with the Grim Reaper. Same deal—she ate something she shouldn't."

"Peanuts?"

"Yep—but she had one of those pen whatchamacallits she stuck into her leg and came back from the brink."

"You think she was deliberately poisoned then too?"

"Who knows? Her people hushed it right up at the time—Georgia being the peanut state and all. Didn't want the voters finding out she was violently allergic to one of the state's biggest exports. I only know about it because I got talking to an agent who was on her security detail at the time. You know how it is—one cop to another—strictly off the record."

"But if an attempt was made on her life at the time, shouldn't it have been investigated? The Bureau should have gotten involved."

"They did. Your people were very discreet about it. They just put it down to an unfortunate accident. Someone at the restaurant got fired. And before you ask, yes I did follow up on that. It was an assistant chef. Who was a woman."

"Must have been very frustrating for you."

"The case is still open. I go back to it once in a while, on my own time. Occasionally the ex-congresswoman's family kicks up a stink and then I'll get permission from the boss to dedicate some proper resources to it. But I guess if our man doesn't wanna be found he's just gonna stay hidden."

21

Ingrid hung up and looked down at the pad on her desk. This time the arrows were inside the cube pointing out. She tore off the page of scribblings and wrote a note on a fresh page to remind herself to follow up what Barbara Highsmith's legal specialism had been before she became District Attorney. But right now she had a restaurant manager to track down.

It was easier than she expected. Darryl Wyatt's ex-girlfriend picked up almost immediately. Ingrid quickly introduced herself.

And the woman hung up.

Ingrid called back and the voicemail kicked in right away. She left another message, imploring the woman to call her back. Without more information about Darryl Wyatt, Ingrid felt her investigation would go nowhere at all.

As she sat at her desk, staring at her phone, willing it to ring, Ingrid felt the first pang of hunger. She checked the time—it was ten minutes after eight. She wondered if the kitchen would still be open. There were plenty of personnel in the building, and would be right through the night. Surely someone on duty would be able to fix her a sandwich? She quickly made her way to the cafeteria, her hunger growing with every step, her cell phone gripped tightly in her hand. If Wyatt's ex-girlfriend did call back, Ingrid sure as hell didn't want to miss her.

When she arrived, Ingrid discovered the cafeteria in darkness. She'd half expected to see a group of drivers or counter-terror agents huddling around a corner table discussing the latest ballgame over a cup of coffee. Or maybe playing a game of cards. The lights flickered on as she stepped over the threshold. She called toward the kitchen, on the other side of the counter. "Hey! Anyone home? Hello?"

No welcoming greeting called back to her. As she approached the counter she could see the coffee machine was lifeless, the glass jug that seemed permanently full during the day, empty and upside down. For a moment she thought she heard movement from within the kitchen. She called out again. Again there was no reply. Maybe she could fix herself a sandwich. She slipped behind the counter and pushed at the door that led into the kitchen. It was locked. Her fantasy of freshly-seared tuna salad on whole wheat dissolved in an instant. Instead, she headed for the vending machine and got herself a Snickers bar. Just as she was tucking it into a pocket, her phone started to vibrate. It was an out of area number. She answered and gave her name.

"Sorry I hung up before," the woman on the other end told her. "I guess I panicked."

"That's quite all right, Miss Townsend. This call must be costing you a fortune, shall I call you back?"

"It's OK—has he killed again?" She swallowed. "Only if he has, I'm not sure I want to know about it."

"What makes you think that?" Ingrid would have expected the woman's first question to have been, "have you found him?"

"I… I guess… I wasn't totally surprised when it happened the first time."

Ingrid hurried around the tables and out of the cafeteria. She took the stairs back to her office. Now she had Bella Townsend on the line, she didn't want to risk losing the connection due to bad reception in the elevator.

"It'd be really helpful for me if you could explain why you felt that way."

"Where do I begin?"

"How about we start when you first met Mr Wyatt?"

"Or whatever his goddamn name is." Townsend took a noisy breath. "You know he only got that job because of me?"

"There's absolutely no way you should blame yourself."

"I'm just so mad I let myself be sucked in like that."

"How did you meet him?"

"You want the whole, drawn out story?"

"I'd like to know everything I can about Wyatt, you're the only person who knew him well."

"I'm not sure I really knew him at all. But I can certainly tell you how we met. He was a customer at the restaurant. I helped him get to his table—his leg was in a splint, he was on crutches. I felt sorry for the guy. Not only had he busted his leg, but his date didn't turn up." There was the noisy breath again. "There he was all dejected and stoic, trying to make a joke out of a bad situation. He told me it was a blind date. 'She must have taken one look at me and run!' he said. He was kinda cute. Handsome even. I guess he charmed me. When he spoke to me it was as if I was the only person in the room. That never happens to me." She fell silent. Ingrid could hear her breathing at the other end of the echoey line. "With hindsight I realize that the whole thing was an act. He wanted me to feel sorry for him. His ankle probably wasn't even sprained, he probably never even had a date. What a pushover I must have seemed."

"You were just in the wrong place at the wrong time." Ingrid got back to the office, she threw the slightly melted Snickers bar onto her desk and sank down onto her chair.

"Tell me about it. So, anyway, long story a little shorter, we started dating."

"How long before he got the job as maitre d'?"

"Clifford, the previous maitre d', left unexpectedly just a couple weeks after I first met Darryl."

"Can you give me Clifford's last name?" Ingrid grabbed her notebook.

"Sure, it's… Quigley. Why?"

"Do you know what happened to make him leave so suddenly?"

"He just upped and left."

"Without an explanation?"

"We got a postcard from him from Hawaii, saying he needed a break."

"Was he a postcard kinda guy?"

"Actually no—it wasn't Cliff's style at all. I was surprised when we received it… Wait a minute… are you investigating Cliff's disappearance or something?"

"The detectives who investigated the case at the time didn't talk to you about Mr Quigley?"

"They never even asked me about Clifford. Jesus, you don't really think—"

"I'm sure Clifford's just fine. I'm just covering all the bases." Ingrid made a note to follow up. A name like Clifford Quigley had to be pretty straightforward to track down. "Was Darryl Wyatt good at his job?"

"He was a complete professional. When we first started dating, I thought his charm was dedicated to me. What a joke! He could turn it on like a kitchen faucet. The female patrons loved him. Some of the male ones too. Barbara Highsmith was particularly enamored."

"How did that make you feel?"

"Is this relevant to your investigation?"

"Humor me, if it's not too intrusive."

There was a long pause. "I was jealous as hell at first. But he still came home with me at the end of a shift. So I got over myself."

"You don't think he was seeing anyone else?"

"Thanks a lot."

"I'm sorry to be so blunt, but we are talking about a murderer."

"It's kinda hard reliving my own stupidity."

"You weren't stupid. He was manipulative. In a sense, there was nothing you could do. He's an expert at getting what he wants."

"Well he didn't get everything he asked for."

"He didn't?"

"He wanted keys to my apartment. I told him no way. I wasn't going down that road again."

"Did you visit him in his apartment?"

"No—I thought at the time that he was ashamed of it, like maybe it was in a bad neighborhood. I felt for the guy. Now I realize he just didn't want anyone to know his address."

"Do you think he was seeing anyone else?"

"I don't know. I guess now I know what he was capable of, I suppose it's possible. Why do you want to know?"

"Just trying to build up a picture of the guy. Detective Trooe has sent me the photograph you took of Wyatt. Is it a good likeness?"

"I guess. He didn't always have the beard. He could grow one real fast. I preferred it when he shaved. He was a good looking guy. Well-groomed too. Always spent a lot of time on his appearance. Which is why he never stayed over, I guess—didn't want me to see what he looked like first thing in the morning. How vain is that? I used to tease him about it."

"Did he share the joke with you?"

"He hated me even mentioning it. I soon learned not to."

"What do you mean?"

"Darryl had... an underdeveloped sense of humor. He wasn't very good at laughing at himself. Whenever I tried to tease him about it, he'd get really angry with me."

"Violent?"

"You've spoken to Detective Trooe?"

"He said Wyatt hit you a few times."

"More than a few. But he always said it was my fault. Like I'd driven him to it. After a while, I started to believe him." She let out a sigh. "I know what you're thinking… if it was so bad, why not end it?"

"I'm thinking nothing of the sort. Wyatt was manipulating you. He knew exactly what he was doing." She flipped over to a fresh page in her notebook. "While you were together, did Wyatt ever talk about his family?"

"He didn't like to. Every time I tried, he'd change the subject. I just supposed he'd had a big fight with them at some point and lost contact."

"And what about his friends?"

"He wasn't local. His friends were all back home."

"And where was that?"

There was another long pause. "Some place out west. But now I think about it, he never actually told me where. He told me only what he wanted me to know. Looking back I can't trust a single goddamn word he said." She sucked in a noisy breath. "Look, if he has done something like that again, can you make sure you catch the bastard this time?"

"I'm working on it."

"Good. You need anything else from me, just call. I hate the thought of him being out there some place. Still makes me feel uneasy."

"Thanks for your time." Ingrid hung up and spent a moment staring at her phone. She was no expert—the sum total of her knowledge wouldn't even fill a single lecture in Psychology 101—but from the way Bella Townsend had just described Darryl Wyatt's character traits, he had exhibited some of the hallmarks of a narcissistic sociopath.

She knew an agent working at the Behavioral Analysis Unit at Quantico, a guy she did her training with. She should run through Wyatt's profile with him, get a professional opinion.

But right now she wanted to track down Clifford Quigley. If her assessment of Wyatt's psychological profile was even halfway accurate, Barbara Highsmith wouldn't have been his first victim. And she sure as hell wouldn't be his last.

22

The two a.m. security check of the third floor finally pried Ingrid from her desk. She hadn't managed to track down Clifford Quigley, but she had discovered a John Doe who'd turned up dead just a few days after Darryl Wyatt's first visit to the restaurant. The unidentified male was found over the state border in South Carolina and ended up in a morgue over a hundred miles away. It was possible the man lying in the chiller drawer wasn't Clifford Quigley, but Ingrid knew she'd feel a lot easier once she'd found out one way or the other. She tried calling the local cops in South Carolina, but discovered the officer she needed to speak to wasn't available. She made a note to try him again the next day.

Before she left the building, Ingrid put in a call to Mike Stiller, her one remaining contact at Bureau headquarters, to ask him to delve as deeply as he could into the history of ex-congresswoman Highsmith, especially the FBI investigation of the earlier poisoning attempt. Stiller had higher security clearance than Ingrid and he might just uncover something she couldn't. By the time Ingrid returned to her hotel, it was already three in the morning. Less than five hours before she needed to head back to Grosvenor Square.

Early the next morning, when she shoved her hastily purchased breakfast on her desk, Ingrid couldn't help wondering if a fold-up bed tucked away some place in the building might be a good idea. She kept a sleeping bag in a drawer just in case she had to stay over, a bed might make things a little more comfortable.

Isaac arrived before Jennifer, presumably still eager to impress.

"You want another crack at using those victim support skills of yours?" Ingrid asked.

"Absolutely. Yes please."

"Great—we have a missing person case to investigate."

"The one in Kilburn?"

"Jennifer told you about it?"

"Not exactly." He looked down at his feet. "I overheard her taking down the details."

"Nothing wrong with paying attention. Don't worry about it."

Ingrid actually felt a little sorry for him. He didn't know Angela Tate would be accompanying them to the interview. He had no idea what was in store for him. If he could handle whatever awkward questions Tate might throw at him, he'd be able to cope with anything else that might come up in the course of his embassy work. After dealing with an investigative reporter with a fearsome reputation of getting to the truth, however deeply it was buried, anything else would be child's play.

Ingrid steeled herself for Tate's arrival. She'd already decided to meet the journalist at the gate—it was too dangerous to have her setting foot inside the office. God only knew what precious nugget of information Tate might manage to glean from somebody's desk. Or their trash can. The landline rang at a quarter before ten. Sure enough, Tate had arrived. She was certainly keen. Ingrid puffed out a breath and grabbed her jacket and purse.

"Ready, Isaac?"

They reached the lobby and found Angela Tate sitting in the main reception area. Her hair was a little wilder than usual and she'd chosen a particularly deep shade of red lipstick. It looked a little like dried blood. Tate must have wrangled her way inside the building, despite Ingrid's strict instructions to the Marine manning the desk. Tate was obviously in a combative mood. It didn't bode well for Isaac. Like a lamb to the slaughter.

"Agent Skyberg. I'm so glad you finally found me a window." Tate's gaze shifted to Isaac. "And who's this charming young man?"

Isaac opened his mouth, but no words came.

"This is Isaac Coleman. He'll be accompanying us today." Ingrid smiled first at Tate then at Isaac. He still seemed completely lost for words.

Tate reached out her hand toward him. "I'm DCI Jane Tennyson—Special Branch. Here in an observational capacity only."

Ingrid glared at her. What the hell did she think she was doing? It was

bad enough having to include the reporter in an investigation, but introducing herself to Isaac as a cop? She'd better not try that with their
interviewee. "Shall we?" Ingrid tore her admonishing stare from Tate's
face and ushered them outside onto the sidewalk. Less than a minute later
the embassy car arrived to dispatch them to Kilburn.

Once they were settled in the car—Isaac had insisted he sit up front
with the driver—Tate pulled out a notebook. "So what case are we starting
with today? Unexplained death perhaps? Is that possible, statistically?
Would you expect to get two in a single week? I do hope a visit to Fisher
Krupps is on our itinerary."

Ingrid lowered her voice. "What kind of stunt was that?"

"Stunt?"

"Introducing yourself as a cop?"

"A purely fictional one."

"Makes no difference."

"What possible harm can it do? It was only a bit of fun." She dragged a
hand through her hair and tilted her head back. "My little joke was totally
wasted on you anyway." She glanced out the window. "So, is the first stop
Fisher Krupps?"

"Let's just see how we get on with our initial interview, shall we?"

"Initial interview?"

"A missing persons case."

Tate turned in her seat to face Ingrid. "Tell me you're joking. Do you
mean I've schlepped all the way to Grosvenor Square for a missing
person? I presume a child's disappeared." She stared into Ingrid's face.
"Something serious."

Ingrid said nothing.

"Oh please."

"I don't have much detail yet. I do know it's a male aged thirty-seven
who's gone missing. Besides, you said you wanted 'warts-and-all' access.
That's just what you've got. Welcome to my world."

"But your world also contains a City trader who died in suspicious
circumstances. Why can't I observe you on that investigation? Maybe we
should rearrange for another day."

"One time offer."

"Need I remind you just how indebted to me you are?" Tate didn't
bother to lower her voice.

Ingrid glanced toward Isaac. Thankfully he was too busy talking to the
driver to eavesdrop on her conversation. "You're making this really difficult for me."

"Them's the breaks. Perhaps you should never have come to me asking for help. Perhaps I should have refused to have anything to do with your highly dubious scheme. No wait, I don't mean dubious do I? I mean illegal."

Two weeks ago Ingrid had thought long and hard before asking Tate for help, she was well aware of the journalist's reputation for ruthlessness. At the time she'd had little choice but to get her involved. Right now she was deeply regretting the decision. The way things were going, she wasn't entirely sure her debt would ever be repaid. "We'll speak to the wife of the missing man. I'm already breaking the rules letting you come along."

"Don't worry—I'll behave myself."

Ingrid wasn't sure Tate even knew how.

They arrived at the house a couple of blocks south of Kilburn High Road just ten minutes later. Before they got out of the car, Ingrid held on to Tate's arm. "You are here in an observational capacity only—we are clear on that? I'll be doing the talking."

"Don't fret. Do as much talking as you like. Quiet as a mouse, that's me."

23

After a half hour of quietly observing the interview, barely making a note in her reporter's pad, Angela Tate stood up. "Would you excuse us for a moment, madam?" She put a hand under Ingrid's elbow and dragged her to her feet and all the way to the front door. "My God—what are we all doing here wasting our time? If I didn't know better, I'd think you set this whole thing up. A little crumb to throw to the annoying journalist."

Isaac hurried down the hallway toward them, his face crumpled in confusion.

"Don't say a word," Tate warned him. "You might look decorative, but my God you're as useless as a sunhat in a monsoon." She stared at Ingrid. "Is this really how you spend an average day? Doing something this... mind-bogglingly boring?"

"Most of my work is mundane, procedural. I'm sorry to disappoint."

"Oh sure. You're not telling me this investigation isn't something that pretty boy couldn't handle on his own?"

"Wait a minute!" Isaac said. Tate had obviously hit a nerve.

"You're right. Isaac can handle this one from here." Ingrid turned to her eager apprentice. "Are you OK with that?"

"Absolutely!" He eyed Tate defiantly.

Brave boy, Ingrid thought.

"Get as many details as you can about where her husband might have taken himself off to. Be as sympathetic as you can."

"Don't worry—I won't let you down."

"Good. You OK to get back to embassy on public transportation?"

"Sure."

Ingrid and Tate quickly exited the property. Once outside, Tate lit a cigarette.

"I can't believe that's the sort of thing you'd normally investigate." She shook her head and took a long drag on her cigarette as they walked back to the car.

"Where can I drop you?" Ingrid asked as she opened a rear passenger door.

"What?"

"Back at the *Evening News* building?"

"You're not getting rid of me that easily. Let's just agree that performance in there was the rather tedious short before the main feature. You want to know where to drop me? How about Fisher Krupps, EC3?"

Ingrid's phone started buzzing in her pocket. She checked the screen: an "out of area" number. She really didn't want to speak to Marshall right now, not with Tate breathing down her neck. "Excuse me, would you? Feel free to wait in the car."

Tate stood her ground, staring at Ingrid through a cloud of cigarette smoke. Ingrid answered her phone and marched up the street.

"This really isn't a good time."

There was a pause at the other end of the line, then, "In that case, I'll keep the information to myself."

"Mike?"

"Expecting somebody else?"

"What time is it there?"

"Do you want to know what I found out about Barbara Highsmith or not?"

"Please, I do—but I'm not at my desk. Could you also email the details?"

"You do know I'm not your personal Stateside secretary, huh? You only ever check in with me when you've got a problem."

Although Ingrid accepted that was true, she also knew that Special Agent Mike Stiller loved a challenge. "You know how much I appreciate any help you can give me." She turned to see what mischief Tate was getting up to. The reporter was leaning against the hood of the embassy sedan, staring at her cell phone.

"OK—as long as we're clear how much you owe me. There's a lot of stuff here, so I'll just give you the edited highlights." He took a deep breath. "Barbara Highsmith, born Barbara Jane Reese, grew up in a nice middle class home, attended Wellesley College for her first degree—she majored in English—and then went on to study law at Harvard. Didn't graduate top of the class, but she was in the top third. After law school she went to work for a law firm in Boston, lasted there four years before switching sides to go work in the District Attorney's office. In Philadelphia." Finally Stiller took a breath.

In the brief lull, Ingrid took the opportunity to interrupt. "Anything interesting in her medical records?" The medical records of an ex-congresswomen were highly classified—only an agent with Stiller's security clearance could access them.

"Are you referring to the peanut allergy?"

"Dig up anything interesting about the earlier allergic reaction that nearly killed her?"

"The investigation was snuffed out pretty much before it began. Foul play was dismissed as a possibility right away."

"It was? Why?"

"The agents were directed to drop it. By people close to the congresswoman herself. I can't find out any more than that. There's nothing on file. And I had to call in a couple favors from the D.C. field office to find out that much."

"It happened in Washington?"

"You didn't know that?"

"My information is as sketchy as yours."

"Thanks for the vote of confidence in my intel gathering skills."

"I know you're the best agent there is for intel—why do you think I keep hassling you for information?"

"Because you got nobody else?"

"There must be something more about it you can find out."

"The general consensus is it was hushed up because she didn't want to jeopardize her re-election prospects. Doesn't do to have a secret peanut allergy leak out if you want to retain your seat representing the peanut capital of the USA."

"I guess not." She glanced up at Tate again. The journalist seemed to be behaving herself. "Did you find any link between Wall Street and Highsmith? Any Wall Street traders in her past?"

"Not that I've been able to find."

"Oh."

"The legal firm she worked for specialized in tax law, I think that's the closest she got to the world of high finance. Helping corporations pay as little tax as possible. What angle are you working, anyway?"

"It's not so much an angle as a wild stab in the dark." It didn't look like she was going to be able to establish a direct link between Matthew Fuller and Barbara Highsmith. Maybe the poisoning thing was a just a coincidence. But coincidences made Ingrid feel uncomfortable. She glanced toward Tate, who was mid-yawn. When Tate saw her, the reporter tapped a finger against her wrist. Ingrid held up her hand. "So apart from the tax attorneys, nothing else financial?"

"I said there was no link to Wall Street. If you'd read her file on the database a little more carefully, you would have discovered she worked as an Assistant US Attorney."

"I thought she was at the District Attorney's office."

"She was. Then she moved on to the US Attorney's office in Washington state."

Dammit. Ingrid had conflated the ex-congresswoman's sojourn at the district attorney's with the time she'd devoted to the US Attorney's Office. How had she missed that? "So she was dealing with federal cases?"

"For seven years in total. Started out in Spokane then transferred to Seattle two years later. Could be she dealt with plenty of finance-related cases. But it would have been small beer. Nothing newsworthy."

"Equally it could be just what I'm looking for. Can you get me a list of all her cases during her time at the US Attorney's Office?"

"Oh come on, Skyberg. I got my own work to do, you know."

"I promise this is the last request I'll make."

"Oh sure."

"Is that a yes?"

The line went very quiet.

"OK."

"Great—call me when you have the list." She hung up before Stiller had a chance to say goodbye, or complain, and started wandering back toward Tate, trying to work out how the hell she was going to get rid of her.

Tate ground the stub of her second cigarette under a boot. "What was that all about?"

"I can't say."

"Off the record."

Ingrid raised her eyebrows.

"Truly. Cross my heart."

Ingrid doubted Tate had one. "I can't go into the details. I was just checking some information with a colleague of mine back at Bureau HQ."

"Something to do with the Fisher Krupps trader?"

"Not at all," she lied.

"So—what was it then?"

"Another case—I told you, I can't give you the details." Her phone, still in her hand, started to buzz again.

"You are popular." Tate eyed the phone.

"Maybe we should forget all about this."

"I've cleared my diary for the day. I'm an optimist. I'm sure I'll pick up something of interest during our time together. But right now I could murder a bacon sandwich."

Ingrid turned away again and glanced at the screen. It was a call she couldn't ignore.

24

"Detective Fraser, thank you so much for getting back to me." Ingrid tried to keep her voice controlled and even, but she was inwardly cursing him for previously ignoring her calls. "What can you tell me?"

"Nothing. There have been no new developments."

"You haven't even identified the victim?" Ingrid walked down the street, further away from Tate.

"It's proving more difficult than we thought."

"Still nothing back from Latvian police about the tattoo?"

"You're assuming she had a record."

"What about the media over there—have the police been liaising with the newspapers and TV?"

"I haven't seen any evidence of it. She's not a priority for them. We don't even know for sure that she was Latvian."

I know. "Extend your inquiries to include Lithuania and Estonia then."

"I'll have a word with the SIO." From the noncommittal tone of Fraser's voice, Ingrid doubted he'd do anything of the sort.

"Maybe I should speak to him." She'd actually already tried that approach. The senior officer running the case was ignoring her calls too. It was possible Fraser knew that. "Are you in the incident room? Is the SIO there with you now?"

"He... er..."

Ingrid could hear mumbling in the background.

"He's just had to step out. Important meeting."

"I don't understand, if you have nothing new to tell me, why are you even calling?"

"To be honest… to stop you calling me. You have to believe I'll get in touch if something of interest comes up."

"How about the house-to-house inquiries? Do any of the neighbors remember seeing a man at the address?"

"Nope."

"And none of them recognize the man in the photograph I sent you?"

Fraser drew in a noisy breath.

"What is it?"

"When no one confirmed a sighting of a man, we wound down the house-to-house interviews. We're concentrating our efforts elsewhere."

"Are you saying that the woman's neighbors haven't even *seen* the photograph?"

Another rasping inhale.

Goddammit.

"Why aren't you treating her murder as a priority? Is it because she's an immigrant?"

"Of course not! We take all homicides very seriously. It's not like America. We don't have this sort of thing happening every day of the week. Thank God."

"Where are you concentrating your efforts?"

"The boss is due to fly out to Latvia on Sunday morning. He's liaising with the police force in Riga."

"That's it?" It sounded like an excuse for a weekend away to Ingrid.

"We're still looking at the CCTV footage from the area around her flat. Nothing of interest has come up so far." He let out a long sigh. "Look, we're all as frustrated as you are with the lack of progress on this case. But it doesn't mean we've given up on finding out who killed her.

Ingrid hoped he meant what he said. She hung up and opened the search app on her cell. Tate was striding toward her.

"And what was that call about?"

"Another ongoing case."

"That you can't share."

Ingrid looked up from her phone. "Actually, I can. But I need some help first."

"From me?" Tate threw what was left of her third cigarette into the gutter. Ingrid nodded back at her. "Fire away!" The reporter rubbed her hands together.

"Do you have a chain of copy shops here in the UK? I need to find one —fast."

Forty minutes later, Ingrid and Tate were walking out of a Kall Kwik copy shop on Wembley High Road, laden down with a box each of 250 color copies of Darryl Wyatt's photograph.

"Where to now?" Tate said as they shoved the boxes onto the front seat of the car.

Ingrid leaned in and punched an address into the sat nav. The driver shifted uncomfortably in his seat a little but offered no word of protest.

"Actually—before we go anywhere," Tate said, "I need to find some lunch." She slammed shut the door and grabbed Ingrid's arm around the elbow. "My God you need feeding up. Let's get you something substantial to eat, shall we?"

Lunch took a lot longer than Ingrid would have liked, and mostly consisted of her deflecting Tate's intrusive questions about her life in London and her work in the FBI. By the time they were back in the car and turning off Lordship Lane, the traffic was starting to get heavy—mainly moms picking up their kids from kindergarten and the first signs of the evening rush hour—it was Friday afternoon after all—and the embassy driver seemed a little irritated.

"You know, you still haven't told me where we're going," Tate said as she wriggled to get comfortable in the plushly upholstered rear seat of the sedan. "Though I've got to admit, I could get used to having my own personal driver. What a treat!"

The car pulled into the curb a few minutes later and Tate peered out the window. "What are we doing in Dulwich?"

"Something I guess you've done plenty of over the years."

Tate arched a single eyebrow.

"A little doorstepping."

"Really? Let me at 'em. I thought I might die of boredom."

Ingrid reached into the front seat, pulled a sheaf of color copies from one of the boxes and handed them to Tate, who was practically limbering up on the sidewalk like a marathon runner, she was so keen to start. She looked at the photograph of Darryl Wyatt. "I'm already sick of this bloke's face. What's the score—asking people if they recognize him, if so when did they last see him, etcetera etcetera… Does he have a name?"

"I doubt he'd be using the one I have on record for him."

"So, if they happen to put a name to the face, I get bonus points."

"You only get those if they give you an address for him."

"I'm glad you're not my boss."

Ingrid pointed to the Latvian's building. A little blue and white police tape had gotten caught in the branches of a nearby tree and was fluttering in the breeze. "We'll start there. With the other apartments in the building, then work outwards."

Tate was already halfway up the path leading to the front door before Ingrid finished speaking. She rang all five buzzers, leaning her hand against them until she got a response. An intercom crackled and a distant voice hollered at her. Ingrid decided to give the reporter some space and tried the neighboring property. She knocked on the door and a dog started barking almost immediately. A deep, menacing bark. She heard an internal door open and close. The barking got louder for a moment then faded. A few seconds later the front door opened a few inches.

"Where's the bloody fire?" The woman holding onto the door was dressed in sweatpants and a hoodie with bright white sneakers on her feet.

Ingrid flashed her badge at her and held up one of the copied sheets.

"Not more bloody coppers. I've already told you, I don't know anything and I haven't seen anything. I mind my own business." She started to close the door.

"Please ma'am, just take a quick look."

"You're a Yank."

"FBI, from the American embassy, ma'am."

"So who's this then?" She pointed to the sheet. "One of your Most Wanted?" She let out a little snort of laughter.

"He is, as a matter of fact. The sooner we track him down the safer we'll all sleep in our beds." Ingrid had grown sick of the subtle, softly, softly approach. She decided to try scaring the crap out of this woman. See if that made her pay attention. So far it seemed it might just be working.

"What's he supposed to have done?" The woman jabbed a finger at the photograph.

"Murder."

"Of her next door?"

"You know the deceased?"

"No—but I've seen her around. Said hello a couple of times." She scrutinized Ingrid's face. "Why's the American embassy getting involved? She wasn't American. Not with that accent."

"This man is the prime suspect in a murder investigation in Georgia."

"And you think he's come all the way over here?"

"It's one line of inquiry we're pursuing."

"God you sound just like the policewoman I spoke to yesterday. Do you all get the same training?"

"Please, ma'am, take a good look at his face. It's possible he's clean shaven now, maybe his hair's a different color. He could be wearing glasses."

The woman stared a little longer at the color copy, then started shaking her head. "I've not seen him."

"Is there anyone else in the house who might have?"

"My husband. But he doesn't pay attention to anything outside work and football. I'm lucky if he even notices me."

"Please keep the photo and ask him, would you?" Ingrid handed her a card too. "Call me anytime if you think of something."

The woman closed the door just as Tate approached from the next door property.

"Any luck?" Ingrid asked her.

"The only person to answer their buzzer was half deaf. I popped a few photocopies through the main letter box anyway. I scribbled my phone number and 'have you seen this man' on the back of each one."

"Don't you think asking them to contact the embassy would have been more appropriate?"

Tate shrugged. "Didn't occur to me." She reached into her purse and pulled out her pack of cigarettes. "I heard most of what you told that woman."

"So?"

"Who did this one kill in Georgia? I'm guessing it's got to be quite a high profile case for the FBI to get involved."

"We take every homicide just as seriously as any other. High profile doesn't come into it."

"Sure, sure. So who was it?"

"Just some woman in a restaurant." She'd already revealed too much.

"Another stabbing?"

Ingrid wondered if she should lie. It wouldn't help her investigation to have Tate sniffing around the ex-congresswoman's death. She decided to be as vague as possible. "That's right. I haven't received the case file yet—I don't know all the details."

"Maybe when you do, we can have a follow-up interview?"

"Sure, why not?" As if that would ever happen.

Tate looked down at the cigarettes and shoved them back in her purse. Then she quickly moved on to the next house. "We'd better get stuck in, or we'll be here all night."

Ninety minutes, and at least three dozen properties later, Ingrid met Tate back at the car. "Anything to report?" Ingrid asked her.

"Most people were either out or chose not to answer. I shoved the picture through their letterboxes anyway. You never know, someone might get in touch. What about you?"

"Same story. It was worth a try."

"Yes—and it kept me out of your hair for a while. But I'm not that easily deterred. We've done everything we can here. You can tell me all about the dead trader while we drive to Fisher Krupps."

Ingrid pursed her lips and shook her head. She pointed at her watch. "Five-thirty. End of my working day. You've had all the access you're going to get."

25

Ingrid had only managed to get rid of Angela Tate after promising to update her with any progress on the City trader case, just as soon as it happened.

"Be warned—I will hold you to that. If I don't hear from you, I shall make your life absolute hell," she'd said.

Ingrid didn't doubt that for a second. She knew well enough not to cross Tate. If she were being entirely honest with herself, she would have to admit she was a little in awe of the journalist's single-mindedness. And maybe even a little intimidated.

When she returned to the embassy, after dropping Tate at the *Evening News* building on Blackfriars Road, Ingrid decided to check in with DI Mbeke.

"Have I caught you still on duty?" Ingrid asked him after she'd almost hung up—the call rang out for what seemed like ages.

"Actually I was just heading out of the building." He sounded slightly out of breath.

"Any news?"

"I was going to leave it until Monday."

Ingrid sat up in her chair.

"It's not earth shattering. We still haven't located Hernandez. But we have confirmed that aconite was used to kill Fuller. The lab found traces of it in his liver and kidneys."

"What about the washroom?"

"Nothing. Which presumably means the poison was in the soap dispensers."

"Which the killer removed. Right under our noses."

"Wait a minute—I hadn't arrived at that point."

"OK—I admit it—I was the law enforcement officer he made a fool of."

"I didn't mean—"

"No offense taken. I'm just still so mad at myself about it."

"But why would he take that risk?"

"Maybe it was his only opportunity to remove the evidence."

"He could have just left the poison there. Wreaked more havoc."

"He did what he came to do."

"You're still certain Fuller was the intended victim?"

"It's the explanation that makes the most sense."

"Then why not leave as soon as Fuller was dead? We still have that hour and a quarter to account for between Fuller's death and the footage of Hernandez making his escape. Why did he hang around for so long?"

"Maybe he enjoys the thrill." Ingrid tried to recall her Psychology 101: narcissistic sociopaths take great pleasure in watching the drama they've created unfold. Especially when it makes them feel so much smarter than the investigating officers. He must have been there, silently mocking them. Mocking her. Ingrid thought of Darryl Wyatt standing in the restaurant, watching Barbara Highsmith gasping her last breaths. "During your interviews of Fuller's colleagues, did anyone mention seeing a cleaner hanging around the area while Fuller was actually dying?"

"Don't forget, no one discovered Fuller for a little while. He was lying in the corridor outside the main trading area. It wasn't until someone visited the toilet that anyone even knew he was in trouble."

"Where the hell is Hernandez? You really have to put all your efforts into finding him."

"You think?"

"Sorry. I'm really not telling you how to do your job."

There was a silence at the other end of the line. Had she really offended him so much?

"Listen, I'll be working right through the weekend," Mbeke eventually said. "I'm just popping out of the station now to get a bite to eat. Would you like to join me?"

Ingrid paused. It didn't *sound* like he was asking her out on a date.

"We could discuss the case in… slightly more pleasant surroundings."

"The case? Sure, why not? I can be with you in less than thirty minutes."

"Good, great. I'll text you the address of the restaurant."

———

By the time Ingrid and Mbeke had ordered their meal, they'd already raked over pretty much everything about the investigation that they'd discovered so far. Ingrid updated Mbeke on the Savannah poisoning case and he ran through how the City of London Police were liaising with other forces up and down the country to try to track Hernandez down.

"Without a photograph, or any consistent description of the man, we're not holding out much hope," Mbeke told her.

"Nobody on staff recognized the photograph I sent you?"

"Don't you think you would have been the first to know if they had? No one notices the cleaners."

"Apart from the other cleaners."

"None of them is comfortable speaking to us. I think the cleaning agency might be running some sort of immigration scam. I've got some colleagues looking into it. But whatever they find, it isn't exactly going to encourage any of the employees to tell us anything." Mbeke was leaning his chin in his hands, his elbows planted on the table. He stared into Ingrid's eyes, his gaze almost uncomfortably intense.

Ingrid started playing with the corner of her napkin, just for something else to focus on. "I guess it's possible Hernandez has left the country already."

"It's impossible to say. Hernandez probably isn't his real name. If he has left, I would imagine he's got alternative paperwork for a different identity. Border control can't help us."

Ingrid wondered if maybe the suspect *was* smarter than the law enforcement agents investigating the case. She was certainly feeling decidedly dumb right now.

Mbeke sniffed loudly and sat up straight. "This is my first murder case, and I'm completely lost. I don't have a single promising lead to follow up. I feel useless. I can't help thinking there's something blindingly obvious that I'm missing."

"If there is, then I'm missing it too."

A waiter approached their table holding a steaming bowl of pasta in each hand. Following the ritual of the black pepper grinding and the parmesan shaving, Ingrid and Mbeke ate in silence for a few minutes. They'd pretty much exhausted all case-related avenues of conversation. Then they both awkwardly started to speak at the same time.

"You first," Ingrid insisted.

"I was just going to ask you about your life back in the US. A pathetic attempt at small talk." He smiled at her.

Ingrid sensed this was the time to bring her fiancé into the conversation. But the thought of even mentioning Marshall's name right now reminded her she was still mad at him. "Oh there's not much to talk about, really. I pretty much live for the job. Sad, I know."

"Not at all. I'm guilty of the same thing myself. You can ask my ex-wife!"

"Oh—I'm sorry."

"It was all my fault. In the end it came down to choosing between the job and my marriage."

"Do you ever regret choosing your career ahead of your love life?" Ingrid was aware just how career-focused she and Marshall were.

Mbeke raised his eyebrows.

"I'm sorry—that was too personal."

"Not at all, I just wasn't expecting it. When it came down to it, I couldn't imagine doing anything else for a living. But I could see myself single again. I guess I'm just too selfish to be in a relationship."

This was all getting a little too intense. Ingrid attacked the bowl of linguine with her fork as if she were trying to harpoon the prawns in their sea of cream sauce.

"What about you?" Mbeke asked.

Ingrid was afraid he might ask that. "Oh I love the job too. It's in my DNA."

"Literally? Your dad was a policeman?"

She laughed. "My dad was a hog farmer."

"Some people might say those two professions are closely related."

Ingrid laughed again, more out of embarrassment than amusement. Time to bring in the cavalry, much as it pained her to do so. "But my fiancé's dad was a cop. A sheriff, as a matter of fact."

"Your fiancé?"

She nodded and shoved another forkful of pasta in her mouth to avoid the need to speak. She couldn't help but notice Mbeke's shoulders sag a little. He stared down at his meal and chased a button mushroom around the bowl.

"Marshall and I are both married to the job, I guess," she said, attempting to fill the awkward silence. "Maybe dating a fellow cop is the answer. We understand the issues. The missed dates, the forgotten birthdays."

"How long have you been engaged?"

"Just over a year. But we started dating two years before that. And we've known one another forever—since Academy training at Quantico."

"You joined the FBI at the same time?"

Ingrid nodded, regretting having brought the subject up. She tried to remember what Marshall had been like eight years ago. Her one abiding memory of him then was his old fashioned Southern charm. He was popular with all the female trainees. When he asked her out five years later, he not only impressed her with his charm, but with his tireless hard work and ambition. They had both wanted to make a difference back then. She wasn't sure either of them had achieved anything close.

"I can see you're a bit uncomfortable talking about it. Now it's my turn to apologize for being too personal."

"Oh, not at all. I was just lost in a little reminiscence."

"And the long distance thing is working out OK for you?"

Ingrid thought about why she'd agreed to take on the embassy job in the first place. She'd needed time to work out what she wanted in her life. She'd hoped a little space and distance from her old job, and from Marshall, would help her in the decision-making process. But she still hadn't worked out what it was she wanted. Thinking about it now, she hadn't really missed Marshall in the five months she'd been away. "Oh it's working out fine."

Mbeke frowned at her, making it quite clear he didn't believe her.

Ingrid wondered just how much she and Marshall truly needed one another. What they continued to get out of their relationship. As she smiled blandly across the table at Mbeke, she knew she had some serious thinking to do.

26

"And what happened after that?" Natasha McKittrick had agreed to come apartment hunting with Ingrid. She should never have mentioned her brief supper with Mbeke to the detective inspector. Now McKittrick just wouldn't let it go.

"We pretty much agreed on a strategy to implement going forward. All resources are now focused on finding Hernandez."

She grabbed Ingrid's shoulder. "You do realize Mills can never find out about your date. He'll be devastated."

"For crying out loud! How many more times have I got to say it? It wasn't a date. I don't go on dates!" Ingrid turned back toward the real estate agent's window. "I've got a new home to find." She glanced at the details of the two or three rentals that were both in the right price range and more or less a fifteen minute motorcycle ride from the embassy. None of them screamed 'pick me!' at her. Maybe this was a mistake. Perhaps staying at the hotel made more sense.

"I can't understand why you'd voluntarily walk away from four star luxury and twenty-four-hour room service," McKittrick said, somehow reading Ingrid's mind. "Not to mention having someone else wash and iron your clothes for you."

"The novelty wears off after a while."

"Does this mean you're planning on staying in the UK? Only you've never actually said how permanent your posting is."

"The Bureau will pay rent for the first six months, so maybe I'm here that long."

"And what does Marshall think about that?"

Ingrid turned away and marched to the door of the realtor's. "Are you helping me find an apartment or not?"

"Oh my God—you haven't told him yet, have you?"

"I haven't had the chance—every time I call he's busy."

"Time to take the bull by the horns—why not call him right now?"

Ingrid ignored her and stepped through the door, leaving McKittrick stranded on the sidewalk. After a few moments the detective slunk into the office, her head angled toward the floor.

"I'm sorry—I genuinely didn't realize this was an issue for you."

"It isn't—I'll call Marshall when I'm good and ready. I may not even find an apartment." She headed toward the desk beneath the 'lettings' sign and waited for the agent to get off the phone. He smiled up at her.

"How can I help you two ladies today?"

Behind her, McKittrick let out a little groan and mumbled 'Ladies' in a sarcastic tone.

"In the window—you have details of a couple of apartments I'd be interested in seeing."

"Sure, no problem." He got up. "Care to show me which ones?"

After an extended, and clearly, as far as McKittrick was concerned, tedious few minutes of small talk, the agent took Ingrid's details and they headed off in his logo-emblazoned Mini to the first apartment in Maida Vale. Ingrid had selected the area because it was a straight run from there to the embassy along Edgware Road. She'd be door to door in ten minutes most days. The small talk continued in the car until McKittrick put a stop to it when the agent asked them if it was their first home together.

"I'm not her partner," the detective told him firmly. "I'm just here to make sure she doesn't get ripped off."

Ingrid was more than capable of ensuring that for herself, but she let McKittrick continue to harangue the guy for the rest of the ten minute car ride and throughout the viewing of the first apartment. It was actually quite entertaining to watch McKittrick ask the agent a series of awkward questions about both the property and the lease that he struggled to answer.

They finally exited the two-bedroom duplex on Elgin Avenue and the detective let rip. "Do you really think anyone would be desperate enough to live in a place like that? It's barely fit for human habitation."

"The rental market in this area is highly competitive," the agent said. "Properties are snapped up before we can even print out the details."

"OK—show us one of those," Ingrid chimed in.

"I'm sorry?"

"One of the highly-sought after residences that everyone is clamoring for."

"It's not quite as simple as that. We've got people on waiting lists. I can't just let you jump the queue."

"Oh, come on. I bet you've got something so new it hasn't even made it onto your books yet." Ingrid treated him to her most fulsome smile. Then she pulled her badge from her purse. "I'll be a very reliable tenant."

He wrinkled his nose while he considered her request. "Oh, what the hell." He reached into a pocket and pulled out a set of keys. "I only got the instruction yesterday. Haven't seen the property myself yet. It won't have been cleaned or anything."

"I think I have the imagination to see beyond a little dirt."

"It's in a mansion block—all services included in the rent. Fully furnished. About five minutes away. On the Maida Vale—St John's Wood borders." He said it like it was meant to impress her.

"Sounds perfect."

It was a little more than five minutes, the property was on the far eastern edge of the area Ingrid had identified, but as soon as she walked through the apartment door she knew she had to have it. It was on the top floor, which meant it was light and airy and had fantastic views right across Regent's Park. Leading off the square lobby area were five doors. The one right opposite the apartment door led into a large, high-ceilinged living area, sparsely furnished, white walled and wooden floored. Just the way she liked her apartments. She stood at the southern-facing of the two windows and gazed toward the park. Between the two windows was a door. Ingrid tried the handle—it was locked.

"Do you have the key?"

The real estate agent produced a key from a pocket and opened the door. It led out onto a small roof terrace. Ingrid stepped outside and inhaled. This was why she had to get out of the hotel: she needed to see the sky when she woke in the morning—to get a sense of space. She turned back toward the agent, he was barely inches away, literally breathing down her neck. "Can I have a little time to think about it?"

He looked at his watch. "I have another appointment at one."

"Plenty of time then." Ingrid waited for him to go back inside. She could stay up here all day.

McKittrick joined her. "I'm guessing you're sold on it?"

"Is it that obvious?"

"Might want to lose the big soppy grin that's been on your face since we set foot over the threshold, if you're going to stand any chance of negotiating a good deal."

"Don't worry—my dad taught me how to haggle."

"I look forward to seeing you in action."

Ingrid walked to the rail at the edge of the roof terrace and surveyed the horizon through one-eighty degrees. Already her head felt clearer than it had in weeks.

"What's next for you today? Going back to work?" McKittrick asked.

"How did you guess?"

"You are in the middle of two investigations with so many loose ends you could crochet them together and make a hat. What else are you going to do on a glorious Saturday afternoon?"

"You know me so well."

"What can you usefully do on the weekend anyway?"

"Go through the files again, read up a little more on Darryl Wyatt, the ex-congresswoman, the City trader. Maybe find something I've missed."

"You're still convinced there's a connection between the dead Latvian and the trader?"

Ingrid closed her eyes and enjoyed the warmth of the sun on her face for a moment. "Convinced is too strong a word. I'm keeping an open mind."

"Have you worked out what his motive might have been for killing the Latvian woman?"

"She was accessing his bank account back in the US. Getting a little too close to his former identity. She was a security risk, I guess."

"But if he's... what did you tell me earlier... a narcissistic sociopath?"

Ingrid nodded.

"And that means he's a meticulous planner..."

Ingrid nodded again.

"Then why leave his bank details lying around for the Latvian to discover?"

"I don't have that worked out yet. Which is why I need to go back to base and do some more digging."

"All work and no play."

"I'll fit in a little parkour before the end of the day. A few easy moves."

"And that's your idea of fun?"

"Closest I'll ever get to flying. Maybe you should give it a try."

"I'll stick to taking the stairs and getting off the tube a couple of stops early for my exercise, thanks very much. I don't know how you fit it all in. Oh no, wait, I remember—you don't have a social life."

"Gee thanks."

The real estate agent was knocking on the glass and pointing at his wristwatch.

"Time for some deal making." Ingrid rubbed her hands together.

"This I've got to see." McKittrick grabbed Ingrid's arm as she started to head back to the roof terrace door. "I really think you should take a break from work. Maybe it'd give you a fresh perspective. A new look at everything on Monday might really help you crack the case."

Ingrid wondered what might be coming next. Hopefully not another invite to a goddamn awful flea market. She'd tried it once and vowed never to do it again. "What do you suggest?"

"Funny you should say that."

The realtor banged on the glass again.

"All right!" McKittrick hollered at him. "A few colleagues have arranged an unofficial team building exercise for tomorrow—it's an excuse to let off a bit of steam, really. I wouldn't mind having you come along for moral support."

"You think you'll need it?"

"Even off the job, they still think of me as their boss, they can be a bit guarded around me."

"You could just not go."

"They've gone to the trouble of inviting me. I can't say no. I'd appreciate a little company." She started walking toward the door. "God—I'm not going to beg."

"OK. I'll come."

"Fantastic! I owe you one."

Having a detective inspector of the Metropolitan Police in your debt had to be a good thing. Ingrid stopped before they went inside. "Wait a minute. Will Ralph Mills be there?"

"Don't worry—I'll make sure he doesn't get anywhere near you. I know what trouble you have keeping your hands off him."

27

Ingrid's digging into the case files on the FBI database all Saturday afternoon and most of the evening produced no new leads. She was still waiting for Mike Stiller to get back to her about Barbara Highsmith's cases from her Assistant US Attorney days. Mike worked long hours, but she couldn't ask him to give up his weekend for her. So—reluctantly—she left the embassy with as many loose ends as she had before she embarked on her marathon trawl of the records.

After a light thirty-minute parkour session on the south bank of the Thames near Waterloo railway station—it was pretty much a playground for free-runners—she headed back to her hotel for another boring room service dinner and a night in front of the TV. She really did need to get something else to do outside of work: there were only so many walls a girl could scramble over for entertainment.

More than once she pulled her phone from her purse and considered calling Marshall. But what was there to say? "Hey, honey, I've just found myself a great new apartment. Oh and I've decided to stay on in London for a little while longer." She could hear his whine of complaint clearly enough in her head without having to suffer the real thing.

With a little time to think, she was also beginning to regret accepting McKittrick's invitation to attend her 'bonding day'. The thought of spending that much time with Detective Constable Ralph Mills made her feel more uncomfortable than she knew it should.

So he was a nice guy.

So he made her laugh.

So he reminded her of her very first junior high school crush. She stopped the thought right there, switched channels on the TV and distracted herself with some dark Danish cop show. She struggled to concentrate on the subtitles until sleep finally got the better of her. Investigating two murders in one week had taken its toll.

The next day she skipped her five-mile morning run and spent the time fueling up on a healthy breakfast before embarking on whatever it was McKittrick had planned for her. She had arranged to meet the detective at Kentish Town Tube station in north London and arrived there a little after ten.

"*Now* will you tell me what we're going to be doing?" Ingrid asked McKittrick when the detective finally turned up fifteen minutes later than planned.

"First of all—we're getting on a train." She strode away, toward the entrance of the overground station. "We, my dear, are going to the country."

"Wouldn't it be better if we drove?" Ingrid followed her in.

"Might not feel up to getting behind a wheel afterwards." She strode away.

"After what?" Ingrid joined McKittrick on a bench. The platform was empty apart from a mom and dad struggling to keep two toddlers under control at one end, and a guy in sweats who appeared from the entrance and immediately started some weird T'ai Chi routine, fixing his gaze on the opposite platform.

"I don't want to spoil the surprise." McKittrick looked first at the boisterous young family then the man, who was now balancing on one leg. "Let's make sure we don't get in the same carriage as the Munsters or the weirdo, all right?"

"Can you at least tell me if I'm dressed suitably for the occasion?"

McKittrick looked at the leather biker jacket, the jeans and the biker boots. "I suppose you'll do. But I'm not sure you needed the back pack. What's in there, anyway?"

"Just a flask of water. Some fruit. Something to read. First aid kit."

"My God, you do like to come prepared." McKittrick glanced down at the small purse slung over her shoulder. "Must be your FBI training." She smiled, a twinkle in her eye.

The train came quickly and their journey lasted less than forty minutes. Four people were waiting for them outside the station when they arrived: Detective Constable Ralph Mills, a detective named Cath Murray from the

London Crime Squad Ingrid had met for the first time a couple of weeks ago, a smiling petite Indian woman, and a scowling, pink-faced blonde woman who seemed to be a little self-conscious about the few extra pounds she was carrying. Mills looked surprisingly muscular dressed in track pants and tight tee shirt. It was the first time Ingrid had seen him not wearing his trademark brown suit.

"Ingrid, hi!" Mills called out to her. He nodded toward McKittrick. "Boss." His smile was wide and generous, Ingrid couldn't help but beam back at him. "Now, you've met Cath, I know... but this is Manisha Kapoor..."

"Please, call me Nisha. It's a pleasure—we've heard so much about you," the Indian woman said as she shook Ingrid's hand. Her comment was rewarded with a sharp dig in the ribs from Mills.

"And this is Jane O'Brien," he said, gesturing toward the self-conscious woman, "who I used to work with at Catford Borough Command a few years back. My first job in CID, as a matter of fact."

"And you've come such a long way, pet," Jane O'Brien said. "All the way to the H-S-C-C." This remark, for some reason, was met with guffaws of laughter from Murray and Kapoor.

"What did I miss?" Ingrid asked.

"Nothing at all. They're all a bit over-excited." He glared at them. "They were like this all the way here. They don't get out much." He smiled at her and turned away. "I've booked a cab. Should be here any minute."

Right on cue, a few moments later, a mini-van pulled into the quiet station's small forecourt and Mills opened the side door. "All aboard the Skylark," he said, inexplicably.

Ingrid feared the day ahead might turn out to be long and arduous. No wonder McKittrick wanted a little support. Ingrid already felt like she was missing all the in-jokes. Judging by the glowering look on the detective inspector's face, she supposed McKittrick was too.

"We were talking on the train," Murray said, when they had all settled into the taxi. "We think you should maybe compete with one arm tied behind your back. You'll have an unfair advantage otherwise."

"I will?" Ingrid looked at McKittrick for guidance. "I still don't know what we're doing today."

"Paintballing!" they all said in unison.

Swell. Ingrid forced a smile. "Sounds like fun."

After five minutes on the road from the station, the mini-van turned off onto a muddy track and pulled through a ranch-style, wide wooden archway. It then bumped along a rough unmade road for about a half mile before depositing them at the opening of a long narrow marquee. Ingrid watched the taxi leave wishing she were still on board. *Paintballing* for God's sake. Definitely *not* her idea of fun. A man dressed in army fatigues stepped out of the marquee to greet them.

"Hello! You're a bit late. Your opposition have already gone into the forest. Not to worry. Let's start off by grouping you into pairs."

Mills glanced at Ingrid but made no move.

"Nisha!" McKittrick said. "How's your aim?" She marched over to the Indian woman and threw a mischievous smile back at Ingrid.

Cath Murray had looped her arm through Jane O'Brien's.

Mills cleared his throat. "A fait accompli."

Ingrid was feeling decidedly set up. What did McKittrick think she was doing?

A sudden throaty wail sounded from somewhere in the distance.

"What the hell was that?" Murray asked.

"Primal Scream. We have a men's warrior course on at the moment. Like a boot camp for your emotions," the man in fatigues explained.

"Stupid bastards," McKittrick said. "Haven't they got better things to do on a Sunday?"

Ingrid was thinking just that about this whole excursion. She could have been enjoying a ten mile run right now. She reached across to a long table at the entrance of the marquee and picked up a glossy brochure. Flicking through it, she discovered the establishment also offered a wild food foraging course, basket weaving and whittling, and archery using traditional Navajo bows and arrows. As if anyone in England would know the first thing about it. The paintballing arm of the operation seemed incongruous to say the least.

"Right, first of all you need to sign a health and safety form indemnifying Nature's Playground against any claims for injuries." The group leader handed them all a clipboard with a sheet of paper attached that contained such tiny small print it was impossible to decipher in the gloom of the forest.

Ingrid signed her form using a false name and quickly handed it back. The man in the fatigues gave her a bright orange bib and a half-inch diameter length of bamboo. Ingrid inspected what she supposed was a weapon. A small trigger was attached to one end of the stick, next to the trigger was a circular chamber. "What is this?" She inspected the trigger more closely. The whole contraption looked lethal. No wonder they had to sign a form.

"It's based on an Cherokee blowpipe. Originally we used a completely authentic design, but discovered that most punters don't have the necessary puff to send the paint pellets much further than a couple of feet. With the pneumatic pump," he said, pointing at the chamber, "everyone can achieve a range of twenty-five to thirty feet. It levels the playing field."

Ingrid slipped the orange vest over her head. It was so bright, they might as well have painted a target on her chest.

"A blowpipe? You're not serious," Cath Murray said. "Where are the unfeasibly large bazookas?" For some reason that comment elicited hearty guffaws from her teammate, Jane. "I wore my Ellen Ripley white vest especially for the occasion. Jesus, Ralph what have you got us into?"

Everyone turned to glare at Mills. He held his hands up in surrender. "Let's make the best of it, shall we? You never know—we might actually enjoy ourselves."

The organizer ran them through an all too brief demonstration on how to fire and reload the blowpipe, and told them their prey were three other couples, dressed in bright green vests.

"One clean shot to a member of the opposition's back or chest retires them from the game. Last person standing wins for the team."

"What's the prize?" Murray asked.

"The satisfaction of a job well done."

Murray, Kapoor and O'Brien groaned.

"Let's make it a bit more interesting then, shall we?" Murray said. "The couple with the most 'kills' gets to… enjoy an intimate Sunday lunch at a venue of their choice."

Mills glared at her.

Ingrid made eye contact with McKittrick, who quickly looked away. McKittrick was so going to pay for this.

28

The three teams split up and fanned out across the forest. After fifteen minutes or so, Ingrid and Mills had covered a lot of ground. The unnerving sound of grown men howling at the sky had even subsided a little. So far they hadn't spotted a member of the opposition.

"We should maybe slow down. Start to circle back a little." Ingrid pulled the vest over her head and shoved it in a pocket. "No point in advertising our presence."

"Isn't that cheating?" Mills said. He seemed genuinely alarmed at the idea.

"Do you want to win?"

"Not especially."

"What?"

"I just want to have a bit of fun."

"Nothing wrong with doing both."

They doubled-back and stopped in a small clearing. Ingrid held a finger to her lips. They listened. After a few moments Mills shrugged at her.

"What do we do now? Just wait for someone to stumble past? That doesn't seem very sporting."

"How are your tree climbing skills?"

"Wait in ambush for them? Shouldn't we be using our highly tuned detective tracking skills?"

"I left my eyeglass and deerstalker at home."

Mills looked around the clearing. "None of these trees look particularly climbable. I suppose… I mean, we could use the opportunity to get to know one another a bit better."

"Tell me you weren't part of this whole goddamn set up."

"No!" His hand shot up to his mouth, the word had come out a little loud. "No, not at all," he whispered. "But as we are both here… where's the harm in being friendly?"

Ingrid was just about to remind him how inappropriate that would be, given she was an engaged woman and all, when a sharp crack echoed around the forest: the sound of a tinder dry branch snapping. She pointed in the direction of the sound and Mills nodded back at her. They crept to the side of the clearing and slipped behind the thick gnarled trunk of an oak tree.

They waited.

After a couple of minutes Mills started to get restless. Ingrid laid a hand on his arm and looked up into his eyes. She felt the muscles in his forearm flex. He held on to her gaze for a moment longer than she was expecting. But, never one to look away first, Ingrid continued to stare back at him. An unexpected and unwanted thrill ran up her spine.

Another crack sounded. Much louder this time. Coming from directly ahead of them. Ingrid lifted the strange blowpipe contraption to eye-level and steadied herself. She saw a figure dash between two trees. Too fast to get a shot. The figure wasn't wearing a vest either. Without the hi-vis marker it was impossible to identify their opponent. Could it be one of their own team? The individual was too tall to be McKittrick, too fast to be Jane and too broad-shouldered to be Kapoor or Murray. From this distance, Ingrid couldn't even work out if it were a man or a woman. She continued to stare hard in the direction of the movement until her eyes started to water. She pointed behind where the figure was standing, away from the clearing and raised her eyebrows at Mills. He shrugged back at her.

She leaned in close and lowered her voice. "We should try to circle around and come at them from behind—use the element of surprise."

Mills nodded.

They started to move further into the forest, using the trees for cover, both taking extra care to step over twigs and fallen branches as quietly as possible. Continuing this way for two hundred yards or so, Mills stopped, forcing Ingrid to pull up sharply. Her forward momentum sent her crashing into him. For a moment she felt the intense heat coming off his body like steam. She quickly withdrew. They both stood there, staring at one another. Motionless. Listening. Ingrid's heart was pounding. She wasn't entirely sure why.

Another sharp noise sounded out, not the same as before. This was more like a splintering, creaking sound. Then it came again. Emanating from some place above their heads. Ingrid looked up to see an arrow sticking out of the trunk of the tree right next to them, fifteen or so feet up.

"What the fu—"

Another arrow whizzed past them. The quill close enough to brush Ingrid's cheek before it slammed into a tree trunk not two feet from her head. She dropped to the ground, dragging Mills down with her. They half crawled, half snaked along the ground, scrambling onto the other side of the tree that had been hit. Now Ingrid's heart was banging so hard and so fast she thought it might stop. She drew in a deep, slow breath. She listened. Heard footsteps crashing over the undergrowth. She couldn't tell if they were heading toward them or retreating. She tried to speak, but her mouth was so dry her tongue had stuck to the roof of her mouth. She swallowed.

"Hey! I don't know what you think you're playing at, but this isn't a game. Put the bow and arrows down and your hands above your head. You picked on the wrong people to have a little fun with."

"Police!" Mills shouted. "Stop pissing about now and this doesn't have to go any further. Step into the clearing and make yourself known."

The footsteps had slowed, but they were louder now.

Ingrid whispered to Mills, "How fast can you run?"

"As fast as I have to."

"If he doesn't cooperate, we need to head back to base, just as fast as possible. Don't run in a straight line, zig-zag and change direction as often as you can." She pulled herself up into a crouch. "OK, this is your last chance," she hollered, "make yourself visible and put down your weapon."

The footsteps stopped.

Ingrid and Mills looked at one another.

Moments later, another arrow hit the tree right next to them.

Dammit. "Ready?"

Mills nodded back at her.

They both sprinted away from their temporary refuge, Mills heading left, Ingrid going right, creating so much noise herself, it was impossible to tell if the shooter was in pursuit.

Until another arrow flew past her head.

This one was so close it nicked the skin of her right temple. Now she knew two things: he *was* following and for the moment at least, she was his target. Some crazy sky-howler had gone berserk with a lethal weapon in his hands.

She carried on crashing through the forest, trying her damnedest to keep her pace up while zigging and zagging her way around trees, sticking to the most densely wooded areas. She leaped over a fallen trunk and landed heavily on the other side on a mulch of leaves and moss, the surface too slippery to keep her footing. She thumped onto the ground, her right hip and shoulder taking the worst of the impact. She lay there for a moment, just listening for footsteps behind her. When she didn't hear any, she scrambled to her feet.

Big mistake.

An arrow hit her shoulder, skidding off the thick leather strap of her backpack, and deflecting upward, narrowly missing her face. She ran, faster than she'd ever run before. Pumping her arms, willing her weary thigh muscles to carry her further. On and on, she went, forcing her numb brain to remember to adjust her direction every few strides.

Her lungs were screaming at her to stop, but she blundered blindly on. Hoping she was still headed in the right direction, disoriented by the number of times she'd adjusted her course. Her limbs started to feel loose and weak. Still she managed to maintain her speed.

At last she reached the marquee. Mills was already there, a cell phone stuck to his ear, a grim expression on his face. When he saw her his mouth fell open.

"Jesus Christ! You're bleeding!"

She collapsed at his feet.

29

Although Ingrid was unable to persuade Mills not to phone for emergency medical assistance, she at least managed to convince the two EMTs that arrived thirty minutes later that their time would be better spent elsewhere, attending real emergencies. They took a look at the wound on her temple, decided it didn't need stitches and stuck on a dressing. Before they left they examined her shoulder and told her it was badly bruised, but nothing was broken.

After she'd made it back to the marquee, Mills had refused to leave her side, like some kind of loyal rescue dog, when all she wanted was a little time alone to properly get her breath back. To gather her thoughts. To try and work out how some crazy guy had managed to get his hands on a bow and a seemingly endless supply of arrows.

As far as she could tell—no one was telling her very much of anything —the local cops had tried, in vain, to secure the area. The adventure facility was just too big to cordon off. Given that the lunatic with the lethal weapon hadn't hung around to take pot shots at anyone else, she had to presume he had made his escape long before the police arrived. But did that mean he was still out there, lying in wait for some other innocent member of the public to cross his path?

The staff at Nature's Playground had confirmed that one of their Navajo bows was missing, together with around a dozen arrows. All the customers who had been on the archery shooting range had been accounted for. So they were certain the person responsible had nothing to do with their organization.

"Shame they didn't keep their weapons better secured," Mills had complained to no one in particular.

Forty yards or so away, a uniformed officer from the local Hertford-shire force was speaking earnestly with a plain clothes colleague, glancing in Ingrid's direction every now and then. They were keeping her out of their conversations, like some kind of frail invalid. But she was suffering from no more than a superficial head wound and extreme fatigue. Mills had been fielding any approach by the local officers and sending them away again, acting like a one man human shield. He couldn't protect her from their interview forever. Everyone else in their party had been inter-viewed and made statements. Not that they would have seen anything.

With some effort, Ingrid struggled to her feet. Immediately Ralph Mills hurried to put a supportive hand under her elbow. His concern would have been touching if it hadn't been irritating the hell out of her for the past half hour.

"It's OK, Ralph—I think I've got this." She pulled away her arm, but maintained a fixed grin as she did so—she didn't want to hurt his feelings. Her legs were very weak, but she managed to limp over to the plain clothes detective from the Hertfordshire force. "I guess you need to speak to me."

The detective scrutinized her through narrowed eyes then glanced in Mills' direction. "You sure you're up to it? Wouldn't want to overtax you."

"I'll survive. I'd prefer to get through your questions sooner rather than later—I wouldn't mind getting myself into a hot bath."

"Of course. Shall we talk in the car? You can take the weight off."

"I'd like to stand. Sitting down for so long doesn't work well for me." She smiled and took a closer look at the detective. He was in his fifties at least, had a tired face, thinning gray hair and his back was stooped as if a great burden were bearing down on him.

"Can you give me a description of your attacker?"

"I didn't see him. I didn't stick around to find out what he looked like."

"You're sure it was a man?"

"An assumption on my part. He or she was pretty damn fast. And not a bad shot. Thankfully not quite good enough though." She paused for a moment, reliving the moment the fourth arrow struck her shoulder. Imme-diately the area just below her shoulder blade felt a little more tender. "I did see a figure between the trees shortly before the shooting started. He was just a blur. I think that was a man, just from the way he moved. He was pretty well camouflaged against the trees. So I guess he was wearing green, or gray, or maybe light brown clothes."

"Height? Build?"

Ingrid closed her eyes and imagined herself back in the thicket of trees just south of the clearing. "I only saw him for a split second. Average height and build, I guess—not what you want to hear, I realize."

"And you think this may have been your attacker?"

"I have no idea."

The detective let out a weary sigh.

"I'm sorry I can't be more definite. It all happened so fast."

"Is there anything else you remember about the attack that might be relevant?"

Ingrid tried hard to think of something, some nugget of information she could give the guy. In the heat of pursuit her mind was focused on nothing more than survival. Her observational skills pretty much deserted her. She felt a little ashamed she couldn't be more helpful.

The cop handed her his card. "Anything else occurs to you, however unlikely... I don't need to tell you that... just call me, anytime." He turned away and trudged back toward his uniformed colleague.

"Detective!" Ingrid called after him. "Am I free to go?"

He turned slowly back. "Do we have your contact details?"

Ingrid nodded.

"We'll be in touch." He dismissed her with a cursory wave of his hand.

McKittrick and Mills, who had been keeping their distance while Ingrid was talking to the cop, both approached her.

"I've just been talking to one of the PCs," McKittrick said. "They've done a quick search of the area and found no arrows."

"Well they need to do a slower one." It wasn't possible a crazy man wielding a bow and arrow would tidy up after himself. "They just haven't looked hard enough."

"Forensics will be a nightmare," Mills added. "Too many pairs of feet trampling through the area. I don't envy them."

"Do you want someone to stay with you tonight?" McKittrick said and glanced in Mills' direction.

"What, you think someone should sleep on the floor of my hotel room like a guard dog?"

"I was more thinking along the lines of the futon in my spare room." McKittrick raised her eyebrows.

"Thanks for the offer. But I'll be just fine by myself. I don't know why you're assuming he was targeting me in particular."

"No one else was shot at."

"He probably saw Mills and me and decided I'd be the easier prey to hunt down. Slower and weaker."

"Had no idea who he was taking on, did he?" Mills smiled at her.

Ingrid was mad she'd gotten hit at all. If she'd been in optimum shape the guy wouldn't have come close. And if she'd really been in form, she would have outrun him, circled back, climbed a tree and ambushed the bastard.

"I'll order us a cab to the station," Mills said.

"Sod that. I'll get one of the uniforms to drive us back. It's the least they can do," McKittrick said and marched off toward the nearest cop car.

"I feel like I abandoned you," Mills said. "I should have come with you."

"And give him twice the target to aim at? Forget about it. In the circumstances, we did the only thing we could."

"Even so." Mills sniffed and looked down at the ground.

"Stop beating yourself up. It doesn't help." She touched him lightly on the arm. "Believe me, I've had plenty of experience."

He smiled at her and nodded, then, seemingly instinctively, he craned his neck down and planted a kiss on the top of her head. Taken completely off guard, Ingrid reared away from him and stumbled backward. Mills' expression suddenly turned from sympathy to something approaching horror.

"God. I'm so sorry," he blurted, "I don't know what I was thinking. I just… You looked so… I wasn't thinking."

Ingrid didn't know what to say. So she said nothing. She turned her head to see McKittrick waving at her from a patrol car twenty or so yards away. Ingrid hurried toward her without risking a backward glance at Mills.

30

"My God—what the hell happened to you?" Sol Franklin stood at his front door and stared at Ingrid open-mouthed.

Without thinking, Ingrid raised a hand to her head. "It's nothing. Someone got a little out of control with a bow and arrow."

"They did what?"

"Are you going to invite me inside, or should I tell you all about it in your front yard?"

Sol pulled the door wide open and ushered her inside. "Isaac's here already, tucking into the hors d'oeuvres."

Poor bastard. Ingrid remembered her initiation dinner at the Franklins like it was yesterday. Sol took enormous pleasure in torturing new recruits with his wife's cooking. If Isaac managed to get through to dessert, he'd pass the Assistant Special Agent in Charge's test with honors. Unfortunately, Ingrid would be forced to endure the same menu. She hoped she could blame her injury for her lack of appetite and Madeleine Franklin would accept the excuse.

By the end of the first course of mushroom pulp on carbonized toast—not the way Mrs Franklin had described it—Ingrid had told the little gathering all about her outdoor adventure.

"And the local cops don't have any leads?" Sol asked.

"Short of the guy handing himself in, I don't think they stand a chance of getting anywhere. They have closed down the facility for the time being. They were breaking every health and safety code in the book, apparently."

429

"Do you think he was targeting you specifically?" Isaac asked as he placed his fork deliberately in the middle of his plate, signaling he was done. To his credit, he'd managed to ingest the whole of his mushroom mush.

"How could he be? I didn't even know where I was headed until I arrived there."

"Maybe he was following you." Isaac dabbed at his mouth with a linen napkin and leaned a little closer toward Ingrid, who was sitting opposite him.

"I think that's a little fanciful."

"But not impossible?"

"As good as." The thought had crossed Ingrid's mind. But since she'd been in the UK, only a half dozen cases had resulted in the arrests of suspects. Ingrid knew for a fact four of those were back in the US and the other two were both in custody here in London. She'd dismissed the idea that someone was targeting her specifically almost as soon as it had occurred to her. "It's not like I've made any enemies."

"Oh I don't know, I can get pretty pissed at you from time to time." Sol smiled broadly at her.

"You look so pale," Madeleine Franklin said. "Do you think maybe you should be in the hospital?"

"No, ma'am, really, I'm just fine. I'm just so sorry I don't have much of an appetite." She offered a weak smile while Sol shot her an admonishing glare.

Uncomfortable with so much attention focused on her, Ingrid was keen to change the subject. "Say, Isaac, did you get a chance to follow up on the missing person case on Friday?"

Before he could answer, Madeleine Franklin got to her feet and announced that the main course would follow imminently. Ingrid saw Isaac stiffen slightly. "I suggest you stop talking about work by the time I come back in."

"Need a hand, my love?" Sol said it with the demeanor of a man who is permanently banned from the kitchen. He hadn't moved a muscle—he knew before he asked what his wife's answer would be.

"Did you manage to pull up the phone records?" Ingrid asked Isaac.

"He hasn't used his cell phone for three straight days. Or his bank cards."

"You think it's time to call in the local cops?" Ingrid asked him.

"Can I do that?" Isaac glanced at Sol for guidance.

"Sure you can," Ingrid answered. "This is your case now."

Isaac straightened his back and sat a little taller. "OK—I will."

"Just keep me posted."

"Of course. I'll get onto the local Borough Command first thing in the morning."

"If he survives the next two courses," Sol mumbled to Ingrid. "In the lull before the oncoming storm, I'm going to smoke a cigarette very slowly. I'll see you good people later."

"You OK here on your own for a while?" Ingrid asked Isaac. "I need to speak to Sol about something."

"Sure—just come back before the food arrives."

Ingrid smiled at him and squeezed his shoulder as she walked past. Isaac Coleman was shaping up OK, especially if he graciously made his way through the main and dessert. Ingrid headed for the kitchen and Madeleine pointed to an open back door. Through the gap Ingrid saw Sol leaning on a wooden rail at the far end of his deck.

"Don't be long," Madeleine said, and dabbed at her brow with a napkin. She peered into the oven and sighed.

Ingrid hurried to join Sol and stood at the rail with him—staring out into a darkening backyard.

"Has he passed the test?" she asked him.

"Too early to call. He didn't play with his first course like you did. So he gets some Brownie points for that." He turned and peered into her face. "Does it hurt?"

"I'll survive."

"That's not what I asked."

"You know me, takes more than a lunatic playing cowboys and injuns to keep me down."

"How's the City trader case coming along?"

"Still waiting for the cops to locate the missing cleaner. I don't hold out much hope."

"You don't think the cops are up to the job?"

"They don't really stand a chance. Hernandez could be anywhere. I'm still trying to figure out why Matthew Fuller was targeted. I'm sure if we could just persuade Witness Protection to reveal his former identity—"

"We've been through this already. You know what I think about it. He was a kid when his name changed and the family moved house. Too young to make any enemies. Especially the kind who would spend the next twenty or so years hunting him down. You're chasing your tail on that one. It's not a percentage shot."

"But we've played all the percentage shots already. And we're losing the game."

"Maybe I'll run it past the DSAC. Let her make the decision."

"Thanks, Sol," Ingrid said begrudgingly. She knew there was as much chance of Amy Louden agreeing her request as Isaac asking for a second helping of his main course.

Sol took an extra long drag on his cigarette, then stubbed it out in an old champagne bucket filled with sand. "We'd better get back in there, give the poor kid some moral support."

"Hey," Ingrid said, "I forgot to tell you... I found myself a perfect apartment."

"I didn't even know you were looking."

"It was a spur of the moment thing, I guess."

"Sick of hotel gourmet cooking, huh?"

"Something like that."

"I'm glad to hear it."

"You are?"

"It means you're planning to stay on at the embassy. And that makes me very happy."

31

The next morning Ingrid felt remarkably good, considering what she'd been through the day before. She was at her desk by eight. Isaac didn't show up until well after nine.

"You survived the night," Ingrid declared when he shuffled to his desk. "For moments at dinner it was pretty much touch and go."

"I've got a strong constitution." He laid a hand gently on his stomach.

"You certainly have. I've got to admit, I was impressed."

He gave her an uncertain smile and lowered himself gingerly to his seat.

Ingrid then spent the next three hours chasing Mbeke, Fraser and the detective from the paintballing place for updates. When she eventually tracked them all down, she discovered they had nothing new to report.

At midday she received the call she'd been hoping for.

"Mike—you got something?"

"You wanted a list, I got you a list."

"And so fast too." Ingrid knew Mike Stiller wouldn't just put the information she'd requested in an email. He needed praise far too much for that. She just needed to remember to heap some on him at every given opportunity. "You are a miracle worker, Agent Stiller."

"You know me, I try to squeeze in three miracles before breakfast."

Ingrid had to remind herself that it was still only seven a.m. in D.C. He must have been working on her request over the weekend. Things had to be difficult at home, with Mary or the kids, for him to need to escape to the office quite so much. "What can I say—I owe you majorly." She waited for him to continue in his own good time.

He cleared his throat then made a gulping sound. Knowing Mike it was probably his fourth latte of the morning. "So... Barbara Highsmith." He swallowed another gulp of coffee. "The ex-congresswoman handled thirty-two financial cases in total while she was working as an Assistant US Attorney. That's an average of just under five a year. Seems she specialized."

Great.

"Any stand-out cases I should pay closer attention to?"

"You haven't exactly been clear what I was supposed to be looking for."

"A defendant who had some reason to want to finish her off."

"I guess at the time, any one of them might have wanted to wreak revenge. But bearing a grudge over twenty years later? You'd think the rage would have subsided after all that time."

"Unless it was festering while he was inside."

"I don't have time to analyze all thirty-two cases for you."

"No, of course not. And I don't expect you to. Email over the files and I'll start on the analysis myself."

"Oh... OK." He'd managed to convey a whole world of disappointment with just two words.

"Did any of the cases involve Witness Protection?" Ingrid asked.

"Wait a minute, I'll check." Less than thirty seconds later he had an answer for her. "We have a grand total of three witnesses who traded key evidence for immunity from prosecution and a new identity."

"Can you give me their names?" She grabbed a pen and pad from her desk drawer.

Mike spelled out each one for her. "But wouldn't it help to know their new identities too?"

"In a perfect world. The guy who's death I'm investigating here in London was in Witness Protection, but the Marshals Office are refusing to let me know anything about his former life."

"You want me to speak to them?"

"Would you?"

"I have a buddy in the Marshals Service. He owes me a couple favors. What's the guy's new name?"

Ingrid gave him Matthew Fuller's details, cursing herself for not thinking of asking Mike for help before. He'd been a Fed so long, he had contacts in pretty much every law enforcement agency there was.

"Leave it with me."

"Thanks, Mike." Ingrid was trying very hard to contain her excitement. Knowing Matthew Fuller's former identity might crack the whole case wide open.

"Is that it?"

"Before you go, can you tell me the names of the convicted defendants in the Witness Protection cases?"

Again, Stiller spelled out the names for her. Then made his excuses and hung up.

Ingrid set to work, searching the database for information about the three defendants. By the time she'd discovered the fate of the third, she felt like banging her head against the desk. If she didn't already have a throbbing headache, she would have done just that.

All three defendants were dead. Two had died after they'd completed their sentences, the third had died in custody, shot dead by a prison guard after attempting to attack the deputy governor. The prisoner went down only after the third bullet was pumped into his chest. Ingrid stared at the screen as she tried to picture the incident. The prisoner must have known his act was suicide, plain and simple. There was a phrase the Behavioral Analysis Unit was fond of using in those circumstances: suicide by cop.

Ingrid continued to stare at her computer monitor. Her last behavioral training session had taken place almost twelve months ago at Quantico. She tried to recall any details that might be relevant. The subject of 'suicide by cop' had come up more than once. She was pretty sure, that according to the Behavioral Analysis guys, sociopaths were much more likely to choose that option of suicide than any other. They were still determined to make their mark, to bend law enforcement officers to their will, right up until the end. She looked at the details of the inmate: Henry Ellis.

If he'd still been alive he would be sixty years old by now. Too old to fit the description they had for Darryl Wyatt in any case. But possibly the right profile in terms of his psychology. And sociopathy often ran in families.

She continued to study the details of the case and discovered that Henry Ellis' crime involved a Ponzi-style scheme that swindled dozens of innocent investors out of millions of dollars. He used the money from each tranche of new investors to pay out to the existing ones at fabulous rates of return, generating an investment frenzy and an endless supply of greedy, if decidedly gullible, investors. The original investor gave evidence against Ellis in return for immunity from prosecution. Then, with his family, he disappeared, courtesy of the Witness Protection Program.

It was way too early to expect Mike Stiller to have contacted his buddy in the US Marshals Office, but Ingrid had to at least try him. She tapped his number into her cell. He answered after the first ring. "Mike, you got any news for me?"

"Hey, I just got off the phone. I'm feeling a little harassed here."

"I'm just eager to get some place with this goddamn case."

"Take it easy, you're sounding a little… stressed."

"Stressed? No way. Just enthusiastic."

"Answer me one question."

"Anything."

"How much do you owe your successful career in the Bureau to yours truly?"

"You know I owe you everything, Mike. It goes without saying."

"Sometimes it's nice to hear it."

"So… your buddy in Witness Protection?"

"Matthew Fuller's name, aged seven, was Matthew Brite. His dad testified against a Henry Ellis, some Ponzi investment scam."

A chill ran across Ingrid's shoulders.

It was the information she had been hoping for. Finally she had a connection between Barbara Highsmith and Matthew Fuller: Highsmith the highly successful, career-focused prosecuting attorney, Fuller the son of the man whose testimony the whole case depended on.

"David Brite is dead, you know that?" Mike said.

"Matthew's dad? Yes—he died in an accident."

"You make it sound straightforward."

"Are you going to tell me that it wasn't?"

"He died while water-skiing, if you can believe it."

"Is that relevant?"

"Did you know the reason for death was asphyxiation?"

"He drowned, I guess."

"No—his asthma inhaler was empty when he tried to use it. He died of an asthma attack."

"Are you suggesting his inhaler was tampered with?"

"I'm just putting two and two together and making plenty. Think about it: the prosecuting attorney in the Ellis case is dead, the star witness is dead, the witness' son is dead. Seems a pretty comprehensive wipeout to me."

"But Henry Ellis is dead too. He didn't kill those people."

"I'm looking at his details right here." Mike's tone sounded decidedly smug.

"What is it?"

"How much do you owe me?"

"Give me a break, Mike." Ingrid's head was pounding.

"Ellis had a son, Cory, born 1979."

Ingrid did the math. "He'd be thirty-four now."

"Don't tell me, that just happens to be the same age as your suspect."

"Mike! You are a genius."

"I know."

"Thank you so much." Ingrid looked up to discover Jennifer looming over her desk, a panicked expression on her face. "Listen Mike, something's come up. I'll call you back." She slammed down the phone. "What is it?"

"You've got blood running all down your face."

32

"How many more times will I have to patch you up, huh?" The embassy doctor was standing in the doorway of the office, wagging a finger at Ingrid.

As far as she could recall, she'd never even asked for his assistance. She threw an accusatory glance at Jennifer, who quickly looked away.

Ingrid then managed to force herself to sit still through the doctor's examination, an endless list of questions and finally the application of a fresh dressing. All in all, she was incapacitated for well over an hour.

Eventually he snapped off his latex gloves. "Now please—take it easy, will you? How's the shoulder?"

"A little sore, but fine. It's nothing more than a big ugly purple bruise."

"I've a mind to sign you off active duty."

"That really won't be necessary."

"There's nothing wrong with admitting you're hurt, you know."

"I'm just sitting at my desk—what possible harm can I come to?"

The doctor turned to Jennifer. "Can I rely on you to make sure she does exactly that?"

Jennifer nodded meekly at him, but avoided Ingrid's gaze. When finally he exited the office, the clerk said, "I only did what was right. I'm not going to apologize for that. You need somebody looking out for you."

Ingrid immediately got back on the phone to Mike Stiller.

"What was the problem?"

"Just an open head wound."

"Yours?"

"Yep."

"You OK?"

"Right as rain. Couple Tylenol and I'll be fully restored."

"Something else you want to discuss?"

"I've been thinking... if you were Ellis' son, why wait so long to avenge your dad's death? Henry Ellis died in 1992, David Brite was killed in 2003."

"Cory Ellis was only thirteen when his dad died. What did you expect him to do? Quit school and go on the rampage?"

"But the ex-congresswoman was murdered just last May, *twenty* years after Henry Ellis committed suicide. Cory Ellis must be an exceptionally patient man."

"Maybe we could describe him as goal-oriented and extremely focused. Determined, single-minded."

Mike Stiller had just set out more character traits for a narcissistic sociopath. Ingrid got a little fidgety. She had a link connecting Highsmith and Fuller and a profile that fit the one she'd sketched of Darryl Wyatt. Cory Ellis had to be her man.

"Wait a minute," Mike said.

"What is it?"

"What a tragedy."

"What have you found out?"

"Mary Ellis, Henry's widow, Cory's mom, also committed suicide, May 15th 2001."

The date was significant, Ingrid was sure. If her head had been a little clearer, she might have remembered why before Mike Stiller chimed in.

"The ninth anniversary of Henry Ellis' death," he said, a note of smugness creeping into his voice.

Ingrid sat very still. She tried to concentrate. The date of Henry Ellis' death wasn't the one she was thinking of. Then, despite the anvil pounding in her head, it came to her. "That's the day Barbara Highsmith was killed."

"It was?"

"When did David Brite have his fatal accident?"

Mike tapped in something to his keyboard. Ingrid waited. "Same date," he told her after a few moments.

"That's one way to mark the anniversary of your parents' deaths."

At the other end of the line Mike Stiller let out a breathy whistle.

"Can you send me everything you have from the Marshals Office?"

"Sure. Who knew a stupid Ponzi scheme could cause so much havoc?"

"It wouldn't have been the first time. Or the last."

"Listen, I'll send you everything I've got. But you should take it easy, you hear? Open head wounds don't heal without a little help."

"No need to worry about me." She hung up and stared for a little while at the phone. Something was niggling at her, but the harder she tried to pin it down, the more elusive it became. She waited for Mike's email to arrive, and tried to get a little more comfortable at her desk.

Just a couple of minutes later, a cascade of emails and attachments arrived courtesy of Agent Stiller. Ingrid set to work. After an hour or so of going through both Matthew 'Brite' Fuller's records and those of his mother and father, her eyes started to swim a little. She closed them and relaxed back in her seat. Maybe it was time for another couple Tylenol.

———

Ingrid snapped open her eyes. The stabbing pain in her temple was so intense that she saw black dots in front of her eyes. It took her a few moments longer to realize her head was resting on her arms and her arms were leaning flat on her desk. She blinked. Someone had thoughtfully draped her jacket over her shoulders. Her mouth was connected to her sleeve by a trail of drool. She managed to lick her lips.

Slowly, painfully slowly, she pushed up off the desk and sat up straight. The room spun a little. She waited for it to stop before trying to move again.

Both Jennifer's and Isaac's desks were empty. They'd obviously left silently, not wanting to disturb her. Given how stiff her limbs felt and how sharp the pain in her temple, she might have welcomed a little gentle prodding. Then she noticed an old-fashioned alarm clock sitting on the corner of her desk. It was set to go off in five minutes. Next to the clock was a bottle of Evian, two white, oval-shaped pills and a note telling her to take it easy. Jennifer Rocharde had thought of everything.

Ingrid's cell started to buzz. She watched it creep a little further across her desk with every vibration. She peered at the screen before picking it up.

Crap.

It was the real estate agent. She was supposed to be moving into her apartment today. She grabbed the phone.

"Hi." The word came out as a croak.

"Ms Skyberg?"

She was so used to having her name prefaced with "Agent" she was momentarily at a loss how to respond.

"I'm here outside the property. Have been since six-thirty." His voice sounded weird, a little higher pitched than she remembered it. He was obviously very pissed at her.

"I'll be there in ten minutes, I swear."

She shrugged into her jacket, grabbed her purse and headed for the women's restroom. A splash of cold water turned out to be even more restorative than she'd hoped.

She headed for the basement parking lot, her stiff legs getting a little looser with every stride.

33

Getting out onto Park Lane and then around Marble Arch at the northeast corner of Hyde Park was no problem at all. Ingrid maneuvered the bike around stationary buses and black taxis, and quickly turned left into Edgware Road, made it fifty yards north, then stopped. Suddenly nothing seemed to be moving up or down the street. There was barely enough space for bicycles to squeeze through the gaps and most of the cyclists had taken to the sidewalk. All she could do was sit and wait. She pulled her phone from a pocket and sent an apologetic text to the realtor. He responded with a text back: *no worries*.

The bike crept forward by tiny increments for the next twenty minutes. More than once, Ingrid considered abandoning it at the side of the road. But she was still faster on two wheels than two legs—especially given the soreness in her shoulder and the throbbing pain in her head. Frustrated as hell, she continued to make very slow progress for another ten minutes, until she passed under the Marylebone expressway. Then, as if by magic, the gridlock ceased. Glancing across the street, Ingrid noticed an ambulance and two smashed up cars. The snarl-up had been caused by an accident in the southbound lane, and then compounded by rubberneckers on the northbound curious to see what had happened. Ingrid had slowed down herself to take a good look at the wreckage at the side of the road. She quickly chastised herself and accelerated toward Maida Vale.

Five minutes later she was climbing off the bike in the forecourt of the apartment block. She took off her helmet and gloves, stored them in the box on the bike and surveyed the parked vehicles for a red, white and blue Mini. There wasn't one. She jogged out onto the street. No Mini there either. And no sign of the realtor on the sidewalk.

Dammit.

He must have gotten tired of waiting for her. So much for his laid back response to her text. She checked her phone. She definitely hadn't missed a call. She returned to the bike and glanced at the main entrance of the building. An envelope was wedged inside one of the long brass door handles. Ingrid pulled it free and discovered her name was scribbled on the front. She tore it open and shook out a set of keys, three in total. Two for the apartment itself and one for the main entrance. She peered inside the envelope expecting to see a note, but there wasn't one.

She thought about going straight up to remind herself just how great the view was, but it was already after eight p.m., so she decided to return to her hotel to check out.

The journey to Marylebone was much easier than the one to Maida Vale. No sign of the road traffic accident at all. Less than a half hour after leaving the apartment block, she was stuffing her handful of possessions into a small suitcase.

She opened the safe inside the closet and pulled out its contents: her passport, a little under $1000 in cash, and her engagement ring. She slipped the ring onto her finger. It felt cold. And a little loose. She must have lost weight since she last wore it. Staring down at the cluster of diamonds set in white gold, she pictured Marshall on one knee—in the middle of his favorite restaurant—reciting a little speech he'd obviously rehearsed. It had to be one of the few times she'd actually detected a flicker of vulnerability in his expression. He'd looked so earnest, so serious, so needy. And the most handsome she'd ever seen him. She wasn't sure how long it had taken her to say yes, but long enough for all the other diners to stop eating and stare at them. With that kind of audience anticipation, she couldn't really say no.

They had been engaged for over a year now. She'd have to agree to a date for the wedding soon. But she couldn't think about that right now. She took off the ring and slipped it into her purse. Immediately she felt a little lighter.

She sank onto the bed. What was she doing? She hadn't even told Marshall about the apartment yet. And here she was, getting excited about her first night there. Thinking about waking up in the morning to glorious views. She wondered if she should call him right then. Tell him she was planning to stay on in London—at least for the next little while. She pulled her cell from her purse, then just stared at the screen.

Tomorrow. She'd tell Marshall tomorrow.

With her daypack on her back and the suitcase strapped to the back of the bike, Ingrid rode the short distance to the embassy, picked up the sleeping bag she kept in the large drawer beneath her desk, then headed north to her new home.

When she finally got inside the building she discovered the elevators were out of order. She struggled over to the stairway with her suitcase and stood looking up at the first flight. A sudden and overwhelming fatigue enveloped her. The eight-story trek to the top floor felt like an attempt on Everest. She took a deep breath and started to climb. By the time she'd reached the halfway point she texted McKittrick, suggesting a little company and a large bottle of tequila seemed like a nice way to welcome her into her new home.

The final flights seemed to go on forever, but she finally made it to the apartment door, fumbled a little with the keys, and practically fell into the hallway.

The apartment was way too hot, like a tropical plant house. Her head pounded. The heating had to be on. The realtor had promised all the appliances would be checked before she moved in. Presumably, whoever checked the radiators had forgotten to turn them off. She dumped her bags in the hall and headed for the bathroom, where she remembered seeing the gas-fired heater on her earlier visit.

Sure enough, the heater was busy distributing kilowatts to all the chunky white radiators in every room. She searched for an off switch, but couldn't find anything that looked right. She did find a red dial, which she gave a good hard yank counter-clockwise. Half the dial came off in her hand, the plastic fracturing in a jagged diagonal line.

Her head throbbed a little harder. Her breathing quickened. She needed to get some cool evening air into the apartment. As she turned toward the window, she noticed something shiny lying in the bath. She bent down and reached out a hand. In an instant her head started to spin. She straightened up and leaned against the wall, wondering if the dizziness was a result of her head injury or the lack of air. She took a couple of deep, steadying breaths and turned again toward the window. She unscrewed the latch and tried to push the top sash upward. It wouldn't budge. It looked painted shut.

Goddammit.

Maybe she could open the door onto the roof terrace. She spun around and started to head for the hall, but the sudden movement made her dizziness worse. She grabbed onto the doorframe with both hands, but her head started to buzz. She took a deep breath and stepped out into the hall.

Her sense of balance abandoned her completely. Her legs buckled and she sprawled across the floor. She tried to get up again, but her limbs felt so weak. Her eyes started to close and there was nothing she could do to keep them open. She laid her head on the floor—her flushed cheek found some relief against the cold floorboards—and drifted into unconsciousness.

34

An intense pressure squeezed Ingrid's arms. Her head lolled from side to side. She couldn't seem to stop it. There was more pressure across her chest, as if something were pressing down on her. She tried to open her eyes.

She saw her dad, his arms open wide, just waiting for her to run into them. But how could she run when she couldn't move her legs? In the distance she heard a voice she recognized. A woman's voice, far, far away.

Natasha? What was Natasha McKittrick doing here in Minnesota? Was she on vacation?

"Ingrid! Wake up!"

Ingrid's head lolled again, faster than before. She was shaking. No—being shaken. Why couldn't Natasha just let her sleep? She was so tired. The pressure on her arms subsided. It started up again around her wrists. Then the floorboards started to slide beneath her. Who was moving the floor? She heard a door slam behind her. The floor felt wonderfully cold. Colder than it had before.

She didn't know this place. Where did her dad go? This wasn't Minnesota.

Cold liquid splashed across her face. What was that smell? Tequila? She heard Natasha's voice again, urgent and loud. What was she saying? Ingrid opened her eyes. Even though she could have sworn they were already open.

This time she didn't see her dad. Where was she? "Natasha?"

"Oh thank God. Stay with me, Ingrid."

Ingrid managed to prop herself up on an elbow. She had seen this place before, but couldn't recall when.

"The ambulance is on its way."

"I'm so hot."

McKittrick helped Ingrid to her feet and they limped out through a set of doors and into a stairwell. They sank down onto the first step. "That's it," McKittrick said, "big deep breaths."

Moment by moment, Ingrid's head cleared a fraction more. Her apartment. *That's* where she was. "What happened?"

"I'm not sure. How're you feeling?"

"Like crap." She tried to swallow. "Thirsty."

McKittrick fished around in her purse and pulled out a half full bottle of mineral water. Ingrid gulped down the lot. Then threw it all back up again two seconds later. All over her friend's shoes.

"I'm sorry."

"In the circumstances, I don't think that really matters."

Ingrid grabbed the banister rail and managed to haul herself up to her feet. She blinked hard a few times and dragged a sleeve across her mouth. She swayed left then right.

"Sit down, for God's sake." McKittrick put a hand under Ingrid's elbow to support her.

"I don't understand. What happened?"

"Let's not worry about that for now, shall we?"

A siren sounded in the distance. "You called the police?"

"No—I'm hoping that's the ambulance."

Ingrid pulled her arm away from McKittrick's. "I don't need an ambulance. I feel better already." She lurched to one side and reached out a hand for the banister rail.

"Tough. You're going to hospital even if I have to arrest you first." McKittrick punched a number in her phone. "This is Detective Inspector Natasha McKittrick, HSCC, area team four. I'm going to need police and fire brigade. I think there might be a gas leak." She pulled the phone from her ear. "Ingrid—could you smell gas when you arrived?"

"What? No—there's no leak. What are you saying?"

"Did you hear that?" McKittrick said into the phone. "I'd hazard a guess at carbon monoxide." She listened for a moment to the person on the phone. "I might not be here when they arrive, I've got to take my friend to the hospital. But if anyone needs to speak to me, you can give them this mobile number." She hung up.

"Carbon monoxide?" Ingrid's words continued to slur, no matter how hard she tried to speak normally.

A loud bang echoed up the stairwell. Then a door slammed. A minute or so later the door into the stairwell opened and an EMT ran through. He took one look at Ingrid and called out to his colleague, who was still in the lobby. A gurney appeared in the doorway.

"I'm not getting on that thing. I can walk." Ingrid stumbled forward a couple of steps and her legs gave way.

The next thing she was aware of was a flashlight shining in her eyes. "You're going to be just fine," a soothing female voice told her. Then sleep overcame her again.

———

When she woke up Ingrid could feel something digging into her nostrils. She raised her hand to her nose, but another hand stopped her before she reached it.

"Leave that just where it is."

Ingrid fought to focus on the face that the voice was coming from. Natasha McKittrick. She blinked and took in her surroundings. A hospital room. The blanket felt heavy against her legs. Light was coming in from a large window to her left. She had a gray plastic clip on one of her fingers and a tube of clear liquid feeding into her left arm.

"What day is it?" She struggled to get the words out, her mouth was so dry.

"Here." McKittrick lifted a plastic beaker to her lips and Ingrid took a sip of water. "It's Tuesday, you've been in overnight."

Ingrid tried to sit up. "My apartment." Memories of the night before were drifting in and out of her mind in a muddled mess.

McKittrick helped raise the pillows behind her and Ingrid pulled herself up. "Do you need the nurse or anything?"

"Not right now. Tell me what happened." She was having trouble focusing, so she closed her eyes. When she opened them again, the chair McKittrick had been sitting in was empty. She glanced toward the door. Through the porthole window she saw the detective speaking to a uniformed cop. A moment later the door opened and McKittrick came back in carrying a Pret A Manger plastic bag.

"Hey—you're with us again." She dumped the bag on a tall bedside cabinet and pulled out a cardboard cup. "I went for decaf—hope you don't mind. I didn't want your heart rate setting off any alarms. There's a pot of muesli and yogurt there for you when you're ready."

Ingrid smiled up at her. "Thank you."

"Don't mention it."

"I fell asleep earlier. I didn't mean to."

"Go right ahead and drift off again, if you need to."

Ingrid blinked a few times and wriggled upwards in the bed. She puffed out a breath.

"The color's come back into your face. You look a bloody sight better than you did earlier."

"What time is it?"

"Two in the afternoon."

"Why is there a cop outside the room?"

"Protection."

"What?"

"You really don't remember what happened?"

"It's a little hazy." She gave her friend a weak smile.

McKittrick sat down on the edge of the bed. "You may want to get comfortable. It could take a while." She handed Ingrid the coffee. "The fire brigade have done some analysis, and it was definitely carbon monoxide poisoning. The flue leading out of the boiler in your bathroom had come loose, and instead of the waste gases going straight outside, they all leaked into the flat."

"That doesn't explain the cop."

"I'll make allowances for your slowness, given you've only just come round. But I'm warning you now, my patience might wear a bit thin—I've been up most of the night." She pulled another cup from the Pret bag and took a sip. "The friendly neighborhood bobby is outside because three of the four screws that were meant to fix the flue in place had been removed." She stared into Ingrid's eyes. "Not come loose with general wear and tear, not rusted away... removed deliberately."

A sudden memory of the shiny objects she had seen in the bathtub popped into Ingrid's head. "Someone tried to..."

"Kill you... bump you off... do you in... yes." McKittrick put her coffee on the bedside cabinet. "Second attempt on your life in as many days. Even the Met aren't going to ignore that."

"Contact Sol Franklin—he can send someone from the embassy."

"You saying our boys can't handle it?"

"Only thinking of your budgets."

"Sod that! Besides, I've already spoken to Sol, he was in earlier with a huge bunch of inappropriate flowers. The nurses weren't at all happy with him."

Ingrid drank a little of her caffeine-free, and frankly, pointless black coffee while she considered who the hell might want to kill her. "I've got to get out of here." Pulling the blanket from her legs she noticed the tube that had been anchoring her to a drip was gone. All that remained was a cannula leading into a vein in her arm with transparent adhesive tape. She wondered how bad the bleeding would be if she just yanked it out.

"Stay exactly where you are."

"I need to find out who did this." She sat very still for a moment, the sudden movement had made her head spin. "How did they know about the apartment? Or the paintballing thing on Sunday? I didn't even know where I was going until we arrived."

"As it happens, I've been giving it some thought. I've had a bit of time on my hands, sitting here, listening to you snore."

"I don't snore."

"Well all last night you did. Thank God you're in a private room."

"And what did you come up with?"

"He must have followed you. To the paintballing place on Sunday and to your apartment yesterday evening."

Ingrid screwed up her face as a wave of nausea swept over her then gradually subsided.

"Jesus—should I fetch someone?"

"Oh God—I just remembered—I threw up on your shoes last night."

"It's OK—I wasn't that fond of them anyway."

"Sorry." Ingrid sniffed. "Whoever sabotaged the boiler would have needed to reach the apartment way ahead of me, just to have enough time to do what they did. They couldn't have followed me."

"Glad to see the gray cells have started firing. I suppose he must have already known about the flat."

"He?"

McKittrick raised her eyebrows. "You said it was a bloke who fired arrows at you."

"You should speak to the real estate agent."

"Tried that. He didn't show up for work today."

"He didn't?"

McKittrick shrugged. "Gone AWOL. I don't think he's our man, though."

"I really do need to get out of here."

"The registrar's doing his rounds later this afternoon. If he says you're good to go, fine. Otherwise you're here for another night."

"Better make sure I pass the test. I'll have that yogurt now."

"I should warn you, you might get a call from Marshall at some point." McKittrick couldn't look her in the eye.

"You told him?"

"I didn't—but someone at the embassy must have. I called your colleagues to find out who your next of kin was—I guessed, as he's only your fiancé, it wouldn't be Marshall. The hospital insisted on having a name."

Ingrid shuddered slightly.

"You cold? Want another blanket?"

"It's my mom."

"I know that now. Svetlana Skyberg. Now that's got a good old American ring to it."

"It's a Russian name."

"I would never have guessed."

"Should I expect a call from her too?" Ingrid shuddered again.

McKittrick shrugged back at her. "Judging by the look on your face, I'm guessing you don't want to speak to her?"

Ingrid shook her head.

"If she calls," McKittrick said, "I'll take it."

———

A half hour later Detective Constable Ralph Mills arrived with a bunch of magazines shoved under one arm. He hesitated at the door, too awkward to come straight in.

In a rush, Ingrid remembered the way she'd recoiled from the kiss he'd planted on the top of her head on Sunday. Thinking about it now, the kiss was as chaste as a grandson pecking his grandmother's cheek. She had completely overreacted. She needed somehow to make amends.

"I was expecting the doctor," she told him as he closed the door. The words came out like a criticism, not as she'd intended at all.

"Sorry to disappoint." He handed her the magazines. "I wasn't sure what you'd like, so I bought a range." He offered her the merest hint of a smile.

"That was very thoughtful of you. Thank you."

Ingrid fanned the glossy monthlies out across the bedclothes. *Parkour and Free Running*, *Motorcycle Monthly*, and *Rolling Stone*. Not a bad selection. She wasn't even sure she'd have chosen as well for herself. His insight into her personality unnerved her.

"And if you don't like any of these, you can read the paper." He laid the late afternoon edition of the *Evening News* on top of the magazines.

As Ingrid stared at the paper, she couldn't stop her mouth dropping open.

"What's wrong? Are you OK?" Mills asked her.

Two portraits dominated the front page of the paper. The one on the left was the photograph of Darryl Wyatt taken by his girlfriend, sent to Ingrid by Detective Trooe in Savannah. The one she and Angela Tate had distributed to dozens of properties surrounding the dead Latvian's apartment. The picture on the right was some sort of artist's impression of the same face, but this one had much darker hair and clean-shaven chin and cheeks. Ingrid checked the byline, even though she didn't really need to: Angela Tate.

The headline: *Have you seen this man?* was followed by a brief reminder of how the cherry-headed Latvian woman was murdered. Ingrid continued to read, fighting hard to keep her head clear, and discovered a witness living in the same apartment block had confirmed seeing a man fitting the description of Wyatt visiting the Latvian's apartment regularly for the last few months. He even occasionally stayed over.

"What is it?" Mills asked again.

The clincher came in the next paragraph. A fact that Ingrid had not revealed to Tate: the witness had also confirmed he'd seen a distinctive rose tattoo on the man's left forearm.

"He's definitely here." Ingrid swung her legs over the side of the bed. "There's no doubt now." The facts about Cory Ellis and his connection to both Matthew Fuller and Barbara Highsmith swam up through layers of murky memories and finally surfaced in her mind. "Darryl Wyatt. Cory Ellis. Whatever he's calling himself now."

"Who?"

"Help me find my clothes. I've got to get out of this place."

35

Mills finally located Ingrid's clothes in a large green plastic sack shoved into the bottom of the bedside cabinet. Just as he was handing them over to her, the door opened. McKittrick marched in. A man in smart suit pants and a short sleeved shirt trailed after her. The man raised both eyebrows in an exaggerated expression of surprise.

"I do hope you weren't thinking of going anywhere, Ms Skyberg," he said.

"First of all, it's *Agent* Skyberg, and I am thinking of getting the hell out of here."

"I'll be the judge of that."

The resident—McKittrick had apparently dragged him all the way from the Emergency Room—spent the next five minutes running through tests: checking her blood pressure, temperature, oxygen absorption and reflexes, before finally giving her the OK to be discharged.

"A nurse will be along in a while to remove the cannula," he explained.

"Can't you take it out for me?" Ingrid lifted her arm toward his face.

"I'm afraid matron wouldn't allow that."

"All right—I'll rip it out myself." Ingrid tugged on the adhesive transparent tape and managed to loosen a corner. "I've got to get back to work."

"Stop that! Good grief." The resident quickly washed his hands, donned a pair of disposable gloves from a dispenser above the bed, and carefully unpeeled the adhesive tape. When the cannula was out he told

Ingrid to apply pressure to a folded dressing on the needle site for a minute or so.

"*Now* you can get the hell out of my hospital. But there is absolutely no way you're returning to work. I'm discharging you into the care of a responsible adult on the clear understanding that you rest for the remainder of the day." He looked from Ingrid to McKittrick and back again.

"He means you, Natasha. How responsible are you feeling?" Ingrid peered at the needle puncture. It oozed a little more blood. She pressed the dressing again.

"Well I'm definitely an adult—that'll have to be good enough. We'll get you fixed up at mine, in the spare room."

"I'd be perfectly fine on my own."

"I didn't hear that," the resident said, and left the room.

———

Ingrid and McKittrick were sitting in a taxi stuck in traffic, just a few hundred yards from the hospital when Ingrid decided to make her escape. She reached for the door handle.

McKittrick grabbed her arm. "What the bloody hell do you think you're doing?"

"I need to get to work. I'll pick up another cab."

"You've been released into my care."

"Jennifer's perfectly capable of looking out for me in the office. I've already taken up far too much of your time. You need to get back to work too."

"No way. I'm not letting you out of my sight."

"But I need access to the Bureau database. I know who killed Matthew Fuller. And the Latvian woman. I need to put together a profile of the perp to try and work out where he might be now."

"Fine. But not today."

"Tomorrow might be too late."

"Tough. Call someone. Get your boss to handle it for you."

"It's my case. I've worked damn hard on it."

"You're in no fit state. You're coming home with me and resting. You can watch a bit of television maybe. But mostly, you're going to be lying down and dozing. Carbon monoxide poisoning isn't something you can just shrug off."

"I've had a night in the hospital. I'm fine now."

"Are you still talking? I'm not listening anymore."

"At least let me make a couple of phone calls."

"OK—but make them quick."

Ingrid found her cell phone buried deep in the bottom of her purse and scrolled through the contacts list until she found the name she was looking for. She hit call and waited. And waited. The call was finally answered just as she was about to give up.

"Agent Skyberg, so good of you to get back to me." The sarcasm in Angela Tate's tone was unmistakable. "I've been leaving you messages all morning."

Ingrid glanced at McKittrick, who was staring out of the window. "I've been a little… tied up."

"Seems those flyers worked a treat."

"Have you reported all the information to the investigating team?"

"Of course I have. The witness is probably giving his official statement as we speak."

"Who is this witness?"

"Bloke who lives in the upstairs flat in the same block as the Latvian woman. He'd been away for a few days. Couldn't believe what had been going on in his absence. I got the impression he was rather fond of the woman."

"He gave you the description of the man?"

"He noticed him coming and going. He'd asked Mary about her new boyfriend a couple of times, but she never wanted to talk about him."

"This neighbor knew her name?"

"Only her first name."

"And the name of the boyfriend?"

"Nope."

"How was he so sure the man he'd seen was the same as the one in the photograph?"

"He wasn't one hundred percent. But the likeness was close enough for him to call me."

McKittrick cleared her throat nosily. Ingrid turned to her.

"I'll take that bloody thing away from you. Hurry up and finish the call."

"Who's that?" Tate asked.

"Don't worry about it."

"So—is he your man? You never mentioned a tattoo to me."

"Maybe. I need to do a little more research to be sure."

McKittrick cleared her throat again. Ingrid held up a finger and mouthed "one minute" at her.

"When was the last time the neighbor saw the man?"

There was a pause at the other end of the line. "Last Tuesday evening. That's when he left for his holidays."

"Can you give me the neighbor's details? I'd like to speak to him myself."

Tate told Ingrid his name and flat number. "Though you might want to wait a while. He's rather tied up with the police at the moment. Perhaps you should liaise with them." Tate hung up.

As Ingrid stared down at her cell phone, trying to work out the significance of the timing of Darryl Wyatt's last visit to the property, McKittrick snatched it from her hands.

"That's enough. You already look paler. No work. And that's final."

"I have another call to make."

"It can wait."

"I don't think it can."

"What was that all about anyway?" McKittrick waved Ingrid's phone in the air.

"According to the witness, my suspect returned to the property several hours after he killed her. I don't understand why."

"To clean up after himself, I expect. Didn't you say no forensic evidence was found at the flat?"

"It's more fundamental than that. If I'm right and the man responsible for the Latvian's death also killed Matthew Fuller..." Ingrid's head was just too fuzzy to figure everything out.

"Yes?"

"Bear with me here—"

"Wait a minute... how is this any different from you sitting at your desk working through things? I shouldn't even be talking to you about it."

"Matthew Fuller is on his hit list, he comes all the way to London to kill him. He watches him die a terrifying, painful death. Why not leave the country straight after? You've achieved your goal. Why stick around long enough to discover that your Latvian girlfriend is trying to screw money out of your old bank account in the US?"

McKittrick shrugged. "Maybe he had another reason to stick around."

"Like what?"

"I don't know. I really shouldn't be encouraging you. Let's talk about it later, once you've settled into the spare room."

"For God's sake! I'm not an invalid."

"Actually, right now that's exactly what you are."

"What possible reason could he have to stay in the UK?"

McKittrick shook her head. "Maybe he's not finished yet."

"What?"

"Is it possible there's someone else on his hit list?"

"Huh?" The fuzziness in Ingrid's head was starting to feel a little worse.

"Maybe he's planning to kill someone else here."

The thought hadn't even occurred to Ingrid. "Someone else?"

"Isn't that possible?"

"I guess. But it'd have to be someone connected to the original trial of his father. All the other deaths were." Ingrid blinked hard, trying to recall all the details of the killings. "In each case, the method of killing was connected to the victim's weakness, a vulnerability."

"Any other similarities?"

"We've spoken about the cases. I'm having a little trouble recalling—" Ingrid hated to admit that her injuries were affecting her ability to do her job.

"Right that's it—let's talk about something else. This is too taxing."

"No, wait." Ingrid struggled hard to remember something she'd discovered that linked David Brite's murder to Barbara Highsmith's. After a few moments it came to her. "The date. Two of the victims were killed on the anniversary of the suspect's parents' deaths. May 15th."

"That's tomorrow. So Matthew Fuller's murder broke the pattern."

Did two kills constitute a pattern? "You think maybe he's planning to kill someone else on the 15th?"

"You're the one who can't work out why he hung around after the City trader's death. I'm just brainstorming with you."

"I need my phone."

"Later. All this talking has already made you a bit sweaty. You really are supposed to be taking it easy."

"Please. It won't take long, I promise. I need to find out who else was involved in Henry Ellis' trial. Whether it's possible they're here in the UK."

Reluctantly, McKittrick handed Ingrid her cell. Ingrid found Mike Stiller in her contacts list and waited for him to pick up.

"Hey, what happened to you?" he said as soon as she'd managed a 'hello'. "You haven't hassled me for more information for over eighteen hours. I was beginning to feel a little unloved."

"I've been in the hospital."

"Jeez—that open head wound of yours?"

"No… something else. It doesn't matter. I'm feeling much better now." She threw McKittrick a look.

"Is this going to take long? Only I've got a meeting to get to ten minutes ago."

"No time at all. I won't have access to the Bureau database for a while —I'm supposed to be convalescing—could you send me everything you can on the Henry Ellis investigation? I'm certain now his son is my suspect. And I know he's right here in London."

"What?"

"Come on, Mike, just this one favor for today."

"How long have you been in the hospital?"

"I don't understand."

"I guess you didn't get a chance to finish your research into Ellis, huh?"

"I didn't. That's why I'm asking for this favor now. Please, Mike."

"I really gotta get going."

"OK—send me the information after your meeting."

"You're wrong."

"What?"

"About Cory Ellis being your suspect. And he certainly isn't in London right now."

"Quit kidding around, Mike. Just send me the information, will you?"

"There's no point. Cory Ellis died in 2002."

36

Ingrid woke up in the middle of the night with a desert-dry mouth. In the half-light, she managed to make out the glass of water sitting on the floor beside the bed. She grabbed it and downed the lot, but it did nothing to quench her thirst.

She wandered to McKittrick's kitchen, her head full of questions she couldn't answer. She'd been so sure about Cory Ellis, and his connection to Matthew Fuller and Barbara Highsmith. It had all fitted together so perfectly. Maybe a little too perfectly. At least she knew that a man fitting Darryl Wyatt's description had been seen at the Latvian's apartment. The Fuller and Highsmith murders may not be linked, but Highsmith's killer seemed to be in London. McKittrick had called the team investigating the Latvian's death on Ingrid's behalf, giving them all the information Ingrid had managed to piece together with Mike Stiller's help.

Just before she'd retired for the night, McKittrick had given Ingrid back her phone. Ingrid thought about calling Mike Stiller again. But all she could have done was whine to him about how certain she'd been and how disappointed she was her theory hadn't panned out.

She refilled her glass from the faucet, and stood at the sink for a moment, enjoying how good the coolness of the tile floor felt beneath her feet. She thought about the kitchen in her own apartment and wondered when she'd be able to set foot in it again. Whether she ever would. She made a mental note to try calling the realtor in the morning.

The morning seemed an eternity away. She hoped she'd be able to get back to sleep, but she knew she'd be endlessly reliving events and running through the hasty plan she'd put together a few hours ago to apprehend her attacker. Under McKittrick's strict supervision, she'd arranged for a security contact of hers, Nick Angelis, who worked for what was effectively a private MI5 and MI6 combined, to follow whoever might still be following her. Angelis had been trailing marks for the past two decades. If there was a mark to spot, Angelis would spot him. In the meantime, there were two cops sitting in an unmarked car parked outside McKittrick's building. It felt like overkill, but Sol and McKittrick had made it quite clear they weren't prepared to take any chances.

Ingrid padded back to bed and discovered that her cell phone was buzzing on the floor. It would be Marshall again. He'd tried her at least a half-dozen times already. She almost felt a little sorry for him. In her sleepy daze, she found herself scooping the cell from the floor and answering the call.

"Hey, Marsh."

"Honey... I've been worried about you."

"I texted you back."

"I needed to hear your voice."

"Well here I am."

"How are you?"

"Fine."

"Come on, honey—you can tell me how it really is."

"I'm a little tired maybe. But it is three in the morning here."

"I'm sorry—I've been trying you for hours. I just had to speak to you. Satisfy myself you were OK. I feel better now."

Well good for you. Ingrid regretted picking up the call.

"I think you should come home," he said, his voice a little whiny. "I miss you. I want to protect you. You must have been so scared."

Scared? Fear hadn't really come into it. Maybe when she had time to sit back and consider just how close she'd come to death, she might get a little terrified. But right now she was too goddamn frustrated that her theory about Cory Ellis had come to nothing. Marshall was wasting his time if he thought he could *scare* her into returning to the US.

"Do the police have any leads?" Marshall asked.

"They're working on several lines of inquiry. No one's really telling me very much of anything—I'm the frail victim in this scenario."

"What do you think? You must have a hunch."

"I really haven't been in London long enough to make any enemies. I'm no threat to anyone." Her head had started pounding again. She let out an exaggerated yawn. "Listen, Marsh, I'm really exhausted—I've got to get some rest. It's what the doctor ordered."

"Sure, sure. I feel so much better for hearing your voice. Goodnight, baby."

Ingrid hung up and tossed her cell into her purse that was sitting on her neatly folded clothes on a chair in the corner of the room. It wasn't until she got back under the quilt that she realized she didn't remember seeing her engagement ring since she'd slipped it into her purse at the hotel.

———

Showering and dressing early the next morning, Ingrid was eager to start her day. When she emerged from the spare room she was surprised to see McKittrick already perched at the breakfast bar in the kitchen, nibbling at a slice of toast.

"There's coffee in the cafetière. I can make you a fresh pot if you'd rather."

"This is fine—thank you."

"That shirt really suits you. I never wear it—you can keep it if you like." McKittrick popped the final corner of toast into her mouth. "Have you spoken to your spook man yet this morning?"

"I don't have to—Angelis knows exactly what to do."

Twenty minutes later Ingrid was standing outside McKittrick's building waiting for an embassy car to convey her to work. She looked up at the tall, white stucco Victorian house. There had to be at least six apartments inside. McKittrick's was on the second floor. Ingrid saw her looking out of the living room window, like an anxious mother waiting for the school bus to arrive to take her child to its first day at school. Ingrid waved and smiled at her, giving her the thumbs up. Her head still hurt like hell, and her brain was fuzzy if she tried to concentrate too hard, but she was playing down the symptoms in order to be freed from what felt like house arrest.

The thirty minute journey from Kentish Town to Grosvenor Square was without incident, much to Ingrid's dismay. She'd been hoping for a little action. She wanted to flush out her attacker and be done with it. When she disembarked from the black sedan in the parking lot beneath the embassy, she phoned Nick Angelis to find out what he'd seen.

"Anything?" she asked.

"Not a sign."

"Is it possible you missed him?"

"If he's good enough to be able to follow you across London without me spotting him then we are dealing with a very talented individual indeed. Better than anyone currently working for the CIA, Mossad or MI6. Trust me—no one followed you this morning. Give me a call as soon as you want to leave the embassy and I'll do the same again."

"Thanks, Nick."

"You really don't have to thank me. I'm not having anyone hurt you again."

Ingrid hung up. She was a little surprised to hear Angelis sound quite so paternalistic. She didn't like it one bit.

She took the elevator to the third floor—her one concession to her impaired fitness—and tried to slip into the office and behind her desk without anyone noticing.

She failed.

"Ingrid!" Jennifer jumped up and hurried toward her. "How're you feeling? Can I get you anything?"

Ingrid waved her away. "I'm fine. Really."

Isaac hurried from his desk too. "Did you like the flowers? Agent Franklin let Jennifer and I choose them."

"They were just beautiful—thank you." Ingrid hadn't even laid eyes on the flowers Sol delivered to her hospital room. Hopefully somebody some place was enjoying them on her behalf.

"Do you know who tried to kill you?" Isaac said.

Jennifer shot him a look.

"I mean, you must have some idea, right?"

"I don't think it's anything you need to concern yourself with," Ingrid told him.

"Maybe we could help—look into the cases you've handled since you've been here. Work out who might be targeting you."

"That won't be necessary, Isaac. I'd appreciate it if you both got back to work. It's what I'm trying to do."

Jennifer grabbed Isaac's arm and forcibly marched him back toward his own desk. Although Ingrid was grateful for Jennifer's intervention, she did feel a little like an invalid. It wasn't a feeling she planned on getting used to.

37

For the next two hours, Ingrid laboriously researched the cases Barbara Highsmith worked while she was an Assistant US Attorney. If Cory Ellis hadn't murdered the ex-congresswoman, it was just possible that the answer to who had was right here in the files, waiting to be discovered. If Ingrid dug deep enough, she might just find it. But as she struggled to concentrate, fighting the fuzziness in her head, she felt she was making no progress at all. She switched databases and brought up Barbara Highsmith's details again. Maybe it was time to get back to basics. She was just starting to jot down a few notes about Highsmith's early life when her cell phone rang. She answered hesitantly, not wanting to have another awkward conversation with Marshall.

"Hey it's Mike."

Ingrid let out a sigh.

"Are you sitting down? You need to be when you hear this. How's that head wound of yours?"

"It's the least of my worries. What is it, Mike?"

"You know how I like to be thorough? How good I am at my job? How I can't leave something I'm investigating half-assed and incomplete?"

Ingrid really wished she could dispense with the 'boosting Mike Stiller's ego' section of the conversation just this once. Nevertheless, she played along. "You Mike, as has been well established, are something of an investigative genius. A god among men. A professional in a world of amateurs. A—"

"OK! You coulda stopped at the 'god' part. I've been looking into your suspect's file a little more closely. I wondered if he'd kept the family tradition of suicide going. I was curious, I guess."

Ingrid presumed he must also be very, very bored with whatever he was supposed to be working on. "And did he? Was it pills? Hanging? Or maybe he jumped in front of a subway train?"

"You sound a little pissed."

"I just got out of the hospital yesterday, give me a break."

"All right—take it easy."

"So how did he die?"

"According to eye witnesses, in September 2002, Cory Ellis paddled into Possession Sound in a sea kayak and was never seen again."

"He drowned?"

"Presumed drowned. Declared dead after seven years."

Ingrid swallowed. "His body was never found?" She snatched a breath.

"Nope. Never found."

Ingrid closed her eyes and let the news sink in for a moment.

"You still there?"

"Sure." The game was still on. She tried to remember what theory about Cory Ellis she and McKittrick had been discussing just before she'd called Mike and discovered Ellis was supposedly dead. But her foggy brain just wouldn't cooperate.

Dammit.

"Mike, OK if I call you back in a little while? This news has sent me into a bit of a tailspin."

"Just as long as you rehearse your speech of infinite gratitude and endless thanks first."

She hung up. Now she really was pissed. If Mike Stiller hadn't told her Cory Ellis was dead in the first place, she might not have wasted all morning trying to identify an alternate candidate for Highsmith's killer. Sometimes Mike tried just a little too hard to be indispensable. Ingrid looked up at Jennifer, who was hovering nearby her desk.

"Are you OK?" She walked around Ingrid's desk and stood next to her, touching her gently on the shoulder. "Only you had your eyes closed just now, I thought maybe you were in pain. Can I get you some painkillers?"

Anything that might make her head even a little less clear was something Ingrid wanted to avoid. "How about a strong black coffee?"

Jennifer was staring over Ingrid's shoulder at her computer monitor. "A long black, right?"

"Make it a double espresso. I need a jump start."

"If you're sure." The clerk couldn't seem to take her eyes from the screen.

"What is it?"

"Why are you looking into Barbara Highsmith?"

"It's connected to a case I'm investigating."

"Which case?" Jennifer sounded a little affronted there was something going on she didn't know about.

Ingrid didn't know where to start. She decided not to. "It's a little complicated."

Jennifer continued to read what was on the screen. "She's dead?"

"She was murdered last May."

"Oh my God."

"You knew her?"

"No. Not exactly." Jennifer ran back to her own desk and yanked open a drawer. She pulled out a thick hardback book and flipped to the index at the back. When she'd found what she was looking for, she waved the front cover at Ingrid. It featured a dramatically lit portrait of Ambassador Frances Byrne-Williams sitting at her desk right here at the embassy. Jennifer dumped the heavy tome on Ingrid's desk and stabbed a finger at the entry for Barbara Highsmith in the index. There were at least a dozen page references.

"Frances is a huge fan of Barbara Highsmith. She didn't mention anywhere in the book that the congresswoman was dead." Jennifer then quickly checked the date of publication at the front of the book. "This edition was printed November 2011. I guess it wasn't updated." She shook her head. "I've read so much about her, how she was an inspiration to Frances, more of a mentor, really, that I feel like I do know her."

"How did they meet?"

"At Wellesley College. Frances was doing some part-time teaching there when Barbara Highsmith was a visiting lecturer."

"When?"

"I'm sorry?"

Ingrid had just remembered the conversation she'd had with McKittrick about Cory Ellis, specifically, why he hadn't left town straight after murdering Matthew Fuller. The fact that he hadn't finished what he came to the UK to do. "Which year were they both at Wellesley College?"

Jennifer flipped back to the index then leafed through the pages until she found a section on the ambassador's college years. "They were both there for the academic year 2003–2004. Why do you need to know, anyway?"

Ingrid worked out Cory Ellis would have been twenty-four at the time. Was it possible he'd made some connection between the two women? Could he have been in Massachusetts at the same time?

"What is it, Ingrid? Can I help with anything?" Jennifer was wearing her concerned girl scout expression. Ingrid was getting a little sick of it.

Then Isaac jumped up from his desk. "What's happening? Anything I can do to help?"

Ingrid wanted to shout at them to shut up and sit down. All she needed was just a little time and space to think. "Jennifer—you can get me that coffee I asked for?"

Jennifer nodded meekly.

"And Isaac—find out anything you can about possible links between Ambassador Byrne-Williams and Barbara Highsmith outside of their college connection. Anything at all. Though I'm most interested in any link the ambassador may have to Washington state."

"Washington State?"

"Any connection to the US Attorney's Office there."

Isaac hesitated.

"You understand what I'm asking you to do?"

"Sure. I'm on it."

Both Jennifer and Isaac slunk away from Ingrid's desk. Ingrid leaned back in her chair and exhaled. Was it possible Cory Ellis did plan to kill someone else in London? Could the ambassador be the next victim on his list?

38

After the double espresso had been duly delivered by an unsmiling Jennifer and drunk in two gulps by Ingrid, a good thirty minutes had passed. So far Isaac had found no connection between Highsmith and Byrne-Williams except for Wellesley College. Ingrid's own search was just as unsuccessful. She got Jennifer on the case too.

"Can I ask why we're looking for a separate link?"

Ingrid decided not to go into the details. At this stage, the ambassador's possible connection to her investigation was so tenuous she didn't want to risk saying it out loud and triggering an overreaction. "It's just a little theory I'm working on."

"Hey—did you know Highsmith was poisoned by peanuts?" Isaac called over to Jennifer.

"She was?"

"She had an allergy."

"Poor Frances. She must have been so devastated when she found out."

"*And* her killer is still on the loose." Isaac seemed a little too ghoulish in his revealing of the facts.

"Is that the investigation you're working on?" Jennifer asked Ingrid. "Are you looking for Barbara Highsmith's killer? Does that mean he's here in London?"

"I can't go into the details right now." Ingrid glared at Isaac, who seemed completely oblivious. "We're still looking for a link, remember," she told him. "Details about the murder are irrelevant."

"Not if he's planning to poison someone else," Isaac said.

If Frances Byrne-Williams had nothing to do with the Henry Ellis case, there was no reason to think she would be on Cory Ellis' hit list. But it was possible they just hadn't found the link yet. Ingrid grabbed her cell from her desk and headed for the door. "Carry on with that research," she told Isaac and Jennifer as she left the room.

Halfway down the corridor she called Sol. Running her crazy theory past him was the sanity check she needed. If he felt the ambassador was in any danger, he could decide to contact the Regional Security Officer, who in turn could ramp up Byrne-Williams' security detail.

Her call went straight to voicemail. She thought about leaving a message, but it was just too complicated to explain. Instead, she called DI Mbeke. He was more than due an update.

"Ingrid. You've been very quiet," Mbeke said in place of a simple 'hello'.

"I've been a little tied up." She then proceeded to tell the detective inspector everything she'd learned about the Henry Ellis case, his son Cory, the very definite connection between the Fuller and Highsmith poisonings, and the possibility that Cory Ellis was still in the country because he hadn't finished yet.

"How long have you known all this?"

"Is that relevant?"

"I thought we were sharing everything, as and when."

"Like I say, I've been tied up. It was impossible to call any sooner." Ingrid really didn't need to be given a hard time by Mbeke.

"And you think this Cory Ellis is still here in London?"

"I'm saying it's a possibility. We've discovered a link between the woman he poisoned in Savannah and…" She hesitated. Could she even voice her theory to Mbeke?

"Yes?"

"The ambassador."

"Your ambassador?"

"It seems Highsmith was something of a mentor for Frances Byrne-Williams."

"But have you found a connection between the ambassador and the original Ellis fraud investigation?"

"Not yet. We're working on it."

"But you've raised the ambassador's protection level while you do your research?"

"The whole thing seems a little far-fetched to me. I figured I should have a more robust connection before I go spreading panic."

"Better to be safe than sorry, surely."

Ingrid had been wrestling with that question for a while now. She really needed to locate Sol. "You think?"

"I suppose I'd do it just to cover my own arse. Imagine if you did nothing and something happened to her."

"Point taken."

"I have a little news of my own," Mbeke said.

"You do?"

"Two things. Patience Toure has contacted me. Initially all she would tell me was what a good man Miguel Hernandez was, how she was sure he wouldn't hurt anyone. How she didn't want to get him in any trouble. Eventually she told me she was calling about the picture on the front of the *Evening News*."

"She'd already seen that photograph."

"Not the photograph—the artist's impression. She said maybe it looked a bit like Hernandez. With some more encouragement from me, she was prepared to admit that it looked a lot like him. She apologized for not recognizing him before, told me he'd always been very good to her, then rang off."

"So we have a motive for Ellis to kill Fuller, and a witness confirming the man seen at the Latvian's apartment was also the cleaner at Fisher Krupps. It's all fitting together."

"But we're still no closer to finding the perpetrator."

"I've created a profile of Cory Ellis that you might be interested in taking a look at. Might help you work out where he could be holed up. I'll email it to you."

"I suppose I should liaise with the team investigating the Latvian's murder. You're sure Ellis is responsible for that death too?"

"As far as I can be. Let me contact the team first. Like I said before, I've been a little tied up. I need to bring them up to speed."

"Are you all right?"

"Why wouldn't I be?"

"You're slurring your words a bit."

"I am?"

"I wasn't going to mention it."

"I had a night at the hospital. But I'm fine now."

"You don't sound fine."

"Fully recovered. Right as rain. One hundred percent."

"I hope you're managing to convince yourself."

"What was the other thing you wanted to tell me?"

There was a long pause, as if Mbeke had forgotten. "Actually, it's some good news for once. The maintenance man, Colin Stewart, has been released from hospital. He's made a full recovery."

Ingrid couldn't quite believe just how good that news seemed. She felt like she needed something to go right. "That's great. Really great. Thank you for telling me. "

"My pleasure." He said goodbye and hung up.

As she'd already walked as far as the elevator, Ingrid decided to pay Sol a visit.

She stepped out onto the fifth floor and hurried to his office. His door was open and the office was empty. She tried calling him again. Got the voicemail again. Patrick Mbeke's words had started to haunt her a little. What if she did nothing and something bad happened to the ambassador? Without Sol acting as her sounding board she felt lost and adrift. The fact that her head was still so foggy didn't help the rational decision making process one little bit. She headed back to her office.

"Have you found any other connections between Highsmith and the ambassador?" she asked before she was even through the door.

Isaac and Jennifer shook their heads.

"Maybe it would help if you could tell us why we're looking for one," Jennifer unhelpfully suggested.

"Do you think the peanut poisoner wants to kill the ambassador?" Isaac asked. He glanced at Jennifer who scowled back at him. It seemed to Ingrid as if they'd discussed the matter between themselves and then agreed not to raise it. Isaac had just broken ranks.

Ingrid took a deep breath. "I don't want to rule anything out."

"We should tell the RSO—Frances' protection should be increased," Jennifer said.

With the risk that Jennifer or Isaac might act unilaterally and contact the head of diplomatic security without her knowledge, Ingrid had no choice but to do something herself. "It's OK—I've got this covered. You carry on looking for a link, I'll deal with the RSO."

In Sol Franklin's absence, she headed for his boss' office. Thankfully, when she arrived, she discovered Amy Louden, the Deputy Special Agent in Charge, sitting behind her desk. Taking her time, making sure to enunciate as clearly as possible, Ingrid outlined in brief what she had discovered so far.

"You think there's a clear and present danger?"

"That I can't say. We don't have a concrete reason why Cory Ellis might consider the ambassador a target. But I thought it better not to take any chances." As Louden stared at her and said nothing, Ingrid was acutely aware that the potential threat she'd just outlined must have sounded crazy to any rational individual. She tensed, waiting for Louden's final verdict.

"You've done the right thing. I'll have a quiet word with the RSO, the ambassador need never know anything about it."

Ingrid rocked backward on her heels. She hadn't anticipated such a sympathetic hearing. She supposed that now a potential threat had been raised, maybe Louden was just covering her own ass. She couldn't just ignore it. It was hard to tell if the Deputy was pissed at her, or genuinely pleased she'd brought the matter to her attention.

"Well done, Ingrid."

"Thank you, ma'am."

"Close the door on your way out."

By the time Ingrid stepped out of the elevator onto the third floor, she could already sense something had changed. As she passed fellow Feds, Marines and Diplomatic Security agents in the corridor, she felt each of them had a little more purpose in the way they moved. A tangible sense of urgency had somehow filled the air. Amy Louden sure worked fast. The RSO must have set some protocol in motion immediately. Ingrid couldn't help wondering if it was all a terrible overreaction.

She returned to the office and slumped heavily into her chair, her limbs as exhausted as her brain. She was starting to question the wisdom of returning to work so soon. She shook her head in an attempt to clear the cobwebs from it and only succeeded in making herself feel slightly dizzy and a little nauseous. She closed her eyes and took a few deep breaths.

"Man, it's harder to get into this building than the goddamn White House," a voice called from the other side of the room. Ingrid's tired brain had started to play tricks on her. That voice didn't belong here. She opened her eyes and turned her head slowly toward the doorway.

No way.

With a suit carrier slung over his shoulder, a huge grin plastered across his face, Marshall Claybourne sauntered toward her.

39

Marshall dumped his bags on her desk, leaned over and planted a kiss on her open mouth.

"Hey, honey, aren't you pleased to see me?"

Ingrid glanced over his shoulder to see Jennifer and Isaac staring at them, their jaws dropped lower than hers. "What are you doing here?" she managed to say in an urgent whisper, once she'd recovered the power of speech.

"I'm not sure that's any sort of welcome, honey."

She jumped up and grabbed his hand, then marched him straight out the office. She dragged him all the way down the corridor and into a small kitchen area before she let go. Once she had, he took the opportunity to wrap his long arms around her, pinning her arms to her sides, and scooped her off her feet. He squeezed her hard and rocked her from side to side. Eventually he returned her to the ground and kissed her again.

She took a good look at him. He'd gained a few pounds since she'd last seen him five months ago. His sandy hair was a little thinner too, at the temples. There were definitely more lines around his eyes and mouth. As they stood there for a moment, looking each other up and down, she supposed he was thinking the same thing about her. Sprinkled across his nose, Ingrid noticed the start of dark golden summer freckles. Somehow it still seemed kind of cute.

"Aren't you pleased to see me?" He looked a little crestfallen.

"I'm just so surprised you came all this way."

"I'd be a pretty crap fiancé if I didn't come see you after some lowlife tried to kill you. I love you, baby." He kissed her on top of her head. "You're using a new shampoo. I like it."

Marshall hadn't been this attentive even before she left the US. It was unnerving her. She wasn't sure she would have jumped on a plane and crossed the Atlantic if the same thing had happened to him. Which made her feel as guilty as hell.

He searched her face some more. "You look a little tired, honey. I can't believe you're back at work so soon."

"Wouldn't you be?"

He grinned at her. "I guess."

"I still can't believe you've just dropped everything and come all this way. I told you on the phone last night that I was perfectly fine."

"I was already at the airport when I spoke to you. You think I was just going to stay home when somebody tried to kill you?"

"When did you leave D.C.?" It suddenly occurred to her that Marshall may have found out about her continuing investigation into the Darryl Wyatt case.

"I just said—I was at the airport when we spoke. Why?"

Ingrid thought it through. There was no way he could have found out about the progress she was making on the case. She'd only found out herself that Cory Ellis might still be alive a few hours ago. She couldn't help but smile. Marshall couldn't have known about the case and yet here he was, in his six feet three, two hundred and ten pound glory. In exactly the right place at exactly the right time, slap bang in the middle of a minor crisis that needed solving. It was quite a knack.

"What's going on around here, anyway?" he said, "has there been a terrorist threat? There were so many armed Marines manning the reception I thought there'd been an invasion."

Ingrid really couldn't face the prospect of explaining everything she'd discovered. As soon as she'd finished, she knew Marshall would insist on taking over. She stared at the floor and said nothing.

"Honey? What is it?"

"There's probably some stuff you should know." Ingrid then spent the next ten minutes bringing Marshall partially up to speed. Although she confirmed a man fitting the description of Darryl Wyatt had been seen visiting the dead Latvian, she stopped short of revealing what she knew about the Henry Ellis case and the connection to Matthew Fuller's death. She felt she had to keep a little something back for herself.

"And the ambassador has a direct link to Barbara Highsmith?" Marshall asked once she was through with her little speech.

"She does. But I'm not one hundred percent convinced that makes her his next target."

"Does she have an allergy?"

"No—not as far as I know."

"But he may choose a similar method. He could be right here in the embassy cafeteria. Or maybe working in the kitchen of the official residency. Has anyone interviewed the kitchen staff?"

"We literally just got the ambassador's protection ramped up moments ago. Nothing else has happened. Not yet."

"We should put the kitchen and cafeteria into lockdown. Plus the kitchen at the residence."

We?

As Ingrid had feared, Marshall was taking over. It was second nature to him. She wasn't even sure she blamed him. But she sure didn't have to like it. "Just because he once poisoned someone in a restaurant, doesn't make that his M.O. I mean, look at what he did to the Latvian woman."

"You still think that was him?"

"I'm certain."

"How long have you known about Wyatt's presence here?"

"What's that got to do with anything?"

"Why didn't you tell me?"

"Wait a minute. I tried right at the beginning. You crapped all over my theory." Her earlier vaguely warm feelings toward her fiancé were rapidly cooling. It wouldn't be long before she was just plain mad at him again.

"But I'm listening now. What a stroke of luck I should be here when this all kicked off." He was grinning at her like a big idiot. "Aren't you pleased for me, honey? All the hard work, all the promotions and the commendations, they're all for you, you know. For us." His smile grew wider. "I'm making a better future for us both."

It had never felt that way to Ingrid and she certainly didn't want to think about their future together right now. She wasn't sure they even had one.

"I booked into the same hotel as you for my stay. I wanted to get you all moved into my suite while I'm here, but someone must have screwed up with the reservations or something. The manager said you moved out a couple days ago. I told him he didn't know what the hell he was talking about. Stuck to his story though. Fool."

This was not the way Ingrid had intended telling Marshall she was planning to extend her stay, but in the circumstances, she could hardly *not* mention it. She took a deep breath. "I moved into my own apartment."

"What?"

"The heater with the leaky flue that nearly killed me? That was in *my* bathroom."

"I assumed it was a friend's house."

She shook her head.

"Well, heck, honey. When were you planning on telling me?" He stepped back from her and narrowed his eyes. "Does this mean you're making the job permanent?"

"No! I don't know. Not permanent. But I do want to stay for at least another six months."

"And when the hell were you gonna share that with me? What about the wedding? Are you expecting us to get married and then live four thousand miles apart?" His cheeks had started to flush.

"No! I'm not expecting anything—" She pulled up short. They couldn't have this conversation here. She didn't even know for sure how she wanted the conversation to go. They had a job to do. They needed to focus on it. Bring their personal relationship into the equation, and things would get too messy to work around. "We can talk about everything later, when all this is over. Sitting down, in a calm environment. I'll buy you dinner, huh? The biggest steak in London, how about that?"

His face softened a little. He opened his arms wide. "I'm sorry, honey, you've been through a traumatic experience. I should be a little more understanding. It's OK now—I'm here to protect you." He took a step forward, but Ingrid was too fast for him, she ducked sideways and away, and left him hugging nothing but air.

He quickly recovered and clapped his hands together. "I need to get started." He turned on his heels and headed back toward the office.

"Where are you going?"

"I'll need some help. But I don't want to exhaust you. What's the name of the skinny black kid sitting in the corner?"

"Kid? He's a twenty-three-year-old grown man. You need to treat him with some respect. His name is Isaac."

"Good, I'll use him as my assistant for the time being. I need to speak to the RSO, find out exactly how secure the ambassador is. And we'll need to stop any food that's come from the kitchen being consumed by her."

"Or anyone else," Ingrid interjected.

"What?"

"If you genuinely think it could be poisoned, no one should be eating it."

"No, of course not. I'll see to that. Plus we have to interview all the staff." He shook his head. "My God—it's a huge job."

"You really think Wyatt is right here inside the embassy?"

"He got himself pretty embedded in the restaurant in Savannah."

"But security is so tight. There's no way he could be here."

"Why take chances? Who do I need to talk to? I've got to get the kitchen staff isolated."

"I thought you were here to see me."

"You need to take it easy. I'll keep coming back to check on you. OK, honey?" He pecked her on the top of the head.

"You're wrong about this, I'm sure of it." Ingrid was controlling the urge to punch her fiancé square in the jaw.

"We'll see, I guess." He smiled at her, screwing up his eyes the way he did when he wasn't really smiling at all.

He marched her back to her desk, grabbed Isaac and headed for Deputy Louden's office. Ingrid was pretty sure Amy Louden wouldn't go for Marshall's scheme. She was content to let him fall flat on his face. It'd make a nice change.

As she watched him hurrying away, an awestruck Isaac trailing behind him, Ingrid decided she'd get back to basics. If Cory Ellis was still in London because he had someone else to kill, maybe studying exactly who was involved in his father's arrest and conviction would yield some piece of information that might actually help her track him down.

40

"So that's your fiancé, huh?" Jennifer stared at Ingrid, her expression hungry with the need for information.

Ingrid blinked. She sat back down at her desk.

"How long have you been engaged?"

"I'm sorry, Jennifer, I'm just too busy for a girlie chat."

"Me too. I'm really busy." Jennifer flicked through a stack of Post-It stickers to prove it. "There's a message here for you." She unstuck the little yellow note from the pile and read it aloud. "Please call DC Fraser."

"Did he say what it was about?"

"He couldn't have—or I would have written it down."

Ingrid quickly found his number on her phone and dialed.

"I thought you'd lost interest," Fraser said when he picked up.

"I've been a little... indisposed. Do you have news about the case?"

"We think we've identified her. Name of Marija Jansons, family haven't heard from her since January. Her brother's flying over tomorrow to make the formal ID. You can speak to him if you like."

"Thanks. Thanks for letting me know. I appreciate that." Ingrid took a deep breath. "I guess you've been pretty busy getting lots of calls about the picture on the front of the *Evening News* yesterday?"

"Not as busy as I might have expected."

"I have a name for the murder suspect, but I doubt very much he's using it now." Ingrid went on to repeat everything she'd told Mbeke.

Apart from the current presumed threat to the ambassador. There was no way Fraser should know about that.

"So you think he's killed, what... three people?"

"It could be more."

"Jesus. And he's not left the country yet?"

"That's the hunch we're working with at the moment. It's possible he's not finished yet."

"Bloody hell. I'll need you to put all that in writing. And you should probably speak to the DCI too."

"Sure." *But it won't be anytime soon.*

She threw her phone on the desk and thought about the dead woman. Marija Jansons had gotten involved with the wrong man. Ingrid supposed Bella Townsend in Savannah was damn lucky to be alive. If she'd stumbled across something she shouldn't have, presumably Ellis wouldn't have hesitated to dispatch her in much the same way. What Ingrid still had trouble understanding, was the fact that Ellis had left the details of his old bank account accessible to Jansons in the first place. The man was a meticulous planner. That just seemed too sloppy. It didn't fit with his profile. Every move he made was deliberate, carefully prepared in advance. Maybe Marija Jansons was smarter than he'd given her credit for.

Her cell phone buzzed. She glanced at the screen as it gently vibrated against the desk. It was McKittrick, no doubt wanting to know how she was doing. Ingrid hesitated before picking up.

"I'm fine," she said, before McKittrick even got a chance to inquire after her health.

"That's nice. So am I. That's not why I called. I've just got off the phone. I've been talking to a certain chief inspector working on an attempted murder case I think you might be interested in."

"Oh yeah, whose?"

"Whose? Yours, you daft cow!"

Although Ingrid's sore temple and fuzzy head had been bothering her all morning, she hadn't given much thought to what had caused them in the first place. "They finally found some of those goddamn arrows?"

"What? No. No, I'm talking about the investigation into the *second* attempt on your life. The arrows I can't help you with."

"So what do you have?"

"I'm trying to tell you."

"Have they identified a suspect?"

"Not exactly. They've been speaking to the other estate agents who were working with your lettings man on Monday afternoon."

"Has he turned up yet?"

"No—they didn't have any new information on him, but they did tell the chief inspector that a bloke with an American accent—claiming to be your husband, can you believe it—tipped up shortly before five p.m. He and the lettings agent left shortly afterwards. That was the last anyone saw of them."

"My husband?"

"The theory the DCI's working on is that this mysterious American chap—seemed to know all about you, by the way—lured the agent somewhere, somehow got him out of the way, then presumably went to the flat, tampered with the boiler, left the keys on the main door, where you found them, and... well, you know the rest."

"'Got the agent out of the way,' you just said. You think the guy's dead?"

"I'd put money on it. Expect a call from DCI Renton later this afternoon. He wants to ask you some more questions. In the meantime, you've got to work out who this American bloke might be. Someone so intent on bumping you off, that he's not at all worried about collateral damage. Poor bloody agent just happened to be in the wrong place at the wrong time."

Ingrid's breath got caught in her throat as she tried to speak. She coughed and tried again. "Did the realtors provide a description of the guy?"

"They were a bit sketchy about the details. But they were both certain he was just under six feet tall and quite slim. But he was wearing a baseball cap too low for them to get a proper look at his face."

"I guess they didn't see his left arm?"

"You mean the rose tattoo? They didn't mention it. So you are thinking what I'm thinking—that it was Darryl Wyatt?"

"Darryl Wyatt, Cory Ellis, Miguel Hernandez. Whatever the hell he's calling himself today."

"I thought Cory Ellis was dead."

"There have been some... developments."

"He's alive?"

"He could be."

"And you didn't think to tell me?"

"It's been a little hectic around here." Ingrid glanced up at Jennifer, who quickly looked away. "Marshall turned up about an hour ago."

"He did what?"

"He's right here at the embassy. He's taken over the investigation."

"Can he do that?"

"It's complicated. And too long a story to get into right now."

"At least nothing untoward has happened so far today. Unless there's something else you're not telling me."

"What's special about today?"

"Bloody hell—don't you remember? I think it's fair to say you may have lost your edge. Should you even be at work? "

"What are you talking about?"

"Today's the 15th of May. The killer's preferred kill date. You didn't think I paid attention, did you?"

Ingrid gasped in a breath. How could something like that slip her mind? She had to shape up, and fast.

"So with Marshall on the scene, I suppose you won't be staying at my place again tonight? I was planning to go to Marks and Spencer and pick up a few treats for dinner."

Ingrid thought about the suite Marshall had booked at the hotel. The way she felt right now she couldn't even bear to look at his face. "Thanks —I'd like that. I'll call you later to let you know when I'm leaving." She hung up and carefully placed the cell back on the desk. She sat very still and pondered what McKittrick had just told her. She'd never known her brain feel this sluggish. But then she'd never suffered carbon monoxide poisoning before. She took a deep breath and considered the facts calmly and objectively.

An American man, same height and build as the man seen at Marija Jansons' apartment, lured away the realtor, most probably to his death, in order to get into Ingrid's apartment to tamper with the boiler. He knew all about the apartment. He must have been following her since she set off from her hotel last Saturday to go apartment hunting with McKittrick. If he stayed around long enough to remove the poisoned soap from the restroom, there was every chance he'd seen her at the murder scene at Fisher Krupps. Had he been following her ever since then? Had he been watching her when she visited Marija Jansons' apartment?

Ingrid tried hard to remember who she'd seen on the street that evening. She was pretty sure there were only two other people around. A dog walker and some guy washing his car. Ellis could have been either of them.

Then it struck her.

Maybe Ellis hadn't been careless with his bank details. Maybe he wanted Jansons to access the account to test the response it provoked. Then sure enough, less than an hour after the account was accessed, the

FBI agent he'd seen at Fisher Krupps turned up at the apartment in Dulwich, using some lame story to get inside.

Ingrid suddenly felt very stupid. And, if she allowed herself a moment's self-indulgence, not a little scared.

41

Ingrid grabbed her phone and jumped up from her desk. She hurried out of the office, trawling through her contacts list as she went.

"Nick?"

"Hey—I didn't expect to hear from you so soon. Are you on the move? Want some back-up?"

Ingrid sucked in a breath, trying to calm her nerves. "Not yet, I'll call again later. Just thought I'd update you on developments." She briefly explained the investigation she'd been working on and who she thought was responsible for the two attempts on her life. She then gave him as detailed a description of Ellis as she could. "But I'm just going by the eye witness report that resulted in the artist's impression on the front page of yesterday's *Evening News*."

The line went very quiet. Ingrid could hear Angelis breathing. "Are you OK about this?"

"Sure."

"I read the article. I know what he did to that woman. The man's a vicious bastard. Do you have protection where you are right now?"

"Of course not. Ellis won't be here inside the embassy." Ingrid quickly remembered that was exactly where Marshall was supposing Ellis, or as far as he was concerned, Darryl Wyatt, was right now. Her stomach somersaulted. She coughed as a reflux of acid tried to make it all the way up into her mouth. Whatever Ellis had been planning and wherever he intended to execute that plan, it was likely to happen today. Ingrid felt as if time was running out.

"Presumably this Ellis bloke will have changed his appearance again?"

"He has a distinctive rose tattoo on his left forearm."

"So as long as he's wearing a tee shirt I won't have any problems."

"It was worth mentioning."

Angelis sniffed. "Of course it was. Don't mind me, I'm just worried about you."

"I'm fine. There are dozens of armed Marines patrolling the building."

"I can come in—I don't have much on today. I wouldn't be any bother. Just sit me in a corner with a good book."

"That won't be necessary. But thanks for offering."

Ingrid made her way back to the office, frustrated Sol still wasn't answering his phone. She got there to discover Marshall sitting at her desk, tapping away at her keyboard. Jennifer was leaning over the desk, thrusting her breasts toward him.

Dear God.

"Is there anything else I can help you with, Marshall?" Jennifer said.

"No—that's all for now. Thank you." Marshall looked up and smiled at Ingrid, who was hovering in the doorway. She felt like turning right around and leaving again. Instead, she marched purposefully toward her desk.

"Where's Isaac?" she asked and watched as Jennifer sashayed back to her own desk.

"I sent him on an errand to find Sol Franklin. We can't get him on his cell," Marshall said.

"You do know Isaac doesn't actually work for you?"

"For today he does. I squared it with DSAC Louden."

"So what do you want with Sol?"

"The DSAC said Sol would be able to authorize any extra manpower I'll need to maintain security at the cafeteria and kitchen."

"How long has Isaac been gone?" She glanced at her watch. Her tone was a little harsher than she'd intended.

"What's wrong, honey?" Marshall grabbed her hand.

Ingrid tugged it away and glanced up at Jennifer. The clerk was watching them closely. Now was neither the time nor the place to list all her grievances.

Marshall stood up. "I guess you want your desk back. I'm heading to the kitchen soon to start interviewing the staff."

"You're just fine where you are. Sit down." With that, Ingrid spun around and left. She tried Mike Stiller on her cell phone and headed in the direction of Sol's office.

"Hey, Mike. How many miracles is it so far today?"

"Whatever it is you want, make it quick. I do actually have other work to do."

"I'm looking for a connection between Ambassador Frances Byrne-Williams and the original Henry Ellis investigation."

"The ambassador? You've got to be kidding me. Are you saying she's mixed up in all of this somehow?"

"Actually I'm trying to prove the opposite. I don't think she is. But I do think Cory Ellis is still right here in London and he hasn't finished what he came here to do." She reached the elevator as the doors opened. A half dozen Marines marched out, heading toward her office. No doubt they were on some fruitless mission for Marshall.

"You know how impossible it is to prove a negative?" Mike said. "I guess you could look at all the main players involved in the investigation. See how many of them are still alive, see if any could conceivably be in the UK."

"OK—I guess Cory Ellis would have targeted the man who actually killed his father."

"The prison guard?"

"Can you find out what happened to him?"

"What's the matter? Your computer stop working?"

"I'm not at my desk. It's been... commandeered by somebody working the Byrne-Williams angle."

"OK—you remember the name of the guard?"

Ingrid struggled to remember. Amazingly, the name popped into her head. Maybe her mind was finally clearing a little. She spelled the name out to Mike Stiller and stepped out of the elevator on the fifth floor. She reached Sol's office. Again it was unoccupied. Only this time she noticed Sol's cell phone sitting in the middle of his desk. No wonder she wasn't having any luck calling him. Maybe he'd just popped out to the restroom. She heard a whistle at the other end of the line. "Mike?"

"Well, as you may have already guessed, the guard responsible for killing Henry Ellis is no longer with us."

"How'd he die?" Ingrid wondered if Ellis had plumped for poison.

"He was shot dead. Three shots to the chest, two to the face. Point blank range."

That didn't match Ellis' profile at all. To be so close to the victim at the time of death? Plus he carefully planned and executed the killings. That just sounded like a wild shooting spree. And how did it have anything to do with a weakness or vulnerability in the victim? At the end of a gun, everyone is vulnerable.

"Perpetrator was never found."

"Can you tell me anything about the guard himself? I'm looking for some kind of weakness he might have had. Something that maybe most people didn't know about him."

"It's hardly likely to turn up in the police report, if nobody knew about it."

Ingrid felt like she was flailing. She reminded herself that, despite his claims, Mike Stiller wasn't actually a miracle worker.

"But I can tell you something about the poor schmuck," Mike said.

Ingrid waited. Knowing Mike he would want to pause a beat for an imaginary drum roll.

"The guard was shot in his bed, naked, handcuffed to the headboard."

42

"The guard had a sex addiction?"

"Maybe, but that's not the perceived weakness I was shooting for. According to the regular bartender at the local gay bar, on the night he died, the guard picked up some dark handsome stranger and took him home with him. Something he never did. Because of his job, he was always real cautious. Seems the dark stranger made him an offer he couldn't refuse."

"Ellis?"

"Can you think of any more likely candidates?"

"How did Ellis even know he was gay?"

"All he had to do was follow him for a few nights. If the perpetrator is as smart as you seem to think he is, it wouldn't exactly have taxed his intellect to discover the guard's little secret."

"What year was this?"

"Two-thousand five."

"And the date?" Ingrid had a feeling she knew the answer already.

"May 15th. Just like Highsmith and David Brite." Mike paused again. "Wait a minute. That's today's date."

Ingrid closed her eyes.

"OK—let's look at exactly what we've discovered so far," Mike said. "Holy crap."

"What is it?"

"I've got a meeting I should be getting to."

Ingrid took one last look around Sol's office and left the room. Where the hell was he? "Any help you can give me, Mike, you know I appreciate it."

"I've only got a coupla minutes."

"We have four victims either directly or indirectly involved in the Henry Ellis investigation. The investor who testified against him, the investor's son, the prosecuting attorney and the prison guard who shot him dead." Ingrid was more convinced than ever that there was no connection between Cory Ellis and Frances Byrne-Williams. She should go and speak to Marshall about it.

She headed for the cafeteria in the basement.

"Listen, I'll call you back," Mike whispered down the line. "My boss just walked in the room."

Ingrid reached the entrance to the cafeteria. A Marine was standing sentry. She waved her security pass at him, followed by her badge. Eventually, he stood to one side and let her enter.

All the harsh overhead lights had been turned on in the cafeteria. Ingrid recognized some of the counter staff sitting at the tables, sipping at cans of soda, nibbling on candy bars and potato chips. All of them looking royally pissed off. Then there were lots of faces she didn't recognize, judging by the way they were dressed, they had to be kitchen staff. They looked severely pissed off too. None of them, however, looked in any way tense or guilty. No one was trying to leave. They just seemed resigned to their fate, as if this sort of thing happened every day.

"Excuse me." A woman dressed in a white tunic and checkered pants stood up and touched Ingrid on the arm. "Do you have any idea how long this is going to take? Only I have some slow-cooking pot roasts in the ovens. Pretty soon, they're going to start burning."

"I'll look into that for you," Ingrid said, without the slightest intention of doing any such thing. She needed to find Marshall, try to convince him again how wrong he was. At the far end of the cafeteria was a small office used by the restaurant manager. From what Ingrid could see through the window in the door, it seemed Marshall was using it to interview the kitchen and cafeteria staff. Another armed Marine was guarding the door.

Ingrid's cell phone started to buzz in her pocket. She pulled it out and answered quickly.

"When are we going to get our cell phones back?" one of the kitchen staff asked, the tone of her voice somehow managing to be accusatory and defeatist at the same time.

Ingrid ignored her. "Mike, did you get out of your meeting?"

"I'm joining them in five minutes. Now, where were we?"

"Trying to work out the identities of other possible victims on Ellis' list."

"Sure. If we work backwards, I guess we should look at who the arresting officers were. Who was investigating Henry Ellis before he even got arrested."

"Was it a cop or a Federal agent? Should have been a Fed, in that kind of fraud case, shouldn't it?"

"Just looking that up now."

Ingrid's left ear was suddenly filled with the sound of nasal breathing coming all the way from Washington D.C.

"Holy shit."

"What have you found?" Ingrid started to edge closer to the small room Marshall was occupying, and the six feet something Marine standing to attention outside.

"Tell me you're sitting down."

"Please don't make me go through all of that again. Is it someone you know? Someone I know?"

"I can't believe it, but here it is in black and white."

"Goddammit, Mike, who?"

"Special Agent Solomon Franklin."

Ingrid stopped in her tracks. "Sol? You're sure?"

"He led the team of investigating agents. It looks like it was quite a coup for him at the time. Got a juicy promotion out of it."

"I've got to go, Mike." She hung up and tried Sol's cell phone again. It switched to voicemail. Just like it had every other time she'd attempted to speak to him today. The phone was probably still on the desk in his empty office.

Ingrid marched up to the Marine guarding Marshall's interview room. "I need to speak to SSA Claybourne," she declared, "right now."

"He's a little busy."

She flashed her embassy ID and her FBI badge. The Marine wasn't impressed. Ingrid stepped to one side and banged a fist against the door, and kept on banging until the armed guard physically restrained her. Marshall turned around and yanked open the door.

"What the hell is it?"

43

Ingrid pushed into the makeshift interview room, glanced at the man dressed in white tunic and checkered pants sitting very upright in front of the desk, then turned her attention to Marshall.

"For God's sake, what do you think you're doing?" Marshall was trying to keep his booming voice down and failing.

"You need to stop this charade right now." Ingrid could feel the Marine's hot breath blasting against the back of her neck. He was standing just inches away. In theory, one word from Marshall and he could have her bundled away.

"Charade? What the hell are you talking about?" Marshall glanced at his interviewee, a hint of embarrassment on his face. "These interviews are highly sensitive. They have to be handled in the right way."

"And I'm telling you to stop."

Marshall grabbed her arm, walked her past the Marine and straight out the office. He didn't let go until they were in the corridor outside the cafeteria. "Were you deliberately trying to humiliate me in there?"

"I can't worry about hurting your feelings, you're wasting your time interviewing these people. The ambassador is not the target."

"You have nothing to back that up."

"The target is Sol Franklin and I have plenty to back it up but no time to explain. We've got to find Sol. I haven't been able to reach him for hours. The killer will strike today. Maybe he already has." Ingrid drew down an unsteady breath. "We can't waste any more time."

Much to her amazement, Marshall seemed to be considering what she'd said. He was chewing the inside of his cheek as if it were a plug of tobacco. Then he shook his head decisively. "If I didn't know better I'd think you were trying to… sabotage this operation. Just because I've come here and—"

"Taken over?"

"Exactly."

"You seriously think I'd put the ambassador's life in jeopardy out of… some petty resentment?"

He shrugged at her. "I know you never say anything, but it's got to be hard seeing me get promoted over and over. It's only human. I don't even blame you." He gave her a patronizing smile with the corner of his mouth.

She wanted to slap it.

"Listen, Marshall. I am one hundred percent sure about this. I need the manpower you've been assigned to search the building for Sol."

"You think the suspect intends to poison Sol?"

"Poison? No!" She hadn't had time to consider what method Ellis might use. "I don't know how he plans to do it. Just that he will. We have to find Sol." She grabbed Marshall's thick arms and squeezed them, hoping that might somehow make him take her more seriously.

"I love you, honey, but you're just not making any sense. You obviously came back to work too early. Why don't you go back to the hotel and I'll join you there just as soon as I can."

"Goddammit, I don't have time to argue with you. You have to help me."

"Explain to me properly why I should, and I'll consider it."

"I've already told you—we don't have time."

"I'm not going to let some crazy, half-assed theory get in the way of my investigation. Take it up with Louden if you're not happy about it."

Ingrid let go of his arms and strode away. She called Louden. Maybe the Deputy would agree to some resources to help her search. The call switched straight to voicemail. Ingrid wasn't going to get any help there.

Time was against her. Left to search on her own, it would be practically impossible to find Sol. He could be anywhere in the building.

She ran toward the elevator, not really knowing where she would go when she got there. She passed another armed Marine guarding the door to the stairwell.

"What are you doing here?" she asked him.

He stood a little taller and raised his chin. Ingrid showed him her embassy ID and FBI badge. "Please, tell me why you're here."

"To ensure none of the kitchen or cafeteria staff leaves the basement. There's a man stationed at every exit."

"Really?"

"Orders from above." He looked toward the ceiling.

Typical. Marshall Claybourne overkill. Trying to prove how much power he could yield. What a waste of resources.

"I'm guessing it's OK for me to leave the basement?"

"Yes, ma'am." He opened the door for her.

Ingrid got through the door, heard it clang shut behind her, and wondered what the hell she was going to do next.

Sol had to be inside the building. No way would he go anywhere without his cell. If Ellis really was within the embassy, was it possible he'd forcibly taken Sol some place? Wouldn't somebody have noticed? Sol would have put up too much of a fight. It was much more likely that wherever Sol had disappeared to, he'd gone of his own accord. But then what had happened? And it still didn't explain what his cell was doing on his desk.

Ingrid was finding it hard to believe that Cory Ellis was working within the embassy. But then he had gotten on the cleaning staff at Fisher Krupps without any problems. Maybe he'd done the same thing at the embassy. She'd seen all the cafeteria and kitchen staff, and none seemed to fit his description. Perhaps he was part of maintenance and engineering, or the janitorial team.

She had to remind herself that it was still possible Ellis wasn't on staff at all and was planning to kill Sol outside of the embassy. Some place Sol was more vulnerable and exposed. The fact that she couldn't track him down made her fear that something had already happened to him.

An audacious attack within the walls of one of America's most prestigious embassies fitted Cory Ellis' profile too—how much of a coup would it be to kill a Federal agent right inside one of the most secure buildings in London?

Ingrid hesitated. Should she head up or down? She tried hard to fit together everything she knew about how Ellis operated when he was working through one of his kill plans. The method of execution would have something to do with a weakness he had discovered about Sol.

Ingrid wasn't sure she knew Sol well enough herself to have discovered any weaknesses. Maybe he didn't have any.

The creak of a door opening sounded from the floor below. Someone coming in from the parking lot, presumably. She waited for whoever it was to make their way up the stairs and pass her. But no one came. Maybe they'd gone down instead of up.

She waited a few more moments then shut her eyes tight and pictured Sol in as much detail as she could. What immediately sprang to mind?

What did she see, hear, feel?

She snapped her eyes back open. The strongest sense of Sol she had was his aroma. He always stank of cigarettes. Plus he had the worse smoker's cough she'd ever heard. Surely his Achilles' Heel had to be more significant than a nicotine habit. But then if it was something else she had absolutely no idea what it could possibly be.

She tried to picture where he was most likely to go for a smoke. Apart from the courtyard out back and Grosvenor Square itself, she was at a loss. He had mentioned some place inside the building he'd found for himself. A little niche, he'd said. But where?

Another noise sounded from below. This time she heard someone moan. The long, low moan of pain.

Ingrid's immediate thought was of Sol. She flew down the stairs to the lower floor. The small landing area leading out into the basement parking lot was empty.

She heard the moan again.

She raced down another two flights.

Then she saw him.

Not Sol.

Isaac. He lay in the doorway leading to the third basement level, clutching his stomach with both hands. The heavy fire door had trapped him where he lay. His pants and his shoes were covered in thick dark blood. A pool of blood was spreading across the floor. His eyes flickered open and he looked toward her. He moaned again.

Ingrid bent down low and put her head close to his. "It's OK, buddy. You're going to be OK. We'll get you some help." She started to move away.

Isaac moaned again. Louder and more insistent this time. "Sol," he managed to whisper.

Ingrid had retrieved her cell from a pocket and was dialing for assistance. Her fingers fumbled with the phone. "It's OK—help'll be on its way real soon."

"You... gotta... help Sol."

"What about Sol?"

"He's... killing him." Isaac looked down at his hands, both of them slick with red. He swallowed. "Help... him."

"Where? Where is he?"

Isaac's eyes closed. His head lolled heavily to one side.

Oh no, dear God.

Ingrid looked at her phone. She wasn't sure who she could call to get the response she needed. Everything would take just too long to explain.

Then she remembered the armed Marine two floors up.

There was nothing she could do for Isaac now. But she might still be able to save Sol.

44

She sprinted up the four flights of stairs and threw open the door. "I need you to come with me. Now."

"Ma'am?"

Ingrid flashed her badge at him, just in case he'd forgotten her from ten minutes ago. "Come with me."

"I have orders to secure the stairway on this level. The kitchen and cafeteria staff are in lockdown."

"I realize that. But I'm ordering you to come with me."

"Supervisory Special Agent Claybourne outranks you. I'm staying exactly where I am."

Screw this.

"Give me your gun."

The Marine's hand automatically flew toward the holster in his belt. "Step away, ma'am."

Ingrid puffed out a frustrated sigh. She didn't have time to argue with him. Still looking him square in the eye, she brought up her knee hard and fast and slammed it right into his crotch. As he doubled over, she kicked him hard under the chin. His head snapped backward at the same time his knees buckled. He fell to the floor like a puppet with its strings cut, folding in on himself.

Ingrid prodded him with the toe of her boot. He was out cold. She popped open his holster and yanked out a Glock 27. Not the model she was used to. But it would do just fine.

She shoved open the door to the stairway and clattered back down toward the level three basement, her feet only lightly touching the edges of the steps.

She quickly reached Isaac. Why the hell did Ellis have to hurt him? He must have just been in the wrong place at the wrong time. More collateral damage Ellis didn't give a crap about.

Ingrid blinked hard and pushed open the door, unable to avoid jarring Isaac's body. In the dim basement light, she could just make out a trail of blood smeared along the floor. It led away from the door, deep into the corridor beyond. The corridor that carried all the services to the rest of the building. Thick insulated pipes ran along the low ceiling as far as she could see.

Ingrid struggled a little for breath, it was so hot and airless down there. She stepped over Isaac Coleman's dead body and gently let the door rest once again against his ribs.

She checked that the chamber of the Glock 27 had a round in it. She hated relying on a weapon she hadn't personally tested, but she didn't have a lot of choice. She held the gun outstretched in both hands, two index fingers resting lightly on the trigger. A gentle squeeze would be sufficient to let off the first round. She hoped to hell she wouldn't have to use it.

She continued to tread slowly and carefully, glancing down at the trail of blood every now and then, but mostly keeping eyes front, staring into the gloom, watching for movement.

Now she knew where she was headed, her destination was obvious. The only place inside the building not fitted with smoke detectors was the bunker on basement level three. It had its own water, power and oxygen supply. And it was never used. Sol's little smoking 'niche' was a nuclear fallout shelter.

The bunker had to be at least another hundred yards ahead of her. Its entrance was set into the wall of another corridor that ran perpendicular to this one. Cory Ellis could be anywhere between there and here. Assuming he was here at all. It was quite possible he'd done what he'd come to do, watched Sol die a slow and painful death, and escaped completely without detection.

Ingrid blinked the moisture from her eyes. She wasn't sure if it was caused by sweat or tears. She glanced up toward the ceiling, at the thick pipes covered in insulating foam. It really was hot down there.

After a few more yards she stopped for a moment and listened. All she could hear was the deep, insistent thrum of the generators.

She picked up a little pace, conscious Sol could very well be struggling for his last breaths just a hundred or so feet away. She forced a little more air into her lungs and continued down the corridor, keeping her eyes fixed on the end, now just thirty or so yards away, occasionally glancing left and right toward maintenance access doors as she passed each one. Sweat was dribbling between her breasts and making her shirt stick to her back.

Finally she reached the last few yards of the corridor. She pressed herself against the wall and edged sideways, barely daring to breathe, not wanting to make too much noise. She got to the end of the corridor, where it met the one running perpendicular to it.

From her position, she could just make out the innocuous painted wooden door set in the wall of the corridor beyond. The door that led to the fortified bunker. She struggled to remember the layout on the other side.

As far as she could recall, the door opened onto a square, ten feet by ten feet, interior room. The bunker itself was situated on the other side of a twelve-inch thick titanium reinforced hatch that looked like something from a ship or a submarine—a circular handle set into its center, a punch code security pad on the wall to the right.

Ingrid steadied her breath for a moment.

She had no idea whether Ellis would be armed. He could quite easily have overpowered a Marine the same way she had.

Only one way to find out.

Gun in one hand, she inched forward and reached the wooden door. She bent her head in close. She listened. The blood pumping in her ears pretty much drowned out anything else. She tried to swallow, but her mouth was too dry. Her lips were stuck to her teeth.

She pushed down on the handle. When the latch released, she pushed open the door wide and shuffled sideways, pressing her back flat against the corridor wall. No sound came from within. She waited another couple of seconds then stepped through the doorway. Gun outstretched, she swung left, then right.

The anteroom was empty.

The shiny reinforced hatch leading into the bunker itself was ajar. Ingrid stepped toward it. She peered through the gap.

She couldn't see much, but about thirty feet away, half obscured by shelves of dried goods and eight-gallon water containers lining both sides of a narrow corridor, she could see into another room, beyond another submarine-style shiny metal door that was open wide. She'd never seen inside the interior room before. She could just make out a figure stooping low, his legs straddling a large object on the floor.

Ingrid slowly opened the hatch in the anteroom wider and stepped into the long, thin corridor that stored the supplies. As carefully as she could, she started walking down the shelf-lined passage, toward the inner room, her eyes fixed on the stooping figure she could see through the open hatch. It was definitely a man. He straightened suddenly.

Ingrid froze.

How had he heard her? She'd been so quiet.

The man started to turn.

"Show me your hands. Now!" she yelled, running along the remainder of the corridor toward the open hatch and the interior room. "Hands over your head!"

He didn't move.

"I won't ask you again."

He turned a little more, one hand gripping his thigh, the other behind his back. As he moved, Ingrid caught a glimpse of Sol's lifeless body lying at his feet.

"Get away from him."

"What are you going to do, Agent Skyberg?" Slowly, he turned to face her.

He didn't look like the photograph or the artist's impression. His hair was cut in a short crop, close to his scalp. His chin and cheeks were covered in two days' blonde stubble.

"Hands over your head!" she said again.

He smiled at her.

She suddenly felt vulnerable, standing in the middle of the room, and backed up closer to the hatch, keen not to get locked inside.

"You really think I'm going to do what you say? Haven't you done your research? You should stop wasting your breath." He let out a little laugh. "Your friend here stopped wasting his a short time ago."

"Step away from him."

"You shoot me, I win. I've done everything I came here to do. You don't shoot me, you die." He pulled his right arm from behind his back, his right hand wrapped around the handle of a ten-inch screwdriver.

She couldn't let him have what he wanted. Suicide by cop? No way.

He jabbed the screwdriver toward her. But he was still more than ten feet away. He stepped closer.

"Drop your weapon."

"Haven't we just been through that? Weren't you listening to me? I guess I should make allowances—the carbon monoxide still preventing the oxygen getting to your brain, huh?" He smiled again. "I was pretty pissed when your friend turned up to save you, but then if she hadn't, I guess we wouldn't be enjoying this moment together now, would we?"

The sweat from Ingrid's forehead was sliding into her eyes. She didn't dare blink.

"Drop your weapon."

"Isn't that getting a little tired?"

"This is your last warning."

He laughed at her and took a deep breath, his shoulders almost shrugging up to his ears. Then he exhaled and his whole body seemed to go limp.

A second later he launched forward, hurling himself toward her.

Ingrid squeezed the trigger. She saw the effect of the bullet before she heard the deafening crack. Ellis jerked backward, but didn't fall. A long moment passed. The screwdriver slipped from his hand. Then he came at her again.

She fired.

He stalled. Dropped to his knees. Pitched forward. He landed just a couple of feet from her. Blood started oozing onto the floor beneath him. His arms and legs twitched.

Ingrid turned back toward the door and searched for the panic button, her eyes still misted with sweat. She located the big red plunger switch and thumped her fist against it.

A piercing wail erupted from loudspeakers in the corridor outside. Ingrid skirted around Ellis' twitching body and kneeled next to Sol. She kept her gun trained on Ellis' back.

But Cory Ellis wasn't going anywhere.

And neither was Sol.

45

Three days later

Marshall opened the door, but refused to look at Ingrid as she entered the room. He was still pissed at her for being right. The way things were between them at the moment, it seemed he might never be able to forgive her. The fact that she'd broken off their engagement the night before seemed much less important to him than what he perceived as her attack on his professional capabilities.

She couldn't worry about Marshall's feelings. She was right and he was wrong. They both needed to move on.

Right now she had to stay focused. She was about to conduct the most important suspect interview of her career.

She stood at the viewing window and stared at Cory Ellis. He was staring right back at her. Beneath his tee shirt, his entire right side, all the way from his shoulder to his hip, was covered in strapping and bandage. Even though Ingrid hadn't been on a shooting range for over six weeks, her aim had still been accurate enough to miss the major arteries and his heart and lungs. His shoulder blade would need a lot of reconstructive surgery. But that wasn't her problem. She'd been determined he wouldn't use her the same way his father had used the prison guard. Suicide by cop was never going to be an option.

"I could have gotten him to talk. I just needed a little more time," Marshall said.

He'd been telling her that for the last two days. But Louden had lost patience and given in to Ellis' demands: he was pleading the fifth unless Ingrid interviewed him herself.

The door to the observation room opened and the Deputy Special Agent in Charge, Amy Louden, came in. She nodded to Ingrid and Marshall, settled herself in a chair, and stared toward the prisoner.

"They're always much smaller than you think they're going to be," Louden said, turning to Ingrid.

"Ma'am?" Ingrid glanced at Ellis, who was grinning toward the glass now.

"In my experience, at any rate." Louden raised her eyebrows expectantly. "Shall we get this started? I have a feeling it may take some time. Remind me—what's the current estimated death toll?"

Ingrid opened her mouth to speak, but Marshall beat her to it.

"We've identified at least five people connected to the imprisonment of Ellis' father who have died either in unexplained accidents or unsolved homicides," he said.

"Are we expecting to add to that list?"

"At the moment we'd like to get confirmation he's responsible for those killings. He might volunteer further information in the course of questioning."

"And the killings here in London?"

"As far as we know, in addition to the City trader, there were two fatalities outside of embassy property—the Latvian woman and the realtor. We're not pursuing those as a priority. We'll liaise with our London colleagues, of course." Marshall glanced at Ellis. "But there's no way we're handing him over. He's coming back to the US to face trial."

Louden had tilted her head impatiently. Ingrid winced a little inside. Marshall was stating the goddamn obvious. The DSAC turned away and leaned her elbows on the table in front of her. "When you're ready, agent."

Ingrid did her best to cover the discreet earpiece wedged into her left ear with her hair. But it wasn't really long enough to do the job. She stepped out into the corridor and took a deep breath. She hadn't interviewed a suspect on her own for nearly a year. She wanted to ensure Ellis wouldn't pick up on any potential weakness in her technique. If she went into that room presenting anything other than supreme confidence, he'd be able to detect it in a heartbeat. She straightened her collar, tugged at the bottom of her jacket and opened the door.

Striding into the room, she stared into Ellis' face and didn't take her eyes off him as she lowered herself onto the plastic and metal chair opposite his, determined not to be the one to blink first.

After a few seconds Ellis smiled at her. "OK—you win." He dropped his gaze toward the single handcuff tethering his one functioning hand to the table. "Where would you like to start, Ingrid?"

"How about the beginning?"

"Why be so conventional? Why don't I talk to you about Sol Franklin, huh? Wouldn't you like to hear how he pleaded with me to spare his life? Or maybe I should tell you all about how he and his fellow agents harassed my family for months before my father's arrest?"

"Was that when you decided you'd kill him? All those years ago? Most teenagers would have been dating girls and hanging out at the mall."

"Most teenagers weren't hounded out of high school."

"What is this? Am I meant to feel sorry for you?"

"Not as sorry as I feel for you."

Ingrid maintained a neutral expression.

"I mean," he continued, "it can't be easy for you carrying all that pain around. There's no escaping it, is there?"

"I think you may be mistaking me for somebody else."

"Not at all. I can see the suffering in your eyes."

"Don't let this slip out of your control," Marshall murmured into her earpiece.

She thought about removing the device from her ear. A running commentary from Marshall wasn't going to help anyone.

"How naive do you think I am, Ellis? I know what you're trying to do. This isn't *Silence of the Lambs*, we're not playing a game of quid pro quo. Either you're going to tell me what you've done, or you're not. It doesn't really matter to me one way or the other." She relaxed back into her chair. "We have enough forensic evidence to convict you of at least two murders. Your DNA has been detected on the clothes of Isaac Coleman. Plus there's all the evidence found at the restaurant in Savannah. Two murders is more than enough to put you away."

Ellis tilted back his head and yanked at the metal cuff. "You can't deny it. Something happened to you. When you were a child maybe. Or a teenager, like me. You must have lost someone like I did. I can see it in your eyes."

She studied his face. There was no expression there to read. Ellis was on a fishing expedition. Everyone had pain some place in their past. If he thought he could unnerve her with a carnival fortune teller's trick, he was sorely mistaken.

"Stay focused, agent," Marshall said in an urgent whisper.

Ingrid supposed he was putting on a show for Louden. She wished he would shut the hell up.

"What I'd be interested in knowing," Ingrid said, leaning forward a little, "is why it took you so long to do anything. I mean, your dad was shot dead in 1992, and yet you waited a whole *decade* before you acted."

The muscles in his jaw flexed and bulged. It was the first real sign she was having some impact.

"Oh wait, maybe it took your *mother's* suicide for you to finally grow a pair, huh? Two parents who chose to end their lives. That's got to make you feel pretty unloved and abandoned, I guess."

Ellis blinked slowly at her but said nothing.

"Nice of your mom to end it all on the anniversary of your dad's death. I guess she was just thinking of you. You'd only have one day in the year to truly dread."

He licked his lips.

"Even then, you still waited to make your move. It couldn't have taken you that long to track down the prison guard. But then I guess it was a big step—your first kill. Must have taken you months to summon the… I was going to say courage… but there's nothing brave about shooting an unarmed man in the face at point blank range."

"You know nothing about it."

"But that's why I'm here, isn't it? For you to enlighten me." She pulled the miniature speaker from her ear and laid it on the table. "You have my undivided attention."

Ellis stared into her face, searching. Ingrid stared right back at him.

"No," he said emphatically. He blew out a breath. "I've changed my mind. You don't get to know. I won't give you the satisfaction. I'm not telling you anything." He stared toward the mirror set into the wall. "This interview is terminated."

46

Frustrated as hell, Ingrid scooped up the earpiece and marched out the room. She threw open the door into the observation room.

"That went well," Marshall said. "Maybe the combative approach wasn't the right one after all." He was clearly trying to embarrass her in front of the DSAC.

She ignored him. "I'm certain he'll come around, ma'am."

Louden raised her eyebrows.

"If we leave him to stew a while, the need to boast about his achievements will overwhelm him. He'll be begging to speak to me again."

"How long are we going to let Ellis dictate the timetable?" Marshall said, his face and the tips of his ears reddening. "Maybe someone else should have a crack at him."

Deputy Louden tensed as he raised his voice. "The BAU guys have profiled him. I assume you've read their report?"

Both Ingrid and Marshall nodded back at her. Ingrid had been surprised and hesitantly self-satisfied that their profile matched the one she'd compiled almost point for point.

Louden turned to face Marshall. "So I suppose you know Agent Skyberg's approach is the one they've recommended?"

"Yes, ma'am." Marshall was balling his fists and breathing fast. Ingrid knew that if he didn't shout at someone or punch a wall soon, he risked exploding.

"He still hasn't requested a lawyer," Louden said. "Ensure someone asks him if he's still happy with that situation."

"I get the feeling he wants a one on one... a gladiatorial contest." Ingrid regretted making the interview sound like a boxing match as soon as the words left her mouth.

"I think you're absolutely right," Louden said. "Are you happy to continue to be his opponent?"

"Absolutely, ma'am."

"Let's hope he decides to start talking again soon." With that Louden left the room.

As soon as the door closed behind her, Marshall turned to Ingrid. "Are you trying to sabotage my career?"

Ingrid started to move toward the door. Marshall blocked her path.

"Come on, Marsh, let's not get things out of proportion."

"You can call me SSA Claybourne while we're in a work environment."

The way he was acting, Ingrid sure as hell didn't want to be in any other kind of environment with him. She was waiting for him to relieve his pent up frustration by shouting at her. "About last night... we didn't really finish the conversation—"

"I am *not* discussing that matter here. Besides, there's nothing more to discuss."

"I never intended to hurt you. I just couldn't let things go on—"

"Shut. Up." He turned and flung open the door. Ingrid watched him stride down the corridor.

She felt relieved that the termination of their fourteen month engagement had gotten to him a little. She also felt a little sorry for him. He disappeared around the corner and she let out a long breath and sucked in another. Right now she had more important matters to focus on. She returned to her desk and reread the case files.

Less than ninety minutes later, Ellis told the Marine guarding him that he wanted to speak to Agent Skyberg again. Louden, Marshall and Ingrid reconvened in the observation room ten minutes after that.

"You're confident you can handle this?" Louden asked.

"One hundred per cent." Ingrid tried to make her tone convincing. Everything depended on whether Ellis had truly decided to cooperate. If he had, Ingrid supposed she wouldn't be much more than an over-qualified note taker. But if he still wanted to play games, there wasn't much she could do to stop him.

She entered the interview room without the earpiece she'd been wearing earlier. Ellis had made it a condition of their meeting. Which was fine by Ingrid. She was relieved to be free of Marshall's unhelpful interjections.

She sat down slowly and rested her hands in her lap, keeping her upper body as relaxed as she could. All her tension had transferred to her thighs, which had started to twitch. Thankfully they weren't visible beneath the table.

"I guess you're wondering why I changed my mind and decided to talk to you?" he said.

"I'm not, but feel free to enlighten me."

"A sense of completion. I've achieved everything I set out to. I think that deserves a little celebration."

"I left the balloons and party poppers at home."

"We can make our own fun."

Ingrid's legs twitched a little harder under the desk. She wanted to get this over with. Fun and games Cory Ellis style she could do without.

"Where shall we start?"

"Why not be conventional and choose the beginning?"

"Way back then?"

"I don't mean the first kill. When did you decide there would be any kills at all? Was it after your mom committed suicide?"

Ellis tilted his head sideways and stared hard into her face. The muscles in his cheeks flexed. Any mention of his mother seemed to hit a nerve. "There wasn't a specific tipping point. I'm sure I don't have to tell you that these things fester and ferment over time. Must have been the same for you, with the loss you suffered."

Ingrid had already decided that if Ellis started to make things personal, she'd terminate the interview. She ignored the comment. "OK, let's move on to your first kill."

"I made a plan for every single one long before that."

"You drew up a list?"

He nodded back at her. "I like to be thorough. I worked out an exact plan for each one back then too. Obviously, I had to adjust and amend the details over the years. But it was good to start out with a blueprint, a framework. The outcome was the same, no matter the exact execution method."

"Each one based on what you saw as a weakness in the victim?" Although it was petty, Ingrid wanted Ellis to confirm another of her theories.

"I had to make it a little challenging for myself. There would have been no fun in gunning them down with a semi-automatic, now would there?"

"So, getting back to the prison guard."

"Thomas Greerson. That name haunted me right through my teenage years."

"That was 2002. Exactly a year after your mom's death."

He tensed again, this time across his shoulders. "No better way to honor her memory, wouldn't you say?"

Ingrid held his gaze. Raised an eyebrow. "And when you shot Greerson in the chest and the face... how did that make you feel?"

"I'm giving you a comprehensive list, not participating in a counseling session. It's none of your goddamn business how I felt."

Ingrid leaned forward in her seat. "OK—tell me about David Brite."

"He was called David Fuller when I killed him." Ellis' nostrils flared as if he'd just smelled something unpleasant. "If Brite had kept his mouth shut, none of this would have had to happen." His eyes sparked with an intensity Ingrid hadn't seen before. "Brite was making a fortune. And it was my dad who made it possible."

"He was breaking the law."

"No one really got hurt. Lots of people were making a lot of money."

"It wasn't sustainable." Ingrid wondered just how deluded Ellis was about his dad's illegal investment scheme.

Ellis shrugged.

"So you killed David Brite in 2003. What happened in 2004?"

"Nothing."

"But you had a plan."

"I was busy making a living. I worked on Wall Street 2004 through 2007."

"Really?"

"Have you any idea how expensive these operations can be? I had to get some cash together."

"So what happened in 2008?"

"Plenty."

Ingrid shifted in her seat. She'd meant to remain perfectly still, hoping to appear supremely in control. So far she felt as if she'd been wriggling around in her chair like a five year old. Ellis, meanwhile had barely moved. Mostly he seemed relaxed, almost Zen-like in his repose.

"I could see what was around the corner," he continued. "The crash was so inevitable it's amazing it took anyone by surprise. Time to get out of finance. I'd made enough not to have to work again. Enough to dedicate myself to my… mission."

For a moment Ingrid thought he was going to say 'art'.

"Who did you kill in 2008?"

He pulled a face. "Highsmith was asking for it. To have the audacity to run for Congress after what she did to my dad? She might as well have waved a red flag. Taunting me that way."

"Her allergic reaction in the restaurant in D.C.? That was you?"

"Would have killed her then if her aide hadn't been carrying a spare EpiPen. How could I have known a thing like that?" He shook his head, the bitterness fierce in his eyes. "No aide to save her the second time." In an instant the bitterness transformed into something approaching glee. "But I'm skipping ahead. You want strict chronology, I'm sure." He leaned back in his seat and yawned. "In 2009 I eliminated the FBI agent who was second in command in Sol Franklin's team. Agent Franklin had left the country by then, so I went for the next best thing—his able lieutenant. Not the order I'd planned originally, but over the years I've learned to be flexible. Sometimes you have to improvise." He stared into her eyes. "Were you quite close to Sol? I saw a little tension around your eyes just then, when I mentioned his name. Was he a mentor maybe? A father figure?" He searched her face.

Ingrid was determined not to react. When Ellis realized he wasn't going to get the response he wanted, he eventually looked away.

"There I go, skipping forward again," he said. "Where were we?"

"Twenty-ten."

"Oh yes, 2010 it was the turn of the reporter from the local paper. That bitch hounded my mom after Dad was convicted. She wouldn't quit. Finding new angles to write about, anything to twist the knife just a little more." He shook his head. "Then I found out why she was so diligent in her work. Her dad was one of the investors who lost money. It was a personal vendetta. Got so bad Mom couldn't take it anymore. We moved towns. Ended up some place Mom had no friends, no job, no life. All she did was look after me." He looked down toward the table. Ingrid thought she'd detected a slight moistening of his eyes. "She could have been so much more." He sat motionless for a few moments and said nothing. Then his head snapped back up and the gleeful glint was back in his eyes. "I guess we're nearly through. I dispatched the defense attorney in 2011."

"The attorney who defended your dad?"

"He had to be the most incompetent lawyer ever to pass his bar exams.

Assuming of course he actually did. A better lawyer may have gotten my dad off."

There was no doubting Ellis' dedication to his task. He certainly had been thorough.

"So, we're practically up to date." Ellis sniffed. "That bitch Highsmith last year. And Sol Franklin just three days ago. A complete set."

"What about Matthew Fuller?"

"He was a bonus I wasn't expecting. He hadn't actually made it onto my list. He was only a kid at the time of the conviction. I came here to eradicate Franklin. But when I discovered Matthew Brite was in London too—some people really are careless with what they post to their social media accounts—it seemed too good an opportunity to pass up. Especially when I discovered he was suffering from OCD. Got my creative juices flowing."

"So you got yourself a job at Fisher Krupps?"

"Do you know how easy it is to get into all sorts of places when everyone sub-contracts their cleaning and maintenance work? You should maybe check who else you have working here at the embassy. You might be surprised. Shocked, even." He glanced over Ingrid's shoulder toward the glass. Ingrid pictured Marshall scrambling for the phone, demanding a list of all the staff.

"And that's it," Ellis said. "A full lid. I'll of course provide methods, dates, times. Everything you need for the complete picture."

"What about everyone else who got killed along the way?"

"Collateral damage. Unavoidable."

"Do you even remember them all?"

"Sure—I can make you another list. The only one I truly regret is Marija. She was a great gal. But I needed to test the FBI response, as I'm sure you've worked out by now. Marija was the best way of doing that." He slumped back in his seat. "A shame, but unavoidable." He flashed a smile at Ingrid. "I guess we're done. I won't say it's been a pleasure, Agent Skyberg. But I do rather admire your determination, not to mention your apparent cockroach-like indestructibility. I hope there are no hard feelings between us. You were getting in the way just a little too much. I couldn't have you jeopardizing what I'd come here to do. And ultimately, you didn't. So it all worked out for the best." He smiled more broadly at her.

Ingrid scraped back her chair and got to her feet. "I would maybe tone down the smugness, if I were you."

"Oh please, allow me a little self-congratulation. Twelve years ago I had quite a to-do list. And I've achieved everything I set out to. How many people can say that about their miserable lives?"

"Not quite everything." Ingrid smiled down at him. "And there's absolutely nothing you can do about it now." She pulled out her phone and scrolled through her photo gallery.

Ellis frowned up at her, his chest rising and falling a little more rapidly. But he said nothing.

"Oh come on," Ingrid said. "You're dying to know what I'm talking about. Admit it."

He glared at her.

"Now that you've… unburdened yourself, I thought it was the least I could do to keep you up-to-date with the latest developments. I thought you might appreciate that."

"What could you possibly have to say that would interest me?"

"Something that'll change your whole perspective. It'll certainly destroy your sense of… completion."

"Don't bother trying to play games—you're no good at it."

"I wouldn't dream of playing games with you. I just thought you'd be interested to know Assistant Special Agent in Charge Franklin says hi."

Ellis started to laugh, but as the pain in his shattered shoulder took hold, the laughing abruptly stopped. "Really? Is that the best you can do? And you expect me to believe you?"

"Sol Franklin regained consciousness a little before you did on Wednesday afternoon."

"You're lying."

"Now I expected you to say that. So I came prepared."

She turned her phone around and showed Ellis a picture of Sol Franklin smiling up at the camera from his hospital bed with a copy of yesterday's *Washington Post* lying across the bed covers. It had taken all of Sol's will power and determination to pose for the photograph. He was completely exhausted afterward. But it had been worth it for this moment. Worth it to witness the bewildered, distraught look on Ellis' face.

"I guess you didn't achieve what you set out to do after all," Ingrid said. "And you never will."

DEEP HURT
AN INGRID SKYBERG THRILLER BOOK 3

He killed his daughter. Now he's taken his son.

In the next Ingrid Skyberg Thriller, Ingrid must track down a pilot who has gone AWOL from a US Air Force base in rural Suffolk. Accused of murdering his baby daughter, he's now abducted his eight-year-old son. Can she find him in time to save the boy?

READ DEEP HURT NEXT

DEEP HURT

BOOK THREE

EVA HUDSON

1
_____

Ingrid Skyberg reached the stairway in her apartment building and stupidly looked up at the dozen or so flights ahead of her. The action meant she lost momentum completely. It was a bad habit she'd gotten into after her daily five-mile run, and that brief pause made the final climb seem ten times harder. Nevertheless, ignoring the burn in her thighs and calves, she pushed on up, two steps with each stride, her breath labored, but her mind gloriously clear.

Triumphantly, she reached the top floor and punched the air. Just as she was putting her key in the lock, her cell phone buzzed. She answered the call without looking at the screen to see who was calling. Big mistake.

"Ingrid? Is that you?" Svetlana Skyberg's Russian accent was still unmistakable even after nearly forty years in the US.

"Who else would it be? You're calling me on my cell." Ingrid turned the key and kicked open the apartment door. Speaking to her mother instantly made her feel like a petulant teenager. She tried to subdue the irritation the sound of her mother's voice always provoked. "Everything all right? You OK?" Ingrid hadn't spoken to her in months.

"Me? Of course I am OK. Why wouldn't I be?"

The indestructible Svetlana Skyberg: two packs of specially imported unfiltered cigarettes a day for the last forty years and still going strong. Ingrid shut the apartment door with her behind and wandered into the kitchen. She pulled a fresh bottle of water from the fridge. "Then why are you calling?" A split second later, she remembered. How could she have forgotten? Svetlana only contacted her when… Ingrid got a sinking feeling in her stomach.

Oh no, not again.

"Have you seen TV? It is on the news in England?"

"I don't own a TV."

"Why not? Is FBI not paying you enough to buy a TV now?"

"Mom… tell me why you're calling."

"They found another house."

Ingrid closed her eyes and made a low moaning sound.

"What? You're complaining? You don't even know what I am going to tell you. You need to know. You must listen to me."

"Please, Mom. I don't have time for this. I have to get ready for work."

"So now you can't spare five minutes for something so important?"

Ingrid knew the amount of time she spent speaking with Svetlana was irrelevant—as soon as she put the phone down she'd replay the events of eighteen years ago over and over. It was the anger and resentment, swiftly followed by guilt and remorse, that would go on for hours afterwards.

"Three girls, they found this time. Alive. You hear me? *Alive.*" She took a deep breath. Ingrid pictured her sucking on one of her long cigarettes. "What am I saying? They are not girls. Not now. They are full grown women. One of them is thirty-two. For God's sake, Ingrid—don't you see what I'm saying? She is Megan's age."

A chill ran across Ingrid's shoulders and down her arms. Her hands started trembling. She was still sticky with sweat from her run, but suddenly so cold. "Have they identified them?"

"Not yet. Already they have given the police their ages. But not names. Or maybe the police are not telling the news people."

Ingrid wandered into the living room and rested one hand on the back of the beaten up old leather couch to steady herself. Was it possible? Could Megan Avery still be alive? Her mouth had gone dry. "What else do the news reports say? Have they apprehended the perpetrator?"

"You mean have they arrested the stinking bastard who did this? What's the matter with you, sounding so much like a cop? You're speaking to your mother. We are talking about your friend."

"I'm an FBI agent, how do you want me to sound?"

"Like a goddamn human being for once."

Ingrid pulled the phone from her ear and considered hanging up. She could hear her mother still speaking at the other end, the words indistinct, the sound just an annoying buzz in the distance, but the tone of her voice was unmistakably angry. Like a wasp trapped inside a jar. They always had this effect on one another, Svetlana had an uncanny knack of pressing all of Ingrid's buttons. It wasn't even the words themselves, her accusatory tone was enough to make Ingrid want to scream at her. And yet her mother was the picture of charm itself with her friends back home. She saved her criticism for her only child. Ingrid had never been able to do anything right in Svetlana's eyes.

"Did they say if the women are unharmed?" Ingrid asked, cutting across whatever venomous statement her mother was in the middle of.

"How can they be unharmed? They have been held against their will for years and years. God knows what tortures they have suffered."

"Are they in the hospital?"

"The police sent them all straight to the nuthouse for assessment. It's not *their* brains that need testing. It's that goddamn evil bastard's."

Ingrid walked shakily to the door leading out onto the roof terrace of her apartment. After struggling for a moment with the stiff key, she stumbled outside and drew in a deep breath. "You still haven't answered my questions: have the police arrested him?" She paced to the end of the roof, the wooden deck creaking beneath her feet. "Are they looking for anyone else?"

"The police have not arrested anyone. They are searching the house. Like they're going to find him hiding in a closet somewhere. They did find some vicious dogs tied up in the yard." She mumbled something in Russian Ingrid couldn't make out.

Then she fell silent.

Ingrid didn't want to ask any more questions. She didn't want to know anything else about the case. They'd been through this too many times already in the last three or four years. Svetlana would call her about the latest case of recovered abductees. The rescued women would then be identified, and once it was clear Megan Avery wasn't one of them, the phone calls from Svetlana would cease. Until the next time.

Ingrid braced herself for what was inevitably coming next.

"I'm at Kathleen's house now," Svetlana said. "All night we have watched the news together." She took another long pull on her cigarette.

Here we go.

"I told her she should not get her hopes up. Like she has every other time this has happened."

Ingrid gripped the metal rail at the edge of the roof.

"Kathleen wants to speak to you."

Ingrid closed her eyes and said nothing. Her mother never gave up. Even though Ingrid had made it perfectly clear she couldn't speak to Megan's mom.

"Ingrid? You still there? Ingrid?"

"I'm here." The tremor in her voice took her by surprise.

"Tell me this time you will talk to her. Like a grown up. Like..." She paused. "Like a goddamn human being."

Ingrid wanted to hurl the phone over the side of the building.

"Well?"

"You know I can't. Nothing's changed. I just can't do it."

Svetlana said something in Russian again. This time she didn't mumble. But Ingrid had heard all the Russian curse words her mother could throw at her. They were accompanied by, 'coward', 'no child of mine' and 'your papa would be ashamed'. Bringing Ingrid's dead father into the conversation? That was a low blow. Something Svetlana reserved for special occasions. It had the desired effect: Ingrid's eyes started to sting. "There's nothing I can say to Kathleen that will make things better."

"How can you say that? When have you even tried?"

"No matter what I say I can't justify why I'm alive and Megan is dead."

"We don't know she is dead. Not for sure. Besides, Kathleen has never asked you to justify anything."

"But that's what's in my head. I can't face her. Don't you get that?"

"For once, why not stop thinking about what is in your head and think about what is in hers?"

Ingrid squeezed her eyes shut, forcing out the tears. How could Svetlana be so cruel? Hardly a day went by that Ingrid didn't think of Megan and the loss Kathleen had to endure. But she made no comment. She didn't have the energy to fight.

"Megan's vigil is coming soon. Why not come home for once and light a candle for her?"

Ingrid wiped her damp cheeks with the back of her hand. "I can't." The words came out in a sob.

"Stop feeling so sorry for yourself, like always. I should have known already what your answer would be."

If you knew then why put us both through this?

"If you won't speak to Kathleen, at least promise you will do one thing for her."

"What?" This was new. Normally Svetlana would hang up about now.

"Ask your FBI friends for any information they have about this house and these women. It's no good just watching news on TV. They tell the TV people only what they want them to know."

"You've never asked me for my professional help before."

"I've got more reason to this time."

"I don't understand."

"The house where they found these women is only thirty miles away."

2

After Ingrid had promised her mother she would ask one of her contacts in the Bureau for more information, Svetlana hung up without bothering to say goodbye. Ingrid marched back into the apartment, threw her cell phone on the couch and headed for the bathroom. She hoped the sensation of hot water pummeling her skin and flattening her short hair against her scalp might banish the distressing conversation with Svetlana from her mind.

But instead it gave her time to think. And all she could think about was Megan Avery.

Megan at fourteen, the way she'd looked when Ingrid last saw her: flushed cheeks, sparkling eyes, a little breathless maybe, as she and Ingrid hurried from the carnival to return home before their curfew at ten. Ingrid walked as fast as she could, Megan struggled to keep up. Like Ingrid, she had carried quite a few extra pounds right through her baby fat years and into her teens. Megan's mom liked to cook and enjoyed spoiling them. Ingrid never complained. She took after her father when it came to her appetite. Svetlana had always eaten like a bird. Another memory popped into her mind: Svetlana poking a talon-like finger into the soft flesh of her upper thigh, a disgusted look on her face, her voice shrill and harsh as she told her just how lazy she was.

Ingrid scrubbed shampoo into her scalp with both hands, her eyes squeezed shut, and started humming some dumb pop song she'd heard on the radio the day before. Anything to shut out the other sounds that had begun playing in her head: the high-pitched and slightly out of tune carnival steam organ melody, the distant screams of the people on the roller coaster. She hummed a little louder. Then the shampoo reminded her of the sickly sweet smell of the cotton candy they had eaten. It was an aroma she'd tried to avoid ever since. It brought on the rush of memories faster than anything else.

She quickly rinsed out the suds and turned off the shower. She stepped out of the bathtub and stood dripping on the floor. Disoriented for a moment, she'd forgotten where she'd left her bath towel. In that instant she was back in the bathroom of her childhood home.

The house that was only thirty miles from where those women were found. So close to where Megan had been taken. Was it possible she could still be alive? For years Ingrid had held on to that hope. It was the reason she'd been so determined to join the FBI. After Megan disappeared, everything Ingrid had done had been carefully planned to get her another step closer to her goal. She worked hard in high school and college, got herself fit, made endless sacrifices in her personal life, until finally she was accepted into the Academy at Quantico. She had dreamed of heading up her own team and one day tracking down the man who'd snatched away her best friend. A tiny part of her also harbored the fantasy that somehow Megan was still alive and Ingrid would be the one to liberate her from her prison.

But over the years she'd slowly begun to realize what a forlorn hope it was, that in all likelihood Megan had been abused and murdered within hours of being abducted. And in time Ingrid had learned how to live with that realization.

After her conversation with Svetlana, a glimmer of that same hope had come back to torment her. She was compelled to find out anything she could about this latest case for her own peace of mind: not just because her mother had asked her to.

Just forty minutes after stepping out of the shower, Ingrid was making her way from the basement parking lot of the ugly six-story concrete building situated on the western side of Grosvenor Square in Mayfair to the FBI's Criminal Division office on the third floor. She had extra purpose to her step as she hurried along the rosewood-paneled corridor. When she reached the twenty by thirty foot, low-ceilinged room, she was surprised to discover it was empty. Jennifer Rocharde, the administrative clerk and currently the only other member of the Criminal Division team, wasn't sitting at her desk.

With Jennifer out of the way, Ingrid considered calling Mike Stiller, her most reliable contact within the Bureau. But it was still only four-thirty a.m. on the East Coast. Mike was keen, but even he wouldn't be working that early in the morning. She didn't want to leave him a voicemail message—her request for information would need careful handling.

For the next three hours she struggled to complete a report for her most recent case. The Metropolitan Police investigation into the armed mugging of an American tourist had been relatively straightforward, but writing up her assessment of their work had proved more difficult than she'd expected. She found it almost impossible to concentrate on anything other than what might be happening with another investigation that was being played out over four thousand miles away. A cursory check of the major news sites online hadn't revealed much more than Svetlana had told her. Without hard facts, all the reporters and so-called experts could do was speculate. It was worse than no news at all.

At a quarter before twelve she reached for her cell phone and out of the corner of her eye noticed that Jennifer had risen to her feet.

"Hey," the clerk said, scooting around her desk on the other side of the office and hurrying toward Ingrid's, "I'm going for coffee. Can I get you anything?"

"That'd be great." Ingrid was relieved Jennifer was going out, which meant she didn't have to. There was no way she wanted an audience for her potentially awkward phone conversation with Mike Stiller.

"Let me guess," the clerk said, studying Ingrid's face carefully, "double espresso."

"It's that obvious I need caffeine, huh?"

Mildly embarrassed, the young clerk pushed her long, strawberry-blond hair behind her ears and nodded. "If I'm not out of line mentioning it, you've seemed awfully quiet this morning. Is everything OK?"

"Nothing a few early nights wouldn't fix," Ingrid lied. She forced a cheerful smile and watched Jennifer turn on her sensible heels and leave the office. She waited another couple of minutes before picking up the phone. Jennifer wouldn't be gone long. Ingrid hoped she'd have enough time to persuade Mike Stiller to agree to help her. Given what had happened three months ago, he might take a lot of persuading.

3

Since Ingrid had first started working at the embassy, back in December, she'd relied on intel from Mike Stiller more times than she cared to admit. As the weeks turned into months, she had discovered that when it came to the collation of information, working around the system—circumventing the strictest of Bureau protocols—was sometimes the only way to get things done. That wasn't something she would even have considered doing before her move overseas. But so far, her new pragmatic approach seemed to be working out just fine: Mike felt indispensable and Ingrid got to see higher classified intel that her level two security clearance would normally have given her access to.

She scrolled through her contacts list for his number and hesitated when she found it. After what had happened a couple of months ago, Mike might decide he never wanted to help her again.

Ingrid's break-up with her fiancé might make the conversation very uncomfortable. Mike was probably closer to Marshall than he was to her. Marshall may have asked him to choose sides. This was the first time she'd needed a favor from her old D.C. field office colleague since she'd ended her engagement, so there was no way of knowing if he'd agree to help her or not.

There was only one way to find out. She hit the call button and hoped for the best. Mike answered right away, no doubt eager to feel both busy and indispensable even before seven a.m. Eastern Standard Time.

"Agent Stiller—how are you this fine and pleasant August morning?" Ingrid was struggling to inject an upbeat tone into her voice.

"It's seventy-five in the shade and humidity's set to reach eighty-five percent by two p.m. The office air conditioning has stopped working, my iced tea has no sugar in it and I've got an appointment with the dental hygienist at lunchtime. So I'm just peachy." He let out a weary sigh to emphasize the tragic nature of his situation. "Thank you for having the courtesy to inquire about my well-being, but I'm sure that's not why you're calling."

"You know me so well."

"Listen, I don't have a lot of time."

"I'll be real quick."

"I don't just mean now. I've got a lot on my plate at the moment. If you need a favor, you might have to ask some other pliable schmuck."

Mike had to have been talking to Marshall.

"You know I wouldn't be asking if the circumstances didn't call for your skills and expertise." She continued to keep her tone as light as she could.

"I have a new boss. The regime here isn't as… relaxed as it used to be."

It seemed to Ingrid a pretty lame excuse. Why didn't he just come right out and admit his loyalties lay with his old friend, Marshall Claybourne?

"Hey, I'm not asking you for classified information, just a little heads up on a current case. It's really important."

Mike didn't say anything. Normally his curiosity would have gotten the better of him.

"Just a couple phone calls to your contacts in the Minneapolis field office," she said.

"All our calls are monitored now."

"You're kidding me."

"The new boss is pretty tough. Takes no prisoners, you know what I mean?"

"Come on, Mike, it can't be—"

"It's Marshall, OK?"

"What?"

"The new boss—it's Marshall. Started last month. He's busy trying to prove himself right now. I'm sure he'll mellow with time."

"But I thought he was your friend."

"I guess only when I was useful to him."

Ingrid wondered if maybe he was getting at her, but quickly dismissed the notion. Marshall's demands would be in a whole different league to hers. Obviously the breaking off of their engagement had done nothing to diminish his determination to haul himself up the greasy pole. She didn't know if she felt relieved or disappointed that the end of their relationship had affected him so little.

"Listen, I'm sorry it didn't work out for you guys," Mike said after a long pause.

"It was in the cards. You and me can still be friends, right?"

"Sure we can. But getting you intel? It's just not possible. Right now I gotta keep my nose clean. Marshall already got two agents transferred. And I like working here."

Ingrid wasn't sure what to say. Mike was still her best hope of getting all the information she needed, as fast as she needed it.

"Hey, are you OK?" he asked her.

"Fine." She could already hear Svetlana's mocking tone when she told her that the one time she'd asked for Ingrid's help, she'd failed to deliver. "If you can't help me, then I guess I do have to find somebody else who… I mean I need to…"

"You sure you're OK? You don't sound fine. What's going on?"

"I should let you get back to work. I don't want you getting crap from Marshall on my account." Her voice wavered and she let out an involuntary sob.

"I'm so sorry—I didn't realize you were so cut up about Marshall."

"God, I'm not! No way!"

"It's OK—I understand. You guys were together for a long time."

"It's not Marshall, I swear."

"Then what the hell…?"

Ingrid took a moment to compose herself. "I guess you must know about the case in Blue Earth County? The rescued abductees?"

"It's impossible to avoid it." She could hear him breathing noisily at the other end of the line. "Wait a minute, don't you come from around there?"

This was the part she'd been dreading. In the two years she'd worked with Mike out of the D.C. office, she'd managed to avoid the subject of Megan Avery entirely, even when she'd surprised him by putting in a transfer request to the Violent Crimes Against Children Unit. "The house where they found the girls is thirty miles from my home town." She could feel her throat tightening. "Megan, my best friend, was abducted eighteen years ago. I need to know if she's one of the women they found." She stalled and took a breath.

"Jesus Christ. I had no idea. Tell me what you need."

Ingrid swallowed, grateful Mike hadn't asked her for any more details about Megan's disappearance. "All the information the local feds gather in as close to real time as you can get it. Including any audio or video interviews the witnesses, victims, or suspects participate in. I don't want to get information from FBI reports, I want the facts straight from the source."

"That's gonna be tough."

"I wouldn't ask if it didn't mean so much to me."

"Sure. I understand."

"Can you do it?"

Mike didn't answer right away. Ingrid wondered if maybe Marshall had just stepped into the office.

"Mike?"

"I'll make some calls. I can't promise anything—it might take a little while to set up. You want me to send files to your private email account?"

"Please. This is strictly between you and me." Ingrid swallowed again. Just mentioning Megan's name to Mike had been tougher than she'd imagined. "As soon as you get positive IDs for any of the three women, you will let me know?"

"You didn't even need to ask."

"Thanks, Mike." She hung up and leaned back in her seat. She'd been squeezing her cell phone so tightly it had left deep indentations in her right hand. She concentrated hard on forcing the muscles in her neck and shoulders to relax.

Mike Stiller had never let her down before. She prayed this time would be no exception. She planted a hand across her forehead and leaned her elbow on the desk. All she could do now was wait.

"Jeez—I guess you really need this, huh?" Jennifer said as she appeared at the door. "Sorry I was so long. The line at the cafeteria took forever. I think the espresso machine isn't working properly." She carefully placed the small cardboard cup on Ingrid's desk.

Before Ingrid had a chance to drink any coffee her landline started to ring. She stared at the phone for a moment, trying to get her head together.

"Want me to get that?" Jennifer asked.

"It's OK." The words came out louder and harder than she'd meant. "Hey—thanks for the coffee."

The clerk smiled back at her and returned to her desk. Ingrid answered the call.

"Agent Skyberg, US embassy."

"Hello, this is the duty sergeant, calling from Holborn Police Station, I've been asked to inform you about an incident that happened earlier today at a hotel in Bloomsbury."

Ingrid grabbed pen and paper from her desk. "Give me the details, sergeant."

"I don't have them all, this is a courtesy call, more than anything."

"Give me what you got."

"American family, husband went on the rampage, attacked his baby daughter and left her for dead."

"Left her? Has he been apprehended?"

"No. He snatched his eight-year-old son and took the boy with him. He's still on the loose."

Ingrid's pen remained poised over the notebook. "When did this happen? How long has he been out there?" She heard the rustling of paper.

"Haven't been given an exact time—earlier this morning."

"And what about the wife? Where is she?"

"At the hospital."

"He attacked her too?"

More rustling.

"No, that doesn't appear to be the case."

"Is there someone else I can speak to who has more information?"

"Sorry, no, not at the moment. The bulk of the team are at the hotel. The rest are at the hospital."

"Which hospital?"

The sergeant gave her the address and hung up.

Ingrid grabbed her jacket from the back of the chair and her purse from the drawer beneath the desk. Over the last eight months she'd gotten used to being the last to find out about incidents when they occurred, but had never received such limited information about a case before. She tried not to read too much into it, and headed for the door.

4

Ingrid parked her motorcycle on Chenies Street and walked three blocks north to the rear entrance of University College Hospital. Although she'd never before set foot inside the building during her eight months in London, she had often been struck by its appearance. It looked more like a skyscraper office block than a hospital: seventeen stories of tinted green windows and pearly white cladding towering over the intersection between Euston and Tottenham Court Roads. She supposed from the top few floors the patients must get a pretty impressive view of the whole of London.

A plain clothes detective was waiting for her just inside the entrance when she arrived.

"Agent Skyberg?" the muscular man in the cheap gray suit asked Ingrid as she glanced around the expansive reception area.

She nodded back at him. Unruly tufts of shortish dark blond hair stuck out from his scalp at different angles. His face was covered in stubble and the shirt beneath his jacket was a little crumpled. Ingrid suspected he'd had an unplanned early start.

"I'm Detective Sergeant Brad Tyson, I believe our duty sergeant has passed on the details of the case to you." He guided her toward a wide corridor to the right of the entrance, three elevators on each side.

"Actually, the details were a little sketchy." Ingrid saw no point in criticizing the duty sergeant's reticence. She didn't want her relationship with the investigating team to start off on the wrong foot.

"Let me bring you right up to speed, then." After pressing the 'up' button of the express elevator he stood back and studied her face for a moment. "If you think that's strictly necessary, in the circumstances."

"Why wouldn't it be?"

"I've had the embassy's role explained to me. I know when an American citizen is involved in a crime—victim or perpetrator—you like to keep an eye on the investigation, offer assistance, write your report, etcetera, etcetera."

He had just made her job sound almost an irrelevance, but Ingrid did her best to ignore his dismissive tone. She said nothing, just nodded at him encouragingly so that he might actually get to the point.

"But with the Air Force so closely involved in this case, I suppose the US government is pretty well represented already."

"Air Force? What do you mean?"

Before Tyson could answer, the elevator doors opened to reveal a crush of bodies crammed inside. Ingrid and the detective stepped to one side as the occupants started to pile out. Two or three were on crutches, a couple more, hooked up to IV machines, clutched packs of cigarettes in their spare hands. A man in a wheelchair rolled out without looking where he was going. Ingrid wondered how they'd all managed to breathe in such a confined space.

"It's a very busy hospital," Tyson said by way of explanation.

Ingrid and Tyson eventually managed to make it into the elevator, followed by another twenty or so people. Most of them were carrying bags of apples and grapes and a variety of less healthy snacks, with magazines and newspapers tucked under their arms. All of them had weary expressions on their faces.

During the ascent, Tyson made banal small talk and Ingrid played along, just as keen to be discreet. But once the elevator stopped at the eleventh floor and Tyson pushed a path to the front, Ingrid following in his wake, the doors had barely closed before she repeated her earlier question. Her tone more urgent this time.

"Tell me exactly who is involved in this investigation."

"I assumed you knew."

Ingrid now suspected the details she'd been given earlier weren't so much sketchy as deliberately vague. "Let's assume I know nothing at all and start over, shall we?"

"The US Air Force have sent one of their Security Forces officers." Tyson headed down the stark white, brightly-lit corridor and Ingrid followed. The further they walked from the elevator lobby, the more she could detect the familiar aroma of every hospital she'd ever visited. It was a mix of sterilizing alcohol, disinfectant and something non-specific—a smell Ingrid always associated with illness and disease.

"You're telling me the man we're looking for is a serving officer?" she asked as they pushed through a set of double doors.

"First Lieutenant Kyle Foster, stationed at RAF Freckenham in Suffolk."

"And exactly what authority does this Security Forces officer have?"

"I'll introduce you to the Major shortly. He can tell you himself."

"He's already here?" Ingrid stopped walking, forcing Tyson to do the same. "You informed the Air Force before you contacted the embassy?"

Tyson looked at her indignantly, as if she were questioning his competence personally, rather than the protocol of the Metropolitan Police in general.

"We needed good quality photographs of Foster and his son. We had to contact the base first."

"And you couldn't inform the embassy at the same time?"

"You'll have to bring up any complaints with DCI Radcliffe. He's the senior investigating officer." He started walking again.

"Wait a minute." Ingrid wanted more information before she walked all over whatever relationship the military policeman had managed to establish with the investigating team. "How long has the 'Major' been here?"

Detective Sergeant Tyson slowly came to halt and turned to face her, an irritated expression on his face. "An hour or so, why?"

"You've given him all the facts of the case?"

"Only as far as we know them. We're still waiting to speak to Mrs Foster to find out exactly what happened this morning."

"You haven't spoken to her yet?"

He took a step backwards and looked up at the ceiling, his irritation clearly mounting. "She's been too distraught. Wanted to be at Molly's side. In case she came round."

"Her daughter's still alive?"

Tyson narrowed his eyes. "You didn't even know that?"

"I told you—the details I've been given are sketchy at best."

"Molly's sustained head injuries. She's unconscious. Hooked up to so many machines you can barely see her for all the leads and wires."

"Is she going to be all right?"

Tyson shrugged. "Doctors can't tell us that. Not yet."

"I'd like to speak to Mrs Foster. She's an American citizen. She needs to know the embassy will help any way we can."

"You'll have to go to the back of the queue. DCI Radcliffe's going to interview her soon. With Major Gurley."

"The MP?"

"I think he prefers to be called a Security Forces officer."

Ingrid didn't give a damn what he preferred. As far as she was concerned all armed services cops were cut from the same cloth. "I want to be part of that interview."

Tyson shook his head. "Not my decision to make—you'll have to speak to the DCI about it." He continued down the corridor, marching toward another set of double doors.

As Ingrid hurried to catch up she wondered just how much access DCI Radcliffe was planning on giving her. It seemed the Air Force MP had everything sewn up. She needed to make him understand just what the pecking order should be here.

Tyson pushed through the doors and pointed to a couple of chairs lined up against the corridor wall. "Make yourself as comfortable as you can. There's a vending machine just through those doors. The coffee's drinkable, but the tea is disgusting. And however desperate you get, don't be tempted by the soup—croutons or not, it tastes like dishwater."

"You really just expect me to sit and wait?"

The detective shrugged. "Sit down, stand up. It's up to you."

"Take me to the SIO—I need to speak to him."

"He'll speak to you when he can. He's tied up right now." He tried to move past Ingrid, but she blocked his path.

"Tied up doing what?"

"I'm not sure that's any of your business."

"OK—where's the Security Forces guy?"

"Major Gurley's with the DCI."

"Great—I can meet them both at the same time." Ingrid hurried to the first door along the corridor and tried the handle: it was locked. She moved on to the second. "You could just tell me where they are. Save me interrupting someone else's meeting." Before she reached the second door, another, diagonally opposite, opened abruptly and a very tall man dressed in gray and white camouflage battledress stood in the doorway, his head turned towards the room. Ingrid rushed over to him. "Major Gurley?"

He spun around to face her. He was late thirties, with a tanned complexion and blond buzz cut. His features were chiseled, his jawline lean, his eyes pale blue. He wore a puzzled expression, but the quizzical smile faded once he glanced towards Tyson.

Ingrid stuck out a hand. "I'm Agent Ingrid Skyberg, from the FBI's Legal Attaché program at the embassy. I've been assigned to this case."

Bemused, his gaze switching quickly from Ingrid to Tyson and back again, Gurley shook her hand. "Pleasure to meet you, agent."

He was joined in the doorway by an ashen-faced man in his early fifties dressed in a suit that looked far too expensive to afford on a cop's salary.

Ingrid introduced herself again.

"DCI Paul Radcliffe." His mouth twitched upwards at the corners. "I think you may have had a wasted journey."

"This is a matter for the US Air Force Security Forces, agent. No need for the FBI to get involved," Gurley said. "I've got it covered." He gave her a warm smile. If it hadn't been for the content of what he'd just said, Ingrid might almost have believed it was genuine.

She didn't smile back.

"Now, I can provide you with an update each day, or a digest every forty-eight hours, if you'd prefer. Though I'd hope we can have First Lieutenant Foster safely in custody by the end of today."

"Police custody," Radcliffe added, either for Gurley's benefit or hers.

"Of course," Gurley turned his smile on Radcliffe. This time there was no mistaking its insincerity. Ingrid supposed the DCI wasn't fooled by it for a moment.

"If you could excuse us, detectives." Ingrid turned first to Radcliffe, then quickly to Tyson. She could be as polite as Gurley if that was the game he had chosen to play. She started to walk away. When the tall military policeman didn't follow she said, "Major Gurley? If you have a moment?"

"Please—call me Jack," he said and with two long strides was standing beside her.

"I don't know whose orders you're following, but after the Metropolitan Police Force, the FBI has jurisdiction. If anyone has had a wasted journey, it's you. I'm sorry you've traveled all the way from Suffolk unnecessarily." She forced a smile. "Naturally, I can give you regular updates."

"There seems to be a misunderstanding here. I'm sure a short phone call to the Special Agent in Charge at the embassy can clear everything up for you. My orders come direct from the Pentagon," Gurley said.

"I believe the misunderstanding is yours, Major." Ingrid was doing her best to tamp down her rising anger. How dare he patronize her like this? Who the hell did he think he was? As she reached into her purse for her cell phone—she was more than willing to 'clear things up' at the embassy

—a woman in a dark blue pant suit pushed through a set of swing doors into the corridor. She rushed over to the two detectives.

Ingrid edged a little closer to them.

"The ICU team have taken Molly down for another scan, sir," the woman said. "Mrs Foster can give you twenty minutes."

5

Ingrid hurried to the detectives, eager to make her case before Gurley did. "I'm sure you won't have a problem if I sit in on the interview, chief inspector," she said. "In a purely observational capacity, of course."

Radcliffe looked at the MP who was standing with his feet wide apart, his long arms folded across his chest.

"Major Gurley and I have a few wrinkles to iron out in terms of exactly who has authority here, but I wouldn't want you to delay your interview on our account," Ingrid quickly said before Gurley had a chance to respond.

"Just as long as you do. I don't really care which one of you represents the US government, but keep your personal quarrels out of my investigation."

"Absolutely." Ingrid nodded toward Gurley, who managed to dip his head in agreement.

"I don't want a peep out of either of you, clear?"

"Crystal," Gurley said.

Radcliffe led them down another corridor, stopping when he reached a uniformed officer standing beside a closed door with a notice above it that read, 'ICU Room 4'.

"Everything all right, constable?" the DCI asked the squat man wearing a dark blue stab-proof vest over his uniform.

"Nothing to report, sir. The team got Molly out and away without incident. PC Lewis has accompanied her to the MRI room on the first floor."

543

Ingrid noticed the officer had a night stick, pair of cuffs and Taser attached to his belt. "You're guarding the little girl?" she asked Radcliffe. "You think Foster is likely to come back and try to attack her?"

"I'm not taking any chances." He opened the door and let the female detective enter the room first.

Ingrid followed close behind them. The room was bright—sun streamed in from a large window to the right of the door. Opposite the door, next to a collection of monitors, was a vacant space where Molly's bed must have stood just a few minutes earlier. Somehow the emptiness felt more distressing to Ingrid than the sight of a small child lying unconscious in a hospital bed. She looked away toward the window and focused on the woman standing to one side of it. She was wearing a light blue and yellow summer dress, a bright orange sweater wrapped across her shoulders. She gave the impression of someone who had dressed in a hurry, which was hardly surprising, Ingrid thought, given the circumstances. The woman turned slowly away from the window and seemed to recoil as she took in the scene at the door. Seeing a group of people standing there, including one in military uniform, must have been a little overwhelming for her.

The female detective, who Ingrid supposed was the Fosters' family liaison officer, hurried to Mrs Foster's side and held her arm as she led her to a large recliner armchair in the corner of the room. Ingrid saw Foster's face for the first time and noticed her eyes were bloodshot, her cheeks blotchy. She couldn't have been older than thirty-five. The woman slowly eased herself into the chair and continued to stare at the group standing awkwardly just inside the room.

"You'd better get on and ask your questions," she said, her voice shaky. "As soon as they bring Molly back from her scan I want you all out of here."

DS Tyson ducked out of the room. He returned moments later carrying a chair in each hand. He set them down opposite the armchair, as the family liaison officer introduced both detectives to Mrs Foster. She glanced toward the door, at Ingrid and Gurley, a deep frown etched into her forehead. DCI Radcliffe introduced Ingrid. Then Gurley.

"And Major Gurley you already know, I presume," he said.

Carrie Foster nodded at them both but wouldn't make eye contact. "Can we please get this over with?"

Radcliffe and Tyson sat down, leaving the FLO to crouch beside Mrs Foster's chair. Gurley leaned against the wall next to the window, Ingrid stood behind the two detectives.

"We'll be as swift as we can," Radcliffe told Mrs Foster. "Our main priority is getting Tommy back. We need to locate your husband as soon as possible. But we really need to know exactly what happened this morning, to get some idea what we're dealing with."

Carrie Foster opened her eyes wide, her gaze fixed on the ragged Kleenex she was holding.

"First off, do you mind telling me why you're here in London?" Radcliffe asked.

The woman looked up at him, a puzzled expression on her face. "It was a mini-vacation. Sightseeing, you know? Apart from our trips home, it was the first time we'd left the base." She shook her head. "I should never have agreed to it. It was way too stressful to take on something like that."

"For you?"

"No! For Kyle. All of us crammed into that small hotel room." She wiped her nose with the disintegrating Kleenex. "The kids were overexcited. Really noisy, you know?"

"And that was a problem?"

"Noise is one of the triggers for Kyle."

"Triggers?"

"You know he's being treated for PTSD?"

Ingrid sensed Radcliffe stiffen slightly. He threw a glance toward Gurley, who remained expressionless.

"Let's assume we know nothing at all. We'd much rather hear the facts from you," Radcliffe said.

Carrie Foster continued. "Kyle was diagnosed around eighteen months ago. But he's not been right for a lot longer than that."

"He's still been on active duty during that time?"

"He's been going to counseling sessions at the base. His doctor says it's under control."

Ingrid made a mental note to speak to the Air Force doctor about Kyle Foster's condition.

"OK. Let's go back to the events of this morning. I realize how difficult it is for you to go over things again. But I really need you to tell us everything you remember."

Carrie Foster sniffed. "It's all right—I understand." She snatched a breath.

"Can we start right at the beginning?" Radcliffe said. "Who woke up first?"

"Kyle showered and dressed before the kids woke up. He seemed fine. A little tired maybe—he didn't sleep that well. You see, he has these nightmares. Has done ever since he came back from Afghanistan. Once a bad dream wakes him, he finds it really hard to get back to sleep."

"So everything was all right before your children woke up?"

"Yes. Peaceful. Happy, even. Kyle was singing in the shower."

"What happened after that?"

"Molly woke up. It was time for a feed. She started to cry just as soon as her eyes were open. Her crying woke Tommy. Right away he sprang out of bed—a little A-frame bed the hotel had fixed up alongside ours. Then he started to jump up and down on it. Like I say, he was excited. Kyle told him to stop, but he just bounced even harder. Jumping higher and higher. Until the bed collapsed underneath him."

"Was he hurt?"

"No—Tommy thought the whole thing was hilarious. Then he climbed on our bed and bounced on that instead. Kyle shouted at me to do something. He swore at me. But Tommy doesn't listen to a thing I tell him. I was holding Molly by then, trying to pacify her. Trying to stop her crying." She blinked slowly. "That's when it happened." A sob escaped from her mouth.

"Take your time, Mrs Foster."

The FLO took her hand and squeezed it tight.

"Kyle started yelling at Molly to shut up. When she didn't he snatched her from my arms and started shaking her. So hard. I tried to grab her back. But he shoved me away and I hit something. I have a big bruise halfway up my thigh." She rubbed her leg with a fist, staring blankly into space. She was clearly back in that hotel room. Reliving the events of the morning.

"Can you tell us what happened next?" Radcliffe said gently.

"Kyle carried on shaking her. Until the crying stopped." She swallowed. "Then he threw her on the bed. I mean *threw* her." Her eyes were moist.

The FLO grabbed a pack of Kleenex from a pocket and handed it to Mrs Foster.

"Thank you." Carrie Foster pulled out a tissue and dabbed her eyes. "Then Kyle ran out. Said he couldn't breathe and needed to get air. As soon as I could, I locked the door behind him, and I called for the ambulance."

Jack Gurley shifted his position, straightening his back then crossing one ankle over the other before leaning back against the wall.

"He came back just before the EMTs arrived."

"How long before, would you say?"

She shrugged. "Seconds maybe. I don't know. Not long."

"He managed to get back into the room, even though you'd locked the door."

"I opened it when the manager came. The other guests had complained to him about the noise. Kyle had been shouting. I might have been screaming. I don't remember. I guess they were worried what was going on."

Radcliffe leaned closer to Mrs Foster. He lowered his voice. "Where was Molly when the ambulance crew arrived?"

"In my arms. She wasn't moving. Or making a sound. I thought she was... I mean I thought..." She sobbed again. "One of the EMTs asked me what happened. I hesitated. I didn't want to believe what Kyle had done. I just looked at him."

"What did you tell the paramedic?"

"I said Kyle had shaken Molly and she'd gone quiet. The other EMT started to move toward Kyle, his hands up, telling him to take it easy. I guess Kyle panicked." Her eyes widened even more as she stared at the floor. "He had the EMT moving closer on one side and the hotel manager stepping into the room from the hallway." Another sob escaped her throat. "That's when he grabbed Tommy. Picked him up and ran right out the door. Barging into the manager as he went." She shook her head. Then looked up at Radcliffe, staring into his face. "Why didn't anyone try to stop him?"

Radcliffe gave her a half-shrug. "No one really knows how they're going to react in a situation like that," he said soothingly. "It all happened so fast, they probably didn't even work out what was going on until it was too late."

"Someone should have stopped him." She turned her stare toward the window and Major Gurley. "You've got to find them. I want my little boy back."

Gurley tensed but said nothing. Mrs Foster turned back to the DCI.

"Is there anywhere your husband might have taken Tommy?" Radcliffe asked her.

She shook her head numbly. "He doesn't know London. Where would he go? Do you think he's hurt Tommy? Why did he take him? If he wanted to run away, why take my boy with him?"

6

The door into Molly Foster's hospital room opened and her mother jumped to her feet. She ran to Molly's bed as it was wheeled back in. Molly looked smaller than Ingrid had expected. She seemed tiny lying in the adult-sized bed. Her short curly hair spread across the pillow each side of her pale face. Her lips were almost colorless.

"Is she OK? What did the scan show?" Carrie Foster asked the ICU nurse dressed in a crisp white short-sleeved tunic and dark pants.

The nurse gave her a warm smile and laid a reassuring hand on her arm. "The swelling in her skull hasn't got any worse. We'll know more when the radiologist has studied the scans. He'll speak to the consultant and then the consultant will come and explain everything to you."

"How long before that happens?"

"Hopefully before the end of the day."

"What? That's hours away."

The nurse helped the porters position the bed into place and reattached the monitors. She switched the tube feeding oxygen into the little girl's nostrils from a portable cylinder tucked beneath the bed to a supply coming out of the wall above it. Ingrid was relieved to discover the child was breathing without the aid of a respirator.

"I'm sorry, Carrie," the nurse said when she'd finished her tasks. "We have one radiologist covering for two of his colleagues at the moment. It won't affect Molly's care in any way. You don't need to worry about that."

Carrie Foster stroked her daughter's forehead. She seemed to have forgotten the detectives were even in the room. Major Gurley stood in silence at the foot of the bed with Radcliffe. After a moment DS Tyson cleared his throat.

"We'll leave it for now, Mrs Foster," Radcliffe said. "But we will need to speak to you again later."

The female FLO ushered them all towards the door and closed it behind them.

Once outside, Ingrid took DCI Radcliffe to one side asked him for an update on what was being done to locate First Lieutenant Foster and his son.

"I've already updated Major Gurley." He glanced back towards the room. Gurley was peering through the round window set into the upper third of the hospital room door. "Perhaps you could liaise with him?" He turned to walk away. Ingrid scooted in front of him.

"I'd rather hear it from you."

"Look, I told you before, whatever's going on with the embassy and the US Air Force is no concern of mine. You get things sorted out between yourselves."

"I'm about to call my boss to resolve the situation. I'd like to be able to give him a progress report at the same time."

Radcliffe puffed out an impatient sigh. "I've posted officers at the major train terminals and Victoria Coach Station. We're going through CCTV footage from the streets surrounding the hotel. We've questioned all the guests present at the hotel when the initial response officers arrived. And we have statements from the hotel manager and receptionist."

"Do their accounts match up with what Carrie Foster just told us?"

"Of course. Why wouldn't they?"

"Just being thorough." Ingrid looked back towards Gurley. He was speaking with DS Tyson. Tyson was nodding gravely. She wanted to know what they were talking about. "And what about the EMTs... the ahh... paramedics? You've spoken to them?"

"They were just finishing their shift when they picked Molly up. We've managed to interview one of them, and before you ask, yes, his account matches Mrs Foster's."

"Do you have CCTV footage from inside the hotel?"

"It's a small, family-run establishment. Three star. They don't have cameras recording their guests' every move." He beckoned to his detective sergeant and tapped a finger against his wristwatch. "I suggest you resolve your issues sooner rather than later with Major Gurley. I see no point in you replicating each other's duties."

Ingrid watched as Tyson shook Gurley's hand, then hurried toward his senior officer. Gurley disappeared into the mens' restroom.

Radcliffe handed her a scrap of paper. "The hotel is only about five minutes away on foot," he told her. "Ask for Brian, he's the Crime Scene Manager. He'll walk you through events, as we understand them, in situ. Help you to picture what happened." He glanced down at the note. "Pass that on to Gurley if he's got the gig, would you? I don't want to be endlessly repeating myself." He gave what seemed to Ingrid a reluctant smile and briskly walked away.

Ingrid seized her moment. She snatched her cell phone from her purse and called her immediate boss at the embassy, Assistant Special Agent in Charge Sol Franklin.

"Hey, Sol. Do you have a couple minutes?" she asked as soon as he picked up.

"For you...?"

"What do you know about this case in Bloomsbury?"

"The Air Force guy who ran amok?"

"I feel like I've walked into it completely blind. The intel I got from the Met was severely lacking, to say the least. I get the feeling they were surprised I even showed up."

"Have you met Major Gurley yet?"

"You know about him?"

There was an extended pause. "I didn't know in time to warn you, if that's what you mean. I only just got off the phone from the Legal Attaché himself."

"You did?" Sol hardly ever spoke to the head of the FBI program at the embassy. He normally received his instructions from his next in command, Deputy Special Agent in Charge, Amy Louden.

What the hell was going on?

"You're telling me the Legat is involved with this investigation personally?"

"He just got off the phone from the Pentagon. I gather there was a rather fraught—my word, not the Legat's—discussion with the Chief of Staff of the Air Force."

The Legal Attaché and the Chief of Staff? With such big hitters taking a personal interest in the case, Ingrid was surprised Sol hadn't taken it on himself. "Listen, I realize you can't give me all the details of your conversation, so I'm not even going to ask, but can you at least tell me who should be liaising with the cops here?"

Another pause.

"Sol—just spit it out. If I'm off the case, I'm off the case. I can live with that."

"That would be far too straighforward."

"I don't understand." Ingrid kept her eyes peeled on the door to the men's restroom. She wanted to get this resolved before Gurley reappeared.

"A US pilot on the run in a host nation doesn't look that good… politically."

"Politically? Maybe I would give a crap if a fourteen-month-old girl wasn't in a coma and an eight-year-old boy hadn't been abducted." She turned around and started walking, concerned if she stayed still a moment longer she might feel the need to punch somebody.

"You don't need to get involved with all the political BS," Sol said. "That's my job."

"So why are you even telling me about it?"

"Because I need to explain the strategy the Legal Attaché and the Air Force big cheese cooked up between them."

Ingrid didn't like where she thought this might be heading. She pulled up abruptly.

"You and Major Gurley better start to play nice with one another. You've got to work together on this. Show a US government united front."

Ingrid let out a groan. "I'm not taking orders from that arrogant son of a—"

"You don't have to."

"As much pleasure as it might give me telling him what to do, I don't think he'd agree to follow my orders either."

"Working *together*, didn't I say? You're going to cooperate with one another. Gurley has his chain of command, you have yours. But on the ground you two liaise with the local cops as a *team*."

"I like to work alone."

"I don't care. My hands are tied on this one."

"For God's sake, Sol."

"No point in arguing. Just don't let me down."

It wasn't that long ago Ingrid had saved Sol Franklin's life. She wasn't about to disappoint him now. She never could. But the thought of working with an opinionated military cop? She felt a wave of heat pass from her chest up into her throat.

A moment later Sol said a brusque goodbye and hung up.

"I'm guessing you just had the exact same conversation as me." A Texan accent. A voice so close to her ear she felt Gurley's warm breath against her skin.

She pulled away and wheeled around to face him. "Jesus! What are you doing creeping up on me like that?"

"Don't tell me, your boss at the embassy, huh?" he said, undeterred. "Major General Walker called me himself. Might have considered it an honor." He raised a sandy-blond eyebrow at her. "Under different circumstances." He ran a hand over his buzz cut and put a hat on his head. "Looks like we're stuck with one another. I suggest we make the best of it. Sooner we track Foster down, faster we can get back to normal." He held out his hand. Reluctantly, Ingrid shook it.

He smiled a wily smile at her, moving just one corner of his mouth. "As long as we're clear on one thing."

"And that is?"

"We both agree that for practical purposes, on the ground… I'm in charge."

Ingrid practically had to break into a jog to keep up with her companion's lengthy strides. When they'd made it out of the hospital and onto the noisy, bustling Euston Road, she'd made it quite clear there was no way she'd be taking orders from Gurley. He'd merely laughed in her face. After that they continued the journey to the Fosters' hotel in a hostile silence. Gurley was at least right about one thing, Ingrid thought: a swift resolution to the situation would be best for all parties concerned.

The hotel was situated in a side street just off Russell Square—a favorite location for American tourists on a budget. The slightly down-at-heel, three-star establishment took up four row houses in the middle of a Georgian terrace. Three of the front doors were sealed shut. The shabby exterior looked in need of urgent redecoration.

Ingrid led the way and quickly found a uniformed police constable chatting to a woman behind the reception desk. "We're looking for Brian, the Crime Scene Manager," Ingrid said and flashed her badge at him. He pointed her toward the stairs.

"Second floor. You can't miss it."

They tramped up four shallow flights of stairs, still not speaking to one another, and discovered another uniformed policeman on the second floor landing. He directed them to the other end of a dimly-lit corridor. Ingrid peered into the gloom, only just managing to make out two Tyvek-suited crime scene examiners standing outside an open door, talking to a woman dressed in a dark suit and vivid pink shirt. On her feet the woman was wearing overshoe bootees.

Ingrid hurried towards them. She waved her badge in the air by way of introduction and asked for Brian, the CSM. The woman, who was a detective constable, handed Ingrid and Gurley a pair of bootees each.

"I'm not sure they're big enough," the detective said, her gaze working its way slowly from Gurley's feet to his face. "You are rather a tall specimen."

Gurley glanced down at the small blue bootees and quickly rejected them. "It's OK, I can see all I need from out here," he said.

Ingrid couldn't help but feel a little irritated at Gurley's attitude. It seemed as if he'd decided this exercise was a waste of his time and wasn't prepared to participate. She peered into the room.

"That's Brian's arse, right there," the detective told her and pointed to a man crawling on his hands and knees beneath a low couch.

Ingrid slipped the bootees over her shoes and entered the room, taking care to step on the plastic platforms laid out twelve inches apart to get to the other side. "Brian? I'm Agent Skyberg... from the embassy."

The CSM made a little groan then carefully backed out of the confined space without hitting his head. He wriggled backwards like a man who had learned the hard way not to move too quickly in tight spaces. With some effort, he heaved himself vertical and looked Ingrid up and down. "I was expecting a bloke," he said, unapologetically.

"Sorry to disappoint."

"Oh no, not at all. You'll do nicely." He smiled a lascivious smile at her and Ingrid prepared herself for a barrage of double entendres and inappropriate remarks about her appearance. "What do you need to know, my lovely?"

She was still tuning her ear to the various regional accents in the UK, trying to get a grip on most of them. She quickly decided "Brian the CSM" was Welsh. Most probably south Wales, if she had to choose. She rapidly outlined everything Carrie Foster had told her about what happened that morning. "Is this scene consistent with her statement?"

Brian stuck out his bottom lip and surveyed the room, nodding as he turned his head left then right. "That could work." Then he started to shake his head. "Bloody domestics. I've seen the aftermath of too many of them over the years. They never get any easier to deal with, especially when there's kiddies involved. Bloody tragedy." He stared into Ingrid's face. "You got kids have you?" His gaze dropped to the small triangle of bare flesh that was visible above her shirt.

"I don't."

"Then you wouldn't understand."

"Oh I think I can empathize just fine."

"No—that's what I thought until I had one of my own. Turns your world upside down. Got five of the little buggers now. Love them all more than life itself. How could he do something like that to his own baby girl?"

Ingrid glanced around the room, taking in the built-in closet, the couch, the broken A-frame bed, and finally the kingsize. The room was in need of urgent redecoration, even more so than the exterior of the hotel. She wondered what the room rate was for a run-down place like this. Maybe First Lieutenants in the US Air Force got paid a lot less than she imagined. She completed another 360 degree turn and tried to work out if anything seemed out of place. From Carrie Foster's description of what happened, Ingrid felt sure something was missing. Then she worked out what it was. "Has your team removed any large items of furniture?"

"No. Only small ones. Why do you ask?"

She turned back toward the door. "Hey, Major Gurley." Gurley was busy talking to the detective in the bright pink blouse. He looked up, a slightly guilty expression on his face. "How tall would you say Carrie Foster was?"

He shrugged back at her. "Bit shorter than you, maybe."

"That's what I thought." Ingrid scanned the room again. But there was no solid piece of furniture at the right height that would cause a bruise on her mid-thigh. She'd been expecting a table, a desk or a low bureau. But nothing fitted the bill. "Detective, have you seen a list of the injuries sustained to Mrs Foster and her daughter?" she asked the pink-shirted woman.

"A list was emailed to my phone a little while ago," she said. "I haven't had chance to look at it properly yet."

"Do you think you could look at it now?" *And stop flirting with my colleague.*

The detective quickly located the file on her smart phone. "What am I looking for exactly?"

"Did the doctors confirm a large bruise on Mrs Foster's thigh?"

The cop scanned the email. "Yes—here it is. Large hematoma. Left thigh, eight inches below pelvis."

Ingrid made a note of the details and studied the room more closely. There really was very little floor space, no wonder tempers had been fraying. Four human beings in such a cramped environment would have tested the most patient of souls. She tried to put herself in Kyle Foster's place, bringing to mind the mild, self-diagnosed version of Post-Traumatic Stress Disorder she'd been suffering from on and off since Megan was taken. She closed her eyes and could immediately recall the sickly sweet caramel aroma of cotton candy. The distant sound of carnival organ music grew louder the harder she concentrated. Her breathing became shallower as her heart started to pound. Then her temperature increased as if someone had turned on a heater. She could absolutely understand Foster's need to flee. It felt claustrophobic in there. But to hurt his daughter? If it had all been getting too much for him, why not just run? But then Ingrid supposed in his head he wasn't so much hurting his daughter as making the noise go away.

"You OK?"

Ingrid felt the CSM's elbow nudge her arm. She snapped open her eyes. Sweat had begun trickling down her back, and was prickling at the nape of her neck. She had to get out of that room. "I'm fine," she told the CSM, even though it was obvious she was anything but.

"Are we done here?" Gurley called from the doorway.

Ingrid needed to speak to Carrie Foster again. If the facts surrounding her injury were already being called into doubt, what else about her statement might prove unreliable?

8

A black embassy sedan was waiting for them when Ingrid and Gurley emerged from the hotel. Ingrid asked the driver to drop her on Gower Street so she could pick up her motorcycle: she didn't want to add to the embassy's growing pile of unpaid parking tickets. As she stood on the sidewalk and watched the limousine merge into the long line of traffic, the relief of getting away from Gurley for a while was greater than she'd expected.

Although the traffic from Bloomsbury to Mayfair was heavy all the way, on the bike Ingrid managed to arrive at the embassy parking lot ahead of Major Gurley. She took the opportunity to visit Sol's office on the fifth floor, but when she got there his desk was empty. She called him and discovered he was heading up the welcoming committee in the Criminal Division office two floors below.

"An update, if you wouldn't mind, agent?" he said when she got there.

Ingrid started to lay out everything she'd learned in detail, interrupted occasionally by the beep of Sol's cell phone. When she stopped abruptly halfway through her account, Sol turned around to see what had caused the sudden halt.

"Major Gurley, you made it," he said and extended a hand. "I'm Sol Franklin. Ingrid you've met, of course." He put his arm around Gurley's wide back and guided the MP to Jennifer's desk. "And this is the most indispensable member of the FBI program here at the embassy. Jennifer

Rocharde. Anything on any of our databases you need to find, Jennifer is the person to find it. We'd be quite lost without her."

"Pleasure to be acquainted with you, miss." Gurley nodded toward Jennifer and immediately her cheeks flushed bright pink.

"Now, where were we?" Sol sat on the edge of Jennifer's desk and folded his arms.

Ingrid continued to tell him what she'd discovered, turning to the Major sporadically for his input.

It never came.

"You haven't said very much, Major. What's on your mind?" Sol said when Ingrid had finished.

"May I speak frankly, sir?"

"Wouldn't have it any other way. And please—call me Sol."

"I'm concerned we're wasting time. The clock's running down. We should be out there searching for Foster. We're making polite conversation while the trail's going cold."

Ingrid wondered why the hell Gurley had even agreed to come to the embassy if he felt so strongly about it.

"We should be following standard US Air Force procedure: apprehend the man who's gone AWOL, ASAP. Foster's had survival training—in the event of being shot down in enemy territory. If he's gone to ground, it's going to be one hell of a job to track him down."

"And you feel you're the man for the job?" Sol's tone was patient, if a little condescending.

"Due respect, sir. I know I am."

Sol smiled up at Gurley's blank face. "As a matter of fact, I've spoken to your superiors at the base and they agree. They have full confidence in your abilities. They want you and Agent Skyberg to share your expertise with the Met. But you have to understand, the Met does have some experience in apprehending fugitives."

"To be truly effective, I've found it's better if I work alone." He glanced at Ingrid. "No disrespect, agent. I'm making no comment on your skills in these matters."

For a man who didn't mean to disrespect anyone, Gurley was doing a good job at demonstrating the complete opposite. Why was he making things difficult when the investigation had barely begun?

"Working alone just isn't practical on this case," Sol said. "I was under the impression that had been explained to you. The Pentagon has agreed to Bureau involvement."

Gurley shook his head and stared down at the floor.

"But both you and Agent Skyberg must work closely with the Metropolitan Police Force. They have the best intel in this kind of situation. Their PR department are liaising with the major news outlets to get the story out there. The officers manning the phones in the police incident room have already received calls from people claiming they've seen Kyle and Tommy Foster."

"Claiming? What does that mean?"

"None of the sightings has been confirmed at this time."

"You see? Their intel isn't worth a shi—" Gurley glanced at Jennifer and didn't finish his sentence.

"Is Carrie Foster making a statement herself?" Ingrid asked.

"At the press conference. Hopefully that'll happen tomorrow morning. She'll be pleading for the safe return of her son. Trying to appeal to her husband's sense of duty, loyalty. Playing on his conscience—if he has one. And if all that fails to elicit the desired response, she'll be appealing to the great British public."

"So that more crackpots and loony toons call the police and waste even more time? You really think that's gonna help any?" Gurley thumped the desk with his fist and made Jennifer jump. "I'm sorry, miss."

Ingrid could see Sol struggling to control his reaction to Gurley's obstructiveness. "I know this operation is outside your normal working procedures, but we have to be flexible and adapt. We've got to pull together." He looked from Gurley to Ingrid. "Can we agree to that at least?"

"Not a problem for me," Ingrid said.

"I don't have any choice, do I?"

"We'll reconvene here tomorrow after the press conference."

The muscles in Gurley's jaw were working overtime. "Where is this police incident room?"

"Holborn Police Station," Jennifer told him.

He looked at her blankly.

"Around two miles from here," Ingrid said.

"If that's where all this valuable intel will come from, why are we here instead of there?"

Ingrid supposed it was a good point, but knew that Sol would have had his own reasons to bring Major Gurley to the embassy, presumably to get some measure of the man.

"I'm sure that will be your next stop, Jack—may I call you Jack?"

Gurley nodded but didn't seem enthusiastic about the idea.

"But first I'd like to discuss First Lieutenant Foster's service history with you."

"I don't actually know the man."

"But since you were informed of this morning's tragic events, you must have read his personnel file?"

"I've perused it. Dry facts and figures tend not to help in these situations."

"Before you left the base, I'm guessing you had a chance to speak to the doctor who's treating him for PTSD?" Ingrid asked.

"She wasn't available. I'm still waiting for a call."

"But you've read his medical report?"

Jennifer handed Ingrid a sheaf of papers held together in the top left-hand corner by a paperclip.

"What's this?" she asked the clerk.

"I only just finished putting it together. It's everything we have on Kyle Foster."

"That's Defense Department classified information. You have no authority to look at that." Gurley reached out a hand, but Ingrid was too fast for him, she snatched away the report.

"I can print you one too, if you'd like, Major?" The clerk smiled at him.

Gurley hadn't taken his eyes off Ingrid as she leafed through the pages. "That won't be necessary, thank you, Miss Rocharde."

"Did you know Foster has been flying drone missions for the last two years?" Ingrid said. She scanned down to the bottom of the page.

Dear God.

"You've read this, Sol?"

Her boss nodded gravely at her.

"It says he was responsible for the deaths of at least twenty-two women and children in a single mission in February 2011." She swallowed and turned the page. The more she read, the more she wished she hadn't. "The targets were meant to be arms silos and fuel depots, but the missiles ended up hitting a school in a village just outside Hajjah. She looked directly at Gurley. "You knew about the civilian casualties in the drone attacks?"

Gurley let out a breath and clenched his jaw, as if he'd been expecting the question. "You're always going to get collateral damage in a war situation."

"According to the report these people were on their way to a family *wedding*."

"You know as well as I do that shit happens."

"Did you tell Radcliffe about all this?"

"It wasn't relevant to his investigation."

"How can you say that? The police need to know what kind of man they're dealing with." Ingrid flipped through the pages to get to Kyle Foster's medical reports and discovered his PTSD was formally diagnosed at the end of 2011. She remembered Carrie Foster telling them he'd been suffering for quite a while longer than that. She skimmed through the remainder of the report. "It doesn't say what caused his condition," she said when she'd finished. "Was it his time in Afghanistan, or the drone missions he's carried out since moving to the UK?"

Gurley shrugged. "It's not likely to be one isolated incident. How is that relevant, anyway?"

"It might help us work out what his triggers are likely to be."

"You heard what his wife said—loud noises, crying, screaming—that's what set him off this morning. God knows what little thing might trigger the next attack. We've just got to hope Tommy is behaving himself." He glanced at Jennifer before continuing. "We have to accept the longer they're out there, the more chance there is Tommy will be his next victim."

9

Ingrid stared at her vibrating phone, suspecting it was Svetlana rather than Mike Stiller, wondering whether she could face speaking to her. She answered just before the call diverted to voicemail. "Hi, Mom. Before you ask, I don't have any news yet. And yes, I did put in a request with one of my old colleagues." She hit the speakerphone option on her cell and rested it on the counter between the sinks in the ladies' washroom. "All we can do now is wait." She put her hands under the faucet then ran her wet fingers through her messy hair in an attempt to restyle it.

"Oh we can do plenty more than just wait," Svetlana said. "You think you know what I'm going to say before I get a chance to open my mouth? Well you're wrong. I'm calling to beg you to speak to Kathleen. She's been talking about you all day. She got out the photograph albums this morning. She showed me the pictures of you and Megan. The two of you looked so happy."

We were. But I ruined all that.

"I can't go through this again with you, Mom. Please stop asking me. My answer isn't going to change."

"Where's your conscience?"

Locked in a secure file cabinet at the bottom of Lily Lake, just where the psychotherapist told me to put it.

"I didn't raise you to be so heartless."

You didn't raise me at all.

Ingrid hung up and tossed the phone into her purse. The door into the restroom opened and a uniformed policewoman walked in. Ingrid reapplied her lipstick and gave herself a long hard stare in the mirror. She was looking tired. Her eyes were a little bloodshot and dark shadows had started to appear underneath them. She ran her fingers though her short blond hair again, but it was well past restyling. She could take some consolation from the fact she was spending the evening in Holborn Police Station rather than on a much anticipated date with Detective Constable Ralph Mills—at least he wouldn't see just how crappy she looked. She corrected a smudge of lipstick with the tip of her little finger and fished around in her purse for some concealer to deal with the dark circles beneath her eyes. Before she found the tube of makeup her phone started to vibrate again. She pulled it out, saw it was Ralph calling and couldn't decide whether or not to answer.

What the hell.

"I just got your message," he said, as soon as Ingrid picked up.

"I'm really sorry. I wouldn't cancel if it wasn't important."

"That's why I'm calling. There's no need to cancel. I'm walking up Theobalds Road as we speak."

That was just around the corner. "I really can't leave right now."

"That's why I'm coming to you. I've got two pizzas and half a dozen chilled beers. I went for a quattro formaggi and pancetta with mozzarella and rocket. How does that sound?"

"I don't know—I really need to work."

"I can help. I do know my way around an incident room. See you in five." He hung up.

Ingrid stared at her phone. She was tempted to call him back, but she was ravenous, and a big part of her really wanted to see him. She'd been on a few dates since she'd ended her fourteen month engagement with Marshall Claybourne. Feeling a little on the rebound, she'd wanted to get Marshall out of her system, so she'd dated men who didn't really mean that much to her. But Ralph was different. She'd wanted their first date to go well. For once she actually cared what impression she made. But an impromptu meal in a busy corner of a station house? It wasn't an auspicious start to a relationship. Not that Ingrid was even sure that was what she wanted from him. She dug into her purse again, found the tube of concealer she'd been looking for, plus some mascara and eyeshadow. She did the best she could to enliven her tired features. The female PC emerged from one of the cubicles just as Ingrid put the final flourish to her eyelashes.

"Are you working the abduction case?" Ingrid asked her, feeling she couldn't exactly ignore the woman in the cramped restroom.

The policewoman nodded at her via the mirror.

"Taken any promising calls yet this evening?"

"Not so far. I have had two proposals of marriage, a heavy breather and a shed load of abuse though."

"What gets into folk?"

"Your guess is as good as mine."

Ingrid headed for the door. "See you back in there, I guess."

"I've just finished a double shift. I'm going home. If I'm lucky I might just get there before it's time to come back again." She smiled at Ingrid. "Good luck."

"Thanks." Ingrid had a feeling she might need it.

10

Ingrid returned to the incident room. It seemed even busier than when she'd left it. The forty-foot square, open-plan office was jammed with desks, two people answering phones at each one. The large room was brightly illuminated by unflattering fluorescent overhead lighting, more than bright enough to expose all the flaws in her hasty repair job.

She saw Ralph Mills sitting on the edge of a desk, chatting to a detective whose name Ingrid had forgotten. Ralph was dressed in combat pants and a vintage tee shirt, a pair of Timberland boots on his feet. He must have been home to get changed after work. He looked restless, nervously picking the label off a bottle of beer. She was relieved he seemed just as anxious as her about their 'date'. She took a deep breath and marched toward him.

A moment later Ralph spotted her and his anxious expression melted away as he smiled warmly at her. In that instant, Ingrid was reminded, just as she had been many times before when Ralph smiled at her, of Clark Swanson: her very first junior high school crush. Something about that smile made her stomach flip, as if she were thirteen all over again.

She gave him a little smile in return and he jumped up from the desk and hurried toward her.

When he reached her, a long, awkward moment passed, both of them unsure how to greet one another. Finally they simultaneously opted for a safe peck on both cheeks, a sanitized European-style 'hello' that couldn't carry any subtext. He stood back and beamed at her. "You look fantastic."

His dopey grin was infectious. She found herself grinning back at him so hard her cheeks started to ache. "You too."

"I've managed to commandeer a spare desk in a relatively quiet corner of the room."

"Hey, I'm really sorry about this."

"I completely understand. You can't just drop everything. But I've had a quick chat with the incident room manager, I've wangled you the next twenty minutes off."

"A man with influence, huh?"

"I have my uses. Why do you think the boss has put up with me for so long?"

Ralph's senior officer, DI Natasha McKittrick, was the nearest thing Ingrid had to a good friend in London. In fact, Natasha was pretty much the closest friend she'd had in her adult life. After Megan Avery had disappeared, Ingrid had made it a rule not to get too close to people. In each of the field offices she worked in her eight years in the Bureau, she'd done no more than made acquaintances. No real friends. She was grateful Mike Stiller still took her calls.

"Which reminds me," Ralph said, breaking into her thoughts. "The boss says 'hi'."

"You told her about our... this... I mean, tonight?"

"Didn't you?" When he took in the appalled expression on her face, he made a silent 'o' with his mouth. "I just assumed you chatted to her about everything. Thought I'd get in early, try to prevent some of her piss-taking." He sighed. "Needless to say my strategy didn't work—she's been ribbing me about it all day."

Even before Ingrid had made the break from Marshall, McKittrick had done her best to act as Cupid. The detective inspector seemed determined to get the two of them out on a date together. Now McKittrick had finally gotten what she wanted. In the end it was easier for Ingrid to give in to her friend's ham-fisted attempt at matchmaking than continue to pretend she wasn't interested.

"She just won't let up," he said. "She's been worse since you broke off —" He stopped himself, no doubt encouraged to by the admonishing look Ingrid was giving him. "That was out of order. Shouldn't have mentioned it. Sorry."

"It's not like it's a taboo subject or anything. But I'd rather not spend whatever time we've got this evening talking about my ex."

Ralph turned away, suddenly unable to look her in the eye. He ducked between desks, not stopping to look back until he'd reached the promised 'quiet corner'. The small desk was flanked on both sides by long tables occupied by a half dozen cops speaking loudly into their phones. Ingrid joined him and they perched on the edge of the desk, facing toward the wall. Ralph set down the two pizza boxes and pack of beers between them. Ingrid flipped open the lid of the top box.

"So, Natasha's been working you hard today, huh?" She pulled out a wedge of cheesy pizza.

"She's a tough boss. Fair, but tough."

"Sounds like she told you to say that." She smiled. "And is that OK with you? Working hard all the time? No chance for a little fun every now and then?"

"We're having fun now, aren't we?" He pulled off his own triangle of pizza and took a large bite. At the next desk a female cop slammed down the phone and muttered, "bloody pervert". Ralph raised his eyebrows. "Ah, the joys of a public appeal. Shame it has to involve the public." He picked up a bottle of beer, pushed off the top on the side of the desk and handed it to Ingrid. They clinked bottles and Ingrid raised a toast to law enforcement officers everywhere.

"Hear, hear." Ralph took a swig of beer. "I might moan about it, but I do seriously love this job. It's all I ever wanted to do. I suppose it's in my genes."

"Really?"

"My dad was a copper. Detective Inspector Charlie Mills." He picked another corner of the label from his bottle. "In his heyday that name sent chills up and down most old lags' spines." He took another swig. "If he could see me now, eating fancy pizza and drinking beer out of a bottle."

"Pizza too fancy for him is it?"

"Too foreign, definitely."

"A traditional guy, huh?"

"In every sense of the word. Especially at work. Not always a good thing. He wouldn't hesitate beating a confession out of a suspect if he needed a swift conviction. They really were the bad old days."

Ingrid raised her eyebrows.

"Don't get me wrong, I know there are still problems that need sorting inside the Met, but we've made a hell of a lot of progress."

Ingrid hadn't envisaged talking about work quite so much on their first date, but given the surroundings, she didn't really see how they could avoid it. "The guy I'm working with on this case, Jack Gurley?" She turned and looked around the office, expecting to see Gurley standing over someone's desk, waiting to pounce on a confirmed sighting and leap into action, but couldn't spot him anywhere. "I get the impression he's beaten up plenty of prisoners in his time. Different rules in the armed forces, I guess."

"How long are you going to be working with him?"

Was that a fleeting flash of jealousy she detected in Ralph's expression?

"Until we locate the suspect. I guess it could be a while."

"Oh."

"It's OK—I know how to handle the Jack Gurleys of this world."

"I wasn't saying you didn't, I just—"

Ingrid grabbed his hand. He looked down at her hand covering his then looked up into her eyes. He opened his mouth to say something else and Ingrid shoved a corner of her pizza slice into it. She opened the other box and pulled out another slice. "You want some of this too?" she said, waving the triangle of dough laden with thick cheese and pancetta.

Ralph's nose twitched. "Not for me, thanks. Not a big fan of pork."

"You're not?"

"Been that way since I was a kid."

"Come on—not even crispy bacon?"

He shook his head firmly. Ingrid noticed he'd gone a little pale. "Not since half a rotting pig carcass was dumped on our doorstep when I was six years old," he said.

"Who would do a thing like that?"

"Dad never found out. He suspected it was someone he'd put away. Too many potential suspects there to actually pin it on someone." He shook his head. "My God, it was disgusting."

Ingrid looked down at the pizza slice. Ralph's story hadn't put her off one bit. She took a bite. "I was raised on the stuff," she said, in between chews. "My dad was a hog farmer."

"He's retired now?"

"He's dead."

"I'm sorry. What about your mum?"

"Oh she's very much alive—powered by vodka and nicotine."

"Are you close?"

"Not at all. I was a real daddy's girl. He was the kindest man you could ever meet."

"The complete opposite of mine then."

"Do you get along OK?"

"He's dead too."

"Sorry. How did the conversation get so morbid? Let's change the subject, shall we?" She raised her bottle, couldn't think of anything to toast, then took a sip. "Here's to good beer and fine dining."

Ralph raised his bottle too. "And beautiful company." When he realized what he'd just said, his cheeks bloomed crimson. He looked away.

Ingrid couldn't help but smile to herself. It wasn't much of a date, but she had the feeling they would manage to make the best of it.

Across the room someone hollered. Ingrid turned around to see a uniformed cop waving a piece of paper in her hand and running toward DS Tyson who was just coming through the door. Ingrid jumped up and zig-zagged between the tightly arranged desks.

"Cab driver, picked up a man and a boy this morning in Judd Street. Just a couple of hundred yards from the hotel. He said he didn't get a good look at the boy, but the man more or less fits Foster's description," the breathless PC said.

"And where did he drop them?" Tyson asked.

"The man told him to head north. Then asked him to stop just before they reached King's Cross Station."

Gurley appeared in the doorway. "We have a sighting?"

"It looks promising," Tyson told him. "I'll get on to Transport Police, they can check CCTV at the station." He looked at the PC. "What time was this?"

"Around nine a.m."

"We should get down there," Gurley said.

"That was over twelve hours ago." Ingrid shook her head. "He could be anywhere by now. But at least we know which direction Foster was headed. It's a damn sight more than we had five minutes ago."

"She's right," Tyson said. "Let's see what the CCTV comes up with before we go racing round. We can make a start on mapping his movements after he left the hotel."

Ingrid glanced over to the corner of the office. Ralph shrugged back at her and closed the lid of the pizza boxes.

11

The news conference had been arranged by the Metropolitan Police press office, with a lot of unhelpful interference from the embassy and the US Air Force. As Ingrid waited on the steps outside the conference hall just around the corner from New Scotland Yard, she let her mind wander to the end of her 'date' with Ralph Mills.

They had said their goodbyes at Holborn Tube station. Ingrid had explained she had a really early start and Ralph said he did too, even though, by the expression on his face, he looked a little crushed by her announcement. Just as she was about to turn away, Ralph pulled her toward him and planted a kiss on her lips. He tasted of oregano and beer. She felt a rush and flutter in the pit of her stomach, like some schoolgirl on a first date, not an until recently engaged-to-be-married thirty-one-year-old woman.

When they pulled apart again, he looked her square in the eye and for once, he wasn't blushing.

Every time she had remembered that kiss subsequently, Ingrid experienced the same flutter radiating out across her body. So what if it made her feel like a lovestruck teenager?

The sight of Jack Gurley ducking out of a taxi wrenched her from her romantic musings. She was relieved to see he was wearing civilian clothes: a pair of brown pants and a beige shirt with a button-down collar. He still looked like an off duty military cop, but at least it was better than the battledress of the previous day. He spotted her, nodded a restrained 'hello' and paid the cab driver.

They entered the building in silence and followed the last of the journalists and photographers into the main hall. There had been a couple more promising sightings the previous evening, one at the London Aquarium, the other near the London Eye—both locations close to one another on the south bank of the Thames—but as the day approached its end, the number of calls dwindled and eventually stopped. The hope was that a personal appeal by Carrie Foster herself would get more media coverage and in turn lead to a surge in reported sightings.

As the doors closed behind Ingrid and Gurley, Carrie Foster appeared at the other end of the hall, walking unsteadily along a low stage, assisted by a plain clothes female cop—the family liaison officer Ingrid had seen at the hospital. Foster looked more drawn, and much paler than she had the previous day. She was trembling as she placed her bottle of water on the long table. She sat down next to a gray-haired cop in his late fifties who was wearing full ceremonial dress uniform. The Metropolitan Police were obviously very keen to show the world just how seriously they were taking the situation. Next to the uniformed cop sat DCI Radcliffe, looking every bit as sleep-deprived as Foster.

The guy in uniform introduced himself as Assistant Deputy Commissioner Trevor Twyford, then went on to explain how Detective Chief Inspector Paul Radcliffe would be leading the investigation. Twyford outlined the details of the case, referring regularly to a stack of printed notes sitting on the table in front of him, reading from them as if he were discovering the information for the first time. When he was done he opened the floor for questions.

"I hope putting Carrie Foster through this ordeal pays off," Gurley whispered to Ingrid as a dozen arms went up at the front of the hall. "Look at her. She's close to collapse."

"I expect she's tougher than she looks." In Ingrid's limited experience, military wives had to be resilient in order to survive. "Besides, she knows this might really help locate Tommy."

"As long as this press conference doesn't just generate a shit storm of unverifiable sightings."

"Do you have a better strategy?"

"I have some ideas."

"However we may feel about the way the police are handling this, we have to play along. It's delicate politically—you heard what Sol Franklin said yesterday. We're guests in this country and right now one of our compatriots is wanted for attempted murder and abduction. I think, on the surface at least, we follow the Met's lead."

"On the surface? What's that supposed to mean?"

Before Ingrid had a chance to respond, a voice she recognized hollered a question from somewhere near the back of the hall. She might have known Angela Tate would turn up at such a high profile media conference. Ingrid desperately scanned the room to pinpoint the journalist's exact location, just so she could avoid her later, but she couldn't see her anywhere. When Tate didn't get a response from the Assistant Deputy Commissioner right away, she hollered her question again even louder.

"Is the man armed?" she yelled. "You just warned that the public should not approach him—does that mean he's carrying a weapon?"

"We very much doubt that's the case." DCI Radcliffe answered.

"Doubt? You don't know for sure?"

"Kyle Foster wouldn't have had an opportunity to obtain a firearm."

"But you don't know for sure?" she said again.

"Who is that lady?" Gurley asked, "and why the hell doesn't she just shut up and sit down?"

"She's an investigative reporter working for the Evening News—the main London newspaper. She has the ability of a bloodhound to sniff out a story and the tenacity of a Russell Terrier not to let go once she's found it."

"You know her?"

Tate had crossed her path more times than Ingrid would have liked. But she wasn't about to give Gurley a potted history. She raised a finger to her lips. A hush had descended on the room as, with trembling hands, Carrie Foster shuffled through a stack of paper in front of her. She cleared her throat.

"Jesus Christ." Gurley shook his head.

"Yesterday morning, Molly, my beautiful baby girl, almost died. Right now she's hooked up to a hundred and one machines that are helping to keep her alive. But at least I know she's safe. My boy, Tommy, is out there somewhere and he's in danger. I need everyone out there to help the police find him."

Mrs Foster was reading from a sheet in front of her. It seemed so emotive, Ingrid wondered if someone had written the statement for her. It was certainly having the desired effect on the cynical reporters present: they hadn't made a sound.

For the next five minutes, Carrie Foster explained, blow-by-blow, exactly what happened to her and her children the day before. It was the same account she'd given the detectives. Her voice cracked and quavered as she spoke, but she carried on, describing Kyle Foster's PTSD and making it plain just how unstable he had become in recent months.

"But he's still my husband," she said. "I didn't feel I could tell anyone that his condition was getting worse. I so deeply regret now that I didn't. Worst decision of my entire life. If I'd thought for a moment that... that..." Her final words got caught up in a sob. The bottle of water was shoved in front of her. She ignored it and stared directly toward the bank of television cameras. With tears streaming down her face, she said, "Please bring him back to me, Kyle. Please don't hurt my precious boy." Those were her final words before she started to sob uncontrollably.

The family liaison officer jumped up, helped Foster to her feet and led her out of the hall by a side exit.

"We need to get back to the hospital," Ingrid said. "I won't get the chance to speak to Carrie Foster here."

"Is that really necessary? Don't you think she's been through enough already this morning?"

"We still don't know how she got that bruise on her leg. There's something she's not telling us about what Kyle did. Maybe she's protecting him somehow." Ingrid turned towards the exit, eager to make her escape before the few dozen journalists rose from their seats.

But she wasn't fast enough.

"Agent Skyberg!" Angela Tate hollered at her. "I was hoping to bump into you here." The journalist hurried towards them. "My God, you're big," she said to Gurley, uncharacteristically stating the obvious. "So, you're traveling with your own personal bodyguard now, are you, Ingrid?"

Gurley bristled, clearly offended.

"No?" Tate looked from Gurley to Ingrid.

"I'm working with Major Gurley on this case."

"Are you military police?" Tate asked.

"Security Forces, US Air Force, ma'am."

"For God's sake, don't 'ma'am' me! Please, call me Angela." She laid a hand on one of Gurley's forearms.

Was Tate flirting with him? For some reason, the thought appalled Ingrid so much she felt a little nauseous. She started to edge away.

"Would either of you like to give me a quote for the West End Final edition?"

Ingrid arched an eyebrow.

"Oh, please yourself. 'Sources close to the American embassy' it'll have to be then." With that she marched away. "Until next time, Ingrid," she shouted over her shoulder as she pushed through the door.

"Trouble, huh?" Gurley said.

"With a capital 'T'."

"Nothing you can't handle."

Ingrid didn't know quite how to respond. In the day or so that she'd known him, that had to be the nicest thing he'd said to her.

"Let's get to the hospital before Tate and the rest of the pack, shall we?" He strode to the door and held it open for her.

Ingrid led them down a side street she'd discovered cab drivers used as a short cut. As soon as they saw a taxi approaching, Gurley stepped into the road, waving and flapping his long arms. He had to have a wing span of close to seven feet. Not someone to be ignored. The cab screeched to a halt and they jumped in.

Just as they settled back into the seat, Ingrid's cell phone started to ring inside her purse. She yanked it out and peered at the screen and was relieved to discover it wasn't an international call. She answered and turned away from Gurley. "Jennifer, what do you have for me?"

There was silence at the other end as if the clerk were waiting for a formal greeting.

"Jennifer?"

"Hi."

"I'm in kind of a hurry here."

"Sure, sorry. The police have contacted me, they didn't want to disturb you in the middle of the press conference. But I thought you'd like to know right away."

"Yes?"

"There's been another sighting. As a result of Carrie Foster's appeal."

"Already?"

"I guess the story has really captured the public's imagination. I was watching it on the news. She looked so frail. I felt so sorry for—"

"This sighting, the police think it's genuine?"

"Seems that way. A woman working in a laundromat saw a man with a boy dressed in Spiderman pajamas. They were hovering around the driers for a little while, then the man opened one, grabbed some clothes and ran out."

"And the man and boy match Kyle and Tommy Foster's descriptions?"

"I think it was the pajamas that convinced the witness." She paused.

"I guess that's good news, isn't it?" Ingrid said. "Getting warmer clothes for the boy, means his dad is caring for him at least."

Jennifer swallowed noisily. "I wouldn't jump to that conclusion, I haven't told you everything yet."

"What is it?"

"The witness said she thought the boy might be injured."

"What?"

"She was pretty sure she saw blood on his face."

12

Ingrid relayed the details of the call to Gurley. "We should be out there looking for him," he said. "At least get to the laundromat and speak to the witness."

"Don't you see? Speaking to Carrie now is even more important. I want to find out if Tommy was hurt before he left the hotel room or after."

"What difference does it make?"

"If it's happened since it might mean Tommy's in more danger than we thought. It might change how we handle the case."

"As far as I'm concerned Foster's capable of anything. It must have happened after—Carrie Foster would have mentioned it otherwise."

"We speak to her first then work out our next move. Agreed?"

Gurley gave her a begrudging nod and didn't say another word all the way to the hospital.

When the elevator doors opened on the eleventh floor of UCH, Ingrid and Gurley stepped out into the lobby area to discover DCI Radcliffe speaking to a constable in uniform, a grave expression on his face. They waited until he was done before approaching.

"Chief inspector," Ingrid smiled as she strode toward him. "I'm a little surprised to see you here," she said.

"Why wouldn't I be here?" His tone was unmistakably defensive. He shoved his hands in his pockets and leaned toward her.

"I thought you would have handed over the day to day running to a deputy by now." In Ingrid's experience most of the investigative work was done by a team of detective constables led by a detective sergeant or inspector.

"Not this case. Too high profile."

Ingrid glanced behind her as the elevator doors opened again. "The press haven't arrived here yet?"

"I'm in the process of posting officers at the bottom of all the stairways and on each of the lifts on the ground floor, checking visitors' credentials. I'm not having those vultures roaming around, upsetting people."

"Good, you might want to look out for a woman in her fifties with frizzy hair wearing a raincoat and shiny knee-length boots."

"Tate's here?"

"You know her?"

"It's hard to avoid the woman."

Gurley cleared his throat noisily then made a point of looking at the oversized diver's watch on his wrist.

"We really need to speak to Mrs Foster again," Ingrid said.

"She's in with Molly. I don't want her disturbed."

"It wouldn't take longer than five minutes."

"I suppose you've heard about the sighting in the launderette yesterday?"

Ingrid nodded. "We'd like to speak to Carrie about Tommy's injury."

"So would we."

"You haven't yet?"

"She's only just back from the press conference, for God's sake. She needs time with her daughter."

"How is Molly?"

"No change. Which the doctors are taking as a good sign, apparently."

"We can wait to speak to her," Gurley said, much to Ingrid's surprise. "If Tommy sustained his injury after he left the hotel, it could mean Kyle Foster poses a greater threat than we thought."

"You think we haven't worked that out for ourselves?"

"So why wait to speak to her?" Ingrid asked.

Radcliffe bit his top lip as he considered Ingrid's question. "I'll get the FLO to bring Mrs Foster out in ten minutes. I'm not questioning her at Molly's sick bed.

Fifteen minutes later Radcliffe, Ingrid and Gurley were sitting in a cramped room tucked away at the end of a long corridor, opposite Carrie Foster who now looked so pale her skin appeared almost translucent.

"Thank you for speaking to us again, Mrs Foster," Radcliffe said. "I realize reliving your ordeal this morning in front of all those people had to be very hard for you." He leaned in a little closer to her. "Something new has come to light that I really need to speak to you about."

The woman searched the detective's face. "What?"

"Can you recall whether or not Tommy was struggling when Kyle grabbed him yesterday morning?"

Carrie Foster widened her bloodshot eyes. "Why? What's happened?" She held onto the sleeve of Radcliffe's jacket. "Have you found him?"

"Please, there's no need to be alarmed. We haven't located Tommy, not yet. But we have received some information from someone who believes they saw Tommy and your husband yesterday."

"Did he seem OK?"

"The eye witness said she saw blood on Tommy's face."

"Oh my God!" Mrs Foster raised a hand to her mouth. "How bad is it?"

"It really doesn't seem to be that serious. Please—I'm sure there's no need to worry yourself about it."

"How can you say that?" She jumped to her feet.

Ingrid stood too. "Please, Carrie. What you tell us now could really help us find Tommy faster. We all want that."

Mrs Foster's gaze dropped to the floor and she sank back onto her chair. "My poor baby."

"Can you remember if Tommy was hurt *before* he left the hotel room?" Ingrid asked her, keeping her voice quiet and gentle.

Foster continued to stare at the floor. She started to shake her head slowly. "I don't think so. Kyle just scooped him into his arms. Tommy didn't struggle. Why would he? He loves his daddy. I'm pretty sure he was OK. I would have noticed if he'd had blood on his face, I'm certain." She fell silent for a moment then stared up at Ingrid, a look of panic on her face. "Does that mean Kyle has hurt him since then? Is that what you're saying?"

"We don't know that for sure. Maybe he had an accident." Even as Ingrid said the words she realized just how unconvincing they must have sounded to the distraught mother sitting in front of her.

Tears were falling down Foster's face. "What happened? Kyle used to be so kind. I just can't believe what he did to Molly. He was a good man, you know? No one can change that much, can they?"

Ingrid felt Gurley tense slightly as he sat next to her.

"Thank you for your time, Mrs Foster." Radcliffe stood up. "It's been a great help." He waited for Ingrid and Gurley to get to their feet.

Ingrid hadn't had a chance to ask Carrie Foster about the bruise on her leg, but it didn't seem appropriate to bring it up now. She led the way into the corridor, relieved to get out of the airless room.

"After what he did, how can she even think he was a good man?" Gurley said when he'd closed the door behind them.

"It's complicated for her," Ingrid said. "She still remembers the man he was. Before the PTSD. I guess she doesn't want to admit she's married to some kind of monster." She started to head back down the corridor toward the elevators.

"You can find your own way out," Radcliffe said once they'd reached the set of doors leading into the ICU. He disappeared through the doors without waiting for a reply.

"We need to map out Kyle Foster's movements from the time he left the hotel, to see if we can predict where he'll head next." Gurley said.

"I'm sure the police are doing exactly that."

"You heard Radcliffe just now—he pretty much dismissed us. We're meant to be providing our expertise. He doesn't seem that interested in what we might have to offer."

"You're right." Ingrid found herself reluctantly agreeing with Gurley. "We should get back to the embassy and try to convince Sol it's better for us to break free of the Met's investigation. We can be more effective working our own line of inquiry."

"Agreed. Right now I feel like the cops are tolerating us at best."

Welcome to my world.

As they approached the elevator, the doors opened and two uniformed policeman ran out. Ingrid and Gurley looked at one another for a moment, then hurried after the two men. They hung a left, toward the ICU.

The door leading into Molly Foster's room was wide open. There was no sign of the cop who should have been on duty outside.

The two cops ran into the room, with Ingrid and Gurley right behind them. A third cop was inside, anxiously watching the nurse Ingrid had seen the day before check the various machines Molly was hooked up to.

"Is she OK?" the cop asked.

"She's fine. Absolutely fine." The nurse had a worried look on her face.

"I thought he was a doctor. He was dressed in scrubs. He had a stethoscope around his neck."

"What happened?" Ingrid said.

All three cops now turned toward Ingrid and Gurley. "Who the hell are you?" one of them demanded.

Ingrid quickly retrieved her badge. "FBI, American embassy. We've just been interviewing Mrs Foster." She strode toward the bed. "What happened?" she asked the cop again, this time more firmly. She glanced quickly back at the door, wondering where the hell Radcliffe was.

"A man walked right up to the door. He had a hospital ID badge clipped to his pocket. I suppose I should have checked it more closely. I came into the room with him—it's protocol when the nurse isn't around. I was standing next to him the whole time." He lifted a hand to his face. He was trembling. "Have the exits been secured?" he asked the other cops.

One of them nodded. "We've got people at the front and rear. He won't get out of here."

Ingrid stared into the nervous cop's face. "What made you think he wasn't a doctor?"

"There was something about him. Most of the consultants I've seen in here are... you know, cocky. He seemed more unsure of himself. He grabbed the charts attached to the end of the bed, but it didn't look like he was actually reading them. He was too busy looking up at Molly, then at me."

"Who do you think he was?"

"I can't say. For a second I thought it might be her dad. But he didn't look like the photographs I've seen of him."

"Wait a minute," Gurley said. "Are you saying Kyle Foster was right here, in Molly's room?"

"I couldn't say. The man was dressed as a doctor."

"How long ago?"

"Five minutes."

"What did he do?"

"Nothing—he couldn't, could he? Not with me standing right next to him. Like I say, he just looked at her, then glanced at me. Then the nurse came in and he ran for it. It was only then that the penny finally dropped and I realized he wasn't one of the team."

"Why would Foster risk coming here?" Ingrid asked Gurley.

"To finish what he started." Gurley moved toward the door.

"Where are you going?"

"If they've got cops at the exits, I want to be there when they pick the son of a bitch up."

Ingrid ran after him. "You seriously believe Kyle Foster has so completely lost it he'd come into the hospital to try to murder his daughter?"

He paused at the door. "If he has lost it, one thing's certain."

Ingrid tensed, knowing what Gurley was likely to say next.

"We can assume Tommy is already dead."

13

"Wait up a second," Ingrid told Gurley.

Jack Gurley was already halfway through the door. He stopped. The two uniformed cops they'd followed into the room pushed past him and hurried away.

"You know for sure this guy wasn't part of the medical team?" Ingrid directed her question toward the concerned nurse, who was stroking Molly Foster's forehead.

"No one I've seen before in ICU."

"But we don't know for sure it was Kyle Foster. Did you get a good look at his face?"

"Not that good. If it was him, he didn't look like his photo, that's for sure."

"We've just come from the press conference," Ingrid said. "The place was full of unscrupulous reporters looking for a scoop. Any one of them might stoop so low they wouldn't think twice about impersonating a doctor." Ingrid thought it was amazing Angela Tate hadn't already tried something along the same lines. "Describe the man to me."

"About five foot nine or ten, slim build, mid to late thirties," the cop said.

"Did he say anything to you?"

"No, I don't think so."

"You're sure?"

"Erm..." The cop paused, his face had taken on a sudden panicked expression.

A moment later Ingrid discovered why.

DCI Radcliffe was standing in the doorway. "For God's sake, Barlow—he was right here and you let him get away?" Radcliffe didn't bother to even acknowledge Ingrid and Gurley's presence. "Well?"

"That's what we're currently trying to establish," Ingrid said, getting a little frustrated she couldn't get a straight answer from the cop.

"And what the bloody hell is that supposed to mean?"

"Can you please keep your voice down or leave the room?" the nurse said.

"Barlow, come with me."

The hapless cop followed Radcliffe outside. As did Ingrid and Gurley.

"Did the man speak to you?" Ingrid said again.

"He might have said 'good morning'."

"So did he have an accent?"

"Not really."

"So he sounded English?"

"Yes, I suppose he did." He glanced at his superior officer. "The more I think about it... I'd say it was definitely an English accent."

"Just now you weren't even sure whether he'd spoken to you or not, for Christ's sake," Radcliffe said, not bothering to disguise his contempt.

"I've had a moment to think. It was an English accent, sir."

"So it might not have been Foster?" Ingrid asked.

Gurley pulled a folded sheet from the back pocket of his pants. He smoothed out the paper and showed the cop a full color, full length photograph of Kyle Foster dressed in camouflage pants and a light gray tee shirt. The cop turned his head this way and that as he stared at the picture.

"The man I saw had darker hair."

"For God's sake, could it be him?" Radcliffe said.

The nurse came to the door and glared at them. "How do you expect this little girl to recover with all this shouting?"

Gurley showed her the photo too. "Is this the man you saw?"

She stared at the picture for a few moments then said, "I barely got a glimpse of him. The general outline is right, but the man I saw was paler."

"I've got officers stopping people from leaving the building and you're saying it might not even have been Foster?" Radcliffe shook his head. "Un-bloody-believable."

"You got that right." Gurley folded the sheet and returned it to his pocket. "You should still have your officers check any thirty-something males, under six-foot tall, around one hundred sixty pounds, who try to leave the hospital."

"Thank you so much for telling me how to do my job. I would have been quite clueless without your invaluable input."

Ingrid's phone started to chirrup quietly in her purse. She hurried down the corridor before retrieving it. "Sol, if you're calling for an update, we're on our way back to the embassy now."

"No you're not."

"We're not?"

"Another confirmed sighting has just been reported. St Thomas' Hospital. Emergency room. I'll text the address just as soon as I hang up. I want you to speak to the staff there, get some kind of idea of Foster's state of mind."

"Won't the police be doing that anyway? The way things are between us and the cops at the moment, I don't want to tread on anyone's toes."

"Are they giving you a hard time?"

"I've had better."

"Then this break might be just what you need. The doctor who called it in couldn't get through to the incident line at the station house. Luckily for us he's a US citizen, so rather than just giving up and trying again later, he called the embassy. Jennifer spoke to him just a little while ago."

Ingrid hurried back to Gurley as her phone beeped with a new text message. She grabbed his arm. "We have to leave. Right now. I'll explain on the way."

———

———

———

One of the receptionists on the front desk of the Accident and Emergency Department led Ingrid and Gurley to a small room to one side of the main waiting area. This hospital seemed a lot older than the one they were just at. The walls were scuffed at the bottom and paint was flaking off some of the windows.

But the smell was just the same.

Three chairs were arranged around a desk on one side of the room. On the other side was an examining table covered in a long strip of blue paper towel, ready for the next patient. At one end of the table was a lamp attached to the wall on an extending arm. Next to that was a large round magnifying glass. Ingrid saw Gurley looking at the equipment and thought she heard him gulp.

"I hate these places," he said.

The door opened and a young bearded man came in and introduced himself as Dr Daniel Obermast. "I hope I did the right thing calling the embassy." He sat in the chair immediately in front of the desk and gestured for them to take a seat.

"Completely," Ingrid reassured him.

Ingrid sat down but Gurley seemed reluctant to. Maybe he wanted to ensure he could make a fast getaway. He leaned up against a wall.

"You saw the man we want to question with his son?" Ingrid kicked off the interview. There was no point in wasting time on social niceties.

"I did. I'm certain it was him."

"When was this?"

"Yesterday morning. Eleven-fifteen."

"And you treated the boy?"

"I cleaned up his nose a little better than his dad had managed to and put two stitches into the poor little guy's bottom lip."

"Did his dad tell you how he sustained those injuries?"

"Skateboarding."

"You had no reason to doubt that?"

"Not at all. I see so many cases each week. Badly scraped elbows and knees. Dislocated shoulders. And that's just the adults!"

"Any other treatment?"

"I gave him a tetanus shot, as a precaution. Standard procedure."

"And apart from his injuries, how did the boy seem to you?"

"Fine. I guess."

"He didn't seem scared at all? Coerced in any way? He was happy being with his dad?"

The doctor raked his fingernails through his beard and thought for a moment. "There was nothing obvious in his behavior to suggest he was here under duress."

"Could he have been drugged?" Gurley asked.

"Drugged? No way. He was a little tired, I guess."

Gurley pushed himself from the wall and paced across the room. The doctor twisted in his chair to look at him as Gurley then leaned against the other wall.

"Is everything OK? Have I done something wrong?"

"Not at all." Ingrid glanced at Gurley, who had an unmistakable scowl on is face. "What about his dad? How did he seem?"

"Stressed, I guess." The doctor turned back to face Ingrid. "Worried about his son. He said he'd managed to stop his son's nose bleed, but the lip just wouldn't quit. He seemed sorry he hadn't brought him in sooner."

"So he was nervous? Maybe a little jumpy?" Gurley said.

"Yes, but I assumed that was because he was worried about his son." Obermast bent his head closer to Ingrid, almost conspiratorially. "Which is why I doubted myself when I saw the report on the news this morning. I don't normally watch TV, but there's a big screen in the waiting area. It's there to keep the patients occupied. Sometimes they have to wait quite a long time before they get treated," he explained.

"You doubted yourself?"

"The picture they showed on the news only looked a little like the guy I saw. So I talked to Margaret, on reception? She was pretty certain it was the same person. So I called. It was the presence of the boy that convinced me."

Something about the doctor's account didn't feel right to Ingrid. Why would Foster risk taking Tommy to a hospital? He must have known Carrie would get the police involved. He had to have realized by then he was a wanted man. "You said he seemed concerned," Ingrid said.

The doctor nodded.

"In your medical opinion, do you think he could have been suffering from the effects of post traumatic stress disorder?"

"I'm not expert in the field, I can't really say…"

"How about you give us your best professional guess?" Gurley said.

"Well, if you're forcing me to make an assessment…" He glanced at Gurley uncertainly.

"Please—if you wouldn't mind." Ingrid wished Gurley would wipe the frown off his face and sit down. He was clearly spooking their witness.

"If you'd asked me that yesterday, I would have said he just seemed like an anxious parent, worried about his son. Without hesitation."

"But now?"

"Now I know what the man is capable of, it puts his behavior in a whole different light. Maybe he was worried about getting caught. Maybe that's why he seemed so twitchy."

Gurley pushed himself from the wall and stepped toward the doctor, his eyes narrowing. But before he could say anything, there was a loud knock on the door.

"Come in," Obermast said quickly, clearly relieved the interruption had stopped Gurley in his tracks.

The door opened and a nurse dressed in an old-fashioned pinafore dress hovered in the doorway. "So sorry, Daniel, I really didn't want to disturb you, but things are getting a little hectic out there." She threw an apologetic smile in Gurley's direction. "We really need you back on duty."

"I have to go. Was there anything else?"

"Do you think the boy is in danger?" Gurley asked.

The doctor nodded regretfully. "I just wish I'd known about the situation at the time. No way would I have let him take that child anywhere."

14

On their way back to the embassy, Ingrid called Radcliffe to let him know what Obermast had told them. She had to hold her cell away from her ear during his rant about agreed protocol being 'willfully ignored' and how she should understand it was imperative his team were kept in the loop at all times. "It's not your bollocks on the chopping board, Agent Skyberg."

"We do all want the same thing here."

"Really? You're not more interested in point scoring?"

Ingrid decided it was time to do a little ranting herself. "If you think for one second that anyone is treating this as some sort of competition, then you are sorely mistaken. Feel free to make an official complaint about my conduct with the embassy."

Gurley raised his eyebrows and gave her a silent round of applause.

"Dr Obermast and the other clinic staff are ready to speak to your officers, just as soon as they arrive." A moment after she ended the call her phone rang. She glanced at the screen. It was Angela Tate, the demon journalist of Blackfriars Road. Ingrid dismissed the call.

When they got back to the office they found Jennifer standing behind her desk as if she'd been waiting for them to arrive. "I thought we could go through Kyle Foster's last known movements," she said, and pointed to a pile of rolled paper tubes. "I got hold of Ordinance Survey maps of the Greater London area all the way to the M25," she explained. "Plus satellite images of the same region in various resolutions."

"Paper maps?"

"It's quicker than setting up a projector and booking a conference room. Sol requested we go low-tech—he likes maps he can draw all over."

"Where is Sol?"

"He said he'll be here soon."

"We're assuming Foster's still in the area?" Gurley asked.

"We have to start somewhere," Jennifer said.

Gurley started to unfold the maps, while Jennifer unrolled the satellite images.

Once the first map had been smoothed flat on one of the unoccupied desks, Jennifer stuck bright yellow stars onto the few positive sighting locations: the laundromat in King's Cross, the London Aquarium and London Eye on the South Bank and St Thomas' Hospital, less than half a mile away.

"Should I add one to University College Hospital?" She looked from Gurley to Ingrid.

"Radcliffe's team will check the CCTV footage from inside the building and the surrounding streets," Ingrid said. "It's possible we'll never know whether or not it was Kyle Foster in Molly's room."

"So what do we have?" Gurley asked, walking around the desk, staring at the map.

"After they left the hotel, Kyle and Tommy Foster walked just around the corner to Judd Street and hailed a cab heading north but got out after a few blocks at King's Cross," Jennifer said. "Then they went into the laundromat."

"Then there's quite a gap between the laundromat and the next sighting," Ingrid said. "It's what... maybe three miles between King's Cross and the South Bank?"

The clerk nodded. "A little less, maybe."

"And we don't know how they traveled there. On foot, public transport..."

"He wouldn't risk that, not with Tommy's lip bleeding. Safer to get another cab," Jennifer said.

"But we don't have another sighting from a taxi driver." Gurley had started pacing up and down.

"After the aquarium, Foster took Tommy to the hospital, so we have to assume his injury was getting worse by then. And Tommy must have sustained the injury some time between leaving the hotel and arriving at the laundromat."

Gurley stopped suddenly. "What the hell happened to him?"

"Maybe Foster got angry and lashed out?" Jennifer said.

"Or maybe Tommy had an accident," Ingrid suggested, not wanting to dwell on the worst case scenario. "And there haven't been any reliable sightings after Tommy got his lip stitched up at the hospital?"

"None yet," Jennifer said.

"Unless it *was* Foster in Molly's room earlier." Gurley started pacing again. He interlaced his long fingers on the top of his head, flattening the blond buzz cut and somehow making himself look ten years younger.

"It couldn't have been Foster at the hospital," the clerk said, still staring blank-eyed at the map. "That man was alone. If it were Foster, where was Tommy all the time he was there?" Jennifer looked up at Ingrid expectantly, as if she might actually be able to answer that question.

"I guess there are three possible explanations," Ingrid said, "Kyle is alive and Tommy's dead..." She sensed Jennifer stiffen. "...They're both alive and Kyle's found some place safe to stash Tommy..."

Jennifer exhaled.

"Or they're both dead," Gurley said, helpfully providing scenario number three.

Jennifer swallowed hard. "I really don't want to believe that."

"I know this is difficult. Anything involving kids always is." Ingrid had had more than enough experience in her years at the VCAC. "We need you to hang in there."

"I'm sorry, it's just that my baby brother is only ten years old," Jennifer said, her voice shaky. "Mom calls him her little miracle." She sniffed. "Dad calls him his gigantic mistake—but I know he's only kidding. If anything happened to him I don't know what I'd do. Carrie Foster must be going through hell." She sniffed, her eyes had started watering.

"Hey, Jennifer, we're relying on you to be strong for us," Gurley said. "The best way you can help Tommy is by being right where you are and working your butt off." He pulled a folded handkerchief from the back pocket of his pants and handed it to her. "Can you do that for us?"

Jennifer dabbed her nose and nodded rapidly. "Of course I can."

Ingrid caught Gurley's eye and mouthed 'thank you' at him. Maybe the gruff MP wasn't quite as insensitive as she'd thought. "OK," she said, and clapped her hands together. "Let's assume for the sake of argument that both father and son are still alive. If that's the case, Kyle would need to find some place safe for Tommy. So maybe he's taken a cheap rental somewhere, or a room in a budget hotel. Somewhere he could pay with cash without raising suspicion." She turned back to Jennifer. "Do we know how much cash he has on him?"

"Whatever he had in his wallet plus £500 he withdrew from the ATM at Barclays Bank on Russell Square, near the hotel."

"No other traceable activity?"

"No cell phone use, no credit cards. His bank account has now been frozen."

Ingrid looked at another map showing London and its surrounding counties. "Can we even assume he'd stay in the capital? Surely there's too much police activity for him not to leave? Is he familiar with any other location in the UK?"

"As far as we know, he's never been out of Suffolk before," Gurley said. "The only area of the country he really knows is within a forty mile radius of the base."

"I thought we might be needing this." Jennifer unfolded another unwieldy map. This one displayed the whole of England and Wales.

Ingrid studied the distance between central London and mid Suffolk, the location of RAF Freckenham. She was so used to checking dinky little local maps on her GPS app, it was good to get a sense of perspective and distance. Judging by the scale, the Air Force base was around fifty miles from London as the crow flies, which didn't really help any, so Ingrid tapped the details into her trusty app to get the distance by road: seventy-two miles. "That's an awful long way to travel undetected with a small boy when the whole nation is looking for you."

"It would be plain dumb for him to return to the base. What possible reason could he have?" Gurley sucked his teeth.

"A network of people he can trust?" Ingrid suggested.

"Not after what he did," Gurley said.

"I expect Radcliffe has asked the Suffolk cops to watch the train and bus stations close to the base, but it's worth checking, I guess."

"I'll get onto it," Jennifer said.

Gurley returned to studying the map of England and Wales. "If he is on his own…" He lowered his voice. "And if he's gone to ground, living off the land, we might not get any more sightings. We'll just have to track him the old fashioned way."

"Which way is that?"

"Weighing up all the possibilities, trusting your gut, and hoping like hell it doesn't let you down."

"And what's your gut telling you right now?"

"He's going to return to what he knows."

"The base?"

"Not necessarily, but some place related."

Ingrid stared into Gurley's piercing blue eyes. He obviously had a theory. Why didn't he just come right out and tell her? She thought about it for a moment. If Foster returned to what he knew, what was it he knew better than anything else? "Airplanes," Ingrid said, after a beat.

A corner of Gurley's mouth curled into something close to a smile.

"Jennifer, we need a list of all the small airstrips within a..." Ingrid paused, looking at Gurley, "sixty mile radius of London."

"You can't visit every one of them," the clerk said.

"We don't intend to. You're going to call them for us," Gurley smiled at her. "Find out if they've seen anyone hanging around acting suspicious in the past twenty-four hours. If maybe any of their aircraft have been tampered with."

"So I should start from the center and work outwards?"

"See," Gurley said. "I said we couldn't do this without you."

Jennifer beamed up at him then set to work.

Gurley strode to the door.

"You're not staying?" Jennifer's disappointment was obvious.

"I need to get a tracker survival pack together. Want me to get one for you too?" he asked Ingrid.

"This isn't the wilds of Wyoming. You can't go too far in this country without passing a McDonald's or a Domino's Pizza."

"Please yourself. Don't come running to me when you don't have a ground sheet or a bed roll."

"You're suggesting we track him on foot, like stalking a deer or something?"

"It might come to that. Nothing wrong with being prepared." He set off down the corridor for a few steps then hurried back again. "Jennifer? Where should I head for a camping supply store in this city?"

Jennifer frowned at him. "Try Selfridges—on Oxford Street. They sell pretty much everything."

"Is that on the Tube?"

Ingrid found the location quickly on her GPS app. She showed Gurley. "It's just a few blocks away." He stared at the route for a few seconds, nodded his thanks, then disappeared back out the door.

"What do you make of him?" Jennifer whispered, staring at the vacant doorway.

"I really don't know." It was true. Ingrid had assumed he was an unfeeling, tough, arrogant son of a bitch. But he'd shown a different side with Jennifer just now. Maybe she needed to keep an open mind.

Jennifer returned to her mammoth task and Ingrid sat at her desk, hating the fact that all she could do right now was wait for information. From Jennifer's inquiries... from the police... She blinked. There was some other information that she'd already waited far too long for. She shoved her purse over her shoulder, pulled her jacket from the back of her chair and told Jennifer she was going for a walk to clear her head.

15

As Ingrid waited for Mike Stiller at FBI HQ to pick up, she soon discovered she was headed not to the main entrance of the embassy as she'd previously intended, but downstairs toward the underground parking lot. Somehow, on autopilot, her brain had found something useful for her to do while she waited for more news. The call to Mike diverted to his voicemail and she left a terse message.

She was climbing off her Triumph Tiger 800 outside the Fosters' hotel off Russell Square less than fifteen minutes later. She swapped her motorcycle helmet for her purse and locked the box on the back of the bike. Her cell started ringing as she ran up the front steps to the entrance. The call displayed on the screen was an out of area number. An international call. She hoped it was Mike Stiller calling back and not Svetlana on a mission to guilt trip her.

She answered and waited.

"Ingrid? Are you there?" Mike sounded tetchy.

"Did you find anything for me?"

"Not much. I was going to call when I had more information. They found three women in the property, two in their twenties, the third they're guessing is in her thirties."

"Guessing? They don't know?"

"If you let me explain all will become clear. Clearer, at least." He took a deep breath. "So, two women have identified themselves. At present those

599

IDs are being verified. They're not from Minnesota, it's taking a while to track down their next of kin."

"What about the third woman?"

"I'm just coming to that."

Ingrid skipped back down the steps and started to pace up and down the sidewalk.

"The third woman hasn't said a word. She looks older than the other two, and has been there the longest. Neither of the other two women knows anything about her."

"I need to get pictures of the third woman sent to someone in my home town—a lady called Kathleen Avery. She'd recognize Megan in a heartbeat."

"You know the drill. It doesn't work like that. Maybe the local feds can arrange for this Avery lady to visit the medical center the victims are staying at."

"That's not possible. Kathleen Avery hasn't left her house since 1999."

"What is she, sick or something?"

"It's complicated. Ever since Megan disappeared her mother has suffered from agoraphobia. Plus she's morbidly obese. She has serious mobility issues. For her, leaving home just isn't an option."

"Jeez. I don't know what else to suggest."

"There must be something the Bureau can do. What about a DNA test? They could take a sample from Kathleen, compare them with this woman's." Ingrid knew that eighteen years ago, taking DNA samples hadn't been part of regular police procedure in a missing person case. If it had been, making a match now would have been straightforward.

"I'll make some calls."

"And what about the interviews? Can you get me the video recordings?"

"I'm still working on that. It may take a while."

"Can you at least send me a photograph of the mute woman?"

"Sure. I'm attaching it to an email as we speak. But this is for your eyes only—at this stage I can't have you distributing it to anybody else. Is that clear? I shouldn't even be sending it to you."

Ingrid's breath caught in her throat. She wasn't sure she'd recognize Megan after so many years. "Mike?"

"You get it yet?"

"I'm not at my computer—it'll come through on my phone—I'll look at it later. The woman who's not speaking. Is she... heavy?"

"You mean like, morbidly obese?"

"Just heavy?"

"No. All three women were fed strict rations in captivity. Their abductor had specific tastes when it came to body shape and size. They're all pretty skinny."

"Thanks, Mike. You will keep me posted, won't you?"

"Sure—don't I always keep my word?"

"Eventually."

"Harsh! Why do I continue to come to your rescue? You cruel woman."

She appreciated Mike trying to lighten the mood, but she couldn't manage an appropriate retort before she hung up.

As she navigated to the email app on her phone, her mouth became very dry. She found a half bottle of Evian in her purse and finished it. She stared at her phone, paralyzed with dread.

She couldn't bring herself to look at the attachment. She wasn't ready. Not yet. Not to see Megan's face staring back at her after all these years. Instead, she hurried into the hotel.

DS Tyson was inside, chatting to the receptionist. Beyond him Ingrid saw several tables in the lounge-cum-bar area occupied by plain clothes cops interviewing a handful of guests.

Ingrid waited until the receptionist had to answer the phone before she approached Tyson. "Hey, detective, how's it going?"

Tyson spun around and took a moment to respond.

"Agent Skyberg. From the US embassy?" Ingrid prompted.

"Oh I hadn't forgotten you, believe me." He peered toward the hotel entrance. "Where's Lurch?"

"If you mean Major Gurley, he had business elsewhere."

"What can I do for you?"

"Have your CSEs finished up?"

He nodded. "Just this morning. Hotel room door has been secured."

"Made any new discoveries since yesterday afternoon?"

"You will be sent the forensics report when it's ready, you know."

"I can't wait that long."

The receptionist finished her call and Tyson led Ingrid away from the desk, past the groups of guests and cops and through to the empty dining room. He pulled out a couple of chairs and waited for Ingrid to take a seat.

"I thought you interviewed the guests yesterday," Ingrid said and pointed toward the lounge.

"This is the mop-up operation. Mainly the people who weren't around during the first round." He looked at her expectantly.

"The forensics?" Ingrid reminded him.

"You know about the blood in the bathroom?"

Ingrid sat up straighter. "What?"

"Across the tiles above the sink. It was only a trace—someone had obviously tried to clean up. But they didn't manage to get it all."

"Has anyone questioned Carrie Foster about it?"

"Last time I heard, she'd been sedated."

"Sedated?"

"She got wind of the impostor—whoever he was—getting into her daughter's hospital room. She became hysterical, apparently. Can't blame her. What if it was her old man come to finish poor little Molly off? Makes my skin crawl."

"How is Molly?"

"She still hasn't regained consciousness. But the doctors are hopeful."

Ingrid didn't know what a prolonged period of unconsciousness meant in terms of the child's recovery. She decided not to dwell on the subject. "Did the CSEs find anything else?"

"Nope. It's possible the trace of blood belonged to a previous guest—it all depends how well the staff clean the rooms, I suppose."

Ingrid looked through the doorway into the lounge area. Most of the guests had completed their interviews and were starting to leave. Except for one. A purple haired senior was leaning forward in her chair. She'd grabbed the detective's arm sitting opposite her and was squeezing it hard.

"She seems to have something to say for herself."

Tyson followed her gaze. "We haven't gleaned much so far from the other guests. No one seems to have spoken to the Fosters. I think people prefer to keep themselves to themselves in such an intimate sized establishment."

Ingrid rose from her seat. "Let me know if this latest round of questioning uncovers any interesting information." She pulled a business card from her purse and handed it to him.

"Sure, why not? It's not as if I'm busy."

"I really would appreciate it."

He gave her a begrudging smile.

As Ingrid walked toward the dining room exit, the purple haired woman looked up at her. "Good afternoon, ma'am," Ingrid said when she drew level.

"You're American."

"Yes, ma'am. From the US embassy." She extended her hand. "Agent Skyberg."

"Agent? That sounds official. Maybe you want to hear about what I saw yesterday. I'm not sure this young man is taking me at all seriously. It's my age, I expect." From the definite twang in the woman's accent, Ingrid supposed she came from one of the Carolinas.

The woman struggled to her feet, grabbed Ingrid's arm and led her away to another table. She sat down and encouraged Ingrid to do the same. "My name's Merle Simmons."

Tyson walked past their table and pulled a face at Ingrid behind the old woman's back. She ignored him.

"I saw him, you know!" The woman's voice came out in an excited whisper. "He was as close to me as you are now."

"Do you mean Mr Foster?"

"Of course I do!"

"When was this?"

"Yesterday morning. I was on my way down to the dining room. It was clear he'd been too mean to pay the extra supplement."

"I'm sorry?"

"For breakfast. He was carrying a large McDonald's bag. Bringing back food for his whole family, I suppose."

"What time was this?"

"Eight forty-five."

"You're sure?"

"Jim, my husband, and I go down to breakfast the same time every morning."

"I mean you're sure about the McDonald's bag?"

"Why wouldn't I be? Quite unapologetic about it too. He smiled right at me."

"Perhaps I could speak to your husband, confirm the details with him?"

"You don't need to do that, I'm quite in control of my faculties. Besides, Jim's having his nap."

"You didn't see Mrs Foster or the children?"

"Not until we all watched the ambulance people take that poor little baby away." She looked down at Ingrid's hands. "Shouldn't you be making notes? The policeman had a notebook, but once I'd told him what I'd seen, he didn't seem to want to write anything down."

"I have perfect recall." Ingrid smiled and started to get up.

"Is that it?"

"Did you see anything else of the family yesterday morning?"

"Only what I've told you already."

"Then I think we're done—thank you so much for your time."

"What's happening with the little boy? Have you found him yet?"

"Not yet, ma'am, but I'm sure we will real soon." Ingrid wished she could believe that herself.

She left the woman sitting in the lounge and went looking for Tyson. Why would a man who fled his hotel room in a panic, after shaking his baby senseless, return via the nearest McDonald's? It didn't make any sense. She was inclined to believe the old woman had been mistaken.

She found Tyson speaking to the receptionist again.

"You managed to escape her clutches, then?" he said, smirking slightly.

"A quick question. Did the CSIs find any evidence of a—"

"McDonald's bag?"

"Yes—how did you know I was going to say—"

"I've just spoken to the DC who interviewed the batty old cow. No they bloody well didn't find a McDonald's bag. That old lady's got a screw loose."

16

Natasha McKittrick grabbed the last corn chip from her plate as Ingrid started to clear away the dishes. "Any more of that margarita in the fridge?"

"You just drank the last of it."

"Time to break this open then." McKittrick waved the bottle of tequila she'd brought to Ingrid's for their now regular monthly Tex-Mex night. "I can't believe it's this late and you still haven't given me what I came here for."

Ingrid hurried into the kitchen with the dirty dishes to avoid what she knew was coming next. She probably should have canceled dinner with her friend, but after the frustrating afternoon she'd had—they still hadn't come up with a fresh lead by the time she'd left the embassy after nine p.m.—she felt a real need to vent. Now McKittrick was trying to change the subject, Ingrid wished she'd canceled after all.

"You can't escape that easily," McKittrick shouted from the living room. "I mean, fascinating as your new case is—and you must admit, I have been listening patiently—I would like to move on to the main feature."

Ingrid opened the freezer section of the refrigerator and luxuriated in the cool air for a moment.

"You can run but you can't hide." McKittrick appeared at the kitchen door, waving the still unopened bottle of tequila in her fist. "I need shot glasses."

"Maybe you should take it home with you."

"Not until you tell me how your date with Mills went."

"Coffee? Tea?"

"Come on. Spill."

"There's nothing to tell."

"Well he seemed pretty pleased with himself at work this morning, so there must be something."

Ingrid opened a cabinet and retrieved two mugs. "I can't imagine why. We had a bite to eat then said goodbye at Holborn Tube."

"He didn't come back here afterwards?"

"No he didn't. Not that it's any of your business." Ingrid filled the kettle and flipped on the switch.

"I didn't actually think you were serious about the tea." McKittrick slid the unopened tequila bottle onto the kitchen counter. "What's the point of being a matchmaker if I can't even get to enjoy a bit of gossip now and then?"

"Sorry to disappoint you."

Ingrid's cell phone started to vibrate against the kitchen counter. She glanced at the screen, saw it was an out of area number and dismissed the call.

"That's not Mills, is it?"

"Why do you care so much?"

"I've got to work with the grumpy old bugger. Do you know how miserable he's been the last couple of months? When you agreed to go out with him he was like a changed man. Suddenly he was the most attentive detective on the team. Nothing was too much trouble."

"So glad to have helped with morale." Ingrid shoved the phone in a pocket.

"Was it Mills?"

"It was my mom."

"I thought the two of you didn't speak."

The kettle boiled and Ingrid made them both a peppermint tea. "We don't. Only in… special circumstances." She dunked the teabag slowly in and out of the tall mug, staring at the ripples she was creating on the surface of the water. A sudden, overwhelming need to talk about what was going on back home overcame her. "Have you seen the news reports about the three women who were being held captive in Minnesota?" she blurted.

"That's one way of changing the subject."

"I'm serious."

"I'm vaguely aware of it. I try to avoid the news whenever I can. I see enough stuff to depress me at work, without exposing myself to it when I'm off the job."

"The house where they were being held is just thirty miles from my home town. That's why my mom keeps calling me."

"Oh my God—you think one of those women is your school friend?"

Ingrid had told McKittrick about what happened to Megan on one of their drunken nights out, but only given her the sketchiest of details. Now she was regretting bringing the subject up. If she continued, she may never get to sleep tonight. "That's what I'm trying to find out."

"How are you coping?"

"Mostly by trying not to think about it. But the memories keep worming their way into my head, no matter how hard I try to shut them out. Certain sounds and smells take me right back to the moment she was taken and there's absolutely nothing I can do about it."

"Like your runaway pilot." McKittrick peered into her mug at the darkening liquid. She shoved it across the kitchen counter.

"Pilot?"

"Sounds like you're telling me you're suffering from PTSD yourself."

"It really doesn't compare to Foster's. According to his wife, any loud noise can trigger a reaction in him."

"You mean like the crying of his own child?"

"I know—it's tragic." Ingrid took a sip of her tea, decided it wasn't at all what she wanted, and threw the reminder into the sink. She opened another kitchen cabinet and retrieved a couple of shot glasses.

McKittrick grabbed the bottle from the counter and opened it. She poured out two measures. They both downed them in one and she refilled the glasses.

"That's the thing that's been troubling me about his meltdown," Ingrid said.

McKittrick gulped down her second shot.

"Kyle Foster developed his PTSD long after his return from Afghanistan. He was flying search and rescue missions there. His symptoms didn't show until after he started operating drones."

"So?"

"So you'd think his triggers wouldn't be loud noises. It's got to be pretty quiet in some isolated room in the middle of the Air Force base."

"I don't think you can say that. The mind's weird—maybe the drone missions reminded him of his earlier ones in the field and everything's got mixed up in his head. Who knows?"

"Still doesn't seem to fit." Ingrid removed her phone from her pocket and started turning it over and over in her hand, waiting for Svetlana to call again. She couldn't put off speaking to her forever.

"Maybe you should call her back." McKittrick refilled her own glass.

Ingrid put the phone on the counter.

"It was just a suggestion."

"There's something else. On my cell phone. I've been avoiding it since this afternoon. But I need to check it out before I talk to Svetlana."

"Do you have any idea how little sense your making?"

Ingrid took a deep breath and started again. "When I found out about the house in Minnesota, I put in a call to a contact I still have in D.C. This afternoon he sent me a photograph of one of the women. The only one who hasn't been identified."

"Are you telling me you haven't looked at it yet?" McKittrick shoved Ingrid's glass at her.

"What if it's Megan?" Much to her surprise, Ingrid's voice came out in a whisper. "What if it isn't?"

"You have to find out. God, Ingrid, you just have to." McKittrick snatched up the cell phone before Ingrid had a chance to. "Where is it? In your picture roll? Email?"

Ingrid plucked the phone out of her friend's hand. "You don't need to bully me into it." Holding her breath, she scrolled through to Mike Stiller's email and clicked on the attachment. She closed her eyes. She could hear McKittrick's breath quickening beside her. She opened her eyes and stared down at the image. All she saw was a jumble of random features—somehow the picture wouldn't resolve into a face. It seemed her brain was refusing to analyze the information it was receiving.

"Well?"

Ingrid blinked hard, as if she had grit in her eyes. She continued to look without being able to see. She stared at the image a little longer. Finally the random parts settled into a whole. The woman looking back up at her had drawn features, her face framed by lank, dark hair, her eyes lifeless with dark circles underneath. Ingrid shook her head. "I don't know. It's been so long."

McKittrick shuffled closer to her and peered at the image.

"Eighteen years since she was abducted. At least a decade since I last saw a photograph of her." She shoved the phone back into her pocket. "I can't tell. Jesus Christ, I can't even tell." Hot, unwanted tears sprang into her eyes. She turned away. She didn't want to cry in front of McKittrick.

"Bloody hell, it's hardly surprising. God only knows what that woman's been through over the past however many years. She probably looks completely different to the way she looked five years ago, even." She put an awkward arm around Ingrid's shoulders and squeezed. "You've got nothing to beat yourself up about."

If only you knew.

Ingrid emptied her glass and screwed the lid back on the bottle. "You want to take this with you?"

"Let's save it till next time. I might drink it on the way home otherwise."

McKittrick left a quarter hour later and Ingrid felt so restless she considered following her out the door—walking the dark summer streets for a while until she felt able to calm down. Instead she stepped out onto her roof terrace and drew the night air deep into her lungs. After three or four big breaths she pulled her cell from her pocket and called Svetlana.

"So, at least you listened to my message," her mother said in place of a greeting.

Ingrid hadn't. She didn't even realize her mother had left one.

"What have you found out that we don't already know from the TV?"

Ingrid relayed most of what Mike Stiller had told her. She didn't mention the photograph.

"This girl must come see Kathleen."

"That's not possible."

"Then I should go see her."

Ingrid was regretting telling Svetlana as much as she had. "Please, Mom. You have to trust that I know what I'm doing with this. I'm working on something that's going to help. I'll let you know just as soon as I make some progress."

"What? What are you working on? What aren't you telling me?"

"I've told you as much as I can. More than I should have. You have to promise me you'll tell Kathleen and no one else. What I'm doing is strictly unofficial. I could lose my job."

At the other end of the line Svetlana made a grunting sound. As if Ingrid losing her job wouldn't be the worst thing in the world. She'd never thought much of Ingrid's work at the Bureau.

"Is that it?" her mother asked after a long pause.

"There's one more thing." Ingrid hesitated. She wasn't sure whether it was the fact she was asking her mother for a favor—something she'd managed to avoid since elementary school—or the thing she was asking for that was making her feel so damn uncomfortable. "I need you to send me some photographs of Megan. The most recent ones you have. Go to the copy shop and have someone scan them in for you. Then get Bob or Harry to email them to me, can you?"

"You think I don't know how to scan and email? You think I need the neighbors' help for something like this?"

Ingrid dug the fingernails of her right hand into the fleshy part of her palm. It was amazing how the most innocuous of statements could insult Svetlana, then how easily Svetlana's indignation could upset Ingrid. Why wasn't she immune to it by now? "Great, even better, you can do it yourself."

"So, you're finally admitting you've forgotten what your best friend looks like? You wouldn't be having this trouble if you came back every year for the vigil at Kathleen's."

How could she deny what was true? "It's for the investigation, not me personally." As the words came out of her mouth she could plainly hear just how unconvincing they sounded.

"Oh sure."

"Listen, I have to go—there's someone at the door," she lied. "I'll call you again when I have news." She ended the call and went back inside. Without thinking about it, a minute later she was pulling on her running shoes. Two minutes after than she was sprinting down Sutherland Road.

No matter what the time of day, the neighborhood she lived in always felt pretty safe, but even if it hadn't, Ingrid knew she had the speed and skills to get herself out of trouble if she had to. It was something she'd forced herself to get good at after she lost Megan. She pushed her legs a little harder and pumped her arms a little faster, hoping to outrun the memories swarming in her head. Sometimes the technique actually worked.

Tonight it was futile.

She eventually returned to the apartment, her muscles exhausted, but her mind still racing. She went to bed, not hopeful she'd get any sleep, all too aware the alarm would wake her in less than four hours.

Amazingly, she did manage to finally drift off.

Only to be woken by angry banging on the apartment door just two hours later.

17

When Ingrid had asked Gurley exactly how he'd managed to get into her building he'd been evasive, mumbling something about the super letting him in. Except the building didn't actually have staff on site twenty-four hours a day. Ingrid had decided to let it go, concentrating instead on selecting some suitable clothes to throw on when she couldn't quite fully open her eyes.

"Are you drunk?" Gurley had asked when he saw the tequila and glasses on the kitchen counter. He dumped a large backpack by his feet. Its contents clanked and jangled when it hit the tiled floor.

Although Ingrid didn't dignify Gurley's accusation with an answer, she doubted she would have been safe to drive. Mercifully, he told her there was a cab waiting for them. "Where are we headed? An airstrip?" she called through the bedroom door. "Did Foster try to steal a plane?"

Gurley cleared his throat. "I still think that theory was a good one. But no—the sighting was in some place called Willesden. I checked on the map —it's not that far from here. If you could just hurry it up."

They'd made the trip in a little over ten minutes through the empty streets of northwest London. During the cab ride Ingrid had fired questions at Gurley he couldn't answer.

"I just got a call telling me the location. You would have too, if your goddamn phone hadn't been switched off."

Now, at just after four-thirty a.m., they were both leaning against an unmarked police car in a side street just off Willesden High Road that had been sealed off at either end. They'd both refused DCI Radcliffe's offer of a seat inside a car parked further away from the property the team was staking out, not wanting to be so far away from the action. They still felt the police were trying to sideline them.

After fifteen minutes of being ignored by pretty much every law enforcement officer in the vicinity—and there had to be at least two dozen uniformed officers and another dozen detectives—Ingrid was beginning to regret her decision not to wear a sweater beneath her jacket. Eventually Radcliffe approached them, a grim expression on his face.

"We're waiting for the hostage negotiator to arrive." Radcliffe looked as if he hadn't made it into his bed at all the night before. The shirt beneath his crumpled jacket was badly creased and there was a long greasy mark snaking down his tie.

"Why?" Gurley snapped.

"Because none of us has had the appropriate training," he answered in a dismissive tone.

To his credit, Ingrid thought, Gurley didn't react. "I meant, why aren't you just going in? You've evacuated the neighboring houses, right? Foster isn't armed, so why not storm the place with all the manpower you've got?"

"We don't know he isn't armed. Just because he's not likely to have a gun, doesn't mean he hasn't got a weapon. You are a little gun-focused."

Ingrid had to admit Radcliffe had a point. Foster could have easily purchased knives and other tools to use as weapons. They didn't know what they might be dealing with. "Have you made any contact with him at all?" she asked.

"We've got a couple of tech guys inside the property right now, rigging up a speaker system so that we can communicate without the whole street hearing." Radcliffe glanced up at the nearest cordon, just fifty feet or so from where they were standing. A few people had started to gather, eager to know what was going on. So far no journalists appeared to have heard about the incident. "The vultures are circling," Radcliffe said. "I expect pictures have already been sent from onlookers' mobile phones to all the major news outlets. The camera crews will be setting up before you know it."

"All the more reason to settle this swiftly. You have a SWAT team ready to go?" Gurley had started pacing. It seemed to Ingrid that he might go in himself if Radcliffe continued to refuse to.

"We have two vans of Specialist Firearms Command officers at the ready."

"So do it now."

"Save your breath. We're not going in now. And we won't until we've exhausted all other options."

Ingrid shuffled sideways so that she was standing between Radcliffe and Gurley. "Who called it in?"

Radcliffe looked at her, non-plussed for a moment by her question. "One of the other residents in the property. It's an HMO—house of multiple occupancy," he explained. "Houses crammed with lots of rooms that have basic cooking facilities—usually a two-ring hob and a kettle—but with shared bathrooms. They used to be called boarding houses in the old days. Or bedsits. Anyway, some bloke saw the boy coming out of the bathroom on his landing wearing a pair of Spiderman pajamas."

"I assumed Foster had dumped the boy's pajamas when he stole the clothes from the laundromat," Ingrid said.

"Well then you assumed wrong. They haven't been found anywhere."

"Is that resident still around? Can we speak to him?"

"He's been taken to the local leisure center—it's where we're keeping all the people that have been evacuated. I could arrange for a car to take you down there, if you like." He nodded a little too enthusiastically about the idea of sending them some place else.

"You can go, agent," Gurley told Ingrid. "I'm staying right here."

"These... HMOs," Ingrid said, "would the landlords rent the rooms out for cash? No questions asked?"

"Most of the tenants are on benefits... you know, welfare. So generally the rent would be paid by the local council. If any of the landlords can get their hands on actual cash up front, I expect they jump at the chance."

"But how would Foster have gotten the boy in with him, without arousing suspicion? God knows their pictures have been all over the news."

"That's what we'd like to ask the landlord. We're still trying to track him down."

A detective who had been hovering nearby whispered something in Radcliffe's ear.

"Oh—it's a landlady, apparently," Radcliffe said. "At least we're making some progress—we know the gender, if not the location of the owner."

Gurley was shaking his head. "How long before the negotiator arrives? How many hostage situations you got going on this morning, for crying out loud?"

"She'll get here when she gets here."

"A woman?"

Ingrid wheeled around and stared up into Gurley's face accusingly.

"Hey, take it easy, agent. I'm not commenting on her abilities as a nego-tiator, but don't you think after what happened with Foster's wife and daughter… guys in the military don't exactly have a *progressive* attitude when it comes to equality."

"She's the most experienced negotiator on the team." Radcliffe ducked around Ingrid just so he could square up to Gurley, even though he was a good eight inches shorter than the Air Force policeman. "This is my inves-tigation and we're following Met protocols. Is that clear?"

Gurley shook his head resignedly. "Fine. You don't want my help, I'll keep my opinions to myself."

"At last," Radcliffe muttered.

They waited around for another five minutes until eventually the Met negotiator arrived. She disappeared with Radcliffe and two other detec-tives into a nearby unmarked van.

"Is that it? We don't get to hear what she has to say? Oh come on! What happened to close liaison?" Gurley started to make his way toward the van.

"Sir! Please stop," an officer called from a nearby patrol car. "You need to stay where you are."

Gurley ignored him and marched on.

"Hey, come on," Ingrid said. "We can speak to the negotiator later."

Gurley turned and said, "I'm sick of being ignored. I'm making a perfectly reasonable request here. I'm just going to speak to the negotiator. Discuss strategy."

"Please, I have to ask you not to get any closer to the surveillance van," the cop called out.

Gurley spun on his heels. "What you gonna do about it?" He continued toward the van.

With just a nod from the officer, three more cops ran toward Gurley.

"Watch out, Jack!" Ingrid warned.

Gurley glanced over his shoulder, then picked up speed until he was running flat out, his long gangly arms and legs seeming not quite under his control. Just as he was reaching a hand out to the door at the back of the van, one of the cops launched himself at him. The cop flung his arms around Gurley's shoulders, but the big MP barely lost any forward momentum. His fingers wrapped around the handle of the door.

Two more cops landed on him, each one grabbing one of Gurley's arms. With the help of his colleagues, the cop who'd shouted the warning slapped a pair of cuffs on Gurley's wrists. All four of them then proceeded to lead him to a patrol car, even though he wasn't putting up any kind of resistance.

Ingrid ran over to them. "Come on, guys… cuffs? Is that strictly necessary? Tempers just got a little out of control," she said, not quite believing the cops' overreaction. "We'll make sure it doesn't happen again."

But the officer in charge completely ignored her.

Gurley and the group of policemen surrounding him arrived at the car. One of them opened the door and reached up to place his hand on top of Gurley's head. The MP ducked down, bending his knees low and shouted to Ingrid, "For God's sake, Skyberg, don't let them screw this up."

18

As the officer who'd cuffed Gurley walked past her, Ingrid reached out and grabbed his arm. He looked down at her hand and raised an accusative eyebrow. She quickly withdrew it.

"I do hope you're not thinking of giving us any trouble, miss." His tone was patronizing, his demeanor dismissive. Ingrid detected a faint Scottish accent. Edinburgh, if she wasn't mistaken.

"My title is 'agent', and I'm not sure what you've just done to my colleague is entirely legal. Is he under arrest?" She noticed the officer had three stripes on his epaulet. A couple of ranks below Radcliffe.

"Why create all that paperwork for ourselves?" he said, an inappropriate smirk on his face. "We're just letting your friend cool off a wee bit. When this situation is resolved and we no longer consider him a threat to its successful conclusion, he'll be free to go."

"You do know he's a major in the military police? He's a cop, just like you. Can't you show the guy a little more respect?"

"If he'd shown us the same courtesy, you and I wouldn't even be having this conversation." He held her gaze for a long moment, making sure he'd made his point clear, then turned away to speak to a nearby constable.

Ingrid had been dismissed. As she was considering her next move, a loud bang echoed from across the street. She looked toward the source of the noise: a sash window had been flung open in the house under surveillance. A dirty nylon curtain fluttered through the gap. Ingrid stared at it for a while, expecting more activity. None came. Presumably the police negotiator had made contact with Foster and that had sparked a reaction. Everyone in the street was craning their necks up toward the window, all holding their breath, waiting for the next move.

For a full five minutes Ingrid continued to watch nothing happen at the open window. She imagined how frustrated Jack Gurley had to be feeling, handcuffed in the patrol car, watching police officers run up and down the street, and not knowing why. He was so close to apprehending his fugitive and yet not allowed anywhere near the action.

The frustration was getting to Ingrid too. She felt useless. Tommy was less than two hundred yards from her and she couldn't help save him. She hoped he was all right and that Foster wouldn't decide to make some final stand and take his boy down with him if he thought all was lost.

Did the Met negotiator really know what she was doing? Was Kyle Foster even making demands? Maybe they should get Carrie Foster to speak to him. Hearing a familiar voice might make all the difference. Ingrid released the breath she hadn't realized she'd been holding. Kyle Foster talking to his wife could also make matters a whole lot worse. Besides, Ingrid wasn't even sure whether or not Carrie Foster was still under sedation.

She tried calling Radcliffe and wasn't surprised when his cell went straight to voicemail. As approaching the surveillance van to try to speak to him wasn't an option, she walked over to one of the uniformed officers. The man was wearing a Kevlar vest and had an earpiece in his left ear. She showed him her badge. "Any chance you know what's going on in there?"

He shook his head and said, "I'm just waiting for orders." Then he walked away.

Ingrid looked toward the crowd standing at the nearest cordon. Previously silenced by the recent activity at the house, they had started murmuring quietly amongst themselves again.

Except for one woman.

One woman standing close to the barrier had just shouted something at the cop manning the line. Ingrid jogged down to the cordon to see what the woman's problem was.

"I'm seventy-eight years old!" she hollered. "My husband fought for this country. You have no right keeping me from my home."

The cordon cop leaned close to the woman and said something very quietly in her ear.

"What would I do on the hard floor in the leisure center? With my hips? What is the matter with you, suggesting such a thing?"

Ingrid detected the merest hint of a Polish accent, almost eroded away after many years living in London. "Hello, ma'am. Has the officer explained what's going on to you?"

"He says I can't go back to my own house. I've been sitting in the hospital all night at my husband's bedside, on the most uncomfortable chair ever made, and now this policeman wants me to stand in the street for God knows how long."

"It's not safe for you to return right now." Ingrid pointed to the open window. "You see that curtain blowing there? Inside that house is a man the police need to speak to. He has a little boy with him. He's holding the boy hostage." As Ingrid made the statement she realized it wasn't strictly accurate. As far as she knew, Foster had made no demands. And it wasn't at all clear his son was being held against his will.

"Hostage? The poor man has just lost his wife. He's done nothing wrong."

Ingrid stared into the woman's face, realizing she had to be suffering from some form of dementia. She was about to suggest to the cop that he really ought to get the confused old lady somewhere she could rest up until the situation was resolved, when a loud crash sounded from the side-walk outside the house. A bottle had smashed on the hard pavement.

"Dear God." The old woman crossed herself. "I hope he's not smashing the place up. I didn't take a deposit."

Ingrid had already started to walk back toward the house. She stopped. "You know the man in that apartment?" she said, turning back.

"Didn't I just say that? He's lost his wife. That is my house. I want to get back there."

"You rented the room to the man with the boy?" Ingrid asked.

"Who are you anyway? You don't look like a police officer, and you have an American accent. What has all this got to do with you?"

"I work for the American embassy. I'm here because the man and boy are American."

The woman wheezed out a cackling laugh. "Sure they are... and I'm Peruvian."

"What did he tell you?"

"That his wife died and he'll be taking his son back home, just as soon as his family send him the money for his plane ticket."

"And where did he say home was?"

"He did tell me... Iran maybe... or Turkey. I don't remember. And I don't care, as long as I get my rent."

"What does the man look like?"

"I don't know, average. Dark skin, dark hair, average height."

"And the boy?"

"Similar, except his hair is very curly."

Ingrid lifted the blue and white police tape high in the air and guided the old lady beneath it. "I need you to come with me."

"I can go home?"

"You have to speak to some people first."

The uniformed cop ran from the other end of the cordon towards them. "What do you think you're doing?"

"I'll take full responsibility. Call DCI Radcliffe if you don't believe me." The tape had gotten caught in the woman's hair, Ingrid gently lifted it off. But before she got a chance to start walking her down the street, a car screeched to a halt on the other side of the cordon. A familiar figure climbed out.

Ingrid's heart sank.

19

As ever, Angela Tate had managed to arrive at a crime scene ahead of her competitors. Though the sun hadn't yet risen and the street was bathed in a grayish half-light, the journalist spotted Ingrid immediately. She pushed her way to the front of the cordon. Just getting out of the taxi was the overweight photographer who seemed to accompany Tate on most of her assignments. He started arguing with the cab driver.

"Don't run away, agent. Not without a quick comment for the *Evening News*." The reporter stuck out an arm and shoved her digital recorder into Ingrid's face.

"No comment." Ingrid tried to move away but the old woman resisted.

"You're from the newspaper?" She looked Tate up and down. "My husband always used to read the *Evening News*, before his eyesight failed him. So much better than the free papers they give away everywhere now."

"I couldn't agree with you more." Tate gave her an uncharacteristically genuine smile, which faded quickly as she turned back to Ingrid. "Given that you're here, I can only assume the man inside that house is First Lieutenant Kyle Foster."

Ingrid shook her head. "You're wrong."

"How wet behind the ears do you actually think I am? I thought you knew me better than that by now."

"OK—I'll give you a comment," Ingrid said, "but then I really have to go."

Tate looked at her suspiciously.

"Neither Kyle Foster nor his son are in that house."

Tate narrowed her eyes. "You really expect me to believe that?"

"Believe what you like. I've got to get this lady home."

"Yes—yes that's right," the woman said. "I need to go to bed."

Ingrid led the woman to the first patrol car, explained to the cop there that she had new information for DCI Radcliffe about the hostage situation, then waited while he ran to the surveillance van and banged on the door. Radcliffe's pale, sleep-deprived face was thunderous when he emerged from the back of the truck. Nevertheless, he hurried to Ingrid, frowning at the old woman as he approached.

"It's not Foster," Ingrid said, cutting straight to the chase.

"Who's this?"

Ingrid realized she'd never asked the woman her name.

"Katarzyna Tysowski," the old lady said.

"Mrs Tysowski is the landlady of the property. The man she rented the room to looked nothing like Kyle Foster."

"Is that all you have?"

"There's more, but first of all, tell me what was thrown out of the window just now."

"A bottle of whiskey."

"Whiskey? Maybe it wasn't Iran—where he came from," Mrs Tysowski said. Then, at Ingrid's prompting, repeated to the DCI exactly what she'd just told her.

When she was done, Radcliffe let out a low groan. "You're certain?" he asked the old woman.

"I'm not senile."

Ingrid turned to her and smiled. "Please excuse us for a moment, ma'am." She walked up the street a few paces and Radcliffe joined her a moment later. "You have to go in there. Put an end to this now. The press have already arrived. The longer you leave it, the worse—"

Radcliffe cut her off with a raised palm. "Thank you for pointing out the obvious for me." He lifted both hands to his face and stood there in the middle of the street, rocking back on his heels. "This bloody case. I swear to God…"

Five minutes later a team of twenty officers dressed in riot gear stormed into the property. Five minutes after that one of them emerged with a boy in his arms. A female cop wrapped a blanket around the boy's shoulders and carried him to a waiting police car.

"Have you found someone to look after him?" Ingrid asked Radcliffe.

"His mother's on her way." He saw Ingrid's puzzled expression. "Alive and well. Estranged from the boy's father, waiting for the divorce to come through."

"So he had abducted his son?"

"We got that much right, at least." He shook his head. "The whole thing's been a bloody fiasco from start to finish."

Jack Gurley couldn't have put it better himself, Ingrid thought. "I'm guessing you don't have a problem releasing my colleague now?"

"God no—you're welcome to him." He stopped a passing constable and requested Gurley be released immediately.

Jack Gurley emerged from the patrol car, stretching his arms and legs, rubbing his wrists where the cuffs had been. Ingrid quickly brought him up to speed.

"The guy in the house sounds nothing like Foster."

"I think the witness' description relied a little too heavily on the Spiderman pajamas," Ingrid said.

"You're kidding me." Gurley glared at Radcliffe who was now standing on the other side of the street, issuing orders to a group of uniformed officers. "All this manpower for nothing?"

"I know—it's frustrating as hell. But what else could the police do? Ignore it? This was just an unfortunate case of mistaken identity. God knows it's happened to me before."

"But we're no further forward." Gurley shook his head. "I've got to get out of here." He strode across the street, grabbed his heavy backpack, then headed at speed towards the cordon. Ingrid ran after him.

As they reached the line of police tape at the end of the street, Ingrid could see Angela Tate moving fast in her direction, an angry expression on her face.

"Do you think I like standing around in the cold for no bloody reason at all?" the reporter said.

"Not my problem. I gave you a statement—you chose to ignore it," Ingrid told her.

Gurley's cell phone started to ring. He answered the call and turned away, leaving Ingrid to deal with Tate on her own.

"Tell me one thing," Tate said, "off the record."

"You think I'm ever going to believe that, coming from you?"

"I swear."

Ingrid pursed her lips. When she tried to move away, Tate quickly wrapped her fingers around her arm.

"Do you think Tommy Foster is still alive?"

"No comment." She peeled off the reporter's hand only to be grabbed again around the wrist. This time by Gurley. He yanked at her arm and dragged her under the police tape and through the crowd of onlookers.

"What is it, for God's sake?" Ingrid pulled her arm out of his grasp.

Gurley said nothing until they were safely out of Tate's earshot. "We have a lead. A sighting. And this time I can actually trust the intel."

"Why?"

"It came from one of my men at the base."

20

Jack Gurley was forced to duck very low as he ran across the helipad to the waiting Pave Hawk helicopter the US Air Force had sent from RAF Freckenham. Slung across his shoulder was his clanking backpack. Ingrid couldn't help wondering what he'd purchased the day before at the department store. He hadn't volunteered the information and she didn't want to seem so curious that she needed to ask. With just a spare pair of panties, a tee shirt and a toothbrush stuffed into her purse, she was starting to feel a little under-equipped for their trip.

She followed him to the dove-gray chopper. As she approached the big helicopter—it was easily over fifty-foot long—she was reminded of the last time she had flown in one. It was during her first ever case at the embassy. Her stomach lurched a little as she recalled the turbulence they'd endured on the flight back to London, as they tried and failed to outrun a big winter storm. She swallowed hard. At least the weather today was a lot calmer.

Once they were safely harnessed inside, the helicopter rose into the air, and Ingrid spotted Angela Tate standing in the road that led to the helipad in Battersea, looking disheveled and maybe even a little defeated. Ingrid felt a twinge of pity for the reporter.

The feeling soon passed.

The journalist must have followed them all the way from Willesden, no doubt determined to get a better story for the front page of the *Evening News* than a child being snatched by a disgruntled father from his estranged wife. Tate would be on the hunt for bigger headlines and wouldn't stop until she got them. Ingrid was pretty sure that the reporter's expense account wouldn't stretch to hiring a helicopter of her own. For a while at least, their destination would remain classified information.

Gurley tried to fit his long legs into the cramped space, twisting his body one way then the other. He finally resorted to resting his feet on the backpack with his knees up somewhere around head height.

"Maybe you didn't need to bring all that gear," Ingrid said, adjusting her headset so it sat more snugly on her head.

"I wasn't going to leave it behind—I just bought this stuff. Besides, we don't know how Foster is surviving. He's probably living off the land, sleeping outdoors. You might find some of this stuff useful if we have to track him."

"I might?"

"I can get all the supplies I need from the base." He thudded the backpack with the heel of his boot. "Think of this as a small gift from me to you."

Gee, I'm touched.

"On that subject—tracking—I want to make it clear now, I can't have you slowing me down," Gurley told her, his expression solemn. "No offense. It could get very physical."

"I run five miles most days—do you?"

"It's not just about stamina, you need strength too."

"Don't you worry about me." She managed to resist the urge to have him squeeze her biceps just to prove her point.

Gurley didn't comment. His silence told her plenty. Although she might not be capable of overpowering him in an arm wrestling contest, she was damn sure she could outrun him. But there was nothing to gain in getting pissed at his attitude, so she got back on topic. "Assuming this sighting is reliable—"

"It is."

"OK—I guess we'll find out soon enough. Assuming it was Foster, why would he return to Freckenham? Why get anywhere near the base? Do you think he's planning to turn himself in?"

"He could have walked into any station house to do that."

"Not if he thinks he can be tried in the US if he surrenders to US personnel. Maybe he just wants to go home."

"You're still making the mistake of assuming he's thinking rationally. He's gone postal—nothing he does now can be predicted with any measure of accuracy. We don't know what's going through the crazy S.O.B.'s head."

Something didn't fit with the crazed airman picture Gurley was painting. Right now Ingrid couldn't put her finger on it. "So why do you think he's here?"

"Maybe to seek revenge?"

"On who?"

Gurley shrugged.

"You think he really might want to hurt the people on the base?"

"Worst case scenario—maybe some folks in the village too."

"Then we really should inform the local cops." Ingrid didn't want get the Suffolk force involved, but wasn't sure she could keep the new intel from them.

"The local cops were supposed to be keeping the train and bus stations under surveillance. They didn't do a real good job, did they?"

"Assuming this sighting is reliable."

"Like you say—we'll find out soon enough."

The journey from London to Suffolk was uneventful. Ingrid's attempts at engaging Gurley in any conversation that wasn't directly connected to the hunt for Foster were either ignored completely—more than once Gurley feigned sleep—or slapped down as either irrelevant or too damn personal. Silence was just fine with Ingrid. It was a relief to concentrate on the view out the window than make excruciating small talk.

The chopper landed in a designated helicopter zone on the base and a jeep arrived within moments to convey them to a windowless low-rise block situated at the edge of the complex. One of Gurley's sergeants escorted them to a stuffy room at the end of a long corridor. Inside was a man in his late thirties or early forties, a little overweight, dressed in civilian clothes. He was pacing up and down behind a table and four chairs.

"Is that it? Am I going to the police station now?" He had an English accent, with a slight lilt to it. Ingrid supposed he was a local. The man had directed his question at Gurley, ignoring Ingrid completely.

"Mr Cooper?" Gurley said, "Mr Glen Cooper?"

"You know who I am, for God's sake. What's going on here?"

"We need to speak to you, sir."

"Christ, what do you think you're doing? You have no right to hold me like this. Where are the police? I asked the other bloke I spoke to—Lieutenant Grayson—to call them. Where the hell are they? Finally he turned his attention from Gurley to Ingrid. "And who the hell are you?"

Ingrid showed him her badge. "I'm from the American embassy. We're very interested in finding out exactly what you saw this morning."

"Oh, is that right? Well maybe I don't want to tell you. I've done nothing wrong. I've got other deliveries to make. You can't keep me here. It's not legal."

"Why don't you let us worry about what is and isn't legal?" Gurley pulled out a chair from the table and sat down.

"Piss off."

Ingrid sat down too. "The faster you tell us what you saw, the faster you'll get out of here." Ingrid felt sorry for the guy, locked up for the past two hours as if he were a criminal. What the Air Force was doing was illegal, but if it meant that they tracked Foster down sooner, she was willing to be party to a little bending of the rules.

"I know you, I've seen you around the base, you look different out of uniform. Smaller somehow."

"My name's Jack Gurley—I'm a Major in Security Forces. I need you to tell me everything you saw."

"I can't hang around here. I thought I was going to speak to the police. Not bloody Mulder and Scully. I've got a business to run. Deliveries to make."

"You've made that quite clear. Why don't you sit down and tell us what you know?" Gurley folded his arms and tilted his head to one side, the picture of a patient interrogator.

"I'll talk just as soon as that door's unlocked and the armed man outside has been dismissed."

"Not possible." Gurley scraped back his chair and stood up. He hurried around the table and squared up to Cooper. He towered over the man.

Cooper flinched, and raised his arms across his face.

"What? You think this is going to get physical?" Gurley said.

"I know what you Yanks are like, Guantanamo and all that."

"Then you must know how determined we are to get the information we need." Gurley forced a smile.

Ingrid got to her feet, staying on her side of the table, but preparing to launch into action if Gurley did overstep the line. "You say you have a business to run, Mr Cooper?" She maintained a quiet and even tone, despite being sorely tempted to holler at him. "You deliver supplies to the base?"

"And I have been doing for years. You really shouldn't be treating me like this."

"So I'm guessing you rely on the base for a large part of your income. I'm guessing it'd be… significant, in terms of your… profitability, if you lost the RAF Freckenham contract."

Cooper lowered his arms and his shoulders drooped. He stared into Ingrid's face, then down at the floor and shook his head. "That's how you're going to play it. Threatening my business." He looked at Gurley. "She's good. You could learn a thing or two from her, Mulder." He shuffled to the table and sat down opposite Ingrid. "Let's get on with this bloody interview, then, shall we?"

Gurley gave her a begrudging smile as he returned to his seat.

Cooper interlaced his fingers and flexed them outwards, forcing the cartilage to pop noisily. "What do you want to know?"

21

They had been at the base for over thirty minutes, and still hadn't gotten the first nugget of intel from the eyewitness. It was clear to Ingrid that Cooper had been locked up and isolated to maintain first mover advantage. She suspected Gurley wanted to bring Kyle Foster in himself, single-handedly, if he had a choice.

If he thought for one second he could shake her off, he needed to think again.

After Gurley had made a show of rolling up his sleeves, to reveal remarkably pale, almost hairless arms, he planted both elbows on the table and leaned forward. "When did you see him?"

"Just before six o'clock. I was only a few miles from here. Running a bit late... that's a bloody joke, considering what time it is now... anyway, Foster was standing outside the post office, next to the pillar box. Looked as if he was waiting for something."

"Or someone?" Gurley asked.

Cooper shrugged. "How am I supposed to know that?"

"So you recognized him? From the TV reports?"

"I know him. Not well, but enough to recognize him in the street."

"What did you do then?"

"I pulled up and got out of the van."

"Why?"

Cooper paused for a moment. "Actually, I'm not sure. I didn't think about it. By the time I was out of the cab, he was gone."

"Why didn't you call the police right away?" Ingrid asked. Gurley threw her an irritated sideways glance.

"I tried. My phone battery was out of juice. I need to get a new phone, it runs right down after a couple of calls. I just haven't got round to it."

"There are public pay phones in the village. I've seen them," Gurley said.

"But have you ever actually seen anyone use one? You won't have—they've all been vandalized. Quick as BT send an engineer round to fix them, so some little bastard smashes them up again."

"So you continued your journey into the base?" Ingrid asked.

"Seemed like the smart thing to do. I told Lieutenant Grayson I'd seen Kyle. He said he'd phone the police and I should sit tight and wait for them to come out to question me. That was bloody ages ago. And then you two turn up."

"Was Foster alone when you saw him?" Ingrid said. "Was his son with him?"

"Alone. I expected to see Tommy close by, but there was no sign of him. That's not good, is it?" He popped his knuckles again. "My youngest is so upset by it all he's refusing to go to school. Probably just an excuse to bunk off, but you can understand he'd be feeling scared."

"Your son knows Tommy?"

"Lewis plays footie with Tommy every Saturday. It's a little local league, nothing to get excited about, but that doesn't stop some dads taking it very seriously."

"And was Foster one of those dads? Did he push Tommy to do well?"

"God no. He was just pleased Tommy had made a few friends outside of the base."

"Why's that?" Gurley's upper body tensed defensively.

"You'd have to ask him. But I think I know what he meant. Village life can get like that too. Seeing the same people all the time isn't healthy for anyone, is it? That's how tempers fray and arguments start. Well, you tell me, Major. I bet it's like a pressure cooker in here sometimes, isn't it?"

Gurley didn't respond. He just narrowed his eyes and set his jaw.

"So Tommy and Lewis play soccer together. How about you and Foster —are you close?" Ingrid asked.

"What are you getting at?"

"How well do you know him?"

"We have a pint after the match on a Saturday afternoon. But if you're implying that I've done anything wrong... that I'm such a close friend I'd protect him or something... then you're totally barking up the wrong tree. I reported seeing him just as soon as I could."

Ingrid wondered why Cooper had become so defensive. Could he be hiding something? "What was Foster wearing when you saw him?"

"Dark trousers, a pale shirt. Bloody big boots on his feet. US Air Force issue, they looked like."

"Was he clean shaven?"

"He looked like he hadn't had a shave for a day or two. But he didn't exactly have a beard. His hair was greasy, lying flat against his head."

"So maybe he hadn't had access to a bathroom, the past forty-eight hours?" Ingrid asked.

"I suppose not."

"Did he look as if he'd been sleeping outdoors?" Gurley said.

"He looked bloody rough, so he could have been."

"Rough?"

"His clothes were creased and muddy. He seemed exhausted."

"Sounds like you got a pretty good look at him. How long were you staring at him before you opened the door of your truck?" Gurley's tone had changed from general hostility to outright mistrust.

"Wait a minute, I don't like the way this is going."

"What were you planning to do?"

"I wasn't planning anything, I told you, I wasn't thinking at all. I just jumped out of the van."

Ingrid leaned forward, closer to Cooper than Gurley was. She felt as if she needed to get between the two men before tempers flared even more. "Is there anything else you can tell us about the way he looked?"

It took Cooper a moment to tear his gaze away from Gurley's face. Ingrid wasn't even sure he'd heard her question.

"I told you, one second he was there, the next he was gone. I've told you everything there is to tell."

Gurley suddenly stood up and ducked around the table. He crouched next to Cooper, their heads at the same level. "I'm going to ask you this once and I'd advise you to think very carefully before you answer."

Cooper frowned at Gurley, then turned toward Ingrid. She managed to keep her face expressionless. What the hell was Gurley doing?

"Do you know where Kyle Foster is right now?"

"Of course not! How could I? I've been in this place for over two hours."

"Are you protecting Kyle Foster?"

"No! I barely know the bloke. I wish I didn't, now I've found out what he's capable of."

"Did you give him money, or any other kind of assistance when you saw him earlier?"

"What's going on here? I reported the sighting, didn't I? Why would I do that if I wanted to help him?"

"I don't believe you."

"But I'm telling you the truth. For God's sake, what do I have to do to convince you?"

Gurley moved closer to Cooper. "Who then? Who else would want to help him? Who was he waiting for when you saw him?"

"How would I know? I'm not a bloody mindreader." Cooper tried to move his face away, but Gurley clamped a hand around the back of his neck. "Ask Yvonne if she knows anything about it," Cooper said, his voice coming out in a strangled whisper.

"Yvonne?"

"Yvonne Sherwood. The landlady at the Hare and Hounds—the pub I go to on a Saturday afternoon with Foster. She's decidedly chummy with the bloke. If you know what I mean."

22

Ingrid jogged to keep up with Gurley as he strode down the corridor and back outside. "We have to let him go," she said.

"Do we?"

"He's a witness, not a goddamn criminal—he could make a lot of trouble for the embassy if he decided to go to the press. You know how sensitive this whole situation is."

"We will let him go. But there's no harm in having him stew a little longer before we do. That way he might be more reluctant to go to the police when he gets out of here. He won't want to waste any more of his precious time being questioned." Gurley stopped abruptly and called over a Security Forces sergeant who was coming out of the adjacent building. "That guy—Cooper—make sure he gets his phone back and is released in thirty minutes. No, make it an hour. If he talks about filing an official complaint, remind him how valuable the US Air Force contract is to him." He glanced at Ingrid. "That was a nice touch, by the way."

The sergeant saluted Gurley and disappeared into the building they'd just exited.

"Thank you," Ingrid said.

"I had no intention of detaining him. I wouldn't want to make any trouble for you and the embassy."

Ingrid wasn't sure she entirely believed him. She suspected he'd make just as much trouble as he needed, if it got him the right result. "You do know we're supposed to keep DCI Radcliffe informed of what we're doing, if we discover anything new," she reminded him.

"So far we've had an unconfirmed sighting. Geographically we might be a little closer to Foster, but practically? We're no further forward than we were two hours ago."

It seemed like a fine line they were walking, but for the time being, Ingrid was prepared to go along with Gurley's approach. It wasn't as if Radcliffe could offer them much assistance right now, and involving the local cops would only slow them down. "OK—let's go talk to Yvonne Sherwood. Then we can make a decision whether we pass on the information. Maybe she'll tell us nothing useful. No point in wasting anyone else's time."

"Couldn't agree more. We'll take my car. We don't want to roll into the village in an Air Force vehicle. No need to announce our arrival." He set off at top speed once again.

"Do you know her—the manager of the Hare and Hounds?" Ingrid asked, breaking into a jog to catch up with him.

"Never been in there. It doesn't do for members of Security Forces to fraternize with servicemen. Or rather, if any of us showed up, the place would clear in two seconds flat." He smiled at her. Ingrid could have sworn she saw the hint of a twinkle in his eye.

Was Jack Gurley starting to enjoy this mission?

They returned to the jeep and Gurley's sergeant drove them to a large parking lot behind Gurley's quarters. Gurley's car was a pristine condition maroon Oldsmobile. Ingrid would have guessed he'd had it especially imported if she hadn't seen a few of them on the streets of London. She couldn't understand the appeal of something so solid and cumbersome. Until she climbed inside. It was like stepping into an air conditioned ranch house. She sank into the gray and maroon upholstery of the passenger seat and did her best to keep her eyes open.

The eight mile drive into the village took no time at all. Gurley parked on the street rather than using the parking lot of the Hare and Hounds. How he thought the Oldsmobile was any less conspicuous than a regular US Air Force issue jeep, Ingrid hadn't been able to work out during the ride over. On the street or in the parking lot, the car positively glowed with its American credentials. They might as well have made an announcement on a bullhorn when they drove into the center of the village.

"You ready for this?" Gurley asked as he put on the handbrake.

Why was he even asking her that? She wondered if maybe she had fallen asleep at some point during the trip from the base—after all, she'd only managed a couple hours' sleep the night before. "Me? Ready for anything. Always."

"That your personal motto?"

Ingrid smiled. She hadn't thought about it that way before, but maybe it was. Maybe she should get some bumper stickers printed.

When they got inside the Hare and Hounds they found a young bearded man serving drinks. The place was pretty empty—but then it was only eleven-thirty a.m. Ingrid scanned the room. It was decorated in a traditional English country style, horse brasses and leather tack hung from the dark, wooden beams and silver-colored tankards lined high ledges around the walls. She thought it was trying a little too hard to look authentic and wondered if maybe the pub had opened just a few years ago.

"We're looking for your boss, Yvonne Sherwood?" Gurley said.

The man gave him a wry smile. "She's not my boss." He came from behind the bar and hollered into the adjoining room. "Mum! There's some tall bloke asking for you."

"Is he dark and handsome too?" came the muffled reply.

"Well, he's not my type—you'll have to judge for yourself."

Gurley shifted his weight from one foot to the other. He cleared his throat.

The barman returned to the bar. "She'll be with you in a minute. Can I get you a drink?" He glanced at Ingrid and smiled broadly at her, as if he hadn't noticed her before. He leaned his elbows on the bar and rested his chin on a fist. "Now my day just got a whole lot better. What can I get you?"

"Nothing, we're fine, thank you," Gurley said.

A forty-something petite woman with a nice smile and a pink flush to her cheeks appeared at the bar, drying her hands on a dish towel. "You are tall." She looked up into Gurley's face. "And handsome enough, I suppose." She smiled more broadly. "What can I do for you?" She laid her bony hands flat on the bar.

Ingrid stepped forward, her badge already in her hand. "Good morning, ma'am. I'm Agent Skyberg from the US embassy and this is Major Jack Gurley—he works in Security Forces at RAF Freckenham. We'd like to speak to you about Kyle Foster."

The nice smile disappeared so quickly it was as if it had been slapped off the woman's face.

"Why? Has something happened?"

"You know the police are looking for him?"

"Yes, of course I do. I mean has anything new happened. Is he all right?"

"Is who all right, ma'am?"

The two old men drinking nearby had stopped their conversation and shuffled a little closer.

The woman hesitated. "Well, Tommy, of course. Do you have news about Tommy?"

Ingrid stepped right up to the bar and rested her hands very close to Sherwood's. "Is there some place a little more *private* we can speak?"

A flash of panic flitted across the woman's face. "Something has happened, hasn't it?" She lifted a hand to her mouth. "Oh my God!"

Sherwood's son supported her arm and led her into the other main room of the pub—a dining area. He indicated to Ingrid and Gurley to follow. Gurley glanced at Ingrid. Ingrid shrugged back at him. The woman's response had seemed a little extreme, in the circumstances. They hadn't actually explained what it was about Foster they wanted to discuss. She was leaping to her own negative conclusions. Ingrid wondered if that meant the woman had a guilty conscience.

Once they were settled at a corner table, well away from any curious customers, Ingrid started over. "We'd like to speak to you about Kyle Foster because we believe he may try to contact you."

The woman said nothing. Her gaze was focused in the middle distance.

"Has he made contact with you since yesterday morning?"

Yvonne Sherwood's eyes opened wide, her lips parted slightly. After a beat she seemed to recover. "Why would he contact me?"

"We have reason to believe you know First Lieutenant Foster quite well," Ingrid said, not wanting to reveal the details of Glen Cooper's sighting just yet.

"Who told you that?"

"Do you know him?"

"He comes in for a drink now and then. But that's true for a lot of men from the base. Doesn't mean I know them all." She started to scratch her forearm as if something was irritating her skin.

"We believe he may try to return to the area."

"Surely he knows this is the worst place he could come."

"Can you explain what you mean by that?"

"If he doesn't want to get caught, why would he come back here?"

"Perhaps he wants to give himself up."

Sherwood shook her head. "Why would he?"

"But surely that would be better for Kyle, better for Tommy. Better for everyone. Don't you want to see him safely in custody?" Ingrid did her best to keep her expression as neutral as possible. She didn't want to influence the woman's response.

The bar manager swallowed. "Of course. We all want to make sure Tommy's safe. But I was just trying to put myself in Kyle's position."

Gurley leaned back in his chair. His gaze hadn't left the woman's face.

"Can you think why he might come back here?" Ingrid continued.

"I can't imagine, that seems like a stupid thing to do. Are you sure you've got your facts straight? Who told you he was going to come back?"

"We can't share that information with you, I'm afraid, ma'am." Ingrid leaned in a little closer. "How well do you know Kyle Foster?"

Sherwood stopped scratching her arm. Her nails had left long red marks. "I told you. I don't really know him at all. He comes in here every Saturday with some of the other dads from football. They have a couple of drinks. Maybe play some pool. The kids amuse themselves outside—we have a climbing frame and swings in the garden. My son plays for the team too."

Ingrid glanced over her shoulder toward the bar in the other room.

"Not Marcus! My youngest, Luke."

"So does your husband take Luke to the match every week? Maybe he knows Kyle a little better? Maybe we should speak to him."

"I don't have a husband."

"Oh, I'm sorry."

"No need to be sorry—he's not dead or anything. A dead weight, maybe. That's why I got rid of him. Useless lazy sod." Her nostrils flared slightly. "I take Luke to football, Marcus looks after everything here."

"Did you ever get a sense from Foster or Tommy that there might have been problems at home? Anything that might have indicated a recent change in Kyle Foster's state of mind?"

"No, I'm sure everything at home was fine. There's nothing wrong with Kyle Foster's mind." She answered emphatically, without a moment's hesitation.

Ingrid wondered how Sherwood could be so sure if she hardly knew Foster. She glanced at Gurley.

"I know what they keep saying on the news about all that post traumatic whatnot, making a big thing of it," Sherwood said, unprompted. "I heard one of the other dads talk to Kyle about it once. There'd been documentary on the television about PTSD. How it was under-diagnosed in the army. Kyle said he'd seen a few of his Air Force buddies really get it bad."

While she was talking about Foster the expression on her face had softened. It was obvious to Ingrid that she liked the guy.

"Kyle Foster was seen in the village early this morning." Gurley blurted, no doubt getting impatient with the way Ingrid's questioning was going. "There's no point in protecting him, it'll only make things worse. Did he contact you?"

What the hell did he think he was doing?

"I've already told you that he hasn't!"

Ingrid glared at Gurley.

Sherwood stood up. "I think I've answered enough of your questions. I'd like you to leave now."

Reluctantly, Ingrid rose to her feet. She held out a business card to Sherwood, who folded her arms and looked away. Ingrid slipped it onto the table instead. "If he should contact you, it really would be in his best interests if you told us about it. Or the police."

They left the bar and Ingrid strode back to the car. For once, Gurley ambled. Then he turned around and stared at the doorway of the pub, where Yvonne Sherwood and her son were standing, defiant expressions on their faces. He walked the remaining few steps backwards, keeping his gaze fixed on them.

"Thanks for your input," Ingrid said, using all her will power not to raise her voice. "I think we really made some progress with her."

"You know as well as I do she's lying. You saw how uncomfortable she got. Foster could be holed up in her basement right now for all we know."

Ingrid watched Sherwood and her son turn away from the door. There was definitely something about the woman's demeanor that didn't feel right. She seemed too eager to come to Foster's defense. "OK—let's say you're right. Let's say she has heard from Foster."

"You're actually agreeing with me?"

"If you are right, there's only one option open to us."

"I can have a half dozen men here in under fifteen minutes."

"That's not the option I had in mind." Ingrid retrieved her cell from her purse. "I'm calling the local cops."

23

Ingrid and Gurley were waiting outside the Hare and Hounds when the detective sergeant heading up the search of the pub appeared at the door, his head down, his hands buried deep in his pockets.

"Nothing," he said as he approached them.

The search warrant had been arranged quickly. Ingrid and Gurley had stayed in the Oldsmobile, watching the exits of the pub while they waited for the police to arrive. The search itself had taken less than thirty minutes.

"Nothing at all?" Gurley said.

"I did spot a couple of pork pies in the kitchen well beyond their 'best-before' date that environmental health might want to know about. But I don't suppose that's something you'd be interested in." He wrinkled his nose as if the aroma of the offending pies was lingering in his nostrils. "You still haven't told me—what made you think Foster had come back to the area in the first place?"

Gurley shot Ingrid a look. He really should learn to trust her. As if she would say anything to contradict him. She waited with anticipation for his reply.

"A policeman's hunch. I guess you get them all the time too, huh? The key thing is to determine which ones you should pay any attention to. On this occasion I called it wrong."

Ingrid could see Gurley struggling to maintain a light tone. She knew he still thought he was right about Yvonne Sherwood harboring a fugitive.

"Is it possible something could have been missed? Another room inside that your men haven't seen? You were awful fast in there." Gurley asked.

"Do you know how much pressure is on us to track Foster down?" The cop's previously jovial tone disappeared in an instant. Ingrid couldn't blame him, Gurley was more or less accusing his team of being incompetent. "Are you seriously suggesting we wouldn't do a thorough job?"

Gurley held up his hands. "OK, OK—you made your point already."

"We're sorry to have wasted your time on this," Ingrid said, hoping a little polite interjection might diffuse the tension between the two men.

"Do you think maybe I could take a quick look around inside before you pack up and go?"

Gurley just wouldn't quit.

"Unless the proprietor invites you in especially, you're not getting anywhere near the place." The detective shook his head in disbelief and walked away.

"What were they looking for in there? A man hiding in a closet?" Gurley said when the cop was still well within earshot.

"They know what they're doing. Can you just admit that maybe you misjudged Sherwood?"

"And you didn't?"

Ingrid watched the last of the cops trudge out of the pub and back to the police vehicle. "OK—I admit there was something about her that didn't feel right. Maybe she's importing liquor without paying taxes. It's possible she was hiding something. It just wasn't Foster." Ingrid walked around to the passenger side of Gurley's car.

"Are we going somewhere?" he asked her.

"Back to the base."

"What for?"

"There's something I want to take a look at."

———

Back at RAF Freckenham, Gurley parked up behind his quarters. The jeep was already waiting to convey them to the family quarters on the far eastern side of the compound.

"I had my team search the house yesterday, as soon as I was told what Foster had done. They didn't find anything." Gurley said as they stepped inside the Fosters' dinky little two-story house. "What are you looking for?"

"Not a man in a closet."

Ingrid headed for the living room first. A worn couch and armchair took up most of the space, both were angled towards a forty-eight-inch flat screen TV. Framed pictures of the two children adorned the walls. A large plastic crate stuffed with kids toys was shoved in a corner. Beyond the living area was the kitchen. It was big enough to incorporate a small dining table and four chairs. A refrigerator stood in one corner, so tall it almost reached the ceiling. Ingrid pulled open the door. It was pretty much full of groceries. Strange that the Fosters had such a well-stocked fridge when they were planning to go away for a few days. Ingrid wondered if the trip was a last minute decision. Something else they should ask Carrie Foster.

Ingrid opened up the freezer. Apart from the usual cartons of ice cream and frozen vegetables, containers of what she supposed was frozen breast milk were stacked inside.

"How old is Molly?" she asked Gurley.

"Fourteen months," he said quickly.

"Isn't that a little old for breast feeding?"

"Hey—don't ask me. I've managed to avoid that kind of knowledge my whole life." He pulled out one of the containers and held it up to the light as if it might yield some clue. "It looks almost green. Maybe it's really old."

Ingrid checked another container for a date. Stuck on the bottom was a little strip of tape with the digits 07-24 written in thick black Sharpie. "Last month. I guess it keeps frozen as long as any other kind of milk." She screwed up her face. She felt sorry for Carrie Foster having to express the stuff, then label up the container and carefully place it next to the frozen dessert. Ingrid's mom had given her formula just as soon as she could. She grabbed the pot from Gurley's hand and shoved both containers back in the freezer drawer. Then she turned around and headed toward the front door. She paused at the foot of the stairs leading up to the second floor. "Are you OK?"

Gurley nodded back at her unconvincingly.

"Your face looks a little pale. Was it handling the breast milk?"

"Not at all. Just remembered the sight of little Molly lying in that hospital bed."

"We should check to see how she's doing—it's possible Radcliffe wouldn't bother to keep us informed." Ingrid pulled out her cell. She needed to call Radcliffe anyway to give him an update on the local situation. Better that he heard it from her rather than the Suffolk cops. Just as she opened her contacts list the phone vibrated in her hand. An out of area number. She looked at Gurley.

"Hey—you go right ahead. It's not as if we have a man to hunt down here."

Ingrid hesitated for a beat. *Screw Gurley.* She answered the call. Thankfully her gamble paid off: it wasn't Svetlana. "Hey, Mike. I'm in the middle of something right now, can I call you back?"

"It won't take a minute, I was just checking you got the mp3 files I sent you."

"You did?"

"Yep—audio interviews of the two women. I finally got a hold of them. Thought you'd want them right away."

"Thanks Mike. I'll check my email account later. I really appreciate your help."

"Hey—glad to be of service."

She said goodbye and hung up.

"You all done?"

"It's another case I'm working on—I can't just drop everything else."

"You should feel free to go right back to it. I have everything under control here."

Ingrid decided not to remind him about the fruitless search of the Hare and Hounds. She wasn't sure he had anything under control at all. She bounded up the stairs. At the top, straight ahead of her, was the open door leading into the bathroom. The room was small by US standards, but big compared to the tiny shower rooms she'd seen in people's apartments in London. There was a bathtub and a separate shower cubicle, and a sink beside the toilet. Above the sink was a mirrored cabinet. Ingrid opened the door. Inside were the usual items: shaving paraphernalia, deodorant, painkillers, and a small unlabeled bottle of pills. Ingrid reached in for it and checked the reverse—no label there either. She opened the childproof cap and shook a few pills into her hand. Small blue and white capsules rolled around her palm. She returned all but one of them to the bottle and screwed on the lid. She held the capsule between thumb and forefinger, trying to read what was printed in tiny letters on the side. After some serious focusing, she made out a manufacturer's name, a four digit number on one side and a dosage: 30mg, on the other. There was no indication what the drug was called.

"Do you know what it is?" Gurley asked her.

Ingrid had no idea. But she knew a woman who would. Meanwhile, she didn't want Gurley jumping to any conclusions about what they'd found. They didn't even know if the unmarked bottle belonged to Kyle Foster or his wife. "It's a medication for…" She wanted to choose something Gurley wouldn't question. "For severe menstrual cramping."

"Really?"

It seemed Gurley questioned everything no matter what.

"Sure. I take them myself sometimes." She waited for Gurley to turn away before she slipped the single pill into her pants pocket, then followed him into the next room—the kids' bedroom. On one side of the room was a narrow single bed, a Spiderman comforter cover draped over the edge. On the other was a wooden cot, a furry animal mobile suspended above it. On a dresser next to the cot was a baby monitor.

It all seemed so regular. So normal. How could it have gone so wrong?

The final room was the master bedroom. Gurley hesitated at the door. "What was it you were hoping to find in here, anyway?" he asked.

"Don't you think it's worth looking? Just in case we uncover something your team may have missed?" She pushed past him into the room and opened up the closet. Carrie Foster had a lot of shoes, or at least, a lot of shoe boxes. Ingrid glanced along the row of rectangular cardboard containers. The box furthest away from her had a dark stain in one corner. She reached into the closet and grabbed it. The cardboard was wet. She pulled off the lid. Inside was a bottle of vodka, its top a little loose.

Gurley finally made it into the room. "Kyle Foster is a secret drinker?"

"I found it on Carrie's side of the closet."

"Where better for him to hide his nasty little habit?"

"I would think pretty much the worst place ever." Ingrid had no reason to believe it didn't belong to Carrie Foster.

A bang sounded downstairs. "Hello? Carrie? Are you back? Did you know your door is wide open?"

Ingrid shoved the bottle back in its box and shoved the box back in the closet.

24

A few seconds later, a youngish, dark-haired, pale-skinned woman dressed in a light summer dress and baggy cardigan appeared in the hallway.

"Jesus Christ! Who the hell are—" She turned her head and saw Gurley. "Oh, I see." She wrapped her arms around the cardigan, hugging herself as if a sudden chill had blown into the room. "Does this mean? Is Molly...?"

"As far as we know Molly's condition hasn't changed." Ingrid reminded herself again to check in with Radcliffe.

"Should you even be in here? What are you doing here anyhow?" The woman's accent was pure south Boston. "Is this even legal?" She marched over to Gurley. "You can't go rummaging through people's private, personal stuff." She held her head up high. "You got no right to do that."

Ingrid introduced herself quickly, then explained, "We're only here because it may assist us in finding Tommy. Anything that helps track him down is worth doing, wouldn't you say?"

The woman hadn't taken her eyes off Gurley. "I want Tommy to be found as much as anyone. I'm just looking out for Carrie."

"We appreciate that—I'm sure Carrie does too. Maybe I could ask you a few questions?" Ingrid was careful to use the singular pronoun. As she did, she made sure to stare at Gurley and raise her eyebrows, hoping he'd take the hint.

He stood his ground. It was obvious this woman wasn't going to speak freely in front of a member of Security Forces, why wouldn't he just accept that?

"Major Gurley, I don't want to keep you any longer than necessary," Ingrid said. "I can make sure the property is secure when I leave." She nodded expectantly at him. "Didn't you say you had to report to the... ah... general with an update?"

Gurley finally tore his gaze from Carrie Foster's friend and gave Ingrid such a disdainful look it was as if she'd just insulted his family going back three generations.

"Sure—I'll be right back." He slipped past the woman who was now practically scowling at him. She watched him leave before she said another word.

"I don't know what I can tell you that'll help find Kyle and Tommy." She walked over to the window and watched Gurley stride back to the jeep. "Arrogant bastard," she murmured under her breath. She smoothed down a corner of the lilac and pink throw that covered the bed. "I don't know what's gotten into Kyle." She shook her head. "How could he do a thing like that?"

"Did you know they were planning a trip to London?"

"Carrie never mentioned it."

"But you'd say you and Carrie are quite close?"

"I'm the closest thing she's got to a best friend. I don't understand why she never told me about the trip. It's been bugging the crap out of me."

Ingrid was surprised the women were so close: judging by their accents alone they were from different social classes. But she supposed the Air Force threw people together that wouldn't normally mix in civilian life. "You haven't spoken to her since she left?"

"I tried calling when I saw what happened on the news. But I think her cell must be out of juice. It goes straight to voicemail." She shook her head again. "She must be going through hell."

"She's coping. Spending most of her time with Molly."

"Can you get a message to her from me?"

"Sure."

"Tell her we're all thinking of her. We're all praying Molly pulls through."

"I'll let her know." Ingrid smiled at the woman. "It'd help if you told me your name."

The woman opened her eyes wide. "I forgot you didn't know it. Rachelle. Rachelle Carver."

"Shall we go downstairs, Rachelle? Sit down and get a little more comfortable?"

"I can't stay long. My eldest is looking after his two sisters. I only left the house to pick up a few groceries from the commissary."

Ingrid led the way downstairs to the living room.

"Do you mind if we step outside?" the woman asked. "I need a smoke." She was out of the front door and pulling a pack of cigarettes from the pocket of her cardigan before Ingrid had a chance to answer. "Can't do this at home. Mustn't set a bad example, huh?" She offered Ingrid a cigarette.

"Not for me, thanks."

"You can judge me all you like. Doesn't bother me."

"I wasn't judging at all. Every time I tried smoking when I was a teenager, I just threw up," she lied.

"I need all the help I can get." She drew deeply on the cigarette and blew smoke from her nostrils.

"Help?"

"Getting through the next eighteen months of Billy's tour of duty in this shit hole of a country."

"You're having a tough time?" It wasn't the way Ingrid would have described the UK. So far she had a pretty good impression of the place. But then she'd spent most of her time in the capital. Freckenham seemed a nice enough village. She wondered if Rachelle Carver had actually ever ventured far beyond the base.

"I miss my friends, my family. A decent pizza."

"I guess every military wife posted abroad feels the same way."

"You think I'm whining about it?"

"Not at all—I can imagine how difficult it must be. Is it like that for Carrie too?"

She puffed smoke over Ingrid's head. "That's not for me to say."

"I'm just trying to get a picture of her life here."

"Maybe you should ask her."

"She has other things on her mind right now."

Rachelle Carver narrowed her eyes as she exhaled again. She stared at Ingrid through a cloud of smoke. "Carrie doesn't talk about home a whole lot."

"Yet she seems like such a family-oriented person."

Rachelle continued to puff on her cigarette as if she were in a race to finish it, but didn't comment.

"How well do you know Kyle?"

"I only know him through Carrie. So not really that well at all."

"But well enough to form some kind of opinion of him?"

"What are you getting at?"

"Did you like him?"

"I think he must have fooled a lot of people. He seemed like a regular, straight-up kinda guy. If anyone had asked me two days ago, I'd say he adored his wife and kids. Couldn't do enough for them. Just shows you how wrong you can be about somebody." She took another long pull on her cigarette then flicked the glowing butt away. "Maybe he went on one mission too many. Maybe something cracked inside him that couldn't be fixed."

"But you can't blame him for that."

"If you've got a nervous disposition, you shouldn't join the military. My Billy went on three tours in Afghanistan. He's just fine. You can't blame the job for something that happens in your own head."

Ingrid thought Rachelle's little speech sounded less than convincing. As if she were reciting a script rather than telling her what she really thought. Maybe she was just repeating what her husband had told her. "But up until what happened on Monday, Kyle seemed like one of the good guys?" Ingrid asked.

"A regular superhero. For a while there, Carrie and Kyle seemed like the perfect couple. If you want the truth… I was a little jealous of their relationship. I thank God now mine is nothing like theirs."

"Perfect in what way?"

"Every way. Kyle doted on Carrie and Tommy."

"And Molly?"

Rachelle considered her answer. "Sure—I guess. But now that Kyle hurt her so bad… Jeez, I don't know. Who am I to make a judgment?"

"You think maybe Kyle was closer to Tommy than Molly?"

"I've been going over things in my mind since it happened—driving myself half crazy trying to work out why he did what he did. Looking for clues in his behavior, you know?"

"And have you come to any conclusions?"

Rachelle shook her head. "Not really. Except maybe… It's not my place to comment."

"Whatever you tell me is in the strictest confidence."

"I don't know. Feels like I'm betraying Carrie's trust."

"What if you don't tell me something that could have helped find Tommy? Whatever you tell me can only help Carrie right now."

Rachelle took a deep breath. "You swear this is between you and me?"

"You have my word."

The woman raised her eyebrows as if Ingrid's word meant nothing to her.

"After Molly was born I noticed a change in the way Carrie and Kyle were with one another. It was a gradual thing, like they just grew apart. New babies can do that to people sometimes. If I'm completely honest? I guess Carrie started to withdraw from Kyle. I figured they'd work through it. I think Carrie did too. Turns out we were both wrong." She played with the pack of cigarettes, turning it over and over in her hands. "You will give Carrie that message, won't you?"

"Absolutely."

"Maybe I should send something to the hospital. A card or something, can I do that?"

"I think she'd like that. If you want to really help, maybe you could arrange for all the fresh produce in Carrie's refrigerator to be disposed of?"

"The fridge is full of food?"

Ingrid nodded.

"Why would she go grocery shopping if she was going away?"

"I asked myself the same question. Maybe Carrie knew nothing about the trip. Maybe Kyle surprised her."

"I guess." Rachelle shoved the cigarettes into a pocket. "I should be getting back to the kids. Before the third world war breaks out."

Ingrid handed her a business card. "Any time you want to speak to me, if you think of anything that might help us locate Kyle and Tommy, just call."

Rachelle stared down at the card. "You know, Kyle really was a good husband. And a good dad. I can't believe what he did." She glanced over Ingrid's shoulder and tensed for a moment.

Ingrid turned around and saw Gurley approaching. "MPs really are as unpopular as their reputation, huh?"

"I just don't trust the guy."

"Gurley? Why?"

She shrugged and slipped Ingrid's card into her pocket. "Forget I mentioned it. I spoke out of turn. OK?" She hurried away.

25

"What were you talking about?" Gurley eyed Ingrid suspiciously as he approached.

"Do you have a problem with Rachelle?"

"No, why would I?"

"Earlier, upstairs… the atmosphere seemed a little tense."

"Don't know what you're talking about." He stared at Rachelle as she scurried away. "What did she tell you?"

"She just wanted to know how Carrie and Molly were doing. She's concerned."

"And what did you tell her?"

"That Carrie was doing OK, in the circumstances."

"You think so?" He started chewing the inside of his lip.

"I had to be a little upbeat."

"Did you find out anything from her that might help locate Foster?"

"Not really. But she did tell me Carrie and Kyle were the perfect couple before Molly was born."

"She did?"

"Maybe Carrie spent a little too much time with the new baby and Kyle felt excluded. Maybe that was when Kyle's problems started."

Gurley shoved his hands in his pockets.

"Where have you been?" she asked him.

"Speaking to the medical officer."

"The one treating Foster's PTSD?"

He nodded.

"What did she tell you?"

"Not much more than what was in his medical report."

Ingrid wasn't sure she believed him. "Maybe I should speak to her too."

"We're not supposed to be duplicating work."

"She must have been able to give you some background."

"Do you know how many service personnel and their families she treats in a week?"

"Surely not that many suffering from PTSD."

"Foster's been going to regular counseling sessions, making good progress, she said."

"And that's all she had to say?"

"There was nothing more to say."

"What did she make of what happened in London?"

Gurley looked away.

"Major?"

He screwed up his face. "She was surprised. Shocked. He seemed to be doing fine, she said. She thought he had his anger issues under control." He folded his arms. "Just shows you how anyone can make mistakes."

Ingrid wasn't happy that Gurley had interviewed the doctor without her. Was there something he wasn't sharing? "Does the doctor have any inkling what his next move might be?"

"I didn't bother to ask her. I knew she wouldn't know a damn thing about it."

"So, what's next?"

"We both know the manager of the bar was lying."

"About something, maybe."

"So we go back to the village and watch her for a while. See where she goes. See who visits her."

It wasn't the dumbest idea, and in the absence of anything better, Ingrid couldn't really object. "OK—but we limit the surveillance to a couple of hours."

"How about six hours and I'll buy you dinner after?"

"How about four and you promise me you weren't actually asking me out."

"Have no fear of that. You're really not my type. No offense. Four hours and you can buy yourself a pizza, eat it all on your lonesome."

"Deal."

After Ingrid had updated both DCI Radcliffe and Sol Franklin, she and

Gurley returned to the village in a less conspicuous vehicle than his Oldsmobile. Gurley had somehow managed to get hold of a beat up Land Rover that blended right into the rural surroundings. Ingrid insisted she drive and that Gurley slide down in the passenger seat as far as he could and wear a dark knitted hat over his bright blond crew cut. He was a difficult man to disguise.

Ingrid parked forty or so yards from the Hare and Hounds, making sure they had a clear view of the front and rear exits. Unless the pub had some kind of tunnel leading from its basement to a neighboring property, they'd be able to observe anyone leaving or entering the premises. She looked at her watch. "Four hours."

Half an hour into their surveillance, Ingrid's cell phone beeped with a text message. It was from Ralph Mills. She'd been letting his calls go to voicemail since their date on Monday night—she didn't want to be distracted by him in the middle of a manhunt. Not that he'd called her that often. In fact, he'd probably judged the amount of attention he was giving her just about right. His messages had been sweet and funny. He wasn't hassling her for another date, just letting her know she was on his mind. Given she had nothing better to do for the next three and a half hours, she couldn't see any reason not to reply. She didn't want him thinking she wasn't interested. She quickly tapped a message into her phone:

Good thnx, u? on stake out w/ gurley need entertainment

She could sense Gurley was glancing toward her. He was somehow managing to demonstrate his disapproval merely by altering the pattern of his breathing.

Only jokes i know are infantile or adolescent… sorry to disappoint
How about a poem?
There was a young lady from minnesota, who… used up the state's hog feed quota
Is that it?
Her pigs were so big, she needed to dig…
Huh?
Nope sorry… run out of rhymes

Gurley let out a long sigh and shifted in his seat. "If this mission is getting in the way of something more important, I could just complete it without you."

Ingrid turned to look at him. His expression was fixed in a grimace. He really wasn't joking. "From now on, it has my undivided attention. How about that?" She tapped another quick message to Ralph:

Expect u to get it finished by next time i see u

She hesitated before sending. That reply would mean she was suggesting another date. She considered deleting it, but with Gurley breathing down her neck, she hit send before she got to the end of the thought process. Ralph had almost written her a limerick, for God's sake. No one had ever done that for her before. That fact alone was definitely worthy of a second date.

I'll do my best... good luck with mission/gurley

Ingrid's phone buzzed again twenty minutes later: Natasha McKittrick calling. She dismissed the call, not wanting to give Gurley another excuse to question her commitment to the case. Her phone vibrated again to let her know she had a voice message. Dammit, Gurley was making her feel like a misbehaving schoolgirl. She turned away toward the driver window, shoved the phone against her right ear, and listened to the message.

"What have you done to my detective?" McKittrick said, her tone completely deadpan. "He's got the stupidest grin on his face and is practically bloody useless. I've had to send him out for coffee in the hope that the fresh air might blow some sense into him. Call me as soon as you pick this up."

Smiling to herself, Ingrid deleted the voicemail and slipped the phone into a pocket.

"Whoever that was, she has a voice that carries," Gurley informed her. "You might want to let her know."

"Thanks for the tip."

"I'm so glad this operation is giving you plenty of time to organize your social engagements."

Why was Gurley so pissed at her? She wondered if maybe he didn't have much of a social life himself. Working in Security Forces on a base in the middle of the English countryside had to be a pretty lonely existence. Maybe she should feel sorry for the guy.

Three and three-quarter hours later, just as the daylight was starting to fade and Ingrid's behind was aching due to the thin layer of foam between the worn upholstery and the rock hard driver's seat, she turned to Gurley. "I think maybe we should call it a day."

Gurley tapped a big forefinger on his watch. "Fifteen more minutes."

"Nothing's going to happen now." Ingrid adjusted her position and tried to shake some feeling back into her numb right foot.

"You agreed to four hours."

"OK!" She threw up her hands in surrender.

A few minutes later, Yvonne Sherwood appeared at the door of the pub. She was carrying a large sports bag. The woman struggled with the bag to a nearby car and dumped it on the passenger seat.

Gurley mumbled something about patience being a virtue and slid a little further down into his seat. "Remember not to get too close." There was a definite smug tone to his voice.

"I have tailed a few vehicles in my time." Ingrid could tell Gurley was frustrated not to be sitting behind the wheel.

The pub manager's dinky silver car pulled away from the curb and Ingrid started up the Land Rover once there was a distance of fifty or so yards between the two vehicles.

The silver car stopped a minute later outside the convenience store and Yvonne Sherwood jumped out. She looked up and down the street, her gaze lingering in their direction for more seconds than was comfortable.

Ingrid held her breath.

A moment later Sherwood turned away and disappeared inside the store. She re-emerged after a few minutes with a bag of groceries. She shoved the bag onto the passenger seat of the car. Then, instead of getting back behind the wheel, she returned to the store. She pulled something from her purse and headed for the ATM next to the door. She removed the thick wad of cash that came out of the slot, found another card in her purse and repeated the process. They watched her do the same thing with another two cards, then shove all the cash into a pocket.

"Goddammit," Gurley said, when Sherwood headed back to her car. "I knew I was right about her."

26

In the deepening gloom Ingrid and Gurley trailed behind Yvonne Sherwood for fifteen minutes, not daring to put on the headlights of the Land
Rover, edging along the narrow country lanes.

"We're going to lose her, put your foot on the gas." Gurley was leaning
so close to the windshield, his nose was practically pressed up against the
glass.

"Maybe now's the time to call the cops. Get some backup."

"They made their attitude quite clear this morning. I won't have them
swarming all over the countryside and screwing everything up. We call
them when she's led us to Foster."

"If that's where she's going. We're still working on a hunch here. What
if we lose her?" They turned a sharp bend in the road and Ingrid could just
make out the beams from Sherwood's headlights in the distance. It felt
more like luck than judgment.

"Maintain this speed and we won't lose her. We don't need backup. I'm
not sure the local cops could find their own asses with a— What the f—"

Ingrid yanked the steering wheel hard right and stamped on the brake
as an overhanging branch loomed up at the windshield in the twilight. She
yanked the wheel in the opposite direction just a few inches from a dense
thicket on the far side of the road. Her heart lurched in her chest. She felt
as though Gurley was watching her every move, waiting for her to make a
mistake. She was determined not to give him the satisfaction. "You must

work with the cops here all the time. Are you seriously suggesting they can't do their job?"

"I don't work with them a whole lot. They leave us to deal with our men as the Air Force sees fit. They get on with their business and leave us to ours. And that's just the way I like it."

"I'm sure they're really not as bad as you make out." Ingrid didn't know why she was defending the local force, but now she'd started she felt as though she had to follow through. "I've worked with a lot worse police departments Stateside."

"Then maybe the whole world is screwed."

"Yet military cops remain shining examples of perfect policing that everyone else should emulate? You don't have such a great record your-selves. Maybe you should think twice before you start throwing stones."

"I can only judge on what I've seen so far. And it don't impress me much."

"As long as you know I'm calling the cops as soon as we get Foster." Ingrid squeezed the steering wheel harder.

"That's just fine with me."

"Good."

"Great."

After another couple of minutes twisting around tight bends, the road straightened and Ingrid could clearly see the taillights of Sherwood's little Nissan a hundred or so yards ahead of them. Fifty yards later the silver car slowed right down and took a left. Ingrid drove past the dirt track Sher-wood had disappeared down and stopped on the other side of the road. As she came to a halt, the driver side wheels sank into a ditch and the Land Rover lurched sideways.

Gurley huffed out a sigh.

"Maybe you should have brought along the night vision goggles." Ingrid used the flashlight function on her phone to avoid landing in the ditch herself as she climbed out.

They both closed their doors quietly and jogged back to the dirt track. "She might be driving miles down here," Ingrid whispered.

"Lucky we're both in such good shape, wouldn't you say?" Gurley lengthened his stride.

Unlike Gurley's, Ingrid's boots weren't designed for uneven terrain. She did her best to tread carefully and avoid the worst of the exposed stones and random divots underfoot. Right now, straining or twisting her ankle would be nothing short of disaster. Forced to make two strides for every one of Gurley's, she felt a little like a small child trying to keep up with its older sibling. After a few more strides she picked up pace a little and overtook him. As she passed, she noticed his breathing seemed labored. Maybe he wasn't as fit as he'd claimed.

Less than two hundred yards down the track, Ingrid saw the Nissan parked up close to a wide wooden gate. The interior light was on, but there was no sign of Sherwood inside the vehicle. Ingrid shoved out her hand in front of Gurley, who had already slowed down. They ducked sideways into a nearby hedge.

"Where the hell is she?" Gurley whispered.

"Wait a second."

A moment later, the top of Yvonne Sherwood's head appeared above the headrest of the driver's seat. As Ingrid had suspected, the woman had been bending low over the passenger seat, where she'd dumped the heavy sports bag and the groceries earlier. She then climbed out of the car, ran around to the passenger side and, with some effort, heaved the bag out. She hauled it onto her back and immediately seemed six inches shorter.

"What does she have in there?" Gurley leaned out of their hiding place to get a better look. "We have to move in closer."

"Can we just wait for a moment?" Ingrid grabbed his arm and pulled him toward her.

They watched in silence as the petite manager of the Hare and Hounds struggled to the wooden gate with the bag. She fumbled with something where the gate met the gate post, then shook the gate with both hands in frustration. With great effort she heaved the bag over the top of the gate and let it fall on the other side. It landed with a loud metallic clank that echoed down the track. Sherwood then climbed the gate and swung one leg over, sitting on the top for a few seconds, staring toward the muddy field beyond.

She awkwardly swung her other leg over and jumped down the other side. Then she grabbed hold of the heavy bag and dragged it behind her as she stumbled toward the middle of the empty field.

Crouching low, Gurley quickly slipped across the dirt track. He reached the fence that ran alongside the field, and, still keeping his head low, headed toward the gate. Ingrid followed him. Although her eyes were adjusting to the gloom, the darkness seemed to be closing in on them fast. If it hadn't been for the light pink sweat top Yvonne Sherwood was wearing, Ingrid might have lost sight of her all together. She strained her eyes a little harder and managed to figure out the bar manager's destination. Two-thirds of the way across the field was a small trailer. It looked like it had no wheels. Its windows were boarded with wooden planks and the door was hanging half off.

A few feet ahead of Ingrid, a good thirty or so yards from the gate, Gurley stopped. He pulled a small pair of binoculars from a pocket.

"Can you see any sign of life inside that trailer?" Ingrid asked. "Can you see anything at all?"

"I can't see anything happening on the inside and Sherwood is at least fifty feet away from it."

Ingrid peered into the grayness of the night. She could just about make out a lonely figure standing completely still in the middle of the field. "What's she doing?"

"Looking around. Waiting." Gurley moved in closer to the fence and lowered his head. "Stay very still. She's more likely to notice movement."

"Is that so?"

"She's walking again. Headed straight toward the trailer." He slowly scanned the field with the binoculars. "No signs of life anywhere else. She's opened the trailer door now and she's putting the bag inside."

Although Gurley's running commentary was starting to grate, Ingrid wouldn't have known what the hell was happening without it.

"She's not climbing inside the trailer," he continued. "She's walking around it." Gurley watched for a few more moments then, grabbing Ingrid by the arm, dropped suddenly to the ground. "Dammit. She's headed back toward the gate." He lay flat on his belly and dragged Ingrid closer to him.

"We can't stay here. We're too exposed. She'll see us when she drives past," Ingrid hissed at him.

"We can't exactly get up and hightail it back down the track either."

Ingrid peered through the fence into the churned up field. Running along the length of it, parallel to the fence, was a trench, two-foot wide. "Can you wriggle under this wooden bar?" She hit the bottom of the fence with a fist.

"It'd be tight."

"I figure if we time it so that we roll into the ditch when she's climbing over the gate and stay low, she won't notice us."

"You're suggesting we roll into a ditch?"

"You have a better suggestion, then make it fast." Even without binoculars, Ingrid could see Sherwood was striding quickly across the field. She'd reach the gate in no time.

Gurley was already slithering toward the bottom of the fence.

"Deep breath in, Major."

"It's not my stomach I'm concerned about."

As Gurley wriggled closer to the fence, Ingrid noticed for the first time just how big his ass was.

Sherwood grabbed the top of the gate and started to climb.

"OK, you've got to go now," Ingrid told Gurley and watched with alarm as his buttocks got wedged beneath the low wooden strut. "Relax your glutes," she told him.

"Don't you think I'm trying to?"

Ingrid grabbed his ass and started to push.

"What do you think you're doing?"

"Helping." She shoved harder. "Come on, she's on top of the gate now. I've got to get under there too." She took hold of his hip with both hands and pushed with all her strength. Gurley's ass finally submitted and he slid the final few inches into the field. Ingrid quickly followed behind him, rolling into the ditch and onto Gurley's back. She shuffled backwards fast, into her own section of the trench, and was rewarded for her haste with a mouthful of dirt. She spat it out. She was grateful there wasn't a pool of stagnant water at the bottom of the ditch. In fact it was remarkably dry. She exhaled.

They stayed exactly where they were, not daring to move a muscle, until they'd heard the Nissan chug along the track a couple of minutes later. Ingrid lifted her head and shook dirt from her hair. Gurley adjusted his position so that he could prop the binoculars on the edge of the trench and train them toward the trailer.

"I guess all we can do now is wait."

As the cold, silent minutes passed, Ingrid wondered if she should make the most of the forced intimacy and try to get Gurley to open up a little. There was something going on with him that she couldn't put her finger on. But staring at his impassive, motionless back, she quickly decided she'd need a crowbar and a dose of sodium pentothal to make him tell her anything about himself. "Do you think Foster is hiding in an identical ditch on the opposite side of this field, watching the trailer just like us, making sure Sherwood wasn't followed?"

"We can't rule that out."

"That's got to be difficult, with an eight-year-old boy in tow."

"You're assuming Tommy's still alive."

"I'm certain he is." Something about the way Rachelle Carver spoke about Foster had convinced Ingrid that the boy was safe with his dad. She hoped to God she wasn't wrong.

"Must be nice to be so sure about things." Gurley started to lift his head, then froze. "Did you see that?"

"How can you see anything in the dark?"

"Ten o'clock, movement in the bushes. There it is again."

Ingrid saw it this time. A gray shape about a hundred yards away, making a beeline for the trailer. When the figure was just a few dozen feet from the door, Gurley lurched to his feet. He started to race across the field in the darkness, stumbling and tripping as he went, somehow managing to stay upright.

What the hell did he think he was doing? Why hadn't he waited until Foster had disappeared into the trailer? His impatience had completely blown their cover.

Ingrid scrambled to her feet, but rather than follow behind Gurley, she ran in the opposite direction, aiming to approach the trailer from the other side. Hopefully she could stop Foster if he ran away across the field.

She ran as fast as she could without losing her balance. When she was just thirty or so yards from the trailer, Gurley started yelling.

"Stop right where you are, Foster. Put your hands above your head."

From her position, the trailer was now obscuring Ingrid's view. She accelerated forward, stumbling as she went. Just a few feet away she saw a figure come hurtling around the side of the trailer.

It wasn't Gurley.

She picked up speed and hurled herself at the running man, grasping his legs and bringing him crashing to the ground in a classic quarterback tackle.

Gurley caught up with them a few seconds later. "Got you," he yelled. "You sonofabitch!"

27

The man on the ground reared up against the pressure Ingrid was applying to his butt and lower back. Gurley stamped a boot between his shoulder blades.

"You stay just where you are."

He moved his foot upwards and pressed on the man's head, forcing it further into the ground.

"Who the hell are you?" the man managed to say before his voice was muffled by the dirt.

Gurley glanced at Ingrid. The man had spoken with an English accent.

Holy crap.

Ingrid scrambled to her feet. Gurley released the man's head, grabbed his upper arms and hauled him upright as if he were as light as a child. Once he was vertical the man started to cough violently. Grabbing his knees he bent forward. He vomited onto the ground, retching for long moments. Finally he stopped, wiped a sleeve across his mouth and, gasping for breath, managed to stand up straight.

Ingrid grabbed her cell phone, found the flashlight app and shone it into the man's face. He had dark hair and dark eyes, a two inch diagonal scar across his left cheek.

"What are you doing here?" Gurley yelled into his face.

"You're American. Are you from the base?" He wriggled his shoulders. "I think you might have broken something, you know. I could sue."

"We had reason to believe you were a known fugitive." Gurley's tone was unapologetic. "Tell us what you're doing in the middle of a goddamn field in the middle of the night."

"I live here." He pointed toward the dilapidated trailer.

"You do?" Ingrid said.

"I just needed somewhere to put my head down for a couple of nights." He turned more toward Gurley. "The missus chucked me out."

"This is your trailer?"

He shook his head, cleared his throat and spat onto the ground. "I suppose it belongs to the farmer who owns the field. Not sure who that is. But it's not as if I'm doing any harm. He won't even notice."

"So no one knows you're staying here?" Gurley started walking around the trailer.

The man followed him. Ingrid brought up the rear.

"It's not exactly something I want to broadcast. I am squatting, after all. And… well, I don't want my kids to find out. It is a bit of a shit hole." He wiped his mouth again.

Gurley had reached the front of the trailer and was inspecting the door, it was hanging from one hinge. He grabbed it with both hands and yanked it from its flimsy mooring. The door snapped off like a piece of cardboard. Gurley picked up the bag Sherwood had left inside.

"Hang on," the man said, a note of panic in his voice. "That's nothing to do with me. I've never seen it before. If you're trying to plant some evidence on me… you can—"

"Yes?"

"This is my country. You can't just come over here and act as if you own the place. Bloody hell." He started rubbing his back. "You know, I think I am going to make an official complaint. What's your name?"

"I'll tell you when we get to the station house."

"The what?"

"I'm sure the police will want to speak to you. At length." Gurley smiled. Even in the dark, Ingrid could see his even white teeth gleaming. "On the plus side, at least you'll have a leak-proof roof over your head."

"Wait a minute." He peered at the bag in Gurley's hand. "You've got to believe me, that's not mine."

Gurley just stared at the man, clearly enjoying his discomfort.

"Really—I wouldn't lie to you."

Gurley reached up a hand toward the guy's head. The man immediately flinched. Gurley placed his hand on the man's shoulder and squeezed. "I'm feeling generous. So I'll give you the benefit of a doubt."

"And there's no need to tell the police anything, is there?"

Gurley turned his head toward Ingrid. "The police? No—I don't think we need to get the police involved at this stage."

"Cheers, mate—I owe you one."

Ingrid and Gurley left the man where he was and trudged across the field back to the track, Gurley keeping a tight hold of the sports bag. When they returned to the Land Rover, he unzipped it. Ingrid found a pair of nitrile gloves in her purse. She didn't have a pair large enough to stretch over Gurley's hands, so she searched the bag. Inside she discovered a small tent, two bed rolls, bread, cheese and a pint of milk, a change of clothes and a folded wad of bills.

"Seven hundred," Ingrid told Gurley after a quick count.

"Wouldn't get him that far."

"We don't know how much he has on him already. But I guess we can assume he must be running out of cash."

"And maybe getting a little desperate."

"There are kid's clothes in the bag," Ingrid said, doing her best to sound upbeat. "So maybe that means Tommy is still alive."

"Or maybe that's just what Foster wanted Sherwood to believe."

28

Ingrid parked the Land Rover right outside the entrance to the Hare and Hounds. It was just past closing time, so she was forced to bang on the door for a good minute before it opened. Marcus Sherwood stood in the doorway, arms folded defiantly across his chest.

"Jesus. Look at the state of you." He looked Ingrid up and down then past her toward Gurley, who was standing on the sidewalk, the sports bag grasped firmly in his hand.

Ingrid shook the remaining dirt from her clothes. "We're just here to return some property of your mother's."

The young barman glanced down at the bag. "Mum hasn't lost anything. I think you've made a mistake." He started to close the door.

Ingrid shoved her foot over the threshold and grabbed the doorframe with her hand. "We could do this the friendly way, or I can call the police. It doesn't actually make much difference to me. But your mom might prefer to keep this just between ourselves. Why don't you go ask her?" She stepped through the doorway, forcing Sherwood's son backwards.

"There's no need for that." Yvonne Sherwood appeared at the open interior door, a resigned, disappointed expression on her face. "You'd better come in."

Once they'd settled themselves at the same table in the dining area that they'd occupied earlier, Yvonne Sherwood told her son to go to bed.

"I'd rather stay with you. Make sure you're OK," he said.

"I can look after myself. I'll be up soon. If I'm not you can send the search party. All right?" She grabbed his hand and kissed the back of it. It seemed a peculiarly intimate gesture for a middle-aged mother and her grown-up son. But then Ingrid didn't have much to compare it to. Svetlana had never been the demonstrative type.

Once the son was gone, Gurley dragged the heavy bag around the table and unzipped it. "I guess Foster could really have used this stuff, huh?" He gently kicked at the bag with the tip of his boot. "What did he do—give you a list?"

"I don't know what you're talking about." Sherwood scooped a stained cardboard beermat from the table and started to pick at a corner of it.

"Man, it's been a long day," Gurley said. "Why is it so many people don't know what it is I'm talking about?" He turned to Ingrid. "Is it something to do with my accent? Do I talk too fast? Maybe it's my pronunciation?"

The bar manager said nothing, just peeled off a shred of the printed layer from the surface of the beermat.

"Yvonne, you are aware that aiding and abetting a suspect is a criminal offense?" Ingrid kept her voice low. "Perverting the course of justice carries a maximum sentence of life imprisonment."

"That isn't my bag. I've never seen it before."

"Your prints are all over it. And all over the seven hundred pounds inside. We saw you withdraw the cash from the ATM." Gurley sat back in his chair and interlaced his fingers across the back of his head.

"You can't threaten…" Sherwood looked from Gurley to Ingrid.

"There really is no point continuing this charade, ma'am," Gurley told her.

"Where did you find it?" Sherwood stared down at the bag.

"Right where you left it."

"I've never seen it before." She was sounding less convincing each time she repeated the lie.

"Someone got to the trailer before Foster. Seems you didn't choose your drop-off location carefully enough—someone's living there."

"What?"

"Somebody is living in the trailer."

"They've got no right."

"But it's OK for you to drop stuff there for a wanted man, huh?"

She didn't respond.

"Kyle Foster didn't get a chance to pick up what you left him," Ingrid said.

Sherwood closed her eyes.

"Are you ready to start leveling with us?" Gurley kicked at the bag again. Metal clanked against metal.

Sherwood snapped open her eyes at the sound. "The money's still inside?"

At last.

"Everything's inside." Gurley said. "I guess Kyle really needed that cash."

"Have you any idea how much trouble you're in?" Ingrid asked. "You were helping a man accused of attempted murder escape arrest, Yvonne."

"Attempted murder? That's ridiculous. Kyle wouldn't hurt a fly. He's not that sort of man."

"He's a First Lieutenant in the US Air Force. He's flown on dozens of missions. Conducted countless drone attacks. Over the years he must have killed hundreds of innocent civilians. The guy's hardly a peace loving hippy." Gurley jabbed the bag with the heel of his boot.

"He was assigned to search and rescue missions in Afghanistan. And the drone operations are for reconnaissance purposes only."

Gurley gave her a wry smile. "That's what he told you. He couldn't say anything else even if he wanted to."

"OK! But he wouldn't hurt his own flesh and blood. No way. He loves his kids. He'd do anything for them."

Gurley sat up straight. "I'm sure under normal circumstances, he wouldn't deliberately set out to hurt anyone. But under pressure, in the middle of an anxiety attack... in a blind rage? That's a whole different ball game."

"You don't know what you're talking about. Kyle just isn't like that. I've seen him have an attack. Have you?"

Gurley fanned out his thick, long fingers in the air. "Please, enlighten me."

"He doesn't go on the rampage, if that's what you're getting at."

"Really?"

"He gets very subdued, withdrawn, even."

"What brings on an attack—do you know?" Ingrid asked, wondering whether the screaming of his children would have been the thing that triggered the episode on Monday.

"Stillness. Quiet," Sherwood said without hesitation. "He can't stand it. Always has to have the radio on in the car. Or he's constantly whistling some annoying tune. Anything to fill the silence." Sherwood flipped over the beermat and started to peel the printed design off the other side. "He told me that sometimes he even goes into Tommy's room at night just to listen to his noisy breathing. He's a bit of a snorer, Tommy. My Luke is always complaining about him whenever he comes here for a sleepover."

Ingrid glanced at Gurley, wondering if he'd remembered that part of Carrie Foster's account. She had definitely told them it was the noise that triggered Kyle's extreme reaction.

"It's just Kyle's way of handling the problem, I suppose. His coping mechanism," Sherwood continued. "And he has been handling it. He's been doing really well."

"Until Monday morning," Gurley said.

"No!" Sherwood stood up and threw the beermat on the table. "Haven't you been listening to a word I've said? He wouldn't hurt Molly. He couldn't. It's just not in him."

"Due respect, but none of us know exactly what we're capable of, ma'am." Gurley picked up the shredded beermat and folded it in two. Then four. "I mean, I bet before today you had no idea you'd help a suspect evade the law."

Yvonne Sherwood looked to Ingrid, as if she might offer some support. When she said nothing, the woman slumped back into her chair. "He's an innocent man. I'm only interested in justice. You all seem to have made your mind up about him."

"Why are you so certain he's not guilty?" Ingrid said.

"I've already told you—Kyle's just not like that."

"When did he first get in touch with you?" Ingrid leaned further forward in her seat, trying to encourage Sherwood to confide in her.

"Why does that matter?"

"We're trying to piece together his movements. To be frank, we're also trying to work out what might have happened to Tommy."

"Nothing's happened to him. Tommy's fine."

"Have you seen the boy?" Ingrid asked.

"No."

"Spoken to him?"

"No—Kyle told me Tommy wanted to know if Luke was playing football on Saturday. I get the impression Tommy doesn't even realize anything is wrong. You know what boys are like—he probably thinks it's all some big adventure."

The way Sherwood was speaking, it sounded as if Tommy might still be alive. Unlike Gurley, Ingrid didn't believe Foster would lie to Sherwood if he'd seriously hurt the boy. A wave of relief passed over her. Maybe

Rachelle Carver's assessment of Kyle Foster was accurate. Perhaps he did still care about Tommy.

"A big adventure huh?" Gurley threw the beermat back onto the table. "Including the part where Tommy gets a bleeding nose and split lip, courtesy of his father?"

"What?" Sherwood stared at him wide-eyed.

"I thought Foster may have neglected to mention Tommy's injuries to you." Gurley flared his nostrils.

"There has to be some innocent explanation." Despite her words, Sherwood looked genuinely shocked by the news. "Tommy must have had a fall."

Ingrid felt the need to move the conversation in another direction, just in case Gurley's revelation stopped Sherwood talking. "Did Kyle call you on your cell phone?" Ingrid asked.

"He called the public phone, here in the bar."

"And was he using a cell phone?"

"I don't know. Why?"

"It's a way we might be able to trace him." Ingrid leaned even closer to Sherwood. "You do know his best option is to give himself up?"

The woman nodded meekly. "I was hoping to talk him into doing just that. I thought I'd get a chance to speak to him."

"Oh really?" Gurley kicked at the sports bag again. "Would that be before or after you gave him the money?"

"I just want to help him."

"He can't escape, you do realize that?" Gurley said. "There's no place for him to go. The longer this goes on, the worse it gets for him."

Ingrid wished Gurley would shut up, he wasn't helping any. "What was next for Kyle, Yvonne? What was he going to do with the money? Where was he planning on going?"

Sherwood pursed her lips and shook her head so rapidly it looked as if she'd developed a sudden tremor. "He never told me his plans." She looked Gurley square in the eyes and folded her arms. "And that's the God's honest truth. You can arrest me if you want. Threaten me with whatever you like. I still won't tell you anything—I can't tell you what I don't know."

Ingrid glared at Gurley. He didn't seem to notice. He was deliberately ignoring her. His bombastic approach had gotten them nowhere. "Major Gurley, would you mind leaving Yvonne and me to speak alone for a moment?"

He frowned at her, completely taken aback by the suggestion.

"Please?"

"I'll go check on the car," he finally said, and slowly got to his feet. At the door he stopped and turned around, taking a moment to glower at Ingrid, just in case she hadn't picked up on his annoyance.

29

"You're wasting your time if you think I'm going to tell you any more now that he's left the room." Sherwood said. "I don't know where Kyle and Tommy Foster are."

"When he called you, did you hear Tommy in the background?"

The woman thought for a moment, finally uncrossing her arms and relaxing just a little. "I can't be sure, I don't think so."

"But you didn't ask to speak to the boy?"

"Why would I?"

"To check he was OK."

"I had no reason to think he wouldn't be." She let out an irritated sigh. "Kyle Foster is a good man. You don't work in this trade for twenty-odd years without being able to read people."

"Even good people break down. I've been working at the Bureau for long enough to see it happen plenty of times. The nicest folk can do stuff that's completely out of character."

Sherwood shook her head adamantly. "Not Kyle. Molly must have had an accident or something."

"Did Kyle tell you that?"

"He hasn't told me anything about what happened. Only that he didn't hurt Molly."

"Why didn't you try to persuade him to give himself up to the police when he called?"

"Because he told me he didn't do it."

"But he could explain all of that to the police."

Sherwood was shaking her head. "He has Tommy to think about."

"Don't you think Carrie might want Tommy with her?"

"I saw how she was on the news. She doesn't look capable of looking after herself, let alone Tommy."

Ingrid didn't believe what Sherwood was telling her. There was something more to it. Was it possible Yvonne Sherwood was having an affair with Kyle Foster?

"You OK, Mum?"

Ingrid looked up to see Marcus Sherwood standing at the door.

"I thought you'd gone to bed," his mother said.

"As if I'd do that, with you being interrogated down here." He stared at Ingrid. "Where's the other one? Snooping around somewhere?"

"Major Gurley is outside," Ingrid told him.

"Go back upstairs, Marcus. I'll be up soon. I promise." She stared at Ingrid. "I'm sure we're almost finished here."

"Sodding bastard, putting you through this," he said.

"I can assure you Major Gurley was just doing his job. We have to ask these questions," Ingrid said. "The police won't be any different."

"I wasn't talking about Gurley."

"Marcus! Can you please go upstairs?"

"For God's sake, Mum. He's not worth getting into trouble over. Think about Luke. What if you're arrested?"

His mother said nothing. Marcus Sherwood stormed out of the room.

Ingrid sank back in her chair, her eyes wide, her eyebrows raised. She remained silent and waited for Sherwood to comment. After what seemed a very long few moments, she finally did.

"Marcus isn't a big fan of Kyle's."

Ingrid didn't respond.

"Marcus thinks I flirt with Kyle." She tucked a few stray strands of hair behind her ear. "Silly sod. I flirt with every bloke who comes into this place. It's part of the job. It doesn't mean anything. Especially not with Kyle."

Ingrid wriggled forward in her seat again but didn't speak.

Sherwood looked towards the door. "I don't want Marcus to find out about this." She tipped back her head and stared up at the ceiling for a few moments. "I feel so stupid about it now."

Ingrid maintained her silence.

Sherwood puffed out a steadying breath. "A few months ago... Oh God. I'm only telling you this because it might change your opinion of

Kyle…" She took another deep breath. "A few months ago I made a pass at Kyle. I was a bit tipsy. The kids had finally won a match and everyone was celebrating. Kyle and I were getting on really well. I misjudged the situation." She put a hand across her eyes. "I can still picture the shocked expression on his face. He didn't need to say anything—it was clear I'd crossed a line. Kyle might join in with a bit of banter now and then, but he only has eyes for one girl."

Ingrid made no comment.

"You do know I'm talking about Carrie? That's why Kyle arranged the surprise trip to London for her, just to show her how much he cares."

"Actually I'd heard things had been a little… difficult between Kyle and Carrie since Molly was born."

"Who told you that?"

"I really can't divulge—"

"No—I don't suppose you can."

"You don't agree?"

"Kyle mentioned it a few times. He confided in me, I suppose. It's what made me think that he might be interested in…" She shook her head. "What a bloody fool I was." Sherwood leaned in towards Ingrid. "Can this stay just between you and me? I'm only telling you because I want you to understand that Kyle and I became quite close. That's how I know he couldn't do what you say he did."

"Tell me what happened between Carrie and Kyle after Molly was born." While Sherwood was in a confessional mood, Ingrid hoped she could squeeze a little more information from her.

"I'm not a doctor, I couldn't tell you. But I suppose Carrie had a touch of the baby blues. I know she didn't sleep much when they brought Molly home from the hospital. Not for months. I think the sleepless nights took their toll."

"Do you know if Carrie went to see the doctor about it?"

Sherwood was just about to answer when Gurley strode back into the room. Why couldn't he have stayed in the car?

"Yvonne?" Ingrid said gently.

The woman was clearly distracted by the sight of Jack Gurley heading toward her. "What?"

"Did Carrie visit the doctor?"

"Why don't you ask her about it?" she snapped.

Ingrid knew that the interview had come to an end. Gurley's reappearance had seen to that. She got to her feet. "Thank you for your frankness."

"What happens now? Should I expect a visit from the police in the early hours?"

Ingrid was inclined to keep the police out of the picture for now. She was pretty sure they wouldn't get much more out of Sherwood than she had. Although the prospect of prosecution might make the woman more forthcoming, Ingrid decided to hold the threat of police involvement in reserve.

"Not at all. We'll be in touch."

30

On the drive back to the base Ingrid got Gurley up to speed with what Sherwood had told her. "You agree we hold back on informing the police about her involvement?" she asked him when she was done.

"I'd like to keep them out of the picture until we've come up with our own strategy for what we do next."

"We will have to tell them something, though."

"Let's sleep on it, deal with that whole pile of crap in the morning. Agreed?"

"OK." The idea of getting some sleep was suddenly so appealing to Ingrid, right then she might have agreed to anything Gurley suggested. But she knew her day wasn't nearly over. She still had a whole lot of her own crap to confront.

When they reached the base, Gurley personally escorted her to a guest room he'd had prepared for her in advance. As soon as she closed the door behind him, Ingrid collapsed onto the single bed and took a moment to focus on her next task. It was already well after midnight. If she didn't act now, her first chore would have to wait until the morning.

She eased herself upright then carefully retrieved the pill she'd found in the Fosters' bathroom cabinet from her pocket. She then grabbed her cell phone from her purse and called Natasha McKittrick.

"Bloody hell—what time do you call this? Is everything all right?"

"I need a quick favor."

"Where are you?"

"I need you to identify a drug for me."

"Me?" McKittrick exhaled noisily. "What makes you think I can help you?"

The hostility in her friend's tone took Ingrid by surprise. "You told me you were on a prescription drugs bust a little while ago. Sounded to me as if you knew a little something about the subject. Did I get that wrong?"

The line went quiet, but Ingrid could hear McKittrick breathing. "Natasha? Have I said something out of line?"

"No—you woke me up—that's all. I can get a bit tetchy. Sorry."

"Hey, no problem. I'm sending you a photo of the pill now." Ingrid found a sheet of plain white writing paper on the bureau next to the door, carefully placed the small capsule on it so that the writing printed on the side was clearly visible and snapped a couple of shots with her phone. She sent them to McKittrick. "You get them yet?"

"No—where did you find this pill, anyway?"

"Bathroom cabinet of Kyle Foster."

"What does it say on the bottle?"

"The bottle was unmarked—you think I'd be calling otherwise?"

"OK—the pictures have arrived. Give me a second." A few moments later she was back on the line. "It's an anti-depressant. A bit like Prozac with knobs on. You think Foster was taking them for his PTSD?"

"The therapy he's been getting is the cognitive behavioral kind. Do you know if there are any common side effects to these drugs?"

"Like most of this class of drugs: disorientation, fainting, drowsiness maybe."

"Not exactly ideal if you're a pilot."

"Maybe that's why they were in an unmarked bottle. Perhaps he's been getting some unofficial *extra help* with his problem."

"How easy are they to get 'unofficially'?"

"If you have the contacts, it's no problem at all."

Ingrid couldn't imagine how Kyle Foster would have the right connections to get hold of prescription drugs and wondered what other secrets he might be keeping.

"Are they something he'd need to keep taking? Are there any withdrawal symptoms?"

McKittrick paused a beat before answering. "You can't just stop them dead. Otherwise you might suffer severe mood swings, maybe even suicidal thoughts."

Ingrid thought about Tommy. If Kyle Foster were that volatile, it wasn't surprising he'd lashed out at his eight-year-old son. "I don't think the police found any drugs in the hotel room."

"Maybe Foster keeps some with him all the time."

"But if he has stopped taking them... does that mean Tommy is at risk?"

"Foster might not even have any withdrawal symptoms. But it could affect his stability, his judgement." McKittrick yawned.

"I really did wake you up." Ingrid glanced at her watch.

"Nothing shameful about getting to bed early on a school night."

"Sorry to disturb you."

"It's OK. Try not to make a habit of it, will you. Do keep me posted, though."

"We're not making much progress."

"I don't mean with the bloody case. I want to know what's happening with you and my detective constable. What kind of spell have you put on him?"

"I genuinely do not know what you're talking about."

"Oh yeah, right."

"Look—I've got to go. Pleasant dreams." Ingrid hung up before McKittrick had a chance to protest. As she sat staring at the phone, she wondered if she should tell Gurley about her discovery. She quickly decided it was something that could wait until the morning.

She put the phone on the nightstand and started to get ready for bed. In the bathroom she was pleasantly surprised to discover toothpaste, soap and shampoo. The US Air Force knew how to treat their guests.

While Ingrid cleaned her teeth, hoping to let her mind drift, she started to think about the mp3 attachments Mike Stiller had sent her. She'd managed to keep any thought of them buried all day, but now she was on her own, with nothing else to distract her, their presence on her phone was harder to ignore.

She thought about the phone sitting innocently on the nightstand. Now she'd started to consider the content of Mike's email, she knew it would be impossible for her to get to sleep until she'd at least listened to one of the interviews.

She quickly finished up in the bathroom, changed into her tee shirt, turned off all the lights except the one on the nightstand and picked up her phone. Mike's email was easy to find—it was the only one in her private mail account flagged as both urgent and important. She stared long and hard at the mp3 attachments before summoning the courage to open one of them. When she did, the recording started playing automatically. She hit the pause button, not quite ready for what she might hear.

She grabbed a bottle of water from the nightstand, slowly drank a third of it, then hit 'play'.

The first voice she heard was a man's. He had a thick Kentucky accent. He introduced himself, a colleague, and the interviewee for the purposes of the recording. The sound quality wasn't good. There was a low background hum and the voices sounded distant. As Ingrid strained to make out the words, she jotted down a few notes. The start of the interview merely covered the basics: name, date and place of birth and date of abduction. The twenty-eight-year-old woman, Karla Anderson, then quickly went on to describe the basement where she'd been held captive, unprompted by the two agents. She seemed anxious to convey just how bad her living conditions had been for the last fifteen years.

It took Ingrid a little while to notice she had started to cry. It wasn't until tears had actually started to dribble around her jaw and down her neck that the dampness registered. She found a Kleenex in her purse and dabbed her eyes. She wasn't sure whether she was crying in sympathy for the woman's plight or if she'd been imagining Megan Avery in the same house, forced into the same deprivation and depravity.

When the interview moved on to the other women and girls being held, Anderson had nothing to say at all. "First I knew I wasn't there on my own was when I was taken to the hospital in the same ambulance as another girl. Soon as I laid eyes on her I knew she'd been through the same things I had. The pain in her eyes, you know? I could see it plain as day."

"You thought you were alone in the property with your abductor?" a female agent asked.

"He was the only person I spoke to in fifteen years."

"Did you see him?"

"He didn't wear a mask, if that's what you mean."

"Can you give us a description?"

"Why do you need me to do that? You know what he looks like. I can identify him no problem—just tell me when."

The recording fell silent.

"What, what is it?" Anderson asked, the panic in her voice building. "Wait a minute. You have arrested him, right? You do have him locked up?"

"At this time, the suspect is not yet in custody."

"Sweet Jesus. How could you let him get away?"

"Have no doubt, Miss Anderson, we will arrest him. How quickly depends in part on the detail of the description you can give us."

Ingrid heard a muffled sob, then a louder one.

"Please, Karla. We know you've been through so much. But the sooner you give us the information, the faster we can get him behind bars."

"OK. Where should I start?"

"How about height and build?"

"He's skinny… wiry, I guess, only a few inches taller than me, I'm five-foot-six. No, wait. That's how tall I was when I was fourteen. Maybe I grew since then."

Ingrid heard a distant rustling of paper.

"You're five-foot-nine."

"I am?"

"You don't remember the nurse measuring you during the medical exam?"

"I guess I had other things on my mind."

"What else can you tell us about him?"

"He's white, but tanned, like he's spent a lot of years outside. He has tattoos on his arms, from the middle of his forearms right up almost to his shoulders. Old style ones, like you'd see on some old sailor or something. He has greased-back dark hair, going gray a little above his ears. Long sideburns."

"Does he have an accent?"

"Southern. Couldn't say which state, though."

"Did he ever talk about where he came from, originally?"

"He always said he was from everywhere. Real proud of the fact he lived like a gypsy."

"A gypsy?"

"He traveled around the country, always moving from state to state, he said. Until he came here. And decided to settle down."

"What was he? Some sort of salesman?"

"No! He told me he managed the roller coaster at a traveling carnival."

Dear God.

Ingrid closed her eyes. Her head started to buzz. An intense heat rose from the middle of her chest up into her neck and head. She couldn't breathe.

A traveling carnival?

It had to be the same man who took Megan.

31

The next day Ingrid rose early. She was dressed and making her way to the officers' mess for breakfast before seven.

The previous night she had continued to listen right to the end of the mp3 recording, then listened to the whole thing again, just to make sure she hadn't missed anything. Then she'd called Mike Stiller, impressing upon him once again the importance of the DNA test for the third woman.

"I'm still working on it," he'd said. "You have to trust that I'm doing everything I can here." He'd sounded pissed that she'd interrupted the ball game he was watching.

"The more I hear about this case, the more convinced I am that this guy took my friend. Is the investigating team getting any closer to finding him?"

"They're making some progress. That's all they can tell me."

By the time she'd hung up on him and laid her head on the pillow, her mind was swirling with images of carnival men, tattoos, bright lights and contorted half-smiling, half-grimacing faces. She could taste the sweetness of cotton candy at the back of her throat and hear the off-key steam organ music all jumbled up with the screams of people on the roller coaster. It hadn't taken much to transport her back eighteen years and four thousand miles. Mike Stiller had to come through with more information for her. He just had to. The waiting and not knowing whether or not the third victim was Megan was getting harder with each day that passed.

Halfway through breakfast a Security Forces sergeant came to her table and told her Gurley was waiting for her in his office. Five minutes later she arrived at a single-story cinder block building that looked like a bunker from WWII.

She was met at the door by another uniformed sergeant, this one a woman, and led through an outer office to an interior door. The sergeant knocked twice and opened the door without waiting. As Ingrid stepped inside the inner office she saw Gurley sitting behind a wide metal desk, his back to her, his chair facing the wall. He was on the phone, but he wasn't speaking. After a moment he swung around to face her and held up a fore-finger indicating he'd be another minute. Ingrid decided to fill the time by looking at the framed photographs hanging on the wall next to the door. They all featured Gurley posing with high ranking officers, various Secre-taries of Defense, and even one or two ex-presidents. Gurley hadn't struck Ingrid as the boasting kind, so an array of his claims to fame arranged on the wall like a collection of hunting trophies seemed a little out of place.

Gurley slammed down the phone. "Sonofabitch!" He took a breath. "Him, not you," he said, staring at the phone.

"Something to do with the Foster investigation?" Ingrid asked.

"No—Air Force bureaucratic bullshit. I should be used to it by now, but it still pisses me off. It's a waste of time and money." Gurley stood up and stretched his arms above his head. For a moment Ingrid was sure his knuckles would graze the ceiling. "I didn't ask you last night," he said, "did you get a sense from Sherwood that she thinks Foster is likely to stay in the area?"

"I don't think she was lying when she told us she has no idea what Foster's plans are. Without the supplies and the cash from Sherwood, I guess Foster has fewer options."

"I wouldn't be taken in by her story."

"I have done this before, you know. I can get a sense when somebody is lying to me."

"Well, I don't trust her. I'm planning on keeping her under surveillance today, just in case she gets any ideas about helping Foster again."

"I'm not staking out the pub. It'd be a waste of time."

Gurley folded his arms across his broad chest. "I had no intention of asking you to. I'll get a couple of my team to check it out."

"Good, waste their time instead of mine."

The landline on Gurley's desk started to ring. Its tone sounded particu-larly shrill as the noise bounced off the cinder block walls.

"Excuse me." Gurley snatched the handset and turned away from her. "You're saying he's on the line right now?" He glanced over his shoulder at Ingrid. "Of course you should patch him through. Set up a trace on the call, as fast as you can."

Ingrid ran around the desk. "Is it Foster?"

Gurley nodded.

"Put the call on speaker phone."

Gurley narrowed his eyes, clearly reluctant to comply with her request. "He called to speak to his superior officer. His superior officer has transferred the call to me. Foster doesn't know who the hell you are."

"You want me to escalate this? With the embassy? With the Pentagon?"

"This is Major Gurley, Security Forces." He turned another few degrees away from her, the handset pressed hard against his ear. "Major Brown thought it best you speak to me."

Ingrid scanned the phone on the desk and stabbed at the only button that looked remotely like the right one. A crackle of static filled the room. Followed by an irritated sigh from Gurley.

"I know what you're doing. I know you'll be tracing this call, so I'm going to be quick. You have to listen to me without interrupting." Foster's voice was deeper than Ingrid had expected.

"Go on."

"You have to believe that I didn't hurt Molly. I could never hurt her. I love her and Tommy more than anything in the world. Jesus, until I saw the news reports, I thought she was dead. That's why I panicked and took Tommy. I had to get him out of harm's way."

"Tell me what you've done to him," Gurley said.

"I told you not to interrupt. I haven't done anything. Tommy's right here with me. He's safe. I want him to stay that way. In order for that to happen, I need your help. I want to get him to my parents back home. You can arrange that for me, I know you can."

"Let me at least speak to Tommy, know for sure he's all right."

"I don't have time for that. I want him on a flight to the US by the end of tomorrow. He'll need a chaperone. Maybe one of your female officers. My mom and dad will take good care of him."

"We know Tommy was injured. We spoke to the doctor who treated him. What did you do to him?"

"I didn't do anything. Aren't you listening to me? I love my kids."

"I think it's best for Tommy, for you... for everyone... if you give yourself up. We can hear your side of the story then. Take all the... ah... mitigating circumstances into account."

"Story? What do you think this is? I'm not telling tales. Jesus. Why won't you listen to me? I want to make sure Tommy's safe. And Molly. She looked so tiny wired up to all those monitors. I just wanted to scoop her into my arms and protect her. Take her away with me. But I saw the cop guarding her. I figured she was in the best place. That she was safe. But as soon as she can travel I want her to go to my mom and dad's too."

The door opened and the female sergeant from the outer office held up a sheet of paper with the words: *keep him talking, partial location only* scrawled across it.

"A flight to the US and a chaperone will take some organizing, Kyle. It'd be much easier if you and Tommy come to the base, then we can start to put those wheels in motion for you."

Foster didn't reply.

"Kyle?"

"You're lying," Foster said, eventually. Then the line went dead.

"Goddammit!" Gurley slammed down the handset.

A moment later another MP ran in. "He's in northeast England, within a ten mile radius of the center of Newcastle."

Gurley considered the information for a moment. "A ten mile radius?" He paused a beat, glancing up at the ceiling. "That's an area of over three hundred square miles. For crying out loud, you couldn't do any better than that?"

"It took a little while to set up the trace. He hung up too soon."

"I want a trace ready to go next time."

"You think he'll call back?" Ingrid asked.

"We have something he wants: a plane ride home for his son. Of course he'll call back."

"What did you make of all that? He seemed genuinely concerned for Tommy's safety. And his daughter's, for that matter. Do you think he was suggesting they're not safe with Carrie?"

"Yes—I do think the sonofabitch was suggesting that."

Ingrid remembered what Sherwood had told her about Carrie Foster's 'baby blues'. Maybe they were a lot more serious than she'd realized. "At least we solved the mystery of the impostor in Molly's hospital room."

"We were so close to him."

"And now he's over two hundred fifty miles away."

"How'd he get to Newcastle so fast?" Gurley's face had reddened.

"I'd say train, but the local cops should have been liaising with British Transport Police, watching all the local stations and train lines."

"*Should* have been."

"We need to check out the CCTV footage they have, maybe we'll see something they missed."

"So damn close," Gurley said again and thumped the desk with a fist.

The female sergeant ran into the room again, stopped abruptly in front of Gurley's desk and stood to attention.

"Tell me you've pin-pointed his location," Gurley barked.

"No, sir. It's something else." The sergeant glanced at Ingrid, her lips pursed.

"For God's sake, you can speak freely in front of Agent Skyberg!"

"The munitions store have just contacted me. A hand gun and ten rounds of ammunition are missing from their inventory."

32

Ingrid managed to run after Gurley and climb into the passenger seat of the jeep just as he stamped his foot on the gas. He hadn't invited her to join him, but she'd be damned if she let him shut her out. They made the three minute journey in silence—Gurley clearly too mad to talk.

The munitions store was on the other side of the base, a single-story concrete bunker with no windows and one double door made of steel. Gurley stopped the jeep without bothering to park it in the demarcated bay and jumped out. Ingrid made sure she was hot on his heels as the metal door opened and an MP stepped out.

"Sir!" The MP stood to attention.

"At ease. Show me where the gun was taken from," Gurley said, stooping low to get through the doorway.

The MP stepped in front of Ingrid. "I'm sorry, ma'am. Authorized Air Force personnel only."

"Hey, Major Gurley!" she called after him as he disappeared inside. "Tell him I have full authority."

"Not Air Force authority," Gurley shouted back at her.

The MP followed his superior inside and shut the door in Ingrid's face. She slammed a hand against it. Then she took a deep breath and, eager not to feel completely useless, pulled her phone from her purse. She put in a call to Mike Stiller to find out what was happening with the abductee case, got his voicemail and left a curt message, taking her anger with Gurley out on Mike. Which wouldn't help her get the information she wanted any faster. Then she put in another call to the local cops, requesting they make the CCTV footage from the local train stations available for viewing.

After that all she could do was pace up and down outside the steel doors waiting for Gurley to re-emerge. When he eventually did, ten minutes later, he ignored her completely and marched back to the jeep.

"Well?" Ingrid said, running after him. "What did you find out?"

Gurley crunched the gearshift into reverse and drove a fast wide loop to turn the jeep around. "The last inventory was taken at seven p.m. yesterday evening."

"So that means the gun and bullets went missing some time last night."

Gurley didn't respond.

"Then it couldn't have been Foster," Ingrid continued. "He had to be staking out a muddy field in the middle of nowhere last night."

"Sherwood didn't get there until eight-thirty. Foster had plenty of time."

"Oh come on, how could he have entered the base without anyone seeing him and then break into the locked munitions store? Stuff must go missing here all the time."

"We can't rule out the possibility that the suspect is now armed."

"You just spoke to him—did he sound like a man who'd break into an Air Force base? He's just interested in looking out for his kids."

"I don't know what's gotten into you. Why are you so keen to believe Kyle Foster is innocent?"

After talking to Rachelle Carver and Yvonne Sherwood, Ingrid wasn't entirely sure what to think, but she was determined to keep an open mind. "You must have CCTV cameras on the base. Check the footage. You'll see Foster had nothing to do with it."

"The two most useful cameras are out of action. The lenses have been smashed. Glass and small rocks were found at the base of the poles they're mounted on. Foster could easily be responsible for that."

"It still doesn't explain how he got onto the base in the first place."

"What is it with you? Why have you started defending him?" Gurley stamped his foot on the gas and the car lurched forward.

"I'm not—I just don't see why he'd do something like that. Has he even had small arms training?"

"He's a first lieutenant in the US Air Force—of course he has." Gurley took a sharp left turn, slamming Ingrid hard against the passenger door.

Slightly winded, Ingrid grabbed onto the dash and righted herself. "Tell me how he got past the guards on the security gate."

"How big do you think the perimeter fence is here?"

Ingrid shrugged. "A mile… two miles?"

"Ten. We check and repair it on a regular basis, but it's possible there's a hole some place."

"A place that Foster just happens to know about?"

"I'm treating Kyle Foster as an armed suspect who kidnapped his own son. If you want to cast him in a different light, fine. But I'm warning you —I won't have your out of whack judgment affect the way this operation moves forward."

"Guilty till proven innocent, huh?"

"It's the military way."

"Foster has no reason to arm himself."

"Leverage."

"What?"

"You heard what he said. He's started making demands. Making them in possession of a lethal weapon is a whole different ball game."

"But he wants to protect his son, not threaten to hurt him."

"Who says he'll threaten Tommy? Besides, you didn't believe that bull-shit just now, did you? He's trying to pin the blame for what happened to Molly on her mother. Sonofabitch. The 'making sure Tommy's safe' line is a smokescreen. He's just trying to protect his own ass. Please tell me you didn't fall for it."

They drove back the rest of the way to Gurley's office in silence. When they arrived, Ingrid followed him into the building even though he hadn't bothered to invite her. He was on the phone requesting a helicopter to take them to Newcastle before she'd even sat down.

"You think that's really the best way to use our resources?" Ingrid asked when he hung up. She was doing her best not to scream at him for being so gung-ho he hadn't even considered the facts.

"There's no point in looking for him here, is there?"

"But you said yourself—it's a lot of ground to cover. The Northumbria police are in a much better position to search for him."

"While we sit around doing nothing?"

"As soon as they have something solid, then we follow up. In a chopper it wouldn't take that long to get there." Ingrid wasn't sure she was getting through to him at all—his expression was completely blank. "Besides, I'd like to see the CCTV footage from the local train stations. I've already arranged for the force here to make it available to us."

"Why?"

"I'd like to at least check if he has Tommy with him. Wouldn't you?"

Gurley opened his mouth, but couldn't come up with a counter argument. Instead he picked up the phone and barked at his sergeant to find out who the highest ranking police officer in Newcastle was and to get the sorry-assed bastard on the phone.

33

In less than a half hour Ingrid and Gurley were sitting in front of a bank of TV monitors at the local railway hub station. Lined up for their scrutiny on two larger monitors was the footage from the two closest train stations to Freckenham between the hours of eight p.m. and two a.m. the night before. Ingrid had chosen the timeframe without consulting Gurley. She figured Foster was probably watching a muddy field until around nine p.m. and the last scheduled train at either of the local stations was just after midnight. She'd requested a wider timescale for the footage just to play it safe.

"We don't have a lot of time here," Gurley told the technician assigned to operate the equipment for them. "We have some place else to be."

The technician said nothing but made a point of exhaling noisily and shifting in his seat.

"OK, then why don't we start with the footage from nine p.m. onwards?" Ingrid suggested. "We have a pretty good idea where Foster was before that."

The technician quickly found the right point in the footage and hit play on both monitors. The left hand one showed all activity around the entrance of Newmarket station, the other at Kennett, a much smaller station that was closer to the base. At first Ingrid switched her attention between both screens, but as the uneventful scenes played out for half a minute or so, she started to feel a little nauseous. "Let's play these at eight times normal speed, I'll keep my eyes peeled on the left hand monitor, you take the right. OK?"

Gurley grunted his agreement and folded his arms.

After running the footage through from nine p.m. to the final trains at both stations with no sign of a man and a boy, Ingrid asked the technician to stop the playback. "Is it possible for someone to get onto the platforms without using the main entrance at these stations?"

"Possible, but not likely. Security's been tightened up in the last couple of years—to prevent fare evasion. I suppose if someone is really determined to get in they still can, but it'd mean scaling a ten foot wall with barbed wire strung along the top of it."

"Can you get on a train without a ticket?" she asked.

"If you've bypassed the ticket barriers at the entrance you can. The conductor on the train checks that passengers have valid tickets, but he'll also sell you a ticket if you don't have one."

"Can we get a record of any tickets sold on trains last night?"

"You can, but it might take a while."

Gurley let out another grunt. "We're wasting our time here. There's no sign of Foster and Tommy in this footage. Either he didn't use the main entrance—which seems unlikely—or Foster doesn't have Tommy with him anymore." He clapped a heavy hand on the technician's shoulder, making the man jump in his seat. "Thanks for your time. We won't take up any more of it."

"Maybe we can extend the window, start the footage a little earlier," Ingrid said, not wanting to give up just yet.

"I'm leaving, if you want a ride back to base, I suggest you come with me right now."

"Let's give it another fifteen minutes—how will that make a difference to today's schedule?"

Gurley shook his head and frowned at her. "Fifteen and no more."

"So—you want to see the footage from six? Five p.m.?" The technician looked up at her.

"No, same time frame as before—start it at nine but play it at four times normal speed. I saw something early on that bugged me for some reason and I'm not sure why."

The technician did as he was told. Under twenty minutes into the recording Ingrid asked him to freeze the footage on the left hand monitor. She jabbed a finger at the screen. "There, you see that?"

Gurley leaned in closer and peered at the blurry image. "What am I looking for?"

"This guy with the backpack. Can you rewind a few seconds and play at normal speed?"

The technician complied.

"See the way he's walking? Staggering might be a more accurate description. Either he's so drunk he can't walk straight, or that pack on his back is throwing him off balance. He's really struggling to get around."

They all continued to watch the man awkwardly make his way to the ticket counter. His right hand flew up and backwards and he seemed to slap the side of the backpack. He then readjusted the weight on his back.

"Can you get a close-up of his face?" Ingrid asked.

"Sure."

Although the image wasn't clear, what was evident was the color of the man's hair—much darker than Kyle Foster's.

"Could that be him?" Ingrid asked Gurley. "He's the right build and height. He could have dyed his hair." Ingrid stared hard at the screen. "Pull back again, so we can see his whole body." She leaned further forward. "Did you see that?"

"Something moved in that bag," the technician said, a little excitedly, when Gurley didn't respond.

"Hit the pause button again, will you?" Gurley ordered the technician. He turned to look at Ingrid. "Are you seriously suggesting this is Foster and he's stuffed Tommy into the backpack?"

"It could be, couldn't it? The timing fits. Can we get footage from the platform cameras? Which platform would he need if he were planning to head north?"

The technician took a few minutes to cue up the required recordings and fast forward to the correct timestamp. "There are four cameras on the right platform." He tapped the four split screen images in turn with a pen.

They watched in silence as the footage played in real time. They continued to scrutinize the recording for ten minutes until the first train arrived. The man they'd identified hadn't appeared on the platform in that time. At quadruple speed they watched for another five minutes. Another train arrived. Still no sign of the man with the wriggling backpack.

"Where'd he go?" Gurley sounded curious and impatient at the same time.

"Maybe he wanted to cover his tracks a little, took a train some place else, then backtracked," Ingrid suggested.

"We can check the other platforms, give me a second to bring up the relevant recordings."

"What are we trying to prove here?" Now Gurley just sounded pissed.

"This guy may or may not be Foster. Tommy may or may not be inside that bag. It doesn't get us any closer to finding him." He shook his head. "Jesus, what kind of man stuffs an eight-year-old kid into a bag anyway?"

"You're right," Ingrid conceded.

Gurley opened his eyes wide. "I am?"

Ingrid realized she wasn't going to get more definite proof that the man with the backpack was Foster, so decided to withdraw as gracefully as she could. Better to make a concession to Gurley when there was nothing much at stake. "We should try to figure out why Foster's decided to head north. Who does he know up there? Why make such a long journey?" Ingrid was hoping a conversation about Foster's motives might help pinpoint his possible location.

"Let's ask those questions on the way, shall we?"

Ingrid thanked the technician, requested he send her as good a close-up still image of the man with the unwieldy backpack as he could, then she and Gurley made a swift exit.

Halfway back to Freckenham, Gurley's phone rang. He answered on hands-free. A hesitant voice the other end crackled into the car.

"Major Gurley?"

"Yes?"

"Sergeant Willis here, sir. We've had a report sent to us from the local police department in Northumbria that I thought you should know about right away."

"What is it, Willis?" Gurley didn't bother to mask his impatience.

"A flying club in Felton—about twenty miles north of Newcastle—has reported one of their aircraft is missing."

"Missing?"

"Stolen. Must have happened in the last two hours they think."

"And they've only just noticed?" Gurley glanced at Ingrid. "What kind of aircraft?"

"Helicopter, sir. A Eurocopter EC120. First Lieutenant Foster flew choppers in Afghanistan as part of his search and rescue missions."

"Thank you, Willis. I'm well aware of that fact." Gurley ended the call and pulled the car over to the side of the road. He slammed his fists against the steering wheel. "Goddammit! The goddamn sonofabitch could be anywhere by now."

34

After Jack Gurley agreed with Ingrid that a trip to the airfield in Northumberland was a waste of time, he drove her to Bury St Edmunds railway station and left her to get back to London by her own devices. The train journey was a little uncomfortable, and took longer than she would have liked, but she was relieved to be headed back to the embassy without Gurley breathing down her neck.

When she finally returned to her desk, late afternoon, she discovered a rectangular, Fed-Ex labeled box sitting beside her computer monitor.

"Hey, Ingrid, I didn't expect you back so soon," Jennifer said when she walked into the office a moment later, a steaming cup of something herbal in her hand. It smelled as if the clerk had gathered up a few blades of grass from Grosvenor Square and poured boiling water over them.

"When did that arrive?" Ingrid nodded toward the parcel, a hand shoved into each armpit. She circled the desk, not wanting to get anywhere near the package. Certainly not intending to touch it.

"It's OK—security have scanned it," Jennifer told her. "It won't puff white powder into your face when you open it. Or explode. Did you see it's from Minnesota?"

Ingrid didn't need to check the 'from' address—she knew exactly who had sent it and what was inside. Which was why she was so reluctant to touch it and why she had such a sick feeling in her stomach. Jennifer continued to look at her expectantly.

"Aren't you going to open it?" she said, her eyes wide in anticipation.

"Nah, I know what it is."

Jennifer nodded excitedly.

"Just a pair of shoes I asked my mom to pick up for me."

"Oh."

"Sorry to disappoint."

"I didn't mean to pry... I just thought..."

"It's OK, Jennifer. No problem." Ingrid took a deep breath and, using just thumb and index finger, transferred the box from the desk to a drawer beneath it. No wonder Svetlana hadn't sent her the photographs she'd asked for. Not with this ticking time bomb about to arrive any minute. What did she hope it would achieve?

Aware Jennifer's gaze was still trained on her, Ingrid concentrated on keeping the expression on her face as neutral as possible. She'd deal with Svetlana's surprise package when she got home. She grabbed a clean shirt from the bottom drawer of her desk and hurried to the ladies' restroom to change into it, all the time trying to keep thoughts of Svetlana's parcel from her mind. Then she retrieved her cell from her pocket, found DCI Radcliffe's number and hit the call option. As she wasn't sure about the theory she'd come up with on the long train journey back to London, she wanted to speak to the detective in private—and the ladies' restroom was as good a place as any. Radcliffe picked up after several rings.

"You've got a bloody cheek calling me," he said before Ingrid got a chance to say hello. "Why is it I find out Foster's called the base from one of Gurley's men hours after the event? What happened to the timely exchange of information?"

Ingrid silently cursed Gurley. He could have at least warned her one of his team would be speaking to Radcliffe. If she hadn't needed a favor from the chief inspector she would have been tempted to find an excuse to hang up on him. Instead she'd need to beg for forgiveness. "I guess I got a little too involved on the ground to consider the bigger picture. I'm sorry. I assumed Major Gurley would inform you about the situation sooner. It was just a case of miscommunication." The words sounded pathetic enough to her. She could imagine the look of contempt on Radcliffe's face. "There is a bright side," she added.

"Really?"

"Kyle Foster's request for a safe passage for Tommy back to the US at least means the boy is still alive."

"But we don't know that for sure. Without concrete proof I can't tell Mrs Foster."

"What do you make of Kyle Foster's request?"

Radcliffe didn't answer right away. Ingrid couldn't judge if it was because he was carefully considering her question or was too mad at her to respond. "The man is deluded if he thinks anyone will agree to something like that," he finally said.

"But when he calls back, we should at least play along."

"When he calls back I want to be part of the conversation. Do you understand?"

"Of course. Timely exchange of information. I won't let you down again, chief inspector."

"Make sure you don't."

Ingrid pulled the phone away from her face and puffed out a breath. Why did working with local law enforcement always have to be this hard? It was just the same Stateside. She put the phone back to her ear and did her best to stay calm.

"Why are you calling, anyway? Do you have another update for me?"

"I need a favor." She paused a beat and braced herself for his response.

"Of course you bloody well do. I should have guessed."

"Please—just hear me out. I've been working on a theory." Ingrid hesitated. She hadn't said it out loud to anyone yet, and she wasn't sure just how screwy the idea would sound.

"Spit it out, for God's sake—I don't have all day."

"I've talked to a few people now about Kyle Foster and they all tell me what a great dad he is. How they can't imagine him doing anything to hurt his kids."

"So what? We know he flipped. His PTSD got the better of him. Doesn't matter how good a dad he's been in the past."

"But I've seen cases like this before. Usually the father wipes out the whole family then takes his own life. Why bother to take Tommy with him? Why get him treated at the hospital?"

"Why cause Tommy's injuries in the first place?"

Ingrid sucked in a long breath.

Here we go.

"We don't know for sure Kyle was responsible for hurting Tommy."

"What?"

"Shouldn't we at least consider the possibility that Carrie could have hurt him?"

Radcliffe didn't answer, but Ingrid heard him expel an exasperated breath. "You're basing this theory on what exactly?" He didn't wait for a reply before continuing. "Nothing more than a few good words about Foster's character?"

Ingrid hesitated again. She wasn't sure whether she should bring it up, but Radcliffe clearly needed to be persuaded. "We searched Foster's house," she said, quickly.

"We?"

"Major Gurley and I. It's on the base, Gurley has full jurisdiction."

"And?"

"Hidden away in a dark corner of Carrie Foster's closet was a bottle of vodka."

"That's the best you can do? So she likes a drink now and again."

"Hiding booze? Surely that's got to set alarm bells ringing."

"Tell me you've got more than that."

"Someone told me Carrie's been having a hard time since Molly was born. The baby blues, they called it." Ingrid waited for a response, but it didn't come, so she plowed on. "Isn't it worth investigating? Can we really just ignore the possibility Carrie might have hurt Molly too?"

"You're very free and easy with the 'we' pronoun, aren't you? Does Major Gurley agree with your theory?"

I don't give a rat's ass what Gurley thinks.

"I haven't discussed it with him. I thought I'd run it past you first."

"I'm honored."

"I'd like to talk to the consultant at the hospital to discuss Molly's injuries in detail. I was hoping you could arrange an appointment for me —it might speed the whole process up."

"He's a very busy man."

"I'm sure he'd make the time if you convinced him how crucial it was to the ongoing investigation."

Radcliffe let out another exaggerated sigh. "It's too late to set up a meeting for today. And I want to make this quite clear—I'll lead any interview with him. This is my investigation."

"I know that." Ingrid was determined not to apologize to Radcliffe again.

"I'll call you tomorrow and let you know what I've managed to arrange."

Ingrid was just about to hang up when Radcliffe said, "Molly regained consciousness half an hour ago."

"She did? That's fantastic."

"I wouldn't celebrate just yet. It's not clear if any permanent damage has been done."

He hung up before Ingrid had the chance to thank him for letting her know. She made her way back to the office, tapping Gurley's number into her phone, to let him know the good news. She even had a little bounce to her step.

But as she reached the door of the office, she remembered the package her mother had sent, nestling innocently in her desk drawer.

A shiver went up her spine.

35

Ingrid was relieved to finally return home after her sojourn in Suffolk. She didn't leave the embassy until after eight and was looking forward to a good night's sleep in her own bed. Even though she had a feeling she was unlikely to get it. Not with Svetlana's parcel sitting on the coffee table in the living room. She wanted to ignore it, to open it tomorrow. Or the next day. But she knew she couldn't. She knew she wouldn't be able to get any peace at all until she unwrapped the box and inspected each item inside.

First, though, she needed to get changed. She threw on some sweat pants and a baggy tee shirt and left her running shoes by the apartment door. After she had dealt with the package, she might feel the need to hit the well-lit and empty sidewalks of Maida Vale and St John's Wood.

For a moment she pictured herself running across the street in Abbey Road. Her dad had been a big Beatles fan. He would have loved a photograph of her sprinting over the black and white stripes of the crosswalk.

Her breath caught in her throat. She could go for days, or even weeks without missing her dad, but every now and then, a memory of him would catch her off guard and knock her sideways. How she wished he was still around. He'd know exactly what to say when she opened the Fed-Ex box.

Ingrid knew she couldn't ignore it any longer.

She padded slowly into the kitchen, her feet feeling cool on the tile floor, grabbed a bottle of Finnish vodka from the freezer compartment of the tall refrigerator and a glass from the cabinet above the sink, and shuffled into the living room. She slumped down onto the couch and stared at the box in front of her. As she opened the icy bottle of vodka and poured herself a generous measure, she wondered how much of it would be left by the time she'd finished going through the contents of the parcel.

The perforated strip pulled off easily enough and the outer cardboard container peeled away to reveal exactly what she was expecting: a beaten up old sneaker box decorated with hand-drawn flowers and hearts on the lid and around the sides. Very gingerly she lifted one corner of the lid and slid it onto the table.

She took a deep breath and forced herself to look inside.

Lying on top, as if Svetlana had strategically positioned it there, and despite the fact that the parcel had been air freighted all the way from Minnesota, was the most difficult item Ingrid knew she'd have to confront. Using just the tips of her fingers, she pulled out the photo booth strip of four color photographs. Each one was posed individually. Each one featured Ingrid and her best friend in the whole world. She and Megan were pulling faces, sticking out their tongues, tugging on each other's braids and collapsing in fits of laughter as the final flash clicked.

Tears sprang into Ingrid's eyes at the sight of Megan. Especially Megan laughing. The last time Ingrid had seen her face it had been contorted with fear. Tears streamed down Ingrid's face. There was no stopping them. It was the effect Svetlana had probably been hoping for when she'd arranged the contents of the box. It must have taken a while for her mother to unearth it, buried in an unused corner of the basement.

But what did her mother hope would happen when the tears stopped? Did she suppose Ingrid would be calling her right away, desperate to speak to Kathleen Avery? Didn't she know her better than that? She wiped her cheeks with the bottom of her tee shirt and dabbed at her eyes.

Dammit.

She wasn't going to let Svetlana orchestrate her reactions from over 4000 miles away. She picked up the box and shook its contents to get a better look at what was inside without having to actually touch anything. She spotted two of her favorite Mickey Mouse hair grips, Megan had a pair just the same. Then she saw three large metal pins, one featuring Erasure and two decorated with images of a very young George Michael. To one side of those was a length of red and silver ribbon Megan had tied around one of Ingrid's birthday gifts. She shook the box again to see, right at the bottom, wrapped in an almost translucent layer of tissue paper, a lock of Megan's curly brown hair.

A sudden wave of nausea swept up from the pit of Ingrid's stomach.

She grabbed the vodka bottle and took a large mouthful, waiting for the burn of the alcohol to extinguish the taste of vomit at the back of her throat.

Ingrid had snipped off a lock of her own bright, almost white, blond hair and given it to Megan. They had decided exchanging locks of hair was a more meaningful and permanent gesture than mingling blood from cut fingers. They both agreed they should do something that would last forever.

Ingrid took another swig of vodka then slowly reached into the box. But she couldn't bring herself to touch even the tissue paper that surrounded the lock of hair. She wondered if Kathleen Avery still kept Megan's treasure trove contained within a shoe box. Whether she had seen the lock of Ingrid's hair wrapped in tissue paper. The thought of Kathleen sifting through Megan's prized possessions set off another deluge of uncontrollable tears.

When the tears subsided, Ingrid sat very still for a few moments, not quite knowing what to do next. Svetlana was probably waiting for her call. But there was no way she could speak to her mother the way she felt right now. She knew she'd say things she'd regret. She retrieved her cell from the coffee table and scrolled through her contacts list until she found Mike Stiller's number. She hit the call button and waited, hoping she would be able to control any tremor in her voice.

"Hey, Mike. Tell me you have some news. I really need some good news. Tell me the DNA test has been arranged."

"Are you loaded?"

"What?"

"You're slurring your words."

"I am not."

"Have it your own way."

"Well?"

"I don't have any good news to share with you."

"What is that supposed to mean? You have bad news?"

"I planned on calling you tomorrow. What time is it there now?"

"Tell me the news, for God's sake."

"The third woman started talking. She's from Indiana, she's twenty-nine years old. She claims her name is Brenda Lohan." He paused for a moment. "I'm sorry, Ingrid. She's not your friend."

"What do you mean she 'claims' her name is Brenda Lohan?"

"The investigating agents think she may have lifted the name from a magazine they'd given her to read."

"What?"

"They can't find a record of any Brenda Lohan of the right age."

"If she's lying about her identity, maybe she's made up the other stuff too."

"A twelve-year-old girl went missing from Columbus, Indiana in 1995."

"That was the year Megan disappeared."

"Trust me—this woman is not her. Too much of what she said was accurate. About her home town, her school. Everything."

"Except her real name."

"After so many years, maybe she forgot her real name."

"Yeah and maybe she's lying."

"It's not your friend, Ingrid. I know you don't want to hear that but—"

"I'm sorry, Mike. I have to go." She hung up. She couldn't listen to any more. She poured herself another large vodka and drained the glass. Finally she slumped back onto the couch, still clutching her cell phone. She wanted to tell somebody what Mike had told her. But she couldn't tell Svetlana. Not yet. She scrolled to Natasha McKittrick's number and called her. The call went straight to voicemail. She didn't bother leaving a message. She went through the remainder of her contacts list. There were so few people she could share this with. She stopped scrolling when she reached the entry for Ralph Mills. He was a good listener. But could she really burden him with all of this? Could she risk being that vulnerable with him? They hardly knew one another. She hit the 'call' option before she could talk herself out of it.

He answered right away.

"Are you back from the wilds of East Anglia?"

"Uh huh. Listen, do you have a few minutes? I really need to talk something through with you."

"Jesus, what's wrong? You sound awful."

"Do you have the time to—"

"I'm coming over." He hung up.

Ingrid called him back. A phone conversation was one thing. But face to face? She wasn't ready for that. The call diverted straight to voicemail.

Twenty minutes later the intercom was buzzing insistently in the hall.

36

Immediately after Ralph's call, Ingrid drank another glass of vodka then brewed herself a strong coffee. She had just started to drink it when he arrived. She padded unsteadily from the living room to the hall, coffee cup in hand, concentrating hard on walking in a straight line. Although the room wasn't exactly spinning, she was aware her senses were a little dulled. After what Mike Stiller had told her she should have been grateful for the sensation, but she needed to be alert enough not to let her guard down with Ralph. She didn't want to risk doing or saying something she may regret.

As she slowly opened the apartment door she wondered whether it would be best to tell him to turn right around and go back home. But Ralph's anxious expression took her by surprise. She tried to smile at him, hoping to prove he really didn't need to be quite so concerned. But the muscles in her face refused to cooperate.

"It's late," Ingrid said, "I didn't mean for you to come over. We both have work in the morning."

"Actually, I don't start until midday. I can stay up as late as you need me to."

Should he really be staying at all? He followed her inside and closed the door. She stopped at the kitchen.

"Can I get you anything? A coffee? Tea?"

"A cold beer would be great."

"Go on through to the living room. I'll be right in." Ingrid set her coffee cup on the counter and opened the refrigerator. She stood there for a while breathing in the crisp air, wondering again if she'd made a mistake phoning him. She would ask him to leave after he'd finished his beer, she decided. Before would just seem rude.

She shuffled slowly into the living room, bottle of Mexican beer in one hand, her coffee in the other, to find Ralph standing by the window looking out at the view south toward the center of town. She joined him and handed him the beer. He clinked it against her mug.

"Cheers. Great view you've got up here."

Ingrid's apartment was only six floors up, from the end of the roof terrace she could make out some of the major London landmarks. She'd only moved in three months ago and the novelty of the view still hadn't worn off.

"It's my favorite thing about the place."

"Beats my one-bedroom basement flat, that's for sure. I really like the minimalist interior design."

Ingrid glanced at the few items of furniture: the couch, the coffee table and the low, freestanding bookshelf on the other side of the room. "I guess I need to do a little shopping. All this stuff was already here when I moved in."

Ralph took a swig of beer, then said, "So. Tell me what's wrong."

"It doesn't seem so bad now. I feel guilty you've come all the way here."

"No distance at all. Honestly. Any time you feel like you want to talk, I'll be here." He looked toward the couch. "Shall we sit down?"

He pushed off his shoes and curled his long legs under him as he sat down. He patted the leather couch with the flat of his hand. "Come on, sit down and tell me all about it." As Ingrid lowered herself onto the couch she noticed Ralph was staring at the shoebox and its contents on the coffee table.

"What's all this?"

Ingrid blinked. "It's… ah… it's…" Tears prickled her eyelids. *Dammit.* She couldn't cry in front of him. She squeezed her coffee cup a little tighter, sucked down what she hoped was a silent deep breath.

"Bloody hell." He slipped an arm around her shoulders, pulling her toward him until her head was nuzzling his neck. He smelled fresh, an aroma of soap rather than overpowering cologne. She liked it. She let herself be held for a few moments longer, then gently pulled away, her tears now safely under control.

"You remember a little while ago I told you I lost a friend when I was a teenager?" Ingrid said, aware she'd have to continue now she'd started, but not entirely sure how.

Ralph nodded and put his beer on the table. He twisted on the couch to get a better look at her.

"Pretty much ever since it happened I've been hoping that Megan would be discovered some day, alive. For a long while I fantasized I'd be the one to rescue her. But over time I realized that she was most probably dead, killed not long after she'd been abducted."

Ralph held his tongue. Ingrid was grateful he had the sense to know not to speak.

"A few days ago, three women were discovered in a house just outside Jackson, Minnesota. That's only thirty miles from where Megan disappeared." Ingrid drew in a snagging little breath. She wrinkled her nose and swallowed, trying hard to keep fresh tears at bay. "One of the women couldn't be identified. I found out tonight that even though she was abducted the same year, even though her description roughly matches Megan... Oh God... it's not her. It's not my friend." Ingrid sniffed. "I knew it was a long shot. I knew that. But it didn't stop me hoping." She picked up Ralph's beer and took a swig. Then she handed it to him. He hesitated before taking it. "I can get you another," she told him.

"I think maybe you might need it more than me." He put it back on the table. "And these things in the box, they're from your childhood? They remind you of Megan?"

Ingrid nodded. "My mom sent them to me. I think she's trying to make me feel so bad I'll agree to do what she wants."

"And what's that?"

"For years she's tried to bully me into having a long conversation with Megan's mom, Kathleen. But I just can't. I can't face her."

"You don't want to relive it. I understand." Ralph put his hand over Ingrid's. His fingers felt warm and strong.

"It's not that. I relive what happened most days. I can't avoid it. A sound or a smell can trigger the exact same feeling I had at the time. The sickness in my stomach. The fear. The guilt I felt afterwards."

"Guilt? It wasn't your fault."

"But it was."

"Some sick bastard took her. How could you be to blame for that?"

"I ran. I thought she was right behind me. I was slow, but she was even slower. I abandoned her. If I'd stayed I could have protected her."

"You have no way of knowing that. What if he was armed? He might have snatched you both."

"But I *ran*. Don't you get it? I didn't look back. I just kept on running until I was so out of breath I couldn't take another step." An involuntary sob burst out of her mouth. She took a moment to recover. "It was only then that I turned around. And she wasn't there. She wasn't a few steps behind me. She'd gone. And it was my fault." It was the first time she'd admitted that to anyone. Now she had, she wished she could take it back. What must he think of her? "How can I speak to Kathleen when it was all my fault?"

"You can't keep saying that."

Ingrid jumped to her feet. "Why not?"

"Because it's not true. You were just a girl. You did the only natural, instinctive thing you could have done. You expected Megan to do the same."

"But she was heavier than me. And slower. It wasn't as if I didn't know that." She hurried over to the door that led out onto the roof terrace and unlocked it. She stepped outside and immediately the cool breeze enveloped her. August nights in London had been a lot cooler than she was expecting, but she was grateful for that now. She breathed in deep, expecting the tears to come again. But mercifully they didn't. After a moment Ralph stepped out onto the roof. He reached her in a few long strides, wrapped his arms around her and held her tight.

"It's not your fault," he said again, whispering into her ear.

"But it is. How can I face Kathleen when I know what I did? What I didn't do."

Ralph squeezed her tighter. "I lost someone too," he said, continuing to speak in a whisper. "I was even younger than you were when it happened. And for years afterwards I blamed myself."

Ingrid pulled away from him so she could look up into his face. "Who?"

He shook his head. "I shouldn't have brought it up. Totally different circumstances." He started to chew at his bottom lip.

"Who was it, Ralph?"

He wandered over to the edge of the roof, looking out at the view. Ingrid followed him.

"Who, Ralph?"

"My sister." He rubbed his eyes, keeping his face turned away from her. "She killed herself. I was the one who found her in the bathroom."

Ingrid slipped her hand into his and interlaced their fingers. "I'm so sorry."

"I was twelve. For years and years I thought that if I'd come home from school just a few minutes earlier, if I hadn't messed around with my mates in the park first... I could have saved her."

"But you stopped blaming yourself?"

He nodded.

"What changed? What made you think about it differently?"

"Another suicide. I was still a uniformed officer—it was just a few years ago. I was trying to convince a woman that she couldn't have done anything to change the outcome. That if someone is determined to end their own life, there's nothing you can do to dissuade them. Not in the long run."

"And telling her that, you convinced yourself?"

"Not right away. Took a long time before I came round to that way of thinking." He squeezed her hand and started to pull her toward the door. "Let's go back inside. You're shivering."

Still feeling light-headed from the vodka, Ingrid allowed herself to be led through the door and back into the living room. Ralph sat her on the couch and disappeared into the hall. He came back a few moments later with the vodka bottle and two glasses. He poured two generous measures and forced a glass into Ingrid's hand.

"I think you might need this." He watched as she took a sip. He didn't drink anything himself.

Ingrid leaned her head against his shoulder and closed her eyes. "Thank you for listening."

"It's what I came here for." He put an arm around her shoulders, his hand caressing the top of her arm. "You can tell me anything." He hauled her legs over his so that he was cradling her in his arms. He stroked her hair and kissed the top of her head.

Ingrid nodded, her eyes filling again. She raised the glass to her lips, trying to hide her face with it. Ralph settled back on the couch, his arm wrapped around her, his hand stroking her hair.

———

The insistent ring of Ingrid's cell phone woke her. It took a moment before she managed to open her eyes. Her mouth was dry. She was curled up on the couch, wrapped in a woolen throw.

Alone.

She sat up quickly and wished she hadn't. Her head started to pound. She found her phone by her feet. It was four-thirty in the morning. She recognized Gurley's number and quickly swiped the answer button.

"They found the chopper," he said brusquely.

"Have you any idea what time it is?"

"It was abandoned in a field in a place named Aylesbury—that's only forty miles from central London. He's come back to the capital. I was thinking maybe we should stake out the hospital."

Ingrid ran a hand through her hair. She was barely awake. No way was she rushing to UCH on a hunch of Gurley's at this time of the morning. "The location of the helicopter probably isn't even relevant. Foster could be anywhere." She tried to sit tall and straighten out the crick in her neck. Her whole body was sore as hell. "You should get some sleep. We'll think about a strategy in the morning."

"I'm not going to sleep until I have that sonofabitch locked in a cell."

37

Ingrid was early for her meeting. She'd arranged with DCI Radcliffe to meet in the café in the main University College Hospital building. She grabbed herself a half decent Americano and sat at a table by the window hoping to see Radcliffe when he arrived. The café was busy, mostly occupied by patients and visitors, no doubt grateful to escape the wards and consulting rooms for a few brief moments.

With a quarter of an hour to fill, Ingrid's mind naturally returned to the events of the night before. Or rather, the non-events. After she'd put the phone down to Gurley, she'd discovered a hastily written note Ralph had scrawled on the back of an envelope, explaining how it had gotten late, she had fallen asleep and he thought it best to leave, in the circumstances. He'd signed it with his initials. It seemed a little formal, given she'd pretty much poured her heart out to him. Ever since she'd read it she'd been worrying something had happened that she had no memory of. Had she really been that wasted? The vodka bottle had been half full when she started drinking. When she woke up at four-thirty it was empty. Had she just passed out? What did he mean, 'in the circumstances'? Had she said or done something embarrassing? Offended him, maybe?

She buried her head in her hands. She was driving herself crazy asking the same questions over and over. The more she tried to remember of the night, the more her brain stubbornly refused to recall anything more than the feel of his hand on her hair. Or the smell of his skin.

Good God. Had she blown her chance of starting something serious with the only man she'd met in a long time that she actually gave a damn about?

She retrieved her phone from her purse, and, not for the first time that morning, scrolled to his number in her contacts list. Her finger hovered over the call option.

She couldn't do it.

Instead she called Mike Stiller.

"Jesus, Skyberg. It's not even seven a.m. What's the matter with you?"

"Are you seriously telling me I woke you up?"

"As it happens, I'm on my way to the office. But I coulda been wrapped up in bed."

"Sure. You'd live at Bureau HQ if someone put a cot next to your desk."

"I guess you're calling for another update. Even though the woman isn't your friend."

Ingrid took a sip of coffee. "I can't let this one go now. I owe it to Megan's mom to see it through." She owed her a whole lot more besides.

"I do have more news, but you might not want to hear it."

"Nothing you tell me can be worse than what I've been imagining."

"You might want to brace yourself anyways."

Ingrid put down the coffee cup.

"They've started to recover some remains buried underneath the basement floor and in the backyard."

Ingrid swallowed. She'd figured the perp wouldn't have been satisfied with just three abductions. "How many?"

"So far they've identified bones from three different bodies. All female. All probably under forty years of age."

"So far? There could be more?"

"Maybe close to a dozen, according to my sources."

"Jesus, Mike."

"I know."

"And they're still no closer to tracking him down?"

"Getting closer. Maybe. The theory is that somebody's protecting him. When the details about the buried bodies hits the news channels, the hope is whoever's sheltering him will get a bad conscience and come forward."

"That's not much of a lead."

"They're working some other angles—I just don't know what they are yet."

"When you find out, will you tell me right away?"

"I'll do my best." He drew in a sharp breath. "Listen, I know this matters to you, but you gotta keep a little perspective, OK? Don't get obsessed with it, you hear?"

"Don't lecture me, Mike. Just give me what you've got just as soon as you get it." She hung up and shoved the phone back in her purse.

"You're keen."

Ingrid looked up to see Detective Chief Inspector Radcliffe looking down at her. "Can I get you a coffee?" she asked.

"I'm awash with the stuff. I had my first at half-six this morning and I haven't stopped since." He glanced at his watch. "Professor Glynde is expecting us."

"Sure." Ingrid drank the last of her Americano and pushed out her chair. "I really appreciate you setting up this meeting so fast."

"I'm still not entirely sure why I agreed to it."

"You don't want to leave any stones unturned any more than I do."

Radcliffe marched them down to the main reception area of the hospital and they took the elevator to the third floor. He led the way along a corridor with closed half-glazed doors on both sides. Ingrid supposed this floor housed the majority of the administration department.

"Glynde says he can spare us twenty minutes. He's due in theater in just under an hour."

"Busy man."

"Aren't we all." Radcliffe knocked on the door and pushed it open.

Inside, a young woman was standing behind a very organized desk, just a phone, computer and keyboard sitting on top. "DCI Radcliffe?" she asked.

Radcliffe nodded.

"Professor Glynde's expecting you." She grabbed a large gym bag from beneath the desk. "I'm off to lunch now—you'll be taking your own notes at the meeting?"

"We're fine, no need for you to stay." Radcliffe smiled at her and knocked on the interior door just to the right of her desk. This time he actually waited for a response before barging in. "Professor Glynde, thank you for your time." He extended his arm and the two men shook hands. It wasn't until Glynde looked expectantly at Ingrid that Radcliffe remembered his manners. "This is Agent Skyberg, from the American embassy."

"A pleasure." The professor shook her hand, scrutinizing her as closely as she was him. His auburn wavy hair was graying at the temples, he had a pair of wire-framed glasses perched on the end of his nose and his skin was ruddy rather than tanned, as if he sailed on the weekend. His red bow tie completed the hospital consultant look.

He let go of Ingrid's hand and turned to Radcliffe. "I must admit, I thought we'd been through everything in detail during my previous interview, chief inspector."

"Agent Skyberg has some additional questions."

"Fire away. I have to warn you though, I am quite pressed for time."

"I've seen a list of Molly's injuries and there's one in particular that I'd like to speak to you about."

Glynde raised his eyebrows.

"The bruising on Molly's upper arms."

"Consistent with a shaking injury. The child is grabbed by the arms, the attacker squeezing hard against the soft flesh between elbow and shoulder joints. The flesh there bruises fairly readily without too much pressure being applied."

"Have you seen many head injuries caused by shaking?"

"Nothing that's led to a police inquiry."

"But you would definitely say the injuries in this case are consistent with a shaking incident?"

"They are. But I don't have much experience in these kinds of cases. Which is why I invited Dr Ryland to speak to you. He's rather an expert in the field. Given evidence in court and so forth."

"Dr Ryland?" Ingrid said.

"Yes—he should be here any moment. You can continue speaking to him when I duck out. He really is the man who knows all there is to know about cases similar to this one."

"And Dr Ryland is familiar with the details of this case?"

"I've briefed him."

Ingrid was beginning to feel she was being fobbed off. "Do you have Molly's file here?"

Glynde reached over his desk and retrieved a slim folder from the top of a tall pile. He opened it and started to flip through the few pages inside. He stopped at a color photograph of Molly's arms. "What did you want to know about the bruises?"

Ingrid noticed a scale printed at the side of the photo. "Can you tell me the size of the bruises?"

He turned the file around so that it was facing Ingrid. "You can see for yourself. This photograph has recorded the injuries at life size."

Ingrid studied the purple and red marks on Molly's pale arms. "These are finger marks caused by pressure applied to the flesh?"

"They are indeed." The professor glanced at the clock on the wall.

"Wouldn't you say the finger marks were a little small for a man's hands?"

Radcliffe, who had previously been leaning back in his chair, sat forward to get a better look at the photograph.

"It's impossible for me to form an opinion—after all, I don't know the size of the suspect's hands. Perhaps his fingers are abnormally small."

"As far as I can recall, Kyle Foster is average height, average weight." She looked directly at the DCI. "Surely if there were anything abnormal about his hands you would have been made aware of it?"

Radcliffe thought about it for a moment. "The crime scene manager will compare the injuries with Foster's fingerprints in due course."

Ingrid was amazed it hadn't been done already. But then there was no doubt in Radcliffe's mind that Kyle Foster was responsible for his daughter's injuries. Why should there be? All the evidence pointed to Foster. Why would he question the testimony of a distraught mother when the case seemed so cut and dried?

Glynde was looking at the clock again. "Look, I'm sorry I've had to cut this meeting short, but I'm sure Dr Ryland will arrive any moment. Perhaps you could speak to him in the café downstairs?" He stood up.

Reluctantly, Ingrid got to her feet only after Radcliffe had slowly risen from his chair. She could see he was pissed at being asked to leave.

Glynde led them to the door just as a man on the other side opened it.

"Ah... Geoff! I'm afraid I can't stick around. Do you mind taking the reins?"

Ingrid and Radcliffe exchanged an uneasy glance: if anyone was in control it should be one of them.

"Not at all, Roger. Only too pleased to help. It's why I'm here, after all." He turned to Ingrid and Radcliffe.

"You'll have to introduce yourselves. My apologies." Glynde ushered them out of his office, firmly closing the door and then herded them through the outer room and into the corridor beyond. He then practically sprinted away.

"It's all go!" Glynde's colleague stuck out a hand. "Geoff Ryland, at your service." Ryland's appearance was the opposite of Glynde's. He was balding, bearded, gray-skinned and tieless.

Radcliffe quickly introduced himself and Ingrid. He clearly wanted to ensure Ryland knew exactly who was leading the investigation.

"You work here at UCH?" Ingrid asked.

"Did my training here. But no—I'm based at King's College now—the college itself rather than the hospital. I'm involved purely in research these days." He gave Ingrid a sad smile. "Now, Roger tells me you want to discuss shaken baby syndrome." He let out a sigh. "Not that we should call it that, of course. That particular theory has been widely discredited. And my reputation along with it."

38

Rather than have their meeting in the café within the hospital, Dr Ryland suggested they adjourn to a nearby pub. "It is practically lunchtime," he said, as he led them across Tottenham Court Road and down a side street leading to an area that Ingrid had discovered had been dubbed "NoHo" a few years ago.

Once they'd found the pub and Ryland had ordered beer battered fish with thick-cut French fries, a pint of bitter and two orange juices from the bar, they all headed for a corner seat of the large dining area. Ingrid sat down next to Ryland on the dubiously stained upholstery while Radcliffe pulled up a low wooden stool from a nearby table.

"So, little Molly Foster," Ryland said and gulped down a few mouthfuls of beer. "Such a tragic case."

"Professor Glynde suggested you were quite an expert in the field," Ingrid said.

"Certainly I was. As I mentioned before, the subject has been quite controversial over the years. In the mid-2000s a number of cases went to appeal and the original convictions were overturned. Which reflected very badly on me, unfortunately."

"How?"

"I was an expert witness for the prosecution. All the evidence I provided was scientifically sound at the time. But the science itself changed in the intervening years."

Ingrid wondered just how reliable Ryland's opinion was now. Were they wasting their time talking to a doctor about a discredited theory?

"The Crown Prosecution Service changed its guidance on the subject only a couple of years ago—but I'm sure you don't need me to tell you that, chief inspector."

Ingrid looked expectantly at Radcliffe for an explanation. The DCI shifted uncomfortably on his stool. "The CPS guidance says a charge of homicide or attempted murder can't be justified by the presence of head injuries alone. Other evidence needs to be present," Radcliffe told her.

"Such as?"

"Such as an eye witness account of what happened. In this case, Carrie Foster's." The DCI sounded irritated.

Ingrid turned away from him. "How strong would someone need to be to do this kind of damage?" Ingrid was frustrated not to have Molly's file in front of her. "You are familiar with the details of the case?"

"I am—Roger brought me up to speed." He suddenly seemed distracted by something.

Ingrid followed his gaze and saw a waitress approaching with a large oval plate piled high with chunky fries and an enormous hunk of fish covered in dark orange batter. Ryland's eyes widened as he shoved his pint glass out of the way to make room for his lunch.

"Another pint of bitter would go down a treat too." He winked at the waitress then turned to Ingrid and Radcliffe. "Would you like another drink?" He eyed their untouched glasses sitting on the table. "Something stronger than orange juice perhaps?"

"We're both fine." Radcliffe dismissed the waitress with a wave of his hand.

The interview wasn't going the way Ingrid had envisaged. She'd have to keep Ryland on track. But now he had beer battered Moby Dick and two pounds of deep fried potatoes to distract his attention, she wasn't hopeful she'd manage it.

"The person responsible for the attack wouldn't need to be that physically strong at all," Ryland said after he'd thoughtfully chewed and swallowed a large mouthful of greasy fish. Ingrid was surprised he'd even remembered the original question. "Although the infant brain is pretty well protected by the skull at fourteen months, there's still space inside the cranium to allow significant movement of the fragile organ with only the gentlest of shaking. It would need to be prolonged, however." He speared three fat fries onto his fork, dipped them in tomato ketchup and shoved them into his mouth.

"And would prolonged shaking indicate more... premeditation... more intent?" Ingrid waited for him to repeat the chewing and swallowing procedure.

"Impossible to say."

"Really?"

"I would have suggested that in the past, but I've had my fingers burnt making those kind of assumptions."

"So it's possible in a moment of weakness, a fit of rage... in a desperate attempt to stop a baby crying, for example, someone could inflict those injuries *accidentally*?"

"It has been known."

Ingrid stared pointedly at Radcliffe, who took a moment to look up at her. He'd previously been mesmerized by Dr Ryland's eating habits, an expression of mild disgust on his face. He gave her a shrug, his eyebrows raised as if to suggest what Ryland was telling them was of little consequence.

"Though in those cases, in my experience, additional head trauma has been present," Ryland said.

"Meaning?"

"The head has made contact with a hard surface."

"Is there evidence of that in this case?"

"There is some external bruising at the back of the skull. So it's certainly possible."

"Could that kind of injury be the result of an accidental knock to the head?" Ingrid asked.

Ryland nodded thoughtfully. "Though I'm not sure where you're going with this."

"If you wouldn't mind bearing with me just a little longer."

"Not at all." He shoveled more fries into his mouth.

"What if someone were suffering from postpartum depression? Would that make the possibility that the injuries were inflicted without premeditation more likely?"

"Most definitely. In the majority of the cases I've studied, post natal depression has been present. And proven to be a contributory factor."

"Equally, some other type of mental health condition could also trigger this kind of attack, isn't that true?" Radcliffe said, obviously keen to derail Ingrid's theory that Carrie Foster might have been responsible.

"What sort of condition are you talking about?"

"A bout of rage caused by post traumatic stress disorder?"

"Not something I've come across personally. Not really my area. But yes, of course, there have been cases. I've read about them in the papers, just like everyone else."

"But again, that wouldn't point to premeditation," Ingrid suggested.

Ryland put down his cutlery for the first time, picked up his glass and drank the last inch of beer just as the waitress arrived with a fresh pint. He looked from Ingrid to Radcliffe. "Are you two hoping to prove opposing theories?"

Neither of them answered.

"Only, I wouldn't rely on anything I tell you. In these cases I've learnt to have a completely open mind. It has been rather forced upon me by past experience, but nevertheless… either or both of those two syndromes could have triggered an incident of shaking that might have caused Molly Foster's injuries."

"But you wouldn't rule either of them out?" Ingrid pressed her point.

"No—I'm not one for ruling anything out. Not anymore." He stared into space for a moment before quickly recovering to turn his attention back to his now half empty plate.

Radcliffe got to his feet. "Thank you for your time, Dr Ryland. Good of you to come over."

"No trouble at all. Nice to have been asked!" He stood up and slowly reached his right hand behind his back, presumably to grab his wallet from a pocket. He was so slow, in fact, that he still hadn't retrieved it before Radcliffe offered to pay.

From the expression on his face as he called over the waitress and settled the check, Ingrid knew the DCI was seriously pissed.

39

Once they were outside the pub the DCI let rip. "I don't know what you hoped to achieve with that exercise, but I think you'd have to agree your plan failed abysmally. That man is a washed-up excuse for a professional. He's a joke."

"I didn't plan to speak to 'that man' at all—that was Glynde's idea. But you can't totally disregard what he told us. Carrie Foster is strong enough physically, and maybe mentally... compromised enough to have inflicted those injuries on Molly herself. You can't ignore it any longer. You have to at least rule her out of any involvement before you can make any assumptions about her husband."

"We interviewed her extensively. Her statement hasn't wavered."

"You were questioning her specifically about Kyle. About his actions. Have you closely examined hers?"

"She's in no fit state to be put through that kind of interrogation. She wouldn't cope with the ordeal."

"Come on, you know you have to question her again. Kyle Foster insists he didn't hurt Molly."

"Of course he does. He's abducted his son and is evading arrest for the attempted murder of his daughter. What else would you expect him to say?"

"What about the size of the bruises on Molly's arms? How do you explain those?"

Radcliffe didn't answer.

"And there's the vodka hidden in her closet, the fact that people close to her said her mood worsened after Molly was born."

"People? Unless you have medical evidence proving that fact, I'm not interested."

"There's something I haven't told you."

Radcliffe shook his head. "What desperate piece of insignificant information are you going to dredge up now to support your case?"

"I have nothing to gain by proving or disproving Kyle Foster's guilt. How could I? I just want to make sure we look at his side of the story before totally dismissing it. I just want to get at the truth."

"And you think I don't?" He started to walk away.

Ingrid reached out and grabbed his sleeve as she drew level with him. They walked back toward Tottenham Court Road and the hospital. "I don't think that for a second."

"What, then? What haven't you told me?"

"When Major Gurley and I were searching the Foster house we found a bottle of pills in the bathroom cabinet. I've since had them identified as anti-depressants. There was no label on the bottle, so I presume they weren't officially prescribed."

"You're saying they were obtained illegally?"

"That's my presumption. What if they're Carrie's?"

"Why didn't you tell me about them before? Oh wait, I was forgetting, you're somewhat selective with the information you pass on."

"I'm telling you now."

"Because it suits your purpose. They still might be his."

Ingrid threw up her hands. Maybe Kyle Foster had shaken his daughter so hard she lost consciousness, but since Ingrid had spoken to Carrie's friend on the base and Yvonne Sherwood, both telling her what a good father Kyle had been, she felt she should give the guy the benefit of a doubt. He'd seemed so concerned about Tommy's safety when he called the base, wasn't the possibility that his wife was responsible worth at least a little investigation?

As she and Radcliffe walked across the busy intersection, Ingrid tried desperately to come up with something she could tell the DCI that might convince him she wasn't wasting his time.

Nothing came to mind.

They reached the other side of the street and Radcliffe turned to her. "I'm going back to the station. So I suppose this is goodbye." He shook her hand and turned away.

As she watched him walk up Euston Road she saw a steady stream of slow moving pedestrians making their way to the entrance of the hospital. Some of them were in wheelchairs, some using strollers, crutches, a lot of them frail, most of them old.

Then she remembered something. Maybe Radcliffe would dismiss it as irrelevant just as soon as she told him, but she couldn't not mention it. It could make a sliver of difference—and right now she was dealing in tiny increments. She ran after him.

"Hey, chief inspector!"

He didn't hear her, just carried on marching. Or maybe he did and was ignoring her. She picked up her pace and reached him in a matter of seconds. "Please, DCI Radcliffe. There's something else."

He stopped dead and turned to her, a scowl on his face. "Something else you neglected to mention previously?"

"I pretty much dismissed it before, but now maybe it makes more sense."

"Be quick. I really don't want to waste any more of my day."

She snatched a breath and launched into her unprepared speech. "There was a witness at the Fosters' hotel, an American woman. She saw Kyle Foster return to his room when she was on her way down to breakfast on the morning of… the incident."

"The attempted murder, you mean."

"She said she distinctly remembered Foster was carrying a large McDonald's bag."

"I do hope this is leading somewhere."

"According to Carrie Foster, Kyle grabbed Molly from her arms and shook her, violently, flung her onto the bed and stormed out of the room."

"Yes?"

"He was mad. Out of control. He ran. Maybe she thought he wouldn't come back. But he did. Not only that, he came back with *breakfast* for the whole family?"

"According to this witness."

"Why should we doubt it? She was very clear. She said Foster *smiled* at her as he passed. Does that describe a man who practically shook his baby daughter to death only fifteen minutes earlier?"

"I've seen all the evidence collected from the scene. There was no McDonald's bag."

"OK, I don't know what happened to the bag. But I'm sure there must be some CCTV footage from inside the restaurant showing Foster buying breakfast, if you doubt the witness' account."

"You know I can actually hear the faint sound of rustling, you're clutching at straws so desperately."

"I'm just saying Carrie Foster could have hurt Molly while Kyle was out fetching breakfast. She had the opportunity."

The DCI didn't respond.

"Come on—we have this, the hidden booze, the illegally prescribed pills, the small bruises. Doesn't it all add up?"

Radcliffe closed his eyes and shook his head. "Dear God, you just don't give up, do you?"

"Is there any other way to be?"

"All right. But I'm doing the questioning. I'll try to arrange for an interview with Mrs Foster sometime later today."

"Can I observe?"

"I don't want you in the room with me."

"From another room, then."

"We'd need to conduct the interview at the police station for that to be possible."

"Surely you'd want to do that anyway—to record the interview?"

"She won't be answering questions under caution. Let's be quite clear about this—I am *not* arresting her."

"No—of course not."

At last. Ingrid felt she was beginning to get somewhere.

40

"What the hell do you think you're doing?" Jack Gurley towered over Ingrid, she felt his hot breath on her face. His cheeks were scarlet with rage.

Two seconds earlier he'd burst into the observation room next to interview room five in Holborn police station, slamming the door behind him. The uniformed officer assigned to sit with them jumped up from his seat and forced himself between Gurley and Ingrid.

"Take it easy!" he said and raised his hands to Gurley's chest, taking care to leave a good two inches of air between his palms and the angry MP's shirt.

The door opened and another uniformed officer hurried into the room. She had an embarrassed expression on her face, clearly she'd just had the door slammed on her by Gurley.

"Thank you, constable," Ingrid said. "But I think I can manage the situation myself."

"How is it I find out about this interview from your clerk at the embassy?"

"I thought your priority was seeing Kyle Foster behind bars, I didn't imagine you'd be interested in anything more his wife had to say."

"Where's Radcliffe?" he yelled at the male PC standing just inches away from him. "I have to get this thing stopped."

"No way," Ingrid said. "DCI Radcliffe agrees there are enough anomalies in the case to make another interview necessary. With respect, Major, the decision to interview Carrie Foster again wasn't yours to make."

Gurley swore under his breath and kicked a nearby chair. It clattered into the table that was supporting an array of TV monitors. The monitors shook, one of them threatening for a moment to topple onto the floor.

"Take it easy," the male PC said again.

"For crying out loud, is that all you can say?" Gurley marched toward the door, turned, then marched back again. "I want you to know I strongly oppose what you're doing here."

"I think you've made that quite clear."

"Oh I can make it plenty clearer, believe me." He pulled out the chair he'd just kicked and sat down.

The far left-hand monitor on the table showed activity in the interview room. The door opened. The family liaison officer they'd seen at the hospital walked in a few paces ahead of Carrie Foster. They both sat down on a low-backed couch, Carrie Foster leaning forward, her forearms resting on her knees. She looked as exhausted as she had during their previous meeting. After a few moments, DS Tyson and DCI Radcliffe entered the room and shut the door behind them. They sat on a matching couch arranged opposite the other, with just a few feet between the two. It almost looked as if Tyson's knees might bump against the FLO's. Ingrid understood the furniture and ambience of the room was meant to feel casual and unthreatening, but the forced intimacy seemed almost oppressive.

"Look at her," Gurley said, tapping the screen of the next monitor along. It showed a close-up of Carrie Foster's face. "She looks ready to collapse. They shouldn't be putting her through this." He balled his hand into a fist and banged it against his knee. "This shouldn't be happening."

Ingrid pulled out the chair next to him and sat down. The male PC sat next to her. The female PC took up position by the door, presumably ready to hinder any attempt by Gurley to interrupt the interview in the next room.

"Let's just listen to what she has to say, shall we?" Ingrid said.

Gurley didn't answer, just flexed his jaw muscles in response.

Radcliffe's voice boomed through the speakers in the observation room. "Thank you for agreeing to come into the station like this, Mrs Foster. We really appreciate your cooperation."

The PC stretched across Ingrid and lowered the volume control on the small amplifier sitting on the table.

"Do I need a lawyer?" Carrie Foster glanced at the FLO, who gave her a reassuring smile. She ignored it. "I mean, you're all cops after all. Maybe I should have somebody here looking after my interests."

"Good," Gurley muttered. "She won't be a pushover. Radcliffe won't be able to bully her."

"You're not under arrest, Mrs Foster," Tyson said in a soft voice. "You can get up and leave anytime you want. This is just an informal chat."

"Are you recording this?" she looked up toward the ceiling. "Filming it?"

"Only for your benefit. We wouldn't want to mis-remember anything you told us. We don't have to record a single word, if you'd rather have it that way."

Mrs Foster hesitated before answering. "I suppose it's for the best. I wouldn't want you twisting my words."

"We have absolutely no intention of doing that. Why would we?" Radcliffe said, his tone acquiring a harder edge.

"Look—I can't stay here long. I still can't sleep without medication, I've hardly eaten. I don't feel well enough to answer a lot of questions. I shouldn't be away from Molly."

"We only really want you to tell us what happened on Monday morning."

"Again?" Carrie Foster and Gurley said in unison.

"What is this? Anomalies my ass," Gurley said. He started to get up, then changed his mind.

Ingrid did her best to ignore him, concentrating instead on what was going on in the room next door.

"I know it's traumatic for you," Radcliffe was saying, barely managing to sound sympathetic. Ingrid supposed he was eager to get the whole thing over with. "But now that Molly is on the road to recovery, we thought you might feel more able to speak to us."

"The doctors don't know if she'll make a full recovery. There may be long term issues. What if she's permanently brain damaged? What if she can't hear or see properly?" She clasped her hands together. "What am I even doing here? I should get back to the hospital." She stood up.

"We won't keep you long, I promise." Radcliffe managed a faint smile. "Something you tell us now might help track down Kyle."

"Why is it taking you so long to find him?"

"It's just as frustrating for us, believe me. Our priority is to locate Kyle and get Tommy back to you. That's why it's important for us to talk again. You do understand?"

Carrie Foster sat back down. For the next ten minutes she proceeded to list the same sequence of events that she had in her earlier interview.

In the observation room, Ingrid was willing Radcliffe to interject, probe Carrie Foster's account of what happened little more rigorously. But he just sat there nodding silently.

"When you say you attempted to grab Molly back from Kyle, can you describe how you tried to do that? I'm having trouble picturing it," the DCI finally said.

"I pulled at his arms. He was holding Molly close to him while he was shaking her. His grip on her was too tight."

"Where was he holding her, exactly?"

Carrie Foster paused, closed her eyes, as if trying to remember the scene in detail. "He was squeezing her arms."

"At the shoulders? The elbows?"

She lifted her hands in the air, her fingers curled, supposedly miming the actions of her husband. "Upper arms, between her elbows and shoulders."

"That would certainly be consistent with the bruising there," Radcliffe said.

Ingrid thought she saw a flash of panic cross Mrs Foster's face at the mention of Molly's bruises.

"How long was your husband shaking Molly?" Radcliffe asked.

Foster looked down at her hands. She shrugged. "I don't know, a long time maybe. It felt like a long time."

"And all the while you were grabbing at his arms, to try to get Molly back?"

She nodded slowly. "Every time I reached out for her he swung her away from me."

"Still shaking her?"

"Yes! How many times do I have to tell you? He didn't stop shaking her."

The FLO rested a calming hand on Mrs Foster's knee. She angrily batted it away.

"I'm sorry. I really don't mean to upset you," the DCI said. "But you must realize, if we're to build a solid case against your husband, we do need to know even the smallest of details."

"You've got to catch him first. Maybe you should be spending your time doing that."

"Believe me, we are. We've devoted considerable manpower to the operation."

"Oh sure." Gurley said. "And look where it's gotten you."

The uniformed PC sitting next to Ingrid huffed a disapproving sigh.

"You got something to say, officer?"

The PC didn't reply.

"Then keep your goddamn mouth shut."

"Shhh," Ingrid said, still watching the monitors intently.

"What happened next?" Radcliffe said. He had leaned both elbows on his knees, his hands grasped together in front of him.

Carrie Foster let out an unexpected high pitched sob. "Molly went quiet."

"She'd been crying all this time?"

"That's why he was shaking her. To make her stop."

"And then what happened?"

"He shoved her back at me."

The image on the far right-hand monitor showed Radcliffe's forehead pucker into a severe frown. "I thought you said your husband threw Molly onto the bed."

"What?"

"In your earlier statement."

"He did."

"But you just said—"

"He shoved her toward me, I wasn't expecting him to do that, I wasn't ready to take her, so she landed on the bed."

"So he was more throwing Molly at you, rather than deliberately hurling her towards the bed?"

"I don't know what he was doing." She leaned forward, her face inches away from the detective's. "You'd have to ask him that."

41

Without being asked, the family liaison officer got to her feet. Radcliffe glared at her. "Sir, I think it might be time for a break now."

"I'll decide when a break is called for."

"But, sir, Carrie's clearly distressed. Let me at least get her a glass of water."

Carrie Foster started to cry.

"I can't let this go on a minute longer." Gurley got to his feet.

Ingrid grabbed his arm. "Let's wait a few moments, can we? I think Radcliffe might be getting somewhere."

"Sure, if harassing an innocent woman was his aim, he's doing real well."

Ingrid stood up too. "Just a little while longer. Please, Jack."

They both turned their attention back toward the monitors to see the FLO hand Carrie Foster a bottle of water. Mrs Foster's hands were trembling too much to unscrew the top, so the FLO opened the bottle for her.

"Jesus, look at what he's done to her," Gurley said, sitting down again.

"We are grateful for you answering our questions like this, Mrs Foster, I can't express that strongly enough," Radcliffe said gently.

"Are we nearly through?"

"Almost, just another couple of questions and we'll be done." Once again, Radcliffe glanced up at the camera, an admonishing look on his face, as if he were holding Ingrid personally responsible for Carrie Foster's current condition. "In your earlier statement you said that Kyle pushed you away so violently that you bruised yourself on an item of furniture."

"Yes?"

"You didn't mention it just now. When exactly in the sequence of events did this happen? And can you describe the furniture in question?"

"It was... I guess it was the bureau, the wooden bureau set against the wall."

"Really?"

"I think so."

"Only that seems a little high to cause a bruise on your thigh. How tall are you, Mrs Foster?"

"Five-six."

"Exactly, far too high."

Carrie Foster frowned at him. "Maybe it was something else. I wasn't really paying attention to the furniture. Kyle was hurting Molly, it was all I could think about."

"And you sustained this injury when?"

She thought for a moment. "When I tried to grab Molly from him."

"So he what, let go of Molly with one hand to push you?"

"No, he didn't stop shaking her. He kind of... he shoved me with his hip and thigh, sent me off balance and I crashed into something—I guess I don't remember what that was." She raised the bottle of water to her lips with a trembling hand and took a sip. "Is that it?"

"Just one final thing." Radcliffe tilted his head sympathetically. "It has been brought to my attention that you are in possession of a prescription drug—an anti-depressant—that has been illegally obtained."

"What?"

"A bottle of pills was discovered in your bathroom cabinet at home."

"What the hell have you been doing in my house?"

"Strictly speaking, the house is the property of the RAF, leased to the US Air Force. Our American colleagues authorized the search."

Carrie Foster lifted a hand to her mouth.

"Are the pills yours, Mrs Foster?"

"I... don't know anything about any pills."

Ingrid was surprised at her answer. She'd assumed Carrie Foster would say the pills were Kyle's right off the bat.

"Do they belong to your husband?"

Slowly blinking away her tears, Carrie Foster wiped the back of her hand across her cheeks. "I guess they could be—I've never seen any pills."

"The hell with this." Gurley started towards the door. "I'm stopping it right now."

"There's no need," Ingrid called to him. "It's over."

Gurley turned abruptly. "What did you think you were doing?" He pointed a finger into Ingrid's face, his fingertip just a fraction of an inch from her left cheek. She reared backwards, almost losing her balance.

The PC stood up.

"Tell me to take it easy one more goddamn time and I swear..." Gurley yelled at the officer. "You told Radcliffe about the pills?" he said, lowering his hand. "You said they were for menstrual cramping. What's all this anti-depressant crap?"

"Hey—I made a mistake. They were the same color as something I've taken before."

"How'd you even know what they were?"

"I did a little research."

"And when were you planning on sharing that information with me?"

"I guess it slipped my mind."

"Un-fucking-believable."

It was the first time she'd heard Gurley swear. "I'm sorry, OK?"

"You thought they belonged to him, didn't you? But you didn't want to believe he was taking anti-depressants. Didn't fit in with this new theory of yours, huh?"

"Why do you refuse to even question Carrie's innocence?"

Gurley glanced at the PC standing close by. "I'm not having this conversation with you now."

"I just want the truth. Nothing more, nothing less. I thought that's what you wanted too."

"Don't even try to suggest that I don't. How dare you—" He was cut off by the door opening.

Ingrid turned to see Radcliffe standing in the doorway. "Well?" she said. "What are you going to do about her?"

"Give her a lift back to the hospital."

"She contradicted her earlier statement."

"Not significantly."

"She was uncomfortable when you brought up the subject of the bruising. And how could she not know about the pills in her own bathroom cabinet?"

"What do you want me to do?"

"Don't you have enough to arrest her? Insist she answers more questions. You didn't even bring up the issue of the breakfast from McDonald's."

"The what?" Gurley said.

"Nothing—an unconfirmed witness statement. I didn't bring it up because it wasn't relevant," Radcliffe snapped. "I've just put that woman through hell, and wasted my own time in the process. Are you satisfied now?" He stared at Ingrid accusingly.

"Not in the least," she said, holding his gaze. "But I guess that's my problem." Dissatisfaction with Radcliffe's interview technique wasn't the issue. She was frustrated as hell nobody wanted to consider another explanation for Molly's injuries.

Without saying another word, the chief inspector left the room. Gurley followed him out, with Ingrid just a couple of steps behind them.

"Tell me I'm not going to witness a repeat of that performance," Gurley said. "Tell me you have no plans to question Carrie Foster again."

"Perhaps you should be talking to your colleague about that, rather than me." Radcliffe marched away.

"What's going on with you?" Ingrid asked Gurley.

"With me?" He shook his head. "You just don't know when to stop, do you? When to admit you're wrong."

"There's something you're not telling me. How can you be so sure Carrie Foster had nothing to do with her daughter's injuries?"

"You seem to be the only person who isn't. As far as I can see you're in a minority of one."

As they stood in the gleaming, white-walled corridor, the door to the interview room opened and Carrie Foster emerged. She was hanging on to the arm of the family liaison officer for support. She looked from Gurley to Ingrid. "What are you doing here? Was this your idea? I thought you were supposed to be supporting me."

Gurley reached out a hand to her. Carrie Foster ducked away.

"We are here for you," he said, his voice gentle.

"You make me sick. All of you."

The FLO led Mrs Foster away. DS Tyson appeared in the doorway of the interview room. He ignored Ingrid and Gurley and walked away, shaking his head as he went.

"You've managed to alienate just about everyone," Gurley said, contempt in his voice. Then he called after Tyson. "Hey, wait up. I'd like to see the latest intel you have."

Tyson slowed. "I'm on my way to the incident room now."

Ingrid was left stranded in the middle of the corridor. She grabbed her phone and called Sol Franklin.

"Hi Ingrid, any developments?" he said as soon as he picked up.

"No. Nothing worth reporting. I'm calling about something else. I want to make a formal request to investigate this case solo. Major Gurley and I have very different, incompatible methods. His attitude is affecting my ability to do my job."

There was silence for a few moments on the other end of the line.

"Sol?"

"I wanted to talk to you about Major Gurley, as a matter of fact."

Another pause.

"You did?"

"He contacted Louden earlier today. Major Gurley has requested you're taken off the case."

42

Ingrid emerged from Holborn police station in a daze. The rest of her conversation with Sol Franklin had not gone well. She'd let loose a series of grievances about Gurley's behavior that just made her seem whiny and unprofessional. Sol listened patiently to all of her complaints, finally telling her they'd speak in more detail after he'd tried to smooth things out with Louden. She hoped Sol could work his magic and keep her on the case. She'd come too far now not to see it through to its conclusion.

On the other side of the sidewalk she noticed a small gathering of people. It took her a moment to realize they were reporters. A moment after that a familiar figure stepped out of the crowd.

"Ingrid. I'm so glad I didn't miss you." Angela Tate hurried toward her.

Tate was the last person Ingrid wanted to see. She considered making a dash for it. "How did you know I was here?"

"I have my spies at the hospital. They told me Carrie Foster was on the move, accompanied by her FLO and two detectives. It didn't take a genius to work out she was being brought in for questioning. Has she been arrested?"

"How did your... colleagues find out about it?" Ingrid pointed to the handful of journalists, some of them talking on cell phones, others enjoying a cigarette. She saw Tate's photographer chatting to a man holding a large microphone covered in a furry windshield.

"News travels fast, unfortunately. I was rather hoping for an exclusive." She smiled at Ingrid. "Still am, as a matter of fact, with your help."

"No way."

"You haven't answered my question: has Carrie Foster been arrested?"

"I have no intention of speaking to you."

Ingrid could only suppose Foster had been escorted back to the hospital using an alternate exit. Through the parking lot, most probably. Thank God. At least Tate wouldn't get the chance to fire questions at her. "How long have you been waiting here?"

"Long enough to get bloody cheesed off. Come on, Ingrid—throw me a crumb."

"You're wasting your time. There's no story for you."

"Then why are you here? I'm guessing your tall friend is somewhere in the vicinity too." She peered into the entrance of the police station. "Perhaps he'll be a bit more talkative."

"Carrie Foster has not been arrested. That's all you're getting from me."

"Then why bring her to the police station at all?"

"There's no story," Ingrid said again. "Nothing to splash across the front page of tomorrow's *Evening News*. Sorry to disappoint."

"Oh I'm sure you are." Tate pulled a pack of cigarettes from her purse, shook one out and lit it with an antique silver lighter. She exhaled, blowing the smoke behind her. "I do have something else in mind for the headline tomorrow, as it happens."

"I'm not interested."

"No? How about I run it past you? I was thinking of focusing on your absolute lack of competence. Your inability to track down a man and his eight-year-old son. You can't blame this one on the boys in blue. You're all equally culpable. And as far as I can see, equally useless."

Ingrid started to edge away. She was actually inclined to agree with Tate. They had failed at every turn. Especially after getting so close to Kyle Foster in Suffolk. It was pitiful. How was he managing to keep Tommy so well hidden?

"Still nothing to say? Don't you have some embassy approved excuses to reel out?"

Ingrid's phone started to ring. Relieved, she dug it out of her purse and glanced at the screen. It was Natasha McKittrick. "I have to take this."

"Of course you do."

Ingrid answered the phone as she hurried up Lamb's Conduit Street. She wanted to get away. From Tate. From Gurley. If she hadn't felt Tate's gaze boring into her back, she might even have broken into a run. "Hey, it's good to hear a friendly voice."

"I haven't said anything yet." McKittrick sounded decidedly downbeat.

"You just saved me from the clutches of Angela Tate."

"What's that old hack after now?"

"The usual. My soul."

"Tell her nothing." She let out a long sigh.

"What's wrong with you?"

"Mills. Have you seen him recently?"

Ingrid wasn't sure how to answer. She said nothing.

"I'm taking your silence as proof that you have. What happened? I've never seen him like this."

"Like what?" Ingrid worried again that something had happened the previous night that she had absolutely no recollection of.

"I'm used to him moping about when he's seen you, like a lovestruck teenager, too embarrassed even to take the mildest of piss-taking. But today he's just been... weird."

"How?" Now Ingrid was getting really concerned.

"It's hard to describe. He seems... resigned somehow. That's the only word I can come up with."

"About what?"

"About you, I suppose. Like the life's drained out of him. What on earth happened between the two of you?"

"Nothing."

"Something must have. Did you dump him?"

"No! Really—nothing happened. As a matter of fact..." Ingrid wasn't sure she wanted to share this with McKittrick. She certainly didn't want to be teased about it. She wasn't in the right frame of mind.

"What? You have to tell me now."

"Nothing happened between us and I'd really hoped it might."

"Whoa! You're telling me neither of you made a move? Where was this?"

"My apartment, late last night."

"I had no idea you planned to get together yesterday."

Ingrid turned right into Great Ormond Street, not entirely clear where she was headed. "It wasn't planned. I needed someone to talk to, your cell went straight to voicemail. So I called Ralph. It was a spur of the moment thing. He came over. We talked." She picked up speed, hoping to walk off the awkwardness she was feeling.

"And?"

"And nothing—I told you already—nothing happened. I woke up a few hours later and he was gone." She reached the end of the street and stopped.

"You fell asleep on him? As insults go, that's pretty damning."

"I was drunk. He knew that. I hoped he wouldn't take it personally." Ingrid looked up and down the street, unable to decide which direction to take. If she turned right she would loop back around to the police station. "I think I may have blown it with him. That the moment has passed. Like we're destined to be friends and nothing more. He was a shoulder to cry on when I needed it."

"Maybe you should give him a call. Let him know how you really feel."

"The mood I'm in right now, that is the last thing I should do."

"Tate really got to you that badly?"

"No, not Tate. This whole investigation. It's stalled and I'm not sure how to fix it."

"You'll think of something. You always do."

"Gurley's asked Sol to take me off the case."

"That's a bit extreme.

Ingrid's phone beeped in her ear. "I have another call. I should probably get it. Maybe we can talk later?"

"Let's make it over a coffee, I don't want you falling asleep on me."

Ingrid hung up and answered the other call. "Yes?"

"DS Tyson here. We've had a number of new sightings. One is particularly interesting. DCI Radcliffe thinks you should come back to the station straight away."

Ingrid took the right hand turn. "Can you meet me at the entrance out back, in the parking lot? There's somebody I need to avoid."

43

When Ingrid arrived at the incident room she found Gurley leaning awkwardly over a low desk, deep in conversation with DS Tyson. They seemed to be getting along just fine without her. She felt as though she was on the outside, looking in. Gurley's attitude toward her in the observation room made more sense now she'd discovered he was doing his best to have her removed from the investigation. He could cozy up to Tyson all he liked: she wasn't about to let either of them shut her out.

As she approached the desk, Tyson acknowledged her with a nod, and although Gurley turned to face her, he didn't say a word.

"Tell me about the sightings." She addressed the detective sergeant, as if Gurley wasn't there. If Gurley wanted to play games, she would too.

"We've had quite a few conflicting reports. If we took them all seriously we'd have to assume Kyle Foster had perfected the ability of being in two or three places at once. Some of them are from opposite ends of the country."

"And the most promising one?"

"The owner of a convenience store. Said he served a young boy, just over four-foot tall, light brown hair, dressed in clothes that looked a bit too big for him. He was buying milk and Frosties and some paper dishes. The thing that got the shop owner really suspicious was the way the boy spoke. Bloke said he thought the kid had an American accent. Plus the fact he wanted to buy a disposable mobile phone."

Ingrid raised her eyebrows. "It's the first sighting we've had of Tommy in a long while. The boy's still alive." *Thank God.* "Where was this?"

"We're in the middle of trying to trace the call. The caller rang off suddenly. Before he told us his location."

"Do you know why?"

"No idea—I suppose it's possible Foster turned up and threatened him."

"How long ago did he call?"

"About fifteen minutes."

"So you should have a location soon. And Foster has to be pretty close by."

"The man who called in wasn't using a landline. It'll take us a bit longer to get the details of his mobile and address."

"Anything else to report?" Ingrid glanced at Gurley, who continued to ignore her.

"We're just waiting on this. Like I said, it's the most promising sighting we've had in a while."

It felt hot and airless in the incident room. Although the space was large, none of the windows was open. The hostility radiating from Gurley made the atmosphere downright oppressive. "Listen, I need a little air," she said. "I'll be out back. Can you come fetch me when you have news?"

Tyson looked at Gurley before answering. "Of course."

When Ingrid stepped outside she took a deep breath. She wasn't at all certain she could continue to work with Gurley if he carried on behaving the way he was. But she sure as hell wasn't going to leave the investigation without a fight. As she paced up and down between the parked squad cars, her phone chirruped in her purse. She snatched it out and answered without looking at the screen. "You have a location?" She moved toward the rear entrance of the police station.

"Nope. They still haven't found the guy." It was Mike Stiller. "That's not why I'm calling."

"Sorry, Mike. I thought you were somebody else."

"I figured that out already."

"The killer is still on the loose?"

"Yes, but like I said, that's not why I'm calling. They've recovered more bodies. A dozen remains so far. And counting."

The breath caught in Ingrid's throat. It was possible one of them could be Megan. "You have to try to get a match with Kathleen Avery's DNA. You need to get a sample from her."

"The local Feds did that already. Jeez, I was hassling so hard for it, they could hardly refuse."

"It won't be a 100% match—we don't have a sample from Megan's dad." Ingrid remembered the lock of hair at the bottom of the sneaker box. "If it looks promising I can get you a better sample."

"You can? How?"

"Don't worry about that for now. Just look out for a Fed-Ex package from me." A familiar shiver ran up her spine.

"You doing OK?"

"I'm fine. The job's a little… challenging at the moment."

"When is it anything else, huh?"

"I really appreciate your help with this, Mike. I think maybe I've been forgetting to tell you that, I've been so caught up in the detail."

"Hey, don't mention it. I'll call soon as I have more news." He rang off, leaving Ingrid standing in the middle of a police parking lot feeling more than a little lost.

She walked unsteadily to a low brick wall that separated the lot from the back of the police station and sat down, reflecting on what Mike had just told her.

So many bodies.

The killer must have been adding to his collection for at least eighteen years. Ingrid wondered how long his victims had survived before they ended up buried in the yard or beneath the floor of the basement. How much they had suffered before that. She prayed Megan wasn't one of them.

The door to the parking lot opened and Tyson stuck his head through the gap. He stared at her for a moment, a shocked expression on his face. "Are you OK?"

Ingrid stood up, relieved to discover her legs were strong enough to carry her weight. "I'm fine." She swallowed. "Did you get a location for the store?"

"Better than that—Foster's on the phone right now to your tall friend."

Ingrid ran to the door and pushed Tyson aside in her hurry to get back to the incident room. "Can you get a trace on the call?" she said, striding down the corridor.

"We weren't exactly set up for it—we're trying to get something fixed up as quick as we can."

Ingrid slowed to let Tyson catch up with her. "It's OK—the base is monitoring all calls coming into Major Gurley's phone. I'm guessing it was patched through from his landline at Freckenham?"

"No idea—Jack didn't exactly get a chance to tell me."

Tyson's use of Gurley's first name didn't pass Ingrid by. The two of them were getting a little too pally for her liking.

A few moments later, she burst through the incident room door, with Tyson close behind. Gurley turned sharply and glared at her. A plain clothes cop Ingrid hadn't seen before was sitting at the desk next to him with the handset of a landline pressed hard against her ear. She made a circling motion with an index finger, encouraging Gurley to keep Kyle Foster talking. But Foster knew what he was doing—he wouldn't stay on the line for long.

"Sonofabitch!" Gurley exclaimed. "The bastard just hung up on me. Said he'd call back tomorrow." He looked at the detective sitting at the desk. She was nodding and making approving noises into her phone.

"They traced the call to Tring," she said when she'd put down the phone.

"Where the hell is that?" Gurley said.

"It's a village just north of London," the detective explained.

"So he's maybe on his way back to London? To the hospital?" Gurley asked.

"He wouldn't risk it," Ingrid said. "Too many cops."

"Then why come south at all?"

"What did he say to you?" Tyson asked.

"He was making demands again—that Tommy be put on a plane to the US. The guy's got a screw loose."

"What did you tell him?" Ingrid asked.

"What I did before," Gurley said without looking at her. "To give himself up before he made things even worse for himself."

"Why would he change his mind now?"

"I'm not giving in to him."

"We need to at least pretend to agree to his demands—how else are we going to track him down?" Ingrid moved closer to Gurley until he had no choice but to look at her. "What else did he say?"

"He wanted to know how Molly was. I refused to tell him unless he put Tommy on the line."

"You actually spoke to Tommy?"

"No. Foster went quiet after that. Then hung up."

"Couldn't you have given him the information first, then asked to speak to Tommy? The guy's clearly concerned about his daughter." Ingrid felt like shaking Gurley.

"How is that relevant? I kept him on the line long enough to trace the call to some village. How hard can it be to find him there?"

"Except that he's probably already on the move." Ingrid walked away, just in case the temptation to slap Gurley in the mouth became too overwhelming to resist.

She wheeled back around when the landline on the desk rang. Tyson grabbed it. He nodded a couple of times, thanked the caller and threw the handset back onto the cradle. "Unsurprisingly, we've just had confirmation the convenience store is also in Tring."

"How quickly can we get there?" Gurley asked the detective sergeant.

"With blues and twos? Rush hour traffic? It's going to take the best part of an hour. Maybe more."

"We don't have that much time. I'll call the base, get a chopper."

"I can get in touch with the Hertfordshire force. At least get some bodies on the ground." Tyson was already reaching for the phone. "Maybe get the traffic cops in the air too."

"If we're going we should get down to the helipad," Ingrid said.

Gurley scowled at her, but said nothing. She'd expected him to refuse to take her, point blank.

"I'm coming with you." she said, forcing the issue.

"I guess so," Gurley said, reluctantly. "Foster asked for you by name."

"He did what? How does he know my name?"

"He didn't say."

"I don't understand."

"Is there anything you need to tell us, Agent Skyberg?" Tyson took a step toward her.

"No! Why would he ask for me specifically?"

"Has Kyle Foster made contact with you before?" Tyson asked.

"What is this? Of course he hasn't. He must have called the embassy or something—I can get the phone logs checked—see who's been making inquiries in the Criminal Division in the past twenty-four hours." Although she was desperate to find a reasonable explanation, the likelihood of Kyle Foster calling the American embassy seemed pretty remote, even to Ingrid. "Maybe he's been back in touch with Yvonne Sherwood. She could have mentioned my name to him."

Gurley glared at her. "Maybe you can give Sherwood a call. See what she has to say for herself."

44

Even though Gurley's suggestion was clearly meant to be sarcastic, on the way to the helipad in Battersea, Ingrid did try calling Yvonne Sherwood. As soon as she'd introduced herself, Sherwood hung up on her. Each time Ingrid tried after that, her calls went straight to voicemail.

"That's your answer right there," Gurley snapped at Ingrid after her third attempt. "She must have heard from Foster and now she's avoiding you."

"On the plus side, maybe she told him he could trust me. It's possible, isn't it? If he's asking for me specifically."

She and Gurley were sitting in the back of a Metropolitan Police patrol car, the driver and Radcliffe sitting up front. Tyson and another uniformed driver were following behind. Both cars had sirens wailing and blue lights flashing, trying to get through the evening rush hour traffic as fast as possible. Gurley had reluctantly agreed to let the two detectives ride in the US Air Force helicopter to Tring. He couldn't really refuse.

Gurley was still pissed at Ingrid over the Carrie Foster interview and she was mad as hell that he'd tried to have her removed from the investigation. But for the time being at least, they were stuck with one another.

Ingrid decided it was time to clear the air. "Sol told me you've been talking to the chief at the embassy."

"I pretty much guessed that."

"Can we agree on a truce for tonight?"

Gurley continued to stare out the window as the car swerved and slalomed through the heavy traffic.

"Come on, Jack. Meet me half way here. I'm just as pissed as you."

He snapped his head around toward her. "What have I done?"

"If you have a problem with me, you should tell me to my face. Not report me to the boss."

Gurley exhaled noisily through his nose. "I was frustrated. Sometimes it feels like you can be more of an obstruction than a help."

"Is that what you really think?"

"Why have you started taking Kyle Foster's side?"

"I haven't. I told you already. I just want to find out the truth."

"Everyone else accepts Carrie Foster's version of events. They seem happy with the truth as it stands."

Ingrid noticed that DCI Radcliffe had tilted his head sideways into the gap between the passenger and driver seat, obviously trying to listen in. She dropped her voice. "I can't ignore it when things don't add up."

"You are incredible."

"I'll take that as a compliment."

Gurley shook his head. But Ingrid thought she detected the slightest of smiles play across his lips.

"We both want the same thing: to find Foster and recover Tommy, safe and sound."

Gurley nodded.

"So," she said, sticking out her hand, "a truce?"

After a moment's hesitation, Gurley wrapped his hand around Ingrid's and shook on it. "For tonight."

———

The helicopter ride to Tring lasted only fifteen minutes. They landed in a park that had been closed to the public about a half mile from the convenience store Tommy had been in. The area of parkland was enclosed on all sides by stands of tall trees. Through a gap between two of them, Ingrid could make out the main highway that skirted around the little town.

A whole team of detectives and uniformed officers were there to meet them. Ingrid and Gurley were forced to wait around while DCI Radcliffe was debriefed by his opposite number on the Hertfordshire force. When the conversation passed the five minute mark, Gurley lost his patience. He strode over to the two men and stood between them.

"Sorry to break up your cozy chit-chat, detectives, but wouldn't it make more sense to say everything once?" He turned to Ingrid who had followed him over. "After all, my colleague and I are going to be asking you the exact same questions."

The Hertfordshire cop looked at Radcliffe, who gave him a nod.

"What do you have on the ground?" Gurley asked.

The cop stuck out a hand. "DCI Strickland."

"Major Jack Gurley, this is Agent Skyberg, FBI."

Strickland shook Ingrid's hand too. "Pleasure." He gave them both a little smile. Ingrid could sense Gurley's impatience increasing. "We're conducting door to door inquiries on the High Street—where the convenience store is situated. We've got officers—in plain clothes—patrolling the local bus and train stations. Plus a dozen squad cars cruising the vicinity."

"Any new sightings from the public?" Ingrid asked.

"Nothing that's proven particularly reliable."

"What resources do you have in the air?" Gurley asked.

Strickland glanced up at the darkening sky. "Traffic have put a helicopter at our disposal for the rest of the night. It's equipped with powerful searchlights and infra-red equipment. At the moment we've got it flying low over open ground within a five mile radius of the last confirmed sighting."

"Has anyone spoken to the owner of the convenience store?" Gurley asked. He pushed up his sleeves.

"We've interviewed him extensively."

"Did he tell you why he hung up? Did Foster threaten him?"

"Nothing that extreme. Apparently a couple of schoolboys were acting suspiciously at the back of the shop. The owner's had a lot of trouble with shoplifting of late. He rang off so that he could deal with the two lads."

"And you believe him?" Gurley didn't seem convinced.

"I've no reason to doubt him."

"Have you searched his premises?" Ingrid asked.

"We did. Nothing to report."

"What about roadblocks?" Gurley was shifting his weight from one foot to the other, glancing around the park, finally fixing his gaze on a large clump of trees.

"We can't close the roads," Strickland said firmly.

"Why not?"

"Foster's not exactly a threat to the general public."

"What if he's armed?"

"What makes you say that?" Radcliffe suddenly started paying attention. "Is he?"

"I think Major Gurley is just saying that we don't know that he isn't," Ingrid interjected. She attempted to change the subject. "You've got a trace on the cell phone Foster used to call us earlier?" she asked Radcliffe.

"There's no signal. Presumably he's started using a new burner phone and switched the other one off."

Gurley glanced back at the trees. "What if he's gone to ground? You have a lot of woods round here?"

"A fair amount."

"The chopper won't help you find him there. Are you using dogs?"

Strickland let out a snorting laugh. "We really don't have those kind of resources. If we knew where to start looking I could get a couple of dog handlers involved. But without an approximate location they'd be totally wasting their time."

"Jesus." Gurley walked away.

Strickland looked at Radcliffe who shrugged back at him. They both looked at Ingrid. "He's a little frustrated right now," she said, unsure why she was making excuses for his rudeness. "He feels personally responsible for getting Foster back." She gave both detectives a weak smile and hurried after Gurley. "You can't speak to them that way," she said when she caught up with him. "We're all on the same side here. Doing our best with the resources we have."

"We're looking for a man and an eight-year-old boy. How hard can it be? If it were Foster alone I could understand it—the man's been trained to evade capture. But Tommy must be slowing him down, holding him back."

"We must work with the cops now, or risk getting shut out of the investigation completely. They still have access to intel we need."

Gurley rubbed a hand across his face. "Foster's probably miles away by now. Headed God knows where."

"We don't know that. We have to accept the local cops are doing everything they can."

"It's not enough."

Ingrid could quite easily have slapped Gurley across the face. What did he think could be gained by bitching about the cops? It wasn't as if he was coming up with a better strategy of his own.

Out the corner of her eye, Ingrid noticed some activity among the uniformed officers. One of them ran over to Radcliffe and Strickland, who had now been joined by DS Tyson. She started to jog toward the little group. "What's happened?" She made sure to address DCI Strickland, out of courtesy, given this was his patch, and in the hope he might react favorably to the gesture. He didn't answer right away. He was too busy scowling over her shoulder, presumably at an approaching Jack Gurley. "Chief inspector?" she prompted.

"We have CCTV footage of a man and boy, fitting the basic description of Foster and his son, boarding a London-bound train."

Ingrid turned to Radcliffe. "How quickly can you get a team down to the station in London?"

"I'm afraid we're too late for that, agent," Strickland said. "The train was due in at Euston over an hour ago. The best we can do now is get personnel looking at the CCTV recordings for the surrounding area. We might at least be able to discover which direction he was heading in when he left the station."

Behind her Ingrid heard Gurley exhale noisily. She was grateful he didn't make any comment.

"Well, there's no point staying up here," Radcliffe said. "Thanks for all your efforts, Ted. I think it might be time for you to get the troops to stand down." He shook Strickland's hand. "Really appreciate your help."

When just Tyson and Radcliffe remained, Gurley said, "I guess you'll be wanting a ride back?"

"Actually we've arranged alternative transport. Thanks all the same." With that the DCI walked away, closely followed by his number two.

"Wow—I really pissed them off, huh?" Gurley shook his head.

Ingrid was about to reply, when she was interrupted by the trilling of Gurley's cell. He peered down at the number. It was clear he didn't recognize it. He stabbed the answer key. "Major Gurley," he said, "who is this?" He quickly turned away and started walking.

Ingrid ran after him.

"It isn't that straightforward," she heard him say. "What the...?" He glared at his phone.

"Was it Foster?" Ingrid asked him, grabbing his arm.

"Sonofabitch is still making demands."

"The demands haven't changed? He wants safe passage for Tommy?"

"He said he's calling again tomorrow with 'full instructions'. He made one thing very clear."

Ingrid watched the expression on his face turn from anger to something approaching satisfaction. "Well?"

"On no account should we get the police involved."

45

After a restless night, Ingrid arrived at the embassy ahead of Jack Gurley. They had arranged to meet there so that Foster's call could be more easily traced. The technical team assured her the tracking process would kick in just as soon as he called. All she could do now was wait.

She sat at her desk in the Criminal Division for a few minutes enjoying the silence. No phones were ringing, Jennifer wasn't bombarding her with questions, even the air conditioning seemed uncharacteristically quiet. She rested her chin on her hands and closed her eyes, then tried to make her muscles relax and her mind go blank.

It was a mistake.

A sudden image of the house in Jackson filled her mind. She snapped her eyes back open. How many more bodies were they going to recover? What kind of monster were they dealing with? Immediately her head was full of all the messages she'd ignored from Svetlana. Of the shoebox crammed with memories from her past. Of Ralph's silent departure in the middle of the night.

Maybe silence was overrated.

Much to her relief, it was shattered a few moments later by the ringing of her cell. It was DCI Radcliffe.

"You're at work early," she said in lieu of a greeting.

"Did I wake you?"

"Not at all—I'm at the office."

"Is Gurley there with you?"

"No. Why?"

There was a pause. As if Radcliffe didn't believe her.

"What is it?"

"I got back to my desk last night to discover a preliminary forensics report. There's been a new development."

"Forensics? From the hotel? What is it?"

"I don't want to tell you over the phone. Face to face. Without Gurley."

"I can't exclude him from something like that."

"You've had no qualms about excluding us. Gurley's a royal pain in the arse. If you want the information, you meet me on your own. Can you get down to the station now?"

"I have a meeting this morning… with my boss," she lied. "It's the reason I'm here so early."

"Call me when you're out of it. This new evidence—it could be a game changer."

"Can't you even give me a clue?"

"Not over the phone."

"I swear he's not here."

"Call me later." He hung up.

"Who's not here? Who was that?"

Ingrid swiveled in her chair to see Gurley standing in the doorway. She felt her cheeks warm and hoped to God they weren't glowing red. How long had he been standing there? "Radcliffe. You're not too popular with him right now."

"That's why he was calling? To bitch about me?"

"Sometimes it helps to let off a little steam. Unfortunately, he chose me to listen to him vent."

"You want me to call him?"

Ingrid flinched at the thought. She hoped Gurley hadn't noticed. "Best leave him to calm down."

Gurley grabbed a chair from the other side of the office and dragged it to Ingrid's desk. He slumped down on it. Ingrid thought it might collapse under his weight.

"Foster gave no indication what time he'd call?" Ingrid asked Gurley, even though she already knew the answer.

"No. I guess all we can do now is wait." Gurley rested his chin on a fist. "Seems to me it's all we've been doing. Foster has made us look like fools."

"He's a man determined to stay hidden. There's not much anyone can do about that."

Gurley pulled his cell from a jacket pocket and slid it onto the desk. Both he and Ingrid stared wide-eyed at it for the next few minutes in silence. There wasn't anything else to say or do.

When the phone finally rang, the vibration buzzing it across the desk toward Ingrid, she involuntarily jumped in her seat.

"The trace is set up?"

"We've been ready since six a.m."

Gurley snatched up the phone, hit the answer key, and the speaker-phone option, but said nothing.

"The silent treatment makes a change," Foster said. "Aren't you going to spend the next minute trying to persuade me to give myself up?"

Gurley cleared his throat. "I think we're beyond that now, don't you?"

"Pleased to hear it."

Ingrid leaned forward in her chair. It creaked noisily.

"Who's there with you?" Foster demanded.

"This is Agent Skyberg," Ingrid said.

"Good to make your acquaintance, Ingrid. I'm hoping you can drill some sense into Major Gurley's skull."

Ingrid didn't bother to reply.

"I've identified a location for you to pick up Tommy. You'll need to provide the paperwork for travel—I'm sure the embassy can work that out. I don't have his passport. I want Yvonne Sherwood to take him to the airport and ensure he gets on the plane."

"Yvonne is here in London?"

"I haven't told you the location yet."

"I can take Tommy to Heathrow," Ingrid said.

"All due respect, agent, I'd rather have someone I can trust."

"You can trust me."

"I know you're trying to keep me talking, so I'm going to go now. I'll text the location and time shortly. Remember—no police." He hung up.

"Has he lost it completely?" Gurley said. "He thinks we'll let that woman just walk away with Tommy? He's crazy."

The phone beeped. The text gave an address with a west London postal code, a time and another instruction:

Tommy in exchange for Skyberg

. . .

759

Ingrid stared at the words for a moment, unable to quite take in their meaning. A hostage exchange? It seemed almost a quaint notion. It was totally against Bureau protocol. Yet in the circumstances, it seemed like a logical option. If Foster wasn't armed, surely she'd be able to handle it?

"He has lost it," Gurley said, jumping up from his seat. "We can't agree to that. No way."

Ingrid watched him pacing around the room. He reached a bank of metal file cabinets and thumped the first one with his fist. Meanwhile Ingrid was trying to figure out how they could make the whole hostage switch work.

"We'd need to get the police involved," she said. "The Bureau doesn't have the resources here for that kind of operation." She stared at Gurley, as if she were willing him to disagree.

"I understand. But can we at least negotiate some measure of control over their operation?"

"Maybe you should leave that to me."

"Or get your boss involved? Maybe they'd take a little more notice of him?"

Ingrid shook her head firmly. "No way. This isn't something I want Sol to know about. If I do this, it's between you, me and the Metropolitan Police Service." She managed to smile at Gurley, even though a wave of anticipatory nausea was currently making its way from her stomach to the back of her throat.

———

Kyle Foster had chosen a disused industrial estate in Hounslow for their rendezvous. A location that was just three miles from Heathrow Airport. According to Radcliffe, it had been pretty much abandoned in the last recession. As yet, the slow recovery in the British economy hadn't encouraged new tenants to move in. It was so run down that as Ingrid sat next to Gurley in an unmarked embassy car on the main access road, she fully expected to see tumbleweed blow across the street.

"More waiting," Gurley said, not for the first time. They'd been parked there for less than thirty minutes. Ingrid hoped something would happen soon. Otherwise his complaining would become unbearable.

Her phone vibrated in her pocket. She snatched it out and answered quickly.

"All personnel are in position," Detective Sergeant Tyson informed her.

"You're sure everyone's well hidden?"

"It's a bit tricky getting bodies in place in such a deserted location, but we've got some men about to start digging up the road just northwest of your current position, and a fake estate agent and two clients heading for the other entrance right about now. Everyone else is keeping their distance. As promised." He paused. Ingrid could hear him breathing heavily, as if he'd been running. "Are you all right about this?" It was the first time anyone had actually asked her that outright. She was a little taken aback.

"I'm fine. I've worked this kind of operation dozens of times before. I'm an old hand, trust me." It was a gross exaggeration, and she hadn't done anything like it for more years than she cared to count. "Everything's under control my end." Just as she said that, a large muscle in her thigh started to twitch. She convinced herself it was because she hadn't had a long run for too many days now—nothing to do with her mounting anxiety at all.

A minute later Gurley's phone started to ring. He glanced at the screen. "This is it. You ready?"

"As I'll ever be."

Gurley answered, selecting the speakerphone option once again.

"You double-crossing bastards. Yvonne said I could trust you! What is it with you people?"

"You can trust me," Ingrid said, raising her voice.

"This place is crawling with cops!"

"Please, Kyle," Ingrid said. "It's just me and Major Gurley here."

"You think I'm blind? Or stupid?"

"You have to believe me—I had no idea the police were involved." Ingrid winced at the weakness of her lie.

"Bull. Shit. You'll regret this."

46

Following Tyson's directions, Gurley drove quickly around the perimeter of the industrial units and out onto the main drag where they found the detective sergeant standing beside DCI Radcliffe at the open rear doors of a small, white unmarked van.

Ingrid jumped out the car before it came to a complete stop, eager to get to Radcliffe before Gurley had a chance to let rip. "What the hell happened?" she said.

"You tell us. What's he got, this bloke, some sort of sixth sense? You approved our positions before we went into this. What else could we have done?"

Ingrid shook her head. "Foster just told me we'd regret this. He sounded like a man who's been pushed too far. I'm really worried for Tommy now." It was the first time she'd even admitted that to herself.

"Jesus Christ?" Gurley yelled. "Can't you get anything right? You were supposed to be invisible." Gurley was somehow managing to square up to Radcliffe and Tyson simultaneously. Both detectives took a step backwards. Neither man seemed to have the energy for a fight.

"It happens," Radcliffe said resignedly.

"Is that it? We just walk away? Where are the roadblocks?"

"We've got officers trawling the area. If he's close by he won't get far," Tyson said, watching the retreating back of his senior officer as he disappeared into the van.

"OK—I'm getting back in the car, search for myself." Gurley said. He turned to Ingrid. "You coming?"

"Actually, I'd like to stay here, speak to the DCI," Ingrid told him. "Work out what went wrong."

"Fine—you do that. I have nothing more to say to that man."

Ingrid watched Gurley march back to the embassy car, hoping in his anger he wouldn't smash into anything. After he'd accelerated away, tires squealing, she stepped up into the van.

She found Radcliffe sprawled out on a hard bench inside. The man looked exhausted.

"The American Air Force must train their pilots extraordinary well," he said, rubbing a hand across his bloodshot eyes. "We really were careful about the placement of our officers. There shouldn't have been any way for Foster to spot them. You have to believe me." He pulled in his legs and shuffled sideways on the bench, patting the seat beside him. Ingrid perched on the edge.

"It's OK—I haven't come in here to question your tactics. What's done is done. I'm more interested in discussing the new forensics evidence. What exactly do you have?"

Radcliffe seemed a little relieved. "DNA results."

"It's taken this long to get them? I know there can be a backlog, but I thought this request was getting fast-tracked."

"It was fast-tracked. The problem was there were so many samples to analyze. It's been difficult for the lab to differentiate between them. The samples were from the drain in the bathroom sink. As you can imagine, lots of people pass through a central London budget hotel room over the course of a week."

"What exactly did you find?"

"Enough to arrest Carrie Foster."

———

It had taken Ingrid quite a while to convince DCI Radcliffe that Jack Gurley should be permitted to observe Carrie Foster's interview.

"Can you guarantee he'll behave himself this time?" Radcliffe had finally asked.

"I'll make sure of it."

She and Gurley were now sitting in a much better equipped observation room than before. This one had so many monitors and digital video recorders crammed inside, Ingrid felt as though she were sitting in a TV studio. There had to be at least a half dozen cameras in the interview room, each one trained on a different location.

Now that Carrie Foster was being questioned under caution, gone were the ambient atmosphere and soft furnishings. This interview room was starkly decorated: four whitewashed walls and a gray tile floor, the only furniture a wooden table and four chairs.

Sitting next to Ingrid in front of an array of monitors, Gurley turned to her and said, "Radcliffe didn't tell you exactly what they think the forensics will prove?" He kept his voice low so that the lone uniformed officer standing at the door couldn't hear him.

"Trust me, I'm not holding anything back. You know just as much as I do." Ingrid had tried to press Radcliffe for the details, but he'd refused to divulge any further information.

"He's grandstanding. He wants to make the big reveal the same time he confronts Carrie with it. The guy's playing with us."

"That's his prerogative, I guess."

Gurley glared at her.

"Hey—I'm not saying I agree with it." She stared back into Gurley's face. He looked pale. More distressed than angry.

Sudden movement on the monitor screen immediately in front of her refocused Ingrid's attention. Carrie Foster walked unsteadily toward the table. Behind her was the lawyer appointed by the embassy. Both women sat down at the table, tucking their chairs underneath. A close-up of Mrs Foster's face filled the screen directly in front of Gurley. He stared at it without saying a word. Carrie Foster had clearly been crying. Her eyes were red and puffy, the skin around her nostrils raw. Ingrid glanced from the screen to Gurley. He seemed to have grown even paler. She still couldn't shake the feeling he was holding something back from her. She hoped to God it wasn't what she was beginning to think it might be.

Radcliffe and Tyson entered the room and sat down. DS Tyson then proceeded to switch on a digital recorder. He leaned towards it stating the date, time and persons present. Then he sat back in his chair and fixed his gaze on Carrie Foster.

DCI Radcliffe placed both palms flat on the table top. He pursed his lips.

"Whatever it is you're about to say, don't bother wasting your time," Mrs Foster said. "I've told you everything that happened. There's nothing more to discuss." She narrowed her eyes, almost willing Radcliffe to snap back at her. To his credit, he merely slid his hands from the table and rested them in his lap.

"You have been arrested on suspicion of causing cruelty to a minor." He glanced at the lawyer. "Further charges may follow. You understand how serious this situation is?"

"I have made my position perfectly clear. I have nothing to say to you."

Given Carrie Foster's distressed appearance, Ingrid was amazed the woman was holding it together so well. Maybe the team of solicitors the embassy employed were a little too good at their jobs. This one had clearly coached her client very well.

"Of course, as we stated earlier, and as your solicitor has no doubt reminded you, you do have the right to remain silent. But that might not be the best course of action. We have new evidence that we'd like to discuss with you."

DS Tyson passed his superior a file.

"What new evidence?" Carrie Foster snapped. "I told you what happened. Kyle hurt Molly, then snatched Tommy and disappeared. And you still haven't found them."

"I haven't been informed of any new evidence. It should have been disclosed ahead of this interview." The lawyer nodded at the file in Radcliffe's hands.

Gurley shifted in his chair next to Ingrid. "What did I tell you?" He shook his head wearily. "The man's grandstanding." Sweat had started to prickle along his hairline.

"You did arrive rather late, Ms Welland. Perhaps you'd like a few moments now to go through it? We can leave you to discuss it with your client if you'd like?"

"It's OK," Carrie Foster said. "I just want to get this over with. Whatever they have won't change anything. I know what happened."

The lawyer took the slim file from Radcliffe and opened it. It seemed to have only one or two sheets of paper inside. Carrie Foster hadn't taken her eyes off Radcliffe's face.

"I can't imagine what you think you're going to prove, but would you please hurry. I want to get back to the hospital. If anyone's causing cruelty to a minor it's you. Molly shouldn't be in that place without me."

"There are a few... issues we're hoping you'll be able to clear up for us."

47

Ingrid noticed a flicker of emotion in the lawyer's previously mask-like expression as the woman continued to read the notes within the file. Was it surprise, disgust or resignation? Carrie Foster didn't seem to have noticed —she was too busy staring out Radcliffe.

"As I'm sure you know," Radcliffe began, "a number of forensic samples were taken from your hotel room by our crime scene examiners. We have just received an analysis of the DNA tested from the various samples taken from the bathroom. Of particular interest are those recovered from the drain beneath the sink."

Although the monitor Ingrid was staring at showed a close-up of Carrie Foster's face, she didn't react at the mention of the sink. Still the woman refused to look away from Radcliffe's face. But her neck and shoulders definitely seemed to be holding on to a lot of tension.

"It took a while to separate out the various samples. The most interesting results relate to the fine filaments of hair we found."

More tensing of Carrie Foster's neck. She swallowed, visibly but silently.

"You see, the hair samples are definitely yours, Mrs Foster, as we might have expected. But the traces of blood we found clinging to some of those hairs are Tommy's. Tommy's blood on *your* hair—odd isn't it? How do you explain that?"

There was a knock at the door of the interview room. A female detective Ingrid remembered seeing in the incident room appeared just within shot. She was carrying a clear plastic bag. An evidence bag.

"Ah, perfect timing, Alex." Radcliffe took the bag from her and laid it gently on the table. He waited for the detective to close the door behind her before continuing. "We retrieved this from your handbag earlier today."

Inside the evidence bag was a hairbrush. Just a regular hairbrush as far as Ingrid could make out, white plastic bristles, short blue handle. There were long, light brown hairs tangled in a clump at the base of the bristles. She wondered what it had to do with the evidence the police had found in the hotel bathroom.

"I'm surprised you didn't try to get rid of it," Radcliffe said. "I mean, given we didn't find evidence of Tommy's blood on any of the objects we retrieved from the room, and as his blood was attached to *your* hair, it wasn't much of a leap to suspect your hairbrush might have been the weapon used to cause your son's facial injuries."

Carrie Foster set her lips in a hard line.

"Obviously we haven't yet had a chance to analyze the brush for traces of blood, but perhaps you could preempt our findings, Mrs Foster?"

"I have nothing to say."

"It's the trace of Tommy's blood we found that's troubling me the most, as I'm sure you can imagine."

Finally Carrie Foster tore her gaze away from Radcliffe and looked to her lawyer for support.

"My client is asserting her right to remain silent."

"We know Tommy sustained injuries to his face—a split lip and a bloody nose. That much was confirmed by the A & E Department at St Thomas'. When we asked you about them previously you seemed adamant that your son remained unharmed at the time Mr Foster took him from the hotel room. And yet, as I say, we've detected traces of Tommy's blood in the drain."

"No comment." Carrie Foster stared down at her hands. She was clasping them together on the table, as if she were praying.

"Maybe you'll feel more inclined to speak after we've analyzed the hairbrush. I mean, how would you explain any trace of Tommy's blood on that?"

"You won't find any. Why would you?"

"Oh I realize you must have cleaned it several times since Monday. That makes perfect sense. But you'd be surprised just how stubbornly small traces of DNA evidence can cling on to things. Fortunately we'll also be taking samples from the inside of your handbag. I presume that's where you shoved the hairbrush before you left the hotel room? Such presence of mind not to leave it behind. One might say it was calculated."

Ingrid stared at the monitor showing a close-up of Radcliffe's face. His expression seemed almost smug.

"Can we stop this now?" Carrie Foster turned to her lawyer. "I have nothing to add to my previous statement."

"I'm afraid we have more questions for you to refuse to answer." Radcliffe handed the evidence bag to Tyson, who hurried to the door and passed it to the female detective waiting on the other side for it.

"Perhaps you'll feel more like talking if we shift to a slightly different subject," the DCI said.

Mrs Foster frowned at him suspiciously.

"Tell me about the circumstances surrounding your husband's departure from the hotel room."

Her expression switched from suspicion to confusion in an instant. "He snatched Tommy and ran. What else is there to say?"

Radcliffe tilted his head to one side. "I mean his earlier departure."

"After he hurt Molly?"

Radcliffe said nothing.

"He threw Molly onto the bed and rushed past me. He nearly knocked me over. I've already told you that."

"And he returned less than twenty minutes later. A full seven minutes after you called for an ambulance."

"I wasn't exactly taking notice of the time."

"No—of course not. Let me run through some of the events of that twenty-five minute period. According to your account, and what we've been able to piece together with the aid of CCTV footage..." Radcliffe turned to the lawyer. "Details are on the second page." He straightened his spine and pulled back his shoulders, as if he were preparing himself for a long speech. "Shortly after Mr Foster allegedly shook your daughter and threw her onto the bed, he ran out of the hotel room—presumably in somewhat of an agitated state—and then down several flights of stairs, through the reception area and onto the street."

"I guess."

"It's surprising none of the other guests at the hotel can remember witnessing this hurried departure. Not a single one of them."

Carrie Foster shrugged. The tension in her shoulders increased as she leaned away from the table. She looked like a woman bracing herself for a blow.

"Anyway," Radcliffe continued, "Mr Foster then proceeded to walk half a mile south along Southampton Row and arrived at a McDonald's restaurant on High Holborn, where he ordered two breakfast wraps, pancakes and syrup, a raspberry and white chocolate muffin, two black coffees and three bottles of orange juice. He then returned to the hotel, a large McDonald's paper bag under his arm, and made his way to your room."

Mrs Foster dragged down her top lip with her bottom teeth.

"Seems a strange thing to do, really. Purchasing a family breakfast after his supposed violent outburst."

"You've made a mistake."

"CCTV footage from the restaurant in question confirms his movements. Fully time-stamped. No mistake, Mrs Foster."

In the observation room, Gurley had started to shake his head. He let out a long sigh. "Sweet Jesus," he whispered.

Carrie Foster's lawyer closed the file in front of her. "I need to discuss this evidence privately with my client." She glanced at Mrs Foster, who was staring, wide-eyed at the table. She had bitten her top lip so hard it had started to bleed.

Radcliffe started to get to his feet. "Certainly. I'll get one of our constables to escort you to another room."

Tyson leaned toward the digital recorder.

"No!" Foster said and raised a hand to her mouth.

"We really need to talk about this Carrie," the lawyer insisted.

Carrie Foster shook her head. "I just want to get back to the hospital. Please. I need to see Molly."

48

During the unscheduled break, Ingrid and Gurley had sat in the observation room in silence. At one point DS Tyson stuck his head around the door, a self-satisfied grin on his face. Ingrid wasn't sure what he had to be so smug about—it wasn't that long ago he and Radcliffe were certain of Kyle Foster's guilt.

"Can I get you anything?" he asked.

"We're fine, thanks," Ingrid said, answering for them both, unsure if Gurley was capable of saying anything. His face had now lost all its color. He seemed really shaken.

"You're sure?" Tyson frowned at Gurley. "The next session might take a while."

"Really, we're OK." Ingrid just wanted Tyson to leave. His demeanor had started to piss her off.

After fifteen minutes speaking to her lawyer, an unsteady Carrie Foster was led back into the interview room by a female constable and helped onto a chair. She leaned back, tilted her head toward the ceiling and closed her eyes.

In the observation room Gurley murmured something so quietly Ingrid supposed she wasn't meant to hear it. She didn't bother asking him to repeat it.

Ingrid stared at the monitor that showed a close-up of Carrie Foster's face. Her skin was slack. Her eyes seemed blank, her expression resigned somehow.

The two detectives returned to the room and Tyson restarted the digital recorder.

"Now you've had a chance to discuss the new evidence with your solicitor," Radcliffe said, "perhaps you'd like to go over the events of Monday morning again? Tell us what really happened."

The lawyer turned to her client, gently laying a hand on her arm. "You don't have to do this."

"I do. It's been tearing me apart." Carrie Foster blotted her eyes and nose with a Kleenex. "Could I get a glass of water?"

In the next room Ingrid sat up straighter in her chair. She hadn't been expecting a change of heart from Carrie Foster. She craned her neck closer to the screen in front of Gurley. His face now wore a bewildered expression.

A few moments later, the female detective appeared with a plastic jug and four plastic beakers on a tray. She took her time pouring water into each beaker. Carrie Foster drank half a glass, waited for it to be refilled, then took a deep breath.

"It was an accident," she said. The muscles in her face tightened.

Both detectives leaned back in their chairs, a subtle but unmistakable sign that they didn't want to pressure Carrie Foster any further—they were happy to let her make her statement in her own good time.

"Molly just wouldn't stop crying. She's never slept well, ever since she was born. There was no escape from the noise in that tiny hotel room. On Monday morning Tommy was acting out too. I guess he was overexcited to be in a new place, looking forward to visiting the big toy store. He seemed to be making Molly worse. After a while she was pretty much screaming." She closed her eyes. Squeezed them tight shut. "I sent Kyle out to get us some breakfast—asked him to take Tommy with him. But Tommy wasn't dressed yet and Kyle said he'd be much faster if he went alone. We both hoped the promise of food might make Tommy quieten down a little. Tommy loves McDonald's." She drained her glass. Tyson refilled it for her. "Tommy started to bounce up and down on his bed. Higher and higher. I told him to stop, but he wouldn't. I guess I must have had the hairbrush in my hand. I don't really remember. I was just pointing it at him. Not in a threatening way, I swear." She looked at one detective then the other. "You have to believe me, I love my kids." She dabbed her eyes again and leaned towards Radcliffe. "When you have my statement, can I go back to the hospital? Molly really shouldn't be left on her own. She'll get upset."

"Why don't we see where we are when you've finished? Make a judgment then," the DCI said, careful not to make promises he wouldn't be able to keep. "What happened after that?"

"Then Tommy started shouting at me. Taunting me, I guess. Daring me to hit him, almost." She took another drink of water.

Ingrid glanced at Gurley, still he hadn't moved a muscle or said a word. She wanted to ask him what he made of Carrie Foster's statement, but doubted she'd get any kind of sensible response. It was as if he'd gone into a trance, his gaze fixed on the screen, his hands gripping his knees.

Something about the way Carrie Foster spoke was troubling Ingrid. The woman seemed to make every sentence into a question, as if she were doubting herself with each word she uttered. Perhaps she'd hidden the truth for so long, when she actually revealed what really happened, the facts seemed alien to her.

"And then?" Radcliffe asked, when Mrs Foster had returned the beaker to the table.

"Then Molly screamed even louder. I yelled at Tommy to stop shouting. Stop jumping. He wouldn't. Then the bed collapsed. I suppose I lashed out, you know? Forgetting the hairbrush was still in my hand. I caught him right across the face. A second later he was bleeding. Then he started to cry. Then Molly's screaming got louder still. I picked her up from our bed and jiggled her in my arms, but it didn't do any good. Then Tommy ran into the bathroom." She paused, staring down at her hands.

"Did you go after him?"

"Not right away, I wanted to settle Molly first. I couldn't think straight, she was making so much noise. I guess I must have started to shake her. I didn't mean to. I was out of my mind."

The interview room fell silent. All Ingrid could hear was the faint hum of the loudspeakers and the sound of Gurley breathing beside her.

"I'd like to take a break now." Carrie Foster looked at Radcliffe. "Can I take a break?"

"Has anything like this happened before?" Radcliffe asked quietly.

"It was an accident."

"Have there been other accidents?"

Carrie Foster shook her head.

"For the recording, Mrs Foster, I need you to answer verbally."

"No. I get angry sometimes, I suppose. Lose my temper now and then. Mostly I just get a little down."

"Depressed?"

"Doesn't everyone?"

"Those pills in the bathroom cabinet. They're yours?"

She blinked slowly at him. "Kyle got a hold of them for me when I refused to go see the doctor. I didn't ask how he got them. I didn't want to know. But I haven't started taking them. I was mad at him for even suggesting I should. I'm still breastfeeding Molly. I didn't want to have anything in my system that might hurt her."

But 60-proof vodka is just fine, Ingrid thought.

"You haven't seen a doctor about your depression?"

"I thought it would pass, you know? Just as soon as Molly started sleeping through. But I'm still waiting for that to happen." She shook her head. "You've got to believe me—I wouldn't deliberately hurt Molly for the world. It was a terrible, terrible accident." She buried her head in her hands and started to sob.

As Ingrid stared at her, the woman's shoulders and upper body convulsing with with each sob, she still couldn't shake the feeling there was something Carrie Foster wasn't telling the police. What was she hiding?

Radcliffe gave a nod to Tyson, who stated for the record that the interview session was being terminated.

The two detectives got to their feet and left Mrs Foster and Ms Welland sitting silently at the table.

Ingrid slumped back in her chair, a sharp pain radiating across her shoulders where she'd been hunched over leaning forward on the edge of her seat for so long. She opened her mouth, about to make a comment about something in Carrie Foster's statement that really didn't add up, but took another look at Gurley's bereft face and decided to keep it to herself.

The door to the observation room opened and Radcliffe marched in, an almost triumphant swing to his arms. "It seems your suspicions were not unfounded after all."

"I guess I'm a little surprised she decided to confess. She could have chosen to tough it out."

"Perhaps the stress of the situation was just too much for her in the end." He glanced at the monitor. "Doesn't she look like a woman unburdened?"

Ingrid stared at Carrie Foster's face. She looked spent more than relieved. "Are you planning another interview today?"

"I think we'll reconvene tomorrow in all likelihood."

"There's something I'd like you to pursue," Ingrid said.

"Yes?"

"That whole deal with the hairbrush. If she lashed out at Tommy, in a fit of rage, then *accidentally* shook Molly, because she was so 'out of her mind', what compelled her to even think about washing the hairbrush? Trying to get rid of evidence? Doesn't that make her actions seem more premeditated?"

Before Radcliffe had a chance to consider her question, Gurley jumped up from his chair. "For God's sake, what's the matter with you?" he said, spitting out the words. "You got your confession. What more do you want?" He took a stride towards Radcliffe. The DCI stood his ground.

"Actually there's a lot more we need to speak to Mrs Foster about."

"Such as?" Gurley was stooping, his face close to Radcliffe's.

"The DNA analysis revealed something we'd very much like to discuss with her. Although given her confession, it's probably less relevant than might previously have been the case."

"What the hell are you talking about?" The color was creeping back into Gurley's cheeks.

"It seems Kyle Foster is not Molly's biological father."

49

"Can I speak to her?" Ingrid asked. "In my capacity as a representative of the American embassy? Just to let her know we're still here to support her."

"Not possible," Radcliffe said. "And I'm surprised you're even asking. You know better than that."

Ingrid glanced at Gurley. He was staring into space, his face flushed red.

"You're going to release her on bail." Ingrid made it a statement rather than a question.

"In her state of mind? I think it might be better to keep her in custody for her own protection," Radcliffe said.

"The embassy can give her all the protection she needs."

"The solicitor will make her case to the magistrate."

Ingrid felt the sudden need for air. She'd been cooped up in a stuffy room with Gurley for too long. "I'll be outside. I need a few moments to take all this in," she announced, and left the room.

Once outside she walked up and down between the parked vehicles, trying to get some blood pumping in her legs, and tried hard to work out why she wasn't feeling in the least bit satisfied her hunch about Kyle Foster's innocence had been proved right. Maybe there were just too many questions that remained unanswered, especially now, with Radcliffe's latest revelation. As she walked it occurred to her they needed to contact

Kyle Foster urgently. He was so pissed at them the last time he called, Ingrid was worried what he might do next. She found Yvonne Sherwood's number in her cell and called her, but the call went straight to voicemail. She considered leaving a message to let Sherwood know about Carrie Foster's confession, but somehow it didn't seem right to tell Sherwood before Kyle Foster was informed. She needed to discuss what their next move should be with Gurley.

Ingrid hurried back to the observation room to find Gurley slumped against the corridor wall outside, hands on knees.

"Pretty intense, huh?" she said.

He looked her hard in the eye but didn't say a word. Ingrid suspected he was unable rather than unwilling to speak to her.

"I'm going back to the embassy," she told him, suddenly feeling more sorry for the guy than he deserved. He looked so devastated by what he'd just heard. "I think you should come too. We need to work out exactly what we're going to say to Kyle Foster the next time he calls."

"If he calls." Gurley's throat sounded dry as he spoke. He looked up and down the corridor. "Let's get out of here."

They'd exited the police station and had been walking for at least ten minutes before Gurley spoke again. "I guess I owe you an apology. You were right to keep an open mind. I just can't believe Carrie would hurt Molly like that."

"You heard what Carrie said—it was an accident."

"Her own mother?"

"You were prepared to believe her father could hurt her."

Gurley stopped suddenly in the middle of the sidewalk and grabbed Ingrid's arm. "You think Kyle Foster knew Molly wasn't his?"

Ingrid considered the possibility for a moment and quickly rejected it. "I don't think so—every time we've spoken to him he's always referred to Molly as his daughter. He wants to protect her just as much as Tommy."

"But maybe he had to say that. Otherwise we would have been even surer he had motive to hurt Molly."

"You seemed pretty sure he wanted to hurt her anyway."

"I'm not sure about anything anymore." Gurley shrugged his massive shoulders and started walking again. As Ingrid hurried after him her cell vibrated in her pocket. She grabbed it and stared at the screen: it was a cell number she didn't recognize. This time it was her turn to stop in her tracks, getting in the way of pedestrians hurrying along the sidewalk. She hit the answer option and waited.

"Agent Skyberg?"

Gurley mouthed "Who is it?" to her and she mouthed "Foster" back.

"Kyle?" she said.

"I told you no police—why did you go against my wishes? I thought I could trust you."

"Kyle, is Tommy there with you? Is he OK?"

"Tommy's just fine—why wouldn't he be?"

"Absolutely no reason at all. Everything's changed now, Kyle. Your wife has told the police exactly what happened. We know you didn't hurt Molly. We know that for sure now. You don't have to hide out anymore."

"You're lying. This is a trap to get me to give myself up."

"Truly, please believe me—I'm not. Just take Tommy to the nearest hospital, wherever you are, get those injuries looked at again. We can arrange for you both to see Molly. Wouldn't you like that?"

"You lied to me before. Why should I believe you now?"

"It'll be on the news soon, you don't have to take my word for it." Ingrid had no idea when Radcliffe would be making a statement to the media. Maybe she could persuade him to do it sooner rather than later. "Is Yvonne there with you? Maybe I could speak to her."

"She won't be any more convinced by what you're telling me than I am." Foster was starting to sound a little crazy now. Why wouldn't he just take her word for it? She supposed living on his wits, without much sleep or food for the last six days must have taken its toll.

"What can I say to convince you?"

"Nothing—I want to set up the exchange again. Though I swear, if you get the police involved again—"

"Please listen to me, Kyle. There's no need for any of that. Tommy doesn't need to go anywhere. He's safe now. So is Molly. Carrie's in custody. She can't hurt either of them now."

He hung up.

Gurley looked at her expectantly.

"He wants to set up another exchange."

"What's the matter with him?"

"He's just not thinking straight. It's OK—we do as he asks, then I can convince him face to face that he's not in any trouble."

"He abducted his son."

"He was clearly only trying to protect Tommy—he just wanted to get the boy away from Carrie."

"He stole a helicopter."

"In the scheme of things, I think the police might overlook that, don't you?" She was surprised Gurley hadn't brought up the subject of the missing gun and ammunition from the base. She sure as hell wasn't going to mention it.

Her phone beeped. It was a text message from Foster telling her to stand by for further instructions.

50

An hour later Ingrid and Gurley were hunkering down in an anonymous embassy car at another abandoned industrial park. This one was much more run down and older than the first—the buildings were made of red brick rather than prefabricated particle board. No doubt the architects had built them to last, even though by now many of them had started to fall down. Ingrid noticed some of the roofs had collapsed. Most of the windows had no glass in them.

"He'll be calling you, right?" Gurley asked. "My phone is low on juice."

"Mine too. Hopefully the battery will last long enough."

Gurley had pushed back the passenger seat as far as it would go, but his knees still seemed to be butted up against his chin. He adjusted the seat so it reclined at sixty or so degrees and tried to relax his head against the head restraint. He closed his eyes. He started to say something then stopped.

"He'll call when he's ready," Ingrid said. "We can summon a little more patience, can't we?"

"Seems this whole investigation has been about waiting."

"We're so close to the end now. I'm sure I can talk some sense into Kyle." She turned on the radio in the car, keeping the volume low, and retuned it to a news station.

She and Gurley listened in silence for the next five minutes, but there was no mention of Carrie Foster's arrest. The bulletins were full of eye

781

witness reports from Jackson, Minnesota. As the body count increased, so the reporting seemed to get more ghoulish. Ingrid turned off the radio.

"Nothing about the Foster case," Gurley said. "Seems the British media are more interested in something that's happening 4000 miles away."

"Got to keep their audience happy." Ingrid hoped Kathleen Avery wasn't still watching every news report back home. She hated to think of her being exposed to the gruesome details of how each victim had died.

"I guess a head injury sustained accidentally doesn't make for exciting headlines."

"We don't know it was accidental. That's for a jury to decide."

"What?" Gurley turned awkwardly in his seat to face her. "You don't seriously believe Carrie planned to hurt Molly?"

"How can I possibly know one way or the other?" Ingrid really didn't want to have this argument now.

"Come on, you said yourself it was probably an accident."

"I'm not sure what to believe. You've obviously made up your mind." She paused a beat. "But then you were certain she was innocent. Until she confessed." Ingrid had her own suspicions why Gurley was so ready to accept Carrie's version of events, but now really wasn't the time to broach the subject. She reached for the radio dial again, hoping she might find some inoffensive pop station.

Gurley leaned forward and grabbed her hand.

"What the hell?" Ingrid snatched her hand out of his grasp.

"What are you getting at?"

"Can we just focus on the task ahead of us? I'd like a little time to prepare myself, if that's OK with you."

Gurley turned away and stared out at the street. "How long have you known?"

"Known what?" She *really* didn't want to have this conversation now.

"Did Rachelle tell you?"

If she hadn't been certain about her suspicions before, she sure as hell was now. Ingrid stared out through the windshield too. Those street lights that were still working started to flicker into life.

"If you have something you want to confess, maybe you can save it for another time?"

"I know Carrie couldn't hurt Molly deliberately. I just want you to understand that."

"I'm not sure that's necessary."

"Kyle was on a training mission in Iraq. Carrie was lonely. I was in the right place at the right time, I guess." He put a hand to his forehead and sucked in a breath. "The whole thing ended a little under two years ago. It was over before it started. We both knew it was a mistake."

Ingrid didn't respond. What was there to say?

"I promise you I knew nothing about Molly. I had my suspicions, obviously—the timing kind of worked out—but when I asked Carrie about it, she swore to me Molly was Kyle's." He ran a hand over his short hair. "What a fucking mess."

Ingrid sat very still. She tried to recall their first meeting with Carrie Foster at the hospital. There had been something strange about it—a tension she couldn't identify at the time. Then there was Gurley's subsequent refusal to have any doubt about Carrie's account of the incident.

Gurley was right: it was a fucking mess.

"Say something for God's sake." Gurley twisted in his seat again.

There were no words of comfort or reassurance she could give him. She reached up and squeezed his shoulder, looked into his face, trying to muster an expression of sympathy, suspecting she was failing spectacularly.

Her phone beeped.

It was a text from Kyle Foster.

"We're on," she said, "I have the directions."

Gurley blinked hard a few times, as if he were trying to refocus his attention.

"I can't let you go in there on your own," he said after a moment.

"He's not going to hurt me. He has no reason to."

"He could be armed."

"Really?"

Gurley slammed a hand against the dash.

"I really don't think he had anything to do with the missing gun at the base. He didn't have the opportunity."

Gurley turned to the passenger door and opened it. "I'm going in."

"He didn't ask for you." She put a restraining hand on his arm. "Please, Jack. Think about it."

He glanced over his shoulder.

"Maybe Kyle knows about... Maybe you're the last person he wants to see." She braced herself, worried how Gurley would react. She needn't have. He just slumped back in his seat.

"I don't want you going in there without backup."

He still didn't trust her abilities. She would have gotten mad if she'd had the energy. "Tough—we're doing this my way."

"You should have some protection at least."

"I can look after myself."

"Why not have a little extra help?" Gurley shoved an arm behind his back, beneath his jacket. He yanked something from the waistband of his pants. Then held it out to Ingrid.

The Beretta M9 seemed small in his huge hand.

51

Recoiling from the gun, Ingrid pressed her back into the driver door. "What the—"

"Take it."

"No way. Do you have any idea how much crap I'd be in if anyone found me with that?"

"Same for me." He proffered the gun again.

"It's the missing pistol from the munitions store, isn't it?"

"We were hunting a man who tried to kill a fourteen-month-old and had abducted his son. I wanted a little backup."

"And how convenient, to blame Kyle Foster for the theft. You were actually prepared to *frame* him?"

Just when Ingrid thought she was getting a measure of the man, that maybe Gurley wasn't the dick she'd supposed him to be, he threw this at her. What was wrong with the guy? She wanted to punch him in the mouth now more than she ever had. How could he possibly think his actions were in any way justifiable? She was tempted to report him to his superior when this whole thing was done.

"I just wanted to get Tommy back safe and sound," he said. Then added, "By any means necessary." The gun was still balancing on his open palm, his arm outstretched towards her.

"Get that thing out of my sight." She thumped the steering wheel with a fist. "And find some way of returning it to the munitions store. You better make sure it's clear to everyone Kyle Foster had nothing to do with it."

Gurley reluctantly shoved the gun back into his waistband. "You said yourself he sounded like a desperate man. You can't go in there unarmed."

"That's exactly what I intend to do. Foster's instructions are quite clear. I have every intention of following them to the letter. If I can't convince him of Carrie's confession, that we finally believe his version of events, I can at least go along with his plan. That way no one has to get hurt."

Her phone beeped again. The message contained just one word: *now*.

Gurley started to open his door.

"Where the hell do you think you're going?"

"Let me at least walk you to the outside of the building, for God's sake."

"I go alone."

She climbed out the car and hurried to the second building on the right-hand side of the street, as per Foster's instructions. The darkness seemed to be falling more quickly now. She checked her watch: it was a little after eight-thirty. A distant street light was doing nothing to illuminate her path. She stumbled awkwardly over a brick or lump of masonry as she reached the curb. She glanced back towards the car. Much to her relief, Gurley hadn't decided to rush to her aid.

She reached the entrance of the dilapidated building, one of the rotten wooden doors was hanging off its hinges. She shoved it a few inches to one side and squeezed through the gap. As soon as she was through the other side, the light disappeared almost completely. Standing still for a moment in the dark, she hoped her eyes would adjust to the gloom, but apart from a pale glimmer from a distant window, somewhere way over to her left, which cast the faintest of glows onto the uneven, litter strewn floor, she couldn't really make out any detail. Even though she was reluctant to use her precious phone battery, she flipped on the flashlight app and quickly swept it in an arc in front of her. She spotted a doorway on the other side of the high-ceilinged, hundred-square-foot space, switched off the flashlight and slowly made her way towards it, each footfall landing on broken glass or rubble. After a few dozen more steps she reached out her arms, ready to touch the wall she'd been heading for. When she got to it she was surprised the doorway she'd seen wasn't immediately in front of her. She must have deviated from a straight line. She felt along the wall and edged sideways, frustrated progress was so slow.

Her phone beeped.

Another text message from Foster:

. . .

whr the fck ru?

Instead of wasting time fumbling with the phone to text a reply, she located the doorway and moved through it as fast as she dared. She hollered loudly, "I've just crossed the first big room. Can you hear me?"

"Hello?" a distant child's voice answered. "Who are you? Have you—" The child let out a muffled yelp, as if someone had put a hand over his mouth.

"Tommy? Is that you?" Ingrid shouted. "Are you all right?" She stared into a deeper darkness, relieved that Tommy was still alive, but worried now that someone was hurting him. "Tommy?"

As she stood perfectly still, trying to hear his reply, a loud noise, a shuffling, scraping sound, came from somewhere ahead of her. She switched on her phone flashlight again, but there was no one with her in the twenty-foot square room. In the far corner she saw another doorway. With the flashlight trained on the floor, she quickly picked her way over the debris. She reached the door. Through the other side she was relieved to discover a narrow corridor, just as Foster's instructions had described. She called out again, "Kyle? Tommy? I've reached the corridor now. Where are you?" She waited a moment for a reply, but didn't really expect one.

The corridor would be much faster than the previous two rooms to navigate in the dark. All she had to do was reach out both her hands to touch the walls on either side to guide her. She was pretty sure, according to Foster's instructions, her final destination was the room beyond this passageway.

She turned off the flashlight.

After a dozen or so steps another noise, much closer this time, forced her to stop in her tracks.

She felt something scurry over her feet. It was heavy. It had to be a rat.

She continued down the corridor, even faster than she had before. She reached the doorway at the far end and listened.

She heard only the rush of blood and beating of her own heart thump in her ears.

Concentrating hard, Ingrid tried to recall exactly what she was supposed to do once she'd come to the end of the corridor.

Through the doorway she turned right, and, with her fingers lightly touching the rough brickwork of the wall on her right-hand side, followed it until she reached another doorway.

Here she was supposed to wait. Though she was tempted to switch on the flashlight again, she resisted, concerned that in the pitch blackness she might startle Foster with the dazzling bright light.

He might be just feet away from her.

She held her breath and tried to make out the sound of Foster's breathing nearby.

"Kyle? Are you here? Is Tommy with you?" she said, after a few moments.

She listened again.

All she heard was scuttling behind her. More rats, she supposed.

She swallowed hard. The rats themselves weren't a problem. It was the fact she couldn't see them that really bothered her.

She turned her head to the left, then right. But the blackness was absolute.

Behind her the scuttling noise stopped. She exhaled.

"Kyle?"

A split second later she felt an intense pressure across her throat.

Before she could react, a violent shove from behind pushed her face into the rough brick wall. More pressure on her throat, swiftly followed by heavy weight pressing against her body, and she was pinned flat against the wall.

She couldn't move her arms or legs. She couldn't make a sound.

52

"Are you alone?" Though the words were spoken in a harsh whisper, the voice was unmistakably Foster's.

It was impossible for Ingrid to speak, the pressure against her throat was crushing her windpipe.

She managed to nod once.

"You'd better be." Kyle Foster quickly slipped his arm from her throat, grabbed her head by the hair and shoved her left cheek hard against the wall. The rough surface scraped against her skin.

With his spare hand he patted her down, lingering at the pockets. He located her cell phone and threw it onto the ground.

"Please, Kyle." Her voice came out in a murmur, her throat stinging. She coughed. "You're not in any trouble. Carrie has told the police exactly what happened. How she hurt Molly. Why don't you take me to Tommy?"

"You think I would trust you, after you betrayed me before?"

"The police insisted on being part of the operation. It was out of my control." She coughed again. "They're not here now—doesn't that mean anything?"

"Maybe it's a trap." He pressed a knee into her thigh.

"Where's Tommy?"

"You don't need to know."

"Is he with Yvonne?"

"Shut up!" He shifted his weight, leaning more heavily against her. His breathing was rapid and uneven.

Ingrid relaxed her muscles as best she could, hoping Foster might loosen his grip.

He didn't. After a few moments his breathing slowed a little.

"If what you're saying is true, why did Carrie decide to change her story?" he said.

"She had no choice." Ingrid coughed again, her throat felt raw. She tried to swallow. "The police found new evidence."

"I've said all along I wanted to protect Molly and Tommy from her and you didn't believe me. And now you're telling me she's confessed?"

"It's true."

"You'll say anything to get Tommy back. You make me sick."

She couldn't argue with him. The way he was talking, nothing she said would make him trust her. "OK," she said, "just tell me how you want this to work."

He shoved her harder against the wall.

For the first time Ingrid worried what he planned to do to her once he released Tommy.

"Where's Tommy?" she asked again, eager to focus on the reason she was there. "Is he safe? Is Yvonne here with him?"

"Do you have his papers? He needs them for the plane."

"We have an embassy car waiting outside. All the paperwork is inside," she lied. "We've done everything you asked." Ingrid swallowed again. She wasn't sure how much longer she could continue speaking. "You have me now. You can let Tommy go."

He shoved her again. "Shut up! We're doing this my way. When I say."

"You wanted an exchange. You got it. Please. I just want to help you."

"Stop lying to me!" He twisted sideways in an attempt to shove her even closer to the wall.

But this time Ingrid resisted with all the strength she had.

Her efforts threw Foster off balance. He stumbled.

She took her chance.

Driving back both elbows as hard as she could into his torso, she stamped down onto one of his feet. It was enough to knock him further off balance. She used the little momentum she'd gained to spin around and wrap both her arms across his body, pinning his arms to his sides.

He struggled against her.

Now she shoved him against the wall. She knew she wouldn't be able to hold him there for long. He was bigger than her, stronger.

"Kyle—listen to me. Tommy will be safe. We can work together on this."

"Why should I believe you?" He struggled against her grasp.

A strange, high-pitched gulping sound came from behind her. Then a bright light threw her shadow onto the wall. She couldn't turn to see what was there without loosening her grip on Foster. She heard the noise again. More of a sob this time. Then a scream.

Then something barreled into her at speed. The beam of a flashlight bounced around the room, momentarily blinding her. Weak punches hit at her lower back, followed by kicks to her calves. The flashlight clattered to the floor.

"Daddy's right! Stop telling lies!"

"Tom-my!" Her voice cracked between syllables.

"Stop lying." Even though the boy's punches and kicks weren't doing any real damage, they were making it much harder for her to contain Foster.

"Mommy didn't hurt Molly. You're telling lies. Stop it!" The punches came faster and harder for a few moments then eased and gradually stopped. The boy had exhausted himself. He slumped onto the ground. "It's naughty to lie. Mommy didn't hurt Molly." He started to cry.

"It's OK, Tommy," Foster said. "Everything's OK. I'm sure Mommy didn't mean to hurt her."

"Listen to your dad."

Tommy punched her weakly behind her knee. "Let Daddy go!"

Foster wasn't offering any resistance. Ingrid was tempted to release him. "What I said before, it was true. Carrie told the police it was an accident."

"That's true. It was an accident," Tommy said, then sobbed again. "I didn't mean to hurt her." He slid past Ingrid's feet and wrapped himself around his father's legs. "I just wanted to stop her screaming. She was making Mommy cry. She makes Mommy cry all the time. I didn't mean…" His voice was swallowed up by the sobs erupting from his throat, coming faster and louder with each snagging breath he took.

"What?" With his right arm Foster pulled against Ingrid and tried to reach down to his son. "What did you just say?"

Ingrid tightened her grip.

"For God's sake, let me hold my son." Foster strained against her.

"Where's Yvonne?" Ingrid asked.

"She's supposed to be with Tommy."

"I ran away from her," the boy said.

Ingrid let go of Foster and stepped away, out of her reach. Foster dropped to the ground and gathered Tommy into his arms.

"I'm sorry, Daddy."

"Shhh… there's nothing for you to be sorry about."

"But there is. Molly was on the bed, screaming. Like she always does. I could hear Mommy in the bathroom, crying. I told Molly to be quiet. But she wouldn't. So I grabbed her and shook her a little. But she screamed louder. So I shook her some more… I think maybe she hit her head on the back of the bed. I just wanted to…" His voice trailed away.

"It's OK. It's all right, Tommy," Kyle said in a soothing voice.

"That's when Mommy hit me. I let go of Molly then and I hit Mommy back. I punched her in the leg. She shouldn't have hit me. I was just trying to help. I didn't want to hurt anybody."

For the next few moments the only sound that echoed around the room was Tommy's violent sobbing.

"He's lying," Foster said eventually. "Trying to help his mom. He wouldn't hurt his baby sister. He's a good boy." Clearly Foster couldn't believe what his son had just admitted. His voice was shaky, uncertain.

Even in the near-dark, just from the sound of their breathing, Ingrid could tell Foster was squeezing the boy tighter to him.

"I didn't mean to hurt her so bad. It was an accident."

"Shhh, you don't know what you're saying. Be quiet."

"I'm sorry, Daddy."

"It was Carrie," Foster insisted. "It had to be. Molly was just lying so still in Carrie's arms when I got back to the room. But she can get help, right? She's been depressed. That will be taken into account, won't it? Temporary insanity. The stress… the depression she's been suffering from…"

"I'm sorry," Tommy said again between sobs.

"Shhh… I'm not going to lose him," he told Ingrid. "He doesn't know what he's saying."

Ingrid knelt down next to them. "You won't lose him," she said firmly. "That won't happen. Tommy's only eight years old."

"So? He's old enough to be prosecuted. I can't have him go through that."

"He doesn't have to. He's too young."

"You think I'm going to believe you?"

"It's different here than back home. The age of criminal responsibility in the UK is ten years old." She lowered her voice and leaned closer to Foster's head. "The police can't even arrest him."

"What?"

"I swear."

"I don't believe you."

"I wouldn't lie about something like that."

"Why should I trust you?"

"I can call a lawyer right now, if you help me find my cell."

53

A brilliant white light shone in Ingrid's eyes. She held up a hand to shield them from the glare and managed to make out Yvonne Sherwood heading towards them from the doorway, glowing cell phone in one hand, broken brick in the other.

"I'm sorry, Kyle," Sherwood said. "Tommy managed to wriggle out of my arms and run away. He knocked my phone from my hands. It took me a while to find it in the dark." She glared at Ingrid. "Is everything all right?"

"It's fine," Ingrid answered.

"Kyle? What's happened? Why's Tommy crying?"

"It was an accident. I didn't mean to hurt her," Tommy sobbed.

"It's OK, Tommy. It's OK. Shhh…" Foster wrapped his arms around his son more tightly, burying the boy's head beneath his jacket. "Carrie didn't do it," he told Sherwood. "She didn't hurt Molly."

The woman seemed bewildered. "I don't understand. If Carrie didn't—"

"It was Tommy," Ingrid said.

"Kyle?"

"He just said he was trying to make Molly stop crying. He shook her." There was still a tremor in Foster's voice.

"Dear God."

"She says he's too young to face any charges," Foster said, looking at Ingrid. "Do you know if that's true?"

Sherwood shrugged. "Might be. It rings a bell."

"How about you get rid of that brick?" Ingrid said, pointing at the potentially lethal weapon in Sherwood's fist. "Then maybe you can help me find my phone. We need to get out of here."

After locating her cell on the rubble-strewn floor, Kyle Foster gathered his son into his arms and they slowly picked their way across the room. They exited via another corridor and left the building using a different doorway, emerging onto a street on the north side of the derelict warehouse. Sherwood hurried ahead of them to her silver Nissan parked on the other side of the road.

Ingrid sat up front with Sherwood, while Kyle cradled Tommy in his arms on the back seat.

"Are we driving back to the base?" Sherwood asked, peering into the rear-view mirror.

"I want to visit the hospital, see Molly," Foster said. "Show Tommy his sister's going to be just fine."

Ingrid hoped to hell he was right. "I should call some people," she said. "That OK with you, Kyle?" When he didn't answer right away, she twisted in her seat to see him nodding at her, tears streaming down his face.

Ingrid found Gurley's number in her phone. "Jack?"

"What the hell is happening?"

"We've cleared the building. Everyone's just fine. I need you to meet us at the hospital."

"What went down in there?"

She gave him a quick account of what Tommy had admitted then hung up before he could ask her questions. Next she called DCI Radcliffe and repeated the same account.

"You believe him? You don't get the impression he's been coached to admit hurting his sister by Foster?"

Ingrid couldn't believe quite what a cynical bastard Radcliffe was. "I'm certain it's genuine. We're heading for UCH."

"We'll need to take a statement from him."

"Sure. Just not tonight, OK? The kid's exhausted."

Radcliffe reluctantly agreed, then hung up, just moments before Ingrid's cell finally ran out of battery.

———

Ingrid, Yvonne Sherwood and Carrie Foster's family liaison officer stood discreetly beside the door in Molly's hospital room as the little girl giggled and gurgled at the faces her big brother was making at her.

"See?" Sherwood said. "I told you he couldn't hurt either of them. He's a good dad."

"Maybe Carrie's a better mother than either of us have given her credit for too," Ingrid said.

Sherwood didn't comment.

After fifteen minutes, the ICU nurse ushered them all out of the room, insisting they let Molly sleep. Sherwood and the FLO took Tommy in search of something to eat while Ingrid stayed with Kyle Foster just outside the room.

"I think she's going to be OK," he said.

"Tomorrow morning you can speak to the doctors."

"When I saw Molly in Carrie's arms... in the hotel room, she wasn't moving. I just assumed that she was dead, that Carrie had... Carrie's been so down for so long now. I thought... I guess... I just had to get Tommy away from her." He rubbed the back of his hand against his forehead. He looked like he hadn't washed for days, his fingernails and knuckles were grimed with dirt.

Twenty yards or so down the corridor the double doors swung open. Carrie Foster, accompanied by DS Tyson, walked unsteadily towards them. Kyle Foster looked at his wife as she approached, but didn't move.

"I should go, give you a little time together," Ingrid said quietly.

"No, please stay."

"Why?"

"I'm not sure I'm ready to speak to her. A little support would be appreciated."

Carrie Foster quickened her pace. "I want to see Molly. And Tommy," she said as she got closer to the room.

"The nurse said Molly should rest for a while," Ingrid told her.

"Where's Tommy?" she asked.

"Getting something to eat. He's all right," Ingrid said. "Shaken, tired, but he'll be just fine. The FLO and Yvonne are with him."

After a long moment, Carrie Foster shifted her gaze from Ingrid to Kyle. She swallowed. "I'm sorry, Kyle."

They both turned toward the door of Molly's room and peered through the porthole window, saying nothing.

After a while Kyle Foster broke the silence. "Why did you tell the police I hurt her?" His voice was no more than a whisper.

Carrie Foster didn't answer.

"How could you do that?"

"I didn't know what else to do. I had to protect Tommy."

Kyle Foster shook his head. "So did I."

"I panicked. I'm sorry. I should have told them I was responsible right from the start. But I wanted to stay with Molly. If I'd said I'd hurt her they would have taken her away from me. When I saw that EMT staring at you in the hotel room, he had such a suspicious look on his face... the idea of blaming you was the first thought I had. It seemed the easiest option. I couldn't tell them what really happened."

"But you could have told me. We'd have worked something out."

"And what? Have the police arrest Tommy?"

"He's too young to be arrested."

"I didn't know that. You think I would have let all this happen if I knew that? You've got to believe me—I thought I was doing the best thing for everyone."

"Jesus, Carrie. You know how much I love them. How could you tell people I hurt them?" He sniffed. Tears were streaming down his face again.

"Why did you take Tommy?"

"What?"

"Maybe if you hadn't taken him... if you hadn't run..."

"I thought Molly was dead. Tommy had blood on his face... I had to get him away from you."

"I didn't mean to hit him. All I could think about was stopping him hurting Molly." She looked down at the floor. The expression on her face slowly turned from one of remorse to something closer to indignation. She stared up at her husband. "You really thought I'd killed Molly?"

"What else was I supposed to think? Especially when you blamed me for it." Kyle Foster glanced at Ingrid. She wasn't sure what it was he might want her to say, but there was no way she was getting involved. She started to back away.

"I told you already," Carrie said, "blaming you seemed the easiest option. The longer it went on, the more impossible it was for me to change my story. I was terrified of losing Molly."

"Me too." He stared through the window into Molly's room. "What did the doctors tell you? Is she going to be all right?"

"They're hopeful. She'll need more scans. She'll have to be monitored closely, but it's looking much better than it was."

"Thank God." He wiped his cheeks dry with the sleeve of his jacket.

"The police need to interview Tommy. We should both be there when they do. He needs his mom and dad right now."

"Of course." She swallowed. "I want to try to put things right, Kyle." She reached out a hand, but he pulled away. "Tell me you want that too."

He shook his head. "Right now, I just care about the kids, OK? I'll do what I have to for them."

Carrie Foster took a deep breath. "There's something else I need to tell you, about Molly. Something you should hear from me, before you speak to the doctors."

"About her diagnosis?" He sounded panicked.

"No—nothing to do with her condition. Something else."

Ingrid had been slowly edging away from the couple, now she turned around and hurried along the corridor. There was no need for her to witness Kyle's reaction to the bombshell his wife was about to drop. She needed to get to Gurley, head him off at the pass before he came blundering in. As she approached DS Tyson, who'd been keeping a respectful distance, she nodded and said, "Been a long week, hasn't it?"

The detective nodded back at her, his gaze fixed on the Fosters, a grim expression on his face.

"What'll happen to Tommy?"

Tyson hesitated before answering. "He'll need to make a formal statement. Then he might be given a Child Safety Order."

Ingrid looked at him blankly.

"If he is, he'll be placed under the supervision of a youth offending team. But that sort of approach is designed for persistent offenders. I'm not sure it can even be applied to foreign nationals. It's all a bloody awful mess, the whole thing."

Ingrid wasn't about to argue with his assessment.

Along the corridor, the double doors swung open again and Jack Gurley appeared, his face gray, his posture slumped. He looked like a defeated man.

"How's it going with the big reconciliation?" Gurley gestured in the Fosters' direction.

"Not great and I'd say it's about to get a whole lot worse," Ingrid said and quickly walked Gurley back through the doors. "I think Carrie is about to tell Kyle about Molly."

Gurley stopped. "Shouldn't I be around for that? To support Carrie? If Kyle wants to throw a punch at me, maybe I should let him."

"You really think Molly is yours?"

He nodded, letting out a long sigh. "I'll take a DNA test—prove it one way or the other. Maybe afterwards I should ask for a transfer back home."

"Shouldn't you stick around? For Molly's sake?"

"That's not up to me. I'll do whatever Carrie wants me to."

Ingrid wondered at Gurley's reluctance to get involved. He didn't seem like the sort of man who would run away from his responsibilities. "What did you do with the pistol?" she asked, keen to change the subject.

"It's in the glove compartment of the car. Don't worry—I'll deal with it, make sure no one can blame it on Foster."

"Good."

"I screwed up. Least I can do is put it right." He stuck out his hand. "Pleasure working with you, agent." He gave her a wry smile.

Ingrid took his hand in hers. "Likewise." It wasn't exactly a lie, but she wouldn't be in a hurry to repeat the experience. "But you're not quite free of me yet."

He raised his eyebrows.

"There's the whole Bureau debrief ordeal to get through."

"They need me for that?"

"Afraid so."

He shrugged. "Listen, that little chat I had with your chief, about getting you taken off the investigation?"

"It's OK—I won't bear a grudge."

He smiled at her again then led the way toward the elevators. "How about I buy you that pizza I promised you? Prove there's no hard feelings?"

"I'm real tired. Let's take a raincheck on that, shall we?"

He smiled again, his face a picture of relief.

54

The next day Ingrid didn't stir from her bed until noon. She hadn't set an alarm, assuming the bright morning light that streamed into her bedroom would wake her. But she'd slept right through. As she sat up and swung her legs over the edge of the bed, she wasn't sure the extra hours of sleep had been at all restorative. It felt a little shameful sleeping in so late. She reached down and grabbed her phone from the floor and discovered she'd missed a dozen or so calls. She quickly flipped through the list of text messages and worked out who she should call first.

Just as soon as she'd drunk her first cup of coffee.

As she staggered blearily into the kitchen, she listened to a long, rambling voice message from Ralph, telling her how relieved he was that she was safe and asking if she'd perhaps like to meet later, if she was feeling up to it. Ingrid saved his message, smiling stupidly at the phone, surprised at just how much the idea of seeing him appealed to her. She sent him a quick text message, promising to call later.

Then she made coffee.

Just as she was finishing her second large mug, sitting cross-legged outside on the roof terrace, her phone started to ring. It was an international call. Her mother or Mike Stiller. She wasn't sure right now if she wanted to speak to either of them. She drained her coffee and hit the answer button.

It was Mike. For him to be calling her this early D.C. time on a Sunday, it had to be something serious.

He took a while greeting her, asking how she was, how her case was going, was she busy, could she speak, until she had to shout at him to tell her whatever it was he'd called her about. Still he hesitated.

"For God's sake, Mike, all this prevaricating isn't actually helping. Just tell me."

Which was exactly what he proceeded to do for the next ten minutes. He spelled out in detail everything he knew, answering all of Ingrid's questions, even when she interrupted him—which would normally have gotten him so mad he would have hung up on her—and spoke in such gentle tones, at times she wasn't sure she was even speaking to the right man.

When she eventually hung up, even though she'd exhausted all her lines of questioning, drawn out every last morsel of information Mike had for her, Ingrid still couldn't believe what he'd told her. Or maybe she just didn't want to believe it. She stared down at her phone, watching it shake in her trembling hand, and felt her throat tighten. She stood up and walked unsteadily to the edge of her roof terrace. She stared out at the view across London, imagining another vista, another view. One she hadn't seen for many, many years. Maybe too many.

She closed her eyes. She knew what she had to do next, but wasn't sure if she was ready.

After a little while she opened her eyes, wiped the tears from her face and selected a number from her contacts list. She took a quick, deep breath before Svetlana picked up.

"Hey, Mom, it's me. I hope I didn't wake you." She braced herself for a torrent of insults and abuse, but it didn't come. Perhaps it was something about the tone of her voice, in those few words, that stopped her mother's complaints about unanswered calls and ignored messages.

Whatever it was, Svetlana simply said, "Tell me."

Ingrid swallowed and started to relay everything Mike Stiller had just told her. Unlike Ingrid, Svetlana remained quiet on the other end of the line, waiting for a natural pause in her daughter's account before she asked her first question.

"There can be no doubt?" she said, the inflection in the question suggesting she was hoping that there was.

"The samples they tested matched enough of Kathleen's DNA profile to prove the... victim is a close relative. As soon as they get a sample of Megan's hair to test, everything will be confirmed for sure. They found her, Mom. They found Megan."

Svetlana didn't say anything.

"She was so close to home, all this time. So close and we never knew." Ingrid was struggling to contain her tears. She pulled the phone away from her ear for a moment and sniffed sharply. "All these years I thought I could save her."

"Nobody could, Golubushka. Nobody." Ingrid couldn't remember the last time her mother used that name when she was talking to her. It sent a shiver up her spine.

"Are you with Kathleen right now?" Ingrid asked.

"No, I'm in the car on my way over to her house. I should call her."

Ingrid sucked in a breath. "No. Wait. Don't do that. Let me."

"You're sure?"

"I think it's the very least I can do. But she shouldn't be alone when she finds out. Will you call me when you get there, then pass the phone to Kathleen?"

"You don't even have to ask."

"We found her, Mom."

"I'll call you soon. Will you…" She paused.

"What is it?"

"Will you come home now?"

———

After a painful, but thankfully brief conversation with Kathleen Avery, Ingrid managed to book the last seat on the final flight to Minneapolis for the afternoon flight the following day. Then she called Sol Franklin at home to explain the situation, grateful to get through the whole story without breaking down.

"I hate to abandon my post, but I have to go back home. I'll need a week or so."

"Listen to me, you take as long as you need. We can cover for you here. I'll take on your caseload myself if I have to."

"I'm sorry, Sol."

"Nothing to apologize for—we'll manage."

"I need to write up my report on the Foster case."

"I'll speak to Major Gurley, I'm sure between us we can produce something to keep the chief happy."

Ingrid really did feel bad leaving a job half done. But doing the right thing for Megan Avery was more important than anything else.

"Just tell me you're planning on coming back," Sol said.

Ingrid hadn't been thinking that far ahead. She'd just assumed she would return to London. But now Sol had actually raised the possibility she might not, the idea didn't seem that outrageous.

"Ingrid? You are coming back?"

"Sure, sure."

"I'll keep the job open for you as long as I can."

"Thanks, Sol. I'll call you after the funeral, when I have a clearer idea of my plans. OK?"

Sol paused before answering. "That's fine. I know you won't let me down."

Ingrid said goodbye and hung up, feeling unsettled by the conversation. She looked around the living room of her sparsely furnished, rented apartment. She really hadn't personalized it at all. Did that mean in the back of her mind she hadn't been planning on staying? She shook the thought from her head and jumped up from the couch. *Now what?* She'd been working flat out the past week and now had no clue what to do with herself. Instinctively, she headed for the apartment door and found her running shoes there. A long overdue run would make things feel a whole lot better. She strapped her cell phone to her arm, stuck her earphones in her ears and left the building.

It wasn't until she reached the Outer Circle of Regent's Park, just a few dozen yards away from the official residence of the US ambassador, that she realized although her mind had been full of memories of Megan Avery during her run, not all of them had been painful. Thinking of her friend felt different somehow, but she couldn't quite pinpoint what it was that had changed. Previously she had tried and failed to outrun her memories when they came, but now she seemed more able to face them.

She stopped when she got to the entrance of London Zoo and called Ralph Mills.

"Hey, Ralph."

"Hi."

"You got my text."

"I did."

"Good."

"Thanks for getting back to me."

Ingrid had never heard him sound so awkward. She had a feeling the conversation was going to be harder than she'd imagined.

"Listen, about the other night," he said, then stalled.

"I'm sorry," they both said together.

"You have nothing to apologize for," he told her.

"And neither do you." She let out a breath, relieved to have cleared the air. "How about dinner tonight?"

"I was just about to suggest the same thing."

"Great. Pick me up at eight. We'll eat local."

"Look forward to it."

———

After dinner, which they spent talking about pretty much anything except the abduction case in Minnesota, Ingrid and Ralph strolled slowly back to her apartment. As they stood at the apartment door, and he leaned in to kiss her goodnight, Ingrid grabbed both his arms and dragged him over the threshold.

"I really don't want to be alone tonight," she said, then kicked the door shut and carried on through to the living room, figuring that heading for the bedroom right away might just freak him out.

They finished half a bottle of wine while talking about the Molly Foster case, until finally Ingrid had talked herself out. She put down her glass, got to her feet and, grabbing Ralph's hand, led him into the bedroom.

"You're sure about this?" he said, as she started to slowly unbutton his shirt. "I don't want you to think I'm taking advantage of the situation."

"Situation?"

"You're in a vulnerable place right now."

"Don't you think we've moved beyond that?"

"I just want to be sure—"

She put a finger to his mouth then kissed it. "Shut up, dammit."

The next morning, when Ralph left her apartment, his brown hair tousled, the left sleeve of his tee shirt ripped where she had tried to pull it over his head too fast, Ingrid was certain of one thing. She had definitely put her failed engagement to Marshall Claybourne firmly behind her.

A new start was just what she needed.

55

Standing at the end of the snaking security line in Terminal 3 of Heathrow Airport, Ingrid was determined not to get emotional. Ralph had insisted he take her to the airport, and though she hated lingering goodbyes, after the night they had spent together, she felt unable to refuse him. With dry eyes, she grabbed Ralph's face in both her hands, pulling his head toward hers, and planted a kiss on his partly open mouth. They stayed like that for a few moments before Ingrid tore herself away.

"I'll call you," she said.

"If I didn't know better, I'd say that sounded suspiciously like the brush off."

She smiled at him. He smiled his Clark Swanson smile back at her and she felt the inevitable adrenalin rush surge through her body. And it felt good.

On the other side of security, as Ingrid was stuffing her belongings back into her backpack following a particularly thorough search by an officious security employee, her phone started to ring. She retrieved it from her purse and hit the answer option.

"Hey, it's Mike."

Ingrid held her breath. "Tell me they've got him."

"Sorry, not yet, but I just spoke to one of the local agents. They've got a reliable tip-off. They're real hopeful it's gonna lead to something."

"That sounds like the kind of thing I used to say to console family members."

"I'm not bullshitting you. I wouldn't do that. They're real close to a breakthrough, they told me. I believe them, I really do. And you know what a cynical sonofabitch I am."

Ingrid didn't comment.

"As soon as I get any more news, I'll let you know."

"Thanks, Mike." Ingrid hung up wondering if this time she could risk allowing herself to hope for the best.

Before she proceeded to the departure gate, she made one more call.

"Chief inspector."

"Agent Skyberg, so good of you to check in."

"I'm on my way back to the US, I haven't had chance to—"

"It's all right, Sol Franklin has already informed me—a family emergency, I gather."

Ingrid swallowed. "SSA Franklin will be your main point of contact at the embassy in my absence."

"I'm sure we'll muddle through without you."

"Can you tell me what happened when you interviewed Tommy?"

"The boy was distraught, naturally. Clearly remorseful. The US Air Force have agreed to a program of extensive counseling, for both Tommy individually and the family as a whole. He'll be monitored closely, of course, but our forensic psychologist believes this attack was a one-off incident."

Ingrid hoped they were right.

"Have you heard from Major Gurley?" she asked the DCI.

"I haven't been able to contact him. I've been told by his superior officer that after his debrief he was assigned to another base."

"Here or in the US?"

"That wasn't entirely clear. Why?"

"No reason." Maybe Carrie Foster had suggested Gurley make the request for a transfer. She guessed it was something she'd never find out. "Thank you for the update."

"No problem. I hope your family issues are resolved soon."

It was a hope Ingrid hadn't dared wish for herself.

———

She changed planes at O'Hare International and when she finally reached the arrivals hall at St Paul Airport in Minneapolis, she spotted Svetlana standing at a low barrier, fidgeting with a pack of cigarettes.

In the three years since she'd last seen her, Ingrid's mother didn't seem to have changed at all. Her hair was still dyed bright red and she continued to wear the wiry locks piled high on top of her head. For Svetlana, the Soviet gymnast look was clearly impossible to shake. Ingrid surprised herself by smiling at her mother as she approached the barrier. Svetlana didn't seem to notice her own daughter until she was practically standing beside her. Two feet out Ingrid noticed her mother was wearing a pair of glasses on a chain around her neck. They were new. Perhaps she should try wearing them on her face instead, Ingrid thought.

She waved right at her mother. Svetlana jerked to attention, looked Ingrid up and down for a few moments, then said, "You've put on weight."

As soon as they got into the car her mother switched on the local news radio station. "We might hear something new," she explained.

"Nothing about the perpetrator yet?"

"Why?" Svetlana peered at her sideways, a suspicious look in her eyes. "You know something?"

"I just heard the local agents might have a lead."

"They have leads all the time. Each one comes to nothing." She started the car and they drove the next hundred and fifty miles without saying very much at all. But then there wasn't really anything to say. Catching up on each other's news didn't seem appropriate in the circumstances.

When they pulled into Kathleen's drive, just after five in the afternoon, Ingrid was amazed to discover how little the exterior of the house had changed. It must have been repainted over the years, but always in the same color: light blue clapboards with bright white trim. She wondered if time had stood still inside the house too. As soon as she set foot over the threshold, she could see that it had. She supposed Megan's room at the rear of the ranch-style single story building had remained untouched. She expected to find some sort of morbid shrine to her friend. The thought made her feel a little nauseous.

She hesitated in the hallway.

"Go on through," Svetlana told her, slipping a set of keys into her pocket. "Kathleen isn't going to rush out and greet us."

Still Ingrid felt unable to put one foot in front of the other.

"She's been talking about your visit non-stop since yesterday. For God's sake, at least go and say hello." Svetlana shoved Ingrid sharply in the back. Ingrid felt each one of her mother's bony knuckles press against her flesh.

She slowly walked into the living room, feeling all of fourteen again. The couch was pushed up against the wall on the left-hand side, just like it always had been. Kathleen Avery was sitting in the middle of it, her head turned toward the door. Suddenly her face broke into a broad smile.

"Come over here, honey."

Ingrid let out a silent breath of relief. Kathleen wasn't as big as she'd imagined. Morbidly obese, certainly, but it didn't seem she was totally immobile. Ingrid edged toward the couch, staring at Kathleen's flushed cheeks, her short light brown hair peppered with gray. She was wearing a long flowered smock dress over a pair of black leisure pants.

"Don't be bashful. Come sit right next to me." Her voice was just the same, thick like molasses, with a sing-song quality about it. A sudden memory of Kathleen singing lullabies to them when Ingrid stayed over as a child jumped into her head. Something she hadn't thought of in years.

After more coaxing from Kathleen, Ingrid did as she was told and eased herself down onto the soft upholstery of the couch, sliding sideways into the dip that Kathleen was creating in the middle seat cushion. A heavy arm wrapped around Ingrid's waist, pulling her further in. Kathleen planted a kiss on Ingrid's cheek.

"Don't you smell all grown up?"

Ingrid suspected it was the aroma of strong black coffee on her breath and the stink of Svetlana's cigarettes clinging to her hair that was creating the impression of adulthood. The last time Kathleen had laid eyes on her she was still firmly stuck in an awkward adolescence that threatened to go on forever.

Kathleen smelled the same as she always had: of sweet apples and fresh baked pastry. Immediately Ingrid was transported to the late eighties, sitting in the kitchen of this house, devouring a pile of pie and ice cream, wishing Kathleen was her mom and not Svetlana.

Maybe she still did a little.

Kathleen stopped squeezing her for a moment to point a remote at the forty-eight inch TV playing noisily on the other side of the room. "I pretty much have it on twenty-four seven—just in case there's any news." She looked toward the doorway at Svetlana who was hovering there.

"I'm going to the backyard," she announced. "I need a smoke." She marched through the room, glancing at Ingrid as she passed. It was the first time her mother had displayed any hint of tact. She must have guessed Ingrid needed a little privacy to speak to Kathleen. Their phone conversation the day before had been very brief.

"I guess you've been wondering why I haven't come to see you in all these years," Ingrid began.

"We all have our own way of dealing with pain." Kathleen wrinkled her nose, as if she was about to sneeze. Her eyes watered. "I'm not going to make any judgment about the way you dealt with yours." She smiled weakly at Ingrid. "I'm not saying I wouldn't have liked to see you. I'd have loved it, but I can understand how hard it was for you. I really can." Tears fell from her eyes.

"No—there's more to it than that. There's stuff you don't know."

Kathleen sniffed and dabbed her eyes with a lilac lace handkerchief. "Is it something you really need to tell me?"

Ingrid frowned into the woman's flushed face and noticed the deep lines around her eyes and mouth for the first time.

"I mean, it might very well be good for you to say what you've been keeping to yourself all these years, but do you think it would be good for me to hear it?" She wiped her nose with the handkerchief.

Ingrid had to look away. She gazed down at the swirling pattern in the textured carpet. It seemed to move somehow, like waves on the sea. It made her feel a little sick. She felt Kathleen's chubby fingers wrap around her hand. "I just thought I should tell you exactly what I remember," Ingrid said. "What I did." *And what I didn't do.*

"You were both not much more than babies." She sniffed again. "You can't be blamed for what happened."

"I'm so sorry, Mrs Avery."

"It wasn't your fault, do you hear me?"

Tears sprang from Ingrid's eyes and down her cheeks before she even realized she was crying. Kathleen pulled her toward her huge breasts and stroked her hair. She patted a hand against her leg. Sudden sobs issued from Ingrid's mouth, she was unable to keep them under control any longer.

"You let it all out, honey. You let it all out."

They stayed sitting like that for a few moments until Kathleen unexpectedly withdrew her hand and pushed Ingrid away. Ingrid tensed, bracing herself, worried what was going to happen next. What Kathleen might say. She looked at Kathleen's face, expecting to see an expression of disappointment. But Megan's mom turned her face away. She stared intently at the television on the opposite wall.

"Is that him?" Her ruddy face had grown pale.

Ingrid looked at the scene playing out on the huge screen across the room. Two tall FBI agents were bundling a wiry, balding man in his mid-fifties, a mass of tattoos on his scrawny arms, into a waiting police car.

56

Although Ingrid had booked herself a room in a local motel, somehow Svetlana managed to convince her to stay in the family home. Much to Ingrid's relief, her mother led her to a guest room on the top floor at the front of the house, rather than her old room in the attic.

After she'd unpacked, Ingrid checked her phone for all the calls and texts she'd been ignoring since she'd landed in the US. It took her a full fifteen minutes to plow through all of them and when she got to the end there was only one call she wanted to return. She hit a speed dial option.

"Hey, Ralph."

There was a pause at the other end—Ingrid wondered if she'd interrupted something. She hadn't quite oriented herself in terms of days and time. Had she called him in the middle of the night, London time?

"Hello. You arrived," he said.

"I did."

"I'm sorry if I left you a lot of messages. The Kyle Foster story hit the news here this morning and I thought you might want to know about it. Somehow Angela Tate managed to get a scoop. I don't know how she does it."

"Maybe she has friends in high places."

"More likely she has enemies and a lot of dirt on them." He fell quiet again. "Listen, I should come clean—full disclosure and all that... I left you a ton of messages because... well I suppose I just—"

"Does it help to know you're the only person whose call I've returned?"

"It's good to hear your voice."

"I only saw you yesterday."

Another pause. She'd made him feel awkward—not what she'd intended. But to his credit he recovered quickly.

"You left just when things were starting to get interesting."

It wasn't as if she'd had a choice. No need to remind Ralph of that—she didn't want to make him feel uncomfortable.

He cleared his throat. "I saw on the news the police have made an arrest in Minnesota."

"Yes, I was at Kathleen Avery's house when I found out."

"Do you know if he's admitting anything?"

"According to my contact the sonofabitch won't shut up about what he's done."

"At least that'll make the whole process quicker."

"I guess."

"You've spoken to Megan's mum? How'd it go?"

"I think it was OK."

"Better than you were expecting?"

"Much."

"But it was still tough?"

"I didn't tell her exactly what happened—the fact that I ran. It wasn't until I was sitting right next to her that I realized that if I had I would just have been unburdening myself. It wouldn't have helped Kathleen any. It would have been plain selfish."

"You did the right thing."

"I think so. If she asks me for the details, I'll be honest with her. But now is not the right time."

He went quiet again.

"Ralph? Are you OK?"

"I feel like I want to wrap my arms around you, tell you it's going to be all right."

"I guess it never will be. But right now at least it feels a little less hard. I'll take that."

"Has a date been set for the funeral?"

"A week today. I was thinking I'd come back to London right after, but I might stay a while."

"Oh."

A single syllable could hardly ever have conveyed so much disappointment.

"I've got a lot of thinking to do. A lot of talking. And a hell of a lot of fences to mend." Ingrid had expected him to jump right in and tell her she should take just as long as she needed to. But he said nothing. Maybe he was even more disappointed with her decision to stay on than she'd realized.

They said a slightly awkward goodbye and Ingrid made sure she was the first to hang up.

———

The following Monday, with mechanical assistance from the local vehicle hire company together with her own determination, Kathleen Avery managed to get to the cemetery for her only daughter's funeral. It had been the first time she had set foot outside her home in over seven years. One of her six-foot, two-hundred-sixty pound sons pushed her along the paved path from the line of funeral cars to the grave in a super-sized wheelchair designed especially for heavy hospital patients.

Kathleen sat with her back straight and her head held high. She told Ingrid she wanted her to walk with the rest of the family to the graveside, seeing as Megan loved her like a sister. It was all Ingrid could do not to break down into floods of tears every time Kathleen mentioned Megan's name. She'd been feeling a little better with every conversation she'd had with Kathleen over the past week, but the guilt that had burned in her belly for the last eighteen years wasn't going anywhere. She held onto Megan's youngest brother's arm with a tight grip, not completely trusting that her legs would be strong enough to carry her to the mound of earth she could see fifty yards away.

When they reached the graveside, the assembled mourners arranged themselves around the eight foot by four foot hole in strict order of intimacy with the Averys. Even though she hadn't spoken to Kathleen since she'd left home, Ingrid stood right next to her chair, with Svetlana standing on the other side.

Along with her extended family and Ingrid and Svetlana, most of Megan's high school classmates had come to pay their respects. Ingrid felt humbled by the amount of love and compassion on display for Kathleen Avery and regretted that over the years she hadn't felt more able to show some herself.

The short service was both poignant and apt. The reverend was the same one who'd baptized Megan thirty-one years earlier. When he spoke about her in fond and glowing terms he wasn't reciting something her family had told him to say, he was actually remembering Megan's life the way it deserved to be.

When the last of Megan's family and friends had thrown a handful of soil onto her oak paneled, brass handled casket, the entourage slowly made its way back to the cars to return to Kathleen's house for the wake. As the crowd dispersed, Ingrid saw a face she hadn't laid eyes on for so many years she wasn't sure if she'd imagined it. Then the face broke into a smile. A smile she had never forgotten since junior high. Her very first unrequited crush.

It was Clark Swanson.

He gave her a subtle wave and she felt the exact same butterflies in her stomach that she had all those years ago. How was it possible he could still have this effect on her? Maybe it was because now, ironically, Clark Swanson was actually reminding her of Ralph Mills, rather than the other way around.

Clark hurried over to Kathleen and kneeled down so that his face was level with hers. "I'm so sorry, Mrs Avery. I didn't think it was possible to miss Megan more than we had, but today has proved me wrong. She was a beautiful, beautiful girl."

"Thank you, Clark. I appreciate you coming all the way back here for Megan."

"Nothing could have kept me away, ma'am." He glanced up at Ingrid as he got to his feet and nodded at her. "I thought maybe I would gather Megan's classmates together and we could reminisce a little about high school. Share a few of our memories with you, Mrs Avery.

"I'd like that. I'm sure Megan would too." She stared down at the ground, somehow managing to hold back her tears.

Ingrid dropped to her knees and took Kathleen's hand firmly in hers. Then she kissed the back of it. A feeling washed over her that she hadn't been expecting at all.

Ingrid actually felt contented to be back home.

They spent a little while longer together in silence, then Kathleen's eldest son wheeled her away toward the line of waiting cars.

When everyone else had gone, Ingrid crouched low beside the grave and asked Megan Avery to forgive her.

———

I'd like to share a very special short story set between the events of *Deep Hurt* and the next book in the series, *Shoot First*. *Dirty Secret* reveals what Ingrid gets up to with Clark Swanson while she's back in Minnesota and you can get your hands on it, as well as lots of other bonus material, by joining my readers' club.

Visit evahudson.com/readersclub.

In *Shoot First*, the fourth Ingrid Skyberg thriller, Ingrid must make a split second decision that will change her life forever

SHOOT FIRST

AN INGRID SKYBERG THRILLER BOOK 4

A teenage girl disappears after witnessing a gangland murder in Chicago. Nine months later, and heavily pregnant, she arrives in London only to disappear again.

Special Agent Ingrid Skyberg has just two days to find the girl and get her to testify or else a brutal killer walks free. But Ingrid isn't the only person looking for the girl, and a war that started on the streets of Chicago is about to explode in the peaceful English countryside.

Available in paperback and ebook.

Box set published by Venatrix 2021.

Fresh Doubt first published by Two Pies Press 2013.
Kill Plan first published by Two Pies Press 2014.
Deep Hurt first published by Two Pies Press 2014.

Printed in Great Britain
by Amazon

80151597R00466